I0584943

L. (Luise) Mühlbach

Berlin and Sans-Souci

Frederick the Great and his friends

L. (Luise) Mühlbach

Berlin and Sans-Souci
Frederick the Great and his friends

ISBN/EAN: 9783743322226

Manufactured in Europe, USA, Canada, Australia, Japa

Cover: Foto ©Andreas Hilbeck / pixelio.de

Manufactured and distributed by brebook publishing software
(www.brebook.com)

L. (Luise) Mühlbach

Berlin and Sans-Souci

Edition De Luxe

Berlin and Sans=Souci

or, Frederick the Great and his Friends

An Historical Romance

By

Louisa Mühlbach

Translated from the German by

Mrs. Chapman Coleman and Her Daughters

The Chesterfield Society

London ▪ New York

CONTENTS.

BOOK I.

BOOK II.

BOOK III.

BOOK IV.

BERLIN AND SANS-SOUCI;

OR,

FREDERICK THE GREAT AND HIS FRIENDS.

BOOK I.

CHAPTER I.

THE ALCHEMIST'S INCANTATION.

It was a lovely May morning! The early rays of the sun had not withered the blossoms, or paled the fresh green of the garden of Charlottenburg, but quickened them into new life and beauty. The birds sang merrily in the groves. The wind, with light whispers, swept through the long avenues of laurel and orange trees, which surrounded the superb greenhouses and conservatories, and scattered far and wide throughout the garden clouds of intoxicating perfume.

The garden was quiet and solitary, and the closed shutters of the castle proved that not only the king, but the entire household, from the dignified and important chamberlain to the frisky garden-boy, still slept. Suddenly the silence was broken by the sound of hasty steps. A young man, in simple citizen costume, ran up the great avenue which led from the garden gate to the conservatory; then cautiously looking about him, he drew near to a window of the lower story in a wing of the castle. The window was closed and secured with inside shutters; a small piece of white paper was seen between the glass and the shutter. A passer-by might have supposed this was accidental, but the young burgher knew that this little piece of paper was a signal. His light stroke upon the window disturbed

9

for a moment the deathlike silence around, but produced no other effect; he struck again, more loudly, and listened breathlessly. The shutters were slowly and cautiously opened from within, and behind the glass was seen the wan, sick face of Fredersdorf, the private secretary and favorite of the king. When he saw the young man, his features assumed a more animated expression, and a hopeful smile played upon his lip; hastily opening the window, he gave the youth his hand. "Good-morning, Joseph," said he; "I have not slept during the whole night, I was so impatient to receive news from you. Has he shown himself?"

Joseph bowed his head sadly. "He has not yet shown himself," he replied in a hollow voice; "all our efforts have been in vain; we have again sacrificed time, money, and strength. He has not yet appeared."

"Alas!" cried Fredersdorf, "who could believe it so difficult to move the devil to appear in person, when he makes his presence known daily and hourly through the deeds of men? I must and will see him! He *must* and *shall* make known this mystery. He shall teach me *how* and of *what* to make gold."

"He will yield at last!" cried Joseph, solemnly.

"What do you say? Will we succeed? Is not all hope lost?"

"All is not lost: the astrologer heard this night, during his incantations, the voice of the devil, and saw for one moment the glare of his eye, though he could not see his person."

"He saw the glare of his eye!" repeated Fredersdorf joyfully. "Oh, we will yet compel him to show himself wholly. He must teach us to make gold. And what said the voice of the devil to our astrologer?"

"He said these words: 'Would you see my face and hear words of golden wisdom from my lips? so offer me, when next the moon is full and shimmers like liquid gold in the heavens, a black ram; and if you shed his blood for me, and if not one white hair can be discovered upon him, I will appear and be subject to you.'"

"Another month of waiting, of patience, and of torture," murmured Fredersdorf. "Four weeks to search for this black ram without a single white hair; it will be difficult to find!"

"Oh, the world is large; we will send our messengers in every quarter; we will find it. Those who truly seek, find at last what they covet. But we will require much gold, and we are suffering now, unhappily, for the want of it."

"We? whom do you mean by we?" asked Fredersdorf, with a contemptuous shrug of the shoulders.

"I, in my own person, above all others, need gold. You can well understand, my brother, that a student as I am has no superfluous gold, even to pay his tailor's bills, much less to buy black rams. Captain Kleist, in whose house the assembly meets to-night, has already offered up far more valuable things than a score of black rams; he has sacrificed his health, his rest, and his domestic peace. His beautiful wife finds it strange, indeed, that he should seek the devil every night everywhere else than in her lovely presence."

"Yes, I understand that! The bewitching Madame Kleist must ever remain the vain-glorious and coquettish Louise von Schwerin; marriage has infused no water in her veins."

"No! but it has poured a river of wine in the blood of her husband, and in this turbid stream their love and happiness is drowned. Kleist is but a corpse, whom we must soon bury from our sight. The king has made separation and divorce easy; yes, easier than marriage. Is it not so, my brother? Ah, you blush; you find that your light-hearted brother has more observant eyes than you thought, and sees that which you intended to conceal. Yes, yes! I have indeed seen that you have been wounded by Cupid's arrow, and that your heart bleeds while our noble king refuses his consent to your marriage."

"Ah, let me once discover this holy mystery—once learn how to make gold, and I will have no favor to ask of any earthly monarch; I shall acknowledge no other sovereign than my own will."

"And to become the possessor of this secret, and your own master, you require nothing but a black ram. Create for us, then, my powerful and wealthy brother, a black ram, and the work is done!"

"Alas! to think," cried Fredersdorf, "that I cannot absent myself; that I must fold my hands and wait silently and quietly! What slavery is this! but you, you are not in bondage as I am. The whole world is before you; you can seek throughout the universe for this blood-offering demanded by the devil."

"Give us gold, brother, and we will seek; without gold, no black ram; without the black ram, no devil!"

Fredersdorf disappeared a moment and returned with a well-filled purse, which he handed to his brother. "There, take the gold; send your messengers in every quarter; go yourself and search. You must either find or create him. I swear to you, if you do not succeed, I will withdraw my protection from you; you will be only a poor student, and must maintain yourself by your studies."

"That would be a sad support, indeed," said the young man, smiling. "I am more than willing to choose another path in life. I would, indeed, prefer being an artist to being a philosopher."

"An artist!" cried Fredersdorf, contemptuously; "have you discovered in yourself an artist's vein?"

"Yes; or rather, Eckhof has awakened my sleeping talent."

"Eckhof—who is Eckhof?"

"How? you ask who is Eckhof? You know not, then, this great, this exalted artist, who arrived here some weeks since, and has entranced every one who has a German heart in his bosom, by his glorious acting? I saw him a few days since in Golsched's Cato. Ah! my brother, on that evening it was clear to me that I also was born for something greater than to sit in a lonely study, and seek in musty books for useless scraps of knowledge. No! I will not make the world still darker and mistier for myself with the dust of ancient books; I will illuminate my world by the noblest of all arts —I will become an actor!"

"Fantastic fool!" said his brother. "*A German actor!* that is to say, a beggar and a vagabond! who wanders from city to city, and from village to village, with his stage finery, who is laughed at everywhere, even as the monkeys are laughed at when they make their somersets over the camels' backs; it might answer to be a dancer, or, at least, a French actor."

"It is true that the German stage is a castaway—a Cinderella—thrust aside, and clothed with sackcloth and ashes, while the spoiled and petted step-child is clothed in gold-embroidered robes. Alas! alas! it is a bitter thing that the French actors are summoned by the king to perform in the royal castle, while Schönemein, the director of the German theatre, must rent the Council-house for a large sum of money, and must pay a heavy tax for the permission to give to the German public a German stage. Wait patiently, brother, all this shall be changed, when the mystery of mysteries is discovered, when we have found the black ram! I bless the accident which gave me a knowledge of your secret, which forced you to receive me as a member in order to secure my silence. I shall be rich, powerful, and influential; I will build a superb theatre, and fill the German heart with wonder and rapture."

"Well, well, let us first understand the art of making gold, and we will make the whole world our theatre, and all mankind shall play before us! Hasten, therefore, brother, hasten! By the next full moon we will be the almighty rulers of the earth and all that is therein!"

"Always provided that we have found the black ram."

"We will find him! If necessary, we will give his weight in gold, and gold can do all things. Honor, love, power, position, and fame, can all be bought with gold! Let us, then, make haste to be rich. To be rich is to be independent, free, and gloriously happy. Go, my brother, go! and may you soon return crowned with success."

"I have still a few weighty questions to ask. In the first place, where shall I go?"

"To seek the black ram—it makes no difference where."

"Ah! it makes no difference! You do not seem to remember that the vacation is over, that the professors of the University of Halle have threatened to dismiss me if my attendance is so irregular. I must, therefore, return to Halle to-day, or—"

"Return to Halle to-day!" cried Fredersdorf, with horror. "That is impossible! You cannot return to Halle, unless you have already found what we need."

"And that not being the case, I shall not return to Halle; I shall be dismissed, and will cease to be a student. Do you consent, then, that I shall become an actor, and take the great Eckhof for my only professor?"

"Yes, I consent, provided the command of the alchemist is complied with."

"And how if the alchemist, notwithstanding the blood of the black ram, is unhappily not able to bring up the devil?"

At this question, a feverish crimson spot took possession of the wan cheek of Fredersdorf, which was instantly chased away by a more intense pallor. "If that is the result, I will either go mad or die," he murmured.

"And then will you see the devil face to face!" cried his brother, with a gay laugh. "But perhaps you might find a Eurydice to unlock the under world for you. Well, we shall see. Till then, farewell, brother, farewell." Nodding merrily to Fredersdorf, Joseph hurried away.

Fredersdorf watched his tall and graceful figure as it disappeared among the trees with a sad smile.

"He possesses something which is worth more than power or gold; he is young, healthy, full of hope and confidence. The world belongs to him, while I—"

The sound of footsteps called his attention again to the *allée*.

CHAPTER II.

THE OLD COURTIER.

THE figure of a man was seen approaching, but with steps less light and active than young Joseph's. As the stranger drew nearer, Fredersdorf's features expressed great surprise. When at last he drew up at the window, the secretary burst into a hearty laugh.

"Von Pöllnitz! really and truly I do not deceive myself,"

cried Fredersdorf, clapping his hands together, and again
and again uttering peals of laughter, in which Pöllnitz heartily joined.

Then suddenly assuming a grave and dignified manner,
Fredersdorf bowed lowly and reverentially. "Pardon, Baron
Pöllnitz, pardon," said he in a tone of mock humility, "that
I have dared to welcome you in such an unseemly manner.
I was indeed amazed to see you again; you had taken an
eternal leave of the court, we had shed rivers of tears over
your irreparable loss, and your unexpected presence com-
pletely overpowered me."

"Mock and jeer at me to your heart's content, dear
Fredersdorf; I will joyfully and lustily unite in your laughter and your sport, as soon as I have recovered from the
fearful jolting of the carriage which brought me here. Be
pleased to open the window a little more, and place a chair
on the outside, that I may climb in, like an ardent, eager lover. I have not patience to go round to the castle
door."

Fredersdorf silently obeyed orders, and in a few moments Von Pöllnitz was lying comfortably stretched out on
a silk divan, in the secretary's room.

"Ask me no questions, Fredersdorf," said he, breathing
loudly; "leave me awhile to enjoy undisturbed the comfort
of your sofa, and do me the favor first to answer me a few
questions, before I reply to yours."

"Demand, baron, and I will answer," said Fredersdorf,
seating himself on a chair near the sofa.

"First of all, who is King of Prussia? You, or Jordan,—
or General Kothenberg,—or Chazot,—or—speak, man, who is
King of Prussia?"

"Frederick the Second, and he alone; and he so entirely,
that even his ministers are nothing more than his secretaries,
to write at his dictation; and his generals are only subor-
dinate engineers to draw the plans of battle which he has
already fully determined upon; his composers are only the
copyists of his melodies and his musical conceptions; the
architects are carpenters to build according to the plan
which he has either drawn or chosen from amongst old
Grecian models: in short, all who serve him are literally

servants in this great state machine; they understand his will and obey it, nothing more."

"Hum! that is bad, very bad," said Pöllnitz. "I have found, however, that there are two sorts of men, and you have mentioned in your catalogue but one species, who have fallen so completely under the hand of Frederick. You have said nothing of his cook, of his valet-de-chambre, and yet these are most important persons. You must know that in the presence of these powers, a king ceases to be a king, and indeed becomes an entirely commonplace mortal, who eats and drinks and clothes himself, and who must either conceal or adorn his bodily necessities and weaknesses like any other man."

Fredersdorf shook his head sadly. "It seems to me that Frederick the Second is beyond the pale of temptation; for even with his cook and his valet he is still a king; his cook may prepare him the most costly and luxurious viands, but unhappily they do not lead him into temptation; a bad dish makes him angry, but the richest and choicest food has no effect upon his humor; he is exactly the same before dinner as after, fasting or feasting, and the favor he refuses before the champagne, he never grants afterward."

"The devil! that is worse still," murmured Pöllnitz. "And the valet—with him also does the king remain king?"

"Yes, so entirely, that he scarcely allows his valet to touch him. He shaves, coifs, and dresses himself."

"My God! who, then, has any influence over him? To whom can I turn to obtain a favor for me?"

"To his dogs, dear baron; they are now the only influential dependants!"

"Do you mean truly the four-footed dogs?—or—"

"The four-footed, dearest baron! Frederick has more confidence in them than in any two-legged animal. You know the king always trusted much to the instincts of his dogs; he has now gone so far in this confidence, as to believe that the hounds have an instinctive aversion to all false, wicked, and evil-minded men. It is therefore very important to every new-comer to be well received by the hounds, as the king's reception is somewhat dependent upon theirs."

" Is Biche yet with the king? "

" Yes, still his greatest favorite."

" I am rejoiced to hear that! I was always in favor with the Signora Biche; it was her custom to smell my pocket, hoping to find chocolate. I beseech you, therefore, dearest friend, to give me some chocolate, with which I may touch and soften the heart of the noble signora, and thus induce the king to look upon me favorably.

" I will stick a half pound in each of your pockets, and if Biche still growls at you, it will be a proof that she is far more noble than men; in short, that she cannot be bribed. Have you finished with your questions? I think it is now my time to begin."

" Not so, my friend. My head is still entirely filled with questions, and they are twining and twisting about like the fishing-worms in a bag, by the help of which men hope to secure fish. Be pitiful and allow me to fasten a few more of these questions to my fishing-rod, and thus try to secure my future."

" Well, then, go on—ask further! "

" Does Frederick show no special interest in any prima donna of the opera, the ballet, or the theatre? "

" No, he cares for none of these things."

" Is his heart, then, entirely turned to stone? "

" Wholly and entirely."

" And the queen-mother, has she no influence? "

" My God! Baron Pöllnitz, how long have you been away? You ask me as many questions as if you had fallen directly from the moon, and knew not even the outward appearance of the court."

" Dear friend, I have been a whole year away, that is to say, an eternity. The court is a very slippery place; and if a man does not accustom himself hourly to walk over this glassy parquet, he will surely fall. .

" Also there is nothing so uncertain as a court life; that which is true to-day, is to-morrow considered incredible; that which was beautiful yesterday is thrust aside to-day, as hateful to look upon; that which we despise to-day is to-morrow sought after as a rare and precious gem.

" Oh, I have had my experiences. I remember, that

while I was residing at the court of Saxony, I composed a poem in honor of the Countess Aurora of Königsmark. This was by special command of the king; the poem was to be set to music by Hasse, and sung by the Italian singers on the birthday of Aurora. Well, the Countess Aurora was cast aside before my poem was finished, and the Countess Kozel had taken her place. I finished my poem, but Amelia, and not Aurora, was my heroine. Hasse composed the music, and no one who attended the concert, given in honor of the birthday of the Countess Kozel, had an idea that this festal cantata had been originally ordered for Aurora of Königsmark!

"Once, while I was in Russia, I had an audience from the Empress Elizabeth. As I approached the castle, leaning on the arm of the Captain Ischerbatow, I observed the guard, who stood before the door, and presented arms. Well, eight weeks later, this common guard was a general and a prince, and Ischerbatow was compelled to bow before him!

"I saw in Venice a picture of the day of judgment by Tintoretto. In this picture both Paradise and Hell were portrayed. I saw in Paradise a lovely woman glowing with youth, beauty, and grace. She was reclining in a most enchanting attitude, upon a bed of roses, and surrounded by angels. Below, on the other half of the picture—that is to say, in Hell—I saw the same woman; she had no couch of roses, but was stretched upon a glowing gridiron; no smiling angels surrounded her, but a hideous, grinning devil tore her flesh with red-hot pincers.

"Pope Adrian had commanded Tintoretto to paint this picture, to make it a monument in honor of the lovely Cinnia, and to glorify her by all the power of art. Cinnia was a very dear friend of Adrian. He was not only a pope, but a man, and a man who took pleasure in all beautiful things. Cinnia was enchanting, and it was Tintoretto's first duty to paint her picture, and make her the principal object in Paradise. But look you! the Last Judgment by Tintoretto was a large painting, so large that to count even the heads upon it is laborious. The heads in each corner are counted separately, and then added together. It required some years, of course, to paint such a picture; and by the time Tintoretto had completed Paradise and commenced the lower regions, many sad changes had occurred. The fond heart of the seducing Cinnia had withdrawn itself from the pope and clung tenaciously to Prince Colonna. The Holy Father, as we have said before, notwithstanding he was pope, had some human weaknesses; he naturally hated the fair inconstant, and sought revenge. He recommended Tintoretto to bring the erring one once more before the public—this time, however, as a guilty and condemned sinner in hell.

"Dear Fredersdorf, I think always of this picture when I look at the favorites of princes and kings, and I amuse myself with their pride and arrogance. When I see them in their sunny paradise of power and influence, I say to myself, 'All's well for the fleeting present, I'll wait patiently; soon I shall see you roasting on the glowing gridiron of royal displeasure, and the envious devils of this world filled with rapture at your downfall, will tear your flesh to pieces.' Friend Fredersdorf, that is my answer to your question as to whether I have in one short year forgotten the quality of court life."

"And by Heaven, that is a profound answer, which shows at least that Baron Pöllnitz has undergone no change during the last year, but is still the experienced man of the world and the wise cavalier!"

"But why do you not give me my title, Fredersdorf? Why do you not call me grand chamberlain?"

"Because you are no longer in the service of the king, but have received your dismissal."

"Alas! God grant that the Signora Biche is favorable to me; then will the king, as I hope, forget this dismissal. One question more. You say that the queen-mother has no influence; how is it with the wife of the king, Elizabeth Christine? Is she indeed the reigning sovereign?"

"When did you return to Berlin?"

"Now, to-night; and when I left the carriage, I hastened here."

"Well, that is some excuse for your question. If you have only just arrived, you could not possibly know of the important event which will take place at the court to-night. This evening the king will present his brother, Augustus

2

William, to the court as Prince of Prussia, and his successor, I think that is a sufficient answer to your question. As to Queen Elizabeth Christine, she lives at Schönhausen, and might be called the widow of her husband. The king never addresses one word to her, not even on grand festal days, when etiquette compels him to take a seat by her at table."

"Now, one last question, dear friend. How is it with yourself? Are you influential? Does Frederick love you as warmly as he did a year ago? Do you hope to reach the goal of your ambition and become all-powerful?"

"I have ceased to be ambitious," sighed Fredersdorf. "I no longer thirst to be the king of a king. My only desire is to be independent of courts and kings—in short, to be my own master. Perhaps I may succeed in this; if not, be ruined, as many others have been. If I cannot tear my chains apart, I will perish under them! As for my influence over the king, it is sufficient to say, that for six months I have loved a woman to distraction, who returns my passion with ardor, and I cannot marry her because the king, notwithstanding my prayers and agony, will not consent."

"He is right," said Pöllnitz, earnestly, as he stretched himself out comfortably on the sofa; "he is a fool who thinks of yielding up his manly freedom to any woman."

"You say that, baron? you, who gave up king and court, and went to Nurnberg, in order that you might marry!"

"Aha! how adroitly you have played the knife out of my hands, and have yourself become the questioner! Well, it is but just that you also should have your curiosity satisfied. Demand of me now and I will answer frankly."

"You are not married, baron?"

"Not in the least; and I have sworn that the goddess Fortuna alone shall be my beloved. I will have no mortal wife."

"The report, then, is untrue that you have again changed your religion, and become Protestant?"

"No, this time rumor has spoken the truth. The Nurnberger patrician would accept no hand offered by a Catholic; so I took off the glove of my Catholicism and drew on my Protestant one. My God! to a man of the world, his outside faith is nothing more than an article of the toilet. Do you

not know that it is *bon ton* for princes when they visit
strange courts to wear the orders and uniforms of their
entertainers? So it is my rule of etiquette to adopt the
religion which the circumstances in which I find myself
seem to make suitable and profitable. My situation in
Nurnberg demanded that I should become a Protestant, and
I became one."

"And for all that the marriage did not take place?"

"No, it was broken off through the obstinacy of my bride,
who refused to live in good fellowship and equality with me,
and gave me only the use of her income, and no right in her
property. Can you conceive of such folly? She imagined
I would give myself in marriage, and make a baroness of
an indifferently pretty burgher maiden; yes, a baroness of
the realm, and expect no other compensation for it than a
wife to bore me! She wished to wed my rank, and found
it offensive that I should marry, not only her fair self, but
her millions! The contest over this point broke off the
contract, and I am glad of it. From my whole soul I regret
and am ashamed of having ever thought of marriage. The
king, therefore, has reason to be pleased with me."

"You are thinking, then, seriously of remaining at
court?"

"Do you not find that natural, Fredersdorf? I have
lived fifty years at this court, and accustomed myself to its
stupidity, its nothingness, and its ceremony, as a man may
accustom himself to a hard tent-bed, and find it at last more
luxurious than a couch of eider-down. Besides, I have just
lost a million in Nurnberg, and I must find a compensation;
the means at least to close my life worthily as a cavalier.
I must, therefore, again bow my free neck, and enter service.
You must aid me, and this day obtain for me an audience
of the king. I hope your influence will reach that far. The
rest must be my own affair."

"We will see what can be done. I have joyful news for
the king to-day. Perhaps it will make him gay and com-
plaisant, and he will grant you an audience."

"And this news which you have for him?"

"The Barbarina has arrived!"

"What! the celebrated dancer?"

"The same. We have seized and forcibly carried her off from the republic of Venice and from Lord McKenzie; and Baron Swartz has brought her as prisoner to Berlin!"

Pöllnitz half raised himself from the sofa, and, seizing the arm of the private secretary, he looked him joyfully in the face. "I have conceived a plan," said he, "a heavenly plan! My friend, the sun of power and splendor is rising for us, and your ambition, which has been weary and ready to die, will now revive, and raise its head proudly on high! That which I have long sought for is at last found. The king is too young, too ardent, too much the genius and poet, to be completely unimpassioned. Even Achilles was not impenetrable in the heel, and Frederick has also his mortal part. Do you know, Fredersdorf, who will discover the weak point, and send an arrow there?"

"No."

"Well, I will tell you: the Signora Barbarina. Ah, you smile! you shake your unbelieving head. You are no good psychologist. Do you not know that we desire most earnestly that which seems difficult, if not impossible to attain, and prize most highly that which we have won with danger and difficulty? Judge, also, how precious a treasure the Barbarina must be to Frederick. For her sake he has for months carried on a diplomatic contest with Venice, and at last he has literally torn her away from my Lord Stuart McKenzie."

"That is true," said Fredersdorf, thoughtfully; "for ten days the king has waited with a rare impatience for the arrival of this beautiful dancer, and he commanded that, as soon as she reached Berlin, it should be announced to him."

"I tell you the king will adore the Signora Barbarina," said Pöllnitz, as he once more stretched himself upon the sofa pillows. "I shall visit her to-day, and make the necessary arrangements. Now I am content. I see land, a small island of glorious promise, which will receive me, the poor shipwrecked mariner, and give me shelter and protection. I will make myself the indispensable counsellor of Barbarina; I will teach her how she can melt the stony heart of Frederick, and make him her willing slave."

"Dreams, dreams!" said Fredersdorf, shrugging his shoulders.

"Dreams which I will make realities as soon as you obtain me an audience with the king."

"Well, we will see what can be done, and whether—but listen, the king is awake, and has opened his window. He is playing upon the flute, which is his morning custom. His morning music is always the barometer of his mood, and I can generally judge what kind of royal weather we will have, whether bright or stormy. Come with me to the window and listen awhile."

"Agreed," said Pöllnitz, and he sprang with youthful elasticity from the divan and joined Fredersdorf at the window. They listened almost breathlessly to the sweet tones which seemed to whisper to them from the upper windows; then mingling and melting with the perfume of the orange-blossoms and the glorious and life-giving morning air, they forced their sweet and subtle essence into the room with the cunning and hardened old courtiers.

Fredersdorf and Pöllnitz listened as a sly bat listens to the merry whistling of an innocent bird, and watches the propitious moment to spring upon her prey. It was an adagio which the king played upon his flute, and he was indeed a master in the art. Slightly trembling, as if in eternal melancholy, sobbing and pleading, soon bursting out in rapturous and joyful strains of harmony, again sighing and weeping, these melting tones fell like costly pearls upon the summer air. The birds in the odorous bushes, the wind which rustled in the trees, the light waves of the river, which with soft murmurs prattled upon the shore, all Nature seemed for the moment to hold her breath and listen to this enchanting melody. Even Fredersdorf felt the power and influence of this music as he had done in earlier days. The old love for his king filled his heart, and his eyes were misty with tears.

As the music ceased, Fredersdorf exclaimed involuntarily: "He is, after all, the noblest and greatest of men. It is useless to be angry with him. I am forced against my will to worship him."

"Now," said Pöllnitz, whose face had not for one moment lost its expression of cold attention and sly cunning, "how

says the barometer?   May we promise ourselves a clear and
sunny day?"

"Yes, Frederick is in one of his soft and yielding moods.
It is probable he has been some hours awake and has written
to some of his friends—perhaps to Voltaire, or Algarotti;
this makes him always bright and clear."

"You think I shall obtain my audience?"

"I think you will."

"Then, dear friend, I have only to say that I hope you
will give me the chocolate for that noble and soul-searching
hound, the Signora Biche."

CHAPTER III.

THE MORNING HOURS OF A KING.

KING FREDERICK had finished the adagio, and stood leaning against the window gazing into the garden; his eyes,
usually so fierce and commanding, were softened by melancholy, and a sad smile played upon his lips.   The touching
air which he had played found its echo within, and held
his soul a prisoner to troubled thoughts.   Suddenly he
seemed to rouse himself by a great effort to the realities
of life, and, hastily ringing the bell, he commanded Jordan,
the director of the poor and the almshouse, to be summoned
to him.

A few moments later, Jordan, who had been for some
days a guest at the castle of Charlottenburg, entered the
king's room.   Frederick advanced to meet him, and extended both hands affectionately.   "Good-morning, Jordan,"
said he, gazing into the wan, thin face of his friend, with the
most earnest sympathy.   "I hope you had a refreshing
night."

"I have had a charming night, for I was dreaming of
your majesty," he replied, with a soft smile.

Frederick sighed, released his hands, and stepped back
a few paces.   "Your majesty?" repeated he.   "Why do you

lay so cold a hand upon that heart which beats so warmly for you? To what purpose is this etiquette? Are we not alone? and can we not accord to our souls a sweet interchange of thought and feeling without ceremony? Do we not understand and love each other? Forget, then, for awhile, dear Jordan, all these worldly distinctions. You see I am still in my morning-dress. I do not, like the poor kings upon the stage, wear my crown and sceptre in bed, or with my night-dress."

Jordan gazed lovingly and admiringly upon his great friend. "You need no crown upon your brow to show to the world that you are a king by the grace of God. The majesty of greatness is written upon your face, my king."

"That," said Frederick with light irony, "is because we princes and kings are acknowledged to be the exact image of the Creator, the everlasting Father. As for you, and all the rest of the race, you dare not presume to compare yourselves with us. Probably you are made in the image of the second and third persons of the Trinity, while we carry upon our withered and wearisome faces the quintessence of the Godhead."

"Alas! alas, sire, if our pious priest heard you, what a stumbling-block would he consider you!"

The king smiled. "Do you know, Jordan," said he gravely, "I believe God raised me up for this special mission, to be a rock of offence to these proud and worldly priests, and to trample under foot their fooleries and their arrogance? I look upon that as the most important part of my mission upon earth, and I am convinced that I am appointed to humble this proud church, the vain and arrogant work of hypocritical priests, and to establish in its place the pure worship of God."

"Yes, yes," said Jordan, shrugging his shoulders; "if the mass of men had the clear intellect of a Frederick! if their eyes were like those of my royal eagle, to whom it is given to gaze steadfastly at the sun without being dazzled. Alas! sire, the most of our race resemble you so little! They are all like the solemn night-owls, who draw a double curtain over their eyes, lest the light should blind them. The church serves as this double eyelid for the night-owls among men, or, rather, the churches, for the cunning and covetousness of those priests has not been satisfied with one church, but has established many."

"Yes," said the king angrily; "they have sown dragons' teeth, from which bloodthirsty warriors have sprung, who wander up and down, and in mad ambition tear all mankind, and themselves included, to pieces. Listen, Jordan, we have fallen upon a subject which, as you know, has interested and occupied me much of late, and it is precisely upon these points that I have sought your counsel to-day. Be seated, then, and hear what I have to say to you. You know that the pietists and priests charge me with being a heretic, because I do not think as they think, and believe as they believe. Which of them, think you, Jordan, has the true faith? What is truth, and what is wisdom? Each sect believes itself—and itself alone—the possessor of both. That is reason enough, it appears to me, for doubting them all."

"In the same land?"

"Yes, in various places in the same city, we are taught entirely different and opposing doctrines in the name of religion. On one hand, we are threatened with everlasting fire in the company of the devil and his angels, if we believe that the Almighty is bodily present in the elements offered at the sacrament of the Lord's supper. On the other hand, we are taught, with equal assurance, that the same terrible punishment will be awarded us unless we believe that God is literally, and not symbolically, present in the bread and wine. The simple statement of the doctrines of the different churches in the world would fill an endless number of folios. Each religion condemns all others, as leading to perdition; they cannot therefore all be true, for truth does not contradict itself. If any one of these were the true faith, would not God have made it clear, and without question, to our eyes? God, who is truth, cannot be dark or doubtful! If these differences in religion related only to outward forms and ceremonies, we would let them pass as agreeable and innocent changes, even as we adopt contentedly the changes in style and fashion of our clothing. The doctrines of faith, as taught in England, cannot be made to harmonize with those fulminated at Rome. He to whom it would be given to reconcile all opposing doctrines, and to unite all hearts in one pure and simple faith would indeed give peace to the world, and be a Messiah and a Saviour."

"Yes, he would accomplish what God himself, as it appears, has not thought proper to do; his first great act must be to institute and carry out a terrible massacre, in which every priest of every existing religion must be pursued to the death."

"And that is precisely my mission," said the king. "I will institute a massacre, not bodily and bloodily, but soul-piercing and purifying. I say to you, Jordan, God dwells not in the churches of these imperious priests, who choose to call themselves the servants of God. God was with Moses on Mount Sinai, and with Zoroaster in the wilderness; he was by Dante's side as he wrote his 'Divina Commedia,' and he piloted the ships of Columbus as he went out bravely to seek a new world! God is everywhere, and that mankind should reverence and believe in and worship him, is proved by their bearing his image and their high calling."

Jordan seized the hand of the king and pressed it enthusiastically to his lips. "And the world says that you do not believe in God," he exclaimed; "they class you with the unbelievers, and dare to preach against you, and slander you from the pulpit."

"Yes, as I do not adopt their dogmas, I am, to them, a heretic," said the king laughing; "and when they preach against me, it proves that they fear me, and look upon me as a powerful enemy. The enemy of the priests I will be as long as I live, that is to say, of those arrogant and imperious men who are wise in their own eyes, and despise all who do not agree with them! I will destroy the foundations of all these different churches, with their different dogmas. I will utterly extinguish them by a universal church, in which every man shall worship God after his own fashion. The worship of God should be the only object of every church! All these different doctrines, which they cast in each other's teeth, and for love of which they close their doors against each other, shall be given up. I will open all their churches, and the fresh, pure air of God shall purify the musty buildings. I will build a temple, a great illimitable temple, a second Pantheon, a church which shall unite all churches within itself, in which it shall be granted to every man to have his own altar, and adopt his own religious exercises. All desire to worship God; every man shall do so according to his conscience! Look you, Jordan, how pathetically they discourse of brotherly love, and they tear each other to pieces! Let me only build my Pantheon, and then will all men, in truth, become brothers. The Jew and the so-called heathen, the Mohammedan and the Persian, the Calvinist and the Catholic, the Lutheran and the Reformer—they will all gather into my Pantheon, to worship God; all their forms and dogmas will simultaneously fall to the ground. They will believe simply in one God, and the churches of all these different sects will soon stand empty and in ruins." *

While the king spoke, his countenance was illumined; a noble enthusiasm fired his large clear eyes, and his cheeks glowed as if from the awakening breath of some new internal light.

Jordan's glance expressed unspeakable love, but at the same time he looked so sad, so pained, that Frederick felt chilled and restrained.

"How, Jordan! you are not of my opinion?" said he, with surprise. "Our souls, which have been always heretofore in union, are now apart. You do not approve of my Pantheon?"

"It is too exalted, sire, to be realized. Mankind require a form of religion, in order not to lose all personal control."

"No, you mistake. They require only God, only love for this exalted and lofty Being, whom we call God. The only proof by which we can know that we can sincerely love God, lies in a steadfast and strong purpose to obey Him. According to this, we need no other religion than our reason, the good gift of God. So soon as we know that He has spoken, we should be silent and submissive. Our inward worship of God should consist in this, that we acknowledge Him and confess our sins; our outward worship in the performance of all our duties, according to our reason, the exalted nature of God, and our entire dependence upon Him."

* Thiébault, in his "Souvenirs de Vingt Ans," tells of Frederick's plan for a Pantheon.

"It is to be regretted, sire, that this world is not sufficiently enlightened to comprehend you. I am afraid that your majesty will bring about exactly the opposite of that which you design. All these religious sects which, as you say, are so entirely antagonistic, would by this forced union feel themselves humiliated and trampled upon; their hatred toward each other would be daily augmented; their antipathies would find new food; and their religious zeal, which is always exclusive, would burn with fiercer fury. Not only the priests, but kings and princes, would look upon the carrying out of your plan with horror. And shall not this daring step bring terror into the cabinets of kings? A monarch, who has just drawn the eyes of all politicians upon himself, now proposes to take charge of the consciences of his subjects, and bow them to his will! Alas, how would envy, with all her poisonous serpents, fasten upon the triumphal car of a king who, by the great things he has already achieved, had given assurance of yet greater results, and now stoops to tyrannize over and oppress the weak and good, and cast them among the ruins of their temples of worship to weep and lament in despair! No, my king, this idea of a Pantheon, a universal house of worship, can never be realized. It was a great and sublime thought, but not a wise one; too great, too enlarged and liberal to be appreciated by this pitiable world. Your majesty will forgive me for having spoken the honest truth. I was forced to speak. Like my king, I love the one only and true God, and God is truth."

"You have done well, Jordan," said the king, after a long pause, during which he raised his eyes thoughtfully toward heaven. "Yes, you have done well, and I believe you are right in your objections to my Pantheon. I offer up to you, therefore, my favorite idea. For your dear sake, my Pantheon shall become a ruin. Let this be a proof of the strong love I bear you, Jordan. I will not contend with the priests in my church, but I will pursue them without faltering into their own; and I say to you, this will be a long and stiff-necked war, which will last while my life endures. I will not have my people blinded and stupefied by priests. I will suffer no other king in Prussia. I alone will be king.

These proud priests may decide, in silence and humility, to teach their churches and intercede for them; but let them once attempt to play the *rôle* of small popes, and to exalt themselves as the only possessors of the key to heaven, then they shall find in me an adversary who will prove to them that the key is false with which they shut up the Holiest of Holies, and is but used by them as a means to rob the people of their worldly goods. Light and truth shall be the device of my whole land. This will I seek after, and by this will I govern Prussia. I will have no blinded subjects, no superstitious, conscience-stricken, trembling, priest-ridden slaves. My people shall learn to think; thought shall be free as the wanton air in Prussia; no censor or police shall limit her boundary. The thoughts of men should be like the life-giving and beautifying sun, all-nourishing and all-enlightening; calling into existence and fructifying, not only the rich, and rare, and lovely, but also the noxious and poisonous plant and the creeping worm. These have also the right of life: if left to themselves, they soon die of their own insignificance or nothingness—die under the contempt of all the good and great."

"I fear," said Jordan, "that Frederick the Great is the only man whose mind is so liberal and so unprejudiced. Believe me, my king, there is no living sovereign in Europe who dares guarantee to his subjects free thought and free speech."

"I will try so to act as to leave nothing to fear from the largest liberty of thought or speech," said the king, quietly. "Men may think and say of me what they will— that troubles me not; I will amuse myself with their slanders and accusations of heresy; as for their applause—well, that is a cheap merchandise, which I must share with every expert magician and every popular comedian. The applause of my own conscience, and of my friends—thy applause, my Jordan—is alone of value for me. Then," said he, earnestly, almost solemnly, "above all things, I covet fame. My name shall not pass away like a soft tone or a sweet melody. I will write it in golden letters on the tablet of history; it shall glitter like a star in the firmament; when centuries have passed away, my people shall remember me, and shall say, 'Frederick the Second made Prussia great, and enlarged her borders; he was a father who loved his people more than he did himself, and cheerfully sacrificed his own rest and comfort in their service, he was a teacher who spoke to them by word of mouth, and gave liberty to their souls.' Oh, Jordan, you must stand by me and help me to reach this great goal for which I thirst. Remain with me, dear friend, remain ever by my side, and with thy love, thy constancy, thy truth, and thy sincerity, help me to establish what is good, and to punish the evil; to acknowledge and promote what is noble and expose the unworthy to shame and confusion. Oh, Jordan! God has perhaps called me to be a great king; remain by me, and help me to be a good and simple-minded man."

He threw himself with impetuosity on Jordan's breast, and clasped him passionately in his arms. Jordan returned the king's embrace, and silently raised his moist eyes to heaven. A prayer to "Our Father" spoke in that eloquent eye, a heart-felt, glowing prayer for this man now resting upon his bosom, and who for him was not the all-powerful and commanding sovereign, but the noble, loving, and beloved friend, this poet and philosopher, before whose mighty genius his whole soul bowed in wonder and admiration; but suddenly, in this moment of deep and pious emotion, a cold, an icy chill, seemed to shiver and play like the breath of death over his features, and the hot blood, like liquid metal, rushed madly through his veins; he gave a light, short cough; with a quick, abrupt movement, he released himself from the arms of the king. Withdrawing a few steps, he turned away, and pressed his handkerchief to his lips.

"Jordan, you suffer, you are sick," said the king, anxiously.

Jordan turned again to him; his face was calm, and even gay; his eyes beamed with that strange, mysterious, and touching fire of consumption which hides the shadow of death under the rosy lip and glowing cheek; and, less cruel than all other maladies, leaves to the soul its freshness, and to the heart its power to love and hope.

"Not so, sire," said Jordan, "I do not suffer. How can I be otherwise than well and happy in your presence?" As he said this he tried to thrust his handkerchief in his pocket.

The king looked earnestly at this handkerchief. "Jordan, why did you press that handkerchief so hastily to your lips?"

"Jordan forced a smile. "Well," said he, "I was obliged, as your majesty no doubt saw, to cough, and I wished to make this disagreeable music as soft as possible."

"That was not the reason," said Frederick; and, stepping hastily forward, he seized the handkerchief. "Blood! it is drenched in blood," said he, in a tone so full of anguish, that it was evident he recognized and feared this fatal signal.

"Well, yes, it is blood; your majesty sees I am blood-thirsty! Unhappily, I do not shed the blood of your enemies, but my own, which I would gladly give, drop by drop, if I could thereby save my king one hour's suffering or care."

"And yet you, Jordan, are now the cause of my bitterest grief. You are ill, and you conceal it from me. You suffer, and force yourself to seem gay, and hide your danger from me, in place of turning to my physicians and demanding their counsel and aid."

"Frederick the Wise once said to me, 'Physicians are but quacks and charlatans, and a man gives himself up to a tedious suicide who swallows their prescriptions.'"

"No, it was not 'Frederick the Wise,' but 'Frederick the Fool,' who uttered that folly. When the sun is shining, Frederick has no fear of ghosts; but at the turn of midnight, he will breathe a silent 'Father in heaven,' to be protected from them. We have no use for confidence in physicians when we are healthy; when we are ill we need them, and then we begin to hold them in consideration. You are ill, your breast suffers. I entreat you, Jordan, to call upon my physician, and to follow his advice promptly and systematically. I demand this as a proof of your friendship."

"I will obey your majesty, immediately," said Jordan, who now found himself completely overcome by the weakness which follows loss of blood; trembling, and almost sinking, he leaned upon the table. Frederick perceived this, and rolling forward his own arm-chair, with loving and tender care, he placed Jordan within it. He called his servant, and ordered him to roll the chair to Jordan's room, and go instantly for the physician Ellertt.

"It will be all in vain, and I shall lose him," murmured the king. "Yes, I will lose him, as I have lost Suhm, and as I shall soon lose my Cæsarius, the good Kaiserling. Alas! why did God give me so warm a heart for friendship, and then deprive me of my friends?"

Folding his arms, he stepped to the window and gazed thoughtfully and sadly into the garden below, but he saw not its bloom and beauty; his eyes were turned inward, and he saw only the grave of his friend. Suddenly rousing and conquering himself, he shook off the weary spirit of melancholy, and sought comfort in his flute, the faithful companion of all his sufferings and struggles.

CHAPTER IV.

THE PARDONED COURTIER.

FREDERICK commenced again to play, but this time it was not an adagio, but a joyous and triumphant allegro, with which he sought to dispel the melancholy and quench the tears flowing in his troubled heart. He walked backward and forward in his room, and from time to time stood before the sofa upon which his graceful greyhound, Biche, was quietly resting. Every minute the king passed her sofa, Biche raised her beautiful head and greeted her royal friend with an intelligent and friendly glance and a gentle wagging of her tail, and this salutation was returned each time by Frederick before he passed on. Finally, and still playing the flute, the king pressed his foot upon a silver button in the floor of his room, and rang a bell which hung in Fredersdorf's room, immediately under his own.

A few minutes later the secretary entered, but stood quietly at the door till the king had finished his allegro and laid aside his flute.

"Good-morning," said the king, and he looked up at his

favorite with so sharp and piercing a glance that Fredersdorf involuntarily trembled, and cast his eyes to the ground. "You must have been long wide awake, you answer the bell so quickly."

"Yes, your majesty, I have been long awake. I am happy, for I have good news to bring you."

"Well, what is it?" said the king smiling. "Has my god-mother, the Empress Maria Theresa, voluntarily surrendered to the Emperor Charles VII.? Have France and England become reconciled? or—and that seems to me the most probable—has my private secretary mastered the mystery of gold-making, after which he has so long striven, and for which he so willingly offers up the most costly and solemn sacrifices?" The king laid so peculiar an expression upon the word *sacrifice* that Fredersdorf wondered if he had not listened to his conversation with Joseph, and learned the strange sacrifice which they now proposed to offer up to the devil's shrine.

"Well, tell your news quickly," said the king. "You see that I am torturing myself with the most wild and incredible suppositions."

"Sire, the Barbarina reached Berlin last night."

"Truly," said the king, indifferently, "so we have at last ravished her from Venice, and Lord Stuart McKenzie."

"Not exactly so, your highness. Lord Stuart McKenzie arrived in Berlin this morning."

Frederick frowned. "This is also, as it appears, a case of true love, and may end in a silly marriage. I am not pleased when men or women in my service entertain serious thoughts of love or marriage; it occupies their thoughts and interferes with the performance of their duty."

"Your majesty judges severely," murmured Fredersdorf, who knew full well that this remark was intended for his special benefit.

"Well, this is not only my opinion, but I act in consonance with it. I allow myself no relaxation. Have I ever had a love-affair? Perhaps, Fredersdorf, you believe my blood to be frozen like ice in my veins; that I have a heart of stone; in short, that I ceased to be a man when I became a king."

"Not so; but I believe your majesty is too great and too exalted to find any one worthy of your love."

"Folly, folly, sheer folly, Fredersdorf! When a man loves, he does not weigh himself in the scales and find out how many pounds of worth he has; he only loves, and forgets all other earthly things. Now, for myself, I dare not forget that I am a king, and that my time and strength belong to my people. My heart is too tender, and for this reason I fly from love. So should you also flee, you also dare not forget that your life is consecrated to your king. The Signora Barbarina shall not forget that she is in my service; dancing, and not loving, must now occupy her thoughts and actions. I will allow her flirtations and amours, but a true love I absolutely forbid. How can she go through with her ballets, her pirouettes, and *entrechats* gayly and gracefully if a passionate love sits enthroned within her heart? I have promised the English ambassador, who is the cousin of this Lord Stuart McKenzie, that I will separate these lovers. At this moment the friendship of England is of much importance to me, and I shall certainly keep my promise. Write immediately to the director of police that I command him not only to banish Lord McKenzie from Berlin, but to send him under guard to Hamburg, and there place him upon an English ship bound for England. In twelve hours he must leave Berlin.* Is that your only news, Fredersdorf?"

"No, sire," said he, stealing a glance toward the door, which at this moment was lightly opened. "I have another novelty to announce, but I do not know whether it will be acceptable to your majesty. Baron von Pöllnitz—"

"Has sent us the announcement of his marriage?"

"No, sire, he is not married."

At this moment, the Signora Biche began to bay light notes of welcome, and raised herself up from her comfort-

---

* This order was obeyed. Lord McKenzie, the tender lover of the beautiful Barbarina, who had followed her from Venice to Berlin, was immediately on his arrival, banished from Prussia by the special command of the king, and taken to Hamburg; from thence he addressed some passionate letters to his beautiful beloved, which she, of course, never received, and which are preserved in the royal archives at Berlin. (See Schneider's "History of Operas.")

able position on the sofa. The king did not remark her, however; he was wholly occupied with Fredersdorf.

"How! do you say he is not married?"

"No, he has not married," said a plaintive voice from behind the door, "and he prays your majesty, of your great grace, to allow him to dedicate his whole life to his royal master, forgetting all other men and women." The king turned and saw his former master of ceremonies kneeling before the door, and his clasped hands stretched out imploringly before him.

Frederick gave a hearty peal of laughter, while Biche, raising herself with a joyful bark, sprang toward the kneeling penitent, and capered playfully about him; she appeared indeed to be licking the hand in which the sagacious baron held loosely a large piece of her favorite chocolate. At first, the king laughed heartily; then, as he remarked how tenderly Biche licked the hand of the baron, he shook his head thoughtfully. "I have had a false confidence in the true instinct of my little Biche; she seems, indeed, to welcome Pöllnitz joyfully; while a sharp bite in his calf is the only reception which his wicked and faithless heart deserves."

"Happily, sire, my heart is not lodged in my calves," said Pöllnitz. "The wise Biche knows that the heart of Pöllnitz is always in the same place, and that love to my king and master has alone brought me back to Berlin."

"Nonsense! A Pöllnitz can feel no other love than that which he cherishes for his own worthy person, and the purses of all others. Let him explain now, quickly and without circumlocution, if he really wishes my pardon, why, after going to Nurnberg to marry a bag of gold, containing a few millions, he has now returned to Berlin."

"Sire, without circumlocution, the bag of gold would not open for me, and would not scatter its treasures according to my necessities and desires."

"Ah! I comprehend. The beautiful Nurnberger had heard of your rare talent for scattering gold, and thought it wiser to lose a baron of the realm than to lose her millions."

"Yes, that's about it, sire."

"I begin to have a great respect for the wisdom of this woman," said Frederick, laughing. "I think she has a more

reliable instinct than my poor Biche, who, I see, still licks
your hands."

"Oh, Biche knows me better than any man," said Pöllnitz, tenderly patting the greyhound. "Biche knows that
my heart is filled with but one love—love to my king and
master. She knows that I have returned to lay myself as
she does, in all humility and self-abandonment, at the feet
of my royal Frederick, to receive either kicks or favors, as
he may see fit to bestow them; to be equally grateful for
the bones he may throw to me in his pity, as for the costly
viands he may grant in the magnanimity of his great soul."

"You are an absolute and unqualified fool," said the
king, laughing, "and if it was not against my conscience,
and unworthy of human nature, to engage a man as a perpetual buffoon, I would promote you to the office of court
fool. You might, at least, serve as an example to my cavaliers, by teaching them what they ought to avoid."

"I have merited this cruel contempt, this painful punishment from my royal master," said Pöllnitz. "I submit
silently. I will not, for a moment, seek to justify myself."

"You do well in that. You can make no defence. You
left my service faithlessly and heartlessly, with the hope of
marrying a fortune. The marriage failed, and you come
back with falsehood in your heart and on your lips, chatter-
ing about your love for my royal house. You are not
ashamed to liken yourself to a hound, and to howl even as
they do, in order that I may take you back into favor. Do
not suppose, for one moment, that I am deceived by these
professions—if you could have done better for yourself
elsewhere, you would not have returned to Berlin; that not
being the case, you creep back, and vow that love alone has
constrained you. Look you, Pöllnitz, I know you, I know
you fully. You can never deceive me; and, most assuredly,
I would not receive you again into my service, if I did not
look upon you as an old inventory of my house, an inheritance from my grandfather Frederick. I receive you, therefore, out of consideration for the dead kings in whose service
you were, and who amused themselves with your follies;
for their sakes I cannot allow you to hunger. Think not
that I will prepare you a bed of down, and give you gold to

waste in idleness. You must work for your living, even as
we all do. I grant you a pension, but you will perform your
old duty, as grand master of ceremonies. You understand
such nonsense better than I do. You were educated in a
good school, and studied etiquette from the foundation stone,
under Prussia's first king; and that you may not say we have
overlooked your great worth, I will lay yet another burden
upon your shoulders, and make you ' master of the wardrobe.'
It shall not be said of us, that nonsense and folly are neglected at our court; even these shall have their tribute.
You shall therefore be called ' Master of the Robes,' but I
counsel you, yes, I warn you, never to interfere with my
coats and shirts. You shall have no opportunity to make
a gold-embroidered monkey of me. Etiquette requires that
I must have a master of the robes, but I warn you to interest
yourself in all other things rather than in my toilet."

"All that your majesty condescends to say, is written in
letters of flame upon my heart."

"I would rather suppose upon your knees; they must indeed burn from this long penance. I have read you a lecture, à la façon of a village schoolmaster. You can rise, the
lecture is over."

Pöllnitz rose from his knees, and, straightening himself,
advanced before the king, and made one of those low, artistic
bows, which he understood to perfection. "When does your
majesty wish that I should enter upon my duties?"

"To-day—at this moment. Count Tessin, a special ambassador from Sweden, has just arrived. I wish to give him
a courtly reception. You will make the necessary arrangements. Enter at once upon the discharge of your functions."

"I suppose, sire, that my salary also commences so soon
as I begin the discharge of my duties?"

"I said nothing about a salary. I promised you a pension; and, not wishing to maintain you in absolute idleness,
I lay upon you these absurd and trifling duties."

"Shall I not, then, receive two pensions, if I discharge
the two functions?" said Pöllnitz, in a low voice.

"You are an out-and-out scoundrel," said Frederick,
"but I know all your tricks. I shall not follow my father's

example, who once asked you how much it required to maintain worthily a cavalier of rank, and you assured him that a hundred thousand thalers was not sufficient. I grant you a pension of two thousand thalers, and I tell you it must suffice to support you creditably. Woe to you, when you commence again your former most contemptible and miserable life! woe to you, when you again forget to distinguish between your own money and the money of others! I assure you that I will never again pay one of your debts. And in order that credulous men may not be so silly as to lend you money, I will make my wishes known by a printed order, and impose a tax of fifty thalers upon every man silly and bold enough to lend you money. Are you content with this, and will you enter my service upon these terms?"

"Yes, on any conditions which your majesty shall please to lay upon me. But when, in spite of this open declaration of your majesty, crazy people will still insist upon lending me money, you will admit, sire, in short, that it is not my debt, and I cannot be called upon for payment."

"I will take such precautions that no one will be foolish enough to lend you money. I will have it publicly announced that he who lends you money shall have no claim upon you, so that to lend you gold is to give you gold, and truly in such a way as to spare you even the trouble of thanks. I will have this trumpeted through every street. Are you still content?"

"Oh, sire, you show me in this the greatest earthly kindness; you make me completely irresponsible. Woe to the fools and lunatics who are mad enough to lend me money! From this time onward, I shall never know a weary or listless moment. I shall have always the cheering and inspiring occupation of winning the hearts of trusting and weak-minded dunces, and, by adroit sleight-of-hand, transferring the gold from their pockets to my own."

"You are incorrigible," said the king. "I doubt if all mankind are made after the image of God. I think many of the race resemble the devil, and I look upon you, Pöllnitz, as a tolerably successful portrait of his satanic majesty. I don't suppose you will be much discomposed by this opinion.

I imagine you look upon God and the devil in very much the same light."

"Oh, not so, your majesty; I am far too religious to fall into such errors."

"Yes, you are too religious; or, rather you have too many religions. To which, for example, do you now profess to belong?"

"Sire, I have become a Protestant."

"From conviction?"

"So long as I believed in the possibility of marrying several millions—yes, from conviction. These millions would have made me happy, and surely I might allow myself to become a Protestant in order to be happy."

"Once for all, how many times have you changed your religion?" said the king, thoughtfully.

"Oh, not very often, sire! I am forever zealously seeking after the true faith, and so long as I do not find that religion which makes me content with such things as I have, I am forced to change in justice to myself. In my childhood I was baptized and brought up a Lutheran, and I had nothing against it, and remained in that communion till I went to Rome; there I saw the Holy Father, the Pope, perform mass, and the solemn ceremony roused my devotional feelings to such a height that I became a Catholic immediately. This was, however, no change of religion. Up to this time I had not acted for myself; so the Catholic may be justly called my first faith."

"Yes, yes! that was about the time you stole your dying bride's diamonds and fled from France."

"Oh, your majesty, that is a wicked invention of my enemies, and utterly unfounded. If I had really stolen and sold those magnificent brilliants—worth half a million—from my dying love, it would have been sufficient to assure me a luxurious life, and I should not have found it imperative to become a Catholic."

"Ah, you confess, then, that you did not become a Catholic from conviction, but in order to obtain the favor of the cardinals and the Pope?"

"Nothing escapes the quick eye of your majesty, so I will not dare to defend myself. I came back to Berlin then,

a Catholic, and the ever-blessed king received me graciously.
He was a noble and a pious man, and my soul was seized with
a glowing desire to imitate him. I saw, indeed, how little I
had advanced on the path to glory by becoming a Catholic!
I made a bold resolve and entered the Reformed Church."

"And by this adroit move you obtained your object: you
became the favorite of my father the king. As he, unhappily, can show you no further favor, it is no longer prudent to
be a reformer, so you are again a Lutheran—from conviction!"

"Oh, all the world knows the great, exalted, and unprejudiced mind of our young king," said Pöllnitz. "It is to him
a matter of supreme indifference what religious sect a man
belongs to, so he adopts that faith which makes him a brave,
reliable, and serviceable subject of his king and his fatherland."

Frederick cast a dark and contemptuous glance at him.
"You are a miserable mocker and despiser of all holy things;
you belong to that large class who, not from convictions of
reason, but from worldly-mindedness and licentiousness, do
not believe in the Christian religion. Such men can never
be honest; they have, perhaps, from their childhood been
preached to, not to do evil from fear of hell-fire; and so soon
as they cease to believe in hell-fire, they give themselves up
to vice without remorse. You are one of these most miserable wretches; and I say to you, that you will at last suffer
the torments of the damned. I know there is a hell-fire, but
it can only be found in a man's conscience! Now go and
enter at once upon your duties; in two hours I will receive
Count Tessin in the palace at Berlin."

Pöllnitz made the three customary bows and left the room.
The king gazed after him contemptuously. "He is a finished scoundrel!" Then turning to Fredersdorf, who at
that moment entered the room, he said, "I believe Pöllnitz
would sell his mother if he was in want of money. You
have brought me back a charming fellow; I rejoice that
there are no more of the race; Pöllnitz has at least the fame
of being alone in his style. Is there any one else who asks
an audience?"

"Yes, sire, the antechamber is full, and every man de-

clares that his complaint can only be made personally to
your majesty. It will require much time to listen to all
these men, and would be, besides, a bad example. If your
majesty receives fifty men to-day, a hundred will demand
audience to-morrow; they must therefore be put aside;
I have advised them all to make their wishes known in
writing."

"Well, I think every man knows that is the common
mode of proceeding; as these people have not adopted it, it
is evident they prefer speaking to me. There are many
things which can be better said than written. A king has
no right to close his ear to his subjects. A ruler should
not resemble a framed and curtained picture of a god, only
on rare and solemn occasions to be stared and wondered at;
he must be to his people what the domestic altar and the
household god was to the Romans, to which they drew near
at all hours with consecrated hearts and pious memories.
Here they made known all their cares, their sorrows, and
their joys; here they found comfort and peace. I will
never withdraw myself from my subjects; no, I will be the
household god of my people, and will lend a willing ear to
all their prayers and complaints. Turn no man away, Fredersdorf; I will announce it publicly, that every man has the
right to appeal to me personally."

"My king is great and good," said Fredersdorf, sadly;
"every man but myself can offer his petition to your majesty and hope for grace; the king's ear is closed only to me;
to my entreaties he will not listen."

"Fredersdorf, you complain that I will not give my consent to your marriage. What would you? I love you too
well to give you up; but when you take a wife you will be
forever lost to me. A man cannot serve two masters, and I
will not divide your heart with this Mademoiselle Daum;
you must give it to me entire! Do not call me cruel, Fredersdorf; believe that I love you and cannot give you up."

"Oh, sire, I shall only truly belong to you in love and
gratitude, when you permit me to be happy and wed the
maiden I so fondly love."

"I will have no married private secretary, nor will I
have a married secretary of state," said the king, with a

dark frown. "Say not another word, Fredersdorf; put these thoughts away from you! My God, there are so many other things on which you could have set your heart! why must it be ever on a woman?"

"Because I love her passionately, your majesty."

"Ah, bah! do you not love other things with which you can console yourself? You are a scholar and an alchemist. Well, then, read Horace; exercise yourself in the art of making gold, and forget this Mademoiselle Daum, who, be it said, in confidence between us, has no other fascination than that she is rich. As to her wealth, that can have but little charm for *you*, who, without doubt, will soon have control of all the treasures of the world. By God's help, or the devil's, you will very soon, I suppose, discover the secret of making gold."

"He has, indeed, heard my conversation with Joseph," said Fredersdorf to himself, and ashamed and confused, he cast his eyes down before the laughing glance of the king.

"Read your Horace diligently," said Frederick—"you know he is also my favorite author; you shall learn one of his beautiful songs by heart, and repeat it to me."

The king walked up and down the room, and cast, from time to time, a piercing glance at Fredersdorf. He then repeated from Horace these two lines:

> "' Torment not your heart
> With the rich offering of a bleeding lamb.'"

"I see well," said Fredersdorf, completely confused, "I see well that your majesty knows—"

"That it is high time," said the king, interrupting him, "to go to Berlin; you do well to remind me of it. Order my carriage—I will be off at once."

CHAPTER V.

HOW THE PRINCESS ULRICA BECAME QUEEN OF SWEDEN.

PRINCESS ULRICA, the eldest of the two unmarried sisters of the king, paced her room with passionate steps. The king had just made the queen-mother a visit, and had commanded that his two sisters should be present at the interview.

Frederick was gay and talkative. He told them that the Signora Barbarina had arrived, and would appear that evening at the castle theatre. He invited his mother and the two princesses to be present. He requested them to make tasteful and becoming toilets, and to be bright and amiable at the ball and supper after the theatre. The king implored them both to be gay: the one, in order to show that she was neither angry nor jealous; the other, that she was proud and happy.

The curiosity of the two young girls was much excited, and they urged the king to explain his mysterious words. He informed them that Count Tessin, the Swedish ambassador, would be present at the ball; that he was sent to Berlin to select a wife for the prince royal of Sweden, or, rather, to receive one; the choice, it appeared, had been already made, as the count had asked the king if he might make proposals for the hand of the Princess Amelia, or if she were already promised in marriage. The king replied that Amelia was bound by no contract, and that proposals from Sweden would be graciously received.

"Be, therefore, lovely and attractive," said the king, placing his hand caressingly upon the rosy cheek of his little sister; "prove to the count that the intellectual brow of my sweet sister is fitted to wear a crown worthily."

The queen-mother glanced toward the window into which the Princess Ulrica had hastily withdrawn.

"And will your majesty really consent that the youngest of my daughters shall be first married?"

The king followed the glance of his mother, and saw the frowning brow and trembling lip of his sister. Frederick feared to increase the mortification of Ulrica, and seemed, therefore, not to observe her withdrawal.

"I think," said he, "your majesty was not older than Amelia when you married my father; and if the crown prince of Sweden wishes to marry Amelia, I see no reason why we should refuse him. Happily, we are not Jews, and our laws do not forbid the younger sister to marry first. To refuse the prince the hand of Amelia, or to offer him the hand of Ulrica, would indicate that we feared the latter might remain unsought. I think my lovely and talented sister does not deserve to be placed in such a mortifying position, and that her hand will be eagerly sought by other royal wooers."

"And, for myself, I am not at all anxious to marry," said Ulrica, throwing her head back proudly, and casting a half-contemptuous, half-pitiful look at Amelia. "I have no wish to marry. Truly, I have not seen many happy examples of wedded life in our family. All my sisters are unhappy, and I see no reason why I should tread the same thorny path."

The king smiled. "I see the little Ulrica shares my aversion to wedded life, but we cannot expect, dearest, that all the world should be equally wise. We will, therefore, allow our foolish sister Amelia to wed, and run away from us. This marriage will cost her anxiety and sorrow; she must not only place her little feet in the land of reindeers, bears, and eternal snows, but she must also be baptized and adopt a new religion. Let us thank God, then, that the prince has had the caprice to pass you by and choose Amelia, who, I can see, is resolved to be married. We will, therefore, leave the foolish child to her fate."

It was Frederick's intention, by these light jests, to comfort his sister Ulrica, and give her time to collect herself. He did not remark that his words had a most painful effect upon his younger sister, and that she became deadly pale as he said she must change her faith in order to become princess royal of Sweden.

The proud queen-mother had also received this announcement angrily. "I think, sire," said she, "that the daughter of William the Second, and the sister of the King of Prussia, might be allowed to remain true to the faith of her fathers."

"Madame," said the king, bowing reverentially, "the question is not, I am sorry to say, as to Amelia's father or brother; she will be the mother of sons, who, according to the law of the land, must be brought up in the religion of their father. You see, then, that if this marriage takes place, one of the two contracting parties must yield; and, it appears to me, that is the calling and the duty of the woman."

"Oh, yes," said the queen bitterly, "you have been educated in too good a school, and are too thoroughly a Hohenzollern, not to believe in the complete self-renunciation of women. At this court, women have only to obey."

"Nevertheless, the women do rule over us; and even when we appear to command, we are submissive and obedient," said the king, as he kissed his mother's hand and withdrew.

The three ladies also retired to their own rooms immediately. Each one was too much occupied with her own thoughts to bear the presence of another.

And now, being alone, the Princess Ulrica found it no longer necessary to retain the smiles which she had so long and with such mighty effort forced to play upon her lips; every pulse was beating with glowing rage, and she gave free course to her scorn.

Her younger sister, this little maiden of eighteen years, was to be married, to wed a future king; while she, the eldest, now two-and-twenty, remained unchosen! And it was not her own disinclination nor the will of the king which led to this shameful result; no! the Swedish ambassador came not to seek her hand, but that of her sister! She, the elder, was scorned—set aside. The king might truthfully say there was no law of the land which forbade the marriage of the younger sister before the elder; but there was a law of custom and of propriety, and this law was trampled upon.

As Ulrica thought over these things, she rose from her seat with one wild spring. On entering the room she had been completely overcome, and, with trembling knees, she had fallen upon the divan. She stood now, however, like a tigress prepared for attack, and looking for the enemy she was resolved to slay. The raging, stormy blood of the Hohenzollerns was aroused. The energy and pride of her mother glowed with feverish pulses in her bosom. She would have been happy to find an enemy opposed to her, the waves of passion rushing through her veins might have been assuaged; but she was alone, entirely alone, and had no other enemy to overcome than herself. She must, then, declare war against her own evil heart. With wild steps she rushed to the glass, and scrutinizingly and fiercely examined her own image. Her eye was cold, searching, and stern. Yes, she would prove herself; she would know if it were any thing in her own outward appearance which led the Swedish ambassador to choose her sister rather than herself.

"It is true, Amelia is more beautiful, in the common acceptation of the word; her eyes are larger, her cheek rosier, her smile more fresh and youthful, and her small but graceful figure is at the same time childlike and voluptuous. She would make an enchanting shepherdess, but is not fitted to be a queen. She has no majesty, no presence. She has not by nature that imposing gravity, which is the gift of Providence, and cannot be acquired, and without which the queen is sometimes forgotten in the woman. Amelia can never attain that eternal calm, that exalted composure, which checks all approach to familiarity, and which, by an almost imperceptible pressure of the hand and a light smile, bestows more happiness and a more liberal reward than the most impassioned tenderness and the warmest caresses of a commonplace woman. No, Amelia could never make a complete queen, she can only be a beautiful woman; while I—I know that I am less lovely, but I feel that I am born to rule. I have the grace and figure of a queen—yes, I have the soul of a queen! I would understand how to be imposing, and, at the same time, to obtain the love of my people, not from any weak thirst for love, but from a queenly ambition. But I am set aside, and Amelia will be a queen; my fate will be that of my elder sisters, I shall wed a poor margrave, or paltry duke, and may indeed thank God if I am not an old maiden princess, with a small pension."

She stamped wildly upon the floor, and paced the room with hasty steps. Suddenly she grew calmer, her brow, which had been overshadowed by dark clouds, cleared, and a faint smile played upon those lips which a moment before had been compressed by passion.

"After all," she said, "the formal demand for the hand of Amelia has not yet been made; perhaps the ambassador has mistaken my name for that of Amelia, and as he has made no direct proposition, I am convinced he wishes to make some observations before deciding. Now, if the result of this examination should prove to him that Amelia is not fitted to be the wife of his prince, and if Amelia herself— I thought I saw that she turned pale as the king spoke of abandoning her faith; and when she left the room, despair and misery were written upon that face which should have glowed with pride and triumph. Ah, I see land!" said Ulrica, breathing freely and sinking comfortably upon the divan, "I am no longer hopelessly shipwrecked; I have found a plank, which may perhaps save me. Let me consider calmly,"—and, as if Fate itself were playing into her hand, the door opened and Amelia entered.

One glance was sufficient to show Ulrica that she was not deceived, and that this important event had brought no joy to poor Amelia. The lovely eyes of the princess were red with weeping; and the soft lips, so generally and gladly given to gay chat and merry laughter, were now expressive of silent anguish. Ulrica saw all this, and laid her plans accordingly. In place of receiving Amelia coldly and repulsively, which but a few moments before she would have done, she sprang to meet her with every sign of heart-felt love; the little maiden threw herself weeping convulsively into her sister's arms, and was pressed closely and tenderly to her bosom.

"Tears!" said Ulrica lovingly, as she drew her sister to the sofa and pressed her down upon the soft pillows; "you weep, and yet a splendid future is this day secured to you!"

Amelia sobbed yet more loudly and pressed her tear-stained face more closely to the bosom of her sister. Ulrica looked down with a mixture of curiosity and triumph; she could not understand these tears; but she had a secret satisfaction in seeing the person she most envied weeping so bitterly.

"How is this? are you not happy to be a queen?"

Amelia raised her face hastily and sobbed out: "No! I am not pleased to be an apostate, to perjure myself! I am not content to deny my faith in order to buy a miserable earthly crown! I have sworn to be true to my God and my faith, and now I am commanded to lay it aside like a perishable robe, and take another in exchange."

"Ah, is it that?" said Ulrica, with a tone of contempt she could scarcely control; "you fear this bold step by which your poor innocent soul may be compromised."

"I will remain true to the belief in which I have been educated, and to which I have dedicated myself at the altar!" cried Amelia, bursting again into tears.

"It is easy to see that but a short time only has elapsed since you took these vows upon you. You have all the fanaticism of a new convert. How would our blessed father rejoice if he could see you now!"

"He would not force me to deny my religion; he would not, for the sake of outward splendor, endanger my soul's salvation. Oh! it is harsh and cruel of my brother to treat me as a piece of merchandise; he asks not whether my heart or principles can conscientiously take part in his ambitious plans."

Ulrica cast a long and piercing glance upon her sister. She would gladly have searched to the bottom of her soul; she wished to know if this fierce opposition to the marriage was the result of love to the faith of her fathers.

"And you are not ambitious? you are not excited by the thought of being a queen, of marrying a man who will fill a place in the world's history?"

The young girl raised her eyes in amazement, and her tears ceased to flow.

"What has a woman to do with the world's history?" she said; "think you I care to be named as the wife of a king of Sweden? It is a sad, unhappy fate to be a princess. We are sold to him who makes the largest offer and the most favorable conditions. Well, let it be so; it is the fate of all princesses; it is for this we are educated, and must bow

humbly to the yoke; but liberty of conscience should be at
least allowed us, freedom of thought, the poor consolation of
worshipping God in the manner we prefer, and of seeking
help and protection in the arms of that religion we believe
in and love."

"One can be faithful to God even when unfaithful to
their first faith," said Ulrica, who began already to make
excuses to herself for the change of religion she contemplated.

"That is not in my power!" cried Amelia passionately.
"I cling to the religion of my house, and I should tremble
before the wrath of God if I gave it up."

"After all, it is but a small and unimportant difference
between the Reformed and Lutheran Churches," said Ulrica,
much excited, and entirely forgetting that the question had
as yet no relation to herself. "One can be as pious a Christian in the Reformed Church as in the Lutheran."

"Not I; it is not in my power," said Amelia, with the
wilfulness of a spoiled child not accustomed to opposition.
"I will not become a Lutheran. A Pöllnitz may change
his faith, but not the daughter of Frederick William. Did
not the king with indignation and contempt relate to us
how Pöllnitz had again changed his religion and become a
Protestant? Did we not laugh heartily, and in our hearts
despise the dishonorable man? I will not place myself in
such a position."

"Then, my sister, there will be stormy times and stern
strife in our household: the bitter scenes of earlier days
will be renewed. Our royal brother is not less resolute than
our stern father. I fear that his brothers and sisters are
nothing more to him than useful instruments in this great
state machine, and they must bow themselves unquestion-
ingly to his commands."

"Yes, I feel this; I see it clearly," said Amelia, trembling; "and for this reason, dear sister, you must stand by
me and help me. I swear to you that I will not become a
Lutheran."

"Is that your unchangeable resolution?"

"Yes, unchangeable."

"Well, if that is so, I will give you my counsel."

"Speak, speak quickly," said Amelia, breathlessly, and throwing her arms around the slender waist of her sister, she laid her head trustingly upon her shoulder.

"Firstly, the Swedish ambassador has not made a formal demand for your hand; that probably proves that he will first examine and observe you closely, to see if you are suited to be the wife of the prince royal. We have still, therefore, a short delay, which, if wisely used, may conduct you to the desired goal. But, Amelia, prove yourself once more; ask counsel again of your heart and conscience, before you make a final resolve. I will not have you complain of me in future, and say that my foolish and guilty counsel lost you the throne of Sweden."

"Oh, fear not, my beloved sister. I will not be queen of Sweden at the cost of my immortal soul."

"You will not, then, reproach me, Amelia?"

"Never."

"Listen, then. From this moment lay a mask upon your face; that is to say, assume a proud, rude, overbearing tone to all around you—toward your friends, your servants, the court circle, yes, even toward the members of your family. Particularly in the presence of this Swedish ambassador, show yourself to be a capricious, nervous, and haughty princess, who scarcely thinks it worth the trouble to speak a word, or give a friendly glance, to a man in his position. When you speak to him and he attempts to answer, cut short his replies, and command him to be silent; if he strives to win your favor by the most respectful civility, let an unmistakable expression of contempt be written upon your face, and let that be your only answer. Regulate your conduct for a few days by these rules, and I am convinced you will attain your object."

"Yes, yes! I understand, I understand!" said the young girl, clapping her little white hands, and looking up joyously. "I shall, by my pride and passion, freeze the words in the mouth of my lord ambassador, so that the decisive word cannot find utterance. Oh! this will be a precious comedy, my sweet sister, and I promise you to carry out my *rôle* of heroine to perfection. Oh, I thank you! I thank you! I am indeed happy to have found so wise a sister, so

4

brave a comrade in arms, while surrounded with such perils!"

"She would not have it otherwise," said Ulrica, laconically, as she found herself again alone. "If she is without ambition, so much the worse for her—so much the better for me! And now, it is high time to think of my toilet—that is the most important consideration. To-day I must be not only amiable, but lovely. To-day I will appear an innocent and unpretending maiden."

With a mocking smile she entered her boudoir, and called her attendants.

CHAPTER VI.

THE TEMPTER.

PRINCESS ULRICA was earnestly occupied with considerations of her toilet. Amelia had returned to her room, musing and thoughtful.

There were difficulties in the way of the new *rôle* she had resolved to play, and by which she expected to deceive the world. She stood for a moment before the door of her dressing-room, and listened to the voices of her attendants, who were gayly laughing and talking. It was her custom to join them, and take a ready part in their merry sports and jests. She must now, however, deny herself, and put a guard over her heart and lips. Accordingly, with a dark frown on her brow and tightly-compressed lips, she entered the room in which her maids were at that moment arranging her ball toilet for the evening.

"It seems to me that your loud talking is most unseemly," said Amelia, in a tone so haughty, so passionate, that the smiles of the two young girls vanished in clouds. "I will be obliged to you if you will complete your work noiselessly, and reserve your folly till you have left my room! And what is that, Mademoiselle Félicien? for what purpose have you prepared these flowers, which I see lying upon your table?"

"Your royal highness, these flowers are for your coiffure, and these bouquets are intended to festoon your dress."

"How dare you allow yourself to decide upon my toilet, mademoiselle?"

"I have not dared," said Félicien, tremblingly; "your royal highness ordered moss roses for your hair, and bouquets of the same for your bosom and your robe."

"It appears to me," said Amelia, imperiously, "that to contradict me, and at the same time assert that which is false, is, to say the least, unbecoming your position. I am not inclined to appear in the toilet of a gardener's daughter. To prove this, I will throw these flowers, which you dare to assert I ordered, from the window; with their strong odor they poison the air."

With a cruel hand, she gathered up the lovely roses, and hastened to the window. "Look, mademoiselle, these are the flowers which you undertook to prepare for my hair," said Amelia, with well-assumed scorn, as she threw the bouquet into the garden which surrounded the castle of Monbijou; "look, mademoiselle."

Suddenly the princess uttered a low cry, and looked, blushing painfully, into the garden. In her haste, she had not remarked that two gentlemen, at that moment, crossed the great court which led to the principal door of the castle; and the flowers which she had so scornfully rejected, had struck the younger and taller of the gentlemen exactly in the face. He stood completely amazed, and looked questioningly at the window from which this curious bomb had fallen. His companion, however, laughed aloud, and made a profound bow to the princess, who still stood, blushing and embarrassed, at the window.

"From this hour I believe in the legend of the Fairy of the Roses," said the elder of the two gentlemen, who was indeed no other than Baron Pöllnitz. "Yes, princess, I believe fully, and I would not be at all astonished if your highness should at this moment flutter from the window in a chariot drawn by doves, and cast another shower of blossoms in the face of my friend."

The princess had found time to recover herself, and to remember the haughty part she was determined to play.

"I hope, baron," she said, sternly, "you will not allow yourself to suppose it was my purpose to throw those roses either to your companion or yourself? I wished only to get rid of them."

She shut the window rudely and noisily, and commanded her attendants to complete her toilet at once. She seated herself sternly before the glass, and ordered her French maid to cover her head with jewels and ribbons.

The two gentlemen still stood in the garden, in earnest conversation.

"This is assuredly an auspicious omen, my friend," said Pöllnitz to the young officer, who was gazing musingly at the roses he held in his hand. He had raised his eyes from the flowers to the window at which the lovely form of the princess had, for a few moments, appeared.

"Alas!" said he, sighing, and gazing afar off; "she is so wonderfully beautiful—so lovely; and she is a princess!"

Pöllnitz laughed heartily. "One might think that you regretted that fact! Listen to me, my young friend; stand no longer here, in a dream. Come, in place of entering the castle immediately, to pay our respects to the queen-mother, we will take a walk through the garden, that you may allay your raptures and recover your reason."

He took the arm of the young man, and drew him into a shady, private pathway.

"Now, my dear friend, listen to me, and lay to heart all that I say to you. Accident, or, if you prefer it, Fate brought us together. After all, it seems indeed more than an accident. I had just returned to Berlin, and was about to pay my respects to the queen-mother, when I met you, who at the same time seek an audience, in order to commend yourself to her royal protection. You bear a letter of commendation from my old friend, Count Lottum. All this, of course, excites my curiosity. I ask your name, and learn, to my astonishment, that you are young Von Trenck, the son of the woman who was my first love, and who made me most unhappy by not returning my passion. I assure you, it produces a singular sensation to meet so unexpectedly the son of a first love, whose father, alas! you have not the happiness to be. I feel already that I am prepared to love you as foolishly as I once loved your fair mother."

"I will not, like my mother, reject your vows," said the young officer, smiling, and extending his hand to Pöllnitz.

"I hoped as much," said Pöllnitz; "you shall find a fond father in me, and even to-day I will commence my parental duties. In the first place, what brings you here?"

"To make my fortune—to become a general, or field-marshal, if possible," said the young man, laughing.

"How old are you?"

"I am nineteen."

"You wear the uniform of an officer of the life-guard; the king has, therefore, already promoted you?"

"I was a cadet but eight days," said Trenck, proudly. "My step-father, Count Lottum, came with me from Dant-zic, and presented me to the king. His majesty received me graciously, and remembered well that I had received, at the examination at Königsberg, the first prize from his hand."

"Go on, go on," said Pöllnitz; "you see I am all ear, and I must know your present position in order to be useful to you."

"The king, as I have said, received me graciously, even kindly; he made me a cadet in his cavalry corps, and three weeks after, I was summoned before him; he had heard something of my wonderful memory, and he wished to prove me."

"Well, how did you stand the proof?"

"I stood with the king at the window, and he called over to me quickly the names of fifty soldiers who were standing in the court below, pointing to each man as he called his name. I then repeated to him every name in the same suc-cession, but backward."

"A wonderful memory, indeed," said Pöllnitz, taking a pinch of Spanish snuff; "a terrible memory, which would make me shudder if I were your sweetheart!"

"And why?" said the young officer.

"Because you would hold ever in remembrance all her caprices and all her oaths, and one day, when she no longer loved you, she would be held to a strict account. Well, did the king subject you to further proof?"

"Yes; he gave me the material for two letters, which I dictated at the same time to his secretaries, one in French and one in Latin. He then commanded me to draw the plan of the Hare Meadow, and I did so."

"Was he pleased?"

"He made me cornet of the guard," said Trenck, modestly avoiding a more direct answer.

"I see you are in high favor: in three weeks you are promoted from cadet to lieutenant! quick advancement, which the king, no doubt, signalized by some other act of grace?"

"He sent me two horses from his stable, and when I came to thank him, he gave me a purse containing two hundred 'Fredericks.'"

Pöllnitz gave a spring backward. "Thunder! you are indeed in favor! the king gives you presents! Ah, my young friend, I would protect you, but it seems you can patronize me. The king has never made me a present. And what do you desire to-day of the queen-mother?"

"As I am now a lieutenant, I belong to the court circle, and must take part in the court festivals. So the king commanded me to pay my respects to the queen-mother."

"Ah, the king ordered that?" said Pöllnitz; "truly, young man, the king must destine you for great things— he overloads you with favors. You will make a glittering career, provided you are wise enough to escape the shoals and quicksands in your way. I can tell you, there will be adroit and willing hands ready to cast you down; those who are in favor at court have always bitter enemies."

"Yes, I am aware that I have enemies," said Trenck; "more than once I have already been charged with being a drunkard and a rioter; but the king, happily, only laughed at the accusations."

"He is really in high favor, and I would do well to secure his friendship," thought Pöllnitz; "the king will also be pleased with me if I am kind to him." He held out his hand to the young officer, and said, with fatherly tenderness: "From this time onward, when your enemies shall please to attack you, they shall not find you alone; they will find me a friend ever at your side. You are the son of the only woman I ever loved—I will cherish you in my heart as my first-born!"

"And I receive you as my father with my whole heart," said Trenck; "be my father, my friend, and my counsellor."

"The court is a dangerous and slippery stage, upon which a young and inexperienced man may lightly slip, unless held up by a strong arm. Many will hate you because you are in favor, and the hate of many is like the sting of hornets: one sting is not fatal, but a general attack sometimes brings death. Make use, therefore, of your sunshine, and fix yourself strongly in an immovable position."

"The great question is, what shall be my first step to secure it?"

"How! you ask that question, and you are nineteen years old, six feet high, have a handsome face, a splendid figure, an old, renowned name, and are graciously received at court? Ah! youngster, I have seen many arrive at the highest honors and distinctions, who did not possess half your glittering qualities. If you use the right means at the right time, you cannot fail of success."

"What do you consider the best means?"

"The admiration and favor of women! You must gain the love of powerful and influential women. Oh, you are terrified, and your brow is clouded! perhaps, unhappily, you are already in love?"

"No!" said Frederick von Trenck, violently. "I have never been in love. I dare say more than that: I have never kissed the lips of a woman."

Pöllnitz gazed at him with an expression of indescribable amazement. "How!" said he; "you are nineteen, and assert that you have never embraced a woman?" He gave a mocking and cynical laugh.

"Ordinary women have always excited my disgust," said the young officer, simply; "and until this day I have never seen a woman who resembled my ideal."

"So, then, the woman with whom you will now become enamored will receive your first tender vows?"

"Yes, even so."

"And you wear the uniform of the life-guard—you are a lieutenant!" cried Pöllnitz with tragical pathos, and extending his arms toward heaven. "But how?—what did you say?—that until to-day you had seen no woman who approached your ideal?"

"I said that."

"And to-day—?"

"Well, it seems to me, we have both seen an angel to-day!—an angel, whom you have wronged, in giving her the common name of fairy."

"Aha! the Princess Amelia," said Pöllnitz. "You will love this young maiden, my friend."

"Then, indeed, shall I be most unhappy! She is a royal princess, and my love must ever be unrequited."

"Who told you that? who told you that this little Amelia was only a princess? I tell you she is a young girl with a heart of fire. Try to awake her—she only sleeps! A happy event has already greeted you. The princess has fixed your enraptured gaze upon her lovely form, by throwing or rather shooting roses at you. Perhaps the god of Love has hidden his arrow in a rose. You thought Amelia had only pelted your cheek with roses, but the arrow has entered your soul. Try your luck, young man; gain the love of the king's favorite sister, and you will be all-powerful."

The young officer looked at him with confused and misty eyes.

"You do not dare to suggest," murmured he, "that—"

"I dare to say," cried Pöllnitz, interrupting him, "that you are in favor with the brother; why may you not also gain the sister's good graces? I say further, that I will assist you, and I will ever be at your side, as a loving friend and a sagacious counsellor."

"Do you know, baron, that your wild words open a future to my view before which my brain and heart are reeling? How shall I dare to love a princess, and seek her love in return?"

"As to the first point, I think you have already dared. As to the second, I think your rare beauty and wondrous accomplishments might justify such pretensions."

"You know I never can become the husband of a princess."

"You are right," said Pöllnitz, laughing aloud; "you

are as innocent as a girl of sixteen! you have this moment
fallen headlong in love, and begin at once to think of the
possibility of marriage, as if love had no other refuge than
marriage, and yet I think I have read that the god of Love
and the god of Hymen are rarely seen together, though
brothers; in point of fact, they despise and flee from each
other. But after all, young man, if your love is virtuous and
requires the priest's blessing, I think that is possible. Only
a few years since the widowed margravine, the aunt of the
king, married the Count Hoditz. What the king's aunt accomplished, might be possible to the king's sister."

"Silence, silence!" murmured Frederick von Trenck;
"your wild words cloud my understanding like the breath of
opium; they make me mad, drunk. You stand near me like
the tempter, showing to my bewildered eyes more than all
the treasures of this world, and saying, 'All these things will
I give thee'; but alas! I am not the Messiah. I have not
the courage to cast down and trample under foot your devil-
ish temptations. My whole soul springs out to meet them,
and shouts for joy. Oh, sir, what have you done? You have
aroused my youth, my ambition, my passion; you have filled
my veins with fire, and I am drunk with the sweet but deadly
poison you have poured into my ears."

"I have assured you that I will be your father. I will
lead you, and at the right moment I will point out the obstacles against which your inexperienced feet might stumble," said Pöllnitz.

The stony-hearted and egotistical old courtier felt not the
least pity for this poor young man into whose ear, as Trenck
had well said, he was pouring this fatal poison. Frederick
von Trenck, the favorite of the king, was nothing more to
him than a ladder by which he hoped to mount. He took
the arm of the young officer and endeavored to soothe him
with cool and moderate words, exhorting him to be quiet and
reasonable. They turned their steps toward the castle, in
order to pay their respects to the queen-mother. The hour
of audience was over, and the two gentlemen lounged arm
in arm down the street.

"Let us go toward the palace," said Pöllnitz. "I think
we will behold a rare spectacle, a crowd of old wigs who have

disguised themselves as *savans*. To-day, the first sitting
of the Academy of Arts and Sciences takes place, and the
celebrated President Maupertius will open the meeting in
the name of the king. This is exactly the time for the
renowned worthies to leave the castle. Let us go and witness this comical show."

The two gentlemen found it impossible to carry out their
plans. A mighty crowd of men advanced upon them at this
moment, and compelled them to stand still. Every face in
the vast assemblage was expectant. Certainly some rare
exhibition was to be seen in the circle which the crowd had
left open in their midst. There were merry laughing and
jesting and questioning amongst each other, as to what all
this could mean, and what proclamation that could be which
the drummer had just read in the palace garden.

"It will be repeated here in a moment," said a voice from
th' crowd, which increased every moment, and in whose
fierce waves Pöllnitz and Trenck were forcibly swallowed up.
Pressed, pushed onward by powerful arms, resistance utterly
in vain, the two companions found themselves at the same
moment in the open space just as the drummer broke into the
circle, and, playing his drumsticks with powerful and zealous hands, he called the crowd to order.

The drum overpowered the wild outcries and rude laughter of the vast assemblage, and soon silenced them completely. Every man held his breath to hear what the public crier,
who had spoken so much to the purpose by his drum, had
now to declare by word of mouth. He drew from his pocket
a large document sealed with the state seal, and took advantage of the general quiet to read the formal introductory to
all such proclamations: "We, Frederick, King of Prussia,"
etc., etc.

On coming to the throne, Frederick had abolished all that
long and absurd list of titles and dignities which had heretofore adorned the royal declarations. Even that highest of all
titles, "King by the grace of God," had Frederick the Second
set aside. He declared that, in saying King of Prussia, all
was said. His father had called himself King of Prussia, by
the grace of God; he, therefore, would call himself simply
the King of Prussia, and if he did not boast of God's grace,

it was because he would prove by deeds, not words, that he possessed it.

After this little digression we will return to our drummer, who now began to read, or rather to cry out the command of the king.

"We, Frederick, King of Prussia, order and command that no one of our subjects shall, under any circumstances, lend gold to our master of ceremonies, whom we have again taken into our service, or assist him in any way to borrow money. Whoever, therefore, shall, in despite of this proclamation, lend money to said Baron Pöllnitz, must bear the consequences; they shall make no demand for repayment, and the case shall not be considered in court. Whosoever shall disobey this command, shall pay a fine of fifty thalers, or suffer fifteen days' imprisonment."

A wild shout of laughter from the entire assembly was the reply to this proclamation, in which the worldly-wise Pöllnitz joined heartily, while his young companion had not the courage to raise his eyes from the ground.

"The old courtier will burst with rage," said a gay voice from the crowd.

"He is a desperate borrower," cried another.

"He has richly deserved this public shame and humiliation from the king," said another.

"And you call this a humiliation, a merited punishment!" cried Pöllnitz. "Why, my good friends, can you not see that this is an honor which the king shows to his old and faithful servant? Do you not know that by this proclamation he places Baron Pöllnitz exactly on the same footing with the princes of the blood, with the prince royal?"

"How is that? explain that to us," cried a hundred voices in a breath.

"Well, it is very simple. Has not the king recently renewed the law which forbids, under pain of heavy punishment, the princes of the blood to borrow money? Is not this law printed in our journals, and made public in our collections of laws?"

"Yes, yes! so it is," said many voices simultaneously.

"Well, certainly, our exalted sovereign, who loves his

royal brothers so warmly, would not have cast shame upon their honor. Certainly he would not have wished to humiliate them, and has not done so. The king, as you must now plainly perceive, has acted toward Baron Pöllnitz precisely as he has done to his brothers."

"And that is, without doubt, a great honor for him," cried many voices. No one guessed the name of the speaker who was so fortunately at hand to defend the honor of the master of ceremonies. A general murmur of applause was heard, and even the public crier stood still and listened to the eloquent unknown speaker, and forgot for a while to hurry off to the next street-corner and proclaim the royal mandate.

"Besides, this law is 'sans conséquence,' as we are accustomed to say," said Pöllnitz. "Who would not, in spite of the law, lend our princes gold if they had need of it? And who has right to take offence if the state refuses to pay the debts which the princes make as private persons? The baron occupies precisely the same position. The king, who has honored the newly returned baron with two highly important trusts, master of ceremonies and master of the robes, will frighten his rather lavish old friend from making debts. He chooses, therefore, the same means by which he seeks to restrain his royal brothers, and forbids all persons to lend gold to Pöllnitz: as he cannot well place this edict in the laws of the land, he is obliged to make it known by the drummer. And now," said the speaker, who saw plainly the favorable impression which his little oration had made—"and now, best of friends, I pray you to make way and allow me to pass through the crowd; I must go at once to the palace to thank his majesty for the special grace and distinction which he has showered upon me to-day. I, myself, am Baron Pöllnitz!"

An outcry of amazement burst from the lips of hundreds, and all who stood near Pöllnitz stepped aside reverentially, in order to give place to the distinguished gentleman who was treated by the king exactly as if he were a prince of the blood. Pöllnitz stepped with a friendly smile through the narrow way thus opened for him, and greeted, with his cool, impertinent manner those who respectfully stood back.

"I think I have given the king a Roland for his Oliver," he said to himself. "I have broken the point from the arrow which was aimed at me, and it glanced from my bosom without wounding me. Public opinion will be on my side from this time, and that which was intended for my shame has crowned me with honor. It was, nevertheless, a harsh and cruel act, for which I will one day hold a reckoning with Frederick. Ah, King Frederick! King Frederick! I shall not forget, and I will have my revenge; my cards are also well arranged, and I hold important trumps. I will wait yet a little while upon our lovelorn shepherd, this innocent and tender Trenck, who is in a dangerous way about the little princess."

Pöllnitz waited for Trenck, who had with difficulty forced his way through the crowd and hastened after him.

<hr>

CHAPTER VII.

THE FIRST INTERVIEW.

THE ball at the palace was opened. The two queens and the princesses had just entered the great saloon, in order to receive the respectful greetings of the ladies of the court; while the king, in an adjoining room, was surrounded by the gentlemen. A glittering circle of lovely women, adorned with diamonds and other rich gems, stood on each side of the room, each one patiently awaiting the moment when the queens should pass before her, and she might have the honor of bowing almost to the earth under the glance of the royal eye.

According to etiquette, Queen Elizabeth Christine, who, notwithstanding her modest and retired existence, was the reigning sovereign, should have made the grand tour alone, and received the first congratulations of the court; but this unhappy, shrinking woman, had never found the courage to assume the rights or privileges which belonged to her as wife of the king. She who was denied the highest and holiest of all distinctions, the first place in the heart of her husband, cared nothing for these pitiful and outward advantages. Elizabeth had to-day, as usual, with a soft smile, given precedence to the queen-mother, Sophia Dorothea, who was ever thirsting to show that she held the first place at her son's court, and who, delighted to surround herself with all the accessories of pomp and power, was ever ready to use her prerogative. With a proud and erect head, and an almost contemptuous smile, she walked slowly around the circle of high-born dames, who bowed humbly before this representative of royalty. Behind her came the reigning queen, between the two princesses, who now and then gave special and cordial greetings to their personal friends as they passed. Elizabeth Christine saw this and sighed bitterly. She had no personal friend to grace with a loving greeting. No man saw any thing else in her than a sovereign by sufferance, a woman *sans conséquence*, a powerless queen and unbeloved wife. She had never had a friend into whose sympathetic and silent bosom she could pour out her griefs. She was alone, so entirely alone and lonely, that the heavy sighs and complaints dwelling in her heart were ever reverberating in her ears because of the surrounding silence. And now, as she made the grand tour with the two princesses, no one seemed to see her; she was regarded as the statue of a queen, richly dressed and decked with costly lace and jewels, but only a picture: yet this picture had a soul and a heart of fire—it was a woman, a wife, who loved and who endured.

Suddenly she trembled; a light, like the glory of sunshine, flashed in her eyes, and a soft rosy blush spread over her fair cheek. The king had entered the room; yes, he was there in all his beauty, his majesty, his power; Elizabeth felt that the world was bright, her blood was rushing madly through her veins, her heart was beating as stormily as that of an impassioned young girl. Oh, it might be that the eye of the king—that glowing, wondrous eye—might even by accident rest upon her; it might be that Frederick would be touched by her patient endurance, her silent resignation, and give her one friendly word. She had been four years a queen, for four years this title had been a crown of thorns; during all this weary time her husband had not vouchsafed to her poor heart, sick unto death, one single sympathetic word, one affectionate glance; he sat by her side at the table during the court festivals; he had from time to time, at the balls and masquerades, opened the dance with her; never, however, since that day on which he had printed the first kiss upon her lips, never had he spoken to her; since that moment she was to him the picture of a queen, the empty form of a woman.* But Queen Elizabeth would not despair. Hope was her motto. A day might come when he would speak to her, when he would forget that she had been forced upon him as his wife, a day when his heart might be touched by her grief, her silent and tearless love. Every meeting with Frederick was to this poor queen a time of hope, of joyful expectation; this alone sustained her, this gave her strength silently, even smilingly, to draw her royal robe over her bleeding heart.

And now the king drew near, surrounded by the princesses and the queen-mother, to whom he gave his hand with an expression of reverence and filial love. He then bowed silently and indifferently to his wife, and gave a merry greeting to his two sisters.

"Ladies," said he, in a full, rich voice, "allow me to present to you and my court my brother, the Prince Augustus William; he is now placed before you in a new and more distinguished light." He took the hand of his brother and led him to the queen-mother. "I introduce your son to you; he will be from this day onward, if it so please you, also your grandson."

* The king never spoke to his wife, but his manner toward her was considerate and respectful; no one dared to fail in the slightest mark of courtly observance toward Elizabeth—this the king sternly exacted. Only once did the king address her. During the seventh year of their marriage, the queen, by an unhappy accident, had seriously injured her foot; this was a short time before her birthday, which event was always celebrated with great pomp and ceremony, the king honoring the *fête* with his presence. On this occasion he came as usual, but in place of the distant and silent bow with which he usually greeted her, he drew near, gave her his hand, and said with kindly sympathy, "I sincerely hope that your majesty has recovered from your accident." A general surprise was pictured in the faces of all present—but the poor queen was so overcome by this unexpected happiness, she had no power to reply, she bowed silently. The king frowned and turned from her. Since that day, the happiness of which she had bought with an injured foot, the king had not spoken to her.

"How is that, your majesty? I confess you have brought about many seemingly impossible things; but I think it is beyond your power to make Augustus at the same time both my son and my grandson."

"Ah, mother, if I make him my son, will he not be of necessity, your grandson? I appoint him my successor; in so doing, I declare him my son. Embrace him, therefore, your majesty, and be the first to greet him by his new title. Embrace the Prince of Prussia, my successor."

"I obey," said the queen, "I obey," and she cast her arms affectionately around her son. "I pray God that this title of 'Prince of Prussia,' which it has pleased your majesty to lend him, may be long and honorably worn."

The prince bowed low before his mother, who tenderly kissed his brow, then whispered, "Oh, mother, pray rather that God may soon release me from this burden."

"How!" cried the queen threateningly, "you have then a strong desire to be king? Has your vaulting ambition made you forget that to wish to be king is, at the same time, to wish the death of your brother?"

The prince smiled sadly.

"Mother, I would lay aside this rank of Prince of Prussia, not because I wish to mount the throne, but I would fain lie down in the cold and quiet grave."

"Are you always so sad, so hopeless, my son—even now, upon this day of proud distinction for you? To-day you take your place as Prince of Prussia."

"Yes, your majesty, to-day I am crowned with honor," said he, bitterly. "This is also the anniversary of my betrothal."

Augustus turned and drew near to the king, who seized his hand and led him to his wife and the young princesses, saying with a loud voice, "Congratulate the Prince of Prussia, ladies." He then beckoned to some of his generals, and drew back with them to the window. As he passed the queen, his eye rested upon her for a moment with an expression of sympathy and curiosity; he observed her with the searching glance of a physician, who sinks the probe into the bleeding wound in order to know its depth and danger.

The queen understood his purpose. That piercing glance was a warning; it gave her courage, self-possession, and proud resignation. Her husband had spoken to her with his eyes; that must ever be a consolation, a painful but sweet joy. She controlled herself so far as to give her hand to the prince with a cordial smile.

"You are most welcome in your double character," she said, in a voice loud enough to be heard by the king and all around her. "Until to-day, you have been my beloved brother; and from this time will you be to me, as also to my husband, a dear son. By the decrees of Providence a son has been denied me; I accept you, therefore, joyfully, and receive you as my son and brother."

A profound silence followed these words; here and there in the crowd, slight and derisive smiles were seen, and a few whispered and significant words were uttered. The queen had now received the last and severest blow; in the fulness and maturity of her beauty she had been placed before the court as unworthy or incapable of giving a successor to the throne; but she still wished to save appearances: she would, if possible, make the world believe that the decree of Providence alone denied to her a mother's honors. She had the cruel courage to conceal the truth by prevarication.

The watchful eyes of the court had long since discovered the mystery of this royal marriage: they had long known that the queen was not the wife of Frederick; her words, therefore, produced contemptuous surprise.

Elizabeth cared for none of these things. She looked toward her husband, whose eyes were fixed upon her; she would read in his countenance if he were pleased with her words. A smile played upon the lips of the king, and he bowed his head almost imperceptibly as a greeting to his wife.

A golden ray of sunlight seemed to play upon her face; content was written in her eyes; twice to-day her glance had met her husband's, and both times his eyes had spoken. Elizabeth was happier than she had been for many days; she laughed and jested with the ladies, and conversed gayly over the great event of the evening—the first appearance of the Signora Barbarina. The princesses, also, conversed un-

5

ceremoniously with the ladies near them. A cloud darkened the usually clear brow of the Princess Amelia, and she seemed to be in a nervous and highly excited state.

At this moment the master of ceremonies, Pöllnitz, drew near, with Count Tessin, the Swedish ambassador. The princess immediately assumed so scornful an expression, that even Pöllnitz scarcely found courage to present Count Tessin.

"Ah! you come from Sweden," said Amelia, immediately after the presentation. "Sweden is a dark and gloomy country, and you have indeed done well to save yourself, by taking refuge in our gay and sunny clime."

The count was evidently wounded.

"Your royal highness calls this a refuge," said he; "you must, then, think those to be pitied who dwell in my fatherland?"

"I do not feel it necessary to confide my views on that subject to Count Tessin," said Amelia, with a short, rude laugh.

"Yes, sister, it is necessary," said Ulrica, with a magical smile, "you must justify yourself to the count, for you have cast contempt upon his country."

"Ah! your highness is pleased to think better of my fatherland," said Tessin, bowing low to Ulrica. "It is true, Sweden is rich in beauty, and nowhere is nature more romantic or more lovely. The Swedes love their country passionately, and, like the Swiss, they die of homesickness when banished from her borders. They languish and pine away if one is cruel enough to think lightly of their birthplace."

"Well, sir, I commit this cruelty," cried Amelia, "and yet I scarcely think you will languish and pine away on that account."

"Dear sister, I think you are out of temper to-day," said Ulrica, softly.

"And you are wise to remind me of it in this courtly style," said Amelia; "have you taken the *rôle* of governess for my benefit to-day?"

Ulrica shrugged her shoulders and turned again to the count, who was watching the young Amelia with a mixture of astonishment and anger. She had been represented at the Swedish court as a model of gentleness, amiability, and grace; he found her rude and contradictory, fitful and childish. The Princess Ulrica soon led the thoughts of the count in another direction, and managed to retain him at her side by her piquant and intellectual conversation; she brought every power of her mind into action; she was gracious in the extreme; she overcame her proud nature, and assumed a winning gentleness; in short, she flattered the ambassador with such delicate refinement, that he swallowed the magical food offered to his vanity, without suspecting that he was victimized.

Neither the princess nor the count seemed any longer to remember Amelia, who still stood near them with a lowering visage. Pöllnitz made use of this opportunity to draw near with his young *protégé*, Frederick von Trenck, and present him to the princess, who immediately assumed a gay and laughing expression; she wished to give the ambassador a new proof of her stormy and fitful nature: she would humble him by proving that she was not harsh and rude to all the world. She received the two gentlemen, therefore, with great cordiality, and laughed heartily over the adventure of the morning; she recounted to them, merrily and wittily, how and why she had thrown the sweet roses away. Amelia was now so lovely and so spirited to look upon, so radiant with youth, animation, and innocence, that the eyes of the poor young officer were dazzled and sought the floor; completely intoxicated and bewildered, he could not join in the conversation, uttering here and there only a trembling monosyllable.

This did not escape the cunning eye of the master of ceremonies. "I must withdraw," thought he; "I will grant them a first *tête-à-tête*. I will observe them from a distance, and be able to decide if my plan will succeed." Excusing himself upon the plea of duty, Pöllnitz withdrew; he glided into a window and concealed himself behind the curtains, in order to watch the countenances of his two victims. Pöllnitz had rightly judged. The necessity of taking part in the conversation with the princess restored to the young officer his intellect and his courage, and, in the effort to overcome his timidity, he became too earnest, too impassioned.

But the princess did not remark this; she rejoiced in an opportunity to show the Swedish ambassador how amiable and gracious she could be to others, and thus make him more sensible of her rudeness to himself; he should see and confess that she could be winning and attractive when it suited her purpose. The count observed her narrowly, even while conversing with Ulrica; he saw her ready smile, her beaming eye, her perhaps rather demonstrative cordiality to the young officer. "She is changeable and coquettish," he said to himself, while still carrying on his conversation with the talented, refined, and thoroughly maidenly Princess Ulrica.

The great and, as we have said, somewhat too strongly marked kindliness of Amelia, added fuel to the passion of Trenck; he became more daring.

"I have to implore your highness for a special grace," said he in a suppressed voice.

"Speak on," said she, feeling at that moment an inexplicable emotion which made her heart beat high, and banished the blood from her cheeks.

"I have dared to preserve one of the roses which you threw into the garden. It was a mad theft, I know it, but I was under the power of enchantment; I could not resist, and would at that moment have paid for the little blossom with my heart's blood. Oh, if your royal highness could have seen, when I entered my room and closed the door, with what rapture I regarded my treasure, how I knelt before it and worshipped it, scarcely daring to touch it with my lips! it recalled to me a lovely fairy tale of my childhood."

"How could a simple rose recall a fairy tale?" said Amelia.

"It is a legend of a poor shepherd-boy, who, lonely and neglected, had fallen asleep under a tree near the highway. Before sleeping, he had prayed to God to have pity upon him; to fill this great and painful void in his heart, or to send His Minister, Death, to his release. While sleeping he had a beautiful dream. He thought he saw the heavens open, and an angel of enchanting grace and beauty floated toward him. Her eyes glowed like two of the brightest stars. 'You shall be no longer lonely," she whispered; 'my image shall abide ever in your heart, and strengthen and stimulate you to all things good and beautiful.' While saying this, she laid a wondrous rose upon his eyes, and, floating off, soon disappeared in the clouds. The poor shepherd-boy awoke, and was enraptured with what he supposed had been a wild dream. But lo! there was the rose, and with unspeakable joy he pressed it to his heart. He thanked God for this sweet flower, which proved to him that the angel was no dream, but a reality. The rose, the visible emblem of his good angel, was the joy and comfort of his life, and he wore it ever in his heart.—I thought of this fairy tale, princess, as I looked upon my rose, but I felt immediately that I dared not call it mine without the consent of your highness. Decide, therefore; dare I keep this rose?"

Amelia did not reply. She had listened with a strange embarrassment to this impassioned tale. The world—all, was forgotten; she was no longer a princess, she was but a simple young girl, who listened for the first time to words of burning passion, and whose heart trembled with sweet alarm.

"Princess, dare I guard this rose?" repeated Frederick, with a trembling voice.

She looked at him; their eyes met; the young maiden trembled, but the man stood erect. He felt strong, proud, and a conqueror; his glance was like the eagle's, when about to seize a lamb and bear it to his eyrie.

"He goes too far; truly, he goes too far," whispered Pöllnitz, who had seen all, and from their glances and movements had almost read their thoughts and words. "I must bring this *tête-à-tête* to an end, and I shall do so in a profitable manner."

"Dare I keep this rose?" said Frederick von Trenck, a third time.

Amelia turned her head aside and whispered, "Keep it."

Trenck would have answered, but in that moment a hand was laid upon his arm, and Pöllnitz stood near him.

"Prudence," whispered he, anxiously. "Do you not see

that you are observed? You will make of your insane and treasonable passion a fairy tale for the whole court."

Amelia uttered a slight cry, and looked anxiously at Pöllnitz. She had heard his whispered words, and the sly baron intended that she should.

"Will your royal highness dismiss this madman," whispered he, "and allow me to awake his sleeping reason?"

"Go, Herr von Trenck," said she lightly.

Pöllnitz took the arm of the young officer and led him off, saying to himself, with a chuckle: "That was a good stroke, and I feel that I shall succeed; I have betrayed his passion to her, and forced myself into their confidence. I shall soon be employed as Love's messenger, and that is ever with princesses a profitable service. Ah, King Frederick, King Frederick, you have made it impossible for me to borrow money! Well, I shall not find that necessary; my hands shall be filled from the royal treasures. When the casket of the princess is empty, the king must of course replenish it." And the baron laughed too loudly for a master of ceremonies.

CHAPTER VIII.

SIGNORA BARBARINA.

THE princess regarded their retreating figures with dreamy eyes. Then, yielding to an unconquerable desire to be alone, to give herself up to undisturbed thought, she was about to withdraw; but the Princess Ulrica, who thought it necessary that the Swedish ambassador should have another opportunity of observing the proud and sullen temper of her sister, called her back.

"Remain a moment longer, Amelia," said the princess. "You shall decide between Count Tessin and myself. Will you accept my sister as umpire, count?"

"Without doubt," said the count. "I should be greatly honored if the princess will be so gracious. Perhaps I may be more fortunate on this occasion."

"It appears to me," said Amelia, rudely interrupting him, "that 'fortunate' and 'unfortunate' are not terms which can be properly used in any connection between a princess of Prussia and yourself." Amelia then turned toward her sister and gave her a glance which plainly said: Well, do I not play my *rôle* in masterly style? Have I not hastened to follow your counsels? "Speak, sister; name the point which Count Tessin dares to contest with you."

"Oh, the count is a man and a scholar, and has full right to differ," said Ulrica, graciously. "The question was a comparison of Queen Elizabeth of England and Queen Christina of Sweden. I maintain that Christina had a stronger and more powerful intellect; that she knew better how to conquer her spirit, to master her womanly weaknesses; that she was more thoroughly cultivated, and studied philosophy and science, not as Elizabeth, for glitter and show, but because she had an inward thirst for knowledge. The count asserts that Elizabeth was better versed in statecraft, and a more amiable woman. Now, Amelia, to which of these two queens do you give the preference?"

"Oh, without doubt, to Queen Christina of Sweden. This great woman was wise enough not to regard the crown of Sweden as a rare and precious gem; she chose a simple life of obscurity and poverty in beautiful Italy, rather than a throne in cold and unfruitful Sweden. This act alone establishes her superiority. Yes, sister, you are right. Christina was the greater woman, even because she scorned to be Queen of Sweden."

So saying, Amelia bowed slightingly, and, turning aside, she summoned Madame von Kleist, and commenced a merry chat with her. Count Tessin regarded her with a dark and scornful glance, and pressed his lips tightly together, as if to restrain his anger.

"I beseech you, count," said Ulrica, in a low, soft voice, "not to be offended at the thoughtless words of my dear little sister. It is true, she is a little rude and resentful today; but you will see—to-morrow, perhaps, will be one of her glorious sunny days, and you will find her irresistibly charming. Her moods are changeable, and for that reason we call her our little 'April *fée.*'"

"Ah, the princess is, then, as uncertain as April?" said the count, with a frosty smile.

"More uncertain than April," said Ulrica, sweetly. "But what would you, sir? we all, brothers and sisters, are responsible for that. You must know that she is our favorite, and is always indulged. I counsel you not to find fault with our little sister, Count Tessin; that would be to bring an accusation against us all. You have suffered to-day from a shower of her April moods; to-morrow you may rejoice in the sunshine of her favor."

"I shall, however, be doubtful and anxious," said the ambassador, coolly; "the April sun is sometimes accompanied by rain and storm, and these sudden changes bring sickness and death."

"Allow me to make one request," said Ulrica. "Let not the king guess that you have suffered from these April changes."

"Certainly not; and if your royal highness will graciously allow me to bask in the sunshine of your presence, I shall soon recover from the chilling effect of these April showers."

"Well, I think we have played our parts admirably," said Ulrica to herself, as she found time, during the course of the evening, to meditate upon the events of the day. "Amelia will accomplish her purpose, and will not be Queen of Sweden. She would have it so, and I shall not reproach myself."

Princess Ulrica leaned comfortably back in her armchair, and gave her attention to a play of Voltaire, which was now being performed. This representation took place in the small theatre in the royal palace. There was no public theatre in Berlin, and the king justly pronounced the large opera-house unsuited to declamation. Frederick generally gave his undivided attention to the play, but this evening he was restless and impatient, and he accorded less applause to this piquant and witty drama of his favorite author than he was wont to do. The king was impatient, because the king was waiting. He had so far restrained all outward expression of his impatient curiosity; the French play had not commenced one moment earlier than usual. Frederick had, according to custom, gone behind the scenes,

to say a few friendly and encouraging words to the per-
formers, to call their attention to his favorite passages, and
exhort them to be truly eloquent in their recitations. And
now the king waited; he felt feverishly impatient to see and
judge for himself this capricious beauty, this world-renowned *artiste*, this Signora Barbarina, whose rare loveliness and grace enchanted and bewildered all who looked
upon her.

At length the curtain fell. In a few moments he would
see the Barbarina dance her celebrated solo. A breathless
stillness reigned throughout the assembly; every eye was
fixed upon the curtain. The bell sounded, the curtain flew
up, and a lovely landscape met the eye: in the background
a village church, rose-bushes in rich bloom, and shady trees
on every side; the declining sun gilded the summit of the
mountain, against the base of which the little village nestled.
The distant sound of the evening bell was calling the simple
cottagers to "Ave Maria." It was an enchanting picture of
innocence and peace; in striking contrast to this courtly
assemblage, glittering with gems and starry orders—a start-
ling opposite to that sweet, pure idyl. And now this select
circle seemed agitated as by an electric shock. There, upon
the stage, floated the Signora Barbarina.

The king raised himself involuntarily a little higher in
his arm-chair, in order to examine the signora more closely;
he leaned back, however, ashamed of his impatience, and a
light cloud was on his brow; he felt himself oppressed and
overcome by this magical beauty. He who had looked death
in the face without emotion, who had seen the deadly cannon-balls falling thickly around him without a trembling
of the eyelids, now felt a presentiment of danger, and
shrank from it.

Barbarina was indeed lovely, irresistibly lovely, in her
ravishing costume of a shepherdess; her dress was of crimson satin, her black velvet bodice was fastened over her voluptuous bosom by rich golden cords, finished off by tassels
glittering with diamonds. A wreath of crimson roses
adorned her hair, which fell in graceful ringlets about her
wondrous brow, and formed a rich frame around her pure,
oval face. The dark incarnate of her full, ripe lip con-

trasted richly with the light, rosy blush of her fair, smooth
check. Barbarina's smile was a promise of love and bliss;
and, when those great fiery eyes looked at you earnestly,
there was such an intense glow, such a depth of power and
passion in their rays, you could not but feel that there was
danger in her love as in her scorn.

To-day, she would neither threaten nor inspire; she was
only a smiling, joyous, simple peasant-girl, who had returned wild with joy to her native village, and whose rapture
found expression in the gay and graceful mazes of the dance.
She floated here and there, like a wood-nymph, smiling,
happy, careless, wonderful to look upon in her loveliness
and beauty, but more wonderful still in her art. Simplicity
and grace marked every movement; there seemed no difficulties in her path—to dance was her happiness.

The dance was at an end. Barbarina, breathless, glowing, smiling, bowed low. Then all was still; no hand was
moved, no applause greeted her. Her great burning eyes
wandered threateningly and questioningly over the saloon; then, raising her lovely head proudly, she stepped
back.

The curtain fell, and now all eyes were fixed upon the
king, in whose face the courtiers expected to read the impression which the signora had made upon him; but the
countenance of the king told nothing; he was quiet and
thoughtful, his brow was stern, and his lips compressed.
The courtiers concluded that he was disappointed, and began at once to find fault, and make disparaging remarks.
Frederick did not regard them. At this moment he was not
a king, he was only a man—a man who, in silent rapture,
had gazed upon this wondrous combination of grace and
beauty. The king was a hero, but he trembled before this
woman, and a sort of terror laid hold upon him.

The curtain rose, and the second act of the drama began; no one looked at the stage; after this living, breathing,
impersonation of a simple story, a spoken drama seemed
oppressive. Every one rejoiced when the second act was at
an end. The curtain would soon rise for Barbarina.

But this did not occur; there was a long delay; there
was eager expectation; the curtain did not rise; the bell

did not ring. At last, Baron Swartz crossed the stage and
drew near to the king.

"Sire," said he, "the Signora Barbarina declares she
will not dance again; she is exhausted by grief and anxiety,
and fatigued by her journey."

"Go and say to her that I command her to dance," said
Frederick, who felt himself once more a king, and rejoiced
in his power over this enchantress, who almost held him in
her toils.

Baron Swartz hastened behind the scenes, but soon returned, somewhat cast down.

"Sire, the signora affirms that she will not dance, and
that the king has no power to compel her. She dances to
please herself."

"Ah! that is a menace," said the king, threateningly;
and without further speech he stepped upon the stage, followed by Baron Swartz. "Where is this person?" said the
king.

"She is in her own room, your majesty; shall I call
her?"

"No, I will go to her. Show me the way."

The baron stepped forward, and Frederick endeavored
to collect himself and assume a cool and grave bearing.

"Sire, this is the chamber of the Signora Barbarina."

"Open the door." But before the baron had time to
obey the command, the impatient hand of the king had
opened the door, and he had entered the room.

CHAPTER IX.

THE KING AND BARBARINA.

BARBARINA was resting, half reclining, and wholly ab-
stracted, upon a small crimson divan; her rounded arms
were crossed over her breast. She fixed her blazing, glowing eyes upon the intruders, and seemed petrified, in her
stubborn immobility, her determined silence. She had the

glance of a panther who has prepared herself for death, or to slay her enemy.

The king stood a moment quiet and waiting, but Barbarina did not move. Baron Swartz, alarmed by her contemptuous and disrespectful bearing, drew near, in order to say that the king had vouchsafed to visit her, but Frederick motioned him to withdraw; and, in order that Barbarina might not understand him, he told him in German to leave the room and await him in the corridor.

"I do not wish the signora to know that I am the king," said he. As the baron withdrew, Frederick said to him, "Leave the door open."

Barbarina was motionless, only her large black eyes wandered questioningly from one to the other; she sought to read the meaning of their words, not one of which she understood; but her features expressed no anxiety, no disquiet; she did not look like a culprit or a rebel; she had rather the air of a stern queen, withholding her royal favor. The king drew near her. Her eyes were fixed upon him with inexpressible, earnest calm; and this cool indifference, so rarely seen by a king, embarrassed Frederick, and at the same time intoxicated him.

"You are, then, determined not to dance again?" said the king.

"Fully determined," said she, in a rich and sonorous voice.

"Beware! beware!" said he; but he could not assume that threatening tone which he wished. "The king may perhaps compel you."

"Compel me! me, the Barbarina!" said she, with a mocking laugh, and disclosing two rows of pearly teeth. "And how can the king compel me to dance?"

"You must be convinced that he has some power over you, since he brought you here against your will."

"Yes, that is true," said she, raising herself up proudly; "he brought me here by force; he has acted like a barbarian, a cold-blooded tyrant!"

"Signora," said Frederick, menacingly, "one does not speak so of kings."

"And why not?" she said, passionately. "What is your

king to me? What claim has he upon my love, upon my consideration, or even my obedience? What has he done for me, that I should regard him otherwise than as a tyrant? What is he to me? I am myself a queen; yes, and believe me, a proud and an obstinate one! Who and what is this king, whom I do not know, whom I have never seen, who has forgotten that I am a woman, yes, forgotten that he is a man, though he bears the empty title of a king? A true king is always and only a gallant cavalier in his conduct to women. If he fails in this, he is contemptible and despised."

"How! you despise the king?" said Frederick, who really enjoyed this unaccustomed scene.

"Yes, I despise him! yes, I hate him!" cried the Barbarina, with a wild and stormy outbreak of her southern nature. "I no longer pray to God for my own happiness; that this cruel king has destroyed. I pray to God for revenge; yes, for vengeance upon this man, who has no heart, and who tramples the hearts of others under his feet. And God will help me. I shall revenge myself on this man. I have sworn it—I will keep my word! Go, sir, and tell this to your king; tell him to beware of Barbarina. Greater, bolder, more magnanimous than he, I warn him! Cunningly, slyly, unwarned, by night I was fallen upon by spies, and dragged like a culprit to Berlin."

The king had no wish to put an end to this piquant scene; he was only accustomed to the voice of praise and of applause; it was a novelty, and therefore agreeable to be so energetically railed at and abused.

"Do you not fear that the king will be angry when I repeat your words?"

"Fear! What more can your king do, that I should fear him? Yes, he is a king; but am not I a queen? This paltry kingdom is but a small portion of the world, which is mine, wholly mine; it belongs to me, as it belongs to the eagle who spreads her proud wings and looks down upon her vast domains; he has millions in his treasury, but they are pressed from the pockets of his poor subjects; he requires many agents to collect his gold, and his people give it grudgingly, but my subjects bring their tribute joyfully and lay it at my feet with loving words. Look you! look at these two

little feet: they are my assessors; they collect the taxes
from my people, and all the dwellers in Europe are mine.
These are my agents, they bring me in millions of gold;
they are also my avengers, by their aid I shall revenge myself on your barbaric king."

She leaned back upon the pillows and breathed audibly,
exhausted by her wild passion. The king looked at her with
wonder. She was to him a rare and precious work of art,
something to be studied and worshipped. Her alluring
beauty, her impetuous, uncontrolled passions, her bold sincerity, were all attractions, and he felt himself under the
spell of her enchantments. Let her rail and swear to be revenged on the barbarian. The king heard her not; a simple
gentleman stood before her; a man who felt that Barbarina
was right, and who confessed to himself that the king had
forgotten, in her rude seizure, that this Barbarina was a
woman—forgotten that he, in all his relations with women,
should be only a cavalier.

"Yes, yes," said Barbarina, and an expression of triumph
was painted on her lips—"yes, my little feet will be my
avengers. The king will never more see them dance—never
more; they have cost him thousands of gold; because of
them he is at variance with the noble Republic of Venice.
Well, he has seen them for the last time. Ah! it is a light
thing to subdue a province, but impossible to conquer a
woman and an *artiste* who is resolved not to surrender."

Frederick smiled at these proud words.

"So you will not dance before the king, and yet you have
danced for him this evening?"

"Yes," said she, raising her head proudly, "I have
proved to him that I am an *artiste;* only when he feels that,
will it pain him never again to see me exercise my art."

"That is, indeed, refined reasoning," said the king.
"You danced, then, in order to make the king thirst anew
for this intoxicating draught, and then deny him? Truly,
one must be an Italian to conceive this plan."

"I am an Italian, and woe to me that I am!" A storm
of tears gushed from her eyes, but in a moment, as if scorn-
ing her own weakness, she drove them back into her heart.
"Poor Italian," she said, in a soft, low tone—"poor child of

the South, what are you doing in this cold North, amongst these frosty hearts whose icy smiles petrify art and beauty? Ah! to think that even the Barbarina could not melt the ice-rind from their pitiful souls; to think that she displayed before them all the power and grace of her art, and they looked on with motionless hands and silent lips! Ah! this humiliation would have killed me in Italy, because I love my people, and they understand and appreciate all that is rare and beautiful. My heart burns with scorn and contempt for these torpid Berliners."

"I understand you now," said the king; "you heard no bravos, you were not applauded; therefore you are angry?"

"I laugh at it!" said she, looking fiercely at the king. "Do you not know, sir, that this applause, these bravos, are to the *artiste* as the sound of a trumpet to the gallant war-horse, they invigorate and inspire, and swell the heart with strength and courage? When the *artiste* stands upon the stage, the saloon before him is his heaven, and there his judges sit, to bestow eternal happiness or eternal condemnation; to crown him with immortal fame, or cover him with shame and confusion. Now, sir, that I have explained to you that the stage saloon is our heaven, and the spectators are our judges, you will understand that these bravos are to us as the music of the spheres."

"Yes, I comprehend," said the king, smiling; "but you must be indulgent; in this theatre etiquette forbids applause. You have danced to-day before an invited audience, who pay nothing, and therefore have not the right to blame or praise; no one dare applaud—no one but the king."

"Ha! and this rude man did not applaud!" cried she, showing her small teeth, and raising her hand threateningly toward heaven.

"Perhaps he was motionless and drunk from rapture," said the king, bowing gracefully; "when he sees you dance again, he will have more control over himself, and will, perhaps, applaud you heartily."

"Perhaps?" cried she. "I shall not expose myself to this 'perhaps.' I will dance no more. My foot is sore, and your king cannot force me to dance."

"No, he cannot force you, but you will do it willingly; you will dance for him again this evening, of your own free will."

Barbarina answered by one burst of wild, demoniac laughter, expressive of her scorn and her resentment.

"You will dance again this evening," repeated Frederick, and his keen eye gazed steadily into that of Barbarina, who, though weeping bitterly, shook her lovely head, and gave him back bravely glance for glance. "You will dance, Barbarina, because, if you do not, you are lost. I do not mean by this that you are lost because the king will punish you for your obstinacy. The king is no Bluebeard; he neither murders women nor confines them in underground prisons; he has no torture chambers ready for you; for the King of Prussia, whom you hate so fiercely, has abolished the torture throughout his kingdom—the torture, which still flourishes luxuriantly by the side of oranges and myrtles in your beautiful Italy. No, signora, the king will not punish you if you persist in your obstinacy; he will only send you away, that is all."

"And that is my only wish, all that I ask of Fate."

"You do not know yourself. You, who are an *artiste*, who are a lovely woman, who are ambitious, and look upon fame as worth striving for, you would not lose your power, trample under foot your ambition, see your rare beauty slighted, and your enchanting grace despised?"

"I cannot see why all these terrible things will come to pass if I refuse to dance again before your king?"

"I will explain to you, signora—listen. The king (however contemptuously you may think and speak of him) is still a man, upon whom the eyes of all Europe are turned —that is to say," he added, with a gay smile and a graceful bow, "when his bold eye is not exactly fixed upon them, signora. The voice of this king has some weight in your world, though, as yet, he has only stolen provinces and women. It is well known that the king has so irresistible a desire to see you and to admire you, that he forgot his knightly gallantry, or set it aside, and, relying only upon his right, he exacted the fulfilment of the contract signed by your own lovely hand. That was, perhaps, not worthy of a cavalier, but it was not unjust. You were forced to obey. You came to Berlin unwillingly, that I confess; but you have this evening danced before the king of your own free will. This, from your stand-point, was a great mistake. You can no longer say, 'I will not dance before the king, because I wish to revenge myself.' You have already danced, and no matter with what refinement of reason you may explain this false step, no one will believe you if the king raises his voice against you; and he will do this, believe me. He will say: 'I brought this Barbarina to Berlin. I wished to see if the world had gone mad or become childish, or if Barbarina really deserved the enthusiasm and adoration which followed her steps. Well, I have seen her dance, and I find the world is mad in folly. I give them back their goddess—she does not suit me. She is a wooden image in my eyes. I wished to capture Terpsichore herself, and lo, I found I had stolen her chambermaid! I have seen your goddess dance once, and I am weary of her pirouettes and *minauderies*. Lo, there, thou hast that is thine.'"

"Sir, sir!" cried Barbarina menacingly, and springing up with flaming eyes and panting breath.

"That is what the king will say," said Frederick quietly. "You know that the voice of the king is full and strong; it will resound throughout Europe. No one will believe that you refused to dance. It will be said that you did not please the king; this will be proved by the fact that he did not applaud, did not utter a single bravo. In a word, it will be said you have made a *fiasco*."

Barbarina sprang from her seat and laid her hand upon the arm of the king with indescribable, inimitable grace and passion.

"Lead me upon the stage—I will dance now. Ah, this king shall not conquer me, shall not cast me down. No, no! I will compel him to applaud; he shall confess that I am indeed an *artiste*. Tell the director to prepare—I will come immediately upon the stage."

Barbarina was right when she compared the *artiste* to a war-horse. At this moment she did indeed resemble one: she seemed to hear the sound of the trumpet calling to battle and to fame. Her cheeks glowed, her nostrils dilated, a quick and violent breathing agitated her breast, and a nervous and convulsive trembling for action was seen in every movement. The king observed and comprehended her. He understood her tremor and her haste; he appreciated this soul-thirsting for fame, this fervor of ambition, excited by the possibility of failure; her boldness enraptured him. The sincerity and power with which she expressed her emotions, commanded his respect; and while the king paid this tribute to her intellectual qualities, the man at the same time confessed to himself that her personal attractions merited the worship she received. She was beautiful, endowed with the alluring, gentle, soft, luxurious, and at the same time modest beauty of the Venus Anadyomene, the goddess rising from the sea.

"Come," said Frederick, "give me your hand. I will conduct you, and I promise you that this time the king will applaud."

Barbarina did not reply. In the fire of her impatience, she pressed the king onward toward the door. Suddenly she paused, and giving him an enchanting smile, she said, "I am, without doubt, much indebted to you; you have warned me of a danger, and in fact guarded me from an abyss. Truly I think this was not done for my sake, but because your king had commanded that I should dance. Your reasons were well grounded, and I thank you sincerely. I pray you, sir, give me your name, that I may guard it in my memory as the only pleasant association with Berlin."

"From this day, signora, you will confess that you owe me a small service. You have told me it was a light task to win provinces, but to capture and subdue a woman was impossible. I hope now I shall be a hero in your eyes: I have not only conquered provinces, I have captured a woman and subdued her."

Barbarina was neither astonished nor alarmed at these words. She had seen so many kings and princes at her feet to be blinded by the glitter of royalty. She let go the arm of the king, and said calmly and coolly: "Sire, I do not ask for pardon or grace. The possessor of a crown must wear it, if he demands that it should be acknowledged and respected, and the pomp and glare of royalty is, it seems, easily

veiled. Besides, I would not have acted otherwise, had I
known who it it was that dared intrude upon me."

"I am convinced of that," said Frederick, smiling.
"You are a queen who has but small consideration for the
little King of Prussia, because he requires so many agents
to impress the gold from the pockets of his unwilling subjects. You are right—my agents cost me much money, and
bring small tribute, while yours cost nothing and yield a
rich harvest. Come, signora, your assessors must enter
upon their duties."

He nodded to Baron Swartz, who stood in the corridor,
and said in German, "The signora will dance; she must be
received with respect and treated with consideration." He
gave a light greeting to Barbarina and returned to the
saloon, where he found the last act of the drama just concluded.

Every eye was fixed upon the king as he entered. He
had left the room in anger, and the courtiers almost trembled at the thought of his fierce displeasure; but Frederick's
brow was clear, and an expression of peace and quiet was
written on his features. He took his place between the two
queens, muttered a few words of explanation to his mother,
and bowed smilingly to his wife. Poor queen! poor Elizabeth Christine! she had the sharp eye of a loving and jealous woman, and she saw in the king's face what no one, not
even Frederick himself, knew. While every eye was turned
upon the stage; while all with breathless rapture gazed upon
the marvellous beauty and grace of Barbarina, the queen
alone fixed a stolen and trembling glance upon the countenance of her husband. She saw not that Barbarina, inspired by ambition and passion, was more lovely, more enchanting than before. Her eyes were fixed upon the face
of her husband, now luminous with admiration and delight;
she saw his soft smile, and the iron entered her soul.

The dance was at an end. Barbarina came forward and
bowed low; and now something happened so unheard of, so
contrary to court etiquette, that the master of ceremonies
was filled with surprise and disapprobation. The king applauded, not as gracious kings applaud generally, by laying
his hands lightly together, but like a wild enthusiast who

wishes to confess to the world that he is bewildered, enraptured. He then rose from his chair, and turning to the princesses and generals behind him, he said, "Gentlemen, why do you not applaud?" and as if these magical words had released the hands from bondage and given life to the wild rapture of applause which had before but trembled on the lip, the wide hall rang with the plaudits and enthusiastic bravos of the spectators. Barbarina bowed low and still lower, an expression of happy triumph playing upon her glowing face.

"I have never seen a more beautiful woman," said the king, as he sank back, seemingly exhausted, in his chair.

Queen Elizabeth pressed her lips together, to suppress a cry of pain. She had heard the king's words; for her they had a deeper meaning. "He will love her, I know it, I feel it!" she said to herself as she returned after this eventful evening to Schönhausen. "Oh, why has God laid upon me this new trial, this new humiliation? Until now, no one thought the less of me because I was not loved by the king. The world said, 'The king loves no woman, he has no heart for love.' From this day I shall be despised and pitied. The king has found a heart. He knows now that he has not outlived his youth; he feels that he is young—that he is young in heart, young in love! Oh, my God! and I too am young, and love; and I must shroud my heart in resignation and gloom."

While the queen was pouring out her complaints and prayers to God, the Swedish ambassador was confiding his wrath to his king. He wrote to his sovereign, and repeated to him the angry and abusive words of the little Princess Amelia, who was known at the court as the little April *Fée*. She was more changeable than April, and more stormy and imperious than Frederick himself. He painted skilfully the gentle and attractive bearing of the Princess Ulrica. and asked for permission to demand the hand of this gracious and noble princess for Adolph Frederick. After the ambassador had written his dispatches, and sent them by a courier to the Swedish ship lying in the sound, he said to himself, with a triumphant smile: "Ah, my little Princess Amelia, this is a royal punishment for royal impertinence. You were pleased to treat me with contempt, but you did not know that I could avenge myself by depriving you of a kingdom. Ah, if you had guessed my mission, how smilingly you would have greeted the Count Tessin!"

The gentlemen diplomatists are sometimes outwitted.

CHAPTER X.

ECKHOF.

THE reader has learned, from the foregoing chapters, what a splendid *rôle* the French theatre and ballet were now playing at the court of Berlin. A superb house had been built for the Italian opera and the ballet, a stage had been prepared in the king's palace for the French comedies, and every representation was honored by the presence of the king, the royal family, and the court circle. The most celebrated singers of Italy, the most graceful Parisian dancers were now to be heard and seen in Berlin. These things assumed such vast importance, that the king himself appeared as a critic in the daily journals, and his articles were published in the foreign papers. While the king favored the strange actors with his presence and his grace, the German theatre, like a despised step-child, was given over to misery and contempt. Compelled to seek an asylum in low dark saloons, its actors had to be thankful for even the permission to exist, and to plead with Apollo and the Muses for aid and applause. The king and the so-called good society despised them altogether. But this step-child carried under her ashes and ragged garments the golden robes of her future greatness; her cunning step-sisters had cast her down into obscurity and want, but she was not extinguished; she could not be robbed of her future! Only a few propitious circumstances were necessary to enable her to shake the dust from her head, and bring her kingly crown to light.

The king had given Schönemein permission to bring his company to Berlin; and by a happy chance, Schönemein had engaged the young and talented actor Eckhof for the season.

Eckhof was destined to give renown to the German theatre; he was justly called the first and greatest actor in Germany. Alas, how much of misery, how much of humiliation, how many choking tears, how much suffering and care, how much hunger and thirst were then comprised in that one word, a "German actor!" None but a lost or despairing man, or an enthusiast, would enroll himself as a German actor; only when he had nothing more to lose, and was willing to burn his ships behind him, could he enter upon that thorny path. Religion and art have always had their martyrs, and truly the German actors were martyrs in the time of Frederick the Great. Blessings upon those who did not despair, and took up their cross patiently!

The French comedy and the Italian opera flourished like the green bay-tree. The German actors took refuge in the saloon of the Council-house. The lighting up of the Royal Opera-house cost two hundred and seventy-seven florins every night. The misty light of sweltering oil lamps illuminated the poor saloon of the Council-house.

The audience of the German theatre was composed of burghers, philosophers, poets, bankers, and clerks—the people of the middle classes, who wore no white plumes in their hats; they were indeed allowed to enter the opera-house, but through a side passage, and their boxes were entirely separated from those of the court circle. These people of the middle classes seemed obscure and unimportant, but they were educated and intelligent; even then they were a power; proud and independent, they could not be bribed by flattery, nor blinded by glitter and pomp. They judged the king as they judged the beggar, the philosopher as they did the artist, and they judged boldly and well.

This public voice had declared that Eckhof was a great tragedian, who rivalled successfully the great French actor, Monsieur Dennis. This public voice, though but the voice of the people, found entrance everywhere, even in the saloons of the nobles and cabinets of princes. Berlin resounded with the name of Eckhof, who dared to rival the French actor, and with the name of Schönemein, who dared, every time a drama of Corneille or Racine, of Molière or Voltaire, was given in the palace theatre, to represent the same in the

Council-house on the following evening. This was a good idea. Those who had been so fortunate as to witness the performance at the palace, wished to compare the glittering spectacle with the poor caricature, as they were pleased to call it, in the Council-house. Those whose obscure position prevented them from entering the French theatre, wished at least to see the play which had enraptured the king and court; they must be content with a copy, somewhat like the hungry beggar who stands before the kitchen door, and refreshes himself by smelling the roast beef he cannot hope to taste. But there was still a third class who visited the German theatre, not in derision, not from curiosity, not from a desire to imitate the nobles in their amusements, but with the seemingly Utopian hope of building up the German drama. Amongst these were the scholars, who pronounced the dramas of Gottsched far superior to those of Corneille and Racine; there were the German patriots, who would not grant a smile to the best representation of "*Le Malade Imaginaire*," but declared "The Hypochondriac," by Guistorp, the wittiest drama in the world. In short, this large class of men ranged themselves in bold opposition to the favoritism shown to Frenchmen by Frederick the Great. These were the elements which composed the audience in the Council-house.

One afternoon, just before the opening of the theatre, two young men were walking arm-in-arm in the castle court; with one of them we are already acquainted, Joseph Fredersdorf, the merry student of Halle, the brother of the private secretary—he who had been commissioned to seek the black ram, for the propitiation of the devil. In obedience to the command of the secretary, he, with ten other members of this unholy alliance, had been searching in every quarter for this sacrifice. Joseph Fredersdorf, indebted to fortune or his own adroitness, was the first to return from his wanderings, and he brought with him a black ram, on whose glossy coat the sharpest eye could not detect one white hair.

Fredersdorf, and Baron Kleist, the husband of the lovely Louise von Schwerin, were truly happy, and paid willingly some hundred thalers for this coveted object. Indeed, they considered this a very small interest to pay for the large capital which they would soon realize. They were the principal leaders in the secret conspiracy for gold-making, and many other most distinguished nobles, generals, and officers belonged to the society. Fredersdorf was resolved to fathom this mystery; he wished to buy himself free from his service to the king, and wed the woman he had long so passionately loved. Kleist was riotous and a spendthrift; he felt that gold alone would enable him to buy smiles and rapture from this worn-out and wearisome world. Kleist and his beautiful wife required money in large measure; she had been a faithful companion and aid—had stood by honestly and assisted in the waste of her own property; and now they were compelled to confine themselves to the small income of captain of the king's guard.

Joseph laughed, chatted, and jested with his young companion, who walked by his side with modest and downcast eyes. Joseph sometimes put his hand merrily under the dimpled chins of the rosy servant-girls who passed them from time to time, or peeped rather impertinently under the silk hoods of the burgher maidens; his companion blushed and took no part in these bold pastimes.

"Truly," said Joseph, "if I did not have in my pocket a letter from my former room-mate at Halle, introducing you as a manly, brave boy, and a future light in the world of science, I should suspect you were a disguised maiden; you blush like a girl, and are as timid as a lamb which has never left its mother's side."

"I am a villager, a poor provincial," said the youth, in a somewhat maidenly voice. "The manners of your great city embarrass me. I admire but cannot imitate them. I have been always a recluse, a dusty book-worm."

"A learned monster!" cried Joseph, mockingly, "who knows and understands every thing except the art of enjoying life. I acknowledge that you are greatly my superior, but I can instruct you in that science. You have been so strongly commended to me that I will at once commence to unfold to you the real, satisfying duties and pleasures of life."

"I fear," said the youth, "your science is beyond my ability. I have no organ for it. My father is a celebrated physician in Quedlinburg; he would be greatly distressed if

I should occupy myself with any thing else than philosophy and the arts. I myself have so little inclination and so little ability for the enjoyment of mirth and pleasure, that I dare not exchange the world of books for the world of men. I do not understand their speech, and their manners are strange to me."

"But, without doubt, you have come to Berlin to learn something of these things?"

"No, I have come to visit the medical college, and to speak with the learned and renowned Euler."

"Folly and nonsense!" said Fredersdorf, laughing; "keep your dry pursuits for Halle, and give your time and attention to that which you cannot find there, gayety and amusement. I promise to be your counsellor and comrade. Let us begin our studies at once. Do you see that little theatre-bill fastened to the wall? Eckhof appears as Cato to-night."

"Go to the theatre!" said Lupinus, shrinkingly. "How! I go to the theatre?"

"And why not, friend?" said Joseph. "Perhaps you belong to the pietists, who look upon the stage as the mother of blasphemy and sin, and who rail at our noble king because he will not close these houses?"

"No, I do not belong to the pietists," said the youth, with a sad smile, "and I try to serve God, by understanding and admiring His works: that is my religion."

"Well, it seems to me that this faith does not forbid you to enter the theatre. If it pleases you to study God's master-work, I promise to show you this night on the stage the noblest exemplar. Eckhof plays this evening."

"Who, then, is Eckhof?"

Joseph looked at the young man with surprise, and shrugged his shoulders contemptuously.

"You have, indeed, been greatly neglected, and it was high time you should come to me. You do not know, then, that Eckhof is the first tragedian who has dared to set aside the old and absurd dress and manners of the stage, and introduce real, living, feeling men, of like passions with ourselves, and who move and speak even as we do. Now we must certainly enter the theatre; look there, at that great

crowd entering the dark and lowly entrance. Let us remove
our hats reverentially; we stand before the temple of art."
So saying, he drew the young man, who had no longer courage to resist, into the house. "This is Eckhof's benefit.
You see the great tragedian has many admirers; it seems to
me that half of Berlin has come to bring him tribute this
evening."

Lupinus sat silent and confused in the *parterre*, near
Joseph. There was a row of seats slightly elevated and
made of common plank, called *loges;* one of these nearest
the stage was adorned by a golden eagle, from which some
pitiful drapery was suspended; this was called the king's
loge, but, I am constrained to say, it had never been visited
by the king or any member of the royal family. The royal
loge was indeed empty, but the great body of the house was
fearfully crowded, and many an expression of pain was
heard from those who were closely pressed and almost
trampled upon.

"It is fortunate for you that Eckhof appears as Cato to-
night: it is his best *rôle*. Perhaps your learned soul may
be somewhat reconciled to such vanities when you see a
drama of Gottsched, and a hero of the old and classic time."

"Yes, but will not your Eckhof make a vile caricature of
the noble Roman?" sighed Lupinus.

"You are a pedant, and I trust the Muses will revenge
themselves upon you this night," said Joseph, angrily. "I
prophesy that you will become this evening a wild enthusiast for Eckhof: that is always the punishment for those who
come as despisers and doubters. If you were a girl, I
should know that you would be passionately in love with
Eckhof before you slept; you have taken the first step, by
hating him."

Joseph said this thoughtlessly, and did not remark the
deep impression his words made upon the stranger. His
face flushed, and his head sank upon his breast. Joseph
saw nothing of this. At this moment the curtain rose and
the piece began.

A breathless silence reigned throughout the vast crowd;
every eye was fixed upon the stage; and now, with a stately
step and a Roman toga falling in artistic folds from his

shoulders, Eckhof as Cato stood before them. Every thing about him was antique; his noble and proud bearing, his firm and measured step, his slow but easy movements, even the form of his head and the expression of his finely-cut features, were eminently classic. He was the complete and perfect picture of an old Roman; nothing was forgotten. The sandals, laced with red over the powerful and well-formed leg; the white under-garment and leathern girdle, the blue toga, the cut of his hair, every thing brought before you the noble Roman, the son of Liberty, imposing in his majesty and power.

Eckhof was the first who had the courage to clothe his characters in the costume of the time they represented, to make them move and speak simply as men. Eckhof did that for the German stage which some years later Talma introduced on the French boards. Talma was only a copyist of Eckhof, but this fact was not acknowledged, because at that time the German stage had not won for itself the sympathy and consideration of other nations.

As I have said, silence reigned, and from time to time the rapture of applause, which could not be altogether suppressed, was evidenced by thundering bravos. Then again all was still; every eye and every ear were open to the great actor, true to himself and true to nature; who, glowing with enthusiasm, had cast his whole soul into his part; who had forgotten the line separating imagination from reality; who had, indeed, ceased to be Eckhof, and felt and thought and spoke as Cato. At the close of an act, Eckhof was forced to come forward and show himself by the wild the stormy applause and loud cries of the audience.

"Do you not find him beyond all praise?" said Fredersdorf.

Lupinus gazed steadily at the stage; he had only soul, breath, hearing, for Eckhof. His old world had passed away like a misty dream—a new world surrounded him. The olden time, the olden time to which he had consecrated years of study and of thought, to which he had offered up his sleep and all the pleasures of youth, had now become a reality for him. He who stood upon the stage was Cato; that was the Roman forum; there were the proud temples, and the dwelling-houses consecrated by their household gods. There was, then, outside of the world of books and letters, another world of light and gladness! What was it, which made his heart beat and tremble so powerfully? why did his blood rush so madly through his veins? A dark veil had fallen from his face; all around him were life, light, gladness, and rapture. With trembling lips and silent tears he said to himself: "I will live; I will be young; I will turn to Eckhof; he shall counsel me, and I will follow his advice as I would a holy gospel.—Did you not say that you knew Cato?" said he, suddenly awaking from his dream and turning to his companion.

"Cato?" said Fredersdorf. "Do you mean the drama, or that wearisome old fellow himself? or Eckhof, who plays the part of Cato?"

"So it is Eckhof," said Lupinus, to himself; "he is called Eckhof?"

The play was at an end; the curtain fell for the last time, and now the long-suppressed enthusiasm burst forth in wild and deafening applause. The young stranger was silent, his eyes were full of tears; and yet he was perhaps the happiest of them all, and these rapturous tears were a loftier tribute to the great actor than the loudest bravos. The people had passed a happy evening, and common cares and sorrows had been forgotten; but Lupinus felt as if his heart had risen from the dead: he was changed from old age to sunny youth; he had suddenly discovered in himself something new, something never suspected—a glowing, loving heart.

"Well, now I am resolved, wholly resolved," said Joseph, as they forced their way through the crowd. "I no longer hesitate; I give up to you your dry learning and philosophy; you are welcome to your dusty books and your imposing cues. I will be an actor."

"Ha! an actor?" said Lupinus, awaking from his dream and trembling violently.

"Why are you shocked at my words? I suppose you despise me because of this decision; but what do I care? I will be an *artiste;* I shall not be disturbed by the turned-up noses and derisive shrugs of you wise ones. I will be a scholar of Eckhof; so despise me, my learned Lupinus—I give you permission."

"I am not laughing," said Lupinus. "Each one must walk in that path at the end of which he hopes to find his ideal."

"Yes, truly, and so I will go to Eckhof," said Freders- dorf, waving his hat triumphantly in the air.

"Do you know where he dwells?" said the youth.

"Certainly. We are standing now just before his door. See there in the third story, those two lighted windows? That is Eckhof's home."

"What is the name of this street?"

"What is that to you? Has my prophecy really come true, and are you in love with the great actor? Do not let go my arm; do not turn away from me angrily. The Post Strasse is a long way off from where you dwell; you will lose yourself. Let us go together. I will risk no more un- seemly jests with you. Come!"

"He lives in the Post Strasse; he is called Eckhof," said Lupinus to himself, as he took Joseph's arm and walked through the dark streets. "I must see Eckhof; he shall decide my fate."

CHAPTER XI.

A LIFE QUESTION.

It was the morning after Eckhof's benefit. The usually quiet dwelling of the actor resounded with the ringing of glasses and merry songs after the toils and fatigues of the evening. He wished to afford to himself and his comrades a little distraction; to give to the hungry sons of the Muses and Graces a few hours of simple enjoyment. Eckhof's purse was full and he wished to divide its contents with his friends.

"Drink and be merry," said he to his gay companions. "Let us forget for a few hours that we are poor, despised German actors. We will drink, and picture to ourselves that we belong to the cherished and celebrated *artistes* of the French stage, on whom the Germans so willingly shower gold, honor, and even love. Raise your glasses, and drink with me to the success of German art!"

"We will drink also to Eckhof," cried one of the youthful company, raising his glass. "Yes, to the father of the new school of German acting."

"You are that, Eckhof, and you are also our benefactor," said another. "We thank you, that for some months we have not suffered from hunger and thirst; that the good people of Berlin take an interest in the German stage, and treat us with some consideration. Let us, then, drink to our preserver, to the great Eckhof!"

Every glass was raised, and their shouts rang out merrily. Eckhof alone was sad and troubled, and his great dreamy eyes gazed thoughtfully in the distance. His friends observed this, and questioned him as to the cause of his melancholy.

"I am not melancholy, though a German actor has always good reason to be so; but I have some new plans which I wish to disclose to you. You greet me as your benefactor. Alas! how suffering, how pitiful must your condition be, if such a man as I am can have been useful to you! You are all *artistes*, and I say this to you from honest conviction, and not from contemptible flattery. You are greater in your art than I am, only you had not the courage to break through the old and absurd customs of your predecessors. That I have done this, that I have dared to leave the beaten paths, is the only service I have rendered. I have tried to banish from the stage the crazy fools who strutted from side to side, and waved their arms from right to left; who tried to play the orator by uttering their pathetic phrases in weird, solemn sounds from the throat, or trumpeted them through the nose. I have placed living men upon the boards, who by natural speech and action lend truth and reality to the scenes they wish to portray. You, comrades, have assisted me faithfully in this effort. We are in the right path, but we are far from the goal. Let us go forward, then, bravely and hopefully. You think yourselves happy now in Berlin; but I say to you that we dare not remain in Berlin.

This vegetation, this bare permission to live, does not suffice, will not satisfy our honor. I think, with Cæsar, it is better to be the first in a village than the second or third in a great city. We will leave Berlin; this cold, proud, imperious Berlin, which cherishes the stranger, but has no kind, cheering word for her own countrymen. Let us turn our backs upon these French worshippers, and go as missionaries for the German drama throughout our fatherland."

A long pause followed this speech of Eckhof; every eye was thoughtful, every face was troubled.

"You do not answer? I have not, then, convinced you?"

"Shall we leave Berlin now," said the hero and lover of the little company, "even now, when they begin to show a little interest, a little enthusiasm for us?"

"Alas, friend! the enthusiasm of the Berliners for us is like a fire of straw—it flashes and is extinguished; to-day, perhaps, they may applaud us, to-morrow we will be forgotten, because a learned sparrow or hound, a French dancer, or an Italian singer, occupies their attention. There is neither endurance nor constancy in the Berliners. Let us go hence."

"It seems to me that we should make use of the good time while it lasts," said another. "At present, our daily bread is secured for ourselves and our families."

"If you are not willing to endure suffering and want," said Eckhof, sadly, "you will never be true *artistes*. Poverty and necessity will be for a long time to come the only faithful companions of the German actor; and he who has not courage to take them to his arms, would do better to become an honest tailor or a shoemaker. If the prosperity of your family is your first consideration, why have you not contented yourselves with honest daily labor, with being virtuous fathers of families? The pursuit of art does not accord with these things; if you choose the one, you must, for a while at least, be separated from the other."

"That will we do," cried Fredersdorf, who had just entered the room; "I, for my part, have already set you all a good example. I have separated from my family, in order to become the husband of Art, whose sighing and ardent lover I have long been; and now, if the noble Eckhof does not reject me as a scholar, I am wholly yours."

Eckhof seized his hand, and said, with a soft smile, "I receive you joyfully; you have the true fire of inspiration. From my heart I say you are welcome."

"I thank you for the word—and now let us be off. The German actor is in Germany no better than the Jew was to the Romans. Let us do as the Jews: we have also found our Moses, who will lead us to the promised land, where we shall find liberty, honor, and gold."

"Yes," they cried, with one voice, "we will follow Eckhof, we will obey our master, we will leave Berlin and seek a city where we shall be truly honored."

"I have found the city," said Eckhof; "we will go to Halle. The wise men who have consecrated their lives to knowledge are best fitted to appreciate and treasure the true *artiste;* we will unite with them, and our efforts will transform Halle into an Athens, where knowledge and art shall walk hand-in-hand in noble emulation."

"Off, then, for Halle!" said Fredersdorf, waving his hat in the air, but his voice was less firm, and his eye was troubled. "Will the director, Schönemein, consent?"

"Schönemein has resolved to go with us, provided we make no claim for salaries, but will share with him both gains and losses."

"If the undertaking fails in Halle, we must starve, then," said a trembling voice.

Eckhof said nothing; he crossed the room to his writing-table, and took out a well-filled purse. "I do not say that we shall succeed in Halle, that is, succeed as the merchants and Jews do; we go as missionaries, resolved to bear hunger and thirst, if need be, for the cause we love and believe in. Look, this purse contains what remains of my profits from the last two months and from my benefit last night. It is all I have; take it and divide it amongst you. It will, at least, suffice to support you all for one month."

"Will you accept this?" said Joseph, with glowing cheeks.

"No, we will not accept it; what we do we will do freely,

and no man shall fetter us by his generosity or magnanimity, not even Eckhof."

Eckhof was radiant with joy. "Hear, now—I have another proposition to make. You have refused my offer for yourselves, but you dare not refuse it for your children; take this money and divide it equally amongst your wives and children. With this gold you shall buy yourselves free for a while from your families."

After a long and eloquent persuasion, Eckhof's offer was accepted, and divided fairly. He looked on with a kindly smile.

"I now stand exactly as I did when I resolved two years ago to be an actor. Before that I was an honest clerk; from day to day I vegetated, and thanked God, when, after eight hours' hard work, I could enjoy a little fresh air and the evening sunshine, and declaim to the fields and groves my favorite lines from the great authors. It is probable I should still have been a poor clerk and a dreamer, if my good genius had not stood by me and given me a powerful blow, which awakened me from dreaming to active life. The justice of the peace, whose clerk I was, commanded me to serve behind his carriage as a footman; this aroused my anger and my self-respect, and I left him, determined rather to die of hunger than to submit to such humiliation. My good genius was again at hand, and gave me courage to follow the promptings of my heart, and become an actor. He who will be great has the strength to achieve greatness. Let us go onward, then, with bold hearts." He gave his hand to his friends and dismissed them, warning them to prepare for their journey.

"You are determined to go to Halle?" said Fredersdorf, who had remained behind for the last greeting.

"We will go to Halle; it is the seat of the Muses, and belongs, therefore, to us."

Joseph shook his head sadly. "I know Halle," said he. "You call it the seat of the Muses. I know it only as the seat of pedantry. You will soon know and confess this. There is nothing more narrow-minded, jealous, arrogant, and conceited than a Halle professor. He sees no merit in any thing but himself and a few old dusty Greeks and Ro-

7

mans, and even these are only great because the professor
of Halle has shown them the honor to explain and descant
upon them. But, you are resolved—I would go with you
to prison and to death; in short, I will follow you to Halle."

"And now I am at last alone," said Eckhof; "now I
must study my new *rôle;* now stand by me, ye gods, and inspire me with your strength; give me the right tone, the
right emphasis to personate this rare and wonderful Hippolytus, with which I hope to win the stern professors of
Halle!"

Walking backward and forward, he began to declaim the
proud and eloquent verses of Corneille; he was so thoroughly absorbed that he did not hear the oft-repeated knock upon
the door; he did not even see that the door was softly opened,
and the young Lupinus stood blushing upon the threshold. He
stood still and listened with rapture to the pathetic words of
the great actor; and as Eckhof recited the glowing and innocent confession of love made by Hippolytus, a burning
blush suffused the cheek of the young student, and his eyes
were filled with tears. He overcame his emotion, and advanced to Eckhof, who was now standing before the glass,
studying the attitude which would best accord with this
passionate declaration.

"Sir," said he, with a low and trembling voice, "pardon
me for disturbing you. I was told that I should find Eckhof
in this room, and it is most important to me to see and consult with this great man. I know this is his dwelling; be
kind enough to tell me if he is within."

"This is his home, truly, but he is neither a great nor a
wise man; only and simply Eckhof the actor."

"I did not ask your opinion of the distinguished man
whom I honor, but only where I can find him."

"Tell me first what you want of Eckhof."

"What I want of him, sir?" said the youth, thoughtfully; "I scarcely know myself. There is a mystery in my
soul which I cannot fathom. Eckhof has age, wisdom, and
experience—perhaps he can enlighten me. I have faith in
his eyes and in his silver beard, and I can say freely to him
what I dare not say to any other."

Eckhof laughed merrily. "As to his white beard, you

will find that in his wardrobe; his wisdom you will find in the books of the authors, to whose great thoughts he has only given voice; he is neither old, wise, nor experienced. In short—I, myself, am Eckhof."

"You are Eckhof!" said Lupinus, turning deadly pale, and, steping back a few paces, he stared with distended eyes at the actor, whose noble and intellectual face, glowing with youthful fire, was turned toward him.

"I am Eckhof, and I hope you will forgive me for being a little younger, a little browner, and somewhat less wise than the great Cato, in which character you no doubt saw me last night. I dare hope that my confession will not shake your confidence in me; with my whole heart I beg you will tell me how I can be useful to you and what mystery you wish to have explained."

"No, no! I cannot explain," cried the youth; "forgive me for having disturbed you. I have nothing more to say." Confused and ashamed, Lupinus left the room. The actor gazed after him wonderingly, convinced that he had been closeted with a madman.

With trembling heart, scarcely knowing what he thought or did, the student reached his room and closed the door, and throwing himself upon his knees, he cried out in tones of anguish: "Oh, my God! I have seen Eckhof: he is young, he is glorious in beauty, unhappy that I am!" With his hands folded and still upon his knees, he gazed dreamily in the distance; then springing up suddenly, his eyes glowing with energy and passion, he cried: "I must go, I must go! I will return to Halle, to my books and my quiet room; it is lonely, but there I am at peace; there the world and the voice of Eckhof cannot enter. I must forget this wild awakening of my youth; my heart must sleep again and dream, and be buried at last under the dust of books. Unhappy that I am, I feel that the past is gone forever. I stand trembling on the borders of a new existence. I will go at once —perhaps there is yet time; perhaps I may yet escape the wretchedness which threatens me. Oh! in my books and studies I may forget all. I may no longer hear this voice, which is forever sounding in my enraptured ears, no longer see those fearful but wondrous eyes."

With feverish haste and trembling hands he made up his little parcel. A few hours later the post-wagon rolled by Eckhof's dwelling. A young man with pale, haggard face and tearful eyes gazed up at his windows.

"Farewell, Eckhof," murmured he; "I flee from you, but may God bless you! I go to Halle; there I shall never see you, my heart shall never thrill at the sound of your eloquent voice."

Lupinus leaned sadly back in the carriage, comforting himself with the conviction that he was safe; but fate was too strong for him, and the danger from which he so bravely fled, followed him speedily.

CHAPTER XII.

SUPERSTITION AND PIETY.

The goal was at last reached. The black ram for the propitiatory offering was found, and was now awaiting in Berlin the hour of sacrifice.

With what eager impatience, with what throbbing pulses, did Fredersdorf wait for the evening! At last this sublime mystery would be explained, and rivers of gold would flow at his command. Happily, the king was not in Berlin—he had gone to Charlottenburg. Fredersdorf was free—lord of himself.

"And after to-morrow, it will be ever the same," said he to himself joyfully. "To-morrow the world will belong to me! I will not envy the king his crown, the scholar his learning, or youth and beauty their bloom. I shall be more powerful, more honored, more beloved than them all. I shall possess an inexhaustible fountain of gold. Gold is the lord and king of the world. The king and the philosopher, youth, beauty, and grace, bow down before its shrine. Oh, what a life of gladness and rapture will be mine! I shall be at liberty. I shall wed the woman I adore. The sun is sinking; the moon will soon ride triumphantly in the heavens, and then—"

A light rustling on the tapestry door interrupted him; and he turned anxiously toward this door, which led directly to the chamber of the king, and through which he alone could enter. It was indeed Frederick. He entered the room of his private secretary with a bright, gay smile.

"I have come unexpectedly," said the king. His clear, piercing glance instantly remarked the cloud which lowered upon the brow of Fredersdorf. "But what will you have? The King and Fate, as *Deus ex machinâ*, appear without warning and confuse the calculations of insignificant mortals."

"I have made no calculations, sire," said Fredersdorf, confused; "and the presence of my king can never disturb my peace."

"So much the better," said Frederick, smiling. "Well, I have made my calculations, and you, Fredersdorf, have an important part to play. We have a great work on hand, and if you have set your heart upon being at liberty this evening, I regret it; the hope is a vain one. This evening you are the prisoner of your king."

The king said this with so grave, so peculiar, and at the same time so kindly an expression, that Fredersdorf was involuntarily touched and softened, and he pressed his lips warmly upon the hand which Frederick held out to him.

"We must work diligently," said the king. "The time of idleness is past, and also the time consecrated to the Muses. Soon I will lay my flute in its case, and draw my sword from its scabbard. It appears that my godmother, Maria Theresa, thinks it unseemly for a King of Prussia to pass his days elsewhere than in a tented field, or to hear other music than the sound of trumpet or the thunder of cannon calling loudly to battle. Well, if Austria will have war, she shall have it promptly. Never will Prussia yield to her imperious conditions, and never will the house of Hohenzollern subject herself to the house of Hapsburg. My godmother, the empress, can never forget that the Prince-Elector of Brandenburg once, at the table, held a wash-basin for the emperor. For this reason she always regards us as *cavaliere servente* to the house of Hapsburg. Now, by the help of England, Saxony, and Russia, she hopes to bring us under the old yoke. But she shall not succeed. She has made an alliance with England, Russia, and Saxony. I have united with France and Bavaria, for the protection of Charles the Seventh. This, you see, Fredersdorf, is war. Our life of fantasy and dreaming is over. I have given you a little dish of politics," said the king, after a pause. "I wish to show you that I have need of you, and that we have much to do. We must arrange my private accounts, we have many letters to write; and then we must select and prepare the rich presents to be given to the Princess Ulrica on her marriage. Fredersdorf, we cannot afford to be idle."

"I shall be ready at all times to obey the commands of my king. I will work the entire night; but I pray your majesty to grant me a few hours this evening—I have most important business, which cannot be postponed."

"Ah! without doubt, you wish to finish the epistle of Horace, of which we spoke a few days since. If I remember correctly, this epistle relates to the useless offering of a lamb or black ram. Well, I give up this translation for the present; we have no time for it; and I cannot possibly give you leave of absence this evening."

"And yet I dare to repeat my request," said Fredersdorf, with passionate excitement. "Sire, my business cannot be postponed, and I beseech you to grant me a few hours."

"If you will not yield to the earnest wish of your friend, you will be forced to submit to the command of your king," said Frederick, sternly. "I forbid you to leave your room this evening."

"Have pity, sire, I entreat you! I wish but for two hours of liberty. I tell you my business is most important; the happiness of my life depends upon it."

The king shrugged his shoulders contemptuously. "The happiness of your life! How can this poor, short-sighted, vain race of mortals decide any question relating to 'the happiness of life'? You seek it to-day, perhaps, in riches; to-morrow in the arms of your beloved; and the next day you turn away from and despise both the one and the other. I cannot fulfil your wish; I have important work for you, and will not grant you one moment's absence."

"Sire, I must—"

"Not another word! you remain here; I command you not to leave this room!"

"I will not obey this command," said Fredersdorf, completely beside himself with rage and despair. "Will your majesty dismiss me from your service, withdraw your favor, and banish me forever from your presence? I must and will have some hours of liberty this evening."

The king's eyes flashed lightning, and his features assumed so threatening an expression, that Fredersdorf, though completely blinded by passion, trembled. Without a word in reply, the king stepped hastily to the door which led into the corridor. Two soldiers stood before the door.

"You will see that no one leaves this room," said Frederick—"you will fire upon any one who opens the door." He turned and fixed his eyes steadily upon the pale face of the secretary. "I said to you that you were the prisoner of your king to-day. You would not understand my jest. I will force you to see that I am in earnest. The guards stand before this door; the other door leads to my apartment, and I will close it. You shall not work with me to-day; you are not worthy of it. You are a bold rebel, deserving punishment, and 'having eyes see not.'"

Fredersdorf had not the courage to reply. The king stepped hastily through the room and opened the tapestry door; as he stood upon the threshold, he turned once again. "Fredersdorf, the time will come when you will thank me for having been a stern king." He closed the door, placed the key in his pocket, and returned to his room, where Jordan awaited him.

"And now, friend, the police may act promptly and rigorously; Fredersdorf will not be there, and I shall not find it necessary to punish him further. Alas! how difficult it is to turn a fool from his folly! Fredersdorf would learn to make gold through the sacrifice of a black ram; in order to do this, he joins himself to my adversaries, to the hypocrites and pietists; he goes to the so-called prayer-meetings of the godless, who call themselves, forsooth, the children of God! Ah! Jordan, how selfish, how pitiful is this small

race of man! how little do they merit! I took Fredersdorf
from obscurity and poverty. I not only took him into my
service, I made him my confidant and my friend—I loved
him sincerely. And what is my reward? He is ungrateful,
and he hates me with a perfect hatred; he is now sitting in
his room and cursing his king, who has done nothing more
than protect him from the withering ridicule which his
childish and mad pursuit was about to bring upon him.
Jordan, Jordan! kings are always repaid with ingratitude."

"Yes, sire; and God, our heavenly Father, meets with
the same reward," said Jordan, with a painful smile. "God
and the king are the two powers most misunderstood. In
their bright radiance they stand too high above the sons
of men: they demand of the king that he shall be all-wise,
almighty, even as God is; they require of God that He
shall judge and act as weak, short-sighted men do, not
'knowing the end from the beginning.'"

The king did not reply; with his arms folded, he walked
thoughtfully through the room.

"Poor Fredersdorf," said he, softly, "I have slain his
hobby-horse, and that is always an unpardonable offence to
any man. I might, perhaps, have closed my eyes to the mad
follies of these so-called pietists, if they had not drawn my
poor secretary into the toils. For his sake I will give them
a lesson. I will force him to see that they are hypocrites and
charlatans. Happen what will, I have saved Fredersdorf
from ridicule; if he curses me for this, I can bear it cheerfully."

The king was right; Fredersdorf was insane with passion. He cursed the king, not only in his heart, but with his
trembling lips; he called him a tyrant, a heartless egotist.
He hated him, even as an ignorant, unreasoning child hates
the kind hand which corrects and restrains.

"They will discover this mystery; they will learn how
to make gold, and I shall not be there," murmured Fredersdorf, gnashing his teeth; "who knows? perhaps they will
not divulge to me this costly receipt! They will lie to me
and deceive me. Ah! the moon is rising; she casts her
pure, silver rays into this hated room, now become my

prison. Now, even now, they are assembling; now the holy incantation begins, and I—I am not there!" He tore his hair, and beat his breast, and cried aloud.

Fredersdorf was right. As the moon rose, the conspirators, who had been notified by Von Kleist, the husband of the beautiful Louise von Schwerin, began to assemble. The great saloon in which the gay and laughter-loving Louise had given her superb balls and *soirées*—in which her dancing feet had trampled upon her fortune and her happiness—was now changed into a solemn temple of worship, where the pious believers assembled to pray to God and to adjure the devil. The king had forbidden that the churches should be opened except on Sunday and the regular *fête* days. Some over-pious and fanatical preachers had dared to disobey this order. The assemblies had been broken up by force of arms, the people driven to their homes, and the churches closed. Both priests and people were threatened with severe punishment if they should dare to open the churches again during the week.*

The pietists, forgetting the Bible rule, to "give unto Cæsar that which is Cæsar's," refused obedience to the spirit of the command, and assembled together in the different houses of the faithful. Their worship consisted principally in stern resolves to remain obedient to the only true doctrine. To the proud fanatic this is, of course, the faith which he professes, and there is salvation in no other. With zealous speech they railed at the king as a heretic or unbeliever, and strengthened themselves in their disobedience to his commands by declaring it was well-pleasing in the sight of God.

The pietists, who had in vain endeavored to retain the power and influence which they had enjoyed under Frederick William, whom they now declared to have been the holiest and wisest of kings, had become the bitterest enemies of Frederick the Great. The king called their piety hypocrisy, laughed at their rage, replied to their curses by witty words and biting sarcasm; and on one occasion, after listening to an impertinent request, he replied laconically:

* Preuss's "Geschichte Friedrichs des Grossen."

" The cursed priest don't know himself what he wants. Let him go to the devil! "*

This so-called prayer-meeting was to take place to-day in the ball-room of the beautiful Louise, after the regular hour of worship. Only the elect and consecrated would re-main behind to take part in the deeper mysteries, and be witness to the incantation by which the astrologist Pfannen-schmidt would constrain his majesty the devil to appear. No woman was allowed to be present at this holy ordinance, and each one of the consecrated had sworn a solemn oath not to betray an act of the assembly.

Von Kleist had taken the oath, and kept it faithfully. But there is a wise Persian proverb which says: " If you would change an obedient and submissive wife into a proud rebel, you have only to forbid something! If you wish to keep a secret from the wife of your bosom, slay yourself, or tear out your tongue; if you live, she will discover your secret, even though hidden in the bottom of your heart." Louise von Kleist had proved the truth of this proverb. She had discovered the secret which her husband wished to conceal from her. She had soon recovered from the fleeting love entertained at first for the husband chosen for her by the king. She had returned to the levity of her earlier days, and only waited for an opportunity to revenge herself upon her husband. Louise hated him because he had never been rich enough to gratify her extravagant taste and caprices. He had even restrained her in the use of her own means: they were always in want of money, and constantly railing bitterly at each other.

For all this misery Louise wished to revenge herself upon her husband, as beautiful and coquettish women always wish to revenge themselves. She was more than ready to be-lieve the words of that poet who says that " a woman's heart is always girlish and youthful enough for a new love." She wished to take special vengeance upon her husband for dar-ing to keep a secret from her. So soon as she discovered the object of these secret meetings, she informed the king, and implored him to come to her assistance and rescue her husband from those crooked paths which had cost her her

* Busching's " Character of Frederick the Great."

wedded happiness and her fortune. Frederick agreed at once to her proposition, not so much for her sake as because he rejoiced in the opportunity to free Fredersdorf from the mystic suppositions which had clouded his intellect, and convince him of the cunning and hypocrisy of the alchemist Pfannenschmidt.

Every necessary preparation had been made by order of the king. The pious assembly had scarcely met, when Louise called the four policemen who were waiting in a neighboring house, and placed them in a small closet adjoining the ball-room, where every thing which took place could be both seen and heard.

The conspirators had no suspicion. The meeting was larger than ever before. There were people of all classes, from the day laborer to the comfortable burgher, from the honorable officer under government to the highest noble. They prayed earnestly and fervently, and sang hymns to the honor and glory of God. Then one of the popular priests stepped into the pulpit and thundered forth one of those arrogant, narrow-minded, and violent discourses which the believers of those days indulged in. He declared all those lost, condemned to eternal torture, who did not believe as he believed; and all those elected and sanctified who adhered to his holy faith, and who, despising the command of the heretical king, met together for these forbidden services.

All this, however, was but the preparation for the great solemnity prepared for the initiated, who were now waiting with loudly-beating hearts and breathless expectation for the grand result.

And now another orator, the astrologer, the enlightened prophet of God, ascended the pulpit. With what pious words he warned his hearers to repentance! how eloquently he exhorted them to contemn the hollow and vain world, which God had only made lovely and attractive in order to tempt men to sin and try their powers of resistance! "Resist! resist!" he howled through his nose, "and persuade men to turn to you, and be saved even as we are saved—to become angels of God, even as we are God's holy angels." In order, however, to reach their exalted goal, they must make greater efforts, use larger means. Power and wealth were necessary to make the world happy and convert it to the true faith. The world must become wholly theirs; they must buy from the devil the gold which he has hid in the bowels of the earth, and with it allure men, and save their souls from perdition. "We, by the grace of God, have been empowered to subdue the devil, and to force him to give up his secret. To those who, like ourselves, are enlightened by the holy spirit of knowledge, the mysteries of the lower world must be made clear. It is also a noble and great work which we have before us; we must make gold, and with it we must purchase and convert the whole race to holiness!"

When this pious rhapsody was concluded, he called the assembly to earnest prayer. They fell upon their knees, and dared to pray to God that He would give them strength to adjure the devil.

It was not, however, exactly the plan of the astrologer to crown the efforts of the elect with success, and bring the devil virtually before them. As long as his majesty did not appear, the pious must believe and hope in their priest; must give him their love, their confidence, and their gold; must look upon him as their benefactor, who was to crown their future with glory and riches, and bring the world to their feet. In short, he knew it was impossible for him to introduce a devil who could disclose the great secret. The prayers and offerings of the past had failed, and their future sacrifices must also be in vain.

And now, in the midst of solemn hymns, the ram was led to the altar—this rare offering which had cost so much weary wandering and so much precious gold. With pompous ceremony, and covered with a white veil, the black ram was led to the sacrifice. The holy priest Pfannenschmidt, clothed in gold-embroidered robes, stood with a silver knife in his hand, and a silver bowl to receive the blood of the victim. As he raised the knife, the faithful threw themselves upon their knees and prayed aloud, prayed to God to be with them and bless their efforts.

The astrologer, glowing with piety and enthusiasm, was about to sink the knife into the throat of the poor trembling beast, when suddenly something unheard of, incredible, took place. A figure fearful to look upon sprang fiercely from behind the altar, and seized the arm of the priest.

"Spare the offering, let the sacrifice go free!" he said, with a thundering voice. "You have called me, and I am here! I am the devil!"

"The devil! it is truly the devil!" and, with timid glances, they looked up at the giant figure, clothed in crimson, his face completely shaded by a wide-brimmed hat, from which three crimson feathers waved majestically: these, with his terrible club-foot, all gave unmistakable evidence of the presence of Satan. They believed truly in him, these pious children of God; they remained upon their knees and stammered their prayers, scarcely knowing themselves if they were addressed to God or to the devil.

There in the little cabinet stood Louise von Kleist, trembling with mirth, and with great effort suppressing an outburst of laughter. She looked with wicked and mocking eyes upon her husband, who lay shivering and deadly pale at the feet of the devil and the black ram. He fixed his pleading glances upon the fiery monster who was to him indeed the devil. Louise, however, fully understood this scene; she it was who had induced young Fredersdorf to assume this part, and had assisted him in his disguise.

"This moment repays me, avenges me for all I have suffered by the side of this silly and extravagant fool," said Louise to herself. "Oh, I will mock him, I will martyr him with this devil's work. The whole world shall know of it, and, from this time forth, I shall be justified and pitied. No one will be surprised that I am not constant to my husband, that I cannot love him."

Whilst the pious-elect still rested upon their knees in trembling adoration, the priest Pfannenschmidt had recovered from his surprise and alarm. He, who did not believe in the devil, although he daily addressed him, knew that the monster before him was an unseemly jest or a malicious interruption. He must, therefore, tear off his mask and expose him to the faithful.

With passionate energy he stretched out both his arms toward him. "Away with you, you son of Baal! Fly, fly, before I unmask you! You are not what you appear. You are no true devil!"

"How! you deny me, your lord and master?" cried the intruder, raising his hand covered with a crimson glove, against the priest. "You have long called for me. You have robbed these, my children, of their gold in order to propitiate me, and now that I am come, you will not confess me before men! Perhaps you fear that these pious believers will no longer lavish their attentions and their gold upon you, and suffer you to lead them by the nose. Go, go! you are not my high priest. I listened to your entreaties, and I came, but only to prove to my children that you are a deceiver, and to free them from your yoke. Away, you blasphemer of God and of the devil! Neither God nor the devil accepts your service; away with you!" Saying this, he seized the astrologer with a powerful arm, and dragged him toward the altar.

But Pfannenschmidt was not the man to submit to such indignities. With a wild cry of rage, he rushed upon his adversary; and now began a scene which neither words nor colors could portray. The pious worshippers raised themselves from their knees and stared for a moment at this curious spectacle; and then, according as they believed in the devil or the priest, sprang forward to take part in the contest.

In the midst of this wild tumult the policemen appeared, to arrest those who were present, in the name of the king; to break up the assembly, and put an end to the noise and tumult.

Louise, meanwhile, laughing boisterously, observed this whole scene from the cabinet; she saw the police seize the raging astrologer, who uttered curses, loud and deep, against the unbelieving king, who dared to treat the pious and prayerful as culprits, and to arrest the servant and priest of the Lord. Louise saw these counts and barons, these officers and secretaries, who had been the brave adherents of the astrologer, slipping away with shame and confusion of face. She saw her own husband mocked and ridiculed by the police, who handed him an order from the king, written by the royal hand, commanding him to consider himself as under arrest in his own house.   As Louise heard this order read, her laughter was hushed and her brow was clouded.

"Truly," said she, "that is a degree of consideration which looks like malice in the king.   To make my husband a prisoner in his own house is to punish me fearfully, by condemning me steadily to his hateful society.   My God, how cruel, how wicked is the king!   My husband is a prisoner here! that is to banish my beautiful, my beloved Salimberri from my presence.   Oh, when shall we meet again, my love, my adorer?"

BOOK II.

CHAPTER I.

THE TWO SISTERS.

"I HAVE triumphed! I have reached the goal!" said Princess Ulrica, with a proud smile, as she laid her hymn-book aside, and removed from her head her long white veil. " This important step is taken; yet one more grand ceremony, and I will be the Princess Royal of Sweden—after that, a queen! They have not succeeded in setting me aside. Amelia will not be married before me, thus bringing upon me the contempt and ridicule of the mocking world. All my plans have succeeded. In place of shrouding my head in the funereal veil of an abbess, to which my brother had condemned me, I shall soon wear the festive myrtle-wreath, and ere long a crown will adorn my brow."

Ulrica threw herself upon the divan, in order to indulge quietly in these proud and happy dreams of the future, when the door was hastily thrown open, and the Princess Amelia, with a pale and angry face, entered the room. She cast one of those glances of flame, with which she, in common with the king, was wont to crush her adversaries, upon the splendid toilet of her sister, and a wild and scornful laugh burst from her lips.

" I have not, then, been deceived," she cried; " it is not a fairy tale to which I have listened. You come from the chapel?"

" I come from the chapel? yes," said Ulrica, meeting the angry glance of her sister with a firm and steady look. Resolved to breast the coming storm with proud composure, she folded her arms across her bosom, as if she would protect herself from Amelia's flashing eyes. "I come from the chapel—what further?"

"What further?" cried Amelia, stamping fiercely on the floor. "Ah, you will play the harmless and the innocent! What took you to the chapel?"

Ulrica looked up steadily and smilingly; then said, in a quiet and indifferent tone: "I have taken the sacrament of the Lord's Supper, according to the Lutheran form of worship."

Amelia shuddered as if she felt the sting of a poisonous serpent. "That signifies that you are an apostate; that signifies that you have shamefully outwitted and betrayed me; that means—"

"That signifies," said Ulrica, interrupting her, "that I am a less pious Christian than you are; that you, my noble young sister, are a more innocent and unselfish maiden than the Princess Ulrica."

"Words, words! base, hypocritical words!" cried Amelia. "You first inspired me with the thought which led to my childish and contradictory behavior, and which for some days made me the jest of the court. You are a false friend, a faithless sister! I stood in your path, and you put me aside. I understand now your perfidious counsels, your smooth, deceitful encouragement to my opposition against the proposition of the Swedish ambassador. I, forsooth, must be childish, coarse, and rude, in order that your gentle and girlish grace, your amiable courtesy, might shine with added lustre. I was your foil, which made the jewel of your beauty resplendent. Oh! it is shameful to be so misused, so outwitted by my sister!"

With streaming eyes, Amelia sank upon a chair, and hid her face with her trembling little hands.

"Foolish child!" said Ulrica, "you accuse me fiercely, but you know that you came to me and implored me to find a means whereby you would be relieved from this hateful marriage with the Prince Royal of Sweden."

"You should have reasoned with me, you should have encouraged me to give up my foolish opposition. You should have reminded me that I was a princess, and therefore condemned to have no heart."

8

" You said nothing to me of your heart; you spoke only of your religion. Had you told me that your heart rebelled against this marriage with the Crown Prince of Sweden, then, upon my knees, with all the strength of a sister's love, I would have implored you to accept his hand, to shroud your heart in your robe of purple, and take refuge on your throne from the danger which threatens a young princess if she allows her heart to speak."

Amelia let her hands fall from her face, and looked up at her sister, whose great earnest eyes were fixed upon her with an expression of triumph and derision.

" I did not say that my heart had spoken," she cried, sobbing and trembling; " I only said that we poor princesses were not allowed to have hearts."

" No heart for one; but a great large heart, great enough for all! " cried Ulrica. " You accuse me, Amelia, but you forget that I did not intrude upon your confidence. You came to me voluntarily, and disclosed your abhorrence of this marriage; then only did I counsel you, as I would wish to be advised under the same circumstances. In a word, I counselled you to obey your conscience, your own convictions of duty."

" Your advice was wonderfully in unison with your own plans; your deceitful words were dictated by selfishness," cried Amelia, bitterly.

" I would not have adopted the course which I advised you to pursue, because my character and my feeling are wholly different from yours. My conscience is less tender, less trembling than yours. To become a Lutheran does not appear to me a crime, not even a fault, more particularly as this change is not the result of fickleness or inconstancy, but for an important political object."

" And your object was to become Queen of Sweden? "

" Why should I deny it? I accept this crown which you cast from you with contempt. I am ambitious. You were too proud to offer up the smallest part of your religious faith in order to mount the throne of Sweden. I do not fear to be banished from heaven, because, in order to become a queen, I changed the outward form of my religion;

my inward faith is unchanged: if you repent your conduct—if you have modified your views—"

"No, no!" said Amelia, hastily, "I do not repent. My grief and my despair are not because of this pitiful crown, but because of my faithless and deceitful sister who gave me evil counsel to promote her own interests, and while she seemed to love, betrayed me. Go, go! place a crown upon your proud head; you take up that which I despise and trample upon. I do not repent. I have no regrets. But, hark! in becoming a queen, you cease to be my sister. Never will I forget that through falsehood and treachery you won this crown. Go! be Queen of Sweden. Let the whole world bow the knee before you. I despise you. You have shrouded your pitiful heart in your royal robes. Farewell!"

She sprang to the door with flashing eyes and throbbing breast, but Ulrica followed and laid her hand upon her shoulder.

"Let us not part in anger, my sister," said she, softly—"let us—"

Amelia would not listen; with an angry movement she dashed the hand from her shoulder and fled from the room. Alone in her boudoir, she paced the room in stormy rage, wild passion throbbed in every pulse. With the insane fury of the Hohenzollerns, she almost cursed her sister, who had so bitterly deceived, so shamefully betrayed her.

In outward appearance, as well as in character, the Princess Amelia greatly resembled her royal brother: like him, she was by nature trusting and confiding; but, once deceived, despair and doubt took possession of her. A deadly mildew destroyed the love which she had cherished, not only for her betrayer, but her confidence and trust in all around her. Great and magnanimous herself, she now felt that the rich fountain of her love and her innocent, girlish credulity were choked within her heart. With trembling lips, she said aloud and firmly: "I will never more have a friend. I do not believe in friendship. Women are all false, all cunning, all selfish. My heart is closed to them, and their deceitful smiles and plausible words can never more betray me. Oh, my God, my God! must I then be always solitary, always alone? must I—"

Suddenly she paused, and a rich crimson blush overspread her face. What was it which interrupted her sorrowful words? Why did she fix her eyes upon the door so eagerly? Why did she listen so earnestly to that voice calling her name from the corridor.

"Pöllnitz, it is Pöllnitz!" she whispered to herself, and she trembled fearfully.

"I must speak with the Princess Amelia," cried the master of ceremonies.

"But that is impossible," replied another voice; "her royal highness has closed the door, and will receive no one."

"Her royal highness will open the door and allow me to enter as soon as you announce me. I come upon a most important mission. The life-happiness of more than one woman depends upon my errand."

"My God!" said Amelia, turning deadly pale, "Pöllnitz may betray me if I refuse to open the door." So saying, she sprang forward and drew back the bolt.

"Look, now, Mademoiselle von Marwitz," cried Pöllnitz, as he bowed profoundly, "was I not right? Our dear princess was graciously pleased to open the door so soon as she heard my voice. Remark that, mademoiselle, and look upon me in future as a most important person, who is not only accorded *les grandes* but *les petites entrées.*"

The Princess Amelia was but little inclined to enter into the jests of the master of ceremonies.

"I heard," said she, in a harsh tone, "that you demanded importunately to see me, and you went so far as to declare that the happiness of many men depended upon this interview."

"Pardon me, your highness, I only said that the happiness of more than one *woman* depended upon it; and you will graciously admit that I have spoken the truth when you learn the occasion which brings me here."

"Well, let us hear," said Amelia, "and woe to you if it is not a grave and important affair!"

"Grave indeed; it concerns the toilets for a ball, and you

must confess that the happiness of more than one woman hangs upon this question."

"In truth, you are right, and if you came as milliner or dressmaker, Mademoiselle von Marwitz did wrong not to announce you immediately."

"Now, ladies, there is nothing less important on hand than a masked ball. The king has commanded that, besides the masked ball which is to take place in the opera-house, and to which the public are invited, another shall be arranged here in the castle on the day before the betrothal of the Princess Ulrica."

"And when is that ceremony to take place?" said Amelia.

"Has not your royal highness been informed? Ah, I forgot—the king has kept this a secret, and to no one but the queen-mother has it been officially announced. Yes, yes, the Princess Ulrica is to marry this little Prince of Holstein, who will, however, be King of Sweden. This solemn ceremony takes place in four days; so we have but three days before the masquerade, and we must work night and day to prepare the necessary costumes—his majesty wishes it to be a superb *fête*. Quadrilles are arranged, the king has selected the partners, and I am here at his command, to say to your royal highness that you will take part in these quadrilles. You will dance a quadrille, in the costume of Francis the First, with the Margravine of Baireuth and the Duchess of Brunswick."

"And who is to be my partner?" said Amelia, anxiously.

"The Margrave von Schwedt."

"Ah! my irresistible cousin. I see there the hand of my malicious brother; he knows how dull and wearisome I consider the poor margrave."

The princess turned away displeased, and walked up and down the room.

"Did you not say that I, also, would take part in the quadrille?" said Mademoiselle von Marwitz.

"Certainly, mademoiselle; you will dance in Russian costume."

"And who will be my partner?"

Pöllnitz laughed heartily. "One would think that the

most important question was not as to the ball toilet, but as
to the partner; that he, in short, was as much a life-question
as the color and cut of your robe, or the fashion of your
coiffure. So you demand the name of your partner? Ah,
mademoiselle, you will be more than content. The partner
whom the king has selected for you is one of our youngest,
handsomest, most amiable and talented cavaliers; a youth
whom Alcibiades would not have been indignant at being
compared with, and whom Diana would have preferred, perhaps, to the dreaming and beautiful Endymion, had she
found him sleeping. And mark you, you will not only dance
with this pearl of creation, but in the next few days you must
see and speak with him frequently. It is necessary that you
should consult together over the choice and color of your
costumes, and about the dances. If your royal highness will
allow it, he must come daily to arrange these important
points. Alas! why am I not a young maiden? Why can I
not enjoy the felicity of loving this Adonis? Why can I
not exchange this poor, burnt-out heart for one that glows
and palpitates?"

"You are a fool, and know nothing about a maiden's
heart! In your ecstasy for this Ganymede, who is probably
an old crippled monster, you make rare confusion. You
force the young girl to play the part of the ardent lover, and
give to your monster the character of a cool, vain fop."

"Monster? My God! she said monster!" cried Pöllnitz,
pathetically. "Fall upon your knees, mademoiselle, and
pray fervently to your good fortune to forgive you; you have
sinned greatly against it, I assure you. You will confess
this when I have told you the name of your partner."

"Name him, then, at last."

"Not before Princess Amelia is gracious enough to
promise me that she will watch over and shield you; that
she will never allow you a single *tête-à-tête* with your dangerous partner."

"Ah, you will make me the *duenna* of my maid of honor,"
said Amelia, laughing. "I shall be the *chaperon* of my
good Marwitz, and shield her from the weakness of her own
heart."

"If your royal highness declines to give this promise,

Mademoiselle Marwitz shall have another partner. I cannot answer to my conscience if she is left alone, unobserved and unprotected, with the most beautiful of the beautiful."

"Be merciful, princess, and say yes. For you see well that this terrible Pöllnitz will make me a martyr to curiosity. Consent, gracious princess, and then I may perhaps hear the name of my partner."

"Well, then," said Amelia, smiling, "I consent to play Mentor to my maid of honor."

"Your royal highness promises then, solemnly, to be present at every conference between Mademoiselle von Marwitz and her irresistible partner?"

"I promise; be quick! Marwitz will die of curiosity, if you do not tell the name of this wonder."

"Well, now, that I have, so far as it is in my power, guarded the heart of this young girl from disaster, and placed it under the protecting eye of our noble princess, I venture to name my paragon. He is the young lieutenant—Baron von Trenck, the favorite of the king and the court."

Very different was the impression made by this name upon the two ladies. The eager countenance of Mademoiselle von Marwitz expressed cool displeasure; while the princess, blushing and confused, turned aside to conceal the happy smile which played upon her full, rosy lips.

Pöllnitz, who had seen all this, wished to give the princess time to collect herself. He turned to Mademoiselle Marwitz and said: "I see, to my amazement, that our lovely maid of honor is not so enraptured as I had hoped. Mademoiselle, mademoiselle! you are a wonderful actress, but you cannot deceive me. You wish to seem disappointed and indifferent, in order to induce our gracious princess to withdraw her promise to me, and to think it unnecessary to be present at your interviews with Trenck. This acting is in vain. The princess has given her word, and she will most surely keep it."

"Certainly," said Amelia, smiling, "I have no alternative. Queens and princesses, kings and princes, are bound by their promises, even as common men, and their honor demands that they fulfil their contracts. I will keep my word. But enough of jesting for the present. Let us speak now of the solemn realities of life, namely, of our toilets. Baron, give me your model engraving, and make known your views. Call my chambermaid, mademoiselle, and my dressmakers; we will hold a solemn conference."

CHAPTER II.

THE TEMPTER.

As Mademoiselle von Marwitz left the room, Pöllnitz took a sealed note from his pocket and handed it hastily to the princess. She concealed it in the pocket of her dress, and continued to gaze indifferently upon a painting of Watteau, which hung upon the wall.

"Not one word! Still! Not one word!" whispered Pöllnitz. "You are resolved to drive my young friend to despair. You will not grant him one gracious word?"

The princess turned away her blushing face, drew a note from her bosom, and, without a glance or word in reply, she handed it to the master of ceremonies, ashamed and confused, as a young girl always is, when she enters upon her first love romance, or commits her first imprudence.

Pöllnitz kissed her hand with a lover's rapture. "He will be the most blessed of mortals," said he, "and yet this is so small a favor! It lies in the power of your royal highness to grant him heavenly felicity. You can fulfil one wish which his trembling lips have never dared to speak; which only God and the eyes of one faithful friend have seen written in his heart."

"What is this wish?" said the princess, in so low and trembling a whisper, that Pöllnitz rather guessed than heard her words.

"I believe that he would pay with his life for the happiness of sitting one hour at your feet and gazing upon you."

"Well, you have prepared for him this opportunity; you have so adroitly arranged your plans, that I cannot avoid meeting him."

"Ah, princess, how despondent would he be, if he could hear these cold and cruel words! I must comfort him by this appearance of favor if I cannot obtain for him a real happiness. Your royal highness is very cold, very stern toward my poor friend. My God! he asks only of your grace, that which the humblest of your brother's subjects dare demand of him—an audience—that is all."

Amelia fixed her burning eyes upon Pöllnitz. "*Apage. Satanas!*" she whispered, with a weary smile.

"You do me too much honor," said Pöllnitz. "Unhappily I am not the devil, who is, without doubt, next to God, the most powerful ruler of this earth. I am convinced that three-fourths of our race belong to him. I am, alas! but a poor, weak mortal, and my words have not the power to move the heart of your highness to pity."

"My God! Pöllnitz, why all this eloquence and intercession?" cried Amelia. "Do I not allow him to write to me all that he thinks and feels? Am I not traitress enough to read all his letters, and pardon him for his love? What more can he dare hope for? Is it not enough that he loves a princess, and tells her so? Not enough—"

She ceased suddenly; her eyes, which shrank from meeting the bold, reproachful, and ironical glance of the baron, had wandered restlessly about the room and fell now upon the picture of Watteau; upon the loving, happy pair, who were tenderly embracing under the oaks in the centre of that enchanting landscape. This group, upon which the eye of the princess accidentally rested, was an eloquent and decisive answer to her question—an answer made to the eyes, if not the ears of Amelia—and her heart trembled.

Pöllnitz had followed her glances, and understood her blushes and her confusion. He stepped to the picture and pointed to the tender lovers.

"Gracious princess, demand of these blessed ones, if a man who loves passionately has nothing more to implore of his mistress than the permission to write her letters?"

Amelia trembled. She fixed her eyes with an expression of absolute terror upon Pöllnitz, who with his fox smile and immovable composure gazed steadily in her face. He had no pity for her girlish confusion, for her modest and maid-

enly alarm. With gay, mocking, and frivolous jests, he resolved to overcome her fears. He painted in glowing colors
the anguish and despair of her young lover; he assured her
that she could grant him a meeting in her rooms without
danger from curious eyes or ears. Did not the room of the
princess open upon this little dark corridor, in which no
guard was ever placed, and from which a small, neglected
stairway led to the lower *étage* of the castle? This stairway
opened into an unoccupied room, the low windows of which
looked out upon the garden of Monbijou. Nothing, then,
was necessary but to withdraw the bar from these windows
during the day; they could then be noiselessly opened by
night, and the room of the princess safely reached.

The princess was silent. By no look or smile, no con-
traction of the brow or expression of displeasure, did she
show her emotion, but she listened to these vile and dangerous words; she let the poison of the tempter enter her heart;
she had neither the strength nor will to reject his counsel,
or banish him from her presence; she had only the power to
be silent, and to conceal from Pöllnitz that her better self
was overcome.

"I shall soon reach the goal," said Pöllnitz, clapping his
hands merrily after leaving the princess. "Yes, yes! the
heart of the little Princess Amelia is subdued, and her love
is like a ripe fruit—ready to be plucked by the first eager
hand. And this, my proud and cruel King Frederick, will
be my revenge. I will return shame for shame. If the
good people in the streets rejoice to hear the humiliation
and shame put upon the Baron von Pöllnitz, cried aloud at
the corners, I think they will enjoy no less the scandal about
the little Princess Amelia. This will not, to be sure, be
trumpeted through the streets; but the voice of Slander is
powerful, and her lightest whispers are eagerly received."

Pöllnitz gave himself up for a while to these wicked and
cruel thoughts, and he looked like a demon rejoicing in the
anguish of his victims. He soon smoothed his brow, however, and assumed his accustomed gay and unembarrassed
manner.

"But before I revenge myself, I must be paid," said he,
with an internal chuckle. "I shall be the chosen confidant

in this adventure, and my name is not Pöllnitz if I do not realize a large profit. Oh, King Frederick, King Frederick! I think the little Amelia will pay but small attention to your command and your menace. She will lend the poor Pöllnitz gold; yes, gold, much gold! and I—I will pay her by my silence."

Giving himself up to these happy thoughts, the master of ceremonies sought the young lieutenant, in order to hand him the letter of the princess.

"The fortress is ready to surrender," cried he; "advance and storm it, and you will enter the open door of the heart as conqueror. I have prepared the way for you to see the princess every day: make use of your opportunities like a brave, handsome, young, and loving cavalier. I predict you will soon be a general, or a prince, or something great and envied."

"A general, a prince, or a high traitor, who must lay his head upon the block and expiate his guilt with his life," said Trench thoughtfully. "Let it be so. In order to become this high traitor, I must first be the happiest, the most enviable of men. I shall not think that too dearly paid for by my heart's blood. Oh, Amelia, Amelia! I love thee boundlessly; thou art my happiness, my salvation, my hope; thou—"

"Enough, enough!" said Pöllnitz, laughing and placing his hands upon his ears. These are well-known, well-used, and much-abused phrases, which have been repeated in all languages since the time of Adam, and which after all are only lovely and fantastic lies. Act, my young friend, but say nothing; you know that walls have ears. The table upon which you write your letters, and the portfolio in which you place the letters of the princess, to be guarded to all eternity, both have prying eyes. Prudence, prudence! burn the letters of the princess, and write your own with sympathetic ink or in cipher, so that no man can read them, and none but God and the devil may know your dangerous secret."

Trenck did not hear one word of this; he was too happy, too impassioned, too young, to listen to the words of warning and caution of the old *roué*. He read again and again, and with ever-increasing rapture, the letter of the princess; he pressed it to his throbbing heart and glowing lips, and fixed his loving eyes upon those characters which her hand had written and her heart had dictated.

Pöllnitz looked at him with a subdued smile, and enjoyed his raptures, even as the fox enjoys the graceful flappings of the wings, the gentle movements of the dove, when he knows that she cannot escape him, and grants her a few moments of happiness before he springs upon and strangles her. "I wager that you know that letter by heart," said he, as he slowly lighted a match in order to kindle his cigar; "am I not right? do you not know it by heart?"

"Every word is written in letters of flame upon my heart."

With a sudden movement, the baron snatched the paper from the young man and held it in the flames.

"Stop! stop!" cried Frederick von Trenck, and he tried to tear the letter from him.

Pöllnitz kept him off with one arm and waved the burning paper over his head.

"My God! what have you done?" cried the young man.

"I have made a sacrifice to the god of silence," said he solemnly; "I have burnt this paper lest it might be used to light the scaffold upon which you may one day burn as a high traitor. Thank me, young man. I have perhaps saved you from discovery and from death."

CHAPTER III.

THE WEDDING FESTIVAL OF THE PRINCESS ULRICA.

TRULY this perfidious friend had, for one day, guarded the secret of the young lovers from discovery; but, the poison, which Pöllnitz in his worldly cunning prepared for them, had entered into their hearts. For some days they met under strong restraint; only by stolen glances and sighs, by a momentary pressure of the hand, or a few slightly murmured words, could they give expression to their rapture and their passion. The presence of another held their hearts and lips in bondage.

Pöllnitz knew full well that there was no surer means to induce a young girl to grant her lover an interview than to force them to meet before strange witnesses, to bring every word and look into captivity, to condemn them to silence and seeming indifference. The glowing heart bounds against these iron bands; it longs to cast off the yoke of silence, and to breathe unfettered as the wanton air. Princess Amelia had borne two days of this martyrdom, and her courage failed. She was resolved to grant him a private interview as soon as he dared ask for it. She wished to see this handsome face, now clouded by melancholy, illuminated by the sunshine of happiness; those sad eyes "should look up clear, and the sorrowful lips should smile; she would make her lover happy!" She thought only of this; it was her only wish.

There were many sad hours of pain and anguish, sad hours in which she saw her danger, and wished to escape. In her despair and agony she was almost ready to cast herself at the feet of her mother, to confess all, and seek this sure protection against her own girlish weakness; but the voice of love in her heart held her back from this step; she closed her eyes to the abyss which was before her and pressed panting onward to the brink. If Amelia had had a friend, a sister whom she could love and trust, she might have been saved; but her rank made a true friend impossible; being a princess, she was isolated. Her only friend and sister had alienated her heart, through the intrigues by which she had won the crown of Sweden.

Perhaps these costly and magnificent wedding festivities which would have been prepared for her, had she not refused a husband worthy of her birth, aroused her anger, and in her rage and her despair she entered upon dangerous paths, and fell into the cruel snares of Pöllnitz. She said to herself: "Yes, all this honor and glory was my own, but my weak heart and my perfidious sister wrenched them from my grasp. Fate offered me a way of escape, but my sister

cast me into the abyss in which I now stand; upon her rests
the responsibility. Upon her head be my tears, my despair,
my misery, and my shame. Ulrica prevented me from being
a queen; well, then, I will be simply a young girl, who loves
and who offers up all to her beloved, her pride, her rank, and
the unstained greatness of her ancestors. For Ulrica be
honor, pomp, and power; for me the mystery of love, and a
girl's silent happiness. Who can say which of us is most to
be envied?"

These were indeed happy, sunny days, which were prepared for the bride of Adolph Frederick of Holstein, the
Crown Prince of Sweden. *Fête* succeeded to *fête*. The
whole land took part in the happiness of the royal family.
All the provinces and cities sent deputations to congratulate
the king, and bring rich gifts to the princess; she who
had been always cast into the shade by the more noble and
bewildering beauty of her younger sister, had now become
the centre of attraction in all these superb festivities which
followed each other in quick succession. It was in honor of
the Princess Ulrica that the king gave a masked ball in the
opera-house, to which the whole city was invited; for her,
on the evening of her betrothal, every street in Berlin was
brilliantly illuminated with wax-lights, not by command of
the king, but as a free-will offering of the people; for her
the queen, at Schönhausen, gave a superb ball; for her the
Swedish ambassador arranged a *fête*, whose fabulous pomp
and extravagant luxury were supposed to indicate the splendor which awaited her in her new home. Lastly, this ball at
the royal palace, to which not only the nobles, but many of
the wealthy burghers were invited, was intended as a special
compliment to Ulrica.

More than three thousand persons moved gayly through
these royal saloons, odorous with the perfume of flowers,
glittering with wax-lights, the glimmer of diamonds, and
rich gold and silver embroideries—nothing was to be seen but
ravishing toilets and happy faces. All the beauty, youth,
rank, fame, and worth of Berlin were assembled at the palace; and behind these lovely ladies and glittering cavaliers,
the wondering, gaping crowd, of common men, moved slowly
onward, dumb with amazement and delight. The king had

commanded that no well-dressed person should be denied entrance to the castle.

Those who had cards of invitation were the guests of the king, and wandered freely through the saloons. Those who came without cards had to content themselves behind the silken ropes stretched across one side of the rooms; by means of this rope an almost invisible and yet an insurmountable barrier was interposed between the people and the court circle.

It was difficult to preserve the rules and customs of courtly etiquette in such a vast assembly, and more difficult still to see that every man was received and served as the guest of a king, and suitable to his own personal merit. Crowds of lackeys flew through the rooms bearing silver *plateaux* filled with the richest viands, the most costly fruits, and the rarest wines. Tables were loaded with the luxuries of every clime and season, and the clang of glasses and the sweet sound of happy laughter were heard in every direction. The king expressed a proud confidence in his good people of Berlin, and declined the services of the police. He commissioned some officers of his life-guard to act as his substitute and play the host, attending to the wants and pleasures of all. Supper was prepared in the picture-gallery for the court circle.

But what means this wild laughter which echoes suddenly through the vast crowd and reaches the ear of the king, who looks up surprised and questioning to his master of ceremonies, and orders him to investigate the tumult? In a few moments Pöllnitz returned, accompanied by a young officer, whose tall and graceful figure, and whose handsome face, glowing with youth, pride, and energy, attracted the attention of the noblest ladies, and won a smile of admiration from the queen-mother.

"Sire," said Pöllnitz, "a mask in the guise of a thief, and in the zealous pursuit of his calling, has robbed one of the officers who were commanded by your majesty to guard the public peace and property. Look, your majesty, at our young lieutenant, Von Trenck: in the midst of the crowd, his rich, gold-embroidered scarf has been adroitly removed; in his zeal for your service, he forgot himself, and the merry gnome, whom Trenck should have kept in order, has made our officer the target for his sleight of hand. This jest, sire, caused the loud laughter which you heard."

The eyes of the king rested with an expression of kindliness and admiration upon the young man, and the Princess Amelia felt her heart tremble with joy and hope. A rich crimson suffused her cheeks; it made her almost happy to see that her lover was appreciated by her exalted brother and king.

"I have watched and wondered at him during the whole evening," said the king, merrily; "his glance, like the eye of Providence, pierces the most distant and most obscure corner, and sees all that occurs. That he who sees all else has forgotten himself, proves that he is not vain, and that he forgets his own interests in the discharge of his public duties. I will remember this and reward him, not in the gay saloon, but on the battle-field, where, I am sure, his scarf will not be taken from him."

Frederick gave his hand to the young officer, who pressed it warmly to his lips; then turning to the queen-mother, he said: "Madame, I know that this young man has been commended to you, allow me also to bespeak your favor in his behalf; will your majesty have the grace to instruct him in all the qualities which should adorn a noble cavalier? I will make him a warrior, and then we shall possess a nobleman beyond praise, if not beyond comparison."

The king, rising from the table, left his seat and laid his hand kindly upon Trenck's shoulder. "He is tall enough," said Frederick laughing; "for that he may thank Providence; let him not be satisfied with that, but strive to be great, and for that he may thank himself." He nodded graciously to Trenck, gave his arm to the queen-mother, and led her into the ball-room.

CHAPTER IV.

THE crowd and heat of the dancing-saloon were intolerable. All wished to see the quadrille in which the two princesses, the loveliest women of the court, and the most gallant cavaliers were to appear. The music also was a special object of interest, as it was composed by the king. The first quadrille closed in the midst of tumultuous applause, restrained by no courtly etiquette. The partners for the second quadrille advanced to the gay and inspiring sound of pipes and drums.

The Princess Amelia had withdrawn from the crowd into a window recess. She was breathless and exhausted from the dance and the excitement of the last few days. She required a few moments of rest, of refreshment, and meditation. She drew the heavy silk curtains carefully together, and seated herself upon the little *tabouret* which stood in the recess. This quiet retreat, this isolation from the thoughtless crowd, brought peace to her soul. It was happiness to close her weary eyes, and indulge in sweet dreams to the sound of this glorious music; to feel herself shut off from the laughing, heartless crowd.

She leaned her lovely head upon the cushion, not to sleep but to dream. She thought of her sister, who would soon place a crown upon her head; who had sold herself for this crown to a man whom she had never seen, and of whom she knew nothing, but that he was heir to a throne. Amelia shuddered at the thought that Ulrica had sacrificed her religion to this man, whom she knew not, and had promised at God's altar to love and be faithful to him. In the purity and innocence of her girlish heart she considered this a crime, a sacrilege against love, truth, and faith. "I will never follow Ulrica's example," she whispered to herself. "I will never sell myself. I will obey the dictates of my heart and give myself to the man I love." As she said this, a crimson glow overspread her cheeks, and she opened her eyes wide, as if she hoped to see the man she loved before her, and

9

wished him to read in her steady glance the sweet confirmation of the words she had so lightly whispered.

"No, no! I will never marry without love. I love, and as there can be but one true love in a true life, I shall never marry—then—" She ceased and bowed her head upon her bosom, her trembling lips refused to speak the hope and dream of her heart, to give words to the wild, passionate thoughts which burned like lava in her breast, and, like the wild rush of many waters, drowned her reason. She thought that in the eloquence of her great love she might touch the heart of the king, and in the magnanimity of his soul he might allow her to be happy, to place a simple myrtle-wreath upon her brow. She repeated the friendly and admiring words which the king had spoken to her lover. She saw again those wondrous eyes resting with interest and admiration upon the splendid form of the young baron. A happy, playful smile was on her lip. "The king himself finds him handsome and attractive; he cannot then wonder that his sister shares his opinion. He will think it natural that I love him—that—"

A wild storm of applause in the saloon interrupted the current of her thoughts. She drew the curtains slightly apart, and gazed into the room. The second quadrille was ended, and the dancers were now sinking upon the *tabourets*, almost breathless from fatigue.

The princess could not only see, but she could hear. Two ladies stood just in front of the curtains behind which she was concealed, engaged in earnest conversation; they spoke of Frederick von Trenck; they were enraptured with his athletic form and glowing eyes.

"He has the face of a Ganymede and the figure of a Hercules," said one. "I think him as beautiful as the Apollo Belvedere," said the other; "and then his expression is so pure and innocent. I envy the woman who will be his first love."

"You think, then, that he has never loved?"

"I am sure of it. The passion and fire of his heart are yet concealed under the veil of youth. He is unmoved by a woman's tender smiles and her speaking and promising glances. He does not understand their meaning."

"Have you tried these powerful weapons?"

"I have, and I confess wholly in vain; but I have not given up the contest, and I shall renew the attack until—"

The ladies now moved slowly away, and the princess heard no more, but she knew their voices; they were Madame von Brandt and Louise von Kleist, whom the king often called the "loveliest of the lovely." Louise von Kleist, the irresistible coquette, who was always surrounded by worshippers and adorers, confessed to her friend that all her tender glances had been unavailing; that she had in vain attempted to melt the ice-rind of his heart.

"But she will renew her efforts," cried Amelia, and her heart trembled with its first throb of jealousy. "Oh, I know Louise von Kleist! She will pursue him with her tenderness, her glances of love, and bold encouragement, until he admires, falls at her feet a willing victim. But no, no, I cannot suffer that. She shall not rob me of my only happiness—the golden dream of my young life. He belongs to me, he is mine by the mighty power of passion, he is bound to me by a thousand holy oaths. I am his first love. I am that happy woman whom he adores, and who is envied by the beauteous Louise von Schwerin. He is mine and he shall be mine, in spite of the whole world. I love him, and I give myself to him."

And now she once more looked through the curtains and shrank back in sweet surprise. Right before her stood Trenck—the Apollo of Louise von Kleist, the Hercules and the Ganymede of Madame von Brandt, the beloved of the Princess Amelia—Trenck stood with folded arms immovable, and gazed piercingly in the crowd of maskers. Perhaps he sought for Amelia; perhaps he was sorrowful because she had withdrawn herself.

Suddenly he heard a soft, low voice whispering: "Do not move, do not turn—remain standing as you are; but if you hear and understand me, bow your head."

Frederick von Trenck bowed his head. But the princess could not see the rapturous expression which illuminated his face; she could not know that his breath almost failed him; she could not hear the stormy, tumultuous beating of his heart.

" Do you know who speaks? if you recognize me, incline your head."

The music sounded loud and clear, and the dancing feet, the gay jest, and merry laughter of five hundred persons gave confidence and security to the lovers. Frederick was not content with this silent sign. He turned toward the recess and said in low tones: " I know the voice of my angel, and I would fall upon my knees and worship her, but it would bring danger and separation."

" Still! say no more," whispered the voice; and Trenck knew by its trembling tones, that the maiden was inspired by the same ardent passion which glowed in every fibre of his being. That still small voice sounded in his ears like the notes of an organ: " Say no more. but listen. To-morrow the Princess Ulrica departs for Sweden, and the king goes to Potsdam; you will accompany him. Have you a swift horse that knows the way from Potsdam to Berlin, and can find it by night? "

" I have a swift horse, and for me and my horse there is no night."

" Four nights from this you will find the window which you know open, and the door which leads to the small stair, only closed. Come at the hour of eleven, and you will receive a compensation for the scarf you have lost this evening. Hush—no word; look not around, move onward indifferently; turn not your head. Farewell! in four days—at eleven —go! "

" I had to prepare a coat of mail for him, in order that he might be invulnerable," whispered Amelia tremblingly; exhausted and remorseful, she sank back upon the *tabouret.* " The beautiful Kleist shall not ravish my beloved from me. He loves me—me alone; and he shall no longer complain of my cruelty. I dare not be cruel! I dare not make him unhappy, for she might comfort him. He shall love nothing but me, only me! If Louise von Kleist pursues him with her arts, I will murder her—that is all! "

CHAPTER V.

A SHAME-FACED KING.

THE king laid his flute aside, and walked restlessly and sullenly about his room. His brow was clouded, and he had in vain sought distraction in his faithful friend, the flute. Its soft, melodious voice brought no relief; the cloud was in his heart, and made him the slave of melancholy. Perhaps it was the pain of separation from his sister which oppressed his spirit.

The evening before, the princess had taken leave of the Berliners at the opera-house, that is, she had shown herself to them for the last time. While the prima donna was singing her most enchanting melodies, the travelling carriage of Ulrica drove to the door. The king wished to spare himself the agony of a formal parting, and had ordered that she should enter her carriage at the close of the opera, and depart, without saying farewell.

The people knew this. They were utterly indifferent to the beautiful opera of "Rodelinda," and fixed their eyes steadily upon the king's *loge*. They thus took a silent and affectionate leave of their young princess, who appeared before them for the last time, in all the splendor of her youth and beauty, and the dignity of her proud and royal bearing. An unwonted silence reigned throughout the house; all eyes were turned to the box where the princess sat between the two queens. Suddenly the door was thrown open, and the young Prince Ferdinand rushed, with open arms, to his sister.

"My dear, dear Ulrica!" he cried, weeping and sobbing painfully, "must it then be so? Do I indeed see you for the last time?" With childish eagerness he embraced his sister, and leaned his head upon her bosom. The princess could no longer control herself; she mingled her tears with those of her brother, and drawing him softly out of view, she whispered weeping and trembling words of tenderness; she implored him not to forget her, and promised to love him always.

The queen-mother stood near. She had forgotten that she was a queen, and remembered only that she was a mother about to lose her child forever; the thought of royal dignity and courtly etiquette was for some moments banished from her proud heart; she saw her children heart-broken and weeping before her, and she wept with them.*

The people saw this. Never had the most gracious smile, the most condescending word of her majesty, won their hearts so completely as these tears of the mother. Every mother felt for this woman, who, though a queen, suffered a mother's anguish; and every maiden wept with this young girl, who, although entering upon a splendid future, shed hot tears over the happy past and the beloved home. When the men saw their wives and children weeping, and the prince not ashamed of his tears, they also wept, from sympathy and love to the royal house. In place of the gay jest and merry laughter wont to prevail between the acts, scarcely suppressed sobs were the only sounds to be heard. The glorious singer Salimberri was unapplauded. The Barbarina danced, but the accustomed bravos were hushed.

Was it the remembrance of this touching scene which moved the king so profoundly? Did this eternal separation from his beloved sister weigh upon his heart? The king himself knew not, or he would not acknowledge to himself what emotion produced this wild unrest. After laying his flute aside, he took up Livy, which lay always upon his writing-table, and tried to read a chapter; but the letters danced before his eyes, and his thoughts wandered far away from the old Roman. He threw the book peevishly aside, and, folding his arms, walked rapidly backward and forward.

"Ah me! ah me! I wish this were the day of battle!" he murmured. "To-day I should be surely victorious! I am in a fierce and desperate mood. The wild roar of conflict would be welcome as a sweet home song in a strange land, and the shedding of blood would be medicinal, and relieve my oppressed brain. What is it which has drawn this veil over my spirit? What mighty and mysterious power has stretched her hand over me? With what bounds am I

* Schneider's " History of the Opera and the Royal Opera-House."

held a helpless captive? I feel, but I cannot see them, and cannot tear them apart. No, no! I will be lord of myself. I will be no silent dreamer. I will live a true life. I will work, and be a faithful ruler, if I cannot be a free and happy man."

He rang the bell, and ordered the ministers to assemble for a cabinet council.

"I will work, and forget every thing else," he said, with a sad smile, and he entered his cabinet with this proud resolve.

This time the king deceived himself. The most earnest occupation did not drive the cloud from his brow: in fact, it became more lowering.

"I cannot endure this," he said, after walking backward and forward thoughtfully. "I will put a stop to it. As I am not a Ulysses, I do not see why I should bind my eyes, and stop my ears with wax, in order not to see this bewildering siren, and hear her intoxicating song. In this sorrowful and pitiful world, is it not a happiness to meet with an enchantress, to bow down to the magic of her charms, and for a small half hour to dream of bliss? All other men are mad: why should I alone be reasonable? Come, then, spirit of love and bliss, heavenly insanity, take possession of my struggling soul. Let old age be wise and cool, I am young and warm. For a little while I will play the fool, and forget my miserable dignity."

Frederick called his servant, and sent for General Rothenberg, then took his flute and began to play softly. When the general entered, the king nodded to him, but quietly finished his adagio; then laid the flute aside, and gave his hand to his friend.

"You must be Pylades, my friend, and banish the despondency which oppresses the heart and head of thy poor Orestes."

"I will be all that your majesty allows or commands me to be," said the general, laughing; "but I think the queen-mother would be little pleased to hear your majesty compare yourself to Orestes."

"Ah, you allude to Clytemnestra's faithless love-story, with which, truly, my exalted and virtuous mother cannot be associated. Well, my comparison is a little lame, but my despondency is real—deeply seated as my friendship for you."

"How! your majesty is melancholy? I understand this mood of my king," said Rothenberg. "It only takes possession of you the day before some great deed, and only then because the night before the day of triumph seems too long. Your majesty confesses that you are sad. I conclude, therefore, that we will soon have war, and soon rejoice in the victories of our king."

"Perhaps you are right," said the king, smiling. "I do not love war, but it is sometimes a necessary evil; and if I cannot relieve my godmother, Maria Theresa, of this mortal malady of pride and superciliousness without a general blood-letting, I must even play the physician and open a vein. The alliance with France is concluded; Charles the Seventh goes to Frankfort for coronation; the French ambassador accompanies him, and my army stands ready for battle, ready to protect the emperor against Austria. We will soon have war, friend, and I hope we will soon have a victory to celebrate. In a few weeks we will advance. Oh, Rothenberg! when I speak of battle, I feel that I am young, that my heart is not of stone—it bounds and beats as if it would break down its prison walls, and found a new home of glory and fame."

"The heart of my king will be ever young; it is full of trust and kindliness."

Frederick shook his head thoughtfully. "Do not believe that, Rothenberg; the hands that labor become hard and callous, and so is it with the heart. Mine has labored and suffered; it will turn at last to stone. Then I shall be condemned. The world will forget that it is responsible; they will speak only of my hard heart, and say nothing of the anguish and the deceptions which have turned me to stone. But what of that? Let these foolish two-legged creatures, who proudly proclaim that they are made in the image of God, say what they please of me; they cannot deprive me of my fame and my immortality. He who possesses that has received his reward, and dare utter no complaint. Truly Erostratus and Schinderhannes are celebrated, and

Eulenspiegle is better known and beloved by the people than Socrates."

"This proves that Wisdom herself must take the trouble to make herself popular," said Rothenberg. "True fame is only obtained by popularity. Alexander the Great and Cæsar were popular, and their names were therefore in the mouths of the people. This was their inheritance, handed down from generation to generation, from father to son. So will it be with King Frederick the Second. He is not only the king and the hero, but he is the man of the people. His fame will not be written alone on the tablets of history by the Muses; the people will write it on the pure, white, vacant leaves of their Bibles; the children and grandchildren will read it; and, centuries hence, the curious searchers into history will consider this as fame, and exalt the name of Frederick the Great."

"God grant it may be so!" said the king solemnly. "You know that I am ambitious. I believe that this passion is the most enduring, and that its burning thirst is never quenched. As crown prince, I was ever humiliated by the thought that the love, consideration, and respect shown to me was no tribute to my worth, but was offered to a prince, the son of a powerful king. With what admiration, with what enthusiasm did I look at Voltaire! he needed no high birth, no title, to be considered, honored, and envied by the whole world. I, however, must have rank, title, princely revenues, and a royal genealogical tree, in order to fix the eyes of men upon me. Ah, how often did I remind myself of the history of that great prince, who, surrounded by his enemies, and about to surrender, saw his servants and friends despairing and weeping around him! He smiled upon them, and uttered these few but expressive words: 'I feel by your tears that I am still a king.' I swore then to be like that noble man, to owe my fame, not to my royal mantle, but to myself. I have fulfilled but a small portion of my oath. I hope that my godmother, Maria Theresa, and the Russian empress, will soon afford me more . enlarged opportunities. Our enemies are indeed our best friends; they enrage and inspire us."

"In so saying, sire, you condemn us all, we who are the

most faithful, submissive, and enthusiastic friends of your highness."

"You are also useful to me," said the king. "You, for example, your cheerful, loving face does me good whenever I look upon it. You keep my heart young and fresh, and teach me to laugh, which pleasant art I am constantly forgetting in the midst of these wearisome and hypocritical men. I never laugh so merrily as when I am with you at your table, where I have the high privilege of laying aside my royalty, and being a simple, happy man like yourself. I rejoice in the prospect of this evening, and I am impatient as a young maiden before her first ball. This evening, if I remember correctly, I am invited by General von Rothenberg to a *petit souper*."

"Your majesty was kind enough to promise me that you would come."

"Do you know, Rothenberg, I really believe that the expectation of this *fête* has made the hours of the day so long and wearisome. Now, tell me, who are we to have? who takes part in our gayety?"

"Those who were selected by your majesty: Chazot and Algarotti, Jordan and Bielfeld."

"Did I select the company?" said the king, thoughtfully; "then I wonder that—" He stopped, and, looking down, turned away silently.

"What causes your majesty's wonder?" said the general.

"I am surprised that I did not ask you to give us Rhine wine this evening," said the king, with a sly smile.

"Rhine wine! why, your majesty has often told me that it was a slow poison, and produced death."

"Yes, that is true, but what will you have? There are many things in this incomprehensible world which are poisonous, and which, for that reason, are the more alluring. This is peculiarly so with women. He does well who avoids them; they bewilder our reason and make our hearts sick, but we do not flee from them. We pursue them, and the poison which they infuse in our veins is sweet; we quaff it rapturously, though death is in the cup."

"In this, however, your majesty is wiser than all other

men: you alone have the power to turn away from or withstand them."

"Who knows? perhaps that is sheer cowardice," said the king; he turned away confused, and beat with his fingers upon the window-glass. "I called the Rhine wine poison, because of its strength. I think now that it alone deserves to be called wine—it is the only wine which has bloom." Frederick was again silent, and beat a march upon the window.

The general looked at him anxiously and thoughtfully; suddenly his countenance cleared, and a half-suppressed smile played upon his lips.

"I will allow myself to add a conclusive word to those of my king, that is, a moral to his fable. Your majesty says Rhine wine is the only wine which deserves the name, because it alone has bloom. So I will call that society only society which is graced and adorned by women. Women are the bloom of society. Do you not agree with me, sire?"

"If I agree to that proposition, it amounts to a request that you will invite women to our *fête* this evening—will it not?" said the king, still thrumming on the window.

"And with what rapture would I fulfil your wish, but I fear it would be difficult to induce the ladies to come to the house of a young bachelor as I am!"

"Ah, bah! I have determined during the next winter to give these little suppers very often. I will have a private table, and women shall be present."

"Yes, but your majesty is married."

"They would come if I were a bachelor. The Countess Carnas, Frau von Brandt, the Kleist, and the Morien, are too witty and too intellectual to be restrained by narrow-minded prejudice."

"Does your majesty wish that I should invite these ladies?" said the general; "they will come, without doubt, if your majesty commands it. Shall I invite them?"

The king hesitated a moment to reply. "Perhaps they would not come willingly," said he; "you are unmarried, and they might be afraid of their husbands' anger."

"I must, then, invite ladies who are not married," said Rothenberg, whose face was now radiant with delight; "but

I do not know one unmarried lady of the higher circles who carries her freedom from prejudice so far as to dare attend a bachelor's supper."

"Must we always confine our invitations to the higher circles?" said the king, beating his parade march still more violently upon the window.

Rothenberg watched him with the eye of a sportsman, who sees the wild deer brought to bay.

"If your majesty will condescend to set etiquette aside, I will make a proposition."

"Etiquette is nonsense and folly, and shall not do the honors by our *petits soupers;* pleasure only presides."

"Then I propose that we invite some of the ladies from the theatre—is your majesty content?"

"Fully! but which of the ladies?" said the king.

"That is your majesty's affair," said Rothenberg, smiling. "You have selected the gentlemen, will it please you to name the ladies?"

"Well, then," said the king, hesitating, "what say you to Cochois, Astrea, and the little Petrea?"

"Sire, they will be all most welcome; but I pray you to allow me to add one name to your list, the name of a woman who is more lovely, more gracious, more intellectual, more alluring, than all the prima donnas of the world; who has the power to intoxicate all men, not excepting emperors and kings, and make them her willing slaves. Dare I name her, sire?"

"Certainly."

"The Signora Barbarina."

The king turned his head hastily, and his burning eyes rested questioningly upon the face of Rothenberg, who met his glance with a merry look.

Frederick was silent; and the general, making a profound bow, said solemnly: "I pray your majesty to allow me to invite Mesdames Cochois, Astrea, and Petrea, also the Signora Barbarina, to our *petit souper.*"

"Four prima donnas at once!" said the king, laughing; "that would be dangerous; we would, perhaps, have the interesting spectacle of seeing them tear out each other's eyes. No, no! to enjoy the glories of the sun, there must be no rival suns in the horizon; we will invite but one enchantress, and as you are the host, you have the undoubted right to select her. Let it be then the Signora Barbarina." *

"Your majesty graciously permits me to invite the Signora Barbarina?" said Rothenberg, looking the king steadily in the face; a rich blush suffused the cheeks of Frederick. Suddenly he laughed aloud, and laying his arm around the neck of his friend, he looked in his radiant face with an expression of confidence and love.

"You are a provoking scamp," said Frederick. "You understood me from the beginning, and left me hanging, like Absalom, upon the tree. That was cruel, Rothenberg."

"Cruel, but well deserved, sire. Why would you not make known your wishes clearly? Why leave me to guess them?"

"Why? My God! it is sometimes so agreeable and convenient to have your wishes guessed. The murder is out. You will invite the beautiful Barbarina. You can also invite another gentleman, an artist, in order that the lovely Italian may not feel so lonely amongst us barbarians."

"What artist, sire?"

"The painter Pesne; go yourself to invite him. It might be well for him to bring paper and pencil—he will assuredly have an irresistible desire to make a sketch of this beautiful nymph."

"Command him to do so, sire, and then to make a life-size picture from the sketch."

"Ah! so you wish a portrait of the Barbarina?"

"Yes, sire; but not for myself."

"For whom, then?"

"To have the pleasure of presenting it to my king."

"And why?"

"Because I am vain enough to believe that, as my present, the picture would have some value in your eyes," said Rothenberg, mockingly. "What cares my king for a portrait of the Barbarina? Nothing, sans doute. But when this picture is not only painted by the great Pesne, but is also the gift of a dear, faithful friend, I wager it will be

* Rodenbeck: "Journal of Frederick the Great."

highly appreciated by your majesty, and you will perhaps be gracious enough to hang it in your room."

"You! you!" said the king, pointing his finger threateningly at Rothenberg, "I am afraid of you. I believe you listen to and comprehend my most secret thoughts, and form your petition according to my wishes. I will, like a good-natured, easy fool, grant this request. Go and invite the Barbarina and the painter Pesne, and commission him to paint a life-size picture of the fair one.* Pesne must have several sketches, and I will choose from amongst them."

"I thank your majesty," cried the general; "and now have the goodness to dismiss me—I must make my preparations."

As Rothenberg stood upon the threshold, the king called him. "You have guessed my thoughts, and now I will prove to you that I read yours. You think I am in love."

"In love? What! I dare to think that?" said the general; and folding his hands he raised his eyes as if in prayer. "Shall I dare to have such an unholy thought in connection with my anointed king?"

The king laughed heartily. "As to my sanctity, I think the holy Antonius will not proclaim me as his brother. But I am not exactly in love." He stepped to the window, upon the sill of which a Japanese rose stood in rich bloom; he plucked one of the lovely flowers, and handing it to the general, he said: "Look, now! is it not enchantingly beautiful? Think you, that because I am a king, I have no heart, no thirst for beauty? Go! but remember that, though a king, I have the eyes and the passions of other men. I, too, am intoxicated by the perfume of flowers and the beauty of women."

---

* This splendid picture of Barbarina hung for a long time in the king's cabinet, and is still to be seen in the Royal Palace at Berlin.

CHAPTER VI.

THE FIRST RENDEZVOUS.

THE night was dark and still; so dark in the garden of Monbijou, that the keenest eye could not detect the forms of the two men who slipped stealthily among the trees; so still, that the slightest contact of their clothing with the motionless leaves, and the slightest footstep in the sand could be heard. But, happily, there was none to listen; unchallenged and unseen, the two muffled figures entered the avenue, at the end of which stood the little palace, the summer residence of the queen-mother. Here they rested for a moment, and cast a searching glance at the building, which stood also dark and silent before them.

"No light in the windows of the queen-mother," whispered one; "all asleep."

"Yes, all asleep, we have nothing to fear; let us go onward." The last speaker made a few hasty steps forward, but his companion seized him hastily by the arm, and held him back.

"You forget, my young Hotspur, that we must wait for the signal. Still! still! do not stamp so impatiently with your feet; you need not shake yourself like a young lion. He who goes upon such adventures must, above all things, be self-possessed, cautious, and cool. Believe me, I have had a long range of experience, and in this species of love adventure I think I might possibly rival the famous King Charles the Second, of England."

"But here there is no question of love adventure, Baron Pöllnitz," said his companion impatiently, almost fiercely.

"Not of love adventure, Baron Trenck! well, may I dare to ask what is the question?"

"A true—an eternal love!"

"Ah! a true, an eternal love," repeated Pöllnitz, with a dry, mocking laugh. "All honor to this true love, which, with all the reasons for its justification, and all the pathos of its heavenly source, glides stealthily to the royal palace, and hides itself under the shadow of the silent night. My good young sentimentalist, remember I am not a novice like yourself; I am an old fogy, and call things by their right names. Every passion is a true and eternal love, and every loved one is an angel of virtue, beauty, and purity, until we weary of the adventure, and seek a new distraction."

"You are a hopeless infidel," said Trenck, angrily; "truly he who has changed his faith as often as you have, has no religion—not even the religion of love. But look! a light is shown, and the window is opened; that is the signal."

"You are right, that is the signal. Let us go," whispered Pöllnitz; and he stepped hastily after the young officer.

And now they stood before the window on the ground floor, where the light had been seen for a moment. The window was half open.

"We have arrived," said Trenck, breathing heavily; "now, dear Pöllnitz, farewell; it cannot certainly be your intention to go farther. The princess commissioned you to accompany me to the castle, but she did not intend you should enter with me. You must understand this. You boast that you are rich in experience, and will therefore readily comprehend that the presence of a third party is abhorrent to lovers. I know that you are too amiable to make your friends wretched. Farewell, Baron Pöllnitz."

Trenck was in the act of springing into the window, but the strong arm of the master of ceremonies held him back.

"Let me enter first," said he, "and give me a little assistance. Your sophistical exposition of the words of our princess is entirely thrown away. She said to me, 'At eleven o'clock I will expect you and the Baron von Trenck in my room.' That is certainly explicit—as it appears to me, and needs no explanation. Lend me your arm."

With a heavy sigh, Trenck gave the required assistance, and then sprang lightly into the room.

"Give me your hand, and follow cautiously," said Pöllnitz. "I know every step of the way, and can guard you against all possible accidents. I have tried this path often in former years, particularly when Peter the Great and his wife, with twenty ladies of her suite, occupied this wing of the castle."

"Hush!" said Trenck; "we have reached the top—onward, silently."

"Give me your hand, I will lead you."

Carefully, silently, and on tip-toe, they passed through the dark corridor, and reached the door, through which a light shimmered. They tapped lightly upon the door, which was immediately opened. The confidential chambermaid of the princess came forward to meet them, and nodded to them silently to follow her; they passed through several rooms; at last she paused, and said, earnestly: "This is the boudoir of the princess; enter—you are expected."

With a hasty movement, Trenck opened the door—this door which separated him from his first love, his only hope of happiness. He entered that dimly-lighted room, toward which his weary, longing eyes had been often turned almost hopelessly. His heart beat stormily, his breathing was irregular, he thought he might die of rapture; he feared that in the wild agitation of the moment he might utter a cry, indicative as much of suffering as of joy.

There, upon the divan, sat the Princess Amelia. The hanging lamp lighted her face, which was fair and colorless. She tried to rise and advance to meet him, but she had no power; she extended both her hands, and murmured a few unintelligible words.

Frederick von Trenck's heart read her meaning; he rushed forward and covered her hands with his kisses and his tears; he fell upon his knees, and murmured words of rapture, of glowing thanks, of blessed joy—words which filled the trembling heart of Amelia with delight.

All this fell upon the cold but listening ears of the master of ceremonies, and seemed to him as sounding brass and the tinkling cymbal. He had discreetly and modestly withdrawn to the back part of the room; but he looked on like a worldling, with a mocking smile at the rapture of the two lovers. He soon found, however, that the *rôle* which he was condemned to play had its ridiculous and humiliating aspect, and he resolved to bear it no longer. He came forward, and with his usual cool impertinence he approached the princess, who greeted him with a crimson blush and a silent bow.

10

"Pardon me, your royal highness, if I dare to ask you to decide a question which has arisen between my friend Trenck and myself. He did not wish to allow me to accompany him farther than the castle window. I declared that I was authorized by your royal highness to enter with him this holiest of holies. Perhaps, however, I was in error, and have carried my zeal in your service too far. I pray you, therefore, to decide. Shall I go or stay?"

The princess had by this time entirely recovered her composure. "Remain," said she, with a ravishing smile, and giving her hand to the baron. "You were our confidant from the beginning, and I desire you to be wholly so. I wish you to be fully convinced that our love, though compelled for a while to seek darkness and obscurity, need not shun the eye of a friend. And who knows if we may not one day need your testimony? I do not deceive myself. I know that this night my good and evil genius are struggling over my future—that misfortune and shame have already perhaps stretched their wings over my head; but I will not yield to them without a struggle. It may be that one day I shall require your aid. Remain, therefore."

Pöllnitz bowed silently. The princess fixed her glance upon her lover, who, with a clouded brow and sad mien, stood near. She understood him, and a smile played upon her full, red lip.

"Remain, Von Pöllnitz, but allow us to step for a moment upon the balcony. It is a wondrous night. What we two have to say to each other, only heaven, with its shining stars, dare hear; I believe they only can understand our speech."

"I thank you! oh, I thank you!" whispered Trenck, pressing the hand of Amelia to his lips.

"Your royal highness, then, graciously allowed me to come here," said Pöllnitz, with a complaining voice, "in order to give me up entirely to my own thoughts, and force me to play the part of a Trappist. I shall, if I understand rightly my privileges, like the lion in the fairy tale, guard the door of that paradise in which my young friend revels in his first sunny dream of bliss. Your royal highness must confess that this is cruel work; but I am ready to undertake it, and place myself, like the angel with the flaming sword, before the door, ready to slay any serpent who dares undertake to enter this elysium."

The princess pointed to a table upon which game, fruit, and Spanish wine had been placed. "You will find there distraction and perhaps consolation, and I hope you will avail yourself of it. Farewell, baron; we place ourselves under your protection; guard us well." She opened the door and stepped with her lover upon the balcony.

Pöllnitz looked after them contemptuously. "Poor child! she is afraid of herself; she requires a *duenna*, and that she should have chosen exactly me for that purpose was a wonderful idea. Alas! my case is indeed pitiful; I am selected to play the part of a *duenna*. No one remembers that I have ears to hear and teeth to bite. I am supposed to see, nothing more. But what shall I see, what can I see in this dark night, which the god of love has so clouded over in compassion to this innocent and tender pair of doves? This was a rich, a truly romantic and girlish idea to grant her lover a rendezvous, it is true, under God's free heaven, but upon a balcony of three feet in length, with no seat to repose upon after the powerful emotions of a burning declaration of love. Well, for my part I find it more comfortable to rest upon this divan and enjoy my evening meal, while these two dreamers commune with the night-birds and the stars."

He threw himself upon the seat, seized his knife and fork, and indulged himself in the grouse and truffles which had been prepared for him.

CHAPTER VII.

ON THE BALCONY.

WITHOUT, upon the balcony, stood the two lovers. With their arms clasped around each other, they gazed up at the dark heavens—too deeply moved for utterance. They spoke to each other in the exalted language of lovers (understood only by the angels), whose words are blushes, sighs, glances, and tender pressures of the hand.

In the beginning this was their only language. Both shrank from interrupting this sweet communion of souls by earthly material speech. Suddenly their glances fell from heaven earthward. They sought another heaven, and other and dearer stars. Their eyes, accustomed to the darkness, met; their blushes and their happy smiles, though not seen, were understood and felt, and at the same moment they softly called each other's names.

This was their first language, soon succeeded by passionate and glowing protestations on his part; by blushing, trembling confessions on hers. They spoke and looked like all the millions of lovers who have found themselves alone in this old world of ours. The same old story, yet ever new.

The conduct, hopes, and fears of these young lovers could not be judged by common rules. Theirs was a love which could not hope for happiness or continuance; for which there was no perfumed oasis, no blooming myrtle-wreath to crown its dark and stormy path. They might be sure that the farther they advanced, the more trackless and arid would be the desert opening before them. Tears and robes of mourning would constitute their festal adorning.

"Why has Destiny placed you so high above me that I cannot hope to reach you? can never climb the ladder which leads to heaven and to happiness?" said Trenck, as he knelt before the princess.

She played thoughtfully with his long dark hair, and a burning tear rolled slowly over her cheek and fell upon his brow. That was her only answer.

Trenck shuddered. He dashed the tear from his face with trembling horror. "Oh, Amelia! you weep; you have no word of consolation, of encouragement, of hope for me?"

"No word, my friend; I have no hope, no consolation. I know that a dark and stormy future awaits us. I know that this cloudy night, under whose shadow we for the first time join our hands will endure forever; that for us the sun will never shine. I know that the moment our glances first met, my protecting angel veiled her face and, weeping, left me. I know that it would have been wiser and better to give your heart, with its treasures, to a poor beggar-girl on the street, than to consecrate it to the sister of a king—to the poor Princess Amelia."

"Stop, stop!" cried Trenck, still on his knees, and bowing his head almost to the earth. "Your words pierce my heart like poisoned daggers, and yet I feel that they are truth itself. Yes, I was indeed a bold traitor, in that I dared to raise my eyes to you; I was a blasphemer, in that I, the unconsecrated, forced myself into the holy temple of your heart; upon its altar the vestal flame of your pure and innocent thoughts burned clearly, until my hot and stormy sighs brought unrest and wild disorder. But I repent. There is yet time. You are bound to me by no vow, no solemn oath. Oh, Amelia! lay this scarcely-opened flower of our first young love by the withered violet-wreaths of your childhood, with which even now you sometimes play and smile upon in quiet and peaceful hours; to which you whisper: 'You were once beautiful and fragrant; you made me happy—but that is past.' Oh, Amelia! yet is there time; give me up; spurn me from you. Call your servants and point me out to them as a madman, who has dared to glide into your room; whose passion has made him blind and wild. Give me over to justice and to the scaffold. Only save yourself from my love, which is so cowardly, so egotistic, so hard-hearted; it has no strength in itself to choose banishment or death. Oh, Amelia! cast me away from your presence; trample me under your feet. I will die without one reproach, without one complaint. I will think that my death was necessary to save you from shame, from the torture of a long and dreary existence. All this is still in your power. I have no claim upon you; you are not mine; you have listened to my oaths, but you have not replied to them; you are free. Spurn me, then, you are bound by no vow."

Amelia raised her arm slowly and solemnly toward heaven. "I love you! May God hear me and accept my oath! I love you, and I swear to be yours; to be true and faithful; never to wed any other man!"

"Oh, most unhappy woman! oh, greatly to be pitied!" cried Trenck. Throwing his arms around her neck he laid his head upon her bosom. "Amelia, Amelia! these are not tears of rapture, of bliss. I weep from wretchedness, from anguish, for your dear sake. Ah, no! I will not accept your oath. I have not heard your words—those heavenly words which would have filled my heart with light and gladness, had they not contained your fatal condemnation. Oh, my beloved! you swear that you love me? That is, to sacrifice all the high privileges of your rank; the power and splendor which would surround a husband of equal birth—a throne, a royal crown. Beware! when I once accept your love, then you are mine; then I will never release you; not to the king —not even to God. You will be mine through all time and all eternity; nothing shall tear you from my arms, not even your own wish, your own prayers. Oh, Amelia! do you see that I am a madman, insane from rapture and despair! Should you not flee from a maniac? Perhaps his arm, imbued with giant strength, seeking to hold you ever to his heart, might crush you. Fly, then; spurn me from you; go to your room; go, and say to this mocking courtier, to whom nothing is holy, not even our love, who is surprised, at nothing—go and say to him: 'Trenck was a madman; I summoned him for pity; I hoped by mildness and forbearance to heal him. I have succeeded; he is gone. Go, now, and watch over your friend.' I will not contradict your words; so soon as you cross the threshold of the door, I will spring from the balcony. I will be careful; I will not stumble; I will not dash my head against the stones; I will not be found dead under your window; no trace of blood shall mark my desperate path. My wounds are fatal, but they shall bleed inwardly; only upon the battle-field will I lie down to die. Amid the roar of cannon I shall not be heard; I dare call your name with the last sigh which bursts from my icy lips; my last words of love will mingle with the convulsive groans of the dying. Flee, then! flee from wretchedness and despair. May God bless you and make you happy!"

Trenck drew aside reverentially, that she might pass him; but she moved not—her eyes were misty with tears, tears of love, of heavenly peace. Amelia laid her soft hand upon his shoulder. Her eyes, which were fixed upon his face, had a wondrous glow. Love and high resolve were written there. " Two of the brightest stars in yonder heavens did wander in our sphere." Trenck looked upon her, and saw and felt that we are indeed made in the image of God.

"I seek no safety in flight. I remain by your side; I love you, I love you! This is no trembling, sighing, blushing, sentimental love of a young maiden. I offer you the love of a bold, proud woman, who looks shame and death in the face. In the fire of my anguish, my love has become purified and hardened; in this flame it has forgotten its girlish blushes, and is unbending and unconquerable. I have baptized it with my tears; I have taken it to my heart, as a mother takes her new-born child whose existence is her condemnation, her dishonor, her shame; whom she loves boundlessly, and blesses even while weeping over it! I also weep, and I feel that condemnation and shame are my portion. I also bless my love; I think myself happy and enviable. God has blessed me; He has sent one pure, burning ray of His celestial existence into my heart, and taught me how to love unchangeably, immortally."

" Oh, Amelia, why cannot I die now?" cried Trenck, falling powerless at her feet.

She stooped and raised him up with a strong hand. " Rise," she said; " we must stand erect, side by side, firm and cool. When you kneel before me, I fear that you see in me a princess, the sister of a king. I am simply your beloved, the woman who adores you. Look you, Trenck, I do not say 'the young girl;' in my interior life I am no longer that. This fearful battle with myself has made me old and cautious. A young girl is trembling and cowardly. I am firm and brave; a young girl blushes when she confesses her love; I do not confess, I declare and glory in my passion. A young girl shudders when she thinks of dishonor and misery, of the power and rage and menaces of her family; when with prophetic eye she sees a herald clad in mourning announcing her dark fate. I shudder not. I am no weak maiden; I am a woman who loves without limit, unchangeably, eternally."

She threw her arms around him, and a long and blessed pause ensued. Lightly whispered the wind in the tops of the lofty poplars and oaks of the garden; unnumbered stars came out in their soft splendor and looked down upon this slumbering world. Many slept, forgetful alike of their joys and their griefs; some, rejoicing in unhoped-for happiness, looked up with grateful and loving hearts; others, with convulsive wringings of the hands and wild cries of anguish, called upon Heaven for aid. What know the stars of this? they flash and glimmer alike upon the happy and the despairing. The earth and sky have no tears, no sympathy for earthly passions. Amelia released herself from the arms of her lover and fixed her eyes upon the heavens. Suddenly a star fell, marking its downward and rapid flight with a line of silver; in a moment, in the twinkling of an eye, it was extinguished.

"An evil omen!" cried she, pointing upward. With a mysterious sympathy, Trenck had looked up at the same moment.

"The heavens will not deceive us, Amelia; they warn us, but this warning comes too late. You are mine, you have sworn that you love me; I have accepted your vows. May God also have heard them, and may He be gracious to us! Is it not written that Faith can remove mountains? that she is more powerful than the mightiest kings of the earth; stronger than death—that conquerors and heroes fall before her? Let us, then, have faith in our love; let us be strong in hope, in patience, in constancy."

"My brother says we shall soon have war. Will you not win a wreath of laurel upon the battle-field? who can know but the king may value it as highly, may consider it as glorious, as a princely crown? All my sisters are married to princes; perhaps my royal brother may pardon me for loving a hero whose brow is bound by a laurel-wreath alone."

"Swear to me, Amelia, to wait—to be patient, to give me time to reach this goal, which you paint in such heavenly colors."

"I swear!"

"You will never be the wife of another?"

"I will never be the wife of another."

"Be it prince or king; even if your brother commands it?"

"Be it prince or king; even if my brother commands it, I will never obey him."

"God, my God! you have heard our vows." While speaking, he took Amelia's head in his hands softly and bowed it down as if it were a holy sacrifice which he offered up to Heaven. "You have heard her oath: O God, punish her, crush her in your wrath, if she prove false!"

"I will be faithful to the end. May God punish me if I fail!"

"And now, beloved, you are mine eternally. Let me press our betrothal kiss upon your sweet lips; you are my bride, my wife. Tremble not now, turn not away from my arms; you have no other refuge, no other strong fortress than my heart, but it is a rock on which you can safely build; its foundation is strong, it can hold and sustain you. If the storm is too fierce, we can plunge together into the wild, raging sea, and be buried in the deep. Oh, my bride, let me kiss your lips; you are sanctified and holy in my eyes till the glorious day in which life or death shall unite us."

"No, you shall not kiss me; I embrace you, my beloved," and she pressed her soft full lips, which no untruthful, immodest word had ever desecrated, to his. It was a kiss holy, innocent, and pure as a maiden's prayer. "And now, my beloved, farewell," said Amelia, after a long pause, in which their lips had been silent, but their hearts had spoken to each other and to God. "Go," she said; "night melts into morn, the day breaks!"

"My day declines, my night comes on apace," sighed Trenck. "When do we meet again?"

Amelia looked up, smilingly, to the heavens. "Ask the stars and the calendar when the heavens are dark, and the moon hides her fair face; then I expect you—the window will be open and the door unbarred."

"The moon has ever been thought to be the friend of lovers," said Trenck, pressing the hand of the princess to his heart; "but I hate her with a perfect hatred, she robs me of my happiness."

"And now, let us return to Baron Pöllnitz, who is, without doubt, impatient."

"Why must he always accompany me, Amelia? why will you not allow me to come alone?"

"Why? I scarcely know myself. It seems to me we are safer when watched over by the eye of a friend; perhaps I am unduly anxious; a warning voice whispers me that it is better so. Pöllnitz has become the confidant of our love, let us trust him fully; let him know that, though traitors and meriting punishment in the sight of men, we are not guilty in the sight of God, and have no cause to blush or look down. Pöllnitz must always accompany you."

"Ah, Amelia!" sighed Trenck; "you have not forgotten that you are a princess. Love has not wholly conquered you. You command. It is not so with me. I submit, I obey, and I am silent. Be it as you will: Pöllnitz shall always accompany me—only promise me to come ever upon the balcony?"

"I promise! and now, beloved, let us say farewell to God, to the heavens, to the soft stars, and the dark night, which has spread her mantle over us and allowed us to be happy."

"Farewell, farewell, my happiness, my love, my pride, my hope, my future! Oh, Amelia, why cannot I go this moment into battle, and pluck high honors which will make me more worthy of you?"

They embraced for the last time, and then stepped into the room. Pöllnitz still sat on the divan before the table. Only a poor remnant of the feast remained; his tongue had been forced to silence in this lonely room, but he had been agreeably occupied with the game, fruits, jellies, and wine which were placed before him; he had stretched himself comfortably upon the sofa, and was quietly enjoying the blessed feeling of a healthy and undisturbed digestion. At last he had fallen asleep, or seemed so; it was some moments before Trenck succeeded in forcing him to open his eyes.

"You are very cruel, young friend," said he, rising up; "you have disturbed me in the midst of a wondrous and rapturous dream."

"Might I inquire into this dream?" said the princess.

"Ah, your royal highness, I dreamed of the only thing which would ever surprise or enrapture me in this comical and good-for-nothing world. I dreamed I had no creditors, and heaps of gold."

"And your dream differs widely from the reality?"

"Yes, my gracious princess, just the opposite is true. I have unnumbered creditors, and no gold."

"Poor Pöllnitz! how do you propose to free yourself from this painful embarrassment?"

"Ah, your royal highness, I shall never attempt it! I am more than content when I can find some soothing palliatives for this chronic disease, and, at least, find as many louis d'ors in my pocket as I have creditors to threaten me."

"And is that now your happy state?"

"No, princess, I have only twelve louis d'ors."

"And how many creditors?"

"Two-and-thirty."

"So twenty louis d'ors are wanting to satisfy your longing?"

"Yes, unhappily."

The princess walked to her table and took from it a little roll of gold, which she handed to the master of ceremonies. "Take it," said she, smiling; "yesterday I received my pin-money for the month, and I rejoice that I am in a condition to balance your creditors and your louis d'ors at this time."

Pöllnitz took the gold without a blush, and kissed the hand of the princess gallantly. "Ah! I have but one cause of repentance," sighed he.

"Well, what is that?"

"That I did not greatly increase the number of my creditors. My God! who could have guessed the magnanimous intentions of my royal princess?"

CHAPTER VIII.

THE FIRST CLOUD.

DRUNK with happiness, revelling in the recollection of this first interview with his lovely and exalted mistress,

Frederick von Trenck rode slowly through the lonely highways toward Potsdam. It was not necessary for him to pay any attention to the road, as his horse knew every foot of the way. Trenck laid his bridle carelessly upon the neck of the noble animal, and gave himself up entirely to meditation. Suddenly night waned, the vapors melted, light appeared in the east, and the first purple glow was succeeded by a clear, soft blue. The larks sang out their joyous morning song in the heavens, not yet disturbed by the noise and dust of the day.

Trenck heard not the song of the lark, he saw not the rising sun, which, with his golden rays, illuminated the landscape, and changed the dew-drops in the cups of the flowers into shimmering diamonds and rubies; he was dreaming, dreaming. The sweet and wondrous happiness of the last few hours intoxicated his soul; he recalled every word, every smile, every pressure of the hand of his beloved, and a crimson blush suffused his cheek, a sweet tremor oppressed his heart, as he remembered that she had been clasped in his arms; that he had kissed the pure, soft, girlish lips, whose breath was fresher and more odorous than the glorious morning air which fanned his cheeks and played with his long dark hair. With a radiant smile and proudly erected head, he recalled the promise of the princess. She had given him reason to hope; she believed in the possibility of their union.

And why, indeed, might not this be possible? Had not his career in the last few months been so brilliant as to excite the envy of his comrades? was he not recognized as the special favorite of the king? Scarcely six months had passed since he arrived in Berlin; a young, poor, and unknown student, he was commended to the king by his protector, the Count von Lottum, who earnestly petitioned his majesty to receive him into his life-guard. The king, charmed by his handsome and martial figure, by his cultivated intellect and wonderful memory, had made him cornet in his cavalry guard, and a few weeks later he was promoted to a lieutenancy. Though but eighteen years of age, he had the distinguished honor to be chosen by the king to exercise two regiments of Silesian cavalry, and Frederick himself had expressed his content, not only in gracious but affectionate words.* It is well known that the smile of a prince is like the golden rays of the sun: it lends light and glory to every object upon which it rests, and attracts the curious gaze of men.

The handsome young lieutenant, basking in the rays of royal favor, was naturally an object of remark and the most distinguished attentions to the circle of the court. More than once the king had been seen to lay his arm confidingly upon the shoulder of Trenck, and converse with him long and smilingly; more than once had the proud and almost unapproachable queen-mother accorded the young officer a gracious salutation; more than once had the princesses at the *fêtes* of the last winter selected him as their partner, and all those young and lovely girls of the court declared that there was no better dancer, no more attentive cavalier, no more agreeable companion than Frederick von Trenck —than this youthful, witty, merry officer, who surpassed all his comrades, not only in his height and the splendor of his form, but in talent and amiability. It was therefore to be expected that this proud aristocracy would seek to draw the favorite of the king and of the ladies into their circle.

Frederick von Trenck was of too sound and healthy a nature, he had too much strength of character, to be made vain or supercilious by these attentions. He soon, however, accustomed himself to them as his right; and he was scarcely surprised when the king, after his promotion, sent him two splendid horses from his own stable, and a thousand thalers, † at that time a considerable sum of money.

This general adulation inspired naturally bold wishes and ambitious dreams, and led him to look upon the impossible and unheard of as possible and attainable. Frederick von Trenck was not vain or imperious, but he was proud and ambitious; he had a great object in view, and all his powers were consecrated to that end; in his hopeful, sunny hours, he did not doubt of success; he was ever diligent, ever watch-

* " Mémoires de Frédéric Baron von Trenck," traduits par lui-même sur l'original allemande.
† Ibid.

ful, ever ready to embrace an opportunity; ever expecting some giant work, which would, in its fruition, bring him riches and honor, fame and greatness. He felt that he had strength to win a world and lay it bound at his feet; and if the king had commanded him to undertake the twelve labors of Hercules, he would not have shrunk from the ordeal. Convinced that a glorious future awaited him, he prepared himself for it. No hour found him idle. When his comrades, wearied by the fatiguing service and the oft-repeated exercises and preparations for war, retired to rest, Trenck was earnestly engaged in some grave study, some scientific work, seated at his writing-table surrounded with books, maps, and drawings.

The young lieutenant was preparing himself to be a general, or a conquering hero, by his talents and his great deeds; to subdue the world and its prejudices; to bridge over with laurels and trophies the gulf which separated him from the princess. Was he not already on the way? Did not the future beckon to him with glorious promise? Must not he, who at eighteen years of age had attained that for which many not less endowed had given their whole lives in vain—he, the flattered cavalier, the scholar, and the officer of the king's guard—be set apart, elected to some exalted fate?

These were the thoughts which occupied the young man, and which made him forgetful of all other things, even the danger with which the slow movements of his horse and the ever-rising sun threatened him.

It was the custom of the king to attend the early morning parade, and the commander, Captain Jaschinsky, did not belong to Trenck's friends; he envied him for his rapid promotion; it angered him that Trenck had, at a bound, reached that position to which he had wearily crept forward through long years of service. It would have made him happy to see this young man, who advanced so proudly and triumphantly upon the path of honor and distinction, cast down from the giddy height of royal favor, and trampled in the dust of forgetfulness. He watched his young lieutenant with the smiling cunning of a base soul, resolved to punish harshly the smallest neglect of duty.

And now he had found his opportunity. A sergeant, who was a spy for the captain, informed him that Trenck's corporal had told him his master had ridden forth late in the night and had not yet returned. The sergeant had watched the door of the house in which Trenck resided, and was convinced that he was still absent. This intelligence filled the heart of Captain Jaschinsky with joy; he concealed it, however, under the mask of indifference; he declared that he did not believe this story of Trenck's absence. The young man knew full well that no officer was allowed to leave Potsdam, even for an hour, without permission, particularly during the night.

In order, as he said, to convince the sergeant of the untruth of this statement, he sent him with some trifling commission to Lieutenant von Trenck. The sergeant returned triumphantly; the baron was not at home, and his servant was most anxious about him, The captain shrugged his shoulders silently. The clock struck eight; he seized his hat, and hastened to the parade.

The whole line was formed; every officer stood by his regiment, except the lieutenant of the second company. The captain saw this at a glance, and a wicked smile for one moment played upon his face. He rode with zealous haste to the front of his regiment and saluted the king, who descended the steps of the castle, accompanied by his generals and adjutants.

At this moment, to the right wing of the regiment, there was a slight disturbance, which did not escape the listening ear of the captain. He turned his head, and saw that Trenck had joined his company, and that his horse was panting and bathed in sweat. The captain's brow was clouded; the young officer seemed to have escaped the threatened danger. The king had seen nothing. Trenck was in his place, and it would be useless to bring a charge against him.

The king, however, had seen all; his keen eye had observed Trenck's rapid approach, and his glowing, heated countenance; and as he rode to the front, he drew in his horse directly before Trenck.

"How comes it that your horse is fatigued and sweating? I must suppose he is fresh from the stable, and his master just from his bed. It appears, however, that he has been delayed there; I see that he has just arrived upon the parade-ground."

The officer murmured a few incomprehensible words.

"Will you answer me?" said the king; "is your horse just from the stable—are you directly from your bed?"

Frederick von Trenck's head had been bowed humbly upon his breast, he now raised it boldly up; he was resolved; his fierce eyes met those of the king. "No, your majesty," said he, with a cool, composed mien, "my horse is not from the stable—I am not from my bed."

There was a pause, an anxious, breathless pause. Every eye was fixed observantly upon the king, whose severity in military discipline was known and feared.

"Do you know," said the king at last, "that I command my officers to be punctual at parade?"

"Yes, sire."

"Do you know that it is positively forbidden to leave Potsdam without permission?"

"Yes, your majesty."

"Well, then, since this was known to you, where have you been? You confess that you do not come from your dwelling?"

"Sire, I was on the chase, and loitered too long. I know I am guilty of a great misdemeanor, and I expect my pardon only from the grace of my king."

The king smiled, and his glance was mild and kindly. "You expect also, as it appears, under any circumstances, a pardon? Well, this time you shall not be disappointed. I am well pleased that you have been bold enough to speak the truth. I love truthful people; they are always brave. This time you shall go unpunished, but beware of the second offence. I warn you."

Alas! what power had even a king's warning over the passionate love of a youth of eighteen? Trenck soon forgot the danger from which he had escaped; and even if remembered, it would not have restrained him.

It was again a cloudy, dark night, and he knew that the princess expected him. As he stood again upon the balcony, guarded by the watchful master of ceremonies; as he listened to the sweet music of Amelia's voice and comprehended the holy and precious character of her girlish and tender nature; as he sat at her feet, pouring out the rich treasures of his love and happiness, and felt her trembling small white hand upon his brow; as he dreamed with her of a blessed and radiant future, in which not only God and the night but the king and the whole world might know and recognize their love—how could he remember that the king had ordered the parade at seven in the morning, and that it was even now impossible for him to reach Potsdam at that hour?

The parade was over when he reached his quarters. A guard stood before his door, and led him instantly before the king. Frederick was alone in his cabinet. He silently dismissed his adjutant and the guard, then walked for some time backward and forward through the room, without seeming to observe Trenck, who stood with pale but resolved countenance before the door.

Trenck followed every movement of the king with a steady glance. "If he cashiers me, I will shoot myself," he said in a low tone. "If he puts me to the torture, in order to learn the secret of my love, I can bear it and be silent."

But there was another possibility upon which, in the desperation of his soul, Trenck had not thought. What should he do if the king approached him mildly and sorrowfully, and, with the gentle, persuasive words of a kind friend, besought him to explain this mystery?

This was exactly the course adopted by the king. He stepped forward to the poor, pale, almost breathless youth, and looked him steadily in the eyes. His glance was not threatening and scornful, as Trenck had expected, but sad and reproachful.

"Why have you again secretly left Potsdam?" said the king. "Where do you find the proud courage to disobey my commands? Captain Jaschinsky has brought serious charges against you. He tells me that you often leave Potsdam secretly. Do you know that, if punished according to the law, you must be cashiered?"

"Yes, I know, sire. I also know that I will not outlive this shame."

11

A scornful glance shot from the king's eye. "Do you intend to make me anxious? Is that a menace?"

"Pardon, sire. It is not in my power to make you anxious, and I do not dare to menace. Of what importance to your majesty is this atom, this unknown and insignificant youth, who is only seen when irradiated by the sunshine of your eye? I am nothing, and less than nothing, to your majesty; you are every thing to me. I will not, I cannot live if your highness withdraws your favor from me, and robs me of the possibility of winning a name and position for myself. That was my meaning, sire."

"You are, then, ambitious, and thirst for fame?"

"Your majesty, I would gladly sell one-half of my life to the devil if he would insure me rank and glory for the other half, and after death an immortality of fame. Oh, how gladly would I make this contract!"

"If such ambition fires your soul, how can you be so foolish, so inconsiderate, as to bring degradation and shame upon yourself by carelessness in duty? He who is not prompt and orderly in small things, will neglect the most important duties. Where were you last night?"

"Sire, I was on the chase."

The king looked at him with angry, piercing eyes. Trenck had not the courage to bear this. He blushed and looked down.

"You have told me an untruth," said the king. "Think again. Where were you last night?"

"Sire, I was on the chase."

"You repeat that?"

"Your majesty, I repeat that."

"Will you solemnly declare that this is true?"

Trenck was silent.

"Will you declare that this is true?" repeated the king.

The young officer looked up, and this time he had the courage to meet the flaming eye of the king. "No, sire, I will not affirm it."

"You confess, then, that you have told me an untruth?"

"Yes, your majesty."

"Do you know that that is a new and grave offence?"

"Yes, your majesty, but I cannot act otherwise."

"You will not, then, tell me the truth?"

"I cannot."

"Not if your obstinacy will lead to your being immediately cashiered, and to your imprisonment in the fortress?"

"Not then, your majesty. I cannot act differently."

"Trenck, Trenck, be on your guard! Remember that you speak to your lord and king, who has a right to demand the truth."

"Your majesty may punish me, it is your right, and your duty, and I must bear it," said Trenck, trembling and ghastly pale, but firm and confident in himself.

The king moved off for a few moments, then stood again before his lieutenant. "You will report to your captain, and ask for your discharge."

Trenck replied not. Perhaps it was not in his power. Two great tears ran slowly down his cheeks, and he did not restrain them. He wept for his youth, his happiness, his honor, and his fame.

"Go!" repeated the king.

The young man bowed low. "I thank you for gracious punishment," he said; then turned and opened the door.

The eyes of the king had followed him with marked interest. "Trenck!" cried he; and, as he turned and waited silently upon the threshold for the new command, the king stepped forward hastily and held out his hand.

"I am content with you! You have gone astray, but the anguish of soul you have just now endured is a sufficient punishment. I forgive you."

A wild cry of joy burst from the pale lips of the youth. He bowed low over the king's hand, and pressed it with passionate earnestness to his lips.

"Your majesty gives me my life again! I thank you! oh, I thank you!"

The king smiled. "And yet your life must have but little worth for you, if you would sign it away so readily. Once more I have forgiven you, but I warn you for the future. Be on your guard, monsieur, or the lightning will fall and consume you." * And now the king's eye was threaten-

* The king's own words. See Trenck's " Mémoires."

ing, and his voice terrible in anger. "You have guarded
your secret," he said; "you did not betray it, even when
threatened with punishment worse than death. Your honor,
as a cavalier, demanded that; and I am not surprised that
you hold it sacred. But there is yet another kind of honor,
which you have this day tarnished—I mean obedience to
your king and general. I forgive you for this; and now I
must speak to you as a friend, and not as a king. You are
wandering in dangerous paths, young man. Turn now,
while there is yet time; turn before the abyss opens which
will swallow you up! No man can serve two masters, or
strive successfully after two objects. He who wills something, must will it wholly; must give his undivided heart
and strength to its attainment; must sacrifice every thing
else to the one great aim! You are striving for love and
fame at the same time, and you will forfeit both. Love
makes a man soft and yielding. He who leaves a mistress
behind him cannot go bravely and defiantly into battle,
though women despise men who are not gallant and laurel-
crowned. Strive then, Trenck, first to become a hero; then
it will be time to play the lover. Pluck your laurels first,
and then gather the myrtle-wreath. If this counsel does
not suit you, then give up your ambition, and the path to
fame which you have chosen. Lay aside your sword; though
I can promise you that soon, and with honor, you may hope
to use it. But lay it aside, and take up the pen or the ham-
mer; build yourself a nest; take a wife, and thank God for
the gift of a child every twelve months; and pray that the
sound of battle may be heard only in the distance, and the
steps of soldiers may not disturb your fields and gardens.
That is also a future, and there are those who are content
with it; whose ears are closed to the beat of drums and the
sound of alarm-bells which now resound throughout Europe.
Choose, then, young man. Will you be a soldier, and with
God's help a hero? or will you go again 'upon the chase?'"

"I will be a soldier," cried Trenck, completely carried
away. "I will win fame, honor, and distinction upon the
battle-field, and above all I will gain the approbation and
consideration of my king. My name shall be known and
honored by the world."

"That is a mighty aim," said the king, smiling, "and it requires the dedication of a life. You must offer up many things, and above all other things 'the chase.' I do not know what you have sought, and I do not wish to know. I counsel you though, as a friend, to give up the pursuit. I have placed the two alternatives before you, and you have made your choice—you will be a brave soldier. Now, then, from this time onward, I will be inexorable against even your smallest neglect of duty. In this way only can I make of you what you resolve to be—a gallant and stainless officer. I will tell your captain to watch you and report every fault; I will myself observe and scrutinize your conduct, and woe to you if I find you again walking in crooked paths! I will be stern and immovable. Now, monsieur, you are warned, and cannot complain if a wild tempest bursts over your head; the guilt and responsibility will be yours. Not another word! Adieu!"

Long after Trenck had left the room, the king stood thoughtfully looking toward the door through which the tall, graceful figure of the young officer had disappeared.

"A heart of steel, a head of iron," said the king to himself. "He will be very happy, or very wretched. For such natures there is no middle way. Alas! I fear it had been better for him if I had dismissed him, and—" Frederick did not complete his sentence; he sighed deeply, and his brow was clouded. He stepped to his writing-table and took up a large sealed envelope, opened and read it carefully. A sad smile played upon his lips. "Poor Amelia!" said he —"poor sister! They have chosen you to be assistant Abbess of Quedlinburg. A miserable alternative for the Swedish throne, which was in your power! Well, I will sign this paper." He took the pen and hastily wrote his name upon the diploma. "If she is resolved never to marry, she will be one day Abbess of Quedlinburg—that is something. Aurora of Königsmark was content with that, but only after she had reached the height of earthly grandeur."

Frederick was completely unmanned by these painful thoughts. He raised his eyes to heaven, and said in a low tone: "Poor human heart! why has Fate made you so soft, when you must become stone in order to support the disappointments and anguish of life?" He stood bowed down for a long time, in deep thought; then suddenly rising proudly erect, he exclaimed: "Away with such cares! I have no time to play the considerate and amiable father to my family. My kingly duty and service call me with trumpet tones."

CHAPTER IX.

THE COUNCIL OF WAR.

FREDERICK stepped from the room into the adjoining saloon, where his ministers and generals were assembled for a council of war. His expression was calm and clear, and an imposing fire and earnestness lighted up his eyes. He was again the king, and the conqueror, and his voice rang out martially:

"The days of comfort and repose are over; we have reasoned and diplomatized too long; we must now move and strike. I am surfeited with this contest of pen and ink. I am weary of Austrian cunning and intrigue. In these weighty and important matters I will not act alone upon my own convictions; I will listen to your opinions and receive your counsel: I will not declare war until you say that an honorable peace is no longer possible. I will unsheath the sword only when the honor of my throne and of my people demands it, and even then with a heavy heart; for I know what burdens and bitter woes it will bring upon my poor land. Let us therefore carefully read, weigh, and understand the paper which lies upon the table, and fulfil the duties which it lays upon us."

Frederick stepped to the table and seated himself. The generals, the old Dessauer, Ziethen, Winterfeld, and the king's favorite, Rothenberg, with the ministers and councillor of state, placed themselves silently around the table. The eyes of all these experienced men, accustomed to battle and to victory, were steadily fixed upon the king. His youthful countenance alone was clear and bright; not a shadow was seen upon his brow.

There was a pause—a stillness like that which precedes a tempest. Every one felt the importance of the moment. All these wise and great men knew that the young man who stood in their midst, with such proud and calm composure and assurance, held in his hands at this moment the fate of Europe; that the scales would fall on that side to which his sword was consecrated. The king raised his head, and his eyes wandered searchingly from one to the other of the earnest faces which surrounded him.

"You know, messieurs," said Frederick, "that Maria Theresa, who calls herself Empress of Germany and of Rome, still makes war against our ally Charles the Seventh. Her general, Karl von Lothringen, has triumphed over the Bavarian and French army at Sempach; and Bavaria, left, by the flight of the emperor, without a leader, has been compelled to submit to Maria Theresa, Queen of Hungary. She has allied herself with England, Hanover, and Saxony. And these allied powers have been victorious over the army of our ally, King Louis of France, commanded by Marshal Noailles. These successes have made our enemies imperious. They have demanded much; they have resolved to obtain all. Apparently they are the most powerful. Holland has offered money and ships; Sardinia and Saxony have just signed the treaty made at Worms by England, Austria, and Holland. So they have troops, gold, and powerful allies. We have nothing but our honor, our swords, and our good cause. We are the allies of a land poor in itself, and, what is still worse, governed by a weak and faint-hearted emperor; and of France, whose king is the plaything of courtiers and mistresses. Our adversaries know their strength, and are acquainted with our weakness. Look, messieurs, at this letter of George of England to our godmother, Maria Theresa of Hungary; an accident placed it in our hands, or, if you will, a Providence, which, without doubt, watches over the prosperity of Prussia. Read it, messieurs."

He handed General Rothenberg a paper, which he read with frowning brow and scarcely suppressed scorn, and then passed it on to Winterfeld. The king studied the face of every reader, and, the more dark and stormy it appeared, the more gay and happy was the expression of his countenance.

He received the letter again with a friendly smile from the hands of his minister, and pointing to it with his finger, he said: "Have you well considered these lines where the king says, 'Madame, what is good to take, is also good to return'? What think you of these words, Prince von Anhalt?"

"I think," said the silver-haired old warrior, "that we will prove to the English king what Frederick of Prussia once holds cannot be rescued from him."

"You think, then, that our hands are strong enough to hold our possessions?"

"Yes, your majesty."

"And you, gentlemen?"

"We share the opinion of the prince."

"You have expressed precisely my own views," cried Frederick, with delight. "If this is your conclusion, messieurs, I rejoice to lay before you another document. It was above all other things the desire of my heart, as long as it was possible, to preserve the peace of Germany. I have sacrificed my personal inclination and my ambition to this aim. I have united the German princes for the protection of Charles the Seventh. The Frankfort union should be a lever to restore freedom to Germany, dignity to the emperor, and peace to Europe. But no success has crowned this union; discord prevails amongst them. A part of our allies have left us, under the pretext that France will not pay the promised gold. Charles the Seventh is flying from place to place, and our poor land is groaning under the burdens of a crippling and exhausting war. We must put an end to this. In such dire need and necessity it is better to die an honorable death than to bear disgrace, to live like beggars by the grace of our enemies. I have not the insolence and courage of cowardice so to live. I will die or conquer! I will wash out these scornful words of the King of England with blood. Silesia, my Silesia, which I have conquered, and which is mine by right, I will hold against all the efforts of the Hungarian queen. Look, now, at this document; it is a treaty which I have closed with France against Austria, and for the protection of the Emperor Charles. And now, here is another paper. It is a manifesto which Maria Theresa has scattered throughout all Silesia, in which she declares that she no longer considers herself bound by the treaty of Breslau, but claims Silesia and Glatz as her own. Consequently she commands the Silesians to withdraw from the protection of Prussia, and give their allegiance to their rightful inheritor."

"That is an open breach of contract," said one of the generals.

"That is contrary to all justice and the rights of the people," cried another.

"That is Austrian politics," said the king, smiling. "They hold to a solemn contract, which was detrimental to them, only so long as necessity compels it; so soon as an opportunity offers to their advantage, they prove faithless. They do not care to be considered honorable, they only desire to be feared, and above all, they will bear no equals and no rivals in Germany. Maria Theresa feels herself strong enough to take back this Silesia I won from her, and a peace contract is not sacred in her eyes. Austria was and is naturally the enemy of Prussia, and will never forgive us because our father, by the power of his genius, made himself a king. Austria would gladly see the King of Prussia buried in the little Elector of Brandenburg, and make herself rich with our possessions. Will we suffer that, messieurs!"

"Never!" said the generals, and the fire of battle flashed in their eyes.

"The Queen of Hungary has commanded her troops to enter Glatz. Shall we wait till this offence is repeated?"

"If the Austrian troops have made us a visit, politeness requires that we should return the call," said Ziethen, with a dry laugh.

"If the Queen of Hungary has sent a manifesto to Silesia, we must, above all other things, answer this manifesto," said the councillor of state.

"Maria Theresa is so bold and insolent because Bellona is a woman, consequently her sister; but we will prove to her that Dame Bellona will rather ally herself with gallant men than with sentimental women," said General Rothenberg.

"Now, messieurs, what say you? shall we have peace or war?"

"War, war!" cried they all in one breath, and with one movement.

The king raised himself from his chair, and his eagle eye was dazzling.

"The decisive word is spoken," said he, solemnly. "Let it be as you say! We will have war! Prepare yourselves, then, generals, to return the visit of Austria. Ziethen tells us that this is a courtly duty. Our councillor will write the answer to Maria Theresa's manifesto. The Austrians have visited us in Glatz, we will return their call in Prague. Rothenberg thinks that Dame Bellona would incline to our arms rather than to those of the queen, so we will seek to win her by tender embraces. I think the goddess would favor our Prince of Anhalt, they have often fought side by side. Up, then, prince, to battle and to love's sweet courtesies with your old Mistress Bellona! Up, my friends, one and all! the days of peace are over. We will have war, and may God grant His blessing to our just cause!"

CHAPTER X.

THE CLOISTER OF CAMENS.

It was a still, lovely morning. The sun gilded the lofty, giant mountain and irradiated its snow-crowned top with shifting and many-colored light; it appeared like a giant lily, luminous and odorous. The air was so clear and pure, that even in the far distance this range of mountains looked grand and sublime. The spectator was deluded by the hope of reaching their green and smiling summits in a few moments. In their majestic and sunny beauty they seemed to beckon and to lure you on. Even those who had been for a long time accustomed to this enchanting region would have been impressed to-day with its exalted beauty. Grand old Nature is a woman, and has her feminine peculiarities; she rejoices in her *beaux jours*, even as other women.

The landscape spread out at the feet of those two monks now walking in silent contemplation on the platform before the Cloister of Camens, had truly to-day her *beau jour*, and sparkled and glittered in undisturbed repose.

"How beautiful is the world!" said one, folding his hands piously, and gazing up into the valley; "created by wisdom and love, adapted to our necessities and enjoyments, to a life well-pleasing to God. Look now, brother, at the imposing majesty of that mountain, and at the lovely, smiling valley which lies at its feet. There, in the little village of Camens, this busy world is in motion, and from the city of Frankenstein I distinguish the sound of the bells calling to early morning prayer."

"That is, perhaps, the alarm-bell," said the second monk; "the wind is against us; we could not hear the sound of the small bells. I fear that is the alarm-bell."

"Why should the Frankensteiners sound the alarm-bell, Brother Tobias?" said his companion, with a soft, incredulous smile.

"Why, Brother Anastasius, because the Austrians have possibly sent their advance guard to Frankenstein. The Frankensteiners have sworn allegiance to the King of Prussia, and probably desire to keep this oath; they sound the alarm, therefore, to call the lusty burghers to arms."

"And do you truly believe that the Austrians are so near us, Brother Tobias?"

"I do not believe—I know it. Before three days General Count Wallis will enter our cloister with his staff, and, in the name of Maria Theresa, command us to take the oath."

"You can never forget that we were once Austrians, Brother Tobias. Your eyes sparkle when you think that the Austrians are coming, and you forget that his excellency the Abbot Stusche is, with his whole heart, devoted to the King of Prussia, and that he will never again subject himself to Austrian rule."

"He will be forced to it, Brother Anastasius. The star

of the Prussian king has declined; his war triumphs are at an end; God has turned away His face from him, because he is not a true Christian; he is, indeed, a heathen and an infidel."

"Still, still, Brother Tobias! If the abbot heard you, he would punish you with twenty *pater-nosters*, and you know very well that praying is not the business of your choice."

"It is true; I am fonder of war and politics. I can never forget that in my youth I was a brave soldier, and have more than once shed my blood for Austria. You will understand now why I am an Austrian. I declare to you, I would cheerfully say thirty *pater-nosters* every day, if we could be once more subject to Austria."

"Well, happily, there is no hope of that."

"Happily, there is great hope of it. You know nothing about it. You read your holy prayers, you study your learned books, and take but little interest in the outward world. I know all, hear all, take part in all. I study politics and the world's history, as diligently as you study the old Fathers."

"Well, Brother Tobias, instruct me a little in your studies. You are right; I care but little for these things, and I am heartily glad of it. It grieves me to hear of the wrath and contentions of men. God sent us into the world to live in peace and love with one another."

"If that be so, why has God permitted us to discover gunpowder?" said Brother Tobias, whistling merrily. "I say to you that by the power of gunpowder and the naked sword Silesia will soon be in possession of the faithful believer Maria Theresa. Is it not manifest that God is with her? The devil in the beginning, with the help of the Prussian king and his wild army, did seem more powerful than God himself! Only think that the gates of Breslau were opened by a box on the ear! that the year before, Prague was taken almost without a blow! It seemed indeed like child's play. Frederick was in possession of almost the whole of Bohemia, but like a besieged and suffering garrison he was obliged to creep away. God sent an enemy against him who is more powerful than all mortal foes, his army was perishing with hunger. There is no difference between the bravest soldier and the little maiden when they fall into the hands of this adversary. Hunger drove the victorious King of Prussia out of Bohemia; hunger made him abandon Silesia and seek refuge in Berlin.* Oh, I assure you, we will soon cease to be Prussians. While King Frederick is refreshing and amusing himself in Berlin, the Austrians have entered Glatz, and bring us greetings from our gracious queen, Maria Theresa."

"If the King of Prussia hears of these greetings, he will answer them by cannon-balls."

"Did I not tell you that Frederick of Prussia was idling away in Berlin, and recovering from his disastrous campaign in Bohemia? The Austrians will have taken possession of all Upper Silesia before the king and his soldiers have satisfied their hunger. I tell you, in a few days they will be with us."

"God forbid!" said Brother Anastasius; "then will the torch of war burn anew, and misfortune and misery will reign again throughout Silesia."

"Yes, that is true. I will tell you another piece of news, which I heard yesterday in Frankenstein; it is said that the King of Prussia has quietly left Berlin and gone himself into Silesia to look after the Austrians. Would it not be charming if Frederick should make our cloister a visit, just as General Count Wallis and his troops entered Camenz?"

"And you would call that charming?" said Brother Anastasius, with a reproachful look.

"Yes, most assuredly; the king would be taken prisoner, and the war would be at an end. You may rest assured the Austrians would not give the king his liberty till he had yielded up Silesia for ransom."

"May God be gracious, and guard us from war and pestilence!" murmured Brother Anastasius, folding his hands piously in prayer.

The thrice-repeated stroke of the bell in the cloister interrupted his devotions, and the full, round face of Brother Tobias glowed with pleasing anticipations.

"They ring for breakfast, Brother Anastasius," said he;

* Preuss's " History of Frederick the Great."

"let us hasten before Brother Baptist, who is ever the first
at the table, appropriates the best morsels and lays them
on his plate. Come, come, brother; after breakfast we will
go into the garden and water our flowers. We have a
lovely day and ample time—it will be three hours before
mass."

"Come, then, brother, and may your dangerous prophe-
cies and expectations not be fulfilled!"

The two monks stepped into the cloister, and a deep and
unbroken silence reigned around, interrupted only by the
sweet songs of the birds and the light movements of their
wings. The building was in the noble style of the middle
ages, and stood out in grand and harmonious proportions
against the deep blue of the horizon.

It was, without doubt, to observe the beauty and grandeur
of this structure, that two travellers who had toiled slowly
up the path leading from the village of Camens, now paused
and looked with wondering glances at the cloister.

"There must be a splendid view from the tower," said
the oldest and smaller of the travellers to his tall and slender companion, who was gazing with rapture at the enchanting landscape.

"It must indeed be a glorious prospect," he replied with a
respectful bow.

"It affords a splendid opportunity to look far and wide
over the land, and to see if the Austrian troops are really on
the march," said the other, with a stern and somewhat hasty
tone. "Let us enter and ascend the tower."

The youth bowed silently, and followed, at some little distance, the hasty steps of his companion. They reached the
platform, and stood for a moment to recover breath.

"We have reached the summit—if we were only safely
down again."

"We can certainly descend; the question is, under what
circumstances!"

"You mean, whether free or as prisoners? Well, I see
no danger; we are completely disguised, and no one knows
me here. The Abbot Amandus is dead, and the new abbot
is unknown to me. Let us make haste; ring the bell."

The youth was in the act of obeying, when suddenly a

voice cried out: "Don't sound the bell—I will come myself and open the door."

A man had been standing at the upper story, by an open window, and heard the conversation of the two travellers. He drew in his head hastily and disappeared.

"It seems I am not so unknown as I supposed," said the smaller of the two gentlemen, with a quiet smile.

"Who knows whether these monks are reliable and true?" whispered the other.

"You certainly would not doubt these exalted servants of God? I, for my part, shall believe in their sincerity till they convince me of the contrary. Ah! the door is opened."

The small door was indeed open, and a monk came out, and hastily drew near to the two travellers.

"I am the Abbot Tobias Stusche; I am also a man wholly devoted to the King of Prussia, though he does not know me."

The abbot laid such a peculiar expression upon these last words, that the strangers were forced to remark them.

"Do you not know the King of Prussia?" said the elder, fixing his eagle eye upon the kindly and friendly face of the abbot.

"I know the king when he does not wish to be *incognito*," said the abbot, with a smile.

"If the king were here, would you counsel him to remain *incognito*?"

"I would counsel that; some among my monks are Austrian in sympathy, and I hear the Austrians are at hand."

"My object is to look out from your tower after the Austrians. Let us enter; show us the way."

The abbot said nothing, but entered the cloister hastily, and cast a searching glance in every direction.

"They are all yet in the refectory, and the windows open upon the gardens. But no—there is Brother Anastasius."

It was truly Brother Anastasius, who stood at the window, and regarded them with astonished and sympathetic glances. The abbot nodded to him and laid his forefinger lightly upon his lips; he then hastily crossed the threshold of the little door.

The stranger laid his hand upon the shoulder of the abbot, and said sternly, " Did you not give a sign to this monk ? "

" Yes, the sign of silence," answered the abbot; and turning back, he looked calmly upon the strangers.

" Let us go onward." And with a firm step they entered the cloister.

CHAPTER XI.

THE KING AND THE ABBOT.

SILENTLY they passed through the lofty halls and corridors, which resounded with the steps of the strangers, and reached the rooms appropriated to the abbot. As they entered and the door closed behind them, shutting them off from the seeing and listening world, the face of the abbot assumed an expression of the most profound reverence and emotion. He crossed his hands over his breast, and bowing profoundly, he said : " Will your majesty allow me from the depths of my soul to welcome you ? In the rooms of the Abbot Tobias Stusche, King Frederick need not preserve his *incognito*. Blessed be your entrance into my house, and may your departure also be blessed ! "

The king smiled. " This blessed conclusion, I suppose, depends entirely upon your excellency. I really cannot say what danger threatens us. It certainly was not my intention to wander here; to stretch out my reconnoissance to such a distance. But what would you, sir abbot ? I am not only a king and soldier, but I am a man, with eye and heart open to the beauties of nature, and I worship God in His works of creation. Your cloister enticed me with its beauty. In place of mounting my horse and riding back from Frankenstein, I was lured hither to admire your building and enjoy the splendid prospect from your tower. Allow me to rest awhile; give me a glass of wine, and then we will mount the tower."

There was so much of calm, bold courage, so much of proud self-consciousness in the bearing of the king, that the poor, anxious abbot could not find courage to express his apprehensions. He turned and looked imploringly at the companion of the king, who was no other than the young officer of the life-guard, Frederick von Trenck. The youth seemed to share fully the careless indifference of his royal master; his face was smiling, and he did not seem to understand the meaning looks of the abbot.

"Will your majesty allow me, and me alone, to have the honor of serving you?" said his excellency. "I am jealous of the great happiness which Providence has accorded me, and I will not divide it with another, not even with my monks."

Frederick laughed heartily. "Confess, your excellency, that you dare not trust your monks. You do not know that they are as good Prussians as I have happily found you to be? Go, then, if it is agreeable to you, and with your own pious hands bring me a glass of wine, I need not say good wine—you cloistered men understand that."

Frederick leaned back comfortably in his arm-chair and conversed cheerfully, even merrily, with his young adjutant and the worthy abbot, who hastened here and there, and drew from closets and hiding-places wine, fruit, and other rich viands. The cloistered stillness, the unbroken quiet which surrounded him, were pleasing to the king; his features were illuminated with that soft and at the same time imposing smile which played but seldom upon his lips, but which, like the sun, when it appeared, filled all hearts with light and gladness. Several hours passed—hours which the king did not seem to observe, but the heart of the poor abbot was trembling with apprehension.

"And now," said the king, "I am rested, refreshed, and strengthened. Will your excellency conduct me to the tower? then I will return to Frankenstein."

"There is happily a way to the tower for my use alone," said the abbot, "where we are certain to be met by no one. I demand pardon, sire, the way is dark and winding, and we must mount many small steps."

"Well, abbot, it resembles the way to eternal life; from the power of darkness to light; from the path of sin and folly to that of knowledge and true wisdom. I will seek

12

after this knowledge from your tower, worthy abbot. Have you my field-glass, Trenck?"

The adjutant bowed, silently; they passed through the corridor and mounted the steps, reaching at last the platform at the top of the tower.

A wondrous prospect burst upon their view; the horizon seemed bounded by majestic mountains of porphyry—this third element or place of deposit of the enchanting primeval earth, out of which mighty but formless mass our living, breathing, and beautiful world sprang into creation, and the stars sang together for joy. In the midst of these mountains stood the "Giant," with his snow-crowned point, like the great finger of God, reaching up into the heavens, and contrasting strangely with the lofty but round green summits of the range, now gilded by the morning sun, and sparkling in changing rays of light.

The king looked upon this picture with rapture; an expression of prayer and praise was written upon his face. But with the proud reserve which ever belongs to those who, by exalted rank or genius, are isolated from other men, with the shrinking of a great soul, the king would allow no one to witness his emotion. He wished to be alone, alone with Nature and Nature's God; he dismissed the abbot and his adjutant, and commanded them to wait in the rooms below for him. And now, convinced that no one saw or heard him, the king gave himself up wholly to the exalted and pious feelings which agitated his soul. With glistening eyes he gazed upon the enchanting landscape, which glowed and shimmered in the dazzling sunshine.

"God, God!" said he, in low tones; "who can doubt that He is, and that He is from everlasting to everlasting? Who, that looks upon the beauty, the harmony, and order of creation, can doubt of His wisdom, and that His goodness is over all His works?*   O my God, I worship you in your works of creation and providence, and I bow my head in adoration at the footstool of your divine Majesty. Why cannot men be content with this great, mysterious, exalted, and ever-enduring church, with which God has surrounded them? Why can they not worship in Nature's great cathe-

* The king's own words. "Œuvres posthumes," page 162.

dral? Why do they confine themselves to churches of
brick and mortar, the work of men's hands, and listen to
their hypocritical priests, rather than listen to and worship
God in His beautiful world? They cry out against me and
call me an infidel, but my heart is full of love and faith in
my Creator, and I worship Him, not in priestly words, but
in the depths of my soul."

And now Frederick cast a smiling greeting to the lovely
phenomena which lay at his feet. His thoughts had been
with God, and his glance upward; but now his eyes wandered over the perfumed and blooming valley which lay in
the depths between the mountains; he numbered the little
cities and villages, with their red roofs and graceful church-
spires; he admired the straw-thatched huts upon whose
highest points the stork had built her nest, and stood by it
in observant and majestic composure.

"This is all mine; I won it with my spear and bow. It
is mine, and I will never yield it up. I will prove to Maria
Theresa that what was good to take was *not* good to restore. No, no! Silesia is mine; my honor, my pride, and
my fame demand it. I will never give it up. I will defend it with rivers of blood, yes, with my own heart's
blood!"

He took his glass and looked again over the luxurious
valley; he started and fixed his glass steadily upon one
point. In the midst of the smiling meadows through which
the highway wound like a graceful stream, he saw a curious,
glittering, moving mass. At the first glance it looked like
a crowd of creeping ants; it soon, however, assumed larger
proportions, and, at last, approaching ever nearer, the forms
of men could be distinctly seen, and now he recognized a
column of marching soldiers.

"Austrians," said the king, with calm composure. He
turned his glass in the other direction, where a road led
into the valley; this path was also filled with soldiers, who,
by rapid marches, were approaching the cloister. "Without doubt they know that I am here," said the king; "they
have learned this in the village, and have come to take me
prisoner. *Eh bien, nous verrons.*"

So saying, Frederick put his glass in his pocket, descended the steps, and with cool indifference entered the room of the abbot.

"Messieurs," said he, laughing merrily, as he looked at the good-natured and unsuspicious faces of the worthy abbot and the young officer, "we must decide upon some plan of defence, for the Austrians draw near on every side of the cloister."

"Oh, my prophetic soul!" murmured the abbot, folding his hands in prayer.

Trenck rushed to the window and looked searchingly abroad. At this moment a loud knock was heard upon the door, and an anxious voice called to the abbot.

"All is lost, the Austrians are already here!" cried Tobias Stusche, wringing his hands despairingly.

"No!" said the king, "they cannot yet have reached the cloister, and that is not the voice of a soldier who commands, but that of a monk who prays, and is almost dead with terror; let us open the door."

"O my God, your majesty! would you betray yourself?" cried Stusche, and forgetting all etiquette, he rushed to the king, laid his hand upon his arm and held him back.

"No," said the king, "I will not betray myself, neither will I conceal myself. I will meet my fate with my face to the foe."

"Open, open, for God's sake!" cried the voice without.

"He prays in God's name," said the king. "I will open the door." He crossed the room and drew back the bolt.

And now, the pale and anxious face of Brother Anastasius appeared. He entered hastily, closed and fastened the door.

"Pardon," said he, trembling and breathless—"pardon that I have dared to enter. The danger is great; the Austrians surround the cloister."

"Are they already here?" said the king.

"No; but they have sent a courier, who commands us immediately to open all the doors and give entrance to the soldiers of Maria Theresa."

"Have they given a reason for this command?"

"Yes; they say they know assuredly that the King of

Prussia is concealed here, and they come to search the cloister."

"Have you not said to them, that we are not only the servants of God, but the servants of the King of Prussia? Have you not said to them that the doors of our cloister can only open to Prussian troops?"

"Yes, your excellency. I told the soldier all this, but he laughed, and said the pandours of Colonel von Trenck knew how to obtain an entrance."

"Ah! it is Trenck, with his pandours," cried the king, casting a searching glance at Frederick von Trenck, who stood opposite, with pale and tightly-compressed lips; he met the eye of the king boldly, however, and looked him steadily in the face.

"Is Colonel Trenck your relation?" said the king, hastily.

"Yes, your majesty; he is my father's brother's son," said the young man, proudly.

"Ah! I see you have a clear conscience," said the king, laying his hand smilingly upon the youth's shoulder. "But, tell me, worthy abbot, do you know any way to rescue us from this mouse-trap?"

Tobias did not reply immediately; he stood thoughtfully with his arms folded, then raised his head quickly, as if he had come to some bold conclusion; energy and purpose were written in his face. "Will your majesty make use of the means which I dare to offer you?"

"Yes, if they are not unworthy. I owe it to my people not to lay upon them the burden of my ransom."

"Then I hope, with God's help, to serve your majesty." He turned to the monk, and said, with a proud, commanding tone: "Brother Anastasius, listen to my commands. Go immediately to Messner, order him in my name to call all the brothers to high mass in the choir of the church; threaten him with my wrath and the severest punishment, if he dares to speak to one of the brethren. I will prove my monks, and see if they recognize that obedience is the first duty in a cloister."

"While Messner assembles the priests, shall the bell sound for mass?"

"Hasten, Brother Anastasius; in ten minutes we must be all in the church."

"And you expect to save me by celebrating high mass?" said Frederick, shrugging his shoulders.

"Yes, sire, I expect it. Will your majesty graciously accompany me to my dressing-room?"

CHAPTER XII.

THE UNKNOWN ABBOT.

THE bell continued to sound, and its silver tones echoed in the lofty halls and corridors, through which the priests, in their superb vestments and holy orders, passed onward to the church. Surprise and wonder were written upon every face; curious questions were burning upon every lip, restrained, however, by the strong habit of obedience. The abbot had commanded that not one word should be exchanged between the brethren. The abbot must be obeyed, though the monks might die of curiosity. Silently they entered the church. And now the bell ceased to toll, and the grand old organ filled the church with a rich stream of harmony. Suddenly the notes were soft and touching, and the strong, full voices of men rose high above them.

While the organ swelled, and the church resounded with songs of prayer and praise, the Abbot Tobias Stusche entered the great door. But this time he was not, as usual, alone. Another abbot, in the richly-embroidered habiliments of a *fête* day, stood by his side. No one had ever seen this abbot. He was wholly unknown.

Every eye was turned upon him; every one was struck with the commanding and noble countenance, with the imposing brow and luminous eye, which cast searching and threatening glances in every direction. All felt that something strange, unheard of, was passing in their midst. They knew this stranger, glowing with youth, beauty, and majesty, was no common priest, no humble brother.

The command to strict silence had been given, and implicit obedience is the first duty of the cloister. So they were silent, sang, and prayed; while Tobias Stusche, with the strange abbot, swept slowly and solemnly through the aisles up to the altar. They both fell upon their knees and folded their hands in silent prayer.

Again the organ swelled, and the voices of the choristers rose up in adoration and praise; but every eye and every thought were fixed upon the strange abbot kneeling before the high altar, and wrestling with God in prayer. And now the organ was silent, and the low prayers began. The monks murmured mechanically the accustomed words; nothing was heard but sighs of penitence and trembling petitions, which seemed to fade and die away amongst the lofty pillars of the cathedral.

Suddenly a loud noise was heard without, the sound of pistols and threatening voices demanding admittance. No one regarded this. The church doors were violently thrown open, and wild, rude forms, sunbrowned and threatening faces appeared. For one moment noisy tumult and outcry filled the church, but it was silenced by the holy service, now celebrated by these kneeling, praying monks, who held their beads in their hands, and gave no glance, in token of interest or consciousness, toward the wild men who had so insolently interrupted the worship of God. The soldiers bowed their heads humbly upon their breasts, and prayed for pardon and grace. This holy duty being fulfilled, they remembered their worldly calling, and commenced to search the church for the King of Prussia, whom they believed to be hidden there. The clang of spurs and heavy steps resounded through the aisles, and completely drowned the prayers and sighs of the monks, who, kneeling upon their stools, seemed to have no eye or thought for any thing but the solemn service in which they were engaged.

The pandours, in their dark, artistic costumes, with the red mantle fastened to their shoulders, swarmed through the church, and with flashing eyes and scarcely suppressed curses searched in every niche and behind every pillar for Frederick of Prussia. How often did these wild forms pass by the two abbots, who were still kneeling, immovable in rapturous meditation, before the high altar! How often did their swords strike upon the floor behind them, and even fasten in the vestment of the strange abbot, who, with closed eyes and head bowed down upon his breast, had no knowledge of their presence!

The prayers had continued much longer than usual, and yet the abbot did not pronounce the benediction! And now he did indeed give a sign, but not the one expected. He rose from his knees, but did not leave the church; with his companion, he mounted the steps to the altar, to draw near to the holy crucifix and bless the host. He nodded to the choir, and again the organ and the choristers filled the church with melody.

This was something so extraordinary that the monks turned pale, and questioned their consciences anxiously. Had they not committed some great crime, for which their stern abbot was resolved to punish them with everlasting prayer and penitence? The pandours knew nothing of this double mass. They had now searched the whole church, and as the king was not to be found, they rushed out in order to search the cells, and, indeed, every corner of the cloister. The service still continued; the unknown abbot stood before the high altar, while Abbot Stusche took the host and held it up before the kneeling monks.

At this moment a wild cry of triumph was heard without; then curses and loud laughter. The monks were bowed down before the host, and did not seem to hear the tumult. They sang and prayed, and now the outcry and noise of strife was hushed, and nothing was heard but the faint and dying tones of the organ. The pandours had left the cloister; they had found the adutant of the king and borne him off as a rich spoil to their commander, Colonel von Trenck.

The soldiers were gone, it was therefore not necessary to continue the worship of God. Tobias Stusche repeated a *pater-noster*, gave his hand to the unknown abbot, and they turned to leave the church. As they slowly and majestically swept through the aisles, the monks bowed their heads in reverence; the organ breathed its last grand accord, and the glorious sun threw a beckoning love-greeting through the lofty windows of painted glass. It was a striking and solemn scene, and the unknown abbot seemed strangely impressed. He paused at the door and turned once more, and his glance wandered slowly over the church.

One hour later the heavy state-coach of the Abbot of Clostenberg rolled down from Camens. In the coach sat Tobias Stusche with the unknown abbot. They took the road to Frankenstein. Not far from the gate the carriage stopped, and to the amazement of the coachman, no abbot, but a soldier clad in the well-known Prussian uniform, descended. After leaving the coach, he turned again and bowed to the worthy Abbot Stusche.

"I will never forget this bold and noble act of your excellency," said the king, giving his hand to the abbot. "You and your cloister may at all times count upon my special favor. But for your aid, I should this day have been betrayed into a most unworthy and shameful imprisonment. The first rich abbey which is vacant I will give to you, and then in all future time I will confirm the choice of abbot, which the monks themselves shall make." *

"O my God!" exclaimed the abbot, "how rarely must your majesty have met with honest and faithful men, if you reward so richly a simple and most natural act of love!"

"Faithful hearts are rare," said the king. "I have met this blue-eyed daughter of Heaven but seldom upon my path, and it is perhaps for this reason that her grandeur and her beauty are so enchanting to me. Farewell, sir abbot, and greet the brother Anastasius for me."

"Will not your majesty allow me to accompany you to the city?"

"No, it is better that I go on foot. In a quarter of an hour, I shall be there; my carriage and my guard await me,

* In gratitude for this service, the king gave the rich Abbey of Sentus to Stusche, and kept up with him always the kindest intercourse. There are letters still preserved written by the king himself to the abbot, filled with expressions of heart-felt kindness and favor. Frederick sent him from Meissen a beautiful set of porcelain, and splendid stuff for pontifical robes, and rare champagne wine. While in Breslau, he invited him twice to visit him. Soon after the close of the Seven Years' War, Stusche died. The king sent a royal present to the cloister with a request that on the birthday of the abbot a solemn mass should be celebrated. Some years later, Frederick stopped at Camens, and told the abbot to commission the first monk who died to bear his loving greeting to the good Abbot Stusche in Paradise.— (See Rodenbeck.)

and I wish no one to be acquainted with the adventures of this day. It remains a secret between us for the present."

Frederick greeted him once more, and then stepped lightly onward toward the city. The coach of the abbot returned slowly to the cloister.

The king had advanced but a short distance, when the sound of an approaching horse met his ear. He stood still and looked down the highway. This time the Austrian uniform did not meet his eye; he recognized in the distance the Prussian colors, and as the horse approached nearer, he marked the uniform of a young officer of his life-guard. Before Frederick found time for surprise, the rider had reached him, checked his horse with a strong hand, sprang from the saddle, bowed profoundly before the king, and reached him the reins.

"Will not your majesty do me the favor to mount my horse?" said Trenck, calm and unembarrassed, and without alluding by word or smile to the adventure of the day.

The king looked at him searchingly. "From whence come you?" said he sternly.

"From Glatz, where the pandours carried me as a prisoner, and delivered me to Colonel Trenck."

"You were then a prisoner, and were released without ransom?"

"Colonel Trenck laughed merrily when his pandours delivered me to him, and declared I was the King of Prussia."

"Colonel Trenck knows you?"

"Sire, I saw him often in my father's house."

"Go on: he recognized you, then?"

"He knew me, and said laughingly, he had sent to take Frederick, King of Prussia, and not Frederick von Trenck, prisoner. I was free, I might go where I wished, and as I could not go on foot, he presented me with one of his best horses; and now I am here, will not your majesty do me the honor to mount this horse?"

"I mount no Austrian horse," said the king in a harsh tone.

The young officer fixed his glance for one moment, with an expression of regret upon the proud and noble animal, who with dilating nostrils, flashing eyes, and impatient

stamping of the fore-feet, stood by his side, arching gracefully his finely-formed and muscular throat. But this expression of regret soon vanished. He let go the bridle and
bowing to the king he said, "I am at your majesty's command."

The king glanced backward at the noble steed, who,
slender and graceful and swift as a gazelle, was in a moment
so far distant as to be no larger than a flying eagle. He
then advanced toward Frankenstein: both were silent;
neither gave another thought to the gallant horse, who, rider-
less and guided by instinct alone, was far on the way to
Glatz. Once before they reached the city, the king turned
and fixed his eyes upon the open, youthful, and handsome
face of Trenck.

"I believe it would be better for you if this colonel of
pandours were not your relation," said the king thoughtfully;
"there can no good come to you from this source, but only
evil."

Frederick von Trenck turned pale. "Does your majesty
command that I shall change my name?"

"No," said the king after a moment's reflection. "The
name is a holy inheritance which is handed down from our
fathers, and it should not be lightly cast away. But be careful, be careful in every particular. Understand my words,
and think upon my warning, Baron von Trenck."

CHAPTER XIII.

THE LEVEE OF A DANCER.

In Behren Street, which was at that time one of the
most *recherché* and beautiful streets of Berlin, order and
quiet generally reigned. To-day, however, an extraordinary activity prevailed in this aristocratic locality; splendid
equipages and gallant riders, followed by their attendants,
dashed by; all seemed to have the same object; all drew up
before the large and elegant mansion which had for some

time been the centre of attraction to all the courtly cavaliers
of the Prussian capital. Some of the royal princes, the
young Duke of Würtemberg, counts, ambassadors, and generals, were to-day entreating an audience.

Who dwelt in this house? What distinguished person was
honored by all these marks of consideration? Why was
every face thoughtful and earnest? Was this a funeral, and
was this general gloom the expression of the heart's despair
at the thought of the loved and lost? Perhaps the case was
not quite so hopeless. It might be that a prince or other
eminent person was dangerously ill! "It must be a man,"
as no woman was seen in this grand cavalcade. But how account for those rare and perfumed flowers? Does a man
visit his sick friend with bouquets of roses and violets and
orange-blossoms? with rare and costly southern fruits in
baskets of gold and silver? This would indeed be a strange
custom!

But no! In this house dwelt neither prince nor states-
man, only a woman. How strange that only men were there
to manifest their sympathy! In this pitiful and dreary
world a woman who has made a name for herself by her own
beauty and talent is never acknowledged by other women.
Those who owe their rank to their fathers and husbands, are
proud of this accidental favor of fate; they consider themselves as the chosen accomplices and judges of morals and
virtue, and cast out from their circles all those who dare to
elevate themselves above mediocrity. In this house dwelt
an *artiste*—the worshipped prima donna, the Signora Barbarina!

Barbarina! ah! that was an adored and a hated name.
The women spoke of her with frowning brows and contemptuous laughter, the men with flashing eyes and boundless enthusiasm; the one despised and abhorred her, even
as the other exalted and adored her. And truly both had
cause: the women hated her because she stole from them the
eyes and hearts of their lovers and husbands; the men worshipped her as a blossom of beauty, a fairy wonder, a consecrated divinity.

These two parties were as zealous as the advocates of
the white and red rose. The women fought under the ban-

ner of the faded, withered white rose; the men gathered around the flag of her glowing sister, the enchanting Barbarina. This was no equal contest, no doubtful result. The red rose must conquer. At the head of her army stood the greatest of warriors. The king was at the same time Barbarina's general and subject. The white rose must yield, she had no leader.

Possibly Elizabeth Christine desired to lead the army of martyrs; possibly the same rage and scorn swelled in her heart which spoiled the peace of other women. But her modest and trembling lips betrayed nothing of the secret storms of her bosom; her soft and gentle smile veiled her shrouded wishes and the hopes there buried in her heart. One could scarcely believe that this timid, pious queen could worship an earthly object, or yield herself one moment to the bare passion of hate. Truly Elizabeth Christine hated no one, not even Barbarina—this woman who had given the last blow to her tortured heart, and added the passion of jealousy to her despised love. Elizabeth Christine was indeed jealous, but not in the common way; she felt no scorn, she uttered no reproach; silent tears and earnest prayers for strength were her only speech.

The king had given her no occasion to complain of his love for Barbarina; she did not know that he had ever approached her, even spoken to her; she knew, however, with what looks and smiles of rapture he gazed upon her, and she would joyfully have given her life for one such glance or smile. That, however, which was not known to Elizabeth, was fully understood by the whole court. It was known that more than once the Barbarina had supped with the king at the house of General Rothenberg; it was known that the king, every time the Barbarina danced, was behind the curtain, and that he had commanded the court painter, Pesne, to paint her portrait, life size, for him.

Was not this enough to exalt the signora in the eyes of every courtier and every diplomatist to the first rank of beauty and power? Would they not, indeed, have hastened to acknowledge her claims, even had she not been the loveliest and most enchanting creature? She was indeed a queen, a powerful enchantress. Men struggled for one smile, one glance; they bowed down to all her caprices and humors; worship, submission, and obedience were the tribute brought by all. Her house was besieged with visits and petitions as if it were the palace of a fairy queen. Barbarina had her court circle, her levees, her retinue.* All her subjects rendered her a glad and voluntary service, and received no other compensation than a gay smile or friendly word.

All this splendor, consideration, and worship, of which she was the shining centre, seemed to make no impression upon the heart of the proud and self-reliant *artiste;* she was accustomed to it, and moved on in silent majesty; her whole life had been a triumphant march. Like a summer morning glittering in the dew and sunshine, she had had her little griefs and tears, but they resembled the dew-drops in the flower-cups, shining for a moment like costly diamonds, then kissed away by the sun. Barbarina wept when the king separated her from her lover, Lord Stuart, and forced her to fulfil her contract and come to Berlin. She wept no more. Was it because she was too proud? or had the sun of royal favor kissed away her tears?

Barbarina's tears had ceased to flow, but she smiled rarely. She had the grace and imposing beauty of the Roman, and never forgot that she was a daughter of that proud nation who had ruled the world, and, even though disenthroned, preserved her majesty and renown. Barbarina was a glowing, passionate woman, and passion adorns itself with flashing eyes, with a clear and touching pallor and crimson lips, but never with the innocent smile and harmless jest. She was never heard and rarely seen to laugh. Laughter was not in harmony with her proud beauty, but smiles illuminated and glorified it. She was imperial to look upon; but, filled with all sweet charity and gentle grace, womanly and tender; with a full consciousness of her power, she was humble and yielding. In the midst of her humility she was proud, and sure of success and victory; one moment she was the glowing, ardent, and yielding woman; the next the proud, genial, imposing *artiste.* Such was Barbarina; an incomprehensible riddle, unsearchable, unfathomable as the sea—ever changing, but great in every aspect.

* Schneider, "History of the Opera and Opera-Houses in Berlin.

Barbarina had appeared the evening before, but her dance had been interrupted by a sudden indisposition exactly at the moment when the king appeared in the opera-house. No one knew that the king had returned from his mysterious journey to Silesia; every one believed him to be absent, and the ballet had been arranged without any reference to him. Frederick arrived unexpectedly, and changing his travelling-dress hastened to the opera, no doubt to greet the two queens and his sisters. Barbarina was seized with indisposition at the moment of the king's entrance. She floated smilingly and airily over the stage; her small feet seemed borne by the Loves and Graces. Suddenly she faltered, the smile vanished from her lips, and the slight blush from her cheek, and with a cry of pain she sank insensible upon the floor.

The curtain fell, and an intermission of a quarter of an hour was announced. The king, who was conversing with the queen-mother, appeared to take but little interest in this interruption, but Baron Swartz approached and announced that Signora Barbarina was ill and could not appear again during the evening. Frederick gave such an angry exclamation, that the queen-mother looked up astonished and questioning. Elizabeth Christine sighed and turned pale. She comprehended the emotion of her husband; guided by the instinct of jealousy, she read the king's alarm and disappointment, which he tried in vain to hide under the mask of scorn.

"It appears to me," said the king, "that the signora is again indulging in one of her proud and sullen moods, and refuses to dance because I have returned. I will not submit to this caprice; I will myself command her to dance."

He bowed to the two queens, stepped behind the curtain, and advanced to the boudoir of the signora. The door was fastened within. The king stood hesitating for a moment; he heard the sound of weeping and sobbing—the signora was in bitter pain or sorrow.

"She is truly ill," said he.

"She has cramp," suggested Baron Swartz, who had followed the king.

Frederick turned hastily. "Is that dangerous" he asked, in a tone which betrayed his alarm and agitation.

"Not dangerous, sire, but the physician who was with her has declared that absolute quiet was necessary. Will your majesty command that another dancer shall take her place?"

"No," said Frederick; "the *pas* which belongs to Barbarina shall be danced by no other. Salimberri and Astrea shall sing an aria and the house be dismissed. Go to their majesties and say to them I pray they will excuse me; I only came to greet them, and, being much fatigued by my journey, I will now retire."

Bowing to the baron, the king left the opera-house and entered the palace. But in the silence of the night, when all others slept, the soft tones of his flute melted on the air.

Barbarina was ill. For this reason her house was besieged; for this reason every face was clouded. Her adorers were there begging to see her, and thus find comfort and encouragement; each one wished to prove his sympathy by some marked attention. They hoped that these glorious and costly fruits might win for them a smile of gratitude.

The reception-room of Barbarina was like a royal conservatory, only the life-giving and dazzling sun was hidden from view. Barbarina was in her boudoir, and all these gallant cavaliers waited in vain for her appearance. It was the hour of her levee, the hour when her door was open to all who had enjoyed the honor of being presented to her. The courtiers stood in groups and conversed in light whispers over the *on-dits* of the day, and turning their eyes from time to time to the *portière* of purple velvet which separated them from the boudoir of the signora; from that point must the sun rise to illuminate this dusky room.

But Barbarina came not. She lay upon a white silk divan, dressed in the most ravishing *négligée* of white muslin, covered with rare and costly lace. She was dreaming with open eyes, and arms crossed upon her breast. Those flashing eyes were soft and misty; a melancholy expression trembled upon her lips. Barbarina was alone. Why should she not dream, and lay aside for a while her gracious smiles and fiery glance? Of what were those unfathomable eyes dreaming? what signified those sighs which burst from her full crimson lips? Did she know herself, or did she wish to know? Did she comprehend the weakness of her own proud heart, or had she veiled it from herself, ashamed to read what was written there?

At this moment the door opened, and a young girl entered —one of those insignificant, gentle, yielding creatures, generally found amongst the attendants of an *artiste*—a *tête de souffrance*, on whom they exhaust their humor, their scorn, and their passion; the humble companion, kept in the background when blessed with the society of distinguished and wealthy adorers. The companion of Barbarina did not suffer, however, from this hard fate. She was Barbarina's sister, and had followed her from tender love to the cold north. The signora loved her sister fondly; she was the companion of her joys and sorrows; she had no secrets from her, and knew that an open ear and judicious counsel were always to be found with her little sister Marietta.

Barabrina lay, still dreaming, upon the divan. Possibly she did not know that Marietta stood by her side, and laid her hand upon her shoulder.

"Sorella," said she, "get up; many gentlemen are in the saloon, waiting for you."

"Let them wait. I will see no one to-day."

"It is the hour when you are accustomed to receive, Sorella, and if you do not come they will think you are still unwell."

"Well, let them think so."

"They will not only think so, Sorella; they will say so, and make malicious comments."

"What comments?" said Barbarina, raising herself up; "what comments, Marietta?"

"It was indeed unfortunate that your sickness came upon you just as the king appeared," said Marietta.

Barbarina's eyes flashed. "Do you think they will put those things together?" said she. "They will say, perhaps, that Barbarina fainted at the unexpected appearance of the king; that the joy of seeing him overcame her; is that your meaning, Marietta?"

"Yes, that is my meaning," said Marietta, in a low tone.

Barbarina sprang from the divan, trembling and pallid.

13

"They will mock at and scorn me," she cried, raising her arms to heaven as if to call down the lightning to her aid; "they will say I love this cold king!"

"They will say that, Sorella," replied Marietta.

Barbarina seized her hand. "But you, sister! you will not say this; you know that I have sworn to hate him with an everlasting hatred. You know that I have put an evil spell upon him with my tears; that I never can forgive him for the suffering and agony he prepared for me. Think, think, Marietta, how much I have wept, how much I have endured! My life was like a lustrous May morning, a fairy tale of starry splendor; roses and pearls were in my path: he has obscured my stars, and changed my pearls to tears. Woe to him! woe to him! I have sworn to hate him eternally, and Barbarina keeps her oath."

"Yes, you have sworn to hate him, sister, but the world is ignorant of your oath and its cause; their eyes are blinded, and they strangely mistake your hate for love. They see that your glance is clearer, brighter, when the king is by, and they know not that it is hate which flashes from your eyes; they hear that your voice lightly trembles when you speak to him, they do not know that the hatred in your heart deprives you of self-control; they see that you dance with more enchanting grace in the king's presence, they do not understand that these are instruments of revenge—that you wish to crush him by the mighty power of genius, grace, and beauty."

"Yes, yes! just so," said Barbarina, breathing painfully; "you alone know me, you alone read my heart! I hate, I abhor this cold, cruel king, and he richly deserves my hate! He may be wise and great, but his heart is ice. It is true, he is handsome and exalted; genius is marked on his noble brow; his smile is magical, and irradiates his face; his eyes, those great, inexplicable eyes, are blue as the heavens and unfathomable as the sea. When I look into them, I seem to read the mysteries of the great deep, and the raptures of heaven. His voice, when he pleads, is like consecrated music; when he commands, it is the voice of God in thunder. He is great above all other men; he is a hero, a man, and a king!"

"And yet you hate him?" said Marietta, with a mocking smile.

Barbarina trembled. Marietta's question checked her glowing enthusiasm; it rang in her ears like the name-call in the "Somnambulist," and roused her to consciousness.

"Yes," said she, in a low tone, "I hate him, and I will ever hate him! If I loved him, I should be the most wretched of women—I should despise and curse myself. He has no heart; he cannot love; and shame and dishonor rest upon the woman who loves and is not beloved. Frederick loves nothing but his Prussia, his fame, and his greatness. And the world says, that 'the Barbarina loves him.' You see that is impossible, that can never be. I would rather die than love this man without a heart."

"The world is incredulous," said Marietta; "they cannot look into your heart, and you must be silent as to your hatred. You dare not say that you fainted yesterday from scorn and rage at the sudden appearance of the king."

"Think you they will believe that joy overcame me?" cried Barbarina, in wild frenzy. "They shall not believe it; it shall not be!" She sprang like an enraged lioness and grasped a little stiletto which lay upon her toilet-table, and which she had brought as a relic from her beautiful fatherland. "I will not be mocked at and despised," cried she, proudly, dashing off her gold-embroidered white satin slipper, and raising her foot.

"Oh! Barbarina, what will you do?" cried Marietta, as she saw her take up the stiletto.

"This," said she, significantly, sticking the point of the stiletto in the sole of her foot; the blood gushed out and covered her stocking with blood.

Marietta uttered a cry of terror, and rushed to her sister, but Barbarina waved her away; the wound and the flow of blood had brought relief to her wild nature; she was calm, and a ravishing smile disclosed two rows of pearly teeth.

"Be still, Marietta," said she, in a commanding tone, "the wound is not deep, not dangerous, but deep enough to confirm my statement when I declare that, while dancing last evening, I wounded my foot upon a piece of glass from a broken lamp."

"Ah! now I understand you, you proud sister," cried
Marietta, looking up gayly. "You would thus account for
your swoon of yesterday?"

"Yes, and now give me my slipper, and allow me to take
your arm; we will go into the saloon."

"With your bleeding foot, with this open wound?"

"Yes, with my bleeding foot; however, we had better
check the flow of blood a little."

The cavaliers who waited for the signora became ever
sadder and more thoughtful. Barbarina must be indeed ill,
if she allowed her admirers to wait so long, for she was above
all the small coquetries of women; they would not go, however, till they had news of her, till they had seen her sister.

At last their patience was rewarded; the *portière* was
drawn back, and Barbarina appeared, leaning upon the arm
of her sister. She was pale and evidently suffering. She
walked slowly through the saloon, speaking here and there
to the cavaliers, and conversing in the gay, gracious, and
piquant manner in which she excelled. Suddenly, in the
midst of one of these merry interchanges of thought, in
which one speaks of every thing or nothing, Barbarina uttered a cry of pain and sank upon the sofa.

"I believe, I fear that my foot is bleeding again," she
cried. She slightly raised her robe, and lifted up her foot,
that small object of wonder and rapture to all the lands of
Europe. Truly her white satin slipper was crimson, and
blood was flowing freely from it.

A cry of horror sounded from every lip. The gentlemen
surrounded Barbarina, who lay pale as death upon the sofa,
while Marietta knelt before her, and wrapped her foot in
her handkerchief. This was a striking scene. A saloon
furnished with princely splendor, and odorous with the rarest
flowers; a group of cavaliers in their gold-embroidered coats
and uniforms, glittering with crosses and odors; the signora
lying upon the divan in a charming *négligée*, with her bleeding foot resting upon the lap of her sister.

"You are wounded, signora, you bleed!" cried the young
Prince of Würtemberg, with such an expression of horror,
you would have thought he expected the instant death of the
Barbarina.

The lovely Italian looked up in seeming surprise. "Did not your highness know that I was wounded? I thought you were a witness to my accident yesterday?"

"Certainly, I was at the opera-house, as were all these gentlemen; but what has that to do with your bleeding foot?"

"A curious question, indeed! You did not, then, understand the cause of my swooning yesterday? I will explain. I felt a severe pain in the sole of my foot, which passed like an electric shock through my frame, and I became insensible. While unconscious, my blood, of course, ceased to flow, and the physician did not discover the cause of my sudden illness. This morning, in attempting to walk, I found the wound."

"My God, what a misfortune, what an irreparable blow!" cried the cavaliers with one voice; "we can never again hope to see our enchanting dancer."

"Compose yourselves, gentlemen," cried Barbarina, smiling, "my confinement will be of short duration, and will have no evil consequences. I stepped upon a piece of glass which had fallen upon the boards, and piercing the slipper entered my foot; the wound is not deep; it is a slight cut, and I shall be restored in a few days."

"And now," said Barbarina, with a triumphant smile, as she was once more alone with her sister, "no one will mock at me and make malicious comments upon my fainting. In an hour the whole city will hear this history, and I hope it may reach the ears of the king."

"He will not believe it," said Marietta, shrugging her shoulders; "he sent immediately for your physician and questioned him closely as to your sudden indisposition in the theatre. I had just left your boudoir to get you a glass of water, and when I returned I found the king standing before your door and listening to your groans."

A wondrous expression of light and peace shone in her great black eyes. "The king was then behind the curtains, he stood before my door, he wished to speak to me, and you tell me this now, only now, when you might have known—" Barbarina paused, and turned away her blushing face.

"Well, I might have known that the king, whom you hate

so bitterly, had waited in vain at your door, had been turned away by the proud dancer as a common man; this was, indeed, a triumph of revenge," said Marietta, smiling.

"I did not turn him away," said Barbarina, with embarrassment.

"No! you drew your bolt on the inside, nothing more."

CHAPTER XIV.

THE STUDIO.

BARBARINA was right; the wound in her foot was not dangerous. She was ordered to be quiet for some days, and give up dancing. The physician to whom she showed her foot, and declared that she had only just discovered the cause of her sudden swoon, examined the wound with an incredulous smile, and asked to see the shoe, the sole of which must also be necessarily cut, he said; in this way only could he tell if the wound had been inflicted by a piece of glass or nail, and know the size and sharpness of the instrument. Barbarina blushed, and ordered Marietta to bring the shoe; she returned immediately with a slipper, showing a sharp cut in the sole. The physician examined it silently, and then declared that it was a piece of glass which had caused the fainting of the signora; he ordered cooling applications and perfect quiet, and promised restoration in a few days.

The king had commanded the physician to come to him immediately after his visit to Barbarina. He was announced, and as he entered, Frederick advanced to meet him.

"Well," said he, "is the wound dangerous? will the signora be obliged to give up the stage?"

"Ah, surely your majesty cannot believe that the Barbarina has given herself a wound which will destroy her fame and fortune!"

"I do not understand you," said Frederick, impatiently; "do not speak in riddles."

"I repeat, your majesty, the signora would not intentionally have wounded her foot seriously, and thereby destroyed her art."

"Do you believe that she wounded herself voluntarily?"

"I am convinced of it, sire. The signora declares that she stepped upon a piece of glass. I desired to see the slipper; Marietta brought me one, in the sole of which I discovered a cut, but it did not correspond a all with the wound in the foot, and had been evidently just made with a knife. Certainly Barbarina was not wounded while she wore that shoe; moreover, I affirm that the ound was not inflicted by a piece of glass or a nail, but by a stiletto; the wound is three-sided; I am confident she wounded herself with a stiletto I saw in her room."

The king's face grew dark while the physician spoke; he pressed his lips together: this was ever a sign that a storm was raging in his breast which he wished to control.

"Is that all you have to say?"

"That is all, sire."

"Good! You will visit the signora to-morrow, and bring me news of her."

The king was alone, and pacing his room nervously. It was in vain that Biche, his favorite hound, raised herself up and drew near to him. The wise little animal seemed, indeed, to understand the sadness of her master, and looked up at him with sorrowful and sympathetic eyes. Once Frederick murmured half aloud: "She has sworn to hate me, and she keeps her oath." After long thought, he seemed to be resolved, and drew near to the door; he opened it and stood a moment on the threshold, then closed it again, and said: "No! I dare not do that. I dare not do what any other man might do in my place; not I—I am a king. Alas! men think it is a light matter to be a king; that the crown brings no care, no weight to the brow and the heart. Our hearts' blood is often the lime with which our crowns are secured." He sighed deeply, then stood up and shook himself like a lion, when, after a long repose, he rouses himself to new life and action. "Oh! I am sentimental," he said, with a sad smile. "I doubt if a king has a right to dream. Away, then, with sentiments and sighs! Truly, what would Maria Theresa say if she knew that the King of Prussia was a

sentimentalist, and sighed and loved like a young maiden?
Would she not think she had Silesia again in her dress-
pocket?"

While the king struggled with his passion, Barbarina had
a far more dangerous enemy to contend with. Sentimental-
ity is veiled in melancholy, in softened light and faded tints;
but *ennui* has no eye, nor mind, nor heart for any thing.
It is a fearful enemy! Barbarina was weary, oh, so weary!
Was it perhaps impatience to appear again upon the stage
which made the hours so leaden, so long drawn out? She
lay the whole day stretched out upon her sofa, her eyes wide
open, silent, and sighing, not responding to Marietta's loving
words by a glance, or a movement of the eyelash. Marietta
proposed to assemble her friends, but she affirmed that society was more wearisome than solitude.

At the end of three days, Barbarina sprang from her
sofa and tried to walk. "It gives me no pain," said she,
walking through the room.

"Yes, I remember, Arias said the same as she handed the
dagger to her beloved," replied Marietta.

"But I have no beloved," said Barbarina; "no one loves
me, no one understands this poor, glowing, agonized heart."
As she said this, a flood of tears gushed from her eyes, and
her form trembled with a storm of passion.

"Ah, Sorella, how can you say that—you who are so
much loved, so highly prized?"

Barbarina smiled contemptuously, and shook her head.
"Do you call that love? these empty words, this everlasting,
unmeaning praise; this rapture about my beauty, my grace,
and my skill, is this worship? Go, go, Marietta, you know it
is not love, it is not worship. They amuse themselves with
a rare and foreign flower, which is only beautiful because it
has been dearly paid for; which is only wondered at while it
is rare and strange. You know, not one of these men loves
me for myself; they think only of my outward appearance.
I am never more solitary than when they surround me, never
feel so little beloved as when they swear that they love me
boundlessly. O my God! must I shroud my heart, must I
bury it under the snows of this cold north? O God, give me
a heart for my heart, that can love as Barbarina loves!"

She covered her face with her hands, and her tears flowed freely; she trembled and bowed from side to side, like a lily in a storm.

Marietta drew near, and laid her head upon her sister's shoulder; she did not try to comfort her: she knew there were griefs to which words of consolation were exasperation; she knew that passion must exhaust itself before it could be soothed. She comprehended the nobility and energy of Barbarina's nature; those bursts of tears were like clouds in the tropics; the storm must break, and then the sun would shine more gloriously. Marietta was right. In a short time her sister withdrew her hands from her face; her tears were quenched, and her eyes had their usual lustre.

"I am mad," she cried, "worse than mad! I ask of the north our southern blossoms. I demand that their ice shall become fire. Has not a landscape of snow and ice its grandeur and beauty—yes, its terrible beauty when inhabited by bears and wolves?"

"But woe betide us, when we meet these monsters!" said Marietta, entering readily into her sister's jest.

"Why woe betide us? Every danger and every monster can be overcome, if looked firmly in the face, but not too long. Marietta, not till your own eye trembles. Now, sister, enough of this; the rain is over, the sun shall shine. I am no longer ill, and will not be laid aside like a broken plaything. I will be sound and healthy; I will flap my wings and float once more over the gay world."

"Do you know, Sorella, that the higher you fly, the nearer you are to heaven?"

"I will soar, but think not, that like Icarus I will fasten my wings with wax. No, I am wiser, I will fly with my feet; the sun has no power over them: they are indeed two suns. They warm the coldest heart; they set the icy blood in motion, they almost bring the dead to life. You see, sister, I have adopted the style of speech of my adorers; none of them being present, I will worship and exalt myself."

Barbarina said all this merrily, but Marietta felt this gayety was not natural.

"Do you know what I have determined upon?" said Barbarina, turning away, so that her face might not be seen;

"as I cannot dance either to-day or to-morrow, I will find some other mode of employing my time. I will go to Pesne and sit for my portrait."

She had turned away, but Marietta saw that her throat was suffused with a soft flush.

"Will you drive to the palace?" said Marietta.

"Not to the palace, but to Pesne."

"Pesne's studio is now in the palace; the king appointed him rooms there."

"Well, then, I must sit to him in the palace."

"This, however, will be disagreeable to you; you abhor the king, and it will be painful to be under the same roof. You perhaps suppose the king to be in Potsdam: he is now in Berlin."

Barbarina turned suddenly, and throwing her arms around Marietta's neck, she pressed a kiss upon her lips, and whispered: "I know it, Marietta, but I must go."

The sisters went therefore to the new studio of the painter Pesne, which was in the royal palace. The king took great pleasure in the growth and development of works of art. While Pesne was engaged on his great picture of Diana and her Nymphs, the king often visited his studio and watched him at his work. He had closely examined the sketch of the portrait of Barbarina, and, on his return from Silesia, commanded Pesne to arrange a studio in the castle, as he wished to be near him.

Barbarina sprang like a gazelle up the steps; her foot was not painful, or she was unconscious of it. She was impatient, and would scarcely wait to be announced before entering the room. Pesne was there, and welcomed the signora joyfully. Barbarina looked about in vain for her portrait.

"Has misfortune overtaken the portrait as well as the original?" she said, smiling.

"Not so, signora," said Pesne; "the portrait excites as great a *furor* as the original—only, though, because it is a copy."

"I do not understand you."

"I mean, that his majesty is so enraptured with the copy, that since yesterday it has been placed in his study, although I protested against it, the picture not being finished. The king, however, persisted; he said he wished to show the portrait to his friends, and consult with them as to its defects."

Never, in her most brilliant *rôle*, was Barbarina so beautiful as at this moment: her countenance glowed with rapture; her happy smile and glance would have made the homeliest face handsome.

" Then I have come in vain," she said, breathing quickly; " you can make no use of me to-day ? "

" No, no, signora! your face is a star seldom seen in my heaven, and I must grasp the opportunity—have the kindness to wait; I will hasten to the king and return with the picture."

Without giving Barbarina time to answer, he left the room. Why did her heart beat so quickly? Why were her cheeks suffused with crimson? Why were her eyes fixed so nervously upon the door. Steps were heard in the adjoining room. Barbarina pressed her hands upon her heart: she was greatly agitated. The door opened, and Pesne returned, alone and without the picture.

" Signora," said he, " the king wishes that the sitting should take place in his rooms; his majesty will be kind enough to make suggestions and call my attention to some faults. I will get my palette and brush, and, if agreeable to you, we will go at once."

Barbarina gave no reply, and became deadly pale, as she walked through the king's rooms; her steps were uncertain and faltering, and she was forced to lean upon Pesne's arm; she declared that her foot was painful, and he perhaps believed her.

They reached at last the room in which the portrait was placed. There were two doors to this room: the one through which they had entered, and another which led to the study of the king. This door was closed, and Barbarina found herself alone with the painter.

" The king has yet some audiences to give; he commanded me to commence my work. As soon as he is at liberty, he will join us."

" Let us begin, then," said Barbarina, seating herself. " You must allow me to-day to be seated. I think it can make no difference to you, as you are at present occupied with my face and not with my figure."

Pesne declared, however, that this attitude gave an entirely different expression and bearing to the countenance. Barbarina must, therefore, in spite of the pain in her foot, endeavor to stand. She appeared now to feel no pain; she smiled so happily, she spoke so joyously, that Pesne, while gazing at her animated, enchanting, lovely face, forgot that he was there to paint, and not to wonder. Suddenly her smile vanished, and she interrupted herself in the midst of a gay remark. She had heard the door behind her lightly opened; she knew, by the stormy beating of her heart, that she was no longer alone with the painter; she had not the courage or strength to turn; she was silent, immovable, and stared straight at Pesne, who painted on quietly. The king had motioned him not to betray him.

Pesne painted on, from time to time asked Barbarina the most innocent and simple questions, which she answered confusedly. Perhaps she was mistaken; possibly she was still alone with the painter. But no, that was impossible, it seemed to her that a stream of heavenly light irradiated the room; she did not see the king, but she felt his glance; she felt that he was behind her, that he was watching her, although no movement, no word of his betrayed him.

"I will not move, I will not turn, but I cannot endure this, I shall fall dead to the earth."

But now she was forced to turn; the king called her name, and greeted her with a few friendly words. She bowed and looked up timidly. How cold, indifferent, and devoid of interest was his glance, and he had not seen her for weeks, and she had been ill and suffering! And now, she felt again that she hated him bitterly, and that it was the power of this passion which overcame her when she saw the king so unexpectedly. She felt, however, that every tone of his voice was like heavenly music to her ear, that every word he uttered moved her heart as the soft wind ruffles the sea.

The king spoke of her portrait; he said he had made it his study and sought for its faults and defects, as others sought for its advantages and beauties.

"I tremble, then, before the judgment of your majesty," said Pesne.

"I must confess you have some cause to fear," said the king. "I have not looked at the picture with the eye of a lover, but with that of a critic; such eyes look sharply, and would see spots in the sun; no criticism, however, can prevent the sun from shining and remaining always a sun, and my fault-finding cannot prevent your portrait from being a beautiful picture, surpassed only by the original."

"Perhaps, sire, I am myself one of the spots in the sun, and it may be that I grow dark."

"You see, signora, how little I understand the art of flattery; even my best intended compliments can be readily changed into their opposites. Allow me, then, to speak the simple, unadorned truth. You are more beautiful than your picture, and yet I wonder at the genius of Pesne, which has enabled him to represent so much of your rare loveliness, even as I wonder at the poet who has the power to describe the calm beauty of a sunny spring morning."

"That would be less difficult than to paint the signora's portrait," said Pesne; "a spring morning is still, it does not escape from you, it does not change position and expression every moment."

Frederick smiled. "It would be truly difficult to hold the butterfly and force it to be still without brushing the down from its beautiful wings. But, paint now, Pesne, I will seat myself behind your chair and look on."

Pesne seized his palette and brush, and began to paint. Barbarina assumed the light, gracious, and graceful attitude, which the artist has preserved for us in her beautiful portrait. She was, indeed, indescribably lovely; her rounded arms, her taper fingers, which slightly raised the fleecy robe and exposed the fairy foot, the small aristocratic head, slightly inclined to one side, the flashing eyes, the sweet, attractive smile, were irresistible; every one admired, and every glance betrayed admiration.

The face of the king only betrayed nothing; he was cold, quiet, indifferent. Barbarina felt the blood mount to her cheek, and then retreat to her heart; she felt that it was impossible for her to preserve her self-control; she could not bear this cruel comparison of the portrait and the original, but she swore to herself that the king should not have the triumph of seeing her once more sink insensible at his feet; his proud, cold heart should not witness the outbreak of her scorn and wounded vanity. But her body was less strong than her spirit—her foot gave way, she tottered, and turned deadly pale.

The king sprang forward, and asked in a sympathetic and trembling voice why she was so pale; he himself placed a chair for her, and besought her to rest. She thanked him with a soft smile, and declared she had better return home. Would the king allow her to withdraw? A cloud passed over Frederick's face; a dark, stern glance rested upon Barbarina.

"No!" said he, almost harshly; "you must remain here, we have business with each other. Swartz has brought me your contract to sign; it requires some changes, and I should have sent for you if accident had not brought you here."

"Your majesty can command me," said Barbarina.

"We have business and contracts to consider," said the king roughly, "and we will speak of them alone. Go, Pesne, and say to Swartz I await him."

Frederick nodded to the painter, and, seizing Barbarina's hand, led her into the adjoining room, his Tusculum, never before profaned by a woman's foot; open only to the king's dearest, most trusted friends.

CHAPTER XV.

THE CONFESSION.

BARBARINA entered this room with peculiar feelings; her heart trembled, her pulses beat quickly. She, whose glance was usually so proud, so victorious, looked up now timidly, almost fearfully, to the king. He had never appeared to her so handsome, so imposing as in this moment. Silently she took her place upon the divan to which he led her. Frederick seated himself directly in front of her.

"This is the second time," said the king, with a smile, "the second time, signora, that I have had the honor to be alone with you. On the first occasion you swore to me that you would hate the King of Prussia with an everlasting hatred."

"I said that to your majesty when I did not recognize you," said Barbarina.

"Had you known me, signora, you would surely not have spoken so frankly. Unhappily, the world has silently resolved never to speak the truth to kings. You avowed your resolution, therefore, at that time, because you did not know you were speaking to the king. Oh, signora, I have not forgotten your words. I know that you pray to God every day; not for your own happiness, as all chance of that has been destroyed by this cruel king; but for revenge on this man, who has no heart, and treads the hearts of other men under his feet."

"Your majesty is cruel," whispered Barbarina.

"Cruel! why? I only repeat your words. Cruel, because I cannot forget! The words of Barbarina cannot be forgotten. In that respect at least I am like other men."

"And in that respect should your majesty the least resemble them. The little *windspiel* may revenge its injuries, but the eagle forgives, and soars aloft so high in the heavens that the poor offender is no longer seen and soon forgotten. Your majesty is like the eagle, why can you not also forget?"

"I cannot and I will not! I remind you of that hour, because I wish to ask now for the same frankness of speech. I wish to hear the truth once more from those proud lips. Barbarina, will you tell me the truth?"

"Yes, on condition that your majesty promises to forget the past."

"I promise not to remind you of it."

"I thank your majesty; I will speak the truth."

"You swear it?"

"I swear it."

"Well, then, why did you wound your foot?"

Barbarina trembled and was silent; she had not the courage to raise her eyes from the floor.

"The truth!" said the king, imperiously.

"The truth," repeated Barbarina, resolved, and she raised her flashing eyes to the king; "I will speak the truth. I wounded my foot, because—"

"Because," said the king, interrupting her fiercely, "because you knew it was a happiness, a life's joy to the poor, lonely, wearied king to see you dance; because you felt that your appearance was to him as the first golden rays of the sun to one who has been buried alive, and who bursts the bonds of the dark grave. You hate me so unrelentingly, that even on the evening of my return from an exhausting and dangerous journey, you cruelly resolved to disappoint me. I hastened to the theatre to see you, Barbarina, you, you alone; but your cruel and revengeful heart was without pity. You thought of nothing but your pride, and rejoiced in the power to grieve a king, at the sound of whose voice thousands tremble. Your smiles vanished, your enchanting gayety was suppressed, and you seemed to become insensible. With the art of a tragedian, you assumed a sudden illness, resolved that the hated king should not see you dance. Ah! Barbarina, that was a small, a pitiful *rôle!* leave such arts to the chambermaids of the stage. You are refined in your wickedness; you are inexorable in your hate. Not satisfied with this pretended swoon, the next evening you wounded yourself; you were proud to suffer, in order to revenge yourself upon me. You knew that a swoon must pass away, but a wounded foot is a grave accident; its consequences might be serious. The king had returned to Berlin, and had only a few days to refresh himself, after the cares and exhaustions of a dangerous journey; after his departure you would be able to dance again. Ah! signora, you are a true daughter of Italy; you understand how to hate, and your thirst for vengeance is unquenchable! Well, I give you joy! I will fill your heart with rapture. You have sworn to hate me; you pray to God to revenge you upon the King of Prussia who has trampled your heart under his feet. Now, then, Barbarina, triumph! you are revenged. The king has a heart, and you have wounded it mortally!"

Completely unmanned, the king sprang to his feet, and stepped to the window, wishing to conceal his emotion from Barbarina. Suddenly he felt his shoulder lightly touched, and turning, he saw Barbarina before him, more proud, more beautiful, more queenly than he had ever seen her; energy and high resolve spoke in her face and in her flashing eyes.

"Sire," she said, in a full, mellow voice, which slightly trembled from strong emotion—"sire," she repeated, trying to veil her agitation by outward calm, "I have sworn in this hour to speak the truth; I will fulfil my vow. I will speak the truth, though you may scorn and despise me. I will die of your contempt as one dies of a quick and deadly poison; but it is better so to die than to live as I am living. You shall know me better, sire. You have charged me with falsehood and hypocrisy; thank God, I can cast off that humiliating reproach! I will speak the truth, though it bows my head with shame and casts me at your feet. If I could die there, I would count myself most blessed. The truth, sire, the truth! listen to it. It is true I hated you; you humbled my pride. You changed me, the queen of grace and beauty, the queen of the world, into a poor, hired dancer; with your rude soldiers and police you compelled me to fulfil a contract against which my soul revolted. I cursed you. You separated me violently from the man I loved, who adored me, and offered me a splendid and glorious future. It is true I prayed to God for vengeance, but He would not hear my prayer; He punished me for my mad folly, and turned the dagger I wildly aimed at you, against my own breast. Sire, the hate to which I swore, to which I clung as the shipwrecked mariner clings to the plank which may save him from destruction, failed me in the hour of need, and I sank, sank down. A day came in which the prayer of rage and revenge upon my lips was changed, in spite of myself, into blessings, and I found, with consternation and horror, that there was indeed but one step between wild hatred and passionate love, and this fatal step lies over an abyss. I cannot tell you, sire, how much I have suffered—how vainly I have struggled. I have hated, I have cursed myself because I could no longer hate and curse you. The day you left for Silesia, you said, 'I think ever of thee.' Oh! sire, you

14

know not what fatal poison you poured into my ears, with
what rapture and enchantment these words filled my heart.
My life was a dream; I stood under a golden canopy, drunk
with joy and blessed with heavenly peace. I saw these
words, 'I think ever of thee,' not only in my heart, but in
every flower, on every leaf, and written by the sun in the
heavens, and in the stars. I dreamed of them as one dreams
of fairy palaces and heavenly melodies. In the songs of
sweet birds, in the plaudits and bravos with which the world
greeted me, I heard only these celestial words, 'I think ever
of thee.' I lived upon them during your absence, I wrote
them with my glances upon your empty chair in the theatre,
I fixed my eyes upon it, and for love of you I danced to it.
One night I saw in this chair, not only my golden starry
words, I saw two stars from heaven; I was not prepared—
their glance was fatal. No, sire, that was no miserable
comedy, no actor's work. I sank unconscious, and from that
hour I know one does not die from rapture, but sinks insensible. I wept the whole night, God knows whether from
shame or bliss, I cannot tell. The next day—yes—then I
was false and deceitful. I stuck my stiletto in my foot, to
deceive the world; only God might know that the Barbarina
fainted at the sight of the king—fainted because she felt
that she no longer hated, but worshipped him."

She rushed to the door, but Frederick sprang after her;
he drew her back, madly but silently; his eyes were radiant
with joy.

"Remain," said he; "I command you—I, not the king."
He placed his lips to her ear and whispered two words: her
soft cheeks were crimson.

At this moment there was a knock upon the door, the
portière was thrown back, and the wan, suffering face of
Fredersdorf was seen.

"Sire," said he, "your majesty commanded me to summon Baron Swartz; he is here, and waits for your orders."

"Let him enter," said the king; then smiling upon Barbarina, he said, "He comes just in time; we must sign our
contract, Swartz shall act as our priest."

He advanced to meet the intendant, and asked for the
contract between Barbarina and himself. He read it care-

fully, and said, "There are only a few things to alter." He stepped to his desk and added a few words to the contract.

"Signora," said he, turning backward, "will you come here for a moment?"

Barbarina, embarrassed and blushing, drew near. In the back part of the room stood Baron Swartz, watching the king and Barbarina with a sly smile; near him stood Fredersdorf, whose pale and melancholy face was brought out in strong relief by the dark velvet *portière*.

"Read this," said the king to Barbarina, pointing to the words he had just written. "Have you read?"

"Yes, sire."

Frederick raised his head, and slightly turning, his glowing glance rested upon Barbarina, who, ashamed and confused, cast her eyes to the ground.

"Will you sign this?"

"I will, sire," said she, almost inaudibly.

"You bind yourself to remain here for three years, and not to marry during that time?" *

"I do, sire."

"Take the pen and sign our contract.—Come forward, Swartz, and witness this document.—Fredersdorf, is your seal at hand?"

The contract was ready.

"You will say, 'This is a sad contract,'" said the king, turning to Fredersdorf.

"Yes, sad indeed. The king deals as cruelly with the Barbarina as he has done with his poor secretary. This cold king does not believe in marriage."

"No, no! Fredersdorf, I will prove to you that you are mistaken. I have been told that you are ill because I will not allow you to marry. Now, then, Fredersdorf, I will not be hard-hearted. I have to-day made an innocent sacrifice to my hatred of matrimony. The signora has bound herself not to marry for three years. For her sake, I will be gracious to you: go and marry the woman you love, and when

---

* By this contract, Barbarina received an income of seven thousand thalers and five months' liberty during each year; but she was bound not to marry during this term of three years.—SCHNEIDER.

the priest has made you one, you shall take your wife to Paris for the honeymoon, at my cost."

Fredersdorf seized the hand of the king, kissed it, and covered it with his tears. Barbarina gazed at the handsome, glowing face of Frederick with admiration. She understood him fully; she felt that he was happy, and wished all around him to partake of his joy.

CHAPTER XVI.

THE TRAITOR.

BARON VON PÖLLNITZ was ill at ease; for three days he had sought relief diligently, but had no alleviation. He found himself in the antediluvian condition of our great forefather Adam, while he loitered away his time in Paradise. Like Adam, Pöllnitz had no gold. Our good baron found this by no means a happy state, and his heart was full of discontent and apprehension; he felt that he was, indeed, unblessed. What would become of him if the king should not be merciful, should not take pity upon his necessities, which he had to-day made known to him in a most touching and eloquent letter. Up to this time he had been waiting in vain for an answer. What should he do if the king should be hard-hearted and cruel? But no, that was impossible; he must consider it a sacred duty to take care of the old and faithful servant of his house, who had been the favored companion of two of Prussia's kings. Pöllnitz considered that he belonged to the royal family; he was an adopted member; they could not think slightingly of him, or set him aside.

He had exhausted his means, he had borrowed from Jew and Christian; he had, by his gay narratives and powers of persuasion, drawn large sums of gold from the rich burghers; all his friends held his dishonored drafts; even his own servant had allowed himself to be made a fool of, and had loaned him the savings of many years; and this sum scarcely sufficed to maintain the noble, dissipated, and great-hearted cavalier a few weeks.

Alas! what sacrifices had he not already made to this insane passion for spending money; what humiliation had he not suffered—and all in vain! In vain had he changed his religion three times; he had condescended so far as to pay court to a merchant's daughter; he had even wished to wed the daughter of a tailor, and she had rejected him.

"And yet," said he, as he thought over his past life, every thing might have gone well, but for this formidable stratagem of the king; this harsh prohibition and penalty as to relieving my necessities which has been trumpeted through the streets—that ruined me; that gave me fearful trouble and torment. That was refined cruelty for which I will one day revenge myself, unless Frederick makes amends. Ha! there comes a royal messenger. He stops at my door. God be thanked! The king answers my letter; that is to say, the king sends me money."

Pöllnitz could scarcely restrain himself from rushing out to receive the messenger; his dignity, perhaps, would not have sufficed to hold him back, but the thought of the considerable *douceur* he would be expected to pay moderated his impatience. At last his servant came and handed him a letter.

"I hope," said the baron, gravely, "I hope you rewarded the king's messenger handsomely?"

"No, sir, I gave him nothing."

"Nothing!" cried he angrily. "And you dare to say this to my face! you do not tremble lest I dismiss you instantly from my service? you, and such as you are, cast shame upon our race! I, a baron of the realm, and grand master of ceremonies, allow a royal messenger who brings me a letter to go from my door unrewarded! Ass, if you had no money, why did you not come to me? why did you not call upon me for several ducats?"

"If your grace will give me the money, I will run after the messenger. I know where to find him; he has gone to General Rothenberg's."

"Leave the room, scoundrel, and spare me your folly!"

Pöllnitz raised his arm to strike, but the lackey fled and left him alone with his golden dreams of the future.

He hastily broke the seal and opened the letter. "Not from the king, but from Fredersdorf," he murmured impatiently. As he read, his brow grew darker, and his lips breathed words of cursing and scorn.

"Refused!" said he passionately, as he read to the end, and cast the letter angrily to the floor. "Refused! The king has no money for me! The king needs all his gold for war, which is now about to be declared; and, if I wish to convince myself that this is true, I must go to-night, at eleven o'clock, to the middle door of the castle, and there I will see that the king has no money. A curious proposition, indeed! I would rather go to discover that he *had* money, than that he had it not. If he had it, I would find a means to supply myself. At all events, I will go. A curious rendezvous indeed—a midnight assignation between a bankrupt baron and an empty purse! A tragedy might grow out of it. But if Frederick has really no money, I must seek elsewhere. I will make a last attempt—I will go to Trenck."

The trusty baron made his toilet and hastened to Trenck's apartments. The young officer had lately taken a beautiful suite of rooms. He had his reception-rooms adorned with costly furniture and rare works of art. He had an antechamber, in which two richly-liveried servants waited to receive his orders. He had a stable and four splendid horses of the Arabian breed, and two orderlies to attend to them! From what quarter did Trenck obtain the money for all this livery? This was an open question with which the comrades of the young lieutenant were exercised; it gave them much cause for thought, and some of them were not satisfied with thinking; these thoughts took form, some of their words reached the ears of Trenck, and must have been considered by him very objectionable. He challenged the speaker to fight with the sword, and disabled him effectually from speaking afterward.* Trenck was at dinner, and, contrary to custom, alone; he received Pöllnitz most graciously, and the baron took a seat willingly at the table.

"I did not come to dine with you, but to complain of

* Frederick von Trenck's Memoires.

you," said Pöllnitz, cutting up the grouse with great adroitness and putting the best part upon his plate.

"You come to complain of me?" repeated Trenck, a little embarrassed. "I have given you no cause for displeasure, dear friend."

"Yes, you have given me good cause, even while I am your best friend! Why have you withdrawn your confidence from me? Why do I no longer accompany you on that most romantic midnight moonlight path to virtue? Why am I no longer watchman and *duenna* when you and your lady call upon the moon and stars to witness your love? Why am I set aside?"

"I can only say to all this that I go no more upon the balcony."

"That is to say—"

"That is to say that my stars are quenched and my sun has set in clouds. I am, even as you are, set aside."

Pöllnitz gazed at Trenck with so sharp and cunning an eye that the young man was confused and looked down. The baron laughed merrily.

"Dear Trenck," said he, "a lie shows in your face like a spot on the smooth skin of a rosy apple. You are too young to understand lying, and I am too old to be deceived by it. Another point: will you make me believe that this luxury which surrounds you is maintained with your lieutenant's pay?"

"You forget that my father has left me his property of Sherlock, and that I have rented it for eight hundred thalers!"

"I am too good an accountant not to know that this sum would scarcely suffice for your horses and servants."

"Well, perhaps you are right; for the rest I may thank my gracious king. During the course of this year he has presented me with three hundred Fredericks d'or; and now you know the source of my revenue and will not think so meanly of me as to suppose that—"

"That your great love has any thing to do with earthly riches or advancement. I do not believe that I brought in such a charge against you, even as little do I believe that you have been given up! Ah, dear friend, I alone have cause of

complaint; I alone am *set aside*, and why am I thus treated?
Have I not been discreet, diligent in your service, and ready
at all times?"

"Certainly. I can only repeat to you that all is at an
end. Our beautiful dream has faded like the morning cloud
and the early dew."

"You are in earnest?"

"In solemn earnest."

"Well, then, I will also speak earnestly. I will relate to
you something which you do not appear to know. A gardener boy who had risen earlier than usual to protect some rare
flowers in the garden of Monbijou saw two figures upon the
balcony, and heard their light whispers. The boy made
known his discovery to the principal gardener, and he communicated the facts to the chamberlain of the queen-mother.
It was resolved to watch the balcony. The virtuous and
suspicious queen immediately concluded that Mademoiselle
von Marwitz had arranged a rendezvous upon the balcony,
and she was sternly resolved to dismiss the lady at once if
any proof could be obtained against her. Happily, the queen
made known these facts to the Princess Amelia, and I can
readily conceive that the balcony remains now unoccupied."

"Yes, I understand that."

"You can also understand that this event was regarded as
a warning of fate, and great caution and forethought were
exercised. Not only was the balcony given up, but the old
friend and confidant who had played the part of companion and carrier-pigeon was banished and dismissed wholly
from service."

"You may go further still," said Frederick von Trenck.
"You have not stated the whole case. This fortunate providence was a convincing proof of the danger of an engagement which might never hope to be crowned with success.
never exist except under the shadows of silence and gloom,
with bleeding hearts and tearful eyes; this dream of love
was given up at once, fearing that at no distant day both
honor and liberty might be lost in its pursuit. They separated! An eternal farewell was faltered!"

"That is to say, you would now deceive your confidant
and former aid, in order to place yourself more securely—

and some day, perhaps, when suspicion is aroused, you can call him as a witness to prove that all intercourse was long ago given up; he must know it, being the confidant from the beginning. This was a well-conceived plot, but you only seem to forget that Pöllnitz was not the man to be deceived. He has had too much experience, and has studied the hearts of men, and especially of women, too diligently. A woman who is enjoying her first love and believes in its holy power, convinces herself that it can achieve wonders and overcome all obstacles. She does not sacrifice her love to other duties or to danger, not even if she is a common woman, far less if she is a princess. Princess Amelia has not given up her young and handsome lover; she clings to him with a frenzied constancy, which I confess to you, if I had the honor and glory of being her suitor, would fill me with apprehension and regret. No, no, the princess is just now in a paroxysm of youthful passion, and would rather die than resign her love, and she is fantastic enough to believe in the possibility of a legitimate marriage! Poor thing, she expects to mould the world to her wishes, and arms herself, I suppose, with hair-pins! Princess Amelia was forced to give up her interviews upon the balcony, but she sought other means to gratify her passion. This was simple and easy to do. The maid of honor was taken into her confidence. Marwitz swore to guard the secret fearfully till death; a plan was then arranged with her which was truly well conceived. Lieutenant von Trenck must be spoken of as the suitor of Mademoiselle von Marwitz; he must act at the court-balls and *fêtes* as the tender, sighing, and eager lover of the maid of honor; he must at last make a formal declaration, and receive permission to visit her in her rooms. This is now his daily habit, and the good city of Berlin and the short-sighted, silly court are completely deceived, and look upon Frederick von Trenck as the happy bridegroom of Marwitz, and no one guesses that when the young officer is with the maid of honor, the Princess Amelia is also present, and changes the *rôle* with Marwitz."

"I see it is in vain," said Trenck, sighing; "you know all: but if you have any real friendship for me, you will tell me who betrayed us."

Pöllnitz laughed aloud. "You betrayed yourself, my friend; or, if you prefer it, my worldly wisdom and cunning betrayed you. My young and innocent friend, a man like Pöllnitz is not easily deceived; his eyes are sharp enough to pierce the veil of the most charming little intrigue, and probe it to the bottom! I know the Princess Amelia; I have known her too long, not to know that she would not so quickly, and without a struggle, sacrifice her love; and further when I saw at the last court-ball, with what a long and dreary face you stood behind the chair of the poor Marwitz, and with what calm and smiling content the princess watched the *couple amoureuse*, look you, Trenck, then I knew and understood all."

"Well, then, as you understand all, I make no further attempt to deceive you. Yes, God be praised! the princess loves me still. It is indeed the princess whom I meet in the apartment of the maid of honor; to Marwitz are the letters directed which my servant carries every morning to the palace, and from the Princess Amelia do I receive my answers. Yes, God be thanked! Amelia loves me, and one day she will be mine in the eyes of the whole world, even as she is now mine in the eyes of God and the angels; one day—"

"Stop, stop!" cried Pöllnitz interrupting him; "that last sentence must be explained before you rush on with your dithyrambics. You have declared that the princess is yours in the sight of God: what does that mean?"

"That means," said Trenck, "that God, who looks into our hearts, knows the eternity and boundlessness of our love; that means that, under God's heaven, and calling upon His holy name, we have sworn never to forget our love and our faith, and never to form any other alliance."

"So nothing more than that—no secret marriage? Are you never alone with the princess?"

"No, never! I have given her my word of honor never even to ask it, and I will keep my oath. And, after all, the good Marwitz disturbs us not; she gets as far from us as possible: she seems to see us not, and we speak in such low tones, that she does not hear a word we utter."

"Ah! so the Marwitz does not disturb you?" cried Pöllnitz, with a cynical laugh. "*O sancta simplicitas!* and this is an officer of the life-guard? The world is going to destruction; or it is becoming innocent and pure as Paradise. It is time for me to die; I no longer understand this pitiful world."

"I do not understand you, and I will not understand you," said Trenck gravely. "You laugh at me, and call me a silly boy, and I allow it. I know we cannot understand each other in such matters; you cannot conceive what strength, what self-denial, what energy I exert to make myself worthy of the pure, modest, and exalted love which Amelia has consecrated to me. You cannot comprehend how often my good and evil genius struggle for the mastery, how often I pray God to keep me from temptation. No, I have sworn that this love shall wave pure and unblemished, like a glorious banner over my whole life; come death rather than dishonor! And now, friend, explain your meaning: why all these plots and counterplots? What is your object?"

"Nothing more than to warn you to prudence. I do not believe all the world is deceived by your comedy with Marwitz. The king, who appears to see nothing, sees all. He has his spies everywhere, and knows all that happens in his family. Be careful, be ever on your guard."

"I thank you for your warning," said Trenck, pressing the hand of the master of ceremonies. "We must soon separate; you know that in a few weeks we go to Silesia. The king is silently preparing for war."

"I know it, and I pity you."

"Pity me! Ah, you do not understand me. I long for my first battle as a lover does for his first sweet kiss. The battle-field is for me a consecrated garden, where my laurels and myrtles grow. I shall pluck them and weave wreaths for my bride—wedding wreaths. Pöllnitz, on the other side, beyond the bloody battle-ground, lies my title of prince, and Amelia's bridle-wreath."

"Dreamer, fantastic, hopeless dreamer!" cried Pöllnitz, laughing. "Well, God grant that you do not embrace death on the battle-field, or on the other side find a prison, to either of which you have a better claim than to a prince's title. Make use, therefore, of your time, and enjoy these charming interviews. Is one arranged for this evening?"

"No, but to-morrow. The reigning queen gives a ball to-morrow. Immediately before the ball I am to meet the princess. Oh, my friend, to-morrow evening at five think of me! I shall be the happiest and most amiable of mortals. I shall be with my beloved!"

"Alas! how strange is life, and how little do the fates of men resemble! To-morrow, at the hour when you will be so unspeakably happy, I shall be walking in a thorny, a cursed path; I shall be on my way to the usurer."

"To the usurer? That is indeed a sad alternative for a cavalier like the Baron von Pöllnitz."

"But that is still better than imprisonment for debt, and I have only the choice between these two, unless you, dearest friend, will take pity upon me and lend me a hundred louis d'ors."

Frederick Trenck said nothing. He stepped to his desk. The eyes of the baron glittered with joy as he saw Trenck take out a pocket-book, in which he knew by pleasant experience that the young officer sometimes kept gold. His joy was of short duration. No gold was seen. Trenck took out a small, modest, unsealed paper and handed it to him.

"Look at this draft," said he. "Had you come yesterday I could have accommodated you joyfully. To-day it is impossible. I have this morning lent my colonel two hundred ducats, and my purse is empty."

"Well, you must soon fill it," said Pöllnitz, with a coarse laugh. "To-morrow at five you will enjoy your rendezvous, and you will not only speak of God, and love, and the stars, but also a little of earthly things—of pomp and gold, and—Farewell!"

With a gay laugh Pöllnitz took leave, but he no sooner found himself alone upon the street than his face grew black and his eye was full of malice.

"He has no gold for me, but I have his secret, and I will know how to squeeze some gold out of that," murmured Pöllnitz. "Truly I think this secret of Trenck's is worth some thousand thalers, and the king must find the means to pay for it. But stop! The hour of my interesting rendezvous draws near. I am curious to know how I am to be convinced at eleven o'clock, and in the middle of the street, that the king has no gold. I will be punctual, but I have still time to visit a few friends, and seek if possible to win a few louis d'ors at faro."

CHAPTER XVII.

THE SILVER-WARE.

It was a dark, still night. As the clock struck ten the night might really be said to begin in Berlin. The streets were not lighted except by accidental rays from the windows and the carriage-lamps, and the glare of torches carried by the servants who accompanied their masters to places of amusement. By eleven o'clock the streets were deserted. Pöllnitz was therefore sure to meet no one on his way to the castle. He directed his steps to that door which opened upon the River Spree, as Fredersdorf had advised him.

Silence reigned in the palace. The sentinel stepped slowly backward and forward in the courtyard, and in the distance was heard the baying of two hounds, entertaining each other with their melancholy music. The master of ceremonies began to be impatient; he thought that the impertinent private secretary had been indulging in some practical joke or mystification at his expense; but as he drew near to the Spree, he heard the light stroke of oars in the water. Pöllnitz hastened forward, and his eyes, accustomed to the darkness, discovered a skiff drawn up near the Elector's Bridge.

"This is the point! here we must wait," whispered a manly voice.

"I think we will not have to wait long," said another. " I see lights in the windows."

The side of the castle next the Spree was now suddenly lighted; first the upper story, then the lower, and a pale light was now seen in the vestibule.

"Truly, I have not been deceived; something is going on," said Pöllnitz, hastening forward.

As he entered the court, a curious train was seen descending the steps. In front were two servants with torches; they

were followed by twelve *heyducks*, their shoulders weighed
down with dishes, cans, cups, plates, whose silver surface,
illumined by the golden glare of the torches, seemed to
dance and glimmer along the wall and steps like "will o' the
wisps." Two servants with towels brought up the rear, and
behind these the pale, sad face of Fredersdorf was seen.

"You are punctual," said he to Pöllnitz; "you wish to
convince yourself that the king has no gold?"

"Certainly! though this conviction will deprive me of
my last hope, and one does not adopt such a course eagerly."

"I think you will be fully convinced. Come, let us follow the *heyducks*."

He took the arm of the baron, and they soon reached the
border of the Spree. The large skiff, which had been lying
so dark and still, was now lighted by the torches of the servants, who ranged themselves on each side; it was brilliantly
lighted, and great activity prevailed. The twelve *heyducks*,
bending under their heavy burden, entered the skiff, and
piled up the silver-ware, then sprang again ashore.

"We are going to the treasure-room, will you follow us?"
said Fredersdorf.

"Certainly; if not, you may perhaps expect to leave me
here as sentinel."

"That is not at all necessary; there are some soldiers
with loaded muskets in the skiff. Come."

Silently and hastily they all mounted the steps and
reached at last the large room where the royal silver had
been kept; the door was open, but guarded by sentinels, and
Melchoir, who had had the silver in charge, now walked before the door with a disturbed and sad visage.

"May I enter, Melchoir?" said Pöllnitz to his old acquaintance, greeting him with a friendly smile.

"There is no necessity to ask," said Melchoir, sadly.
"My kingdom is at an end, as you see, when the silver is
gone; there is no necessity for a steward, and the old Melchoir will be set aside, with all those who yet remain of
the good old times of the ever-blessed Frederick William!"

Pöllnitz entered the room with Fredersdorf, and his eye
wandered over the rich treasures spread out before him, and
which the *heyducks* were now packing in large sacks.

"Oh, if these plates and dishes could speak and converse with me, what curious things we would have to confide with each other!" said Pöllnitz, twirling one of the plates between his fingers. "How often have I dined from your rich abundance! Under the first pomp-and-splendor-loving Frederick, you furnished me with gala dinners; under the parsimonious Frederick William, with solid family dinners! How often have I seen my smiling face reflected in your polished surface! how often has this silver fork conveyed the rarest morsels to my lips! I declare to you, Fredersdorf, I think a dinner plate fulfils a noble mission; within its narrow bound lie the bone and sinew, as also the best enjoyments of life. But tell me, for God's sake, how can you bear that these rascals should handle the king's silver so roughly? Only look, now, at that *heyduck*, he has completely doubled up one of those beautiful salad-bowls, in order to force it into the mouth of the sack."

"What signifies, dear baron? That said salad-bowl will never again be used for salad, henceforth it is only silver."

"You speak in riddles, and I do not understand you. Well, well, those fellows have already filled their twelve sacks, and this room is now as empty and forlorn as the heart of an old bachelor. Now tell me what you are going to do with all these treasures?"

"Can you not guess?"

"I think the king, who now lives in Potsdam, needs his silver service, and as he does not wish to make a new purchase, he sends to Berlin for this. Am I right?"

"You shall soon know. Let us follow the *heyducks*, the room is empty. Adieu, Melchoir, your duties will be light hereafter; you need not fear the robbers. Come, baron."

They soon reached the skiff, and found that the twelve sacks had been placed beside the huge pile of dishes, plates, etc.

"Alas!" said Fredersdorf, gloomily, "all this might have been avoided if I had already reached the goal I am aiming at; if I had fathomed the great mystery which God has suspended over mankind, upon whose sharp angles and edges thousands of learned and wise men have dashed their brains and destroyed their life's happiness! My God! I have ac-

complished so much, so little remains to be done! let me only
find a sufficiently hardened substance, and the work is done.
I shall have laid bare God's great mystery—I shall make
gold!"

"Do you think ever of this, Fredersdorf?"

"I think ever of this, and shall think only of this as long
as I live. This thought swallows up all other thoughts; it
has destroyed my love, my rest, my sleep, my earthly happiness! But wait, Pöllnitz, only wait; one day I shall lift the
philosopher's stone, and make gold. On that day you will
love me dearly, Baron Pöllnitz. On that day I will not be
obliged to prove to you, as I have just done, that the king has
no money."

"I have seen no proof yet," said Pöllnitz.

"You shall have it now, baron," said Fredersdorf, springing into the skiff. "Will you not go with us? Forward,
forward at once!"

"But what is your destination?"

"Come nearer, that I may whisper in your ear."

Pöllnitz bowed his head.

"We are going to the mint," whispered Fredersdorf.
"All this beautiful silver will be melted. The king will
give no more dinners, he will give battle. The king changes
his dishes and plates into good thalers to feed his brave
army. And now, are you not convinced that the king has
no money to pay your debts?"

"I am convinced."

"Then farewell. Take the rudder, boys, and go forward;
enter the arm of the Spree which flows by the mint, and
there anchor. The mint is our goal."

"The mint is the goal," murmured Pöllnitz, with a grim
look, gazing after the skiff, which moved slowly over the
water, and which, lighted by the torches, shone brilliantly in
the midst of the surrounding darkness. The golden light,
playing upon the rich liveries of the *heyducks* and the tower
of silver in their midst, formed a scene of wonder and enchantment.

Pöllnitz watched them until the torches seemed like little
stars in the distance. "There go all the pomp and glory
of the world, the joys of peace and luxurious rest. The

silver will be melted, iron and steel will take its place. Yes, the iron age begins. Alas! it begins also for me—why cannot I go into the mint and be melted down with these plates and dishes?"

CHAPTER XVIII.

THE FIRST FLASH OF LIGHTNING.

DURING this night Pöllnitz slept but little; when, however, he rose from his couch the next morning, his brow was clear and his countenance gayer than it had been for a long time; he had made his plans, and was convinced that he would succeed.

"I will earn a hundred ducats, said he, smiling to himself, as in a superb toilet he left his dwelling, "yes, a hundred ducats, and I will revenge myself upon the king for that trumpeting and outcry. This shall be a blessed and beautiful morning."

He walked first to the apartment of Colonel Jaschinsky, and announced himself as coming upon most important business. The colonel hastened to meet him, ready to be of service, and full of curiosity.

"Lead me to a room where we are absolutely certain not to be observed or listened to," said Pöllnitz.

They entered the colonel's cabinet.

"Here, baron, we are secure."

"Without circumlocution, then, count, you know the law which forbids officers to make debts?"

"I know it," said Jaschinsky, turning pale, "and I believe that Baron Pöllnitz is well content not to belong to the officers."

"Perhaps you, sir count, may also cease to belong to them?"

"What do you mean by that?" said Jaschinsky, anxiously.

"I mean simply that Colonel Jaschinsky belongs to those
15

officers who are forbidden to make debts, but that he disregards the law."

"You came here, as it appears, to threaten me?"

"No, principally to warn you; you know that the king is particularly severe against his body-guard. You are the colonel of this splendid regiment, and should, without doubt, set the other officers a good example. I doubt if the king would consider that you did your duty, if he knew that you not only made debts, but borrowed money from the officers of your own regiment."

"Take care, Baron von Pöllnitz!" said Jaschinsky, threateningly.

Pöllnitz said, smilingly: "It appears that you are menacing *me*, that is wholly unnecessary. Listen quietly to what I have to say. I have come to arrange a little matter of business with you. Day before yesterday you borrowed two hundred ducats from Baron Trenck. Give me one hundred of them, and I give you my word of honor not to expose you —deny me, and I give you my word of honor I will go instantly to the king, and relate the whole history. You know, count, you would be instantly cashiered."

"I do not know that his majesty would grant a ready belief to the statement of Baron Pöllnitz, and you have no proof to confirm it."

"I have proof. You gave your note for the money. I think that would be convincing testimony."

The count was pale and agitated. "If I give you a hundred ducats, you promise on your word of honor not to expose me to the king?"

"I give you my word of honor; more than that, I promise you to defend you, if any one shall accuse you to the king."

Jaschinsky did not reply; he stepped to his desk and took out two rolls of ducats. "Baron," said he, "here is half of the money I borrowed from Trenck; before I hand it to you I have one request to make."

"Well, speak."

"How did you learn that I borrowed this money?"

"I saw your note which you gave to Trenck."

"Ah! he showed it to you," cried Jaschinsky, with such

an expression of hate, scorn, and revenge, that even Pöllnitz was moved by it.

He took the gold and let it slide slowly into his pocket. "I owe you a hundred ducats; I cannot promise you to return them; but I can promise you that Trenck will never produce your draft, and I will show you how to revenge yourself upon the handsome officer."

"If you assist me in that, I will present you with my best horse."

"You shall be revenged," said Pöllnitz, solemnly. "You can send the horse to my stable; Frederick von Trenck will soon cease to be dangerous to any one; he is a lost man!—And now to the king," said Pöllnitz, as he left the colonel's quarters. "Yes, to the king; I must thank him for the confidence he showed me last night."

The king was making his preparations for war with the most profound secrecy; he worked only at night, and gave up his entire time seemingly to pleasures and amusements. He was daily occupied with concerts, balls, operas, and ballets; he had just returned from seeing the rehearsal of a new opera, in which Barbarina danced; he was gay and gracious.

He received his master of ceremonies jestingly, and asked him if he came to announce that he had become a Jew. "You have tried every other religion at least twice; I know that you have had of late much to do with the 'chosen people;' I suppose you are now full of religious zeal, and wish to turn Israelite. It would, perhaps, be a wise operation. The Jews have plenty of gold, and they would surely aid with all their strength their new and distinguished brother. Speak, then, make known your purpose."

"I come to thank your majesty for the supper you graciously accorded me last night."

"A supper! what do you mean?"

"Your majesty, through your private secretary, invited me to table, with all your splendid silver-ware. Truly the meal was indigestible and lies like a stone upon my stomach; but, I say with the good soldiers, after the lash, 'I thank your majesty for gracious punishment.'"

"You are an intolerable fool; but mark me, no word of

what you have seen. I wished to prove to you that I had no money, and to be freed from your everlasting complaints and petitions. I have therefore allowed you to see that my silver has gone to the mint. It is to be hoped that you will now compose yourself, and seek no more gold from me. Do not ask gold of kings, but of Jews! Kings are poor, the poorest people of the state, for they have no personal property." *

"Oh, that the whole world could hear the exalted and high-hearted words of my king!" cried Pöllnitz, with well-acted enthusiasm. "Thrice blessed is that nation which has such a ruler!"

The king looked at him searchingly. "You flatter me; you want something, of course."

"No, sire, I swear I come with the purest intentions."

"Intentions? You have, then, intentions?"

"Yes, sire, but now that I stand here face to face with you, I feel that my courage fails, and I cannot speak what I intended."

"Now truly," said the king, laughing, "the circumstances must indeed be dangerous which deprive Baron Pöllnitz of the power of speech."

"Words, your majesty, are important things. Once a few words saved me from death; it may be that a few words, spoken this day to your majesty, may bring me into disfavor, and that would be worse than death."

"What were the words which saved you from death?"

"These, sire: '*Va-t-en, noble guerrier!*'"

"This took place in France?"

"In Paris, sire. I was dining in a small hotel in the village of Etampes, near Paris. A very elegant cavalier sat next me and from time to time, as if accidentally, addressed me in a refined and winning way; he informed himself as to my intentions and circumstances. I was an inexperienced youth, and the cavalier was adroit in questioning. This was at the time of the Mississippi speculation of the great financier Law. I had gained that day, in the *Rue Quinquempois*, the sum of four hundred thousand francs. I had this money

* The king's own words.

with me, and after dinner I proposed to go to Versailles. I was not without apprehension, the streets were unsafe, and Cartouche with his whole band of robbers had for some time taken possession of the environs of Paris, and made them the theatre of his daring deeds."

"So you received your new friend trustingly?" said the king, laughing heartily.

"Yes, sire, and we had just agreed as to the hour of our departure, when a little maiden appeared under the window of our dining-room and sang in a loud, clear voice, '*Va-t-en, noble guerrier!*' The strange cavalier rose and stepped to the window to give her a few sous, then went out—and I saw him no more."

"And you conclude from this that the words of the song saved your life? you think that the man with whom you were eating was a poisoner?"

"I thought nothing, sire, and forgot the adventure. A year after, I was standing in the street as Cartouche was being led to execution. All Paris was abroad to see the famous brigand. I had a good place, the procession passed immediately by me, and look you, I recognized in the poor sinner now being led to execution, the elegant gentleman of the *cabaret* at Etampes! He knew me also and stood still for a moment. 'Sir,' said he, 'I dined with you a year ago. The words of an old song gave me notice to leave the *cabaret* immediately. They announced to me that the pursuers were on my heels; your star was in the ascendant, stranger; had I accompanied you to Versailles, you would have lost your gold and your life.' Your majesty will now understand that these words, '*Va-t-en, noble guerrier,*' saved my life."

"I confess it, and I am now most curious to hear the words which you fear will bring my displeasure upon you."

"Sire, I have been for more than forty years a faithful servant of your exalted house. Will you not admit this?"

"Faithful?" repeated Frederick; "you were faithful to us when it was to your advantage: you deserted us when you thought it to your interest to do so. I reproached you with this in former times, but now that I know the world better, I forgive you. Go on, then, with your pathetic appeal."

"Your majesty has often commanded me to make known to you every thing which the good people say of your royal family, and when any one dared to whisper a slander against you or yours, to inform you of it at once."

"Does any one dare to do that?" said the king, with an expression of anguish upon his noble face.

"Yes, sire."

The king breathed a heavy sigh, and walked hastily up and down; then placing himself before the window, and turning his back on Pöllnitz, he said, "Go on."

"Sire, it is lightly whispered that the young Lieutenant Trenck has dared to love a lady who is so far above him in her bright radiance and royal birth, that he should not dare to lift his eyes to her face except in holy reverence."

"I have been told that he was the lover of Mademoiselle von Marwitz," said the king.

"The world and the good Berliners believe that, but the initiated know that this pretended love is only a veil thrown by the bold youth over a highly traitorous passion."

Pöllnitz was silent; he waited for the king to speak, and watched him with a malicious smile. Frederick still stood with his face to the window, and saw nothing of this.

"Shall I go on?" said Pöllnitz at last.

"I command you to do so," said the king.

Pöllnitz drew nearer. "Sire," said he, half aloud, "allow me to say what no one but myself. Baron Trenck visits Mademoiselle von Marwitz every day, but a third person is ever present at these interviews."

"And this third person is—"

"The Princess Amelia!"

The king turned hastily, and the glance which he fixed upon Pöllnitz was so flashing, so threatening, that even the bold and insolent master of ceremonies trembled. "Are you convinced of the truth of what you have stated?" said he harshly.

"Sire," said he, "if you wish to convince yourself, it is only necessary to go this evening between five and six o'clock, unannounced, into the rooms of the Princess Amelia. You will then see that I have spoken truth."

Frederick did not reply; he stepped again to the window,

and looked silently into the street. Once more he turned to Pöllnitz, and his face was clear and smiling.

"Pöllnitz, you are an old fox; but you have laid your foundation badly, and your whole plot is poorly conceived. Look you! I understand this intrigue perfectly. You hate poor Trenck; I have long seen that. You hate him because I honor and promote him, and you courtiers always regard those as your enemies who stand higher in favor than yourselves. Trenck deserves his good fortune, in spite of his youth; he is a learned and accomplished officer, and a most amiable and elegant gentleman. You cannot forgive him for this, and therefore you accuse him. This time you shall not succeed. I tell you I don't believe one word of this silly scandal. I will forget what you have dared to say; but look to it, that you also forget. Woe to you if you do not forget; woe to you if your lips ever again utter this folly to me or to any other person! I hold you wholly responsible. In your own mad, malicious brain is this fairy tale conceived; it will be your fault if it goes farther, and is ever spoken of. Conform yourself to this, sir, and retreat in time. I repeat to you, I hold you responsible. Now go, without a word, and send me my adjutant—it is high time for parade."

"Flashed in the pan, completely flashed," said Pöllnitz to himself, as with a courtly bow and a smiling lip he took leave of the king. "I had hoped at least for a small reward, if it was only to see that I had made him angry. Alas! this man is invulnerable; all my files wear away on him."

Could he have seen what an expression of care and anguish overshadowed the king's face when he was alone—could he have heard the king's sighs and the broken words of sorrow and despair which he uttered, the wicked heart of the master of ceremonies would have been filled with gladness. But Frederick indulged himself in this weakness but a short time; he drew his royal mantle over his aching heart, he cast the veil of sadness from his eyes, and armed them with the might of majesty.

"This rendezvous shall not take place; this romantic adventure shall come to an end. I will it!" said he, with an energy which only those can feel whose will is law, and from whose words there is no appeal.

Frederick took his hat and entered the vestibule, where his staff awaited to accompany him to the parade. The king greeted them all sternly, and, passing by them rapidly, he descended the steps.

"The king is very ungracious," whispered the officers amongst each other. "Woe to him upon whom his anger falls to-day!"

A storm-cloud did indeed rest upon the brow of the king; his eye looked fierce and dangerous. The regiment stood in line, the king drew up in front; suddenly he paused, his face grew black—his eye had found an object for destruction.

"Lieutenant Trenck," said he, in a loud and threatening tone, "you have this moment arrived, you are again too late. I demand of my officers that they shall be punctual in my service. More than once I have shown you consideration, and you seem to be incurable. I will now try the power of severity. Colonel Jaschinsky, Lieutenant Trenck is in arrest, till you hear further from me; take his sword from him, and transport him to Potsdam."

The king passed on; the cloud had discharged itself; his brow was clear, and he conversed cordially with his generals. He did not give one glance to the poor young officer, who, pale and speechless, handed his sword to his malicious colonel, looked with anguish inexpressible toward the castle of Monbijou, and followed the two officers whose duty it was to conduct him to Potsdam.

That afternoon Mademoiselle von Marwitz waited in vain for her lover; that afternoon the Princess Amelia shed her first tears; and, for the first time, entered the ballroom by the side of her royal mother, with dejected mien and weary eyes. The glare of light, the sound of music, the laugh and jest of the gay crowd, filled her oppressed heart with indescribable woe. She longed to utter one mad cry and rush away, far away from all this pomp and splendor; to take refuge in her dark and lonely room; to weep, to pray, and thus exhaust her sorrow and her fears.

Perhaps the king read something of this fierce emotion in the face of the princess. He drew near to her, and taking her hand kindly, he led her away from her mother. "My sister," he said, in a low voice, but in a tone which made the heart of the princess tremble, "my sister, banish the cloud from your brow, and call the smiles to your young, fresh lips. It ill becomes a princess to be seen at a *fête* with a sad visage; melancholy, this evening, will be particularly unseemly. Be on your guard; you must not decline a single dance; I wish this as your brother, I command it as your king. Conform yourself to this. Do you understand fully all that I have said to you, and all that I have not said?"

"I understand all, your majesty," whispered Amelia, with the greatest difficulty keeping back the tears, which, "like a proud river, peering o'er its bounds," filled her eyes to overflowing.

Princess Amelia danced the whole evening, she appeared gay and happy; but it did not escape the watchful eye of the Baron Pölluitz, that her smile was forced and her gayety assumed; that her eye wandered with an expression of terror toward the king, who was ever observing her. Suddenly all was changed, and she became radiant with the fire of youth and happiness. Mademoiselle von Marwitz, while the princess stood near her in the *Française*, had whispered: "Compose yourself, your royal highness, there is no danger. He has been arrested for some small military offence, that is all!" Here were indeed peace and comfort. Amelia had been tortured by the most agonizing fears, and this news was like a messenger of peace and love. A military offence—that was a small affair. A few days of light confinement, and he would return; she would see him again; and those blessed interviews, those glorious hours of rapture, would be renewed.

The princess had deceived herself. Several days elapsed, and Trenck did not return, and she knew nothing more than that he was in Potsdam, under arrest. Eight days had passed on leaden wings, and still he came not. This severe punishment for a small offence began to be resented by Trenck's comrades; they did not dare to murmur, but their countenances were clouded.

"Colonel Jaschinsky," said the king, on the ninth morning, "go to Trenck and counsel him to ask for my forgiveness; say to him, that you believe I will forgive him, if he asks for pardon. You shall not say this officially, only as a

friend. Remark well what he shall answer, and report it to
me strictly."

The colonel returned in an hour, with a well-pleased
smile.

"Well, will he ask for forgiveness?" said the king.

"No, your majesty; he asserts that for a small fault he
has been too harshly punished, and he will not bow so low
as to plead against an injustice."

"Let him remain in arrest," said Frederick, dismissing
Jaschinsky.

The king was alone; he walked up and down with his
arms folded, as was his custom, when engaged in deep
thought. "A head of iron, a heart of fire!" murmured he;
"both so young, so proud, so fond, and all this I must destroy. I must pluck every leaf from this fair blossom. Sad
mission! Why must I cease to be a man, because I am a
king?"

Eight days again went by—eight days of *fêtes*, concerts,
balls. The princess dared not absent herself; she appeared
nightly in costly toilet, with glowing cheeks, and her lovely
hair adorned with flowers, but her cheeks were *rouged*, and
her sad smile accorded but little with her flowers.

The king had carried on diligently but secretly his preparations for war, under the shadow of these luxurious festivities. Now all was ready; he could lay aside his mask and
his embroidered dress, and assume his uniform. The ball-
room was closed, the music silenced, the silver melted into
thalers. The king left Berlin and joined his generals at
Potsdam. On the day of his arrival he commissioned his adjutant, General von Borck, to release Trenck from arrest,
and send him to Berlin with a letter to the queen-mother;
he was to have leave of absence till the next day.

"I will see, now, if they understood me," said Frederick
to himself. "I have given them a hard lesson; if they do
not profit by it, they are incurable, and force me to extremity."

Alas! they had not understood this hard lesson; they
were not wise, not prudent; they would not see the sharp
sword suspended over their heads: their arms were madly
thrown around each other, and they did not grasp this only

anchor of safety which the fond brother, and not the stern king, had extended to them. They were lost! they must go down to destruction!

The next morning, during the parade, Trenck drew near the king. He had just returned from Berlin; his cheeks were glowing from his rapid ride, and in his eyes there was still a shimmer of that happiness with which the presence of his beloved had inspired him.

"Your majesty, I announce myself," said he, in a fresh and gay voice.

The king said nothing. He looked at the handsome, healthy, and radiant youth with a glance of profound sympathy and regret.

Frederick von Trenck saw nothing of this. "Does your majesty command me to join my regiment at Berlin?" said he, in the most unembarrassed manner.

And now the king's eyes flashed with rage. "From whence come you?" said he, sternly.

"From Berlin, sire."

"Where were you before you were sent to Berlin?"

"In arrest, sire."

"Go, then, to your old place—that is to say, in arrest!"

Frederick von Trenck remained in arrest till every preparation was completed. The army was ready to march. The king assembled his officers, and announced to them that they were bound once more to Silesia to bloody battle, and, with God's help, to glorious victory. On that day Frederick von Trenck was released from arrest. The king received him with a gracious smile, and commanded him to remain near him. Trenck's comrades envied him because of the royal favor; because of the friendly smiles and gracious words which, more than once during the day, the king directed to him. No one understood how Trenck could remain sad and silent under all these evidences of royal favor; no one understood how this gallant young officer could enter upon this campaign with bowed head and heavy brow: he should have sat upon his horse proud and erect—not dreaming, not lost in melancholy musing.

No one but the king could comprehend this; his sympathetic soul was touched by every emotion of his young officer, and he had pity for every pang he inflicted. All this vast crowd of men had taken leave of those they loved and cherished. Trenck alone had been denied this solace. They had all received a love-greeting, a blessing, and a last fond kiss—a last tear to encourage them in battle, perhaps in death. Trenck had no kiss, no blessing, no farewell. He had said farewell to fortune, to love and hope; and even now, though marching to battle, perhaps to victory, he had no future. Tears were flowing for him, and tears would be his only inheritance.

BOOK III.

CHAPTER I.

THE ACTORS IN HALLE.

His excellency, Gotshilf Augustus Franke, president of the university at Halle, bore unmistakable marks of anger and excitement upon his usually calm countenance, as, seated at his study-table, he glanced from time to time at a paper spread out before him.

The entrance of two of his friends and colleagues seemed scarcely to interrupt his disagreeable train of thought, as he bade them good morning and thanked them for coming to him so promptly.

"I have requested your presence, my friends," he continued, "to inform you of the receipt of the answer to the petition which we presented to the General Directory."

"Ah, then," cried Professor Bierman, "our troubles are at an end!"

"Not so," said Professor Franke, gloomily; "the wishes of the servants of the Lord do not always meet with the approbation of kings. King Frederick the Second has refused our petition which was presented to him by the General Directory."

"Refused it?" exclaimed the two professors.

"Yes, refused it; he declares that he will not allow the actors to be expelled from Halle, until it can be satisfactorily proved that they have occasioned public disturbances in our midst."

"This is unheard-of injustice," exclaimed Professor Bierman.

"It is a new proof of the king's utter godliness," said

239

Professor Heinrich. "He has already gone so far as to declare that these actors shall receive Christian burial."

"Astounding!" cried the president. "This is a sacrilege, which will assuredly meet a just punishment. But," he continued after a pause, glancing anxiously around, "let us not forget that we are speaking of our king."

"He seems to forget that even kings are but the servants of the Lord. His acts show a determination to destroy the church and its supporters."

"Your remark is, I fear, too true," answered Professor Franke; "but the object of our meeting was not to discuss the king, but to discover, if possible, some means of extricating ourselves from the disagreeable position in which we have been placed by the unexpected refusal of our petition. We were so confident of a different answer to our just demand, and have expressed this confidence so publicly, that, when the result is known, we shall be ridiculed by both citizens and students."

While the worthy professors were still deep in their discussion, they were interrupted by the entrance of a servant, who announced that there was a gentleman at the door, who called himself Eckhof, and who desired to be admitted to President Franke.

"Eckhof!" exclaimed all three, and the two friends looked mistrustfully at Franke.

"Eckhof! Do you receive Eckhof?"

"Does this actor dare to cross your threshold?"

"It appears so," cried Franke, angrily. "He has the boldness to force himself into my presence.—Let him enter; we will then hear how he justifies this intrusion."

As Eckhof entered the room, the three professors remained seated, as if awaiting the approach of a criminal.

Apparently unmoved by this want of courtesy, Eckhof advanced to the president, and, after making a respectful bow, offered him his hand.

Franke, ignoring this movement, asked, without changing his position, to what singular accident he might attribute the honor of this visit.

Eckhof appeared grieved and astonished at the reception, but replied, "I came, your excellency, to ask a favor. My friends have determined to give me a benefit to-night, and we have selected Voltaire's wonderful tragedy, 'Britannicus,' for our performance. The tickets are all sold, two hundred of them to the students. There is, however, one thing wanting to make the evening all I would wish, and that is the presence of your excellency and some of the professors at the representation. Therefore I am here, and have taken the liberty of bringing these tickets, which I beg you will accept for the use of yourself and your brother professors," and, bowing once more, he placed the tickets upon the table before which he was standing.

"Are you so lost, sir, to all sense of propriety," cried Franke, "as to believe that I, the president of the university, a professor of theology, and a doctor of philosophy, would enter your unholy, God-forsaken theatre? No, sir, even in this degenerate age, we have not fallen so low that the men of God are to be found in such places."

"These are very hard and unchristian words, your excellency, Professor and Doctor Franke, words which no Christian, no man of learning, no gentleman should employ. But I, although a poor actor, bearing no distinguished title, will only remember what is becoming for a Christian, and will say, in the words of our Lord, 'Father, forgive them, they know not what they do.'"

"Those holy words become a blasphemy on your lips," said Professor Heinrich, solemnly.

"And still I repeat them. 'Father, forgive them, they know not what they do.' Do you not know that in judging me, you condemn yourselves? I came into your presence, hoping to reconcile the difficulties and misunderstanding which I heard had been occasioned by the theatre between the professors and the students; but you have treated me with scorn and declined my assistance, and nothing remains for me but to bid you farewell, most learned and worthy men."

He bowed ceremoniously, and passed out, without again glancing at the indignant professors, and joined Joseph Fredersdorf, who awaited him below.

"Well, did they accept your invitation?"

"No, my friend, all happened as you predicted; they refused it with scorn and indignation."

"Now you will agree with me that we can hope to do nothing in Halle."

"Yes, you were right, I fear, Joseph; but let us dismiss so painful a subject. We will now go to our rehearsal, and we must perform our tragedy with such care and in such a manner that the thunders of applause which we receive will reach the ears of our enemies."

The three professors were still in the room of the president, in earnest consultation.

"So this miserable Eckhof is to have what he calls a benefit to-night?" said the president.

"Two hundred students will be present," groaned Professor Heinrich.

"And our lecture halls will be empty."

"We must exert our energies and put a stop to these proceedings; it is scandalous that our students have forsaken their studies to run after these actors."

"Truly something must be done, for not only our fame but our purses are at stake."

"This evil cannot continue; we must take prompt measures to root it out," said the president. "The General Directory decided that the actors should not be expelled from Halle, unless it could be proved that they had been the occasion of some public difficulty. It is therefore necessary that such a difficulty should arise. According to Eckhof's account, there will be two hundred students at the theatre to-night. There are still, however, nearly one hundred who will not be present at his performance. Among these there must be some brave, determined, devout young men, who, in the name of God, of science, and of their teachers, would willingly enter the lists against these actors, and create a disturbance. We must employ some of these young men to visit the theatre to-night, and to groan and hiss when the other students applaud. This will be all-sufficient to raise a riot amongst these hot-blooded young men. After that, our course is plain; we have but to send in our account of the affair to the General Directory, and there will be no danger of a second refusal to our petition."

"An excellent idea!"

"I am afraid, however, it will be difficult to find any students who will put their lives in such jeopardy."

"We must seek them among those to whose advantage it is to stand well with the president."

"There are some who receive a yearly stipend through me, and others who live only for science, and never visit the theatre. I name, for example, the industrious young student Lupinus. I shall speak to him, and I am sure he will not refuse to assist us; he is small and not very strong, it is true, but he stands well with the students, and will carry others with him. I know five others upon whom I can count, and that is enough for our purpose. I will give them these tickets which Eckhof left here. He desired that we should make use of them, and we will do so, but to serve our own purpose, and not his."

Having arrived at this happy conclusion, the three professors separated.

CHAPTER II.

THE STUDENT LUPINUS.

YOUNG Lupinus sat quiet and alone, as was usual with him, in his room, before his writing-table, which was covered with books and folios. He was thinner and paler than when we first met him in Berlin. His deeply-sunken eyes were encircled with those dark rings which are usually the outward sign of mental suffering. His bloodless lips were firmly pressed together, and the small hand, upon which his pale brow rested, was transparently thin and white.

Lupinus was working, or appeared to be so. Before him lay one of those venerable folios which excite the reverence of the learned. The eyes of the young man rested, it is true, upon the open page, but so long, and so uninterruptedly, that it was evident his thoughts were elsewhere.

The professors would, no doubt, have been rejoiced had they seen him bent thus earnestly and attentively over this volume. If, however, they had seen what really claimed his

16

attention, they would have been seized with horror. Upon his open book lay a playbill, the bill for that evening, and upon this "thing of horror" rested the eyes of the young student.

"No, no," he said, after a long pause, "I will not go. I will not be overcome by my heart, after the fierce struggle of these two long, fearful months. I will not, I dare not see Eckhof again; I should be lost—undone. Am I not lost even now? Do I not see ever before me those great, burning eyes; do I ever cease to hear his soft, melodious voice, which seems to sing a requiem over my dead happiness? I have striven uselessly against my fate—my life is blighted. I will strive no longer, but I will die honorably, as I have lived. I only pray to God that in my last hour I may not curse my father with my dying lips. He has sinned heavily against me; he has sacrificed my life to his will. May God forgive him! Now," continued Lupinus, "enough of complaints. My resolution is taken; I will not go to the theatre, for I dare not see Eckhof again."

He suddenly seized the playbill, and pressed the spot where Eckhof's name stood again and again to his lips, then tore the paper into many pieces, and threw them behind him.

"So long as I live, I must struggle—I will battle bravely. My heart shall die, my soul awake and comfort me."

Again he bent his head over the great tome, but this time a light knock at his door interrupted him, and the immediate entrance of Professor Franke filled him with amazement.

"My visit seems to astonish you," said the professor, in the most friendly tone. "You think it singular that the president of the university should seek out one of the students. Perhaps it would be so in an ordinary case; but for you, Lupinus, who are the most learned and honorable young man in our midst, we cannot do too much to show our respect and esteem."

"This is an honor which almost shames me," said Lupinus, blushing; "an honor of which, I fear, I am unworthy."

"I desire to give you a still greater proof of my esteem," continued the professor. "I wish to make you my confidant, and inform you of an intrigue which, insignificant as it appears, will be followed by important results."

With ready words, Franke proceeded to explain to Lupinus his own views with regard to the actors; what he considered their wretched influence over the students, and also the ill-advised decision of the General Directory. He then informed Lupinus of his plan for creating a disturbance in the theatre, and requested his assistance in carrying it out.

Lupinus listened with horror to this explanation and request, but he controlled himself, and quietly received the ticket which the president handed him. He listened silently to the further details, and Franke understood his silence as a respectful assent.

When the president had at length taken leave, and Lupinus was again alone, he seized the ticket, threw it on the ground, and trampled it under foot, thus visiting upon the inoffensive ticket the scorn he had not dared exhibit to the president.

"I—I am to be the instrument of this miserable plot!" he cried passionately. "Because I lead a lonely, joyless life, I am selected to execute this infamy. Ah, how little do they know me! how slight a knowledge of the human heart have these learned professors! Eckhof in danger, and I remain silent? Eckhof threatened, and I not warn him? That were a treachery against myself, a crime against art and my own poor heart. If I remain silent, I become an accomplice in this vile conspiracy." At this thought, he took his hat, and hurried from the room.

When he reached the door of Eckhof's lodging, he hesitated. A profound pallor succeeded a burning glow upon his countenance, and he murmured to himself: "No, no; I have not the strength to see him to-day. I should die if his eyes rested upon me. I will go to Fredersdorf."

Joseph Fredersdorf was at home, and received Lupinus with astonished delight.

"The holy one trusts himself in the den of the wicked," he said, with a bright smile. "This is an unheard-of event, which doubtless indicates something important."

"You are laughing at me, but you are right. I am here for a purpose; nothing unimportant would have induced me to come to you after the ungrateful manner in which I declined your friendly advances. But I am sure you will forgive the intrusion when you become aware of the motive which has led me to you."

With hurried words and frequent interruptions from Fredersdorf, Lupinus informed his friend of the president's visit, and its object.

"This is a regular conspiracy," said Joseph, as Lupinus finished. "If it succeed, the punishment of the actors will be the result."

"It must not succeed—we must prevent that. The first thing to be done is to gain over the other students to whom the president has intrusted this plot. We must either do that or prevent them from entering the theatre."

"But if we can do neither?"

"Then we must allow what we cannot prevent, but we must seek to avert the evil consequences. We will address ourselves to the king, and inform him who has occasioned this disturbance, and why it was done."

"The king is just, and happily it is not difficult to see him, especially for me, as my brother is his private secretary. We must be active, and the victory will be ours. And now, my dear friend, for you must allow me to call you so from this day, let us go to my master, Eckhof. He must thank you himself for this kind warning. Come to Eckhof."

"No!" said Lupinus, "it is a matter of no importance to Eckhof, who has given the information. There is much to be done to-day. I will seek to gain over the students; you must hasten to Eckhof."

"And will you not accompany me?"

"No, my friend, not to-day. Let us await the events of this evening. Perhaps I shall ask you to present me to him to-morrow."

"Ah, that would be a real triumph for me!"

"Let us first take care that this plot fails, and the actors are not driven from Halle."

"When we have accomplished this, will you promise to walk arm-in-arm with me three times through the market-place?"

"Not only three times, but as often as you will."

"Now I feel the strength of Samson, and the craft of Delilah. With this reward before me, I will vanquish all enemies."

CHAPTER III.

THE DISTURBANCE IN THE THEATRE.

So dense was the crowd which filled the streets in the neighborhood of the theatre on the evening of Eckhof's benefit, that it appeared as if the entire population of the city of Halle must be unanimous in wishing to do honor to this wonderful *artiste*.

Eckhof owed this triumph to the students; he had been their darling from the time of his first appearance among them, and now he had become the favorite of the entire city, with the exception of the professors.

Had the theatre been three times its actual size, it could scarcely have accommodated all who had made applications for tickets. The *parterre* was given up almost entirely to the students, upon whose countenances was plainly seen their deep interest in the evening's entertainment.

Here and there among them a few earnest faces and darkly flashing eyes might be seen, but they seemed to arrest no eye but that of Lupinus. He had passed every countenance in review, and had instantly recognized by their expression those students who had entered into the plot of the president. He had failed in his effort to discover them before the opening of the theatre, and was, therefore, unable to prevent their attendance.

Professor Franke had informed these students that they might count upon the assistance of Lupinus, and one of them had just whispered to him: "There will be a fierce struggle, and I fear we shall be worsted, as our number is so small. Did you bring your rapier?"

Before Lupinus could answer, he was separated from his questioner by a crowd of students pushing their way forward. It seemed as if these new arrivals had not come to the theatre for mere amusement. They glanced threateningly around them, as if seeking a concealed enemy. In passing Lupinus they greeted him with a few low-spoken words, or a warm pressure of the hand.

These students were the special friends of Joseph Fredersdorf. To them he had confided the danger which threatened the actors this evening, and had demanded their aid in maintaining peace and quiet. They scattered about amongst the crowd of students, and whispered to their friends and acquaintances: "No disturbance this evening. We must be quiet, whatever occurs."

At length this fluttering, whispering crowd were silenced by the ringing of the bell which announced the rising of the curtain.

The piece began, and never had Eckhof displayed such fire, such enthusiasm; the students had never exhibited such rapt and earnest attention. Their excitement was shown by their flashing eyes and glowing cheeks, and the low murmurs of delight which arose occasionally from this dark mass. But at length a moment arrived when it became impossible to suppress the expression of their delight, and forgetting all resolve to the contrary, they called aloud, amid thunders of applause, for their favorite Eckhof, who had just left the stage.

"A disturbance is now unavoidable," said Lupinus to himself, " but Eckhof deserves that we should forget all such miserable considerations. To die for him were to be indeed blessed."

As Eckhof appeared upon the stage, in answer to the repeated calls upon his name, Lupinus gazed upon him with a beaming countenance, and joined the others in their cries of delight.

The unalloyed triumph of Eckhof endured but for one moment, for suddenly, high above the shouts of applause, arose a piercing, derisive whistle, succeeded by hisses and groans.

As if by magic, the aspect of the *parterre* was changed. Every student looked wrathfully at his neighbor, as if determined to discover and punish the rash offender who dared run counter to the general approbation. A few students were endeavoring to calm the rising storm; but renewed hisses and groans made this impossible, and one voice was heard high above the others: "You hissed, sir; I forbid it!"

"And I forbid you to applaud," was the answer. "So long as you applaud, I will hiss. Accommodate yourself to that."

A universal cry of wrath arose as if from one voice. The struggle was inevitable, as Lupinus had foreseen; the *parterre* of the theatre was converted into a battle-ground, and a fierce combat began among these young, hot-blooded students. The manager ordered the lights to be extinguished, and the police to be called in, but for a long time their efforts were ineffectual in subduing the contest.

We will leave the theatre with Lupinus, who, as soon as he could extricate himself from the battling crowd, hurried through the streets, toward the lodging of Fredersdorf.

He found a post-carriage before the door, and Fredersdorf, dressed for a journey, was just leaving the house. As he was stepping into the carriage, Lupinus placed his hand upon his shoulder, and said, "Where are you going, Fredersdorf?"

"To Berlin, to the king."

"The king is not in Berlin; he is in Silesia, with the army."

"I received letters from my brother to-day. The king has gone to Berlin for a few days, and my brother is with him. I will have no difficulty in obtaining an audience. I shall give the king a correct version of this affair. He will perceive that this disturbance was occasioned by the professors, and he will not allow us to be driven from Halle. Farewell, my friend; in four days I return, and you shall hear the result of my journey."

"I intend to accompany you."

"You intend to accompany me?"

"Yes; perhaps you will need a witness; I must be with you. I thought you would have counted on me."

"How could I suppose that Lupinus, the learned student, who will receive his diploma at the end of a few weeks, would tear himself from the arms of his beloved Science, to go with a comedian before the king, and bear witness for the hated and despised actors?"

"Ah, Fredersdorf," said Lupinus; "if you consider Science my beloved, I fear you will soon have occasion to call me a faithless lover."

"What can you mean? How! you also—"

"Let us be off, my friend. We will discuss that in the carriage."

CHAPTER IV.

THE FRIENDS.

Four days after the unfortunate occurrences in the theatre, Fredersdorf and his friend Lupinus returned from their secret journey, the object of which was unknown even to Eckhof. No sooner had they alighted from their travelling carriage, than they proceeded arm-in-arm to Eckhof's lodging. They found him at home and alone, and Fredersdorf saw from his pale countenance and lustreless eyes that his sensitive, easily excited nature had been deeply wounded by the late events.

"I bring you a new pupil, my master," said Fredersdorf, drawing Lupinus forward, who stood deeply blushing before Eckhof.

Eckhof smiled sadly. "A pupil who desires that I should lead him through all the classes and degrees of the school of suffering and humiliation?"

"A young student, Eckhof, who up to this time has been the pride and delight of the university; who, however, now wishes to relinquish this honor, and become one of your followers. In one word, this is Lupinus, who desires to waive his right to the prospective dignity of the title of doctor of medicine, and to become your pupil, and eventually an actor."

"You are kind and tender-hearted as ever, Joseph," said Eckhof, gently. "You know that I bear a wound in my heart, and you seek to heal it with the balm of your friendship, and this kind jest."

"This is no jest, but a reality. Truly, you resemble a

pair of lovers, who have not the courage to believe in their own happiness. Eckhof will not believe that the learned student Lupinus wishes to become his follower and pupil, and Lupinus stands there like a young girl who has received a declaration and does not dare say yes. Speak, Lupinus, and tell this doubter that you have come voluntarily; that I have not pressed you into the service as Frederick William impressed soldiers. Truly, I had trouble enough in divining from your broken words and repressed sighs, your blushes, and your deep admiration for Eckhof, this secret which lay in your bosom. But now that it has been discovered, take courage, my friend, and raise the veil which conceals your desires."

Lupinus remained speechless, only the heaving of his breast betrayed his excitement. Eckhof had compassion on the evident embarrassment of the young student, and approaching him laid his hand gently on his shoulder. Lupinus trembled and grew pale under Eckhof's gentle, sympathetic glance.

"Do you wish really to become an actor?" questioned Eckhof.

"Yes," he replied in a low voice, "I have long wished it, I have struggled with this wish, and thought I had overcome it; but the struggle has been in vain; in vain have I buried myself in books and studies. I will keep up this internal strife no longer, but will follow the inclinations of my heart, which lead me to you. In this new life I shall be happy and contented; and this I can only hope to be, in giving my life to poetry and art."

"Ah, he speaks and thinks as I did," said Eckhof to himself; then turning to Lupinus, he said: "You wish to be an actor; that means, you desire a life of shame and humiliation. No one shall become an actor if I can prevent it. Do you know, young man, that, to become an actor, means to have the whole world, and perhaps even God, arrayed against you?"

"You are unjust, Eckhof," cried Fredersdorf—"unjust to yourself and to the world. You scorn your own triumph, and those who prepared that triumph for you."

"You are right so far, my friend," replied Eckhof sadly.

"But is it not also true that we are persecuted and driven forth? Has it not been proved that for an actor there is no law, no justice?"

"Who knows," said Fredersdorf, smiling, "that we may not still triumph over these miserable conspirators?"

"Are you aware that the theatre has been closed, and our representations forbidden until the decision of the General Assembly, with regard to the late disturbance in the theatre, shall be known?"

"The General Assembly will order the theatre to be opened, and our representations to recommence."

Eckhof heard this with a cutting, derisive laugh. "Dear friend, such an order would render justice to the scorned and oppressed on earth!"

"And they will receive justice; but it must be sought in the right place."

"Where is that place?"

"Where the king is."

"Ah! the king! That may be true in your case, because your brother is his private secretary, but it is not true for me—not true for the German actor."

"Eckhof, you are again unjust. The king is too noble, too free from prejudice, to be deceived by the dust with which these learned professors have sought to blind him. The king knows that they occasioned the late disturbance in the theatre."

"Who has told you that?"

"The king himself."

"You have seen the king?"

"I have. I hope you will allow now, that it is not a good thing for me only that my brother is private secretary to the king. I have seen his majesty, and I informed him of this wretched intrigue of the professors. He might not have put entire faith in the accounts of the actor, Joseph Fredersdorf, but I was accompanied by a responsible witness, who confirmed my words."

"Who was this witness?"

"This is he," said Joseph, drawing Lupinus forward.

"Ah!" said Eckhof, "and I was murmuring and complaining against fate—I, whose friends have shown their love by deeds as well as by words—friends who worked for me whilst I sat with folded hands bewailing my bad fortune. Forgive me, Joseph; forgive me, my young friend; come to my arms, my comrades, my brothers, and say that you will forget my anger and injustice."

He opened his arms, and Joseph threw himself upon his breast.

"And you, my friend," said Eckhof, turning to Lupinus, who stood pale and motionless before him.

Joseph drew them together and exclaimed: "Was I not right? You are like two lovers; Lupinus acts the part of the coy maiden to the life. I do not believe, Eckhof, that you will ever have a wife who will love you more entirely, more tenderly, than our young doctor does."

Lupinus, now folded in the arms of Eckhof, trembled and grew pale at these words from Joseph.

"Love me, love me, my dear young friend," said Eckhof, softly. "Friendship is the purest, the holiest gift of God. It is the love of the souls. Be faithful to me, Lupinus, as I shall be to you."

"I will be faithful so long as I live, faithful beyond the grave," whispered Lupinus.

"You whispering, dreaming lovers, are forgetting me," said Joseph, laughing. "You must not forget, Eckhof, that the future of our friend is awaiting your decision. Shall he give up his studies as I did, and become an actor? It is only proper to tell you that the cases are not quite parallel, for I was a very lazy student, and he is most industrious. I was considered a good-for-nothing, and Lupinus is a miracle of knowledge and learning. Shall he abandon this position and follow you?"

"He must not, indeed," said Eckhof.

"You will not receive me?" said Lupinus, sadly.

"Not at present, dear friend; I wish to be reasonable and careful, and perhaps a little egotistical. If you should leave the university at present, you give the professors a new weapon against me, and it would be said that I had employed arts to seduce you from the paths of science. And, further, we do not know if you have a talent for our profession; that must first be proved. Remain for the present true to your

studies; at the end of a year, during which time you shall
pass your novitiate, we will decide this question."

"It shall be as you say," said Lupinus, earnestly. "I
will first gain my diploma, and then you shall decide my
future, you and no other."

"So be it," said Joseph, "and now let us drink to your
future success, Lupinus, in a glass of champagne, and to the
confusion of the professors, who are awaiting with such
proud confidence the decision of the General Assembly."

CHAPTER V.

THE ORDER OF THE KING.

JOSEPH FREDERSDORF was quite right in saying that the
professors awaited the decision of the General Assembly
with proud confidence. It did not occur to them that it
might be unfavorable to their wishes. A public disturbance
had arisen between the students, occasioned by a performance
in the theatre; this was a sufficient cause for the banishment of the actors. An account of the riot had been already
forwarded by the Senate of the University to the General
Assembly, and the worthy gentlemen who composed this body
did not doubt the fulfilment of their request, that the actors
should be removed from Halle.

President Franke received with the utmost composure
the official dispatch, containing the decision of the General
Assembly, and called an immediate meeting of the Senate for
its perusal. Whilst awaiting the opening of the meeting,
Professor Heinrich was expressing to his friend, Professor
Bierman, his impatience to know the contents of this dispatch.

"I am not at all impatient," replied Bierman. "I am
convinced the decision will be perfectly satisfactory to us;
in fact, that it commands the departure of these actors from
our city."

"Have you no doubts? Do you not fear that the king,

in his hatred for the theologians, and his admiration for these comedians, may decide in their favor rather than in ours?"

"Dear friend, such a doubt would be unworthy the dignity of our position. The king, seeing that the matter has gone so far, must decide in our favor. And here is our worthy president; look at his proud and cheerful aspect, and judge whether the document he holds in his hand can be unfavorable."

"He does, indeed, seem contented," answered Professor Heinrich, as he and his friend moved forward to meet the president.

With great solemnity the senators proceeded to take their seats in the arm-chairs which encircled a high table standing in the centre of the room.

After a moment's silence the president addressed them: "Worthy friends and colleagues, I have to announce to you that the hour has at length arrived which is to end all the doubts and cares that have oppressed our hearts for many months. We have had a bitter struggle; we have striven to preserve the honor of our university and the well-being of the youth committed to our care. The men who work with such noble motives must eventually triumph."

"The decision is, then, in our favor?" asked Professor Heinrich, no longer able to subdue his impatient curiosity. "Your excellency has already read the dispatch of the General Assembly, and are acquainted with its contents."

"I have not read it, and I do not know its contents. But I rely upon our worthy cause, and the king's sense of justice. These comedians were the occasion of a public disturbance—it is, therefore, proper that they should be punished. As justice is on our side, I cannot doubt the result. I have not read this dispatch, for I considered it more in accordance with the dignity of this body that the seal should be broken in your presence, and I now beg that you, Professor Bierman, as the secretary of the Senate, will read to us this dispatch from the General Assembly."

As Bierman broke the seal, all eyes were turned on him, and in this moment of expectation the professors were aware that their hearts beat louder and more rapidly. Suddenly

Professor Bierman uttered a cry, a cry of horror, which awakened an echo in every breast.

"Proceed," commanded the president, with stony composure.

"I cannot," murmured Bierman, as he sank back powerless in his chair.

"Then I will read it myself," cried Professor Heinrich, forgetting all other considerations in his determination to satisfy his curiosity. "I will read it," he repeated, as he took the paper from the trembling hands of his friend.

"Read," said the president, in a low voice.

Professor Heinrich then proceeded to read aloud the following dispatch sent by the General Assembly to the Senate of the University at Halle.

"We find it most unworthy that you, in your complaint against the comedians now in Halle, should endeavor to cast on them the blame of the late disturbance in the theatre. We are well aware of the cause of this disturbance, and now declare that the actors shall not be banished from Halle."

A fearful pause followed this reading. The president perceived that Heinrich was still looking at the paper he held.

"Is that all? Have you finished the dispatch?"

"No, your excellency; there is a note on the margin, in the writing of the king."

"Read it aloud."

"Your excellency, the king has made use of some expressions that I cannot bring my lips to utter."

"The king is our master; we must hear what he has to say in all humility."

"You command me, then, to proceed?"

"I command it."

"'This pack of theologians have caused the whole difficulty. The actors shall continue to play, and Mr. Franke, or whatever else the scamp calls himself, shall make public reparation, by visiting the theatre; and I must receive information from the actors themselves that he has done so.'"

A murmur of horror succeeded the reading of this order. Only President Franke maintained his erect position, and continued looking straight before him at Professor Heinrich, who had just dropped the fatal paper.

"Is that all?" asked the president.

"It is, your excellency."

He bowed gravely, and, rising from his chair, glanced slowly from one face to another. The senators cast down their eyes before this glance, not from fear or shame, but from terror at the fearful expression of the president's countenance.

"If that is all, it is time for me to go," he said solemnly, as he pushed his chair back, and slowly and stiffly walked forward, like an automaton which has been set in motion by machinery.

"This has affected his brain. He will have a paralytic stroke," murmured the senators to one another.

The president did not hear them, nor did he seem to know what he wished. He was now standing motionless a few steps from the table.

The professors were terrified at this spectacle, and only Heinrich had the courage to advance to his side and ask—

"Where do you wish to go, my dear friend?"

"I wish to obey the command of the king—I am going to the theatre," he replied, with a cry of despair, and then fell fainting into the arms of his friend.

Professor Bierman instantly summoned assistance, and the insensible form of the president was borne from the room, and a messenger sent for a physician.

When the professors had become somewhat composed, Bierman announced to them that he had a proposition to make which he hoped would meet with their approval.

"You doubtless agree with me, my friends, in saying that this cruel sentence of the king must not be carried out. Our friend the president would not suffer alone in its fulfilment—the honor of the university would receive an irreparable wound. We must employ every effort to alter this decision. It is, in my opinion, fortunate that our worthy friend has sunk for the time beneath this blow. His illness relieves him from the necessity of an immediate appearance in the theatre; and, whether ill or not, he must remain in his bed until the king can be induced to alter his sentence. We will prepare a petition and send it immediately to the king."

The proposal of Bierman met with entire approval; and the petition was prepared, signed by all the professors, and sent to Berlin by one of their number. The king, however, declined to receive him, and his only answer was that in eight days the Senate would be made acquainted with his final decision.

The professors convinced themselves that there was comfort in this answer. The king evidently did not intend to insist on the execution of the first sentence, or he would simply have ordered its fulfilment.

The professors were hopeful, and no longer opposed the nightly visits of the students to the theatre. A few of them determined to visit the theatre themselves, and see this Eckhof who had caused them so much sorrow and trouble. The students were delighted at this concession, and considered the professors the most enlightened and unprejudiced of the whole body. To show their apreciation of this, they attended their lectures on the following day.

This unexpected result made the other professors falter in their determination. Their temporal good depended very much on the attendance of the students upon their lectures. They found that they must consent to listen to Eckhof and his companions, if they would be heard themselves; and, at length, they determined to make peace with the students and actors, and to visit the theatre.

Peace was now proclaimed, and Eckhof, whose noble and tender heart was filled with joy and gratitude, played "Britannicus" with such power and feeling that he even won applause from the professors.

President Franke was still confined to his room. The terror of a forced visit to the theatre, which would be known as an expiation for his fault, made his nights sleepless and his days most wretched.

At length, however, the answer to the petition arrived, and, to his great relief, he found himself condemned to pay a fine of twenty thalers to the almshouse of Halle; and no further mention was made of his visit to the theatre.

CHAPTER VI.

THE BATTLE OF SOHR.

DEEP silence reigned in the encampment which the Prussians had established near the village of Sohr. The brave soldiers, wearied with their long march, were sleeping quietly, although they knew that the Austrian army, which far outnumbered their own, was hastening toward them, and would attack them within a few hours. This knowledge did not alarm them, they had not so soon forgotten their signal victory over Karl von Lothringen, with his Austrians, Bavarians, and Saxons, at Hohenfriedberg. They did not fear a defeat at Sohr, although the grand duke was now the leader of forty thousand men, and Frederick's army had been so diminished by the forces he had sent to Saxony and Silesia, that it consisted of scarcely twenty thousand men. The Prussian soldiers relied confidently upon the good fortune and the strategic talent of their king; they could sleep quietly, for Frederick watched beside them.

The watch-fires had died out, the lights in the tents of the officers were extinguished. Now and then might be heard the measured tread of a sentinel, or the loud breathing of some soldier dreaming perhaps of his distant home or forsaken bride. No other sounds broke upon the night air. The Prussian army slept. Alas! how many of them were now dreaming their last earthly dream; how many on the morrow would lie with gaping wounds upon a bloody battleground, with staring glassy eyes turned upward, and no one near to wipe the death-drops from their brows! They know not, they care not, they are lost in sleep. There can be no pressing danger, for the king is in their midst—the light has been extinguished in his tent also. He sleeps with his army.

It is midnight, the hour of wandering spirits. Is that a spirit which has just left so noiselessly the tent of the king, and has so quickly vanished in the tent of the adjutant, which adjoins that of the king? No, not vanished, for it has already reappeared; but there are now three of these shadowy

17

beings quietly approaching the white tents of the officers, disappearing for an instant into each tent, then reappearing, and continuing their course.

Where they have been may now be heard a low whispering and moving. Soon another dark figure is visible; it moves cautiously forward toward the soldiers' tents in which it disappears, and from these may be heard the same low whispering, and like a murmuring brook this babbling glides through the entire camp, always following the first three shadows who have gone noiselessly and with the rapidity of the wind through the camp.

Why have these three shadows driven sleep from the encampment? why have they ordered the horses to be prepared? No one has been told to mount, no "Forward!" has been thundered through the camp; and but for the dark figures which may now be seen on all sides, the silence is so profound that one might almost think the camp still buried in sleep.

The Austrians, who can only view the camp from a distance, think, no doubt, their enemy still sleeps.

The silence of the camp is at last broken by a sound like the heavy roll of thunder; and if the moon were now to break through the clouds, it would gleam upon eight field-pieces which are being carefully drawn behind a little elevation in the ground, which lies opposite the defile occupied by the Austrians.

Once again all is silent, and the horizon begins to clear; a few rosy clouds fly across the heavens, the veil of night is raised, the stars pale as the morning arrays herself with hues of purple and gold.

It is morning. Let us look again at the camp of the Prussian soldiers. Are they sleeping? No, no; all are awake; all prepared for action, but all silent and motionless as if bound by a charm.

And here is the enchanter who has awakened all these thousands to life, and still binds them to silence. His countenance is bright and clear, his glance seems to pierce the hill which divides him from the enemy, and to divine the moment of their attack. There is the ruler, whose will is law to all these thousands of men, whose word is now to lead them to death, to a shameful defeat, or to a glorious victory. There is the king. He knows that within a few moments the Austrians will attack his army, but he does not tremble.

The Austrians expect to surprise a sleeping foe; but the king, who is the father of his people, has himself, with his two adjutants, Trenck and Standnitz, awakened them from their slumbers; it was he who directed the placing of cannon at the point upon which the Austrian cavalry is certain to make their descent upon the sleeping camp.

The king was right. Do you not hear the heavy tramp of cavalry, the thunder of those cannon?

The Austrians are pressing through the narrow defile; this is the thunder of their cannon, with which they thought to awaken the Prussians.

Now the king raises his sword; the sign is given. The Austrian cavalry may advance, for the Prussians are now in motion; now rushing forward, pressing toward the defile, before which their enemy are quietly forming their line of battle, although scarcely fearing a conflict, for are the Prussians not sleeping? They expected a bloodless victory.

But the Prussians are awake; it is they who attack the surprised Austrians. They have already driven the cavalry back into the narrow defile. The thunders of their cannon are now heard, and they bear the appalling news to the Austrians that the Prussians are not sleeping.

Karl von Lothringen, you should have known the Prussians better. Did not they out-manœuvre you two short months since? Did not Frederick make a pretence of retreating, in order to draw you on out of your favorable position, and then attack you, and win, in a few short morning hours, a glorious victory? Karl von Lothringen, you should have remembered Hohenfriedberg. You should not have imagined that the Prussians slept while the Austrians stood before them in battle array. The Prussians are indeed awake. Listen to their joyous shouts, look at their flashing swords!

Karl von Lothringen, where are your troops which were intended to attack the enemy in the rear? Where is Trenck with his pandours? where General Nadasti, with his well-disciplined regiments? If your hope is in these, then despair, and thrust your sword in its sheath.

The Prussians have deserted their camp; the enemy is before them; in their pursuit they have left all behind them; they thought not of earthly possessions, but of honor and victory. Every thing was left in the camp. The king's entire camp-furniture, and even the army treasure.

Karl von Lothringen, hope nothing from Trenck and his pandours; nothing from Nadasti and his regiments. They have obeyed your commands; they have pressed into the enemy's camp; they are taking prizes, plundering greedily. What care they for the battle which thunders and roars before them? the cannon-balls do not reach them; they can enrich themselves in the camp of the Prussians whilst these are gaining a glorious victory.

The battle is not yet decided. "If Trenck and Nadasti attack our rear," said the king, "we are lost."

At this moment an adjutant announced to him that Trenck and Nadasti were plundering the Prussian camp.

The king's countenance beamed with delight. "Let them plunder," he said, joyfully, "whilst they are so occupied they will not interfere with our important work. Whilst they plunder, we will conquer."

Yes, the battle is decided; while the Austrians plundered, the Prussians conquered. Karl von Lothringen, overcome with grief and shame, is retreating with his disorganized troops.

The Prussians have gained the day, but it was a fearful victory, a murderous battle between brothers, German against German, brother against brother.

The Duke Albrecht, of Brunswick, has fallen by the side of the king; his brother Ludwig lies covered with wounds in the Austrian camp.

Poor Queen Elizabeth Christine, your husband has conquered, but you have both paid dearly for the victory. The king has lost his tent, his camp-furniture, and eighty thousand ducats, and the baggage of the entire army. You have lost one brother, and the other lies covered with bloody wounds. The king has gained the battle. His is the fame and honor. You, poor queen, you have only a new grief. Yours are the tears and the pain.

CHAPTER VII.

AFTER THE BATTLE.

THE Prussians were resting from their labors, not in comfortable tents or on soft cushions, but on the hard ground, with no protection against sun and wind, and not too distant from the battle-field to hear the heart-rending cries and groans of their dying comrades. But even these cries and groans were to the triumphant Prussians the sign of their glorious victory, and awoke in those who had escaped unscathed through this terrible fire a feeling of deep gratitude.

After these fearful hours of excitement followed a general lassitude, a positive physical necessity for rest. But, alas! there was something which drove sleep from their eyelids, and increased the weariness of their bodies. This was hunger. The pandours had thoroughly plundered the Prussian camp; they had taken not only the baggage of the poor soldiers, but all their provisions.

The Prussians, who had obtained so glorious a triumph in the morning, were now looking forward to a day of fasting, while the Austrians, in spite of their defeat, were consoling themselves with the provisions which they had taken from the Prussians. Happy was he who had a piece of bread in his knapsack, or whose tent had been overlooked or forgotten by the plunderers; but few had been so fortunate, and these in the egotism of hunger refused to share their precious treasure, even with their dearest friend.

King Frederick was not among the fortunate. The victory was his, but his laurel-wreath could not be transformed into bread. He had said in vain to his generals and adjutants, "We will dine." There was nothing to set before the king.

When General Rothenberg brought this disagreeable news to the king, he said, laughing gayly: "Let us imagine ourselves to be Catholics, my friends, for the present, and it will be quite in order that we should fast on the day of a glorious victory. I will be quite contented with a piece of bread, and I suppose that can be found somewhere for the King of Prussia."

But General Rothenberg's order to the royal cook to satisfy the simple demand of his master was in vain. The cook had nothing, neither meat, fruit, nor bread.

"I will not return empty-handed to the king," said Rothenberg, with tears in his eyes. "I would sooner part with my last ducat to the first soldier I meet who has a piece of bread."

The general then passed, with inquisitive glances, through the group of soldiers who were talking over the events of the last few hours. At last he perceived a soldier who was not talking, but was ogling a piece of bread which he seemed preparing to devour. With a hasty spring the general was at his side, his hand upon the bread.

"I will give you two ducats for this piece of bread, my friend."

"Two ducats! what should I do with two ducats?" he asked, with a scornful laugh. "I cannot eat your ducats, general, and my bread is more precious to me than a handful of ducats."

"If you will not give it for gold, then give it for love," cried the general. "For love of your king who is hungry, and has nothing to satisfy his craving."

The countenance of the soldier, which had been so smiling, became earnest, and he murmured thoughtfully to himself, "The king has no bread!"

"The king is hungry," repeated Rothenberg, almost imploringly.

"The king is hungry," murmured the soldier, sadly, as he glanced at the bread in his hand. Then, with quiet determination, he cut the loaf in two pieces, and handing one to the general, he said, "I will give you half of my bread, that is really all I can do for the king. Take it, general, the matter is settled. I will give no more."

"I desire no more," said Rothenberg, as he hurried off with the bread to the newly-erected tent of the king.

The soldier looked smilingly after him, but suddenly his countenance became overcast, he was seized with a fearful idea—suppose the general had deceived him, and the bread

was not for the king? He must know, he must convince himself that the statement was true. He followed the general
rapidly, and soon overtook him. Rothenberg perceived him,
and understood instantly why he had followed him. Smilingly he entered the presence of the king.

"My king, I am here, and bring what you demanded, a
piece of bread."

"Ah, that means renewed strength," said the king, as he
received the bread and commenced eating it with evident
satisfaction. "How did you procure this bread for me, my
friend?"

"Sire, I obtained it of a soldier, who refused to sell it,
but who gladly gave it to me when he heard it was for the
king. Afterward he conceived a doubt that I had deceived
him, and that I had obtained his treasure for my own grati-
fication. He followed me, and I wager he is standing without longing to know if the king is really eating his bread."

"I will gratify his desire," said Frederick, smiling, as he
raised the curtain of the tent, and stood in the opening.

There stood the soldier, staring at the tent, but he trembled when he perceived the king. Frederick nodded to him
most kindly, and proceeded to cut the bread which he held in
his hand.

"I thank you for your bread," he said; "my friend, you
must ask some favor of me. Think what you would wish."

"Oh! I need not think," the soldier cried joyfully. "If
I may wish for something, it shall be the position of magis-
trate in my native land in Prussia."

"When peace is declared, your wish shall be gratified,"
said the king to the delighted soldier, and then bowing graciously, Frederick reëntered the tent.

"Now my friend, my Pylades, we will allow ourselves an
hour of rest, of recreation; I think we have earned it.
Come and read aloud to me."

"What shall I read to your majesty?" asked Rothenberg,
evidently embarrassed.

"You may read from Horace."

"Your majesty does not know—" said Rothenberg, hesitatingly.

"What do I not know?"

"That the pandours have carried off your camp library."

"What! my books too?" demanded the king, and a cloud darkened his brow. "What can the pandours and Croats do with my poor books? Could they not content themselves with my treasure and my silver-ware? Must they take what is so worthless to them, and so precious to me?"

Then, with bent brows, his hands crossed behind him, he paced back and forth in the narrow tent. Suddenly arresting his steps, he glanced around the tent, as if in search of something. "Biche is not here," he said quietly; "bring Biche to me, my friend."

But General Rothenberg did not move.

"Well!" exclaimed the king.

"Sire, they have taken Biche with them also."

"Biche also, my faithful friend, my pet!" cried the king, with much emotion, as he again began his walk. At length, approaching the general, he placed both hands upon his shoulder and looked tenderly into his eyes. "I have my friend," he said gently, "why should I be troubled about my books or my dog? I will send to Berlin and have the books replaced, and I will ransom Biche. They cannot refuse to restore the faithful animal to me."

There was an expression of such anxiety on the king's features, that Rothenberg was much moved.

"I do not doubt, sire," he said, "that your favorite will be returned to you. Your majesty may well trust to that Providence which has vouchsafed you so glorious a victory."

The king replied, smiling: "I will tell you a secret, my friend. I deserved to be overcome in this battle, for I had weakened my army too much by detachments. Nothing but the skill of my generals and the bravery of my troops saved me from a defeat. Something is also due to the avarice of the pandours and Croats; a branch of our laurel-wreath belongs justly to Nadasti and Trenck. It is most fortunate that the courier who brought those last dispatches from Berlin, did not arrive during the battle. He would certainly have been captured by the pandours, and my dispatches lost. My friend, do you not see how Providence marks out for me the path of duty? A king dare not waste a moment in dreams or idle pleasures. I wished to live an hour for myself, when I should have been reading these dispatches. We will go to work; here is the key of the dispatch bag; open it and take out the letters."

The king then seated himself before the common deal table which stood in the centre of the tent, and assorted the papers which Rothenberg handed to him.

"We will first read the letters from our friends," said the king, placing the dispatches and papers on one side. "Here are letters from D'Argens, and from Knobelsdorf, but none from Duhan, or Jordan, or Kaiserling. What does that mean? I fear that all is not right. Ah! here is a letter for you, my friend, in the handwriting of Duhan. He writes to you, and not to me. Read, Rothenberg, and tell me its contents."

The king then opened one of his own letters, but it was evident that it did not occupy his attention. He raised his eyes every few seconds to look at the general, who had become very pale on first opening his letter, and whose countenance now bore an expression of pain. Frederick could no longer endure this silence. He arose hastily, and approached Rothenberg.

"My friend," he said, "Duhan has written something to you that he would not write to me—something most painful. I see by your countenance."

"Your majesty is right; my letters contain most distressing intelligence."

"Ah!" murmured the king, as he turned from Rothenberg, "I fear I have not the strength to support this coming trial." After a pause, he continued: "Now, my friend, tell me, are my mother and sisters well?"

"Sire, the entire royal family are well."

"Your intelligence, then, relates to my friends. Two of them are ill—yes, two. How is Jordan? You do not answer—you weep. How is Jordan?"

"Sire, Jordan is dead."

"Dead!" cried the king, as he sank powerless upon his chair, and covered his face with his hands. "Dead! my best, my dearest friend is dead?"

"His death was as bright and peaceful as his life," said

Rothenberg. "His last word was a farewell to your majesty, his last act was to write to his king. Here is the letter, sire."

The king silently received the letter from Rothenberg. Two great tears ran slowly down his cheeks, and, falling on the letter, obliterated some words of the address. "Jordan's hand wrote these words for the last time; this idle title 'his majesty'—and my tears have washed it away. Jordan! Jordan I am no longer a king, but a poor, weak man who mourns for his lost friend."

He pressed the paper passionately to his lips; then placed it in his bosom, and turned once more to Rothenberg.

"Tell me the rest, my friend; I am resigned to all things now."

"Did you not say, sire, that you had left two friends ill in Berlin?"

"Jordan and Kaiserling. You do not mean that Kaiserling also—oh, no, no! that is impossible! Jordan is dead, and I knew that he must die; but Kaiserling will recover—I feel, I know it."

"Your majesty," said Rothenberg, "if I were a pious priest, I would say Kaiserling has recovered, for his soul has returned to God."

"Kaiserling dead also! Rothenberg, how could you find the courage to tell me this? Two friends lost in a moment of time." The king said nothing more. His head sank upon his breast, and he wept bitterly. After a time he raised his head, and said, as if to himself: "My two friends! They were my family—now I am orphaned. Sorrow will make a desert of my heart, and men will call me cold and heartless. They will not know that my heart is a graveyard, wherein my friends lie buried."

The tears ran slowly down his cheeks as he uttered this death-wail. So deep was the grief depicted on the countenance of the king, that Rothenberg could no longer restrain himself. He rushed to the king, and, sinking on his knees beside him, seized his hands and covered them with tears and kisses.

"Oh, my king, my hero! cease to mourn, if you do not wish to see me die of grief."

The king smiled mournfully, as he replied: "If one could die of grief, I would not have survived this hour."

"What would the world think could they see this great conqueror forgetting his triumphs and indulging such grief?"

"Ah, my friend, you desire to console me with the remembrance of this victory! I rejoice that I have preserved my land from a cruel misfortune, and that my troops are crowned with glory. But my personal vanity finds no food in this victory. The welfare and the happiness of my people alone lie on my heart—I think not of my own fleeting fame."

"The fame of my king is not fleeting. It will live in future years," cried the general.

The king shrugged his shoulders almost contemptuously. "Only death stamps fame upon kings' lives. For the present, I am content to fulfil my duties to the best of my ability. To be a true king, a monarch mus be willing to resign all personal happiness. As for me, Rothenberg, on this day, when I, as a king, am peculiarly fortunate, my heart is wrung by the loss of two dear friends. The man must pay for the happiness of the king. But," said the king, after a pause, "this is the dealing of the Almighty; I must submit silently. Would that my heart were silent! I will tell you something, my friend. I fear that I was unjust to Machiavelli. He was right—only a man with a heart of iron can be a king, for he alone could think entirely of his people."

"How suffering and full of grief must my king be to speak thus! You have lost two dear friends, sire. I also mourn their loss, but am suffering from a still deeper grief. I have lost the love of my king. I have lost faith in the friendship of my Frederick," said Rothenberg, sighing deeply.

"My Rothenberg," said the king, with his deep, tender voice, "look at me, and tell me what men call you, when they speak of you and me?"

"I hope they call me your majesty's most faithful servant."

"No, they call you my favorite, and what they say is true. *Vox populi vox Dei.* Come to my heart, my favorite."

"Ah! my king, my prince, my friend," cried Rothenberg, enthusiastically, as he threw himself into the arms of the king.

They stood long thus, heart pressed to heart; and who that had seen them, the king and ·h· hero, the conquerors of the day, would have imagined that their tears were not the tears of happiness and triumph, but of suffering and love?

"And now," said Frederick, after a pause, "let me again be king. I must return to my duties."

He seated himself   the table, and Rothenberg, after taking from the dispatch-bag a number of documents bearing the state seal, handed the king a daintily perfumed, rose-colored note. The king would not receive it, although a light flush mounted to his brow and his eyes beamed more brightly.

"Lay that on one side," he said, "I cannot read it; the notes of the *Miserere* are still sounding in my heart, and this operatic air would but create a discord. We will proceed to read the dispatches."

CHAPTER VIII.

A LETTER PREGNANT WITH FATE.

THE king was not the only person, in the encampment at Sohr, to whom the courier brought letters from Berlin; the colonel of every regiment had received a securely-locked post-bag containing the letters for the officers and soldiers of his regiment, which it was his duty to deliver. To avoid errors in the distribution, every post-bag was accompanied by a list, sent from the war department, on which each person to whom a letter was addressed must write a receipt.

Colonel von Jaschinsky was therefore compelled to deliver to Lieutenant von Trenck both the letters which were addressed to him. The colonel looked at one of these letters with a most malicious expression; he was not at all curious concerning its contents, for he was well acquainted with them, and knew that as soon as Trenck received it, it would become a sword, whose deadly point would be directed to the breast of the young man.

He knew the letter, for he had seen it before, but he had not delivered it; he had fraudulently withheld it from Trenck, in order to send it to Berlin, to his friend Pöllnitz, and to ask him if he did not think it well suited to accomplish their purpose of making Lieutenant von Trenck harmless, by bringing about his utter destruction. Pöllnitz had not answered up to this time, but to-day Colonel von Jaschinsky had received a letter from him, in which he said: "It is now time to allow the letter of the pandour to work. I carried the letter to the post, and I imagine that I played the part of a Job's messenger to his impertinent young officer, who allows himself to believe that his colonel owes him two hundred ducats. If you have ever really been his debtor, he will certainly be yours from to-day, for to you he will owe free quarters in one of the Prussian forts, and I hope for no short time. When you inform the king of this letter from the pandour, you can also say that Lieutenant von Trenck received a second letter from Berlin, and that you believe it to be from a lady. Perhaps the king will demand this letter, which I am positive Trenck will receive, for I mailed it myself, and it is equally certain that he will not destroy it, for lovers do not destroy the letters of the beloved."

No, lovers never destroy the letters of the beloved. What would have induced Frederick von Trenck to destroy this paper, on which *her hand* had rested, her eyes had looked upon, her breath touched, and on which her love, her vows, her longing, and her faith, were depicted? No, he would not have exchanged it for all the treasures of the world—this holy, this precious paper, which said to him that the Princess Amelia had not forgotten him. that she was determined to wait with patience, and love, and faith, until her hero returned, covered with glory, with a laurel-wreath on his brow, which would be brighter and more beautiful than the crown of a king.

As Trenck read these lines he wept with shame and humiliation. Two battles had been already won, and his name had remained dark and unknown; two battles, and none of

those heroic deeds which his beloved expected from him with
such certainty, had come in his path. He had performed
his duty as a brave soldier, but he had not accomplished such
an heroic act as that of Krauel, in the past year, which had
raised the common soldier to the title of Baron Krauel von
Ziskaberg, and had given to the unknown peasant a name
whose fame would extend over centuries. He had not astonished the whole world with a daring, unheard-of undertaking,
such as that of Ziethen, who had passed with his hussars, unknown, through the Austrian camp. He had been nothing
but a brave soldier—he had done nothing more than many
thousands. He felt the strength and the courage to tear the
very stars from heaven, that he might bind them as a diadem
upon the brow of his beloved; to battle with the Titans, and
plunge them into the abyss; to bear upon his shoulders the
whole world, as Atlas did; he felt in himself the power, the
daring, the will, and the ability of a hero. But the opportunity failed him.

The deeds which he longed to accomplish did not lie in
his path. And thus, in spite of two victorious battles in
which he had fought; in spite of the evident good-will of the
king, he had remained what he was, the unknown, undistinguished Lieutenant von Trenck. With a trembling heart
he demanded of himself that the Princess Amelia would continue to love him if he returned to her as he had departed;
if her proud, pure heart could stand that severest of all tests,
the discovery that she had bestowed her love upon an ordinary, undistinguished man.

"No, no!" he cried, "I have not the courage to return
thus to her. If I cannot distinguish myself, I can die. In
the next battle I will conquer fame or death. And if I fall,
she will weep for me. That would be a far happier fate
than living to be forgotten or despised by her."

He pressed Amelia's letter to his lips, then placed it in his
bosom, and opened the second letter. Whilst he read, an expression of astonishment appeared on his features, and a
smile, half gay, half scornful, played upon his full, fresh lips.
Soon, however, his features grew earnest, and a dark shadow
clouded his youthful brow.

"If I had enemies they could destroy me with this letter," he said, in a low voice. "It could, wild and silly as it is, be made to represent me as a traitor. Perhaps it is a pitfall which has been prepared for me. Is it possible that the authorities should have allowed this letter, coming evidently from inimical Austria, to pass unread through their hands? I will go immediately to my colonel, and show him this letter," said Trenck. "He can then inform the king of it if he think it necessary. Concealment might be more dangerous for me than an open acknowledgment."

And placing this second letter also in his bosom, Trenck proceeded to the tent of Colonel von Jaschinsky, who welcomed him with unusual warmth.

"Colonel," said Trenck, "do you remember the singular letter which I received six months since from my cousin, Baron von Trenck, colonel of the pandours?"

"Ah, you mean that letter in which he invites you to come to Austria, and promised, should you do so, to make you his sole heir?"

"Yes, that is the letter I mean. I informed you of it at the time and asked your advice."

"What advice did I give you?"

"That I should reply kindly and gratefully to my cousin; that I should not appear indifferent or ungrateful for a proposal by which I might become a millionnaire. You advised me to decline going to Austria, but only to decline so long as there was war between Prussia and Austria."

"Well, I think the advice was good, and that you may still follow it."

"You advised me also to write to my cousin to send me some of those beautiful Hungarian horses, and promised to forward my letter through Baron von Bossart, the Saxon ambassador; but on the condition that when I received the Hungarian horses, I should present one of them to you."

"That was only a jest—a jest which binds you to nothing, and of which you have no proofs."

"I!" asked Trenck, astonished; "what proof do I need that I promised you a Hungarian horse? What do I want with proofs?"

Count Jaschinsky looked embarrassed before the open, trusting expression of the young officer. His singular remark would have betrayed him to a more suspicious, a more worldly-wise man, who would have perceived from it the possibility of some danger, from which Jaschinsky was seeking to extricate himself.

"I did not mean," said the count, laughing, "that you needed a proof; I only wished to say that I had no proof that you had promised me a Hungarian horse, and that you need not feel obliged to give me one."

"Yes, colonel, your request and my promise occurred before witnesses. Lieutenant von Stadnitz and Ensign von Wagnitz were present; and if that had not been the case, I should consider my word binding. But at present I have no Hungarian horses, only an answer from my singular cousin, the contents of which I wish to impart to you."

"Ah, the colonel of the pandours has answered you?" asked Jaschinsky, with well-dissembled astonishment.

"Yes, he has answered me, and has written me the most singular letter that one can imagine. Only listen to it."

And Frederick von Trenck hastily pulled out the letter which he had put in his bosom. Entirely occupied with this subject, and thinking of nothing else, he opened the letter and read:

"From yours, dated Berlin, February 12th, I ascertain that you desire some Hungarian horses on which to meet my hussars and pandours. I learned with much pleasure, in the last campaign, that the Prussian Trenck was a brave soldier; as a proof of my consideration, I returned to you at that time the horses which my men had captured from you. If you desire to ride Hungarian horses, you must take mine from me on the field, or come to your cousin, who will receive you with open arms as his son and friend, and accord you every wish of your heart."

Had Trenck looked less attentively at his letter, while reading, he would have perceived that Jaschinsky was paying but slight attention (he was looking attentively on the floor); he quietly approached Trenck, and placed his foot upon something which he evidently wished to conceal. He then stood still, and as Trenck finished reading he broke into a loud laugh, in which the young officer joined him.

" Your cousin is a droll man," said the count, " and under the conditions which he offers you, I will still accept your Hungarian horse. Perhaps you will soon find an opportunity to give it to me, for I believe we are about to attack Hungary, and you can yourself procure the horses. But now, my young friend, excuse me; I must go to the king to give my report. You know he will endure no neglect of duty. After the war council I will see you again."

Trenck took leave, a little surprised at the sudden dismissal. The colonel did not accompany him, as usual. He remained standing in the middle of the tent until he was alone; then stooping down, he drew from under his foot the daintily folded letter that he had concealed while Trenck was present.

Count Jaschinsky had seen what had escaped Trenck. He saw that Trenck, in taking out the letter from his cousin, had let fall another paper, and while Trenck was reading, he had managed to conceal it with his foot. Now he hastily seized this paper, and opened it. A most wicked expression of joy overspread his countenance whilst he read, and then he said, triumphantly: " Now he is lost. It is not necessary to tell the king that Trenck has received a letter from a lady; I will take him the letter itself, and that will condemn Trenck more surely than any conspiracy with his cousin. Away to the king!"

But, as he had already withdrawn the curtain of his tent, he remained motionless, and appeared deep in thought. Then he allowed the curtain to fall, and returned within.

" I think I was on the point of committing a great folly. This letter would of course accomplish the destruction of my hated creditor, but I doubt exceedingly if I would escape unharmed if I handed this ominous writing to the king. He would never forgive me for having discovered this affair, which he, of course, wishes to conceal from the whole world. The knowledge of such a secret would be most dangerous, and I prefer to have nothing to do with it. How can I manage to let this letter reach the king, without allowing him to know that I am acquainted with the contents? Ah, I have it!" he cried, after a long pause, " the means are sure, and not at all dangerous for me."

18

With rapid steps he left his tent, and proceeded to that of the king from whom he prayed an audience.

"Ah! I wager that you come to complain of some one," said the king, as Jaschinsky entered. "There is a wicked light in your eye. Am I not right? one of your officers has committed some folly."

"I leave the decision entirely to your majesty," said Jaschinsky, humbly. "Your majesty commanded me to watch carefully over my officers, especially the Lieutenant von Trenck."

"Your complaint is again of Trenck, then?" asked the king, frowningly. "I will tell you before we begin, unless it is something important I do not wish to hear it; gossip is disagreeable to me. I am well pleased with Trenck; he is a brave and zealous officer, and I think he does not neglect his duties. Consider, therefore, colonel, unless it is a grave fault of which you have to complain, I advise you to remain silent."

"I hope your majesty will allow me to proceed."

"Speak," said the king, as he turned his back on the colonel, and appeared to occupy himself with the books on his table.

"Lieutenant von Trenck received a letter by the post to-day which points, in my opinion, to an utterly unlawful proceeding."

The king turned hastily, and looked so angrily at the colonel that he involuntarily withdrew a step. "It is fortunate that I did not hand him that letter," thought Jaschinsky; "in his anger the king would have destroyed me."

"From whom is this letter?" demanded the king.

"Sire, it is from Baron von Trenck, the colonel of the pandours."

The king appeared relieved, as he replied, with a smile: "This pandour is a cousin of our lieutenant."

"But he is in the enemy's camp; and I do not think it proper for a Prussian officer to request one in the Austrian service to send him a present of horses, or for the Austrian to invite the Prussian to join him."

"Is this in the letter?" asked the king in a threatening tone; and when Jaschinsky answered in the affirmative, he said: "Give me the letter; I must convince myself with my own eyes that this is so."

"I have not the letter, but if your majesty desire, I will demand it from Lieutenant von Trenck."

"And if he has burnt the letter?"

"Then I am willing to take an oath that what I have related was in the letter. I read it myself, for the lieutenant showed it to me."

"Bring me the letter."

Jaschinsky went, and the king remained alone and thoughtful in his tent. "If he were a traitor, he would surely not have shown the letter to Jaschinsky," said the king, softly; "no, his brow is as clear, his glance as open as formerly. Trenck is no traitor—no traitor to his country—I fear only a traitor to his own happiness. Well, perhaps he has come to his reason, I have warned him repeatedly, and perhaps he has at length understood me.—Where is the letter?" he asked, as Colonel Jaschinsky reëntered.

"Sire, here it is. At least I think that is it. I did not take time to glance at the paper, in my haste to return to your majesty."

"Was he willing to give the letter?"

"He said nothing, but drew it instantly from his bosom, and I brought it to your majesty without glancing at it."

The king looked searchingly into the countenance of the colonel. Jaschinsky's repeated assurances that he had not looked at the letter surprised the king, and led him to suspect some hidden motive. He received the letter, and opened it slowly and carefully. He again turned his piercing glance upon the countenance of Jaschinsky; he now perceived the rose-colored letter, which lay in the folds of that one from Colonel Trenck, and he immediately understood the words of the count. This little letter was really the kernel of the whole matter, and Jaschinsky preferred to know nothing of it.

"Wait outside until I call you. I wish to read this letter carefully," said the king, with perfect composure; but when Jaschinsky had disappeared, he hastily unfolded the paper, and, throwing Trenck's letter on the table, he took the other, and looking carefully at it, he said softly, "It is her writing

—yes, it is her writing, and all my trouble has been in vain. They *would* not understand me. They are lost."

And sighing deeply, the king turned again to the letter. "Poor, miserable children, why should I not make them happy? is it impossible to forget prejudice for once, and to allow these two beings to be happy in their own way? So strange a thing is the heart of a woman, that she prefers an orange-wreath to a crown! Why should I force this young girl to be a princess, when she only desires to be a woman? Shall I allow them to fly away into some wilderness, and there create a paradise? But how soon would the serpent creep into this paradise! how soon would satiety, and *ennui*, and repentance destroy their elysium! No, the daughters of the Hohenzollerns must not stoop for happiness; I cannot change it. Fate condemns them, not I. They are condemned, but the sword which is suspended above them must fall only upon his head. His is the guilt, for he is the man. His stake was immense, and he has lost all."

The king then took the letter of Colonel Trenck, and read it attentively. "This letter bears all-sufficient testimony against him; it is the iron mask which I will raise before his crime, that the world may not discover it. I would laugh at this letter were it not for the other, which condemns him. This will answer as an excuse for his punishment."

The king arose from his seat, and placing the letter of the princess in his bosom, and folding the other, he walked hastily to the opening of the tent and called Jaschinsky.

"Colonel," he said, and his countenance was troubled but determined, "you are right. Lieutenant von Trenck is a great criminal, for this letter contains undeniable proof of his traitorous connection with the enemy. If I ordered him before a court-martial, he would be condemned to death. As his crime may have grown out of carelessness and thoughtlessness, I will be merciful, and try if a few years' imprisonment will not work a cure. You can inform him of his punishment, when you return his cousin's letter to him. You did not open this letter when you brought it to me?"

The eye of the king rested with a threatening expression upon the colonel as he asked this question.

"No, your majesty,—I did not open it," replied the colonel.

"You did well," said the king, "for a wasp had crept within it, which might have given you a deadly wound. Go now, and take this letter to Trenck, and take his sword from him. He is under arrest, and must be sent at once to the fortress at Glatz."

"Must it be quietly done?" asked Jaschinsky, scarcely able to conceal his delight.

"No, on the contrary, I wish the whole army, the whole world to know why I have punished Trenck. You can say to every one that Trenck is a traitor, who has carried on an unlawful correspondence with his cousin in Austria, and has conspired with the enemy. His arrest must be public, and he must be sent to Glatz, guarded by fifty hussars. Go now and attend to this business.—He is lost," said the king, solemnly, when he was once more alone. "Trenck is condemned, and Amelia must struggle with her grief. Poor Amelia!"

The generals were waiting outside, among them the favorite of the king, General Rothenberg. They had been summoned to a council by the king, and were awaiting his orders to enter the tent.

But the king did not call them, perhaps he had forgotten them. He walked slowly up and down in his tent, apparently lost in thought. Suddenly he stood motionless and listened. He heard the tramp of many horses, and he knew what it meant. He approached the opening of the tent, and drew back the curtain sufficiently to see without being seen.

The noise of the horses' hoofs came nearer and nearer. The first hussars have passed the king's tent, and two more, and again two, and again, and again; and there in their midst, a pale young man, with a distracted countenance, with staring eyes, and colorless lips, which appear never to have known how to laugh, a young officer, without sword or epaulettes. Is this Trenck, the beautiful, the young, the light-hearted Trenck, the beloved of a princess, the darling of all the ladies, the envied favorite of the king? He has passed the tent of the king; behind him are his servants with his horses and his baggage; and then again hussars, who close the procession, the burial-procession of Trenck's happiness and freedom.

The king seemed deeply moved as he stepped back from the curtain. "Now," he said solemnly, "I have committed my first act of injustice; for I judged this man in my own conscience, without bringing him before a court-martial. Should the world condemn me for this, I can at least say that it is my only fault of the kind."

CHAPTER IX.

THE RETURN TO BERLIN.

PEACE was proclaimed. This poor land, bleeding from a thousand wounds, might now rest, in order to gather strength for new victories. The husband of Maria Theresa had been crowned as emperor, and the conditions of peace had been signed at Dresden, by both Austrians and Prussians. The king and his army returned victorious to their native land. Berlin had assumed her most joyous appearance, to welcome her king; even Nature had done her utmost to enliven the scene. The freshly fallen snow, which covered the streets and roofs of the houses, glittered in the December sunshine as if strewn with diamonds. But none felt to-day that the air was cold or the wind piercing; happiness created summer in their hearts, and they felt not that it was winter. On every side the windows were open, and beautiful women were awaiting the appearance of their adored sovereign with as much curiosity and impatience as the common people in the streets, who were longing to greet their hero-king.

At length the happy hour came. At length the roar of cannon, the ringing of bells, the shouts of the crowd, which filled every avenue leading to the palace, announced that the king had returned to his capital, which, in the last few days, he had saved by a happy manœuvre from being attacked by the Austrians and Saxons. The people greeted their king with shouts; the ladies in the windows waved their handkerchiefs, and threw fragrant flowers into the open carriage in which Frederick and his brothers sat.

As they passed before the gymnasium, the scholars commenced a solemn song, which was at the same time a hymn, and a prayer for their king, their hero, and their father. "*Vivat, vivat Fredericus! Rex vivat, Augustus, Magnus, Felix Pater Patriæ!*" sang the scholars. But suddenly rising above the voices of the singers, and the shouts of the people, a voice was heard, crying aloud, "*Vivat Frederick the Great!*"

The people who had listened silently to the Latin because they did not understand it, joined as with one impulse in this cry, the shout arose as from one throat, "Vivat Frederick the Great!" And this cry spread like wildfire through all the streets, over all the public squares; it resounded from every window, and even from the tops of the houses. To-day Berlin had rebaptized her king. She gave him now a new name, the name which he will bear through all ages, the name of Frederick the Great.

The king flushed deeply as he heard this cry. His heart, which had been sad and gloomy, seemed warmed as by a ray of sunlight. Ambition throbbed within his breast, and awakened him from his melancholy thoughts. No, Frederick had now no time to think of the dead; no time to mourn secretly over the loved, the faithful friends whom he would no longer find in Berlin. The king must overcome the feelings of the friend. His people are here to greet him, to welcome his return, to bestow upon him an immortal name. The king has no right to withdraw himself from their love; he must meet it with his whole soul, his whole heart.

Convincing himself that this was necessary, Frederick lifted his head, a bright color mounted to his cheeks, and his eyes flashed as he bowed graciously to his people. Now he is truly Frederick the Great, for he has conquered his own heart, and he has poured upon the open wound of his private sorrows the balm of his people's love.

Now the carriage of the king has reached the palace gate. Frederick raises his hat once more, and bows smilingly to the people, whose cries of " Vivat Frederick the Great " still fill the air. When for a moment there is silence, a single, clear, commanding voice is heard, "Long live Frederick the Great!"

The king turns hastily; he has recognized the voice of his mother. She is standing on the threshold of the palace, surrounded by the princesses of the royal family. Her eyes are more brilliant than the diamonds which glitter in her hair, and more precious than the costly pearls upon her bosom are the drops which fall from her eyes, tears of pride and happiness, shed in this moment of triumph. Again she repeats the cry taught her by the people, "Long live Frederick the Great!"

The king knew the first tone of that dear voice, and, springing from the carriage, hurried forward and threw himself into his mother's extended arms, and laid his head upon her breast, as he had done when a child, and wept hot tears, which no one saw, which his mother alone felt upon her bosom.

Near them stood Elizabeth Christine, the consort of the king, and in the depths of her heart she repeated the cry of the people, and she gazed prayerfully toward heaven, as she petitioned for the long and happy life of her adored husband. But Frederick did not see her; he gave his arm to his mother, and they entered the palace, followed by his wife and his sisters and brothers.

"Frederick the Great!" This cry still resounds through the streets, and the windows of the palace tremble with the ringing of this proud name. The sound enters the saloons before him; it opens wide the doors of the White Saloon, and when the king enters, the pictures and statues of the Hohenzollerns appear to become animate, the dead eyes flash, the stiffened lips smile, and the motionless heads seem to bow, for Frederick's new name has called his ancestors from their graves—this name, which only one other Hohenzollern had borne before him—this name, which is as rare a blossom on the genealogical trees of the proudest royal families as the blossoms of the aloe. The king greets his ancestors with a happy smile, for he feels that he is no unworthy successor. He has forgotten his grief and his pain; he has overcome them. In this hour he is only the king and hero.

But as the shadows of night approach, and Berlin is brilliant with illuminations, Frederick lays aside his majesty, and becomes once more the loving man, the friend. He is sitting by the death-bed of his friend and preceptor, Duhan. The joyous shouts of the people are still heard without, but the king heeds them not; he hears only the heavy breathing of his friend, and speaks to him gentle words of love and consolation.

At length he leaves his friend, and now a new light springs into his eyes. He is no longer a king, no longer a mourning friend, he is only a young man. He is going to spend an hour with his friend General Rothenberg, and forget his royalty for a while.

Rothenberg seems to have forgotten it also, for he does not come to welcome his kingly guest. He does not receive him on the threshold. No one receives him, but the hall and stairway are brilliantly lighted; and, as he ascends, a door opens, and a woman appears, beautiful as an angel, with eyes beaming like stars, with lips glowing as crimson roses. Is it an angel or a woman? Her voice is as the music of the spheres to the king, when she whispers her welcome to him, and he, at last, thinks he beholds an angel when he sees Barbarina.

CHAPTER X.

JOB'S POST.

BERLIN shouted, huzzaed, sang, danced, declaimed, illuminated for three entire days in honor of the conquered peace, and the return of her great king. Every one but the young Princess Amelia seemed contented, happy, joyous. She took no part in the glad triumph of her family, and the loud hosannas of the people found no echo in her breast. With heavy heart and misty eyes she walked slowly backward and forward in her boudoir. For three days she had borne this terrible torture, this anguish of uncertainty. Her soul was moved with fearful anticipations, but she was forced to appear gay.

For three days, with trembling heart and lips, she had been compelled to appear at the theatre, the masquerades, the balls, and ceremonious dinners of the court. She felt that the stern eye of the king was ever searchingly and angrily fixed upon her. Several times, completely overcome and exhausted by her efforts to seem gay and careless, she sought to withdraw unobserved to her room, but her ever-watchful brother intercepted her, and led her back to her place by her royal mother. He chatted and jested merrily, but his expression was dark and threatening. Once she had not the power to respond with smiles. She fixed her pleading, tearful eyes upon the king. He bowed down to her, and said harshly: "I command you to appear gay. A princess has not the right to weep when her people are happy."

To-day the court festivities closed. At last Amelia dared hope for some hours of solitude and undisturbed thought. To-day she could weep and allow her pale lips to express the wild grief of her heart. In her loneliness she dared give utterance to the cry of anguish rending her bosom.

Where was he? where was Trenck? Why had he not returned? Why had she no news, no love-token, no message from him? She had carefully examined the list of killed and wounded. He had not fallen in battle. He was not fatally wounded. He had not returned with the army, or she would have seen him. Where was he, then? Was he ill, or had he forgotten her, or did he blush to return without his laurels? Had he been taken by the Austrians? Was her beloved suffering in a loathsome prison, while she was laughing, jesting, and adorning herself in costly array? While she thus thought and spoke, burning tears blinded her eyes, and sighs and sobs choked her utterance.

"If he is dead," said she, firmly, "then I will also die. If he is in prison, I will set him at liberty. If he does not come because he has not been promoted and fears I no longer love him, I will seek him out, I will swear that I love him, that I desire only his love, that I will fly with him to some lonely, quiet valley. I will lay aside my rank, my royalty, forget my birth, abandon all joyously, that I may belong to him, be his fond and dear-loved wife."

And now a light sound was heard at the door, and she recognized the voice of her maid asking admittance.

"Ah!" said Amelia, "if the good Marwitz were here, I should not have to endure this torture, but my brother has unconsciously robbed me of this consolation. He has sent my friend and confidante home, and forced upon me a strange and stupid woman whom I hate."

And now a gentle voice plead more earnestly for admittance.

"I must indeed open the door," said the princess, unwillingly drawing back the bolt. "Enter, Mademoiselle von Haak," said Amelia, turning her back in order to conceal her red and swollen eyes.

Mademoiselle von Haak gave a soft, sad glance at the young princess, and in a low voice asked for pardon for her unwelcome appearance.

"Without doubt your reason for coming will justify you," said the princess. "I pray you, therefore, to make it known quickly. I wish to be alone."

"Alas! your royal highness is harsh with me," whispered the young girl. "I was forced upon you. I know it; you hate me because I have taken the place of Mademoiselle von Marwitz. I assure you I was not to blame in this. It was only after the written and peremptory command of his majesty the king that my mother consented to my appearance at court."

"Have you come, mademoiselle, simply to tell me this?"

"No, your royal highness; I come to say that I love you. Even since I had the honor of knowing you, I have loved you. In the loneliness which surrounds me here, my heart gives itself up wholly to you. Oh, do not spurn me from you! Tell me why you are sad; let me bear a part of your sorrow. Princess, I offer you the heart of a true friend, of a sister—will you cast me off?"

The young girl threw herself upon her knees before the princess, and her cheeks were bathed in tears. Amelia raised and embraced her.

"Oh!" said she, "I see that God has not utterly forsaken me. He sends me aid and comfort in my necessity. Will you be, indeed, my friend?"

"Yes, a friend in whom you can trust fully, to whom you can speak freely," said Mademoiselle von Haak.

"Who knows but that may be more dangerous for you than for me?" sighed Amelia. "There are fearful secrets, the mere knowledge of which brings destruction."

"But if I already know the secret of your royal highness? —if I understand the reason of your grief during these last few days?"

"Well, then, tell me what you know."

The maiden bowed down low to the ear of her mistress. "Your eyes seek in vain for him whom you love. You suffer, for you know not where he is."

"Yes, you are right," cried Amelia. "I suffer the anguish of uncertainty. If I do not soon learn where he is, I shall die in despair."

"Shall I tell you, princess?"

Amelia turned pale and trembled. "You will not say that he is in his grave?" said she, breathlessly.

"No, your highness, he lives and is well."

"He lives, is well, and comes not?"

"He cannot come—he is a prisoner."

"A prisoner! God be thanked it is no worse! The king will obtain his liberation. My brother cares for his young officers—he will not leave him in the hands of the Austrians. Oh! I thank you—I thank you. You are indeed a messenger of glad tidings. And now the king will be pleased with me. I can be merry and laugh, and jest with him."

Mademoiselle von Haak bowed her head sadly, and sighed. "He is not in an Austrian prison," she said, in low tones.

"Not in an Austrian prison?" repeated Amelia, astonished, "where is he, then? My God! why do you not speak? Where is Trenck? Who has captured him? Speak! I die with impatience and anxiety."

"In God's name, princess, listen to me calmly, and above all things, speak softly. I am sure you are surrounded by spies. If we are heard, we are lost!"

"Do you wish me to die?" murmured the princess, sinking exhausted upon the divan. "Where is Trenck?"

"He is in the fortress of Glatz," whispered Von Haak.

"Ah! in a Prussian fortress; sent there by the king? He has committed some small fault in discipline, as once before, and as this is the second offence, the king punishes him more severely. That is all! I thank you; you have restored my peace of mind."

"I fear, princess, that you are mistaken. It is said that Baron von Trenck has been arrested for high treason."

The princess became deadly pale, and almost fainted. She overcame this weakness, however, quickly, and said smilingly: "He will then soon be free, for all must know that he is innocent."

"God grant that it may be proved!" said Mademoiselle von Haak. "This is no time to shrink or be silent. You have a great, strong heart, and you love him. You must know all! Listen, therefore, princess. I also love; I also look to the future with hope! My love is calm, for it is without danger; it has my mother's consent and blessing. Our only hope is, that my lover may be promoted, and that the king will give his consent to our marriage. We are both poor, and rely only upon the favor of the king. He is now lieutenant, and is on duty in the garrison of Glatz."

"In Glatz! and you say that Trenck is a prisoner in Glatz?"

"Yes, I received letters yesterday from Schnell. He belongs to the officers who have guard over Trenck. He writes that he feels the profoundest pity for this young man, and that he will joyfully aid him in every way. He asks me if I know no one who has the courage to plead with the king in behalf of this unhappy youth."

"My God! my God! give me strength to hear all, and yet control myself!" murmured Amelia. "Do you know the nature of his punishment?" said she, quietly.

"No one knows positively the duration of his punishment; but the commandant of the fort told the officers that Trenck would be a prisoner for many years."

The princess uttered one wild cry, then pressed both hands upon her lips and forced herself to silence.

"What is the charge against him?" she said, after a long pause.

"High treason. A treasonable correspondence has been discovered between him and his cousin the pandour."

The princess shrugged her shoulders contemptuously. "He will soon justify himself, in view of this pitiful charge! His judges will acknowledge his innocence, and set him at liberty. But why is he not already free? Why has he been condemned? Who were his judges? Did you not say to me that he was condemned?"

"My lover wrote me that Baron Trenck had written to the king and asked for a court-martial and trial."

"This proves his innocence; he does not fear a trial! What was the king's answer?"

"He ordered the commandant to place Trenck in closer confinement, and to forward no more letters from him. And now, princess, you must act promptly; use all your power and influence, if you would save him!"

"I have no influence, I have no power!" cried Amelia, with streaming eyes. "Oh! you do not know my brother; his heart is of stone. No one can move him—neither his mother, his sisters, nor his wife; his purpose is unchangeable, and what he says is fixed. But I will show him that I am his sister; that the hot blood of the Hohenzollerns flows also in my veins. I will seek him boldly; I will avow that I love Trenck; I will demand that he give Trenck liberty, or give me death! I will demand—"

The door was hastily opened, and a servant said, breathlessly, "The king is coming!"

"No, he is already here," said the king, who now stood upon the threshold of the door. "He comes to beg his little sister to accompany him to the court-yard and see the reindeer and the Laplanders, sent to us by the crown princess of Sweden."

The king advanced to his sister, and held out both his hands. But Amelia did not appear to see this. She made a profound and ceremonious bow, and murmured a few cold words of greeting. The king frowned, and looked at her angrily. He saw that she had been weeping, and his expression was harsh and stern.

"Come, princess!" said he imperiously.

But Amelia had now overcome her terror and her confusion. She was resolved to act, and know the worst.

"Will your majesty grant me an audience? I have something important, most important to myself, to say. I would speak more to the heart of my brother than to the ear of my king. I pray your majesty to allow me to speak with you alone."

The king's eyes were fixed upon her with a dark and threatening expression, but she did not look down or tremble; she met his glance firmly, even daringly, and Frederick hesitated. "She will speak the whole truth to me," thought the king, "and I shall be forced to act with severity against her. I cannot do this; I am not brave enough to battle with a maiden's heart."

"Sister," said he aloud, "if you have indeed something to say to your brother, and not to the king, I counsel you not to speak now. I have so much to do and hear as a king, I have no time to act another part. Is what you have to say to me truly important? Does it relate to a rare jewel, or a costly robe?—to some debt, which your pin-money does not suffice to meet?—in short, to any one of those great matters which completely fill the heart of a young maiden? If so, I advise you to confide in our mother. If she makes your wishes known to me, you are sure to receive no denial. It is decidedly better for a young girl to turn to her mother with her little wishes and mysteries. If they are innocent, her mother will ever promote them; if they are guilty, a mother's anger will be more restrained and milder than a brother's ever can be."

"You will not even listen to me, my brother?" said the princess, sobbing violently.

The king threw a quick glance backward toward the door opening into the corridor, where the cavaliers and maids of honor were assembled, and looking curiously into the room of the princess.

"No! I will not listen to you," said he, in a low tone; "but you shall listen to me! You shall not act a drama at my court; you shall not give the world a cause for scandal; you shall not exhibit yourself with red and swollen eyes;

that might be misinterpreted. It might be said that the sister of the king did not rejoice at the return of her brother; that she was not patriot enough to feel happy at Prussia's release from the burdens of war, not patriot enough to despise and forget the enemies of her country! I command you to be gay, to conceal your childish grief. A princess dare not weep, or, if she does, it must be under the shadow of night, when God only is with her. This is my counsel and reproof, and I beg you to lay it to heart. I will not command you to accompany me, your eyes are red with weeping. Remain, then, in your room, and that the time may not pass heavily, I hand you this letter, which I have received for you."

He drew a sealed letter from his bosom, handed it to Amelia, and left the room.

"Let us go," said he, nodding to his courtiers; "the princess is unwell, and cannot accompany us."

Mademoiselle von Haak hastened again to the boudoir. "Has your royal highness spoken to the king?"

She shook her head silently, and with trembling hands tore open the letter given her by the king. Breathlessly she fixed her eyes upon the writing, uttered one wild shriek, and fell insensible upon the floor. This was the last letter she had written to Trenck, and upon the margin the king had written this one word, "Read." The king then knew all; he had read the letter; he knew of her engagement to Trenck, knew how she loved him, and he had no mercy. For this was he condemned. He had given her this letter to prove to her that she had nothing to hope; that Trenck was punished, not for high treason against the state, but because he was the lover of the princess.

Amelia understood all. With flashing eyes, with glowing cheeks, she exclaimed: "I will set him at liberty; he suffers because he loves me; for my sake he languishes in a lonely prison. I will free him if it costs me my heart's blood, drop by drop! Now, King Frederick, you shall see that I am indeed your sister; that I have a will even like your own. My life belongs to my beloved; if I cannot share it with him, I will offer it up to him—I swear this; may God condemn me if I break my oath! Trenck shall be free! that is the mission of my life. Now, friend, come to my help; all that I am and have I offer up. I have gold, I have diamonds, I gave an estate given me by my father. I will sell all to liberate him; we will, if necessary, bribe the whole garrison. But now, before all other things, I must write to him."

"I promise he shall receive your letter," said Mademoiselle von Haak; "I will send it to Lieutenant Schnell. I will enclose it to my mother; no one here must know that I correspond with an officer at the fortress of Glatz."

"No one dare know that, till the day of Trenck's liberation," said Amelia, with a radiant smile.

CHAPTER XI.

THE UNDECEIVED.

SINCE the day Joseph Fredersdorf introduced Lupinus to Eckhof, an affectionate intercourse had grown up between them. They were very happy in each other, and Fredersdorf asserted that there was more of love than friendship in their hearts, that Lupinus was not the friend but the bride of Eckhof! In fact, Lupinus had but little of the unembarrassed, frank, free manner of a young man. He was modest and reserved, never sought Eckhof; but when the latter came to him, his pale face colored with a soft red, and his great eyes flashed with a wondrous glow. Eckhof could not but see how much his silent young friend rejoiced in his presence.

He came daily to Lupinus. It strengthened and consoled him in the midst of his nervous, restless artist-life, to look upon the calm, peaceful face of his friend; this alone, without a word spoken, soothed his heart—agitated by storms and passions, and made him mild and peaceable. The quiet room, the books and papers, the weighty folios, the shining, polished medical instruments, these stern realities, formed a strange and strong contrast to the dazzling, shimmering, frivolous, false life of the stage; and all this exer-

19

cised a wondrous influence upon the *artiste.* Eckhof came often, weighed down with care and exhaustion, or in feverish excitement over some new *rôle* he was studying, not to speak of his anxieties and perplexities, but to sit silently near Lupinus and looked calmly upon him.

"Be silent, my Lupinus," said Eckhof to him. "Let me lay my storm-tossed, wild heart in the moonlight of thy glance; it will be warmed and cooled at the same time. Let thy mild countenance beam upon me, soften and heal my aching heart. Look you, when I lay my head thus upon your shoulder, it seems to me I have escaped all trouble; that only far away in the distance do I hear the noise and tumult of the restless, busy world; and I hear the voice of my mother, even as I heard it in my childish days, whispering of God, of paradise, and the angels. Still, still, friend, let me dream thus upon your shoulder."

He closed his eyes in silence, and did not see the fond and tender expression with which Lupinus looked down upon him. He did not feel how violently the young heart beat, how quick the hot breath came.

At other times it was a consolation to Eckhof to relate, in passionate and eloquent words, all his sorrows and disappointments; all the strifes and contests; all his scorn over the intrigues and cabals which then, as now, were the necessary attendants of a stage-life. Lupinus listened till this wild cataract of rage had ceased to foam, and he might hope that his soft and loving words of consolation could find an entrance into Eckhof's heart.

Months went by, and Lupinus, faithful to the promise given to Eckhof, was still the thoughtful, diligent student; he sat ever in quiet meditation upon the bench of the auditory, and listened to the learned dissertations of the professors, and studied the secrets of science in his lonely room.

But this time of trial was soon to be at an end. Eckhof agreed, that after Lupinus had passed his examination, he should decide for himself if he would abandon the glittering career of science for the rough and stormy path of artist-life. In the next few days this important event was to take place, and Lupinus would publicly and solemnly receive his diploma.

Lupinus thought but little of this. He knew that the events of that day must exercise an important influence upon his future, upon the happiness or unhappiness of his whole life.

The day before the examination Lupinus was alone in his room. He said to himself, "If the faculty give me my diploma, I will show myself in my true form to Eckhof. I will step suddenly before him, and in his surprise I will see if his friend Lupinus is more welcome as—"

He did not complete the sentence, but blushing crimson at his own thoughts, he turned away and took refuge in his books; but the excitement and agitation of his soul were stronger than his will; the letters danced and glimmered before his eyes; his heart beat joyfully and stormily; and his soul, borne aloft on bold wings, could no longer be held down to the dusty and dreary writing-desk; he sprang up, threw the book aside, and hastened to the adjoining room. No other foot had ever crossed the threshold of this still, small room; it was always closed against the most faithful of his friends.

Besides, this little bedroom concealed a mystery—a mystery which would have excited the merriment of Fredersdorf and the wild amazement of Eckhof. On the bed lay a vestment which seemed utterly unsuited to the toilet of a young man; it was indeed a woman's dress, a glistening white satin, such as young, fair brides wear on their wedding-day. There, upon the table lay small white, satin shoes, perfumed, embroidered pocket-handkerchiefs, ribbons, and flowers. What did this signify? what meant this feminine boudoir, next to the study of a young man? Was the beloved whom he wished to adorn with this bridal attire concealed there? or, was this only a costume in which he would play his first *rôle* as an actor?

Lupinus gazed upon all these costly things with a glad and happy heart, and as he raised the satin robe and danced smilingly to the great mirror, nothing of the grave, earnest. dignified scholar was to be seen in his mien; suddenly he paused, and stood breathlessly listening. It seemed to him some one knocked lightly on the outer door, then again louder.

"That is Eckhof," whispered Lupinus. He left the mysterious little room, hastily closed the door, and placed the key in his bosom, then opened the outer door.

Yes, it was Eckhof. He entered with a beaming face, with a gay and happy smile. Lupinus had never seen him so joyous. He clasped his young friend so ardently in his arms, that he could scarcely breathe; he pressed so glowing a kiss upon his cheek, that Lupinus trembled, and was overcome by his own emotion.

"See, Lupinus, how much I love you!" said Eckhof. "I come first to you, that you may sympathize with me in my great joy. Almost oppressed by the sense of heavenly bliss, which seemed in starry splendor to overshadow me, I thought, 'I must go to Lupinus; he alone will understand me.' I am here to say to you, 'Rejoice with me, for I am happy.' I ran like a madman through the streets. Oh! friend, you have not seen my sorrow; I have concealed the anguish of my soul. I loved you boundlessly, and I would not fill your young, pure soul with sadness. But you dared look upon my rapture; you, my most faithful, best-beloved friend, shall share my joy."

"Tell me, then, at once, what makes you happy?" said Lupinus, with trembling lips, and with the pallor of death from excitement and apprehension.

"And you ask, my innocent and modest child," said Eckhof, laughing. "You do not yet know that love alone makes a man wretched or infinitely happy. I was despairing because I did not know if I was beloved, and this uncertainty made a madman of me."

"And now?" said Lupinus.

"And now I am supremely happy—she loves me; she has confessed it this day. Oh! my friend, I almost tore this sweet, this heavenly secret from her heart. I threatened her, I almost cursed her. I lay at her feet, uttering wild words of rebuke and bitter reproach. I was mad with passion; resolved to slay myself, if she did not then and there disclose to me either her love or her contempt. I dared all, to win all. She stood pallid and trembling before me, and, as I railed at her, she extended her arms humbly and pleadingly toward me. Oh! she was fair and beautiful as a pardoning angel, with these glistening tears in her wondrous, dreamy eyes, fair and beautiful as a houri of Paradise; when at last, carried away by her own heart, she bowed down and confessed that she loved me; that she would be mine—mine, in spite of her distinguished birth, in spite of all the thousand obstacles which interposed. One wild day I exclaimed, ' Oh! my God. my God! I am set apart to be an *artiste;* thou hast consecrated me by misfortune.' To-day, I feel that only when 1 am truly happy can I truly create. From this day alone will I truly be an *artiste.* I have now received the heavenly consecration of happiness."

Eckhof looked down upon his young friend. When he gazed upon the fair and ashy countenance, the glassy eyes staring without expression in the distance, the blue lips convulsively pressed together, he became suddenly silent.

"Lupinus, you are ill! you suffer!" he said, opening his arms and trying to clasp his friend once more to his breast. But the touch of his hand made Lupinus tremble, and awakened him from his trance. One wild shriek rang from his bosom, a stream of tears gushed from his eyes, and he sank almost insensible to the floor.

"My friend, my beloved friend!" cried Eckhof, "you suffer, and are silent. What is it that overpowers you? What is this great grief? Why do you weep? Let me share and alleviate your sorrow."

"No, no!" cried Lupinus, rising, "I do not suffer; I have no pain, no cause of sorrow. Do not touch me; your lightest touch wounds! Go, go! leave me alone!"

"You love me not, then?" said Eckhof. "You suffer, and will not confide in me? you weep bitterly, and command me to leave you?"

"And he thinks that I do not love him," murmured Lupinus, with a weary smile. "My God! whom, then, do I love?"

"If your friendship for me were true and genuine, you would trust me," said Eckhof. "I have made you share in my happiness, and I demand the holy right of sharing your grief."

Lupinus did not reply. Eckhof lifted him gently in his arms, and laying him upon the sofa, took a seat near him.

He laid his arms around him, placed his head upon his bosom, and in a soft, melodious voice, whispered words of comfort, encouragement, and love. The young man trembled convulsively, and wept without restraint.

Suddenly he raised himself; the agony was over; his lips slightly trembled, but he pressed them together; his eyes were full of tears, but he shook his head proudly, and dashed them from him.

"It is past, all past! my dream has dispersed. I am awake once more!"

"And now, Lupinus, you will tell me all?"

"No, not now, but to-morrow. To-morrow you shall know all. Therefore, go, my friend, and leave me alone. Go to her you love, gaze in her eyes, and see in them a starry heaven; then think of me, whose star is quenched, who is bowed down under a heavy load of affliction. Go! go! if you love me, go at once!"

"I love you, therefore I obey you, but my heart is heavy for you, and my own happiness is clouded. But I go; to-morrow you will tell me all?"

"To-morrow."

"But when, when do we meet again?"

"To-morrow, at ten, we will see each other. At that time I am to receive my diploma. I pray you, bring Fredersdorf with you."

"So be it; to-morrow, at ten, in the university. Till then, farewell."

"Farewell."

They clasped hands, looked deep into each other's eyes, and took a silent leave. Lupinus stood in the middle of the room and gazed after Eckhof till he had reached the threshold, then rushed forward, threw himself upon his neck, clasped him in his arms, and murmured, in a voice choked with tears: "Farewell, farewell! Think of me, Eckhof! think that no woman has ever loved you as I have loved you! God bless you! God bless you, my beloved!"

One last glowing kiss, one last earnest look, and he pushed him forward and closed the door; then with a wild cry sank upon the floor.

How long he lay there, how long he wept, prayed, and despaired, he knew not himself. The hours of anguish drag slowly and drearily; the moments given to weeping seem to stretch out to eternity. Suddenly he heard heavy steps upon the stairs; he recognized them, and knew what they signified. The door opened, and two men entered: the first with a proud, imposing form, with gray hair, and stern, strongly-marked features; the other, a young man, pale and delicate, with a mild and soft countenance.

The old man looked at Lupinus with a frowning brow and angry glance; the other greeted him with a sweet smile, and his clear blue eye rested upon him with an expression of undying love.

"My father!" said Lupinus, hastening forward to throw himself into his arms; but he waved him back, and his look was darker, sterner.

"We have received your letter, and therefore are we here to-day. We hope and believe it was written in fever or in madness. If we are mistaken in this, you shall repeat to us what was written in that letter, which I tore and trampled under my feet. Speak, then! we came to listen."

"Not so," said the young man, "recover yourself first; consider your words; reflect that they will decide the question of your own happiness, of your father's, and of mine. Be firm and sure in your determination. Let no thought of others, no secondary consideration influence you. Think only of your own happiness, and endeavor to build it upon a sure foundation."

Lupinus shook his head sadly. "I have no happiness, I expect none."

"What was written in that letter?" said the old Lupinus sternly.

"That I had been faithful to my oath, and betrayed the secret I promised you to guard, to no one; that to-morrow I would receive my diploma; that you had promised, when I had accomplished this I should be free to choose my own future, and to confess my secret."

"Was that all the letter contained?"

"No—that I had resolved to choose a new career, resolved to leave the old paths, to break away from the past, and begin a new life at Eckhof's side."

"My child at the side of a comedian!" cried the old doctor contemptuously. "Yes, I remember that was written, but I believed it not, and therefore have I come. Was your letter true? Did you write the truth to Ervelman?"

Lupinus cast his eyes down, and gave his hand to his father. "No," said he, "it was not true; it was a fantasy of fever. It is past, and I have recovered. To-morrow, after I receive my diploma, I will accompany you home, and you, friend, will go with us."

The next day the students rushed in crowds to the university to listen to the discourse of the learned and worthy Herr Lupinus. Not only the students and the professors, but many other persons, were assembled in the hall to honor the young man, of whom the professors said that he was not only a model of scholarship, but of modesty and virtue. Even actors were seen to grace the holy halls of science on this occasion, and the students laughed with delight and cried "Bravo!" as they recognized near Fredersdorf the noble and sharp profile of Eckhof. They had often rushed madly to the theatre; why should he not sometimes honor the university?

But Eckhof was indifferent to the joyful greeting of the students; he gazed steadily toward the door, through which his young friend must enter the hall; and now, as the hour struck, he stooped over Fredersdorf and seized his hand.

"Friend," said he, "a wondrous anxiety oppresses me. It seems to me I am in the presence of a sphinx, who is in the act of solving a great mystery! I am a coward, and would take refuge in flight, but curiosity binds me to my seat."

"You promised poor Lupinus to be here," said Fredersdorf, earnestly. "It is, perhaps, the last friendly service you can ever show him— Ah! there he is."

A cry of surprise burst from the lips of all. There, in the open door, stood, not the student Lupinus, but a young maiden, in a white satin robe—a young maiden with the pale, thoughtful, gentle face of Lupinus. A man stood on each side of her, and she leaned upon the arm of one of them, as if for support, as they walked slowly through the room. Her large eyes wandered questioningly and anxiously over the audience; and now, her glance met Eckhof's, and a deadly pallor covered her face. She tried to smile, and bowed her head in greeting.

"This is the secret from which I wished to fly," murmured Eckhof. "I guessed it yesterday."

"I knew it long since," said Fredersdorf, sadly; "it was my most beautiful and cherished dream that your hearts should find and love each other. Have I not often told you that Lupinus was not your friend, but your bride; that no woman would ever love you as he did? You would not understand me. Your heart was of stone, and her happiness has been crushed by it."

"Poor, unhappy girl!" sighed Eckhof, and tears ran slowly down his cheeks. "I have acted the part of a barbarian toward you! Yesterday with smiling lips I pressed a dagger in her heart; she did not curse, but blessed me!"

"Listen! she speaks!"

It was the maiden's father who spoke. In simple phrase he asked forgiveness of the Faculty, for having dared to send them a daughter, in place of a son. But it had been his cherished wish to prove that only the arrogance and prejudice of men had banished women from the universities. Heaven had denied him a son. He had soon discovered that his daughter was rarely endowed; he determined to educate her as a son, and thus repair the loss fate had prepared for him. His daughter entered readily into his plans, and solemnly swore to guard her secret until she had completed her studies. She had fulfilled this promise, and now stood here to ask the Faculty if they would grant a woman a diploma.

The professors spoke awhile with each other, and then announced to the audience that Lupinus had been the most industrious and promising of all their students; the pride and favorite of all the professors. The announcement that she was a woman would make no change in her merit or their intentions; that the maiden *Lupina* would be received by them with as much joy and satisfaction as the youth *Lupinus* would have been. The disputation might now begin.

A murmur of applause was heard from the benches, and now the clear, soft, but slightly trembling voice of the young girl commenced to read. How strangely did the heavy, pompous Latin words contrast with the slight, fairy form of the youthful girl! She stood adorned like a bride, in satin array; not like a bride of earth, inspired by love, but a bride of heaven, in the act of laying down before God's altar all her earthly hopes and passions! She felt thus. She dedicated herself to a joyless and unselfish existence at the altar of science; she would not lead an idle, useless, musing, cloister-life. With a holy oath she swore to serve her race; to soothe the pain of those who suffered; to stand by the sick-beds of women and children; to give that love to suffering, weeping humanity which she had once consecrated to one alone, and which had come home, like a bleeding dove, with broken wings, powerless and hopeless!

The disputation was at an end. The deacon declared the maiden, Dorothea Christine Lupinus, a doctor. The students uttered wild applause, and the professors drew near the old Lupinus, to congratulate him, and to renew the acquaintance of former days.

The fair young Bride of Arts thought not of this. She looked toward Eckhof; their glances were rooted in each other firmly but tearlessly. She waved to him with her hand, and obedient to her wish he advanced to the door, then turned once more; their eyes met, and she had the courage to look softly upon the friend of her youth, Ervelman, who had accompanied her father, and say:

"I will fulfil my father's vow—I will be a faithful wife. Look, you, Ervelman, the star has gone out which blinded my eyes, and now I see again clearly." She pointed, with a trembling hand, to Eckhof, who was disappearing.

"Friend," said Eckhof, to Fredersdorf, "if the gods truly demand a great sacrifice as a propitiation, I think I have offered one this day. I have cast my Polycrates' ring into the sea, and a part of my heart's blood was cleaving to it. May fate be reconciled, and grant me the happiness this pale and lovely maiden has consecrated with her tears. Farewell, Christine, farewell! Our paths in life are widely separated. Who knows, perhaps we will meet again in heaven? You belong to the saints, and I am a poor comedian, who makes a false show throughout a wild, tumultuous life, with some pompous shreds and tatters of art and beauty, to whom, perhaps, the angels in heaven will deny a place, even as the priests on earth deny him a grave." *

CHAPTER XII.

TRENCK'S FIRST FLIGHT.

"This is, then, the day of his liberation?" said Princess Amelia to her confidante, Mademoiselle von Haak. "To-day, after five months of torture, he will again be free, will again enjoy life and liberty. And to me, happy princess, will he owe all these blessings; to me, whom God has permitted to survive all these torments, that I might be the means of effecting his deliverance, for, without doubt, our work will succeed, will it not?"

"Undoubtedly," said Ernestine von Haak; "we shall and must succeed."

"Let us reconsider the whole plan, if only to enliven the tedious hours with pleasant thought. When the commandant of the prison, Major von Doo, pays the customary Sunday-morning visit to Trenck's cell, and while he is carefully examining every nook to assure himself that the captive nobleman has not been endeavoring to make a pathway to liberty, Trenck will suddenly overpower him, deprive him of his sword, and rush past him out of the cell. At the door he will be met by the soldier Nicolai, who is in our confidence, and will not seem to notice his escape. Once over the palisades, he will find a horse, which we have placed in readiness. Concealed by the military cloak thrown over him, and armed with the pistols with which his saddle-holsters have been furnished, he will fly on the wings of the wind toward Bohemia. Near the border, at the village of Lönnschütz, a second horse will await him. He will mount and hurry on

---

* Eckhof lived to awake respect and love for the national theatre throughout all Germany. He had his own theatre in Gotha, where he was born, and where he died in 1778. He performed the double service of exalting the German stage, and obtaining for the actors consideration and respect.

until the boundary and liberty are obtained. All seems so safe, Ernestine, so easy of execution, that I can scarcely believe in the possibility of a failure."

"It will not fail," said Ernestine von Haak. "Our scheme is good, and will be ably assisted—it must succeed."

"Provided he find the places where the horses stand concealed."

"These he cannot fail to find. They are accurately designated in a little note which my lover, when he has charge of the prison-yard, will contrive to convey to him. Schnell's known fidelity vouches for the horses being in readiness. As your royal highness was not willing that we should enlist accomplices among the soldiers, the only question that need give us uneasiness is this: Will Trenck be able to overcome unaided all obstacles within the fortifications?"

"No," said Amelia, proudly; "Trenck shall be liberated, but I will not corrupt my brother's soldiers. To do the first, is my right and my duty, for I love Trenck. Should I do the second, I would be guilty of high treason to my king, and this even love could not excuse. Only to himself and to me shall Trenck owe his freedom. Our only allies shall be my means and his own strength. He has the courage of a hero and the strength of a giant. He will force his way through his enemies like Briareus; they will fall before him like grain before the reaper. If he cannot kill them all with his sword, he will annihilate them with the lightning of his glances, for a heavenly power dwells in his eyes. Moreover, your lover writes that he is beloved by the officers of the garrison, that all the soldiers sympathize with him. It is well that it is not necessary to bribe them with miserable dross; Trenck has already bribed them with his youth and manly beauty, his misfortunes and his amiability. He will find no opposition; no one will dispute his passage to liberty."

"God grant that it may be as your highness predicts!" said Ernestine, with a sigh.

"Four days of uncertainty are still before us—would that they had passed!" exclaimed Princess Amelia. "I have no doubts of his safety, but I fear I shall not survive these four days of anxiety. Impatience will destroy me.

I had the courage to endure misery, but I feel already that the expectation of happiness tortures me. God grant, at least, that his freedom is secured!"

"Never speak of dying with the rosy cheeks and sparkling eyes your highness has to-day," said Mademoiselle von Haak, with a smile. "Your increasing pallor, caused no doubt by your grief, has given me much pain. I am no longer uneasy, however, for you have recovered health and strength, now that you are again hopeful. As for the four days of expectancy, we will kill them with merry laughter, gayety, and dancing. Does not the queen give a ball to-day? is there not a masquerade at the opera to-morrow? For the last five months your highness has taken part in these festivities because you were compelled; you will now do so of your own accord. You will no longer dance because the king commands, but because you are young, happy, and full of hope for the future. On the first and second day you will dance and fatigue yourself so much, that you will have the happiness of sleeping a great deal on the third. The fourth day will dawn upon your weary eyes, and whisper in your ear that Trenck is free, and that it is you who have given him his freedom."

"Yes, let us be gay, let us laugh, dance, and be merry," exclaimed Princess Amelia. "My brother shall be satisfied with me; he need no longer regard me in so gloomy and threatening a manner; I will laugh and jest, I will adorn myself, and surpass all the ladies with the magnificence of my attire and my sparkling eyes. Come, Ernestine, come. We will arrange my toilet for this evening. It shall be magnificent. I will wear flowers in my hair and flowers on my breast, but no pearls. Pearls signify tears, and I will weep no more."

Joyously she danced through the room, drawing her friend to the boudoir; joyously she passed the three following days of expectation; joyously she closed her eyes on the evening of the third day, to see, in her dreams, her lover kneeling at her feet, thanking her for his liberty, and vowing eternal fidelity and gratitude.

Amelia greeted the fourth day with a happy smile, never doubting but that it would bring her glad tidings. But hours passed away, and still Mademoiselle von Haak did not appear. Amelia had said to her: "I do not wish to see you to-morrow until you can bring me good news. This will, however, be in your power at an early hour, and you shall flutter into my chamber with these tidings, like the dove with the olive-branch."

Mademoiselle von Haak has still not yet arrived. But now the door opens—she is there, but her face is pale, her eyes tearful; and this pale lady in black, whose noble and beautiful features recall to Amelia such charming and delightful remembrances—who is she? What brings her here? Why does she hurry forward to the princess with streaming eyes? Why does she kneel, raise her hands imploringly, and whisper, "Mercy, Princess Amelia, mercy!"

Amelia rises from her seat, pale and trembling, gazes with widely extended eyes at the kneeling figure, and, almost speechless with terror, asks in low tones, "Who are you, madame? What do you desire of me?"

The pale woman at her feet cries in heart-rending accents, "I am the mother of the unfortunate Frederick von Trenck, and I come to implore mercy at the hands of your royal highness. My son attempted to escape, but God did not favor his undertaking. He was overtaken by misfortune, after having overcome almost all obstacles, when nothing but the palisades separated him from liberty and safety; he was attacked by his pursuers, disarmed, and carried back to prison, wounded and bleeding." *

Amelia uttered a cry of horror, and fell back on her seat pale and breathless, almost senseless. Mademoiselle von Haak took her gently in her arms, and, amid her tears, whispered words of consolation, of sympathy, and of hope. But Amelia scarcely heeded her; she looked down vacantly upon the pallid, weeping woman who still knelt at her feet.

"Have mercy, princess, have mercy! You alone can assist me; therefore have I come to you; therefore have I entreated Mademoiselle von Haak with tears until she could no longer refuse to conduct me to your presence. Regardless, at last, of etiquette and ceremony, she permitted me to fall at your feet, and to cry to you for help. You are an

* Trenck's Biography, i., 80.

angel of goodness and mercy; pity an unfortunate mother, who wishes to save her son!"

"And you believe that I can do this?" said Amelia, breathlessly.

"You alone, royal highness, have the power to save my son's life!"

"Tell me by what means, countess, and I will save him, if it costs my heart's blood."

"Conduct me to the king. That is all that I require of you. He has not yet been informed of my son's unfortunate attempt. I must be the first to bring him this intelligence. I will confess that it was I who assisted my son in this attempt, who bribed the non-commissioned officer, Nicolai, with flattery and tears, with gold and promises; that it was I who placed the horses and loaded pistols in readiness beyond the outer palisade; that I sent my son the thousand ducats which were found on his person; that I wrote him the letter containing vows of eternal love and fidelity. The king will pardon a mother who, in endeavoring to liberate her son, left no means of success untried."

"You are a noble, a generous woman!" exclaimed the princess, with enthusiasm. "You are worthy to be Trenck's mother! You say that I must save him, and you have come to save me! But I will not accept this sacrifice; I will not be cowardly and timidly silent, when you have the courage to speak. Let the king know all; let him know that Trenck was not the son, but the lover of her who endeavored to give him his freedom, and that—"

"If you would save him, be silent! The king can be merciful when it was the mother who attempted to liberate the son; he will be inexorable if another has made this mad attempt; and, above all, if he cannot punish the transgressor, my son's punishment will be doubled."

"Listen to her words, princess, adopt her counsel," whispered the weeping Ernestine. "Preserve yourself for the unfortunate Trenck; protect his friends by your silence, and we may still hope to form a better and happier plan of escape."

"Be it so," said the princess with a sigh. "I will bring him this additional sacrifice. I will be silent. God knows that I would willingly lay down my life for him. I would find this easier than to veil my love in cowardly silence. Come, I will conduct you to the king."

"But I have not yet told your royal highness that the king is in his library, and has ordered that no one should be admitted to his presence."

"I will be admitted. I will conduct you through the private corridor and the king's apartments, and not by the way of the grand antechamber. Come."

She seized the countess's hand and led her away.

The king was alone in his library, sitting at a table covered with books and papers, busily engaged in writing. From time to time he paused, and thoughtfully regarded what he had written. "I have commenced a new work, which it is to be hoped will be as great a success in the field of science as several that I have achieved with the sword on another field. I know my wish and my aim; I have undertaken a truly noble task. I will write the history of my times, not in the form of memoirs, nor as a commentary, but as a free, independent, and impartial history. I will describe the decline of Europe, and will endeavor to portray the follies and weaknesses of her rulers.* My respected colleagues, the kings and princes, have provided me with rich materials for a ludicrous picture. To do this work justice, the pencil of a Höllenbreughel and the pen of a Thucydides were desirable. Ah! glory is so piquant a dish, that the more we indulge, the more we thirst after its enjoyment. Why am I not satisfied with being called a good general? why do I long for the honor of being crowned in the capitol? Well, it certainly will not be his holiness the pope who crowns me or elevates me to the rank of a saint—truly, I am not envious of such titles. I shall be contented if posterity shall call me a good prince, a brave soldier, and a good lawgiver, and forgives me for having sometimes mounted the Pegasus instead of the war horse."

With a merry smile, the king now resumed his writing. The door which communicated with his apartments was opened softly, and Princess Amelia, her countenance pale

* The king's own words. "Œuvres posthumes: Correspondance avec Voltaire."

and sorrowful, looked searchingly into the room. Seeing that the king was still writing, she knocked gently. The king turned hastily and angrily.

"Did I not say that I desired to be alone?" said he, indignantly. Perceiving his sister, he now arose, an expression of anxiety pervading his countenance. "Ah, my sister! your sad face proclaims you the bearer of bad news," said he; "and very important it must have been to bring you unannounced to my presence."

"My brother, misfortune has always the privilege of coming unannounced to the presence of princes, to implore pity and mercy at their hands. I claim this holy privilege for the unfortunate lady who has prayed for my intercession in her behalf. Sire, will you graciously accord her an audience?"

"Who is she?" asked the king, discontentedly.

"Sire, it is the Countess Lostange," said Amelia, in a scarcely audible voice.

"The mother of the rebellious Lieutenant von Trenck!" exclaimed the king, in an almost threatening tone, his eyes flashing angrily.

"Yes, it is the mother of the unfortunate Von Trenck who implores mercy of your majesty!" exclaimed the countess, falling on her knees at the threshold of the door.

The king recoiled a step, and his eye grew darker. "Really, you obtain your audiences in a daring manner—you conquer them, and make the princess your herald."

"Sire, I was refused admission. In the anguish of my heart, I turned to the princess, who was generous enough to incur the displeasure of her royal brother for my sake."

"And was that which you had to say really so urgent?"

"Sire, for five months has my son been languishing in prison, and you ask if there is an urgent necessity for his mother's appeal. My son has incurred your majesty's displeasure; why, I know not. He is a prisoner, and stands accused of I know not what. Be merciful—let me know his crime, that I may endeavor to atone for it."

"Madame, a mother is not responsible for her son; a woman cannot atone for a man's crimes. Leave your son to his destiny; it may be a brighter one at some future day,

20

if he is wise and prudent, and heeds the warning which is now knocking at his benighted heart." At these words, the king's glance rested for a moment on the countenance of the princess, as if this warning had also been intended for her.

"It is, then, your majesty's intention to cheer a mother's heart with hope? My son will not be long a captive. You will pardon him for this crime of which I have no knowledge, and which you do not feel inclined to mention."

"Shall I make it known to you, madame?" said the king, with severity. "He carried on an imprudent and treasonable correspondence, and if tried by court-martial, would be found guilty of high treason. But, in consideration of his youth, and several extenuating circumstances with which I alone am acquainted, I will be lenient with him. Be satisfied with this assurance: in a year your son will be free; and when solitude has brought him to reflection, and the consciousness of his crime, when he is more humble and wiser, I will again be a gracious king to him.* Write this to your son, madame, and receive my best wishes for yourself."

"Oh, sire, you do not yet know all. I have another confession to make, and—"

A light knock at the door communicating with the antechamber interrupted her, and a voice from the outside exclaimed: "Sire, a courier with important dispatches from Silesia."

"Retire to the adjoining apartment, and wait there," said the king, turning to his sister.

Both ladies left the room.

"Dispatches from Silesia," whispered the countess. "The king will now learn all, I fear."

"Well, if he does," said the princess, almost defiantly, "we are here to save him, and we will save him."

A short time elapsed; then the door was violently thrown open, and the king appeared on the threshold, his eyes flashing with anger.

"Madame," said he, pointing to the papers which he held in his hand, "from these papers I have undoubtedly learned what it was your intention to have communicated to me. Your son has attempted to escape from prison like a cowardly

* Trenck's Memoirs, i., 82.

criminal, a malefactor weighed down with guilt.   In this attempt he has killed and wounded soldiers, disarmed the governor of the fortress, and, in his insolent frenzy, has endeavored to scale the palisades in broad daylight.   Madame, nothing but the consciousness of his own guilt could have induced him to attempt so daring a flight, and he must have had criminal accomplices who advised him to this step—accomplices who bribed the sentinel on duty before his door; who secretly conveyed money to him, and held horses in readiness for his flight.   Woe to them if I should ever discover the criminals who treasonably induced my soldiers and officers to break their oath of fidelity!"

"I, your majesty, I was this criminal," said the countess. "A mother may well dare to achieve the freedom of her son at any price.   It is her privilege to defend him with any weapon.   I bribed the soldiers, placed the horses in readiness, and conveyed money to my son.   It was Trenck's mother who endeavored to liberate him."

"And you have only brought him to greater, to more hopeless misery!   For now, madame, there can be no mercy. The fugitive, the deserter, has forfeited the favor of his king.   Shame, misery, and perpetual captivity will henceforth be his portion.   This is my determination.   Hope for no mercy.   The articles of war condemn the deserter to death.   I will give him his life, but freedom I cannot give him, for I now know that he would abuse it.   Farewell."

"Mercy! mercy for my son!" sobbed the countess. "He is so young! he has a long life before him."

"A life of remorse and repentance," said the king with severity.   "I will accord him no other.   Go!"

He was on the point of reëntering the library.   A hand was laid on his shoulder; he turned and saw the pale countenance of his sister.

"My brother," said the princess, in a firm voice, "permit me to speak with you alone for a moment.   Proceed, I will follow you."

Her bearing was proud, almost dictatorial.   Her sternly tranquil manner, her clear and earnest brow, showed plainly that she had formed an heroic determination.   She was no longer the young girl, timidly praying for her lover; she was the fearless woman, determined to defend him, or die for him. The king read this in her countenance, it was plainly indicated in her royal bearing; and with the reverence and consideration which great spirits ever accord to misfortune, he did homage to this woman toward whom he was so strongly drawn by sympathy and pity.

"Come, my sister, come," said he, offering his hand.

Amelia did not take his hand; by his side she walked into the library, and softly locked the door behind her. One moment she rested against the wall, as if to gather strength. The king hastily crossed the room, and looked out at the window. Hearing the rustle of her dress behind him, he turned and advanced toward the princess. She regarded him fixedly with cold and tearless eyes.

"Is it sufficient if I promise never to see him again?" said she.

"The promise is superfluous, for I will make a future meeting impossible."

She inclined her head slightly, as if this answer had been expected.

"Is it enough if I swear never to write to him again, nevermore to give him a token of my love?"

"I would not believe this oath. If I set him at liberty he would compromise you and your family, by boasting of a love which yielded to circumstances and necessity only, and not to reason and indifference. I will make you no reproaches at present, for I think your conscience is doing that for me. But this much I will say: I will not set him at liberty until he no longer believes in your love."

"Will you liberate him if I rob him of this belief? If I hurl the broken bond of my promised faith in his face? If I tell him that fear and cowardice have extinguished my love, and that I bid him farewell forever?"

"Write him this, and I promise you that he shall be free in a few months; but, understand me well, free to go where he will, but banished from my kingdom."

"Shall I write at once?" said she with an expression of utter indifference, and with icy tranquillity.

"Write; you will find all that is necessary on my *escritoire*."

She walked composedly to the table and seated herself. When she commenced writing, a deathly pallor came over her face; her breath came and went hurriedly and painfully. The king stood near, regarding her with an expression of deep solicitude.

"Have you finished?" said he, as she pushed the paper aside on which she had been writing.

"No," said she calmly, "it was only a tear that had fallen on the paper. I must begin again." And with perfect composure she took another sheet of paper, and began writing anew.

The king turned away with a sigh. He felt that if he longer regarded this pale, resigned face, he would lose sight of reason and duty, and restore to her her lover. He again advanced to the window, and looked thoughtfully out at the sky. "Is it possible? can it be?" he asked himself. "May I forget my duties as head of my family, and only remember that she is my sister, and that she is suffering and weeping? Must we then all pay for this empty grandeur, this frippery of earthly magnificence, with our heart's blood and our best hopes? And if I now deprive her of her dreams of happiness, what compensation can I offer? With what can I replace her hopes, her love, the happiness of her youth? At the best, with a little earthly splendor, with the purple and the crown, and eventually, perhaps, with my love. Yes, I will love her truly and cordially; she shall forgive the brother for the king's harshness; she shall—"

"I have finished," said the sad voice of his sister.

The king turned from the window; Amelia stood at the *escritoire*, holding the paper on which she had been writing in one hand, and sustaining herself by the table with the other.

"Read what you have written," said the king, approaching her.

The princess bowed her head and read:

"I pity you, but your misfortune is irremediable; and I cannot and will not attempt to alleviate it, for fear of compromising myself. This is, therefore, my last letter—I can risk nothing more for you. Do not attempt to write to me, for I should return your letter unopened. Our separation must be forever, but I will always remain your friend; and if I can ever serve you hereafter, I will do so gladly. Farewell, unhappy friend, you deserve a better fate." *

"That is all?" said the king, as his sister ceased reading.

"That is all, sire."

"And you imagine that he will no longer believe in your love, when he receives this letter?" said the king, with a sad smile.

"I am sure he will not, for I tell him in this letter that I will risk nothing more for him; that I will not even attempt to alleviate his misery. Only when one is cowardly enough to sacrifice love to selfish fears, could one do this. I shall have purchased his liberty with his contempt."

"What would you have written if you had been permitted to follow the promptings of your heart?"

A rosy hue flitted over her countenance, and love beamed in her eyes. "I would have written, 'Believe in me, trust in me! For henceforth the one aim of my life will be to liberate you. Let me die when I have attained this aim, but die in the consciousness of having saved you, and of having been true to my love.'"

"You would have written that?"

"I would have written that," said she, proudly and joyfully. "And the truth of that letter he would not have doubted."

"Oh, woman's heart!" inexhaustible source of love and devotion!" murmured the king, turning away to conceal his emotion from his sister.

"Is this letter sufficient?" demanded the princess. "Shall Trenck be free?"

"I have promised it, and will keep my word. Fold the letter and direct it. It shall be forwarded at once."

"And when will he be free?"

"I cannot set him at liberty immediately. It would be setting my officers a bad example. But in three months he shall be free."

"In three months, then. Here is the letter, sire."

The king took the letter and placed it in his bosom.

* Trenck's Memoirs, i., 86.

And now, my sister, come to my heart," said he, holding out his arms. "The king was angry with you, the brother will weep with you. Come, Amelia, come to your brother's heart."

Amelia did not throw herself in his arms; she stood still, and seemed not to have heard, not to have understood his words.

"I pray that your majesty will allow me to retire," said she. "I think we have finished—we have to other business to transact."

"Oh! my sister," said Frederick, mournfully, "think of what you are doing; do not harden your heart against me. Believe me, I suffer with you; and if the only question were the sacrifice of my personal wishes, I would gladly yield. But I must consider my ancestors, the history of my house, and the prejudices of the world. Amelia, I cannot, I dare not do otherwise. Forgive me, my sister. And now, once more, let us hold firmly to each other in love and trust. Let me fold you to my heart."

He advanced and extended his hand, but his sister slowly recoiled.

"Allow me to remind your majesty that a poor unhappy woman is awaiting a word of consolation in the next room, and that this woman is Trenck's mother. She, at least, will be happy when I inform her that her son will soon be free. Permit me, therefore, sire, to take my leave, and bear her this good news."

She bowed formally and profoundly, and walked slowly across the room. The king no longer endeavored to hold her back. He followed her with a mournful, questioning glance, still hoping that she would turn and seek a reconciliation. She reached the door, now she turned. The king stepped forward rapidly, but Princess Amelia bowed ceremoniously and disappeared.

"Lost! I have lost her," sighed the king. "Oh, my God! must I then part from all that I love? Was it not enough to lose my friends by death? will cruel fate also rob me of a loved and living sister? Ah! I am a poor, a wretched man, and yet they call me a king."

Frederick slowly seated himself, and covered his face

with his hands. He remained in this position for a long time, his sighs being the only interruption to the silence which reigned in the apartment.

"Work! I will work," said he proudly. "This is at least a consolation, and teaches forgetfulness."

He walked hurriedly to his *escritoire*, seated himself, and regarded the manuscripts and papers which lay before him. He took up one of the manuscripts and began to read, but with an impatient gesture he soon laid it aside.

"The letters swim before my eyes in inextricable confusion. My God, how hard it is to do one's duty!"

He rested his head on his hand, and was lost in thought for a long time. Gradually his expression brightened, and a wondrous light beamed in his eyes.

"Yes," said he, with a smile, "yes, so it shall be. I have just lost a much-loved sister. Well, it is customary to erect a monument in memory of those we love. Poor, lost sister, I will erect a monument to your memory. The king has been compelled to make his sister unhappy, and for this he will endeavor to make his people happy. And if there is no law to which a princess can appeal against the king, there shall at least be laws for all my subjects, which protect them, and are in strict accordance with reason, with justice, and the godly principle of equality. Yes, I will give my people a new code of laws.* This, Amelia, shall be the monument which I will erect to you in my heart. In this very hour I will write to Cocceji, and request him to sketch the outlines of this new code of laws."

The king seized his pen and commenced writing. "The judges," said he, hastily penning his words, "the judges must administer equal and impartial justice to all without respect to rank or wealth, as they expect to answer for the same before the righteous judgment-seat of God, and in order that the sighs of the widows and orphans, and of all that are oppressed, may not be visited upon themselves and their children. No rescripts, although issued from this cabinet, shall be deemed worthy of the slightest consideration, if they contain aught manifestly incompatible with equity, or if the strict course of justice is thereby hindered or interrupted;

* Rödenbeck, Diary, p. 187.

but the judges shall proceed according to the dictates of duty and conscience."

The king continued writing, his countenance becoming more and more radiant with pleasure, while his pen flew over the paper. He was so completely occupied with his thoughts that he did not hear the door open behind him, and did not perceive the merry and intelligent face of his favorite, General Rothenberg, looking in.

The king wrote on. Rothenberg stooped and placed something which he held in his arms on the floor. He looked over toward the king, and then at the graceful little greyhound which stood quietly before him. This was no other than the favorite dog of the king, which had been lost and a captive.*

The little Biche stood still for a moment, looking around intelligently, and then ran lightly across the apartment, sprang upon the table and laid its forepaw on the king's neck.

"Biche, my faithful little friend, is it you?" said Frederick, throwing his pen aside and taking the little animal in his arms. Biche began to bark with delight, nestle closely to her master, and look lovingly at him with her bright little eyes. And the king—he inclined his face on the head of his faithful little friend, and tears ran slowly down his cheeks.†

"You have not forgotten me, my little Biche? Ah, if men were true, and loved me as you do, my faithful little dog, I should be a rich, a happy king!"

General Rothenberg still stood at the half-opened door. "Sire, said he, "is it only Biche who has the *grandes* and *petites entrées*, or have I also?"

"Ah, it was then you who brought Biche?" said Frederick, beckoning to the general to approach.

"Yes, sire, it was I, but I almost regret having done so, for I perceive that Biche is a dangerous rival, and I am jealous of her."

* The greyhound had fallen into the hands of the Austrians at the battle of Sohr, and had been presented by General Nadasti to his wife as a trophy. When this lady learned that Biche had been a pet of the king, she at first refused to give it up; and only after several demands, and with much difficulty, could she be induced to return it. Rödenbeck, Diary, p. 126.

† Müchler, "Frederick the Great," p. 350. Rödenbeck, Diary, p. 137.

" You are my best gentleman-friend, and Biche is my best lady-friend," said the king, laughing. " I shall never forget that Biche on one occasion might have discovered me to the Austrians, and did not betray me, as thousands of men would have done in her place. Had she barked at the time when I had concealed myself under the bridge, while the regiment of pandours was passing over, I should have been lost. But she conquered herself. From love to me she renounced her instincts, and was silent. She nestled close to my side, regarding me with her discreet little eyes, and licking my hand lovingly. Ah, my friend, dogs are better and truer than mankind, and the so-called images of God could learn a great deal from them! "

CHAPTER XIII.

THE FLIGHT.

TWO months had passed since Trenck's last attempted escape; two months of anguish, of despair. But he was not depressed, not hopeless; he had one great aim before his eyes—to be free, to escape from this prison. The commandant had just assured him he would never leave it alive.

This frightful picture of a life-long imprisonment did not terrify him, did not agitate a nerve or relax a muscle. He felt his blood bounding in fiery streams through his veins. With a merry laugh and sparkling eye he declared that no man could be imprisoned during his whole life who felt himself strong enough to achieve his freedom.

" I have strength and endurance like Atlas. I can bear the world on my shoulders, and shall I never be able to burst these doors and gates, to surmount these miserable fortress walls which separate me from liberty, the world of action, the golden sunshine? No, no, before the close of this year I shall be free. Yes, free! free to fly to her and give her back this letter, and ask her if she did truly write it? if these cold words came from her heart? No, some one has dared to imitate her writing, and thus deprive me of the only ray of sunshine which enters my dark prison. I must be free in order to know this. I will believe in nothing which I do not see written in her beautiful face; only when her lips speak these fearful words, will I believe them. I must be free, and until then I must forget all other things, even this terrible letter. My thoughts, my eyes, my heart, my soul, must have but one aim—my liberty!"

Alas! the year drew near its close, and the goal was not reached; indeed, the difficulties were greatly increased. The commandant, Von Fouquet, had just received stern orders from Berlin; the watch had been doubled, and the officers in the citadel had been peremptorily forbidden to enter the cell of the prisoner, or in any way to show him kindness or attention.

The officers loved the young and cheerful prisoner; by his fresh and hopeful spirit, his gay laugh and merry jest, he had broken up the everlasting monotony of their garrison-life; by his powerful intellect and rich fancy he had, in some degree, dissipated their weariness and stupidity. They felt pity for his youth, his beauty, his geniality, his energetic self-confidence; his bold courage imposed upon them, and they were watching curiously and anxiously to see the *finale* of this contest between the poor, powerless, imprisoned youth, and the haughty, stern commander, who had sworn to Trenck that he should not succeed in making even an attempt to escape, to which Trenck had laughingly replied:

"I will not only make an attempt to escape, I will fly in defiance of all guards, and all fortress walls, and all commandants. I inhale already the breath of liberty which is wafted through my prison. Do you not see how the Goddess of Liberty, with her enchanting smile, stands at the head of my wretched bed, sings her sweet evening songs to the poor prisoner, and wakes him in the early morning with the sound of trumpets? Oh, sir commandant, Liberty loves me, and soon will she take me like a bride in her fair arms, and bear me off to freedom!"

The commandant had doubled the guard, and forbidden the officers, under heavy penalty, to have any intercourse with Trenck. Formerly, the officers who had kept watch over Trenck, had been allowed to enter, to remain and eat with

him; now the door was closed against them, the major kept
the key, and Trenck's food was handed him through the window.* But this window was large, and the officer on guard
could put his head in and chat awhile with the prisoner.
The major had the principal key, but the officer had a night-
key, and, by this means, entered often in the evenings and
passed a few hours with the prisoner, listening with astonishment to his plans of escape, and his dreams of a happy
future.

But they did not all come to speak of indifferent things,
and to be cheered and brightened by his gay humor. There
were some who truly loved him, and wished to give him counsel and aid. One came because he had promised his beloved
mistress, his bride, to liberate Trenck, cost what it would.
This was Lieutenant Schnell, the bridegroom of Amelia's
maid of honor. One day, thanks to the night-key, he entered Trenck's cell.

"I will stand by you, and assist you to escape. More
than that, I will fly with you. The commandant, Fouquet,
hates me—he says I know too much for an officer; that I
do not confine myself to my military duties, but love books,
and art, and science. He has often railed at me, and I
have twice demanded my dismissal, which he refused, and
threatened me with arrest if I should again demand it. Like
yourself, I am not free, and, like you, I wish to fly from
bondage. And now let us consult together, and arrange our
plan of escape."

"Yes," said Trenck, with a glowing countenance, and
embracing his new-found friend, "we will be unconquerable.
Like Briareus, we will have a hundred arms and a hundred
heads. When two young and powerful men unite their wills,
nothing can restrain them—nothing withstand them. Let
us make our arrangements."

The plan of escape was marked out, and was, indeed, ripe
for action. On the last day of the year, Lieutenant Schnell
was to be Trenck's night-guard, and then they would escape.
The dark shadows of night would assist them. Horses were
already engaged. There was gold to bribe the guard, and
there were loaded pistols for those who could not be tempted.

* Trenck's Memoirs.

These had been already smuggled into Trenck's cell, and concealed in the ashes of the fireplace.

And now it was Christmas eve. This was a grand festal day even for all the officers of the citadel. With the exception of the night-watch, they were all invited to dine with the commandant. A day of joy and rejoicing to all but the poor prisoner, who sat solitary in his cell, and recalled, with a sad heart, the happy days of his childhood. "The holy evening" had been to him a golden book of promise, and a munificent cornucopia of happiness and peace.

The door of his cell was hastily opened, and Schnell rushed in.

"Comrade, we are betrayed!" said he breathlessly. "Our plan of flight has been discovered. The adjutant of the commander has just secretly informed me that when the guard is changed I am to be arrested. You see, then, we are lost, unless we adopt some rash and energetic resolution."

"We will fly before the hour of your arrest," said Trenck, gayly.

"If you think that possible, so be it!" said Schnell. He drew a sword from under his mantle, and handed it to Trenck. "Swear to me upon this sword, that come what may, you will never allow me to fall alive into the hands of my enemies."

"I swear it, so truly as God will help me! And now, Schnell, take the same oath."

"I swear it! And now friend, one last grasp of the hand, and then forward. May God be with us! Hide your sword under your coat. Let us assume an indifferent and careless expression—come!"

Arm in arm, the two young men left the prison door. They appeared calm and cheerful; each one kept a hand in his bosom, and this hand held a loaded pistol.

The guard saluted the officer of the night-watch, who passed by him in full uniform. In passing, he said: "I am conducting the prisoner to the officers' room. Remain here —I will return quickly."

Slowly, quietly, they passed down the whole length of the corridor; they reached the officer's room, and opened the door. The guard walked with measured step slowly before the open door of Trenck's cell, suspecting nothing. The door closed behind the fugitives—the first step toward liberty was taken.

"And now, quickly onward to the side door. When we have passed the sentry-box, we will be at the outer works. We must spring over the palisades, and woe to the obstacle that lies in our path!—advance! forward!"

They reached the wall, they greeted fair Freedom with golden smiles, but turning a corner, they stood suddenly before the major and his adjutant!

A cry of horror burst from Schnell's lips. With one bold leap, he sprang upon the breastworks, and jumped below. With a wild shout of joy Trenck followed him. His soul bounded with rapture and gladness. He has mounted the wall, and what he finds below will be liberty in death, or liberty in life.

He lives! He stretches himself after his wondrous leap, and he is not injured—he recovers strength and presence of mind quickly.

But where is his friend? where is Schnell? There—there; he lies upon the ground, with a dislocated ankle, impossible to stand—impossible to move.

"Remember your oath, friend—kill me! I can go no farther. Here is my sword—thrust it into my bosom, and fly for your life!"

Trenck laughed gayly, took him in his arms as lovingly and tenderly as a mother. "Swing yourself on my back, friend, and clasp your arms about my neck, and hold fast. We will run a race with the reindeer."

"Trenck! Trenck! kill me. Leave me here, and hasten on. Escape is impossible with such a burden."

"You are as light as a feather, and I will die with you rather than leave you."

Onward! onward! the sun sets and a heavy fog rises suddenly from out of the earth.

"Trenck, Trenck, do you not hear the alarm-guns thundering from the citadel? Our pursuers are after us."

"I hear the cannon," said Trenck, hastening on. "We have a half hour's start."

"A half hour will not suffice. No one has ever escaped

from Glatz who did not have two hours' advance of pursuit. Leave me, Trenck, and save yourself."

"I will not leave you. I would rather die with you. Let us rest a moment, and gather breath."

Gently, carefully, he laid his friend upon the ground. Schnell suppressed his cries of pain, and Trenck restrained his panting breath—they rested and listened. The white, soft mist settled more thickly around them. The citadel and the town was entirely hidden from view.

"God is with us," said Trenck. "He covers us with an impenetrable veil, and conceals us from our enemies."

"God is against us—our flight was too soon discovered. Already the whole border is alarmed. Listen to the signals in every village. The three shots from the citadel have announced that a prisoner has escaped. The commanding officers are now flying from point to point, to see if the peasants are doing duty, and if every post is strictly guarded. The cordon is alarmed; the whole Bohemian boundary has been signalled. It is too late—we cannot reach the border."

"We will not go then, friend, in the direction our enemies expect us," said Trenck, merrily. "They saw us running toward the Bohemian boundary, and they will follow in that direction through night and fog. We will fly where they are not seeking us—we will cross the Reise. Do you see there a line of silver shimmering through the fog, and advancing to meet us? Spring upon my back, Schnell. We must cross the Reise!"

"I cannot, Trenck, I suffer agony with my foot. It is impossible for me to swim."

"I can swim for both."

He knelt down, took his friend upon his back, and ran with him to the river. And now they stood upon the shore. Solemnly, drearily, the waves dashed over their feet, sweeping onward large blocks of ice which obstructed the current.

"Is the river deep, comrade?"

"In the middle of the stream, deep enough to cover a giant like yourself."

"Onward, then! When I can no longer walk, I can swim. Hold fast, Schnell!"

Onward, in the dark, ice-cold water, bravely onward, with

his friend upon his back! Higher and higher rose the waves! Now they reached his shoulder!

"Hold fast to my hair, Schnell, we must swim!"

With herculean strength he swam through the dark, wild waters, and dashed the ice-blocks which rushed against him from his path.

Now they have reached the other shore. Not yet safe— but safe from immediate danger. The blessed night conceals their course, and their pursuers seek them on the other shore.

Suddenly the fog is dispersed; a rough bleak wind freezes the moisture in the atmosphere, and the moon rose in cloudless majesty in the heavens. It was a cold, clear December night, and the wet clothes of the fugitives were frozen stiff, like a harness, upon them. Trenck felt neither cold nor stiff; he carried his friend upon his shoulders, and that kept him warm; he walked so rapidly, his limbs could not stiffen.

Onward, ever onward to the mountains! They reached the first hill, under whose protecting shadows they sank down to rest, and take counsel together.

"Trenck, I suffer great agony; I implore you to leave me here and save yourself. In a few hours you can pass the border. Leave me, then, and save yourself!"

"I will never desert a friend in necessity. Come, I am refreshed."

He took up his comrade and pressed on. The moon had concealed herself behind the clouds; the cold, cutting winds howled through the mountains. Stooping, Trenck waded on through the snow. He was scarcely able now to hold himself erect. Hope inspired him with strength and courage—they had wandered far, they must soon reach the border.

Day broke! the pale rays of the December sun melted the mountain vapors into morning. The two comrades were encamped upon the snow, exhausted with their long march, hopefully peering here and there after the Bohemian boundary.

"Great God! what is that? Are not those the towers of Glatz? and that dark spectre which raises itself so threateningly against the horizon, is not that the citadel?"

And so it was. The poor fugitives have wandered round

and round the whole night through, and they are now, alas! exactly where they started.

"We are lost," murmured Schnell; "there is no hope!"

"No, we are not lost!" shouted Trenck; "we have young, healthy limbs, and weapons. They shall never take us alive."

"But we cannot escape them. Our appearance will instantly betray us; I am in full uniform, and you in your red coat of the body-guard, both of us without hats. Any man would know we were deserters."

"Woe to him who calls us so! we will slay him, and walk over his dead body. And now for some desperate resolve. We cannot go backward, we must advance, and pass right through the midst of our enemies in order to reach the border. You know the way, and the whole region round about. Come, Schnell, let us hold a council of war."

"We must pass through that village in front of us. How shall we attempt to do so unchallenged?"

Half an hour later a singular couple drew near to the last house of the village. One was a severely wounded, bleeding officer of the king's body-guard; his face was covered with blood, a bloody handkerchief was bound about his brow, and his hands tied behind his back. Following him, limped an officer in full parade dress, but bareheaded. With rude, coarse words he drove the poor prisoner before him, and cried for help. Immediately two peasants rushed from the house.

"Run to the village," said the officer, "and tell the judge to have a carriage got ready immediately, that I may take this deserter to the fortress. I succeeded in capturing him, but he shot my horse, and I fear I broke a bone in falling; you see, though, how I have cut him to pieces. I think he is mortally wounded. Bring a carriage instantly, that I may take him, while yet alive, to the citadel."

One of the men started at once, the other nodded to them to enter his hut.

Stumbling and stammering out words of pain, the wounded man followed him; cursing and railing, the officer limped behind him. On entering the room, the wounded man sank upon the floor, groaning aloud. A young girl advanced hastily, and took his wounded head in her arms; while an old

21

woman, who stood upon the hearth, brought a vessel of warm milk to comfort him.

The old peasant stood at the window, and looked, with a peculiar smile, at the officer, who seated himself upon a bench near the fire, and drank the milk greedily which the old woman handed him. Suddenly the old man advanced in front of the officer and laid his hand on his shoulder.

"Your disguise is not necessary, Lieutenant Schnell, I know you; my son served in your company. There was an officer from the citadel here last night, and informed us of the two deserters. You are one, Lieutenant Schnell, and that is the other. That is Baron Trenck."

And now, the wounded man, as if cured by magic, sprang to his feet. The sound of his name had given him health and strength, and healed the wound in his forehead. He threw the handkerchief off, and rushed out, while Schnell with prayers and threats held back the old man, and entreated him to show them the nearest way to the border.

Trenck hastened to the stable—two horses were in the stalls. The young girl, who had held his head so tenderly, came up behind him.

"What are you doing, sir?" she said anxiously, as Trenck released the horses. "You will not surely take my father's horses?—if you do, I will cry aloud for help."

"If you dare to cry aloud, I will murder you," said Trenck, with flaming eyes, "and then I will kill myself! I have sworn that I will not be taken alive into the fortress. Have pity, beautiful child—your eyes are soft and kindly, and betray a tender heart. Help me—think how beautiful, how glorious is the world and life and liberty to the young! My enemies will deprive me of all this, and chain me in a cell, like a wild beast. Oh, help me to escape!"

"How can I help you?" said Mariandel, greatly touched.

"Give me saddles and bridles for these horses, in order that I may flee. I swear to you, by God and by my beloved, that they shall be returned to you!"

"You have then a sweetheart, sir?"

"I have—and she weeps day and night for me."

"I will give you the saddles in remembrance of my own

beloved, who is far away from me. Come, saddle your horse quickly—I will saddle the other."

"Now, farewell, Mariandel—one kiss at parting—farewell, compassionate child! Schnell, Schnell, quick, quick to horse, to horse!"

Schnell rushed out of the hut, the peasant after him. He saw with horror that his horses were saddled; that Schnell, in spite of his foot, had mounted one, and Trenck was seated upon the other.

"My God! will you steal my horses? Help! help!"

Mariandel laid her hand upon her father's lips, and suppressed his cries for help. "Father, he has a bride, and she weeps for him!—think upon Joseph, and let them go."

The fugitives dashed away. Their long hair fluttered in the wind, their cheeks glowed with excitement and expectation. Already the village lay far behind them. Onward, over the plains, over the meadows, over the stubble-fields!

"Schnell, Schnell, I see houses—I see towns. Schnell, there lies a city!"

"That is Wunschelburg, and we must ride directly through it, for this is the nearest way to Bohemia."

"There is a garrison there, but we must ride through them. Aha! this is royal sport! We will dash right through the circle of our enemies. They will be so amazed at our insolence, that they will allow us to escape. Hei! here are the gates—the bells are ringing for church. Onward, onward, my gallant steed, you must fly as if you had wings!"

Huzza! how the flint strikes fire! how the horses' hoofs resound on the pavement! how the gayly-dressed church-goers, who were advancing so worthily up the street, fly screaming to every side! how the lazy hussars thinking no harm, stand at the house doors, and fix their eyes with horror upon these two bold riders, who dash past them like a storm-wind!

And now they have reached the outer gate—the city lies behind them. Forward, forward, in mad haste! The horses bow, their knees give way, but the bold riders rein them up with powerful arms, and they spring onward.

Onward, still onward! "But what is that? who is this

advancing directly in front of us? Schnell, do you not know him? That is Captain Zerbtz!"

Yes, that is Captain Zerbtz, who has been sent with his hussars to arrest the fugitives; but he is alone, and his men are not in sight. He rode on just in front of them. When near enough to be heard, he said, "Brothers, hasten! Go to the left, pass that solitary house. That is the boundary-line.* My hussars have gone to the right."

He turned his horse quickly, and dashed away. The fugitives flew to the left, passed the lonely house, passed the white stone which marked the border, and now just a little farther on.

"Oh, comrade, let our horses breathe! Let us rest and thank God, for we are saved—we have passed the border!"

"We are free, free!" cried Trenck, with so loud a shout of joy that the mountains echoed with the happy sound, and reëchoed back, "Free, free!"

CHAPTER XIV.

I WILL.

SWIFTLY, noiselessly, and unheeded the days of prosperity and peace passed away. King Frederick has been happy; he does not even remember that more than two years of calm content and enjoyment have been granted him—two years in which he dared lay aside his sword, and rest quietly upon his laurels. This happy season had been rich in blessings; bringing its laughing tribute of perfumed roses and blooming myrtles. Two years of such happiness seems almost miraculous in the life of a king.

Our happy days are ever uneventful. True love is silent and retiring; it does not speak its rapture to the profane world, but hides itself in the shadows of holy solitude and starry night. Let us not, then, lift the veil with which

* Trenck's Memoirs.

King Frederick had concealed his love. These two years of bloom and fragrance shall pass by unquestioned.

When the sun is most lustrous, we turn away our eyes, lest they be blinded by his rays; but when clouds and darkness are around about us, we look up curiously and questioningly. King Frederick's sun is no longer clear and dazzling, dark clouds are passing over it; a shadow from these clouds has fallen upon the young and handsome face of the king, quenched the flashing glance of his eye, and checked the rapid beating of his heart.

What was it which made King Frederick so restless and unhappy? He did not know himself, or, rather, he would not know. An Alp seemed resting upon his heart, repressing every joyful emotion, and making exertion impossible. He sought distraction in work, and in the early morning he called his ministers to council, but his thoughts were far away; he listened without hearing, and the most important statements seemed to him trivial. He mistrusted himself, and dismissed his ministers. It was Frederick's custom to read every letter and petition himself, and write his answer upon the margin. This being done, he turned to his ordinary studies and occupations, and commenced writing in his "*Histoire de Mon Temps.*" Soon, however, he found himself gazing upon the paper, lost in wandering thoughts and wild, fantastic dreams. He threw his pen aside, and tried to lose himself in the beautiful creations of his favorite poet, all things in nature and fiction seemed alike vain.

Frederick threw his book aside in despair. "What is the matter with me?" he exclaimed angrily. "I am not myself; some wicked fairy has cast a spell about me, and bound my soul in magic fetters. I cannot work, I cannot think; content and quiet peace are banished from my breast! What does this signify? and why—" He did not complete his sentence, but gazed with breathless attention to the door. He had heard one tone of a voice without which made his heart tremble and his eyes glow with their wonted fire.

"Announce to his majesty that I am here, and plead importunately for an audience," said a soft, sweet voice.

"The king has commanded that no one shall be admitted."

"Announce me, nevertheless," said the petitioner imperiously.

"That is impossible!"

Frederick had heard enough. He stepped to the door and threw it open. "Signora, I am ready to receive you; have the goodness to enter." He stepped abruptly forward, and, giving his hand to Barbarina, led her into his cabinet.

Barbarina greeted him with a sweet smile, and gave a glance of triumph to the guard, who had dared to refuse her entrance.

The king conducted her silently to his boudoir, and nodded to her to seat herself upon the divan. But Barbarina remained standing, and fixed her great burning eyes upon his face.

"I see a cloud upon your brow, sire," said she, in a fond and flattering tone. "What poor insect has dared to vex my royal lion? Was it an insect? Was it—"

"No, no," said Frederick, interrupting her, "an angel or a devil has tortured me, and banished joy and peace from my heart. Now tell me, Barbarina, what are you? Are you a demon, come to martyr me, or an angel of light, who will transform my wild dreams of love and bliss into reality? There are hours of rapture in which I believe the latter, in which your glance of light and glory wafts my soul on golden wings into the heaven of heavens, and I say to myself, 'I am not only a king, but a god, for I have an angel by my side to minister to me.' But then, alas! come weary times in which you seem to me an evil demon, and I see in your flashing eyes that eternal hatred which you swore to cherish in the first hour of our meeting."

"Alas! does your majesty still remember that?" said Barbarina, in a tone of tender reproof.

"You have taken care that I shall not forget it. You once told me that from hatred to love was but a small step. If you have truly advanced so far, how can I be assured but you will one day step backward?"

"How can you be assured?" said she, pointing a rosy finger with indescribable grace at the king. "Ah, sire! your divine beauty, your eyes, which have borrowed lightning from Jove and glory from the sun—your brow, where majesty and wisdom sit enthroned, and that youthful and enchanting smile which illuminates the whole—all these make assurance doubly sure! I will not allude to your throne, and its pomp and power! What is it to me that you are a king? For me you are a man, a hero, a god. Had I met you as a shepherd in the fields, I should have said, 'There is a god in disguise!' The fable is verified, and 'Apollo is before me!' Apollo, I adore, I worship you! let one ray from your heavenly eyes fall upon my face!" She knelt before him, folding her hands, extended them pleadingly toward the king, and looked upon him with a ravishing smile.

The king raised her, and pressed her in his arms, then took her small head in his hands, and turning it backward, gazed searchingly in her face.

"Oh! Barbarina," said he, sadly, "to-day you are an angel, why were you a demon yesterday? Why did you martyr and torture me with your childish moods and passionate temper? Why is your heart, which can be so soft and warm, sometimes cold as an iceberg and wholly pitiless? Child! child! do you not know I have been wounded by many griefs, and that every rough word and every angry glance is like a poisoned dagger to my soul? I had looked forward with such delight to our meeting yesterday at Rothenberg's! I expected so much happiness, and I had earned it by a diligent and weary day's work. Alas! you spoiled all by your frowning brow and sullen silence. It was your fault that I returned home sad and heartless. I could not sleep, but passed the night in trying to find out the cause of your melancholy. This morning I could not work, and have robbed my kingdom and my people of the hours which properly belong to them; weak and powerless, I have been swayed wholly by gloom and discontent. What was it, Barbarina, which veiled your clear brow with frowns, and made your sweet voice so harsh and stern?"

"What was it?" said Barbarina, sadly; and resting on the arm of the king, she leaned her head back and looked up at him with half-closed eyes. "It was ambition which tortured me. But I did wrong to conceal any thing from you. I should, without sullen or angry looks, have made known the cause of my despair. I should have felt that I had only to breathe my request, and that the noble and magnanimous heart of my king would understand me. I should have known that the man who had won laurels in the broad fields of science and on the bloody battle-field, would appreciate this thirst for renown; this glowing, burning hate toward those who cross our paths and wish to share our fame!"

"Jealous? you are jealous, then, of some other *artiste*," said the king, releasing Barbarina from his arms.

"Yes, sire, I am jealous!—jealous of your smiles, of your applause; of the public voice, of the bravos, which like a golden shower have fallen upon me alone, and which I must now divide with another!"

"Of whom, then, are you jealous?" said the king.

She threw her head back proudly, a crimson blush blazed upon her cheeks, and her eyes sparkled angrily.

"Why has this Marianna Cochois been engaged? Why has Baron von Swartz put this contempt upon me?" said she fiercely. "To engage another *artiste* is to say to the world, that Barbarina no longer pleases, that she no longer has the power to enrapture the public, that her triumphs are over, and her day is past! Oh! this thought has made me wild! Is not Barbarina the first dancer of the world? Can it be that another prima donna, and not the Barbarina, is engaged for the principal *rôle* in a new and splendid ballet? Does Barbarina live, and has she not murdered the one who dared to do this, to bring this humiliation upon her?"

Tears gushed from her eyes, and sobbing loudly, she hid her face in her hands. The king gazed sadly upon her, and a weary smile played upon his lip.

"You are all alike—all," said he, bitterly, "and the great *artiste* is even as narrow-minded and pitiful as the unknown and humble; you are all weak, vain, envious, and swayed by small passions; and to think that you, Barbarina, are not an exception; that the Barbarina weeps because Marianna Cochois is to play the principal *rôle* in the new ballet, '*Toste Galanti.*'"

"She shall not, she dare not," cried Barbarina; "I will not suffer this humiliation; I will not be disgraced, dishonored in Berlin; I will not sit unnoticed in a *loge*, and listen to the bravos and plaudits awarded to another *artiste* which belong to me alone! Oh, sire, do not allow this shame to be put upon me! Command that this part, which is mine, which belongs to me by right of the world-wide fame which I have achieved, be given to me! I implore your majesty to take this *rôle* from the Cochois, and restore it to me."

"That is impossible, Barbarina. The Cochois, like every other *artiste*, must have her *début*. Baron Swartz has given her the principal part in ' *Toste Galanti,*' and I cannot blame him."

"Oh! your majesty, I beseech you to listen. Is it not true—will you not bear witness to the fact that Barbarina has never put your liberality and magnanimity to the test; that she has never shown herself to be egotistical or mercenary? I ask nothing from my king but his heart, the happiness to sit at his feet, and in the sunshine of his eyes to bathe my being in light and gladness. Sire, you have often complained that I desired and would accept nothing from you; that diamonds and pearls had no attraction for me. You know that not the slightest shadow of selfishness has fallen upon my love! Now, then, I have a request to-day: I ask something from my king which is more precious in my eyes than all the diamonds of the world. Give me this *rôle;* that is, allow me to remain in the undisturbed possession of my fame." She bowed her knee once more before the king, but this time he did not raise her in his arms.

"Barbarina," said he, sadly and thoughtfully, "put away from you this unworthy and pitiful envy. Cast it off as you do the tinsel robes and rouge of the stage with which you conceal your beauty. Be yourself again. The noble, proud, and great-hearted woman who shines without the aid of garish ornament, who is ever the queen of grace and beauty, and needs not the borrowed and false purple and ermine of the stage. Grant graciously to the Cochois this small glory, you who are everywhere and always a queen in your own right!"

Barbarina sprang from her knees with flashing eyes. "Sire," said she, "you refuse my request—my first request— you will not order that this part shall be given to me?"

"I cannot; it would be unjust."

"And so I must suffer this deadly shame; must see another play the part which belongs to me; another made glad by the proud triumphs which are mine and should remain mine. I will not suffer this! I swear it! So true as my name is Barbarina I will have no rival near me! I will not be condemned to this daily renewed struggle after the first rank as an *artiste*. I will not bear the possibility of a comparison between myself and any other woman. I am and I will remain the first; yes, I will!"

She raised herself up defiantly, and her burning glance fell upon the face of the king, but he met it firmly, and if the bearing of Barbarina was proud and commanding, that of King Frederick was more imposing.

"How!" said he, in a tone so harsh and threatening that Barbarina, in spite of her scorn and passion, felt her heart tremble with fear. "How! Is there another in Prussia who dares say, 'I will?' Is it possible that a voice is raised in contradiction to the expressed will of the king?"

Barbarina turned pale and trembled. The countenance of Frederick expressed what she had never seen before. It was harsh and cold, and a cutting irony spoke in his glance and a contemptuous smile played upon his lip.

"Mercy, mercy!" cried she, pleadingly; "have pity with my passion. Forget this inconsiderate word which scorn and despair drew from me. Oh! sire, do not look upon me so coldly, unless you wish that I should sink down and die at your feet; crush me not in your anger, but pardon and forget."

With her lovely face bathed in tears and her arms stretched out imploringly, she drew near the king, but he stood up erect and stepped backward.

"Signora Barbarina, I have nothing to forgive, but I cannot grant your request. The Cochois keeps her *rôle*, and if you have any complaint to make, apply to your chief, Baron Swartz; and now, signora, farewell; the audience is ended."

He bowed his head lightly and turned away; but Barbarina uttered one wild cry, sprang after him, and with mad frenzy she clung to his arm.

"Sire, sire! do not go," she said, breathlessly; "do not

forsake me in your rage. My God, do you not see that I suffer; that I shall be a maniac if you desert me!" and, gliding to his feet, she clasped his knees with her beautiful arms, and looked up at him imploringly. "Oh, my king and my lord, let me be as a slave at your feet; do not spurn me from you!"

King Frederick did not reply; he leaned forward and looked down upon the lovely and enchanting woman lying at his feet, and never, perhaps, had her charms appeared so intoxicating as at this moment, but his face was sad, and his eyes, usually so clear and bright, were veiled in tears. There was a pause. Barbarina still clung to his knees, and looked up beseechingly, and the king regarded her with an expression of unspeakable melancholy; his great soul seemed to speak in the glance which fixed upon her. It was eloquent with love, rapture, and grief. Now their eyes met and seemed immovably fixed. In the midst of the profound silence nothing was heard but Barbarina's sighs. She knew full well the significance of this moment. She felt that fate, with its menacing and unholy shadow, was hovering over her. Suddenly the king roused himself, and the voice which broke the solemn silence sounded strange and harsh to Barbarina.

"Farewell, Signora Barbarina," said the king.

Barbarina's arms sank down powerless, and a sob burst from her lips. The king did not regard it; he did not look back. With a firm hand he opened the door which led into his chamber; entered and closed it. He sank upon a chair, and gave one long and weary sigh. A profound despair was written on his countenance, and had Barbarina seen him, she would have appreciated the anguish of his heart.

She lay bathed in tears before his door, and cried aloud: "He has forsaken me! Oh, my God, he has forsaken me!" This fearful and terrible thought maddened her; she sprang up and shook the door fiercely, and with a loud and piteous voice she prayed for entrance. She knew not herself what words of love, of anguish, of despair, and insulted pride burst from her pallid lips. One moment she threatened fiercely, then pleaded touchingly for pardon; sometimes her voice seemed full of tears—then cold and commanding. The king stood with folded arms, leaning against the other side of the door. He heard these paroxysms of grief and rage, and every word fell upon his heart as the song of the siren upon the ear of Ulysses. But Frederick was mighty and powerful; he needed no ropes or wax to hold him back. He had the strength to control his will, and the voice of wisdom, the warning voice of duty, spoke louder than the siren's song.

"No," said he, "I will not, I dare not allow myself to be again seduced. All this must come to an end! I have long known this, but I had no strength to resist temptation. Have I not solemnly sworn to have but one aim in life—to place the good of my people far above my own personal happiness? If the man and the king strive within me for mastery, the king must triumph above all other things. I must consider the holy duties which my crown lays upon me; my time, my thoughts, my strength, belong to my people, my land. I have already robbed them, for I have withdrawn myself. I have suffered an enchantress to step between me and my duty—another will than mine finds utterance, influences, and indeed controls my thoughts and actions. Alas! a king should be old and be born with the heart of a graybeard—he dare never have a heart of youth and fire if he would serve his people faithfully and honestly! With a heart of flesh I might have been a happier, a more amiable man, but a weak, unworthy king. I should have been intoxicated by a woman's love, and her light wish would have been more powerful than my will. Never, never shall that be! I will have the courage to trample my own heart under foot, and the sorrows of the man shall be soothed and healed by the pomp and glory of the king."

In the next room Barbarina leaned over against the door, exhausted by her prayers and tears. "Listen to me, my king," said she, softly. "In one hour you have broken my will and humbled my pride forever! From this time onward Barbarina has no will but yours. Command me, then, wholly. Say to me that I am never to dance again, and I swear to you that my foot shall never more step upon the stage; command that all my *rôles* shall be given to the Cochois, I will myself hand them to her and pray her to accept them. You see, my king, that I am no longer proud —no longer ambitious. Have mercy upon me then, sire;

open this fearful door; let me look upon your face; let me lie at your feet. Oh, my king, be merciful, be gracious; cast me not away from you!"

The king leaned, agitated and trembling, against the door. Once he raised his arm and laid his hand upon the bolt. Barbarina uttered a joyful cry, for she had heard this movement. But the king withdrew his hand again. All was still; from time to time the king heard a low sigh, a suppressed sob, then silence followed.

Barbarina pleaded no more. She knew and felt it was in vain. Scorn and wounded pride dried the tears which love and despair had caused to flow. She wept no more—her eyes were flaming—she cast wild, angry glances toward the door before which she had lain so long in humble entreaty. Threateningly she raised her arms toward heaven, and her lips murmured unintelligible words of cursing or oaths of vengeance.

"Farewell, King Frederick," she said, at last, in mellow, joyous tones—"farewell! Barbarina leaves you."

She felt that, in uttering these words, the tears had again rushed to her eyes. She shook her head wildly, and closed her eyelids, and pressed her hands firmly upon them, thus forcing back the bitter tears to their source. Then with one wild spring, like an enraged lioness, she sprang to the other door, opened it and rushed out.

Frederick waited some time, then entered the room, which seemed to him to resound with the sighs and prayers of Barbarina. It brought back the memory of joys that were past, and it appeared to him even as the death-chamber of his hopes and happiness. He stepped hastily through the room and bolted the door through which Barbarina had gone out. He wished to be alone. No one should share his solitude—no one should breathe this air, still perfumed by the sighs of Barbarina. King Frederick looked slowly and sadly around him, then hastened to the door before which Barbarina had knelt. An embroidered handkerchief lay upon the floor. The king raised it; it was wet with tears, and warm and fragrant from contact with her soft, fine hand. He pressed it to his lips and to his burning eyes; then murmured, lightly, "Farewell! a last, long farewell to happiness!"

CHAPTER XV.

THE LAST STRUGGLE FOR POWER.

RESTLESS and anxious the two cavaliers of the king paced the anteroom, turning their eyes constantly toward the door which led into the king's study, and which had not been opened since yesterday morning. For twenty-four hours the king had not left his room. In vain had General Rothenberg and Duke Algarotti prayed for admittance.

The king had not even replied to them; he had, however, called Fredersdorf, and commanded him sternly to admit no one, and not to return himself unless summoned. The king would take no refreshment, would undress himself, required no assistance, and must not be disturbed in the important work which now occupied him.

This strict seclusion and unaccustomed silence made the king's friends and servants very anxious. With oppressed hearts they stood before the door and listened to every sound from the room. During many hours they heard the regular step of the king as he walked backward and forward; sometimes he uttered a hasty word, then sighed wearily, and nothing more.

Night came upon them. Pale with alarm, Rothenberg asked Algarotti if it was not their duty to force the door and ascertain the condition of his majesty.

"Beware how you take that rash step!" said Fredersdorf, shaking his head. "The king's commands were imperative; he will be alone and undisturbed."

"Have you no suspicion of the cause of his majesty's distress?" asked Algarotti.

"For some days past the king has been grave and out of humor," replied Fredersdorf. "I am inclined to the opinion that his majesty has been angered and wounded by some dear friend."

General Rothenberg bent over and whispered to Algarotti: "Barbarina has wounded him; for some time past she has been sullen and imperious. These haughty and powerful natures have been carrying on an invisible war with each other; they both contend for sovereignty."

"If this is so, I predict confidently that the beautiful Barbarina will be conquered," said Algarotti. "Mankind will always be conquered by Frederick the king, and must submit to him. So soon as Frederick the *Great* recognizes the fact that the man in him is subjected by the enchanting Barbarina, like Alexander the *Great*, he will cut the gordian knot, and release himself from even the soft bondage of love."

"I fear that he is strongly bound, and that the gordian knot of love can withstand even the king's sword. Frederick, ordinarily so unapproachable, so inexorable in his authority and self-control, endures with a rare patience the proud, commanding bearing of Barbarina. Even yesterday evening when the king did me the honor to sup with me in the society of the Barbarina, in spite of her peevishness and ever-changing mood, he was the most gallant and attentive of cavaliers."

"And you think the king has not seen the signora since that time?"

"I do not know; let us ask the guard."

The gentlemen ascertained from the guard that Barbarina had left the king's room in the morning, deadly pale, and with her eyes inflamed by weeping.

"You see that I was right," said Algarotti; "this love-affair has reached a crisis."

"In which I fear the king will come to grief," said Rothenberg. "Believe me, his majesty loves Barbarina most tenderly."

"Not the king! the *man* loves Barbarina. But listen! did you not hear a noise?"

"Yes, the low tone of a flute," said Fredersdorf. "Let us approach the door."

Lightly and cautiously they stepped to the door, behind which the king had carried on this fierce battle with himself, a battle in which he had shed his heart's best blood. Again they heard the sound of the flute: it trembled on the air like the last sigh of love and happiness; sometimes it seemed like the stormy utterance of a strong soul in extremest anguish, then melted softly away in sighs and tears. Never in the king's gayest and brightest days had he played with such

masterly skill as now in this hour of anguish. The pain, the
love, the doubt, the longing which swelled his heart, found
utterance in this mournful adagio. Greatly moved, the
three friends listened breathlessly to this wondrous development of genius. The king completed the music with a note
of profound suffering.

Algarotti bowed to Rothenberg. "Friend," said he,
"that was the last song of the dying swan."

"God grant that it was the last song of love, not the
death-song of the king's heart! When a man tears love
forcibly from his heart, I am sure he tears away also a piece
of the heart in which it was rooted."

"Can we not think of something to console him? Let
us go in the morning to Barbarina; perhaps we may learn
from her what has happened."

"Think you we can do nothing more to-day to withdraw
the king from his painful solitude?"

"I think the king is a warrior and a hero, and will be
able to conquer himself."

While the king, in solitude, strengthened only by his
genius, struggled with his love, Barbarina, with all the passion of her stormy nature, endured inexpressible torture.
She was not alone—her sister was with her, mingled her
tears with hers, and whispered sweet words of hope.

"The king will return to you; your beauty holds him
captive with invisible but magic bonds. Your grace and
fascinations will live in his memory, will smile upon him,
and lure him back humble and conquered to your feet."

Barbarina shook her head sadly. "I have lost him.
The eagle has burst the weak bonds with which I had bound
his wings; now he is free, he will again unfold them, and rise
up conquering and to conquer in the blue vaults of heaven.
In the rapturous enjoyment of liberty he will forget how
happy he was in captivity. No, no; I have lost him forever!"

She clasped her hands over her face, and wept bitterly.
Then, as if roused to extremity by some agonizing thought,
she sprang from her seat; her eyes were flashing, her cheeks
crimson.

"Oh, to think that *he* abandoned *me;* that I was true to

him; that a man lives who deserted Barbarina! That is a shame, a humiliation, of which I will die—yes, surely die!"

"But this man was, at least, a king," said her sister, in hesitating tones.

Barbarina shook her head fiercely, and her rich black hair fell about her face in wild disorder.

"What is it to me that he is a king? His sceptre is not so powerful as that of Barbarina. My realm extends over the universe, wherever men have eyes to see and hearts to feel emotion. That this man is a king does not lessen my shame, or make my degradation less bitter. Barbarina is deserted, forsaken, spurned, and yet lives. She is not crushed and ground to death by this dishonor. But, as I live, I will take vengeance, vengeance for this monstrous wrong—this murder of my heart!"

So, in the midst of wild prayers, and tears, and oaths of vengeance, the day declined; long after, Barbarina yielded to the tender entreaties of Marietta, and stretched herself upon her couch. She buried her head in the pillows, and during the weary hours of the night she wept bitterly.

With pale cheeks and weary eyes she rose on the following morning. She was still profoundly sad, but no longer hopeless. Her vanity, her rare beauty, in whose magic power she still believed, whispered golden words of comfort, of encouragement; she was now convinced that the king could not give her up. "He spurned me yesterday, to-day he will implore me to forgive him." She was not surprised when her servant announced Duke Algarotti and General Rothenberg.

"Look you," said she, turning to her sister, "you see my heart judged rightly. The king sends his two most confidential friends to conduct me to him. Oh, my God, grant that this poor heart, which has borne such agony, may not now break from excess of happiness! I shall see him again, and his beautiful, loving eyes will melt out of my heart even the remembrance of the terrible glance with which he looked upon me yesterday. Farewell, sister; farewell—I go to the king."

"But not so; not in this *négligée*; not with this hair in wild disorder," said Marietta, holding her back.

22

"Yes, even as I am," said Barbarina. "For his sake I have torn my hair; for his sake my eyes are red; my sad, pale face speaks eloquently of my despair, and will awaken his repentance."

Proudly, triumphantly she entered the saloon, and returned the profound salutation of the two gentlemen with a slight bow.

"You bring me a message from his majesty?" said she, hastily.

"The king commissioned us to inquire after your health, signora," said Algarotti.

Barbarina smiled significantly. "He sent you to watch me closely," thought she; "he would ascertain if I am ready to pardon, ready to return to him. I will meet them frankly, honestly, and make their duty light.—Say to his majesty that I have passed the night in sighs and tears, that my heart is full of repentance. I grieve for my conduct."

The gentlemen exchanged a meaning glance; they already knew what they came to learn. Barbarina had had a contest with the king, and he had separated from her in scorn. Therefore was the proud Barbarina so humble, so repentant.

Barbarina looked at them expectantly; she was convinced they would now ask, in the name of the king, to be allowed to conduct her to the castle. But they said nothing to that effect.

"Repentance must be a very poisonous worm," said General Rothenberg, looking steadily upon the face of Barbarina; "it has changed the blooming rose of yesterday into a fair, white blossom."

"That is perhaps fortunate," said Algarotti. "It is well known that the white rose has fewer thorns than the red, and from this time onward, signora, there will be less danger of mortal wounds when approaching you."

Barbarina trembled, and her eyes flashed angrily. "Do you mean to intimate that my strength and power are broken, and that I can never recover my realm? Do you mean that the Barbarina, whom the king so shamefully deserted, so cruelly humiliated, is a frail butterfly? That the purple hue of beauty has been brushed from my wings? that

I can no longer charm and ravish the beholder because a rough hand has touched me?"

"I mean to say, signora, that it will be a happiness to the king, if the sad experience of the last few days should make you milder and gentler of mood," said Algarotti.

Rothenberg and himself had gone to Barbarina to find out, if possible, the whole truth. They wished to deceive her —to lead her to believe that the king had fully confided in them.

"The king was suffering severely yesterday from the wounds which the sharp thorns of the red rose had inflicted," said Rothenberg.

"And did he not cruelly revenge himself?" cried Barbarina. "He left me for long hours kneeling at his door, wringing my hands, and pleading for pity and pardon, and he showed no mercy. But that is past, forgotten, forgiven. My wounds have bled and they have healed, and now health and happiness will return to my poor martyred heart. Say to my king that I am humble. I pray for happiness, not as my right, but as a royal gift which, kneeling and with up-lifted hands, I will receive, oh, how gratefully! But no, no, you shall not tell this to the king—I will confess all myself to his majesty. Come, come, the king awaits us—let us hasten to him!"

"We were only commanded to inquire after the health of the signora," said Algarotti, coolly.

"And as you have assured us that you have passed the night in tears and repentance, this confession may perhaps ameliorate his majesty's sufferings," said Rothenberg.

Barbarina looked amazed from one to the other. Suddenly her cheeks became crimson, and her eyes flashed with passion. "You did not come to conduct me to the king?" said she, breathlessly.

"No, signora, the king did not give us this commission."

"Ah! he demands, then, that I shall come voluntarily? Well, then, I will go uncalled. Lead me to his majesty!"

"That is a request which I regret I cannot fulfil. The king has sternly commanded us to admit no one."

"No one?"

"No one, without exception, signora," said Algarotti, bowing profoundly.

Barbarina pressed her lips together to restrain a cry of anguish. She pressed her hands upon the table to sustain her sinking form. "You have only come to say that the king will not receive me; that to-day, as yesterday, his doors are closed against me. Well, then, gentlemen, you have fulfilled your duty. Go and say to his majesty I shall respect his wishes—go, sirs!"

Barbarina remained proudly erect, and replied to their greeting with a derisive smile. With her hands pressed nervously on the table, she looked after the two cavaliers as they left her saloon, with wide-extended, tearless eyes. But when the door closed upon them, when sure she could not be heard by them, she uttered so wild, so piercing a cry of anguish, that Marietta rushed into the room. Barbarina had sunk, as if struck by lightning, to the floor.

"I am dishonored, betrayed, spurned," cried she, madly. "O God! let me not outlive this shame—send death to my relief!"

Soon, however, her cries of despair were changed to words of scorn and bitterness. She no longer wished to die—she wished to revenge herself. She rose from her knees, and paced the room hastily, raging, flashing, filled with a burning thirst for vengeance, resolved to cast a veil over her shame, and hide it, at least, from the eyes of the world.

"Marietta, O Marietta!" cried she, breathlessly, "help me to find the means quickly, by one blow to satisfy my vengeance!—a means which will prove to the king that I am not, as he supposes, dying from grief and despair; that I am still the Barbarina—the adored, triumphant, all-conquering *artiste*—a means which will convince the whole world that I am not deserted, scorned, but that I myself am the inconstant one. Oh, where shall I find the means to rise triumphantly from this humiliation? where—"

"Silence, silence, sister! some one is coming. Let no one witness your agitation."

The servant entered and announced that Baron von Swartz, director of the theatre, wished to know if the signora would appear in the ballet of the evening.

"Say to him that I will dance with pleasure," said Barbarina.

When once more alone, Marietta entreated her to be quiet, and not increase her agitation by appearing in public.

Barbarina interrupted her impatiently. "Do you not see that already the rumor of my disgrace has reached the theatre? Do you not see the malice of this question of Baron Swartz? They think the Barbarina is so completely broken, crushed by the displeasure of the king, that she can no longer dance. They have deceived themselves—I will dance to-night. Perhaps I shall go mad; but I will first refute the slander, and bring to naught the report of my disgrace with the king."

And now the servant entered and announced Monsieur Cocceji.

"You cannot possibly receive him," whispered Marietta. "Say that you are studying your *rôle* for the evening; say that you are occupied with your toilet. Say what you will, only decline to receive him."

Barbarina looked thoughtful for a moment. "No," said she, musingly, "I will not dismiss him. Conduct Cocceji to my boudoir, and say he may expect me."

The moment the servant left them, Barbarina seized her sister's hand. "I have prayed to God for means to revenge myself, and He has heard my prayer. You know Cocceji loves me, and has long wooed me in vain. Well, then, to-day he shall not plead in vain; to-day I will promise him my love, but I will make my own conditions. Come, Marietta!"

Glowing and lovely from excitement, Barbarina entered the boudoir where the young Councillor Cocceji, son of the minister, awaited her. With an enchanting smile, she advanced to meet him, and fixing her great burning eyes upon him, she said softly, "Are you not yet cured of your love for me?"

The young man stepped back a moment pale and wounded, but Barbarina stood before him in her wondrous beauty; a significant, enchanting smile was on her lip, and in her eyes lay something so sweetly encouraging, so bewildering, that he was reassured, he felt that it was not her intention to mock at his passion.

"This love is a fatal malady of which I shall never be healed," he said warmly; "a malady which resists all remedies."

"What if I return your love?" said she in soft, sweet tones.

Cocceji's countenance beamed with ecstasy; he was completely overcome by this unlooked-for happiness.

"Barbarina, if I dream, if I am a somnambulist, do not awaken me! If, in midsummer madness only, I have heard these blissful words, do not undeceive me! Let me dream on, give my mad fancy full play; or slay me if you will, but do not say that I mistake your meaning!"

"I shall not say that," she whispered, almost tenderly. "For a long year you have sworn that you loved me."

"And you have had the cruelty to jest always at my passion."

"From this day I believe in your love, but you must give me a proof of it. Will you do that?"

"I will, Barbarina!"

"Well, then, I demand no giant task, no herculean labor; there is no rival whom you must murder! I demand only that you shall make your love for me known to the whole world. Give *éclat* to this passion! I demand that with head erect, and clear untroubled eye, you shall give the world a proof of this love! I will not that this love you declare to me so passionately shall be hidden under a veil of mystery and silence. I demand that you have the courage to let the sun in the heavens and the eyes of men look down into your heart and read your secret, and that no quiver of the eyelids, no feeling of confusion shall shadow your countenance. I will that to-morrow all Berlin shall know and believe that the young Councillor Cocceji, the son of the minister, the favorite of the king, loves the Barbarina ardently, and that she returns his passion. Berlin must know that this is no cold, northern, German, phlegmatic *liking*, which chills the blood in the veins and freezes the heart, but a full, ardent, glowing passion, animating every fibre of our being—an Italian love, a love of sunshine, and of storm, and of tempest."

Barbarina was wholly irresistible; her bearing was proud, her eyes sparkled, her face beamed with energy and enthusiasm. A less passionate nature than that of Cocceji would have been kindled by her ardor, would have been carried away by her energy.

The fiery young Cocceji threw himself at her feet. " Command me! my name, my life, my hand, are yours; only love me, Barbarina, and I will be proud to declare how much I love you; to say to the whole world this is my bride, and I am honored and happy that she has deigned to accept my hand! "

" Of this another time," said Barbarina, smiling; " first prove to the world that you love me. This evening in the theatre give some public evidence, give the Berliners something to talk about: then—then—" said she, softly, " the rest will come in time."

CHAPTER XVI.

THE DISTURBANCE IN THE THEATRE.

DUKE ALGAROTTI and General Rothenberg returned to the castle much comforted by their interview with Barbarina.

" The Barbarina repents, and is ready to take the first step toward reconciliation," said Rothenberg; " I see the end; I will go at once and order my cook to prepare a splendid supper for the evening."

" Do not be hasty," said Algarotti, shaking his head; " you may give your cook unnecessary trouble, and the rich feast might be cold before the arrival of the king."

" Do you believe that? "

" I believe that for a summer cloud or an April shower the king would not withdraw himself to solitude and silence. It is no passing mood, but a life question which agitates him."

" The door has not been opened to-day; Fredersdorf has repeatedly begged for admittance."

The two friends stood sad and irresolute in the ante-room, alarmed at the seclusion and silence of the king. Suddenly the door leading into the corridor was hastily opened, and a man of commanding and elegant appearance stood upon the threshold; you saw at a glance that he was a cavalier and a courtier, while his glowing cheek, his clear, bright eyes, and jovial smile betrayed the man of pleasure and the epicure. This remarkable man, in whom every one who looked upon him felt confidence; whose face, in spite of the thousand wrinkles which fifty years of an active, useful life had laid upon it, still retained an innocent, amiable, and childlike expression—this man was the Marquis d'Argens, the true, unchangeable, never-faltering friend of the king. He had consecrated to him his heart, his soul, his whole being; so great was his reverence for his royal master, that the letters received from him were always read standing. The marquis had just returned from Paris; he entered the anteroom of the king with a gay and happy smile, impatient and eager to see his beloved master. Without looking around, he hastened to the door which led into the cabinet of the king. Rothenberg and Algarotti drew near to him, and greeted him joyously, then told him of the strange seclusion of the king. The countenance of the marquis was troubled, and his eyes filled with tears.

"We must not allow this," he said decidedly; "I will kneel before the door, and pray and plead till the noble heart of the king is reached, and he will have pity with our anxiety. Go, Fredersdorf, and announce me to his majesty."

"Sire," said Fredersdorf, knocking on the door, "sire, the Marquis d'Argens is here and begs for admittance."

No answer was given.

"Oh, sire," said the marquis, "be merciful; have consideration for my eagerness to see you after so long an absence; I have travelled day and night in order to enjoy that happiness a few hours sooner. I wish to warm and solace myself in the sunshine of your glance; be gracious, and allow me to enter."

A breathless silence followed this earnest entreaty. At last the door was shaken, a bolt was drawn back, and the king appeared on the threshold. He was pale, but of that clear and transparent pallor which has nothing in common with the sallow hue of physical weakness; there was no trace of nervous excitement. Smiling, and with calm dignity, he approached his friends.

"Welcome, marquis, most welcome! may joy and happiness crown your return! No doubt you have much to relate to us of your wild and impudent countrymen, and I see that Rothenberg and Algarotti are burning with curiosity to hear an account of your love adventures and rendezvous with your new-baked and glowing duchesses and princesses."

"Ah, your majesty, he approached me with the proud mien of a conqueror," said Rothenberg, gladly entering into the jesting humor of the king. "We are more than ready to believe in the triumphs of the marquis at the court of Louis the Fifteenth."

"The marquis has done wisely if he has left his heart in Paris," said Algarotti. "Your majesty knows that he suffers greatly with heart disease, and every girl whom he does not exactly know to be a rogue, he believes to be an angel of innocence."

"You know," said Rothenberg, "that shortly before his journey, his house-keeper stole his service of silver. The marquis promised to give her the worth of the silver if she would discover the thief and restore it. She brought it back immediately, and the marquis not only paid her the promised sum, but gave her a handsome reward for her adroitness in discovering the robber. As D'Argens triumphantly related this affair to me, I dared to make the remark that the housekeeper was herself the rogue, the good marquis was as much exasperated with me as if I had dared to charge *him* with theft! 'Have more reverence for women,' said he to me, gravely; 'to complain of, or accuse a woman, is a crime against God and Nature. Women are virtuous and noble when not misled, and I cannot see who could have tempted my good house-keeper; she is, therefore, innocent.'"

All laughed heartily, but D'Argens, who cast his eyes to the ground, looking somewhat ashamed. But the king advanced, and laying both hands upon the shoulders of the marquis, he looked into the kindly, genial face with an expression of indescribable love and confidence.

"He has the heart of a child, the intellect of a sage, and the imagination of a poet, by the grace of God," said the king. "If all men were like him, this earth would be no vale of tears, but a glorious paradise! It is a real happiness to me to have you here, my dear D'Argens. You shall take the place of the Holy Father, and bless and consecrate a small spot of earth for me. With your pure lips you shall pray to the house gods for their blessing and protection on my hearth, and beseech them to pour a little joy and mirth into the cup of wormwood and gall which this poor life presses to our lips. My palace of Weinberg, near Potsdam, is finished. I will drive you there to-day—you alone, marquis! As for the others, they are light-minded, audacious, suspicious children of men, and they shall not so soon poison the air in my little paradise with their levities. You alone, D'Argens, are worthy. You are pure as those who lived before the fall. You have never tasted of the ominous and death-giving apple. You will go with me, then, to Weinberg, and when you have consecrated it, you shall relate to me the *chronique scandaleuse* of the French court. Now, however, I must work!—Fredersdorf, are my ministers here?"

"Sire, they have been an hour in the bureau."

"Who is in the anteroom?"

"Baron Swartz, with the *répertoire* of the week."

"Ah! Swartz," said the king, thoughtfully, "let him enter."

Fredersdorf hastened to summon the director, and the king recommenced his careless conversation with his friends. As the baron entered, the king stepped forward to meet him, and took a paper from his hand. He read it with seeming indifference, but his lips were compressed and his brow clouded.

"Who will dance the solo this evening in *Re Pastore?*" he said, at last.

"Signora Barbarina, your majesty."

"Ah! the Signora Barbarina," said the king, carelessly. "I thought I heard that she was indisposed?"

Frederick's eyes were fixed searchingly upon his friends. He perhaps suspected the truth, and thought it natural that, in the disquiet of their hearts, they had sought an explanation of Barbarina.

"Sire," said Rothenberg, "Signora Barbarina has entirely recovered. Algarotti and myself made her a visit this morning, and she commissioned us, if your majesty should be gracious enough to ask for her, to say that she was well and happy."

The king made no reply. He walked thoughtfully backward and forward, then stood before D'Argens, and said, in a kindly tone: "You are so great an enthusiast for the stage that it would be cruel to take you to Weinberg this evening. We will go to the theatre and see Barbarina dance, and to-morrow you shall consecrate my house; and now, adieu, gentlemen—I must work! You will be my guests at dinner, and will accompany me to the theatre."

The king entered his study. "She defies me," said he lightly to himself. "She will prove to me that she is indifferent. Well, so be it; I will also show that I have recovered!"

The theatre was at last opened. A brilliant assembly filled the first range of boxes, and the *parquet*. The second tier and the *parterre* were occupied by the burghers, merchants, and their wives and daughters, who were waiting with joyful impatience for the commencement of the performance. The brilliant court circle, however, was absorbed by other interests. A murmur had spread abroad that "the Barbarina had fallen into disgrace and lost forever the favor of the king." The wild despair of the beautiful dancer was spoken of, and there were some who declared that she had made an attempt to take her life. Others asserted that she had sworn never again to appear on the Berlin stage, and that she would assuredly feign illness in order not to dance. All were looking anxiously for the rising of the curtain, and toward the side door through which the king and his suite were accustomed to enter.

At last the door opened; the drums and trumpets sounded merrily; the king entered, and walked with calm composure to his chair. The bell rang, the curtain rolled up, and the ballet began.

There was at first a dance of shepherds, and shepherdesses, then an interruption by fauns and satyrs, who intermingled in groups with the first dancers and ranged themselves on the side of the stage, waiting for the appearance of the shepherd queen. There was a breathless pause—every eye but the king's was fixed upon the stage.

And now there was an outburst of admiration and enthusiasm. Yes, there she was; rosy, glowing, perfumed, tender, enchanting, and intoxicating, she floated onward in her robe of silver. Her magical smile disclosed her small, pearly teeth and laughing dimples; her great, mysterious black eyes understood the art of flattery and of menace; in both they were irresistible. Noiselessly she floated onward to the front of the stage. Now, with indescribable grace, she bowed her body backward, and standing on tiptoe she raised her rounded arms high over her head, and looked upward, with a sweet smile, to a wreath of roses which she held.

"Wondrous, most wondrous!" cried suddenly a full, clear voice. It was the young state councillor, Von Cocceji, who sat in the proscenium box near the stage, and gazed with beaming eyes on Barbarina.

Barbarina turned toward him, and smiled sweetly. The king frowned, and played rather fiercely with his snuff-box.

"Wondrous!" repeated Cocceji, and threw a threatening, scornful glance upon a thin, wan young man who sat near him, and who dared, in a small, weak voice to repeat the "wondrous" of the young athlete. "I pray you, sir, to refrain from the expression of your applause, or, if that is impossible, choose your own words, and not mine to convey your approbation," said the six-footed giant, Cocceji, to his pallid neighbor.

The latter looked with a sort of horror at the broadshouldered, muscular figure before him, and scarcely daring to breathe loudly, he looked with wide-open, staring eyes at Barbarina, who was now floating with enchanting grace upon the stage. The audience had entirely forgotten the vague rumors of the day—thought no more of the king. Their attention was wholly given to Barbarina and Cocceji, whose eyes were ever fixed threateningly upon his shrinking neighbor. Suddenly, just as Barbarina had completed one of her most difficult *tours* and knelt before the lamps to receive the bravos of the spectators, something flew from the *loge* of Cocceji, and fell exactly at Barbarina's feet.

This offering was no wreath or bouquet of flowers, no costly gem, but a man, a poor, panting, terrified man, who did not yet comprehend how he came to make this rapid journey through the air, nor why Cocceji with his giant hand had seized him and dashed him upon the stage.

Confused and terrified, the poor bruised youth lay for some moments motionless at the feet of Barbarina; then gathering himself up and bowing profoundly to the king, who regarded him in fierce silence, he said aloud: " Sire, I pray for pardon; I am not to blame; Cocceji forbade me, in a proud, commanding tone, to look upon the Signora Barbarina. As I did not choose to obey this arbitrary order, he seized me without warning, and dashed me at the feet of the signora." * The public, recovering from their astonishment, began to whisper, laugh merrily, and gaze ironically at the young man, who stood humble and wan near Barbarina; while Cocceji, turning his bold, daring face to the audience, seemed to threaten every man who looked upon him questioningly. The orchestra was silent. Barbarina stood radiant in grace and beauty, and smiled bewitchingly upon Cocceji.

" Go on," said suddenly the clear, commanding voice of the king, as he nodded to the poor youth, who disappeared behind the curtain. " Go on," said the king again. The music commenced, and Barbarina, raising her garland of roses, swam like an elf over the boards. The audience thought not of her grace and beauty. They were wholly occupied with this curious adventure; they had forgotten her disgrace. They thought only of Cocceji's passionate love, and declared he was jealous as a Turk. So Barbarina had gained her purpose.

* Müchler's " History of Frederick the Great."

CHAPTER XVII.

SANS-SOUCI.

EARLY the next morning a plain, simple equipage stood at the gate of the new park in Potsdam. The king and the Marquis D'Argens entered the carriage alone. Frederick refused all other attendance; even his servants were forbidden to accompany him.

When the carriage stopped he opened the door himself, and springing lightly out, offered his arm to his older and less agile friend. The marquis blushed like a young girl, and wished to decline this offered service of the king.

Frederick, however, insisted upon giving his assistance, and said, smiling: "Forget, D'Argens, for this day, that I am a king; grant me the pleasure of passing the time with you without ceremony, as friend with friend. Come, marquis, enter my paradise, and I pray you to encourage a solemn and prayerful mood."

"Do you know, sire, I have a feeling of oppression and exaltation combined, such as the Grecians may have felt when they entered the Delphian valley?" said D'Argens, as arm in arm with the king they sauntered through the little shady side *allée* which the king had expressly chosen in order to surprise the marquis with the unexpected view of the beautiful height upon which the castle was erected.

"Well, I believe that many oracles will go out from this height to the world," said Frederick; "but they shall be less obscure, shall bear no double meaning; shall not be partly false, shall contain great shining truths. I also, dear D'Argens, feel inspired. I seem to see floating before me through the trees a majestic, gigantic form of air, with uplifted arm beckoning me to follow her. That is the spirit of the world's history, marquis; she carries her golden book on her arm; in her right hand, with which she beckons me, she holds the diamond point with which she will engrave my name and this consecrated spot upon her tables. Therefore, my holy father and priest, I have brought you here to baptize my Weinberg. Come, friend, that form of air beckons once more; she awaits the baptism with impatience."

And now they passed from the little *allée* and entered the great avenue; an expression of admiration burst from the lips of the marquis; with flashing eyes he gazed around upon the magnificent and enchanting scene. Here, just before them, was the grand basin of marble, surrounded with groups of marble statues; farther off the lofty terraces, adorned with enormous orange-trees, rustling their glossy leaves and pearly blossoms in the morning breeze, greeting their king with their intoxicating fragrance. Upon the top of these superb terraces, between groups of marble forms and laughing cascades, stood the little castle of Weinberg, beautiful in its simplicity; upon its central cupola stood a golden crown, which sparkled and glittered in the sunshine.

The king pointed to the crown. "Look," said he, "how it flashes in the sun, and throws its shadow upon all beneath it: so is it, or may it be, with my whole life! May my crown and my reign be glorious!"

The marquis pressed his hand tenderly. "They will be great and glorious through all time," said he. "Your grandchildren and your great-grandchildren will speak of the lustre which played upon that crown, and when they speak of Prussia's greatness they will say: "When Frederick the Second lived, the earth was glad with light and sunshine.'"

Arm in arm, and silently, they mounted the marble steps of the terrace. Deep, holy silence surrounded them, the cascades prattled softly. The tops of the tall trees which bordered the terrace bowed and whispered lowly with the winds; here and there was heard the melodious note of a bird. No noise of the mad world, no discord interrupted this holy peace of nature. They seemed to have left the world behind them, and with solemn awe to enter upon a new existence.

Now they had reached the height; they turned and looked back upon the beautiful panorama which lay at their feet. The luxurious freshness, the artistic forms, the blue and graceful river winding through the wooded heights and green valleys, formed an enchanting spectacle.

"Is not this heavenly?" said Frederick, and his face glowed with enjoyment. "Can we not rest here in peace, away from all the sorrows and sufferings of this world?"

"This is, indeed, a paradise," cried the marquis. He spread out his arms in ecstasy, as if he would clasp the whole lovely picture to his breast; then, turning his eyes to heaven, he exclaimed, "O God! grant that my king may be happy in this consecrated spot!"

"Happy?" repeated Frederick, with a slight shrug. "Say content, marquis. I believe that is the highest point any man attains upon this earth. And now let us enter the house."

He took the arm of the marquis, and then stepped over the golden sand to the large glass door which led to the round saloon. As Frederick opened the door he fixed his great blue eyes steadily upon D'Argens.

"Pray! marquis, pray! we stand upon the threshold of a new existence, which now opens her mysterious portals to us."

"Sire, my every thought is a prayer for you at this moment."

They entered the oblong saloon.

"This is the room which separates me from my friends," said the king. "This side of the house I will dwell; that side is for the use of my friends, above all others, dear marquis, for you. In this saloon we will meet together, and here will be my symposium. Now I will show you my own room, then the others."

In the reception-room, which was adorned with taste and splendor, Frederick remained but a few moments; he scarcely allowed his artistic friend a fleeting glance at the superb pictures which hung upon the walls, and for the selection of which he had sent the merchant, Gotzkowsky, several times to Italy; he gave him no time to look upon the statues and vases of the Poniatowsken Gallery, for which four hundred thousand thalers had been paid, but hurried him along.

"You must first see my work-room," said Frederick; "afterward we will examine the rest."

He opened the door and conducted the marquis into the round library which had no other adorning than that of books; they stood arrayed in lofty cases around this temple of intellect, of art, and science, and even the door through which they had entered, and which the king had lightly pressed back, had now entirely disappeared behind the books, with which it was cunningly covered on the inside.

"You see," said Frederick, "he who enters into this magic circle is confined for life. He cannot get out, and I will have it so. With this day begins a new existence for me, D'Argens. When I crossed the threshold, the past fell from me like an over-ripe fruit."

Frederick's face was sad, his eye clouded; with a light sigh he laid his hand upon the shoulder of the marquis and looked at him long and silently.

"I wish to tell you a secret," said he at last. "I believe my heart died yesterday, and I confess to you the death-struggle was hard. Now it is past, but the place where my heart once beat is sore, and bleeds yet from a thousand wounds. They will heal at last, and then I shall be a hard and hardened man. We will speak no more of it."

"No, sire, we shall not say that you will ever be hardened," cried D'Argens, deeply moved. "You dare not slander your heart and say that it is dead. It beats, and will ever beat for your friends, for the whole world, for all that is great, and glorious, and exalted."

"Only no longer for love," said the king; "that is a withered rose which I have cast from me. The roses of love are not in harmony with thrones or crowns; they grow too high and climb over, or their soft rosy leaves are crushed. I owe it to my people to keep myself free from all chains and make my reign glorious. I will never give them occasion to say that I have been an idle and self-indulgent *savant*. I dedicate to Prussia my strength and my life. But here, friend, here in my cloister, which, like the Convent of the Carmelites, shall never be desecrated by a woman's foot; here we will, from time to time, forget all the pomps and glories of the world, and all its vanities. Here, upon my Weinberg, I will not be a king, but a friend and a philosopher."

"And a poet," said D'Argens, in loving tones. "I will now recall a couplet to the poet-king, which he once repeated to me, when I was melancholy—almost hopeless:

'Nous avons deux moments à vivre ;
Qu'il en soit un pour le plaisir.'"

23

"Can you believe that we have not already exhausted this moment?" said Frederick, with a sad smile. Then, after a short pause, his face lightened and his eye glowed with its wonted fire; a gay resolve was written in his countenance. "Well, let us try, marquis, if you are right; let us seek to extend this moment as long as possible, and when death comes—

> Finissons sans trouble, et mourons sans regrets,
> En laissant l'univers, comblé de nos bienfaits.
> Ainsi l'astre du jour au bout de sa carrière,
> Repand sur l'horizon une douce lumière,
> Et les derniers rayous qu'il darde dans les airs,
> Sont ses derniers soupirs qu'il donne à l'univers."

The marquis listened with rapture to this improvised poem of the king. When it was concluded, the fiery Provençal called out, in an ecstasy of enthusiasm: "You are not a mere mortal, sire; you are a king—a hero—yes, a demigod!"

"I will show you something to disprove your flattering words," said Frederick, smiling. "Look out, dear D'Argens; what do you see, there, directly opposite to the window?"

"Does your majesty mean that beautiful statue in marble?"

"Yes, marquis. What do you suppose that to be?"

"That, sire? It is a reclining statue of Flora."

"No, D'Argens; *that* is my grave!"

"Your grave, sire?" said the marquis, shuddering; "and you have had it placed exactly before the window of your favorite study?"

"Exactly there; that I may keep death always in *remembrance!* Come, marquis, we will draw nearer."

They left the house, and advanced to the Rondel, where the superb statue of Flora was reclining.

"There, under this marble form, is the vault in which I shall lie down to sleep." said Frederick. "I began my building at Weinberg with this vault. But it is a profound secret; guard it well, also, dear friend! The living have a holy horror of death; it is not well to speak of graves or death lightly!"

D'Argen's eyes were filled with tears. "Oh, sire! may

this marble lie immovable, and the grave beneath it be a mystery for many long years!"

The king shook his head lightly, and a heavenly peace was written on his features. "Why do you wish that?" said he. Then pointing to the grave, he said: "When I lie there—*Je serais sans souci!*" *

"*Sans souci!*" repeated D'Argens, in low tones, deeply moved, and staring at the vault.

The king took his hand smilingly. "Let us seek, even while we live, to be *sans souci*, and as evidence that I will strive for this, this house shall be called *Sans-Souci!*'"

* Nicolai, " Anecdotes of King Frederick."

BOOK IV.

CHAPTER I.

THE PROMISE.

IT was a lovely summer day. The whole earth seemed to look up with a smile of faith, love, and happiness into the clear, blue heavens, whose mysterious depths give promise of a brighter and better future. Sunshine and clouds were mirrored in the rapid river and murmuring brook; the stately trees and odorous flowers bowed with the gentle west wind, and gave a love-greeting to the glorious vault above.

Upon the terrace of Sans-Souci stood the king, and looked admiringly upon the lovely panorama spread out at his feet. Nature and art combined to make this spot a paradise. The king was alone at the palace of Sans-Souci; for a few happy hours he had laid aside the burden and pomp of royalty. He was now the scholar, the philosopher, the sage, and the friend; in one word, he was what he loved to call himself, the genial abbot of Sans-Souci.

At the foot of the romantic hill upon which his palace was built Frederick laid aside the vain pomp and glory of the world, and with them all its petty cares and griefs. With every step upon the terrace his countenance lightened and his breath came more freely. He had left the valley of tears and ascended the holy mountain. Repose and purity were around him, and he felt nearer the God of creation.

Sans-Souci, now glittering in the sunshine, seemed to greet and cheer him. These two laconic but expressive words, *sans souci*, smoothed the lines which the crown and its duties had laid upon his brow, and made his heart, which was so cold and weary, beat with the hopes and strength of youth!

He was himself again, the warrior, the sage, the loving ruler, the just king, the philanthropist, the faithful, fond friend; the gay, witty, sarcastic companion, who felt himself most at home, most happy, in the society of scholars, artists, and writers.

Genius was for Frederick an all-sufficient diploma, and those who possessed it were joyfully received at his court. If, from time to time, he granted a coat-of-arms or a duke's diadem to those nobles, " by the Grace of God," it was not so much to do them honor as to exalt his courtiers by placing among them the great and intellectual spirits of his time. He had made Algarotti and Chazot dukes, and Bielfield a baron; he had sent to Voltaire the keys of the wardrobe, in order that the chosen friend of the philosopher of Sans-Souci might without a shock to etiquette be also the companion of the King of Prussia in his more princely castles, and belong to the circle of prince, and princess, and noble.

When Frederick entered Sans-Souci he laid aside all prejudices and all considerations of rank. He wished to forget that he was king, and desired his friends also to forget it, and to show him only that consideration which is due to the man of genius and of letters. Some of his friends had abused this privilege, and Frederick had been forced to humiliate them. There were others who never forgot at Sans-Souci the respect and reverence due to the royal house. Amongst these was his ever-devoted, ever-uniform friend, the Marquis d'Argens. He loved him, not because he was king, but because he believed him to be the greatest, best, most exalted of men. In the midst of his brilliant court circle and all his earthly pomp, D'Argens did not forget that Frederick was a man of letters, and his dear friend; even so, while enjoying the hospitalities of Sans-Souci, he remembered always that the genial scholar and gentleman was a great and powerful king.

Frederick had the greatest confidence in D'Argens, and granted him more privileges than any other of his friends. Frederick invited many friends to visit him during the day, but the marquis was the only guest whose bedchamber was arranged for him at Sans-Souci.

Four years have elapsed since D'Argens consecrated

Weinberg—since the day in which we closed our last chapter. We take advantage of the liberty allowed to authors, and pass over these four years and recommence our story in 1750, the year which historians are accustomed to consider the most glorious and happy in the life of Frederick the Second. We all know, alas! that earthly happiness resembles the purple rose, which, even while rejoicing the heart with her beauty and fragrance, wounds us with her thorns. We know that the sunshine makes the flowers bloom in the gardens, on the breezy mountains, and also on the graves; when we pluck and wear these roses, who can decide if we are influenced by joy in the present or sad remembrances of the past?

Frederick the Great appeared to be gay and happy, but these four years had not passed away without leaving a mark upon his brow and a shadow on his heart; his youthful smile had vanished, and the expression of his lip was stern and resolved. He was now thirty-eight years of age, and was still a handsome man, but the sunshine of life had left him; his eyes could flash and threaten like Jove's, but the soft and loving glance was quenched. Like Polycrates, King Frederick, in order to propitiate fate, had sacrificed his idol. He had thus lost his rarest jewel, had become poor in love. Perhaps his crown rested more firmly upon his head, but his heart had received an almost mortal wound; it had healed, but he was hardened!

Frederick thought not of the past four years, and their griefs and losses, as he stood now upon the terrace of Sans-Souci, illuminated by the evening sun, and gazed with ravished eyes upon the panorama spread out before him.

"Beautiful, wondrous beautiful!" he said to himself. "I think Voltaire will find that the sun is even as warm and cheering at Sans-Souci as at Cirey, and that we can be gay and happy without the presence of the divine Emilie, who enters one moment with her children, and the next with her learned and abstruse books.* Ah! I wish

* Voltaire lived for ten years in Cirey with his friend the Marquise Emilie de Châtelet Samont, a very learned lady, to whom he was much devoted. He had refused all Frederick's invitations because he was unwilling to be separated from this lady. After twenty years of marriage, in the year 1749, the countess gave birth to her first child; two hours after the birth of her son,

he were here; so long as I do not see him, I doubt if he will come."

At this moment the king saw the shadow of a manly figure thrown upon the terrace, which the evening sun lengthened into a giant's stature. He turned and greeted the Marquis d'Argens, who had just entered, with a gracious smile.

"You are indeed kind, marquis," said Frederick; "you have returned from Berlin so quickly, I think Love must have lent you a pair of wings."

"Certainly, Love lent me his wings; the little god knew that your majesty was the object of my greatest admiration, and that I wished to fly to your feet and shake out from my horn of plenty the novelties and news of the day."

"There is something new, then?" said the king. "I have done well in sending you as an ambassador to the Goddess of Rumor; she has graciously sent you back full-handed: let us see, now, in what your budget consists."

"The first, and I am sorry to say the most welcome to your majesty, is this—Voltaire has arrived in Berlin, and will be here to-morrow morning."

The king's countenance was radiant with delight, but he was considerate, and did not express his rapture.

"Dear marquis, you say that Voltaire has arrived. Do you indeed regret it?"

D'Argens was silent and thoughtful for a moment; he raised his head, and his eyes were obscured by tears.

"Yes," said he, "I am sorry! We greet the close of a lovely day, no matter how glorious the declining sun may be, with something of fear and regret; who can tell but that clouds and darkness may be round about the morning? To-morrow a new day dawns and a new sun rises in Sans-Souci. Sire, I grieve that this happy day is ended."

"Jealous!" said the king, folding his arms and walking backward and forward upon the terrace. Suddenly he stood before D'Argens and laid his hands upon his shoulders. "You are right," said he; "a new day dawns, a new sun rises

she seated herself at her writing-table to write an essay on the Newtonian system; in consequence of this she sickened and died in two days. After her death, Voltaire accepted Frederick's invitation to Sans-Souci.

upon Sans-Souci, but I fear the sun's bright face will be clouded and the day will end in storm. Voltaire is the last ideal of my youth; God grant that I may not have to cast it aside with my other vain illusions! God grant that the man Voltaire may not cast down the genius Voltaire from the altar which, with willing hands, I have erected for him in my heart of hearts. I fear the cynic and the miser. I have a presentiment of evil! My altar will fall to pieces, and its ruins will crush my own heart. Say what you will, D'Argens, I have still a heart, though the world has gnawed at and undermined it fearfully."

"Yes, sire, a great, noble, warm heart," cried D'Argens, deeply moved, "full of love and poetry, of magnanimity and mercy!"

"You must not betray these weaknesses to Voltaire," said the king, laughing; "he would mock at me, and I should suffer from his poisonous satire, as I have done more than once. Voltaire is miserly; that displeases me. Covetousness is a rust which will obscure and at last destroy the finest metal! The miser loves nothing but himself. I fear that Voltaire comes to me simply for the salary I have promised him, and the four thousand thalers I have sent him for his journey!"

"In this, sire, you do both yourself and Voltaire injustice. Voltaire is genial enough to look, not upon your crown, but upon the clear brow which it shades. He admires and seeks you, not because you are a king, but because you are a great spirit, a hero, an author, a scholar, and a philosopher, and, best of all, a good and noble man."

"What a simple-minded child you are, marquis!" said Frederick, with a sad smile; "you believe even yet in the unselfish attachments of men. Truly, you have a right to this rare faith; you, at least, are capable of such an affection. I am vain enough to believe that you are unselfishly devoted to me."

"God be thanked for this word!" said D'Argens, with a glowing countenance. "And now let Voltaire and the seven wise men, and Father Abraham himself come; your Isaac fears none of them; my king has faith in me!"

"Yes," said Frederick, "I believe in you; an evil and

bitter thing will it be, if the day shall ever come when I shall doubt you; from that time onward I will trust no man. I tell you, D'Argens, your kindly face and your love are necessary to me; I will use them as a shield to protect myself against the darts and wiles of the false world. You must never leave me; I need your calm, kind eye, your happy smile, your childish simplicity, and your wise experience; I need a Pylades, I well believe that something of Orestes is hidden in my nature. And now, my Pylades, swear to me, swear to me that you will never leave me; that from this hour you will have no other fatherland than Prussia, no other home than Potsdam and Sans-Souci."

"Ah, your majesty asks too much. I cannot adjure my fatherland, I cannot relinquish my Provence. I am the Switzer, with his song of home; when he hears it in his own land, his heart bounds with joy; when he hears it in a strange land, his eyes fill with sorrowful tears. So it is with the 'beau soleil de ma Provence,' the remembrance of it warms my heart; I think that if I were a weak old man, the sight of my beautiful sunny home would make me young and strong. Your majesty will not ask me to abandon my land forever?"

"You love the sun of Provence, then, more than you do me," said Frederick, with a slight frown.

"Your majesty cannot justly say that, when I have turned my back upon it, and shouted for joy when the sun of the north has cast its rays upon me. Sire, let me pass my life under the glorious northern sun, but grant that I may die in my own land."

"You are incomprehensible, D'Argens; how can you know when you are about to die, and when it will be time to return to your beautiful Provence?"

"It has been prophesied that I shall live to be very old, and I believe in prophecy."

"What do you call old, marquis? Zacharias was eighty years of age when his youthful wife of seventy gave birth to her first child."

"God guard me from such an over-ripe youth and such a youthful wife, sire! I shall be content if my heart remains young till my seventieth year, and has strength to love my king and rejoice in his fame; then, sire, I shall be aged and cold, and then it will be time for the sun of Provence to shine upon me and my grave. When I am seventy years of age, your majesty must allow your faithful servant to remember that France is his home, and to seek his grave even where his cradle stood."

"Seventy, marquis! and how old are you now?"

"Sire, I am still young—forty-six years of age. You see I have only sought a plea to remain half an eternity at the feet of your majesty."

"You are forty-six, and you are willing to remain twenty-four years at my side. I will then be sixty-six; that is to say, I will be hard of heart and cold of purpose. I will despise mankind, and have no illusions. Marquis, I believe when that time comes, I can give you up. Let it be so!—you remain with me till you are seventy. Give your word of honor to this, marquis."

"Rather will your majesty be gracious enough to promise not to dismiss me before that time?"

"I promise you, and I must have your oath in return."

"Sire, I swear! On that day in which I enter my seventieth year, I will send you my certificate of baptism, which you will also look upon as my funeral notice. You will say sadly, 'The Marquis d'Argens is dead,' and I—I will go to *ma belle Provence*, and seek my grave." *

"But before this time you will become very religious, a devotee, will you not?"

"Yes, sire; that is, I shall devoutly acknowledge all your goodness to me. I shall be the most religious worshipper of all that your majesty has done for the good of mankind, for the advancement of true knowledge, and the glory of your great name."

"So far, so good; but there is in this world another kind of religion, in the exercise of which you have as yet shown but little zeal. Will you at last assume this mask, and contradict the principles which you have striven to maintain during your whole life? Will you, at the approach of death, go through with those ceremonies and observances which religion commands?"

* Thiébault, vol. i., p. 360.

The marquis did not reply immediately. His eye turned to the beautiful prospect lying at his feet, upon which the last purple rays of the evening sun were now lingering.

"This is God, sire!" said he, enthusiastically; "this is truly God! Why are men not content to worship Him in nature, to find Him where He most assuredly is? Why do they seek Him in houses made with hands, and—"

"And in wafers made of meal and water?" said Frederick, interrupting him; "and now tell me, marquis, will you also one day seek Him thus?"

"Yes, sire," said D'Argens, after a short pause, "I will do thus from friendship to my brothers, and interest for my family."

"That is to say, you will be unfaithful to the interests of philosophy and truth?"

"It will appear so, sire; but no man of intellect and thought will be duped by this seeming inconsistency. If the part which I play seem unworthy, I may be excused in view of my motive—at all events, I do not think it wrong. The folly of mankind has left me but one alternative—to be a hypocrite, or to prepare bitter grief for my relations, who love me tenderly. 'Out of love,' then, for my family, I will die a hypocrite.* But, sire, why should we speak of death? why disquiet the laughing spirits of the Greeks and Romans, who now inhabit this their newest temple by discoursing of graves and skeletons?"

"You are right, marquis—away with the ghastly spectre! This present life belongs to us, and a happy life it shall be. We will sit at the feet of Voltaire, and learn how to banish the sorrows of life by wit and mocking laughter. With the imagination and enthusiasm of poets, we will conceive this

* The marquis returned to Provence, in his seventieth year, and died there. The journals hastened to make known that he died a Christian, recanting his atheistical philosophy. The king wrote to the widow of the marquis for intelligence on this subject. She replied that her husband had received the last sacraments, but only after he was in the arms of death, and could neither see nor hear, and she herself had left the room. The marquise added: "Ah, sire, what a land is this! I have been assured that the greatest service I could render to my husband would be to burn all his writings, to give all his pictures to the flames; that the more we burn on earth of that which is sinful or leads to sin, the less we shall burn in hell!"—Œuvres Posthumes, vol. xii., p. 316.

world to be a paradise. And now tell me what other news you have brought back with you from Berlin."

"Well, sire, Voltaire is not the only star who has risen in Berlin. There are other comets which from time to time lighten the heavens, and then disappear for a season to re-appear and bring strife and war upon the earth."

Frederick looked searchingly upon the marquis. "You speak in riddles—what comet has returned?"

"Sire, I know not what to call it. She herself claims a name, her right to which is disputed by the whole world, though she swears by it."

"She? it is, then, a woman of whom you speak?"

"Yes, sire; a woman whom for years we worshipped as a goddess, or at least as an enchanting fairy—Barbarina has returned to Berlin."

"Returned?" said the king, indifferently; but he walked away thoughtfully to the end of the terrace, and gazed upon the lovely landscape which, in its quiet beauty, brought peace to his heart, and gave him the power of self-control.

The marquis stood apart, and looked with kindly interest upon his noble face, now lighted by the glad golden rays of the sinking sun. Among the trees arose one of those fierce, sighing winds, which often accompany the declining sun, and seem the last struggling groans of the dying day. This melancholy sound broke the peaceful stillness around the castle, and drowned the babbling of the brooks and cascades. As the wild wind rustled madly through the trees, it tore from their green boughs the first faded, yellow leaves which had lain concealed, like the first white hairs on the temples of a beautiful woman, and drove them here and there in wanton sport. One of these withered leaves fell at the feet of the king. He took it up and gazed at it. Pensively he drew near the marquis.

"Look you, friend," said he, holding up the fallen leaf toward the marquis; "look you, this is to me the Barbarina —a faded remembrance of the happy past, and nothing more. Homer was right when he likened the hearts of men to the yellow leaves tossed and driven by the winds. Even such a leaf is Barbarina; I raise it and lay it in my herbarium with other mementoes, and rejoice that the dust and ashes of life have fallen upon it, and taken from it form and color. And now that you know this, D'Argens, tell me frankly why the signora has returned. Does she come alone, or with her husband, Lord Stuart McKenzie?"

"She has returned with her sister, and Lord Stuart is not her husband. It is said that when Barbarina arrived in England, she found him just married to a rich Scotch lady."

The king laughed heartily. "And yet men expect us to listen gravely when they rave of the eternity of their love," said he. "This little sentimental lord called heaven and earth to witness the might of his love for Barbarina. Was he not almost a madman when I seized his jewel, and tore her away from Venice? Did he not declare that he would consider me answerable for his life and reason, if I did not release my prima donna? He wished her to enter, with an artistic *pirouette*, his lofty castle, and place herself, as Lady Stuart McKenzie, amongst his ever-worthy, ever-virtuous, ever-renowned ancestors. And now, Barbarina can stand as godmother by his first born."

"Or he perform that holy office for Barbarina. It is said that she is also married."

"To whom?"

"To the state councillor, Cocceji."

"Folly! how can that be? She has been in England, and he has not left Berlin. But her return will bring us vexation and strife, and I see already the whole dead race of the Coccejis raising up their skeleton arms from their graves to threaten the bold dancer, who dares to call herself their daughter. I prophesy that young Cocceji will become even as cool and as reasonable as Lord Stuart McKenzie has become. Give a man time to let the fire burn out—all depends upon that. This favor his family may well demand of me, and I must grant it. But now let us enter the house, marquis, the sun has disappeared, and I am chilled. I know not whether the news you bring, or the evening air, has affected me. Let us walk backward and forward once or twice, and then we will go to the library, and you will assist me in the last verse of a poem I am composing to greet Voltaire. Do not frown, marquis, let me sing his welcome; who knows but I may also rejoice in his departure? My heart is glad at his coming, and yet I fear it. We must not scrutinize the sun too closely, or we will find spots upon his glorious face. Perhaps Voltaire and myself resemble each other too much to live in peace and harmony together. I think we are only drawn permanently to our opposites. Believe me, D'Argens, I shall not be able to live twenty-four years happily with Voltaire, as I shall surely do with you. Twenty-four years! do not forget that you are mine for twenty-four years."

"Sire, as long as I live I am yours. You have not bought me with gold, but by the power of a noble soul. So long as I live, my heart belongs to you, even when, at seventy, I fly to seek my grave in *belle Provence*. But, my king, I have yet another favor to ask of you."

"Speak, marquis, but do not be so cruel as to ask that which I cannot grant."

"If it shall please Providence to call me away before I have attained my seventieth year, if I die in Berlin, will your majesty grant me the grace not to be buried in one of those dark, damp, dreary churchyards, where skull lies close by skull, and at the resurrection every one will be in danger of seizing upon the bones which do not belong to him, and appearing as a thief at the last judgment? I pray you, let me remain even in death an individual, and not be utterly lost in the great crowd. If I die here, grant that I may be buried where, when living, I have been most happy. Allow me, after a long and active day, to pass the night of immortality in the garden of Sans-Souci."

"It shall be so," said the king, much moved. "There, under the statue of Flora, is my grave—where shall be yours? Choose for yourself."

"If I dare choose, sire, let it be there under that beautiful vase of ebony."

Frederick gave a smiling assent, and taking the arm of the marquis, he said, "Come, we will go to the vase, and I will lay my hand upon it and consecrate it to you."

Silently they passed the statue of Flora, which Frederick greeted gayly, and the marquis with profound reverence then mounted two small steps and stood upon the green circle. The king paused and looked down thoughtfully upon a gravestone which his feet almost touched.

"Be pious and prayerful on this spot," said he; "we stand by the grave of my most faithful friend, who is enjoying before us the happiness of everlasting sleep. Here lies Biche! Hat off, marquis! She loved me, and was faithful unto death. Who knows if I, under my statue of Flora, and you, under your vase, will merit the praise which I, with my whole soul, award to my Biche! She was good and faithful to the end." *

CHAPTER II.

VOLTAIRE AND HIS ROYAL FRIEND.

THE king had withdrawn to his library earlier than usual; he had attended a cabinet council, worked for an hour with his minister of state, and, after fulfilling these public duties, withdrawn gladly to his books, hoping to consume the time which crept along with leaden feet.

The king expected Voltaire; he knew he had arrived at Potsdam, where he would rest and refresh himself for a few hours, and then proceed at once to Sans-Souci.

Frederick regarded this first meeting with Voltaire, after long years of separation, with more of anxiety than of joyful impatience. Voltaire's arrival and residence at Sans-Souci had been the warm desire of Frederick's heart for many years, and yet, as the time for its fulfilment drew near, the king almost trembled. What did this mean? How was it that this friendship, which for sixteen years had been so publicly avowed, and so zealously confirmed by private oaths and protestations, seemed now wavering and uncertain?

About now to reach the goal so ardently striven for, the king felt that he was not pleased. A cold blast seemed to sweep over him, and fill him with sad presentiments.

Frederick was filled with wonder and admiration for the genius of the great French writer, but he knew that, as a man, Voltaire was unworthy of his friendship. He justly

* Nicolai, " Anecdoten."—Heft, p. 202.

feared that the realities of life and daily intercourse would
fall like a cold dew upon this rare blossom of friendship between a king and a poet; this tender plant which, during so
many years of separation, they had nourished and kept warm
by glowing assurances and fiery declarations, must now be removed from the hot-house of imagination, where it had been
excited to false growth by the eloquence of letters, and
transplanted into a world of truth and soberness.

This friendship had no real foundation; it floated like
a variegated phantom in the air, a *fata morgana*, whose glittering temple halls and pillars would soon melt away like the
early cloud and the morning dew. In these "cloud-capped
towers and gorgeous palaces," the two great freethinkers
and genial philosophers of their century intended to cultivate and enjoy their friendship. In these temples of air
they wished to embrace each other, but the two-edged sword
of mistrust and suspicion already flashed between them, and
both felt inclined to draw back.

Both doubted the sincerity of this friendship, and the
less they believed in it the more eloquently they declaimed as
to its ardor and eternity. Each one thought to himself,
"I will enjoy and profit by the fruit of this friendship, I will
yield up the blossoms only." The blossoms, alas! were arti-
ficial, without odor and already fading, though at the first
glance they looked fresh and promising.

Once, in the youthful ardor of his enthusiasm for genius,
Frederick had forgotten himself so far as to kiss the hand
of Voltaire.* The proud and ambitious poet had boasted
loudly of this act of devotion; for this Frederick had never
forgiven him; he should have guarded it as a holy and dangerous secret in the innermost shrine of his heart. Voltaire
was angry with the king because he had lately addressed
some verses to the young poet D'Arnaud, in which he was
represented as the rising and Voltaire as the setting sun.†
And yet they believed they loved each other, and were about
to put their love to the severe test of uninterrupted intercourse.

The king awaited Voltaire with impatience, and now he
heard the rolling of carriage-wheels, then the opening of

* Thiébault.   † Œuvres posthumes.

doors, then the sound of voices. In the first impulse of joy he sprang from his seat and advanced eagerly to meet Voltaire, but reaching the threshold of the door he stood still and considered. "No," said he, "I will not go to meet him —he would mock at me, perhaps boast of it." He turned back to his chair, and took up the book he had been reading. And now some one tapped gently upon the door, a servant appeared and announced "Monsieur Voltaire," and now a figure stood upon the door-sill.

This man, with a small, contracted chest, with a back bowed down by old age or infirmities; this man, with the wonderous countenance, of which no one could decide if it was the face of a satyr or a demi-god; whose eyes flashed with heavenly inspiration at one moment, and in the next glowed with demoniac fire; whose lips were distorted by the most frightful grimaces or relaxed into the most enchanting smiles—this man is Voltaire.

As Frederick's glance met those burning eyes, he forgot all else, his royalty, his dignity, even Voltaire's baseness and vanity; he was to him the spirit of the age, the genius of the world, and he hastened to meet him, opened his arms wide, and pressed him tenderly to his heart. "Welcome, welcome, my lord and master," said the king; "I receive you, as becomes a pupil, in my school-room, surrounded by my books, whose mysterious lessons of wisdom, you, my teacher, will make clear."

"On the contrary, sire," said Voltaire, with a soft voice and a most enchanting smile—"on the contrary, you receive me with all the pomp of royalty seated upon a throne, which is not yours by inheritance, but which you have conquered; upon the throne of knowledge and learning, crowned with the laurels which the gods consecrate to heroes and poets. Alas! my eyes are dazzled by the lustre which surrounds me. I bow in humility before this lordly head adorned by two royal crowns and reigning over two mighty kingdoms. Receive me, sire, as an ambassador from the realm of poets, whose crown you wear with so much grace and dignity."

Frederick smiled kindly. "Let me be only a burgher and your comrade in arms in the republic of letters," said he.

24

"I hold republics generally as impossibilities, but I believe in a republic of letters, and I have a right republican heart, striving after liberty, equality, and brotherly love. Remember this, friend, and let us forget at Sans-Souci that your comrade is sometimes the first servant of a kingdom. And now, tell me how you have borne the fatigues of the journey, and if you have been received at every station with the marked attention I had commanded."

"Yes, sire, everywhere in Prussia I have felt myself almost oppressed, humbled, by your greatness. How great, how mighty, how powerful, must your majesty be, when I am so distinguished, so honored, simply because I enjoy your favor! This honor and this pleasure alone have given me strength for my journey. My friends in Paris thought it absurd and ridiculous for me, in my miserable condition, to attempt so fatiguing a journey. But, sire, I was not willing to die before I had once more sat at the feet of this great and yet simple man, this exalted yet genial philosopher. I wished to revive and quicken my sick heart at this fountain of wit and wisdom. I come, therefore, not as Voltaire, but as the tragic Scarron of your century, and throughout my whole journey I have called myself the 'Invalid of the King of Prussia.' " *

Frederick laughed heartily. "The Marshal of Saxony and yourself are in the same condition with your maladies; in the extremity of illness you have more energy and power than all other men in the most robust health. Voltaire, if you had not come now I should have considered you a bad penny: in place of the true metal of friendship I should have suspected you of palming off plated lead upon me. It is well for you that you are here. You are like the white elephant for whom the Shah of Persia and the Great Mogul are continually at war. The one who is so fortunate as to possess the white elephant makes it always the occasion of an added title. I will follow their example, and from this time my title shall run thus: 'Frederick, by the grace of God, King of Prussia, Prince-Elector of Brandenburg, Possessor of Voltaire, etc. etc.' "

"Your majesty may say, 'of inalienable Voltaire.' I

* Œuvres Complètes de Voltaire. Œuvres Posthumes.

am wiser than the white elephant; no war shall be necessary to conquer or to hold me. I declare myself your majesty's most willing subject joyfully. Let me then be your white elephant, sire, and if the Great Mogul covets and demands me, I pray you to conceal me."

While Voltaire was speaking, he cast a sly glance upon the countenance of the king, his smile disappeared, and his face lost its kindly expression.

Frederick did not, or would not see it. "Not so," said he, gayly; "I will not conceal you, but boldly declare that you are mine."

"I am, nevertheless, the subject of the King of France," said Voltaire, shrugging his shoulders. "When I resolved to leave Paris, they did not deprive me of my title of 'Historian of the King of France,' they only took from me my pension. They knew I must travel by post, and that a title was less weighty for the horses than a pension of six thousand livres; so they lightened me of that, and I come unpensioned to your majesty."

This little comedy was too clear to escape the king, but he seemed not to understand it. A shadow fell upon his brow, and the expression of his face was troubled. He wished to worship Voltaire as a noble, exalted genius, and he was pained to find him a pitiful, calculating, common man.

"You have, then, fallen under the displeasure of my brother Louis, of France?" said he.

"On the contrary, I am assured that I stand in the highest favor. I am, indeed, honored with a most agreeable and flattering commission; and if your majesty allows, I will immediately discharge it."

"Do so," said Frederick, smiling. "Lay aside every weight, that your wings may waft you into the heaven of heavens while at Sans-Souci. You have been relieved of your pension, cast all your ballast into the scale also."

"Sire, the Marquise de Pompadour directed me to present your majesty with her most obedient and submissive greetings, and to assure you of her reverence and heart-felt devotion."

Frederick quietly drew his *tabatière* from his vest-pocket, and slowly taking a pinch of snuff, he fixed his burning eyes upon Voltaire's smiling and expectant face; then said, with the most complete indifference, "The Marquise de Pompadour. Who is she? I do not know her!"

Voltaire looked at the king astonished and questioning.

Frederick did not remark this, but went on quietly: "Have you no other greetings for me? Have none of the great spirits, in which Paris is so rich, remembered me?"

"I shall be careful not to mention any other greetings. All the so-called great spirits appear so small in the presence of your exalted majesty, I fear you will not acknowledge them."

"Not so," said Frederick; "I gladly recognize all that is really great and worthy of renown. Voltaire will never find a more enthusiastic admirer than I am."

"Ah, sire, these words are a balsam which I will lay upon my breast, lacerated by the wild outcries of my critics."

"So the critics have been giving you trouble?" said Frederick.

"Yes, sire," said Voltaire, with the passionate scorn so peculiar to him; "they have bored their insatiable and poisonous teeth into my flesh. They are so miserable and so pitiful, that I seem to myself miserable and pitiful as their victim, and in all humility I will ask your majesty, if such hounds are allowed to howl unpunished, would it not be better for Voltaire to creep into some den, and acknowledge the wild beasts of the forests as his brothers—perhaps they might regard his verses as melodious barkings and howlings?"

"Still the same boisterous hot-head, the Orlando Furioso," cried the king, laughing heartily. "Is your skin so tender still that the needles of the little critics disturb you, and to gratify their malice will you become a mule? If you are driven to abandon the Muses, friend, who will have the hardihood to stand by them? No, no! do not follow in the footsteps of the God of Abraham, Isaac, and Jacob; do not 'visit the sins of the fathers upon the children unto the third and fourth generation;' do not make the public of our day, and of the next century, suffer for the crimes of a few pitiful critics. The persecutions and slanders of the envious are the tribute great merit must always pay to the world at large.

Let them rail on, but do not believe that the nations and the future will be duped by them. Utterly disregarding the criticisms of the so-called masters of art, we of this century admire and wonder at the *chefs-d'œuvre* of Greece and Rome. The mad cry of Æschines does not obscure the fame of Demosthenes; and in spite of Lucian, Cæsar is, and will ever remain, the greatest man the world has ever produced. I guarantee that after your death you will be canonized, worshipped. I humbly entreat you not to hasten the time, but be content to have the apotheosis in your pocket, and to be honored by all those who are too exalted to be envious or prejudiced. I, Frederick, stand foremost in the ranks." *

"Why cannot the whole world be present to hear the words of a king whom I am proud, from this day onward, to call *my* king?" cried Voltaire, passionately. "Sire, I love you ardently! I believe the gods made us for each other. I have long loved you tenderly! I have been angry with you, but I have forgiven you all, and I love you to madness! There was never a weaker, frailer body than mine, but my soul is strong! I dare to say I love you as much as I admire you! †
Verily, I hold this to be as great a conquest as the five other victories your majesty has achieved, and for which the world worships you. From this day I will be like your faithful hound; I will lie at your feet, even though you should spurn me, and declare that you will not be my master and lord. I will still return. Your threshold shall be my home, and I will be content with the crumbs which fall from your table. My fortune and my happiness shall consist in loving you!"

"I will not put your love to so hard a proof," said the king, smiling. "I dare hope to provide you with a more durable dwelling. I promise you shall not be like Lazarus, feeding upon crumbs. You shall be the rich man dispensing them."

Here was a sort of promise and assurance which banished in some degree the nervous anxiety and distrust of Voltaire, and his countenance once more beamed with joy. He suppressed his satisfaction, however, instantly. He did not

* The king's own words.—Œuvres Posthumes.
† Voltaire's own words.

wish to betray to the observant eye of Frederick his selfish and miserly nature, and assumed at once a melancholy look.

"Sire," said he, "I do not resemble Lazarus; and if your majesty does not possess the miraculous power of the young rabbi, Jesus Christus, I fear you will soon have to bury me. But I am as true a believer as any Jew. I trust fully to the magic power of your hand. Was not your marvellous touch sufficient to place beautiful Silesia, a gem of the first water, in the crown of Prussia?—to awaken spirits, sleeping almost the sleep of death, and to call into life on these barbarous northern steppes the blossoms of education and refinement? I believe in the miracles of the Solomon of the North, and I am willing to give my testimony to the whole world."

"Nevertheless, if the French cock crows, you will betray me three times," said the king. "I know you, Voltaire, and I know when you are enraged, nothing is sacred. I fear that here, as elsewhere, you will find provocations. But now, before all other things, what have you brought me? What gift has your muse produced for the poor philosopher of Sans-Souci? I will not believe that you come with empty hands, and that the Homer of France has broken his lyre."

"No, sire, I am not empty-handed! I have brought you a present. I believe it to be the best and most beautiful production of my muse. For twenty years I have swelled with indignation at the tragedy which my good friend, Master Crébillon, made of the most exalted subject of antiquity. With the adroit hands of a tailor he stitched up a monkey-jacket out of the purple toga, and adorned it with the miserable tawdry trifles of a pitiful lore and pompous Gothic verse! Crébillon has written a French Catiline. I, sire, have written a Roman Catiline! You shall see, sire, and you shall admire! In one of my most wretched, sleepless nights, the devil overcame me, and said: 'Revenge Cicero and France! Crébillon has disgraced both. Wash out this stain from France.' This was a good devil; and even you, sire, could not have driven me to work more eagerly than he did. Day and night he chained me to my writing-desk! I feared I should die of excitement, but the devil held on to me, and the spirits of the great Romans stood by my table and tore off the absurd and ridiculous masks which Crébillon had laid upon them. They showed me their true, exalted, glowing faces, and commanded me to portray them, 'that the world at last might feel their majestic beauty, and be no longer deceived by the caricatures of Crébillon!' I was obliged to obey, sire! I worked unceasingly, and in eight days I had finished! Catiline was born, and I was as much exhausted as ever a woman was at the birth of her first-born!'"*

"You do not mean that in eight days you completed the tragedy?" said the king. "You mean only that you have arranged the plot, and will finish the work here."

"No, sire, I bring you the tragedy complete, and I wrote it in eight days. Ah, sire, this is a tragedy you will enjoy! You will see no lovelorn Tullia, no infirm and toothless Cicero; you will see a fearful picture of Rome, a picture at which I myself shuddered. But, sire, when you read it, you must swear to me to read it in the same spirit in which it is written. I have left to my collegian Crébillon all his dramatic plunder; his Catiline is a pure fiction. I have written mine, remembering my province as an historian. Rome is my heroine; she is the mistress for whom I would interest all Europe. I have no other intrigue than Rome's danger; no other material than the mad craft of Catiline, the vehemence and heroic virtue of Cicero, the jealousy of the Roman Senate, the development of the character of Cæsar; no other women than that unfortunate who was seduced by Catiline because of her gentleness and amiability. I know not, sire, if you will shudder at the fourth act, but I, the writer, trembled and shuddered. My tragedy is not formed upon any model, it is new in *nova fert animus* Truly I know the world will rail at me for this, and the small souls gnash their teeth and howl, but my work is written with a great soul, and kindred spirits will comprehend me. The envious and the pitiful I will at last trample under my feet. Jupiter strove with the Titans and overcame them. I am no Jupiter, neither are my adversaries Titans."

While these words, in an irrepressible and powerful stream of eloquence, burst from his lips, Voltaire became another man. His countenance was imposing in its beauty,

* This whole speech is from Voltaire.

his eyes glowed with the fire of inspiration, an enchanting smile played upon his lips, and his bowed and contracted form was proudly erect and commanding. The king gazed upon him with admiration. At length, Voltaire, panting for breath, was silent. Frederick laid his two hands upon his shoulders, and looked into the glowing face with an indescribable expression of love and tenderness.

"Now," said he, "I have again and at last found my Voltaire, my proud, inspired king of poets, my Homer, crowned with immortality! The might of genius has torn away the mantle of the courtier, and in place of pitiful, pliant, humble words, I hear again the melodious, flashing, eloquent speech of my royal poet! Welcome, Voltaire, welcome to Sans-Souci, whose poor philosopher is but king of men, while the spirits are subject unto you! Ah, my all-powerful king and master, be gracious! You possess a wondrous realm, give me at least a small province in your kingdom."

"Sire, you mock at me," cried Voltaire. "I have written Cæsar and Cicero for the theatre. You, however, exhibit on the stage of the world the two greatest men of the greatest century, combined in your own person. I have come to gaze upon this wonder; it is a far loftier drama than mine, and will be surely more nobly represented.* Your majesty represents what you truly are, but where shall I find actors to fill the *rôle* of Cæsar, Cicero, and Catiline; how shall I change the pitiful souls of the *coulisse* into great men; make noble Romans out of these small pasteboard heroes of the mode? I could find no actors for my tragedy in Paris, and it shall never be unworthily represented!"

"We will bring it upon the stage here," said Frederick. "Yes, truly, this new and great work shall announce, like a flaming comet, Voltaire's arrival in Berlin. At the same moment in which the Berlinese see that you are at last amongst them, shall they acknowledge that you are worthy to be honored and worshipped. In four weeks, Voltaire, shall your new tragedy be given in my palace."

"Has your majesty, then, a French company, and such a one as may dare to represent my Catiline?"

* Voltaire's own words.

"For the love of Voltaire will all my courtiers, and even my sister, become actors; and though a Cicero failed you in Paris, in Berlin we will surely find you one. Have we not Voltaire who can take that *rôle*. If no reliable director could be found in Paris, I give you permission to select from my court circle those you consider most talented and most capable as actors, and you can study their parts with them—I myself alone excepted. Ten years ago I wished to have your 'Death of Cæsar' given at Rheinsberg, and I had selected a *rôle;* just then the Emperor of Germany died, and fate called me out upon the great theatre of the world, where I have since then tried to play my part worthily, and I must consecrate to this all my strength and ability. I can play no other part! The two *rôles* might make a rare confusion, and strange results might follow should the King of Prussia of this morning be changed to the Cicero of the evening, utter a fulminating speech against tyrants, and call upon the noble Romans to defend their rights; while this same King of Prussia is a small tyrant, and his subjects are more like pitiful slaves than heroic Romans. I must, therefore, confine myself to the narrow boundaries of a spectator, and applaud you as heartily in your character of Cicero as I applaud you in that of the great Voltaire."

"And is this indeed your intention, sire? My poor tragedy lies in my writing-desk, seemingly dead; will you awaken it to life and light?"

"It shall be given in two months, and you shall conduct it."

Voltaire's countenance darkened; his gay smile disappeared, and lines of selfishness and covetousness clouded the brow of the great poet.

"In two months, sire!" said he, shaking his head. "I fear I shall not be here. I have only come to sun myself for a few happy days in your presence."

"And then?" said Frederick, interrupting him.

"Then I must fulfil one of the darling dreams of my whole life. I must go to Italy, to the holy city of Rome, and kneel upon the graves of Cicero and Cæsar. I must see St. Peter's, the Venus de Medici, and the pope."

"You will never go to Rome," said Frederick. "The

Holy Father will not have the happiness of converting the blasphemous Saul into the pious and believing Paul. You will remain in Berlin; if you do not yield willingly, I must compel you to yield. J will make you my subject; I will bind you with orders and titles; I will compel you to accept a salary from me; and then, should they seek to ravish you from me, I will have a right to withhold you from all the potentates of the world."

Voltaire's face was again radiant. "Ah! sire, no power or chains will be necessary to bind me here; your majesty's command alone would suffice."

"And your duty! My gentleman of the bedchamber dare not withdraw himself for a single day without my permission. I make you gentleman of the bedchamber. I lay the ribbon of my order, '*pour le mérite*,' around your neck, and that I may always have a rope around you, and make you completely my prisoner, I give you an apartment in my palace at Potsdam; and that you may not feel yourself a hermit, you will have every day six covers laid for your friends; and to mock you with the appearance of liberty, you shall have your own equipage and servants, who will obey you in all things with one exception—if you order your valet to pack up your effects, and your coachman to take the road to Paris, they will disobey."

Voltaire heard the words of the king with breathless attention. Sullen suspicion and discontent were written on his face. This did not escape the king; he understood the cause, but he said nothing. Voltaire exhausted himself in words of joy and gratitude, but they had not the ring of truth, and the joy which his lips expressed found no echo in his face.

"I have but one other thing to add," said Frederick, at last. "Can your greatness pardon a poor earthworm, if he dare speak in your presence of so common and villanous a thing as money?"

Voltaire's eyes sparkled; the subject of conversation did not seem disagreeable to him.

"You have relinquished a pension of six thousand livres in France. It is but just that you receive full compensation. Your great spirit is certainly above all earthly considerations, but our fleshy existence has its rights. So long as you are with me, you shall not be troubled by even a shadow of privation. You will therefore receive a salary of five thousand thalers from me. Your lodging and your table cost you nothing, and I think you can be very comfortable."

Voltaire's heart bounded for joy, but he forced himself to seem calm and indifferent.

"Your majesty has forgotten an important matter," said he. "You have named lodging and food, but you say nothing of light and fire. I am an old man, and cannot produce them myself."

"Truly said—I find it quite in order that the great freethinker and poet of this century is troubled for the light which should illuminate him. You shall have twelve pounds of wax-lights every month; I think this will be sufficient for your purposes. As for the other little necessities of life, have the goodness to apply to the castellan of the castle. On the first day of every month he will supply them regularly. The contract is made; you will remain with me?"

"I remain, sire!—not for the title, or the pension, or the order—I remain with you, because I love you. My heart offers up to you the dream of my life, my journey to Italy. Oh, I wish I could make greater, more dangerous sacrifices! I wish I could find a means to prove my love, my adoration, my worship!"

The king laid his hand softly on Voltaire's shoulder, and looked earnestly in his eyes.

"Be as good a man as you are a great poet. That is the most beautiful offering you can bring me."

"Ah! I see," said Voltaire, enraged; "some one has slandered me. Your majesty has opened your ears to my enemies, and already their hellish poison has reached your heart. As they cannot destroy Voltaire the poet, they seize upon Voltaire the man, and slander his character because they cannot obscure his fame. I will advance to meet them with an open visor and without a shield. From their place of ambush, with their poisoned arrows, let them slay me. It is better to die than to be suspected and contemned by my great and worshipped king."

"See, now, what curious creatures you poets are!" said Frederick; "always in wild tumult and agitation; either storming heaven or hell; contending with demons, or revelling with angels! You have no daily quiet, patience, and perseverance. If you see a man who tells you he is planting potatoes, you do not believe him—you convince yourself he is sowing dragons' teeth to raise an army to contend against you. If you meet one of your fellows with a particularly quiet aspect, you are sure you can read curses against you upon his lip. When one begs you to be good, you look upon it as an accusation. No, no, my poet! no one has poured the poison of slander into my ears—no one has accused you to me. I am, moreover, accustomed to form my own conclusions, and the opinions of others have but little weight with me."

"But your majesty is pleased to lend your ears to my enemies," said Voltaire, sullenly; "exactly those who attack me most virulently receive the highest honors at the hands of your majesty. You are as cruel with me as a beautiful and ravishing coquette. So soon as by a love-glance you have made me the happiest of men, you turn away with cold contempt, and smile alluringly upon my rivals. I have yet two dagger-strokes in my heart, which cause me death-agony. If your majesty would make me truly happy, you must cure the wounds with your own hands."

"I will, if it is possible," said the king, gravely. "Let us hear of what you complain."

"Sire, your majesty has made Fréron your correspondent in Paris—Fréron, my most bitter enemy, my irreconcilable adversary. But it is not because he is my foe that I entreat you to dismiss him; you will not think so pitifully of me as to suppose that this is the reason I entreat you to dismiss him from your service. My personal dislike will not make me blind to the worth of Fréron as a writer. No, sire, Fréron is not worthy of your favor; he is an openly dishonored scoundrel, who has committed more than one common fraud. You may imagine what an excitement it produced in Paris when it was known that you had honored this scamp with a position which should be filled by a man of wisdom and integrity. Fréron is only my enemy because,

in spite of all entreaties, I have closed my house upon him.
I took this step for reasons which should have closed the
doors of every respectable house against him.* Sire, I implore you, do not let the world believe for a single day longer
that Fréron is your correspondent. Dismiss him at once
from your service."

The king did not reply for a few moments; he walked
backward and forward several times, then stood quietly before Voltaire. The expression of his eye was stern.

"I sacrifice Fréron to you," said he, "because I will
deny you nothing on this, the day of your arrival; but I repeat to you what I said before, 'be not only a great poet,
be also a good man.'"

Voltaire shook his head, sadly. "Sire," said he, "in
your eyes I am not a great poet, only *un soleil couchant.*
Remember Arnaud, my pupil, whom I sent to you!"

"Aha!" cried the king, laughing, "you have, then, read
my little poem to Arnaud?"

"Sire, I have read it, and that was the second dagger-
stroke which I received on this journey, to which my loving
heart forced my weak and shrinking body; I felt that I must
see you once more before I died. Yes, I have read this terrible poem, and the lines have burned into my heart these
cruel words:

> ' Déjà sans être téméraire,
> Prenant votre vol jusqu'aux cieux,
> Vous pouvez égaler Voltaire,
> Et près de Virgile et d'Homére.
> Jouir de vos succès heureux,
> Déjà l'Apollon de la France,
> S'achemine à sa décadence,
> Venez briller à votre tour,
> Elevez vous s'il brille encore ;
> Ainsi le couchant d'un beau jour,
> Promét une plus belle aurore.' " †

"Yes," said the king, as Voltaire ceased declaiming, and
stood in rather a tragic attitude before him—" yes, I confess
that a sensitive nature like yours might find a thorn in these

* Voltaire's own words.
† Supplément des Œuvres Posthumes.

innocent rhymes. My only intention was to give to the little
Arnaud a few roses which he might weave into a wreath of
fame. It seems I fulfilled my purpose poorly; it was high
time that Voltaire should come to teach me to make better
verses. See, I confess my injustice, and I allow you to punish
me by writing a poem against me, which shall be published
as extensively as my little verse to Arnaud."

"Does your majesty promise me this little revenge in
earnest?"

"I promise it; give me your poem as soon as it is ready;
it shall be published in ' Formey's Journal.' "

"Sire, it is ready: hear it now.*

> ' Quel diable de Marc Antoine !
>   Et quelle malice est le vôtre,
> Vous égratinez d'une main
>   Lorsque vous caressez de l'autre.' "

"Ah," said Frederick, "what a beautiful quatrain Monsieur Arouet has made."

"Arouet!" said Voltaire, astonished.

"Well, now, you would not surely wish me to believe that
this little stinging, pitiful rhyme, was written by the great
Voltaire. No, no! this is the work of the young Arouet,
and we will have it published with his signature."

Voltaire fixed his great eyes for a moment angrily upon
the handsome face of the king, then bowed his head and
looked down thoughtfully. There was a pause, and his face
assumed a noble expression—he was again the great poet.

"Sire," said he, softly, "I will not have this poem published. You are right, Voltaire does not acknowledge it.
This poor verse was written by Arouet, or the ' old Adam,'
who often strikes the poet Voltaire slyly in the back. But
you, sire, who have already won five battles, and who find a
few morning hours sufficient to govern a great kingdom with
wisdom, consideration, and love; you, by one kindly glance
of your eye, will be able to banish the *old Adam*, and call
heavenly hymns of love and praise from the lips of Voltaire."

"I shall be content with hymns of love. I will spare you

* Œuvres Complètes de Voltaire.

all eulogy," cried Frederick, giving his hand warmly to Voltaire.

At the close of the first day at Sans-Souci, the new gentleman of the bedchamber returned to Potsdam, adorned with the order "*Pour le mérite*," and a written assurance from the king of a pension of five thousand thalers in his pocket.

Two richly-liveried servants received him at the gate of the palace; one of them held a silver candelabrum, in which five wax-lights were burning. Voltaire leaned, exhausted and groaning, upon the arm of the other, who almost carried him into his apartment. Voltaire ordered the servant to place the lights on the table, and to wait in the anteroom for further orders.

Scarcely had the servant left the room when Voltaire, who had thrown himself, as if perfectly exhausted, in the arm-chair, sprang up actively and hastened to the table upon which the candelabrum stood; raising himself on tiptoe, he blew out three of the lights.

"Two are enough," said he, with a grimace. "I am to receive twelve pounds of wax-lights a month. I will be very economical, and out of the proceeds of this self-denial I can realize a little pin-money for my niece, Denis." He took the candelabrum and entered his study.

It was curious to look upon this lonely, wrinkled, decrepit old man, in the richly-furnished but half-obscure room; the dull light illuminated his malicious but smiling face; here and there as he advanced it flashed upon the gilding, or was reflected in a mirror, while behind him the gloom of night seemed to have thrown an impenetrable veil.

Voltaire seated himself at his desk and wrote to his niece, Madame Denis: "I have bound myself with all legal form to the King of Prussia. My marriage with him is determined upon. Will it be happy? I do not know. I could no longer postpone the decisive *yes*. After coquetting for so many years. a wedding was the necessary consequence. How my heart beat at the altar! How could I have supposed, seven months ago, when we arranged our little house in Paris, that I should be to-day three hundred leagues from home in another man's house, and this other a ruler!"[*]

* Œuvres Complètes, 301.

At the same moment wrote Frederick, King of Prussia, to Algarotti: "Voltaire is here; he has of late, as you know, been guilty of an act unworthy of him. He deserves to be branded upon Parnassus. It is a shame that so base a soul should be united to so exalted a genius. Of all this, however, I shall take no notice; he is necessary to me in my study of the French language. One can learn beautiful things from an evil-doer. I must learn his French. I have nothing to do with his morals. He unites in himself the strangest oppositions. The world worships his genius and despises his character." *

CHAPTER III.

THE CONFIDENCE-TABLE.

"AND now, friends, let us be joyful, and forget all the cares and sorrows of the world," cried the king, with a ringing laugh; "fill your glasses and strike them merrily. Long life to us, to jest, to joy!"

The glasses were raised, and as they met they rang out cheerily; they were pressed to the lips and emptied at a draught; the guests then seated themselves silently at the table. Frederick glanced at the circle of his friends who sat with him at the round table; his eyes dwelt searchingly upon every laughing face, then turned to the garden of Sans-Souci, which sent its perfumed breath, its song of birds, its evening breeze, through the open doors and windows, while the moon, rising in cloudless majesty, shone down upon them and rivalled with her silver rays the myriads of wax-lights which glittered in the crystal chandeliers.

"This is a glorious evening," said the king, "and we will enjoy it gloriously."

He ordered the servants to close the doors, place the dessert and champagne upon the table, and leave the room.

* Œuvres de Frédéric le Grand.

Noiselessly and silently this command was fulfilled. Frederick then greeted each one of his guests with a kindly nod.

"Welcome, thrice welcome are you all!" said he. "I have longed to have you all together, and now, at last, you are here. There sits Voltaire, whose divine Emile was delivered first of a book, then of a child, and then released from life before he was free to come to Berlin. There is Algarotti, the swan of Italy, who spreads his wings and would gladly fly to the land of oranges and myrtles. There is La Mettrie, who only remains here because he is convinced that my Cape wine is pure, and my *pâtés de foie gras* truly from Strasbourg. There is D'Argens, who sought safety in Prussia because in every other land in Europe there are sweethearts waiting and sighing for him, to whom he has sworn a thousand oaths of constancy. There is Bastiani, who only remains with us while the Silesian dames, who have frankly confessed their sins to him and been absolved, find time and opportunity to commit other peccadilloes, which they will do zealously, in order to confess them once more to the handsome Abbé Bastiani. And lastly, there is my Lord Marshal, the noblest and best of all, whose presence we owe to the firmness of his political principles and the misfortunes of the house of Stuart."

"And there is the Solomon of the North," cried Voltaire —"there is Frederick, the youngest of us all, and the wisest —the philosopher of Sans-Souci. There sits Apollo, son of the gods, who has descended from Olympus to be our king."

"Let us not speak of kings," said Frederick. "When the sun goes down there is no king at Sans-Souci; he leaves the house and retires into another castle, God only knows where. We are all equal and wholly *sans gêne*. At this table, there are no distinctions; we are seven friends, who laugh and chat freely with each other; or, if you prefer it, seven wise men."

"This is then the Confidence-Table," said Voltaire, "of which D'Argens has so often spoken to me, and which has seemed to me like the Round-Table of King Arthur. Long live the Confidence-Table!"

"It shall live," cried the king, "and we will each one honor this, our first sitting, by showing our confidence in

25

each other. Every one shall relate something piquant and strange of his past life, some lively anecdote, or some sweet little mystery which we dare trust to our friends, but not to our wives. The oldest begins first."

"I am afraid I am that," said Voltaire, "but your majesty must confess that my heart has neither white hair nor wrinkles. Old age is a terrible old woman who slides quietly, grinning and threatening, behind every man, and watches the moment when she dares lay upon him the mask of weary years through which he has lived and suffered. She has, alas! fastened her wrinkled mask upon my face, but my heart is young and green, and if the women were not so short-sighted as to look only upon my outward visage, if they would condescend to look within, they would no longer call me the old Voltaire, but would love and adore me, even as they did in my youth."

"Listen well, friends, he will no doubt tell us of some duchess who placed him upon an altar and bowed down and worshipped him."

"No, sire, I will tell you of an injury, the bitterest I ever experienced, and which I can never forget."

"As if he had ever forgotten an injury, unless he had revenged it threefold!" cried D'Argens.

"And chopped up his enemy for pastry and eaten him," said La Mettrie.

"Truly, if I should eat all my enemies, I should suffer from an everlasting indigestion, and, in my despair, I might fly to La Mettrie for help. It is well known that when you suffer from incurable diseases, you seek, at last, counsel of the quack."

"You forget that La Mettrie is a regular physician," said the king, with seeming earnestness.

"On the contrary, he remembered it well," said La Mettrie, smiling. "The best physician is the greatest quack, or the most active grave-digger, if you prefer it."

"Silence!" said the king. "Voltaire has the floor; he will tell us of the greatest offence he ever received. Give attention."

"Alas! my heart is sad, sire; of all other pain, the pain of looking back into the past is the most bitter. I see myself

again a young man, the Arouet to whom Ninon de l'Enclos
gave her library and a pension, and who was confined for
twenty years to the Bastile because he loved God and the
king too little, and the charming Marquise de Villiers and
some other ladies of the court too much. Besides these exalted ladies, there was a beautiful young maiden whom I
loved—perhaps because she had one quality which I had
never remarked in the possession of my more noble mistresses—she was innocent! Ah, friends, you should have
seen Phillis, and you would have confessed that no rose-bud
was lovelier, no lily purer, than she. Phillis was the daughter of a gypsy and a mouse-catcher, and danced on the tight-
rope in the city-gardens."

"Ah, it appears to me the goddess of innocence dances
always upon the tight-rope in this world," said the king.
"I should not be surprised to hear that even your little
Phillis had a fall."

"Sire, she fell, but in my arms; and we swore eternal
love and constancy. You all know from experience the
quality and fate of such oaths; they are the kindling-wood
upon which the fire of love is sustained; but, alas, kindling
and fire soon burnt out! Who is responsible? Our fire
burned long; but, think you my Phillis, whom I had removed from the tight-rope, and exalted to a dancer upon the
stage, was so innocent and _naïve_ as to believe that our love
must at last be crowned with marriage! I, however, was a
republican, and feared all crowns. I declared that Ninon
de l'Enclos had made me swear never to marry, lest my
grandchildren should fall in love with me, as hers had done
with her."

"Precaution is praiseworthy," said La Mettrie. "The
devil's grandmother had also a husband, and her grandsons
might have fallen in love with her."

"Phillis did not take me for the devil's grandfather, but
for the devil himself. She cried, and shrieked, and cast my
oaths of constancy in my teeth. I did not die of remorse,
nor she of love, and to prove her constancy, she married a
rich Duke de Ventadour."

"And you, no doubt, gave away the bride, and swore you
had never known a purer woman!"

"No, sire, I was at that time again in the Bastile, and left it only as an exile from France. When at last I was allowed to return to Paris, I sought out my Duchess de Ventadour, my Phillis of former times. I found her a distinguished lady; she had forgotten the follies of her youth; had forgotten her father, the rope-dancer; her mother, the mouse-catcher. She had no remembrance of the young Arouet, to whom she had sworn to say only '*tu*' and '*toi*.' Now she was grave and dignified, and '*Vous, monsieur,*' was on her fair lip. Thanks to the heraldry office, she had become the daughter of a distinguished Spaniard, blessed with at least seven ancestors. Phillis gave good dinners, had good wine, and the world overlooked her somewhat obscure lineage. She was the acknowledged and respected Duchess Ventadour. She was still beautiful, but quite deaf; consequently her voice was loud and coarse, when she believed herself to be whispering. She invited me to read some selections from my new work in her saloon, and I was weak enough to accept the invitation. I had just completed my 'Brutus,' and burned with ambition to receive the applause of the *Parisiennes*. I commenced to read aloud my tragedy of 'Brutus' in the saloon of the duchess, surrounded by a circle of distinguished nobles, eminent in knowledge and art. I was listened to in breathless attention. In the deep silence which surrounded me, in the glowing eyes of my audience, in the murmurs of applause which greeted me, I saw that I was still Voltaire, and that the hangman's hands, which had burned my '*Lettres Philosophiques*,' had not destroyed my fame or extinguished my genius. While I read, a servant entered upon tiptoe, to rekindle the fire. The Duchess Ventadour sat near the chimney. She whispered, or thought she whispered, to her servant. I read a little louder to drown her words. I was in the midst of one of the grandest scenes of my tragedy. My own heart trembled with emotion. Here and there I saw eyes, which were not wont to weep, filled with tears, and heard sighs from trembling lips, accustomed only to laughter and smiles. And now I came to the soliloquy of Brutus. He was resolving whether he would sacrifice his son's life to his fatherland. There was a solemn pause, and now, in the midst of the profound silence, the Duchess Ventadour in a shrill voice, which she believed to be inaudible, said to her servant: 'Do not fail to serve mustard with the pig's head!'"

A peal of laughter interrupted Voltaire, in which he reluctantly joined, being completely carried away by the general mirth.

"That was indeed very piquant, and I think you must have been greatly encouraged."

"Did you eat of the pig's head, or were your teeth on edge?"

"No, they were sharp enough to bite, and I bit! In my first rage I closed my book, and cried out: 'Madame——! Well! as you have a pig's head, you do not require that Brutus should offer up the head of his son!' I was on the point of leaving the room, but the poor duchess, who was just beginning to comprehend her unfortunate interruption, hastened after me, and entreated me so earnestly to remain and read further, that I consented. I remained and read, but not from 'Brutus.' My rage made me, for the moment, an improvisator. Seated near to the duchess, surrounded by the proud and hypocritical nobles, who acknowledged Phillis only because she had a fine house and gave good dinners, I improvised a poem which recalled to the grand duchess and her satellites the early days of the fair Phillis, and brought the laugh on my side. My poem was called '*Le tu et le vous.*' Now, gentlemen, this is the story of my 'Brutus' and the pig's head."

"I acknowledge that it is a good story. It will be difficult for you, D'Argens, to relate so good a one," said the king.

"I dare not make the attempt, sire. Voltaire was ever the child of good fortune, and his life and adventures have been extraordinary, while I was near sharing the common fate of younger sons. I was destined for the priesthood."

"That's a droll idea, indeed!" said Frederick. "D'Argens, who believes in nothing, intended for a priest! How did you escape this danger?"

"Through the example of my dear brother, who was of a passionate piety, and became in the school of the Jesuits so complete a fanatic and bigot that he thundered out his fierce tirades against all earthly joys and pastimes, no matter how innocent they were. To resemble the holy Xavier and the sanctified and childlike Alois Gonzago, was his highest ideal. In the extremity of his piety and prudery he slipped into the art-gallery of our eldest brother and destroyed Titian's most splendid paintings and the glorious statues of the olden time. He gloried in this act, and called it a holy offering to virtue. He could not understand that it was vandalism. Our family had serious fears for the intellect of this poor young saint, maddened by the fanaticism of the Jesuits. They sought counsel of the oldest and wisest of our house, the Bishop of Bannes. After thinking awhile, the bishop said: 'I will soon cure the young man of this folly; I will make him a priest.'"

"Truly, your uncle, the bishop, was a wise man; he drove out folly with folly. He knew well that no one had less reverence for the churches than those who have built them, and are their priests."

"That was the opinion of my very worthy uncle.. He said, with a sly laugh: 'When he has heard a few confessions, he will understand the ways of the world better!' The bishop was right. My brother was consecrated. In a short time he became very tolerant and considerate, as a man and as a father confessor."

"But you have not told us, marquis, how the fanaticism of your brother liberated you from the tonsure?" said the king.

"My father found I would commence my priestly life with as much intolerance as my brother had done. He therefore proposed to me to consecrate myself to the world, and, instead of praying in the church, to fight for the cross. The thought pleased me, and I became a Knight of Malta."

"Your first deed of arms was, without doubt, to seat yourself and write your '*Lettres Juives*,'" said the king; "those inspiring letters in which the knight of the cross mocks at Christianity and casts his glove as a challenge to revealed religion."

"No, sire, I began my knightly course by entering the land of heathen and idolators, to see if a man could be

truly happy and contented in a land where there was neither
Messiah nor crucifix—I went to Turkey."

"But you carried your talisman with you?" said the
Abbé Bastiani—"you wore the cross upon your mantle?"

"A remark worthy of our pious abbé," said Frederick;
"no one knows better the protecting power of the cross than
the priest who founded it. Tell us, marquis, did your talisman protect you? Did you become an apostate to the true
faith?"

"Sire, I wished first to see their temples and their mode
of worship, before I decided whether I would be an unbelieving believer or a believing unbeliever."

"I think," said Voltaire, "you have never been a believer, or made a convert; you have made nothing but debts."

"That is, perhaps, because I am not a great writer, and do
not understand usury and speculation," said D'Argens, quietly. "Besides, no courtesan made me her heir, and no mistress obtained me a pension!"

"Look now," said the king, "our good marquis is learning from you, Voltaire; he is learning to scratch and bite."

"Yes," said Voltaire; "there are creatures whom all
men imitate, even in their vile passions and habits; perhaps
they take them for virtues."

The face of the marquis was suffused; he rose angrily,
and was about to answer, but the king laid his hand upon
his arm. "Do not reply to him; you know that our great
poet changes himself sometimes into a wicked tiger, and does
not understand the courtly language of men. Do not regard him, but go on with your story."

The king drew back his hand suddenly, and, seemingly
by accident, touched the silver salt-cellar; it fell and scattered the salt upon the table. The marquis uttered a light
cry, and turned pale.

"Alas!" cried the king, with well-affected horror, "what
a misfortune! Quick, quick, my friends! let us use an anti-
dote against the wiles of the demons, which our good marquis maintains springs always from an overturned salt-cellar.
Quick, quick! take each of you a pinch of salt, and throw it
upon the burners of the chandeliers; listen how it crackles
and splutters! These are the evil spirits in hell-fire, are

they not, marquis? Now let each one take another pinch, and throw it, laughing merrily, over the left shoulder. You, Voltaire, take the largest portion, and cast it from you; I think you have always too much salt, and your most beautiful poems are thereby made unpalatable."

"Ah, sire, you speak of the salt of my wit. No one remembers that the tears which have bathed my face have fallen upon my lips, and become crystallized into biting sarcasms. Only the wretched and sorely tried are sharp of wit and bitter of speech."

"Not so," said La Mettrie; "these things are the consequence of bad digestion. This machine is not acted upon by what you poets call spirit, and I call brain; it reacts upon itself. When a man is melancholy, it comes from his stomach. To be gay and cheery, to have your spirits clear and fresh, you have nothing more to do than to eat heartily and have a good digestion. Molière could not have written such glorious comedies if he had fed upon sour krout and old peas, instead of the woodcock, grouse, and truffles which fell to him from King Louis's table. Man is only a machine, nothing more."

"La Mettrie, I will give you to-morrow nothing but grouse and truffles to eat: woe to you, then, if the day after you do not write me just such a comedy as Molière's! But we entirely forget that the marquis owes us the conclusion of his story; we left him a Knight of Malta, and we cannot abandon him in this position; that would be to condemn him to piety and virtue. Go on, dear marquis, we have thrown the salt and banished the demons—go on, then, with your history."

"Well," said the marquis, "to relate it is less dangerous than to live through it. I must confess, however, that the perils of life have also their charms. I wished, as I had the honor to say to you, to witness a religious service in the great mosque at Constantinople, and by my prayers, supported by a handful of gold pieces, I succeeded in convincing the Turk, who had the care of the key to the superb Sophia, that it was not an unpardonable sin to allow an unbelieving Christian to witness the holy worship of an unbelieving Mussulman. Indeed, he risked nothing but the bastinado;

while I, if discovered, would be given over to the hangman, and could only escape my fate by becoming a Mussulman."

"What an earnest and profitable Christian Holy Mother Church would thus have lost in the author of *Les Lettres Juives!*" said Frederick, laughing.

"But what an exquisite harem the city of Constantinople would have won!" cried Voltaire.

"What a happiness for you, my Lord Marshal, that your beautiful Mohammedan was not then born; the marquis would without doubt have bought her from you!"

"If Zuleima will allow herself to be bought, there will be nothing to pay," said Lord Marshal, with a soft smile.

"You are right, my lord," said the marquis, with a meaning side glance at Voltaire, "you are right; nothing is more despicable than the friendship which can be purchased."

"You succeeded, however, in bribing the good Mussulman," said Algarotti, "and enjoyed the unheard-of happiness of witnessing their worship."

"Yes, the night before a grand *fête*, my Turk led me to the mosque, and hid me behind a great picture which was placed before one of the doors of the tribune. This was seemingly a safe hiding-place. The tribune was not used, and years had passed since the door had been opened. It lay, too, upon the southern side of the mosque, and you know that the worshippers of Mohammed must ever turn their faces toward Mecca, that is, to the morning sun; I was sure, therefore, that none of these pious unbelievers would ever look toward me. From my concealment I could with entire comfort observe all that passed; but I made my Turk most unhappy in the eagerness of my curiosity. I sometimes stepped from behind my picture, and leaned a little over the railing. My poor Mussulman entreated me with such a piteous mien, and pointed to the soles of his feet with such anguish, that I was forced to take pity on him and withdraw into my concealment. But at last, in spite of the solemnities, and my own ardent piety, the animal was roused within and overcame me. I was hungry! and as I had expected this result, I had placed a good bottle of wine and some ham and fresh bread in my pocket. I now took them out, spread my treasures upon the floor, and began to breakfast. The Turk looked at me with horror, and he would not have been surprised if the roof of the holy mosque had fallen upon the Christian hound who dared to desecrate it by drinking wine and eating ham within its precincts, both of which were strictly forbidden by the prophet. But the roof did not fall, not even when I forced my Mussulman to eat ham and drink wine with me, by threatening to show myself openly if he refused. He commenced his unholy meal with dark frowns and threatening glances, ever looking up, as if he feared the sword of the prophet would cleave him asunder. Soon, however, he familiarized himself with his sin, and forgot the holy ceremonies which were being solemnized. When the service was over, and all others had left the mosque, he prayed me to wait yet a little longer, and as the best of friends, we finished the rest of my bacon and drank the last drop of my wine to the health of the prophet, laughing merrily over the dangers we had escaped. As at last we were about to separate, my good Turk was sad and thoughtful, and he confessed to me that he had the most glowing desire to become a Christian. The bacon and wine had refreshed him marvellously, and he was enthusiastic for a religion which offered such glorious food, not only for the soul, but for the body. I was too good a Christian not to encourage his holy desires. I took him into my service, and when we had left Turkey, and found ourselves on Christian soil, my Mussulman gratified the thirst of his soul, and became a son of Holy Mother Church, and felt no remorse of conscience in eating ham and drinking wine. So my visit to the holy mosque was rich in blessed consequences; it saved a soul, and my wine and my ham plucked a man from the hell-fire of unbelief. That is, I believe, the only time I ever succeeded in making a proselyte."

"The salvation of that soul will free you from condemnation and insure your own eternal happiness. When you come to die, marquis, you dare say, 'I have not lived in vain, I have won a soul to heaven.'"

"Provided," said Voltaire, "that the bacon with which you converted the Turk was not part of one of the beasts into which the devils were cast, as is written in the Holy

Scriptures. If this was so, then the newly-baked Christian has certainly eaten of everlasting damnation."

"Let us hope that this is not so," said Frederick; "and now, my Lord Marshal, it is your turn to give us a piquant anecdote; or, if you prefer it, an heroic deed from your life, so rich in virtue, magnanimity, truth, and constancy. Ah, messieurs, let us now be thoughtful, cast down our eyes, and exalt our hearts. A virtuous man is about to speak: truly virtue is a holy goddess loved by few, to whom few altars are erected, and who has few priests in her service. My Lord Marshal is consecrated to her altar; you may well believe this when I assure you of it—I, who have been so often deceived, and often tempted to believe no longer in the existence of virtue. My noble Keith has forced me to be credulous. This faith comforts me, and I thank him."

With a glance of inexpressible love he gave his hand to his friend, who pressed it to his breast. The faces of all present were grave, almost stern. The words of the king were a reproach, and they felt wounded. Frederick thought not of them; he looked alone upon the noble, handsome face of Lord Marshal, not remembering that the love and consideration manifested for him might excite the envy and jealousy of his other friends.

"Now, my lord, will you commence your history, or are we too impure and sinful to listen to any of the holy mysteries of your pure life?"

"Ah, sire, there are no mysteries in my simple life; it lies like an open book before the eyes of my king, and, indeed, to all the world."

"In that pure book I am sure that all can learn wisdom and experience," said Frederick. "It is a book of rarest value, in which every nobleman can learn how to be faithful to his king in dire misfortune and to the gates of death. Ah, my lord, there are few men like yourself, who can count it as imperishable fame to have been condemned to the scaffold. The Pretender must, indeed, be a most noble prince, as you were willing to give your life for him."

"He was my rightful king and lord, and I owed him allegiance. That I was condemned for him, and pardoned, and banished from England, I cannot now consider a misfortune, as I have thereby enjoyed the great happiness of being near your majesty. But you must not think too highly of my constancy to 'the Pretender;' it was not pure loyalty, and if I carelessly and rashly cast my life upon a wild chance, it was because the world had but little value for me. In the despair and anguish of my heart I should have called Death a welcome friend. Had I been happier I should have been less brave."

"And will you tell us, my lord, why you were unhappy?"

"Sire, mine is a simple little history, such as is daily acted out in this weary world. We are all, however, proud to think that none have suffered as we have done. There are many living hearts covered as with a gravestone, under which every earthly happiness is shrouded, but the world is ignorant and goes laughing by. My heart has bled in secret, and my happiness is a remembrance; my life once promised to be bright and clear as the golden morning sun. The future beckoned to me with a thousand glorious promises and greeted me with winning, magic smiles. I saw a young, lovely, innocent, modest maiden, like a spring rose, with heaven's dew still hanging untouched upon its soft leaves. I saw and loved; it seemed to me God had sent me in her His most wondrous revelation. I loved, I worshipped her. She was the daughter of a distinguished French noble. I went to Paris, a young and modest man, highly commended to many influential and powerful families of the court. We met daily; at first with wonder and surprise; then, with deep emotion, we heard each other's voices without daring to speak together; and then, at last, I no longer dared to utter a word in her presence, because my voice trembled and I could not control it. One day, as we sat silently next each other in a large assembly, I murmured in low, broken tones: 'If I dared to love you, would you forgive me?' She did not look up, but she said, 'I should be happy.' We then sank again into our accustomed silence, only looking from time to time into each other's happy eyes. This lasted *six* weeks, *six weeks* of silent but inexpressible happiness. At last I overcame my timidity and made known the sweet mystery of my love. I demanded the hand of my Victoire from her father; he gave a cheerful consent, and led me to my beloved. I pressed

her to my heart, drunk with excess of joy. At this moment
her grandmother entered with a stern face and scornful
glance. She asked if I was a Protestant. This fearful
question waked me from my dream of bliss. In the rapture
of the last few months I had thought of nothing but my love.
Love had become my religion, and I needed no other influence
to lead me to worship God. But this, alas, was not sufficient! I declared myself a Protestant. Victoire uttered a
cry of anguish, and sank insensible into her father's arms.
Two days afterward I left France. Victoire would not see
me, and refused my hand. I returned to England, broken-
hearted, desperate, almost insane. In this delirium of grief
I joined 'the Pretender,' and undertook for him and his
cause the wildest and most dangerous adventures, which
ended, at last, in my being captured and condemned to the
block. This, your majesty, was the only love of my life.
You see I had, indeed, but little to relate."

Frederick said nothing, and no one dared to break the
silence. Even Voltaire repressed the malicious jest which
played upon his lip, and was forced to content himself with
a mocking smile.

"What were the words that your father spoke when he
sent you forth as a man into the world? I think you once repeated them to me," said Frederick.

> " Quand vos yeux, en naissant, s'ouvraient à la lumière,
>   Chacun vous souriait, mon fils, et vous pleuriez.
>   Vivez si bien, qu'un jour, à votre dernière heure,
>   Chacun verse des pleurs, et qu'on vous voie sourire."

"You have fulfilled your father's wish," said the king.
"You have so lived, that you can smile when all others are
weeping for you, and no man who has loved can forget you.
I am sure your Victoire will never forget you. Have you
not seen her since that first parting?"

"Yes, sire, I have seen her once again, as I came to
Prussia, after being banished forever from England. Ah,
sire, that was a happy meeting after twenty years of separation. The pain and grief of love were over, but the love
remained. We confessed this to each other. In the beginning there was suffering and sorrow, then a sweet, soft re-

membrance of our love, for we had never ceased to think upon each other. It seems that to love faithfully and eternally it is only necessary to love truly and honorably, and then to separate. Custom and daily meeting cannot then brush the bloom from love's light wings; its source is in heaven, and it returns to the skies and shines forever and inextinguishable a star over our heads. When I looked again upon Victoire she had been a long time married, and to the world she had, perhaps, ceased to be beautiful. To me she will be ever lovely; and as she looked upon me it seemed to me that the clouds and shadows had been lifted from my life, and my sun was shining clear. But, sire, all this has no interest for you. How tenderly I loved Victoire you will know, when I tell you that the only poem my unpoetical brain has ever produced was written for her."

"Let us hear it, my lord," said the king.

"If your majesty commands it, and Voltaire will forgive it," said Lord Marshal.

"I forgive it, my lord," cried Voltaire. "Since I listened to you I live in a land of wonders and soft enchantments, whose existence I have never even guessed, and upon whose blooming, perfumed beauty I scarcely dare open my unholy eyes. The fairy tales of my dreamy youth seem now to be true, and I hear a language which we, poor sons of France, living under the regency of the Duke of Orleans, have no knowledge of. I entreat you, my lord, let us hear your poem."

Lord Marshal bowed, and, leaning back in his chair, in a full rich voice, he recited the following verses:

> " ' Un trait lancé par caprice
> M'atteignit dans mon printemps;
> J'en porte la cicatrice
> Encore, sous mes cheveux blancs.
> Craignez les maux qu'amour cause,
> Et plaignez un insensé
> Qui n'a point cueilli la rose,
> Et qui l'épine a blessé.' *

"And now," said Lord Marshal rapidly, wishing to interrupt all praise and all remark as to his poem; "I have yet

* Mémoires de la Marquise de Créqui.

a confession to make, and if you have not laughed over my verses, you will surely laugh at what I now state. Out of love for my lost mistress, I became a Catholic. I thought that the faith, to which my Victoire offered up her love, must be the true religion in which all love was grounded. I wished to be hers in spirit, in life, and in death. In spirit, in truth, I am a Catholic; and now, gentlemen, you may laugh."

"Sublime!" whispered Voltaire.

"No one will smile," said the king, sternly. "Joy and peace to him who is a believer, and can lay his heart upon the cross, and feel strengthened and supported by it. He will not wander in strange and forbidden paths, as we poor, short-sighted mortals often do. Will you tell us the name of your beloved mistress, or is that a secret?"

"Sire, our love was pure and innocent; we dare avow it to the whole world. My beloved's name was Victoire de Froulay; she is now Marquise de Créqui."

"Ah, the Marquise de Créqui!" said Voltaire, with animation; "one of the wittiest and most celebrated women of Paris."

"She is still living?" said the king, thoughtfully. "would you like to meet her again, my lord?"

"Yes, your majesty, for one hour, to say to her that I am a Catholic, and that we shall meet in heaven!"

"I will send you as ambassador to Paris, my lord, and you shall bear the marquise my greetings." *

"Your majesty will thus be acting an epigram for George of England," said Voltaire, laughing. "Two of his noblest rebels will be cementing the friendship of France and Prussia. Lord Tyrconnel, the Irishman, is ambassador from France to Prussia, and my Lord Marshal Keith is to be ambassador from Prussia to France. Ah, my lord! how will the noble marquise rejoice when her faithful knight shall introduce to her his most beautiful possession—the young and lovely Mohammedan Zuleima! How happy will Zuleima be when you point out to her the woman who loved you so fondly! She will then know, my lord, that you also once had a heart, and have been beloved by a woman."

"I will present my little Zuleima to the marquise," said

* Lord Marshal went to Paris, as an ambassador from Prussia, in 1751.

Lord Marshal; "and, when I tell her that she was a bequest of my dear brother, who, at the storming of Oschakow, where he commanded as field-marshal, rescued her from the flames, she will find it just and kind that I gave the poor orphan a home and a father. I wish first, however, to give Zuleima a husband, if your majesty will allow it. The Tartar Ivan, my chamberlain, loves Zuleima, and she shall be his wife if your majesty consents."

"By all means," said Frederick; "but I fear it will be difficult to have this marriage solemnized in Berlin. Your Tartar, I believe, has the honor to be heathen."

"Sire, he is, in faith, a Persian."

"A fire-worshipper, then," said Frederick. "Well, I propose that Voltaire shall bless this marriage; where fire is worshipped as a god, Voltaire, the man of fire and flame, may well be priest."

"Ah, sire, I believe we are all Persians; surely we all worship the light, and turn aside from darkness. You are to us the god Ormuzd, from whom all light proceeds; and every priest is for us as Ahriman, the god of darkness. Be gracious to me, then, your majesty, and do not call upon me to play the *rôle* of priest even in jest. But why does this happy son of the heathen require a priest? Is not the sun-god Ormuzd himself present? With your majesty's permission, we will place the loving pair upon the upper terrace of Sans-Souci, where they will be baptized in holy fire by the clear rays of the mid-day sun. Then the divine Marianna, Cochois, and Denys will perform some mystical dance, and so the marriage will be solemnized according to Persian rites and ceremonies."

"And then, I dare hope your majesty will give a splendid wedding-feast, where costly wines and rich and rare viands will not fail us," said La Mettrie.

"Look, now, how his eyes sparkle with anticipated delights!" cried the king. "La Mettrie would consent to wed every woman in the world if he could thereby spend his whole life in one continuous wedding-feast; but listen, sir, before you eat again, you have a story to relate. Discharge this duty at once, and give us a piquant anecdote from your gay life."

CHAPTER IV.

THE CONFIDENTIAL DINNER.

"YOUR majesty desires a piquant anecdote out of my own life," said La Mettrie. "Is there any thing on earth more piquant than a truffle-pie? Can any thing deserve more ardent praise, and fonder, sweeter remembrance, than this beautiful revelation of man's genius? Yes, sire, a successful truffle-pie is a sort of revealed religion, and I am its devout, consecrated priest! One day I relinquished, for the love of it, a considerable fortune, a handsome house, and a very pretty bride, and I confess that even now a truffle-pie has more irresistible charms for me than any bride, even though richly endowed."

"And was there ever a father mad enough to give his daughter to the '*homme machine?*'" said the king

"Sire, I had just then written my 'Penelope.' Monsieur van Swiet, of Leyden, a poor invalid, who had been for weeks confined to his bed by a cold, read it, and laughed so heartily over the mockery and derision at the gentlemen doctors, that he fell into a profuse perspiration—a result which neither the art of the physicians nor the prayers of the priests had been able to accomplish. The stiffness in his limbs was healed; in fact, he was restored to health! His first excursion was to see me, and he implored me to suggest a mode by which he could manifest his gratitude. 'Send me every day a truffle-pie and a bottle of Hungarian wine,' I replied. Swiet was greatly amused. 'I have something better than a truffle-pie,' said he. 'I have a daughter who will inherit all my fortune. You are not rich in ducats, but largely endowed with wit. I wish that my grandchildren, who will be immensely wealthy, may have a father who will endow them richly with intellect. Wed my daughter, and present me with a grandson exactly like yourself.' I accepted this proposition, and promised the good Van Swiet to become his son-in-law in eight days; to dwell with him in his house, and to cheer and enliven him daily for a few hours after dinner, with merry, witty conversation, that his liver might be kept in motion, and his digestion improved."

"Just think of this tender Hollander, this disinterested father, who selects a husband for his daughter in order to improve his digestion!"

"Did you not see your bride before the wedding? Perhaps she was a changeling, whom the father wished to get rid of in some respectable manner, and therefore gave her to you."

"I saw my bride, sire, and indeed Esther was a lovely girl, who had but one fault—she did not love me. She had the *naïveté* to tell me so, and indeed to confess that she ardently loved another, a poor clerk of her father's, who, when their love was discovered, a short time before, had been turned out of the house. They loved each other none the less glowingly for all this. I shrugged my shoulders, and recalled the wish of her father, and my promise to him. But when the little Esther implored me to refuse her hand, and plead with her father for her beloved, I laughed and jested no longer, but began to look at the thing gravely. I did go to her father, and informed him of all that had passed. He listened to me quietly, and then asked me, with a fearful grimace, if I preferred prison fare to truffle-pie, every day, at my own table. You can imagine that I did not hesitate in my choice.

"'Well, then,' said my good Swiet, 'if you do not wed my daughter, I will withdraw my protecting hand from you, and your enemies will find a means to cast you into prison. A new book, "*L'Homme Machine*," has just appeared, and every man swears it is your production, though your name is not affixed to the title-page. The whole city, not only the priests, but the worldlings, are enraged over this book. They declare it is a monster of unbelief and materialism. If, in spite of all this, I accept you as my son-in-law, it is because I wish to show the world that I despise it, and am not in the slightest degree influenced by its prejudices and opinions, but am a bold, independent, freethinker. Decide, then! Will you marry my daughter and eat truffle-pie daily, or will you be cast into prison?'

"'I will marry your daughter! I swear that in eight days she shall be my wife!'

"Herr van Swiet embraced me warmly, and commenced his preparations for the wedding immediately. Esther, however, my bride, never spoke to me; never seemed to see me. Her eyes were swollen, and she was half-blind from weeping. Once we met alone in the saloon. She hastened to leave it; but, as she passed by me, she raised her arms to heaven, then extended them threateningly toward me. 'You are a cruel and bad man. You will sacrifice a human soul to your greed and your irresistible and inordinate desires! If God is just, you will die of a truffle-pie! I say not that you will yield up your spirit, for you have none! You will, you must die like a beast—from beastly gluttony!'"

"The maiden possessed the wisdom of a sibyl," said the king, "and I fear she has prophesied correctly as to your sad future. *Hate* has sometimes the gift of prophecy, and sees the future clearly, while Love is blind. It appears to me your Esther did not suffer from the passion of love."

"No, sire, she hated me. But her lover, the young Mieritz, did not share this dislike. He seemed warmly attached to me; was my inseparable companion; embraced me with tears, and forgave me for robbing him of his beloved, declaring that I was more worthy of her than himself. He went so far in his manifestations of friendship as to invite me to breakfast on the morning of my wedding-day, at which time he wished to present me with something sumptuous he had brought from Amsterdam. I accepted the invitation, and as the wedding-ceremony was to take place at twelve o'clock, in the cathedral, we were compelled to breakfast at eleven. I was content. I thought I could better support the wearisome ceremony if sustained by the fond remembrance of the luxurious meal I had just enjoyed. Our breakfast began punctually at eleven, and I assure your majesty it was a rare and costly feast. My young friend Mieritz declared, however, that the dish which crowned the feast was yet to come. At last he stepped to the kitchen himself to bring this jewel of his breakfast. With a mysterious smile he quickly returned, bringing upon a silver dish a smoking pie. A delicious fragrance immediately pervaded the whole room—a fragrance which then recalled the hour most rich in blessing of my whole life. Beside myself—filled with prophetic

expectation—I rushed forward and raised the top crust of
the pie. Yes, it was there!—it met my ravished gaze!—the
pie which I had only eaten once, at the table of the Duke
de Grammont! Alas! I lost the good duke at the battle
of Fontenoy, and the great mystery of this pasty went down
with him into the hero's grave. And now that it was ex-
humed, it surrounded me with its costly aroma; it smiled
upon me with glistening lips and voluptuous eyes. I
snatched the dish from the hands of my friend, and placed it
before me on the table. At this moment the clock struck
twelve.

"'Miserable wretch!' I cried, 'you bring me this pie,
and this is the hour of my marriage!'

"'Well,' said Mieritz, with the cool phlegm of a Hollander, 'let us go first to the wedding, and then this pasty
can be warmed up.'

"'Warmed up!' roared I; 'warm up this pie, whose
delicious odor has already brought my nose into its magic
circle! Can you believe I would outlive such a vandalism,
that I would consent to such sacrilege? To warm a pie!—it
is to rob the blossom of its fragrance, the butterfly of the
purple and azure of its wings, beauty of its innocence, the
golden day of its glory. No, I will never be guilty of such
deadly crime! This pie *thirsts* to be eaten! I will, therefore, eat it!'

"I ate it, sire, and it overpowered me with heavenly
rapture. I was like the opium-eater, wrapped in elysium,
carried into the heaven of heavens. All the wonders of
creation were combined in this heavenly food, which I thrust
into my mouth devoutly, and trembling with gladness. It
was not necessary for Mieritz to tell me that this pie was
made of Indian birds'-nests, and truffles from Perigord.
I knew it—I felt it! This wonder of India had unveiled my
enraptured eyes! A new world was opened before me! I
ate, and I was blessed!

"What was it to me that messenger after messenger
came to summon me, to inform me that the priest stood before the altar; that my young bride and her father and a
crowd of relations awaited me with impatience? I cried
back to them: 'Go! be off with you! Let them wait till

the judgment-day! I will not rise from this seat till this dish is empty!' I ate on, and while eating my intellect was clearer, sharper, more profound than ever before! I rejoiced over this conviction. Was it not a conclusive proof that my theory was correct, that this '*homme machine*' received its intellectual fluid, its power of thought through itself, and not through this fabulous, bodiless something which metaphysicians call soul? Was not this a proof that, to possess a noble soul, it was only necessary to give to the body noble nourishment? And where lies this boasted soul? where else but in the stomach? The stomach is the soul; I allow it is the brain that thinks, but the brain dares only think as his exalted majesty the stomach allows; and if his royal highness feels unwell, farewell to thought." *

The whole company burst out in loud and hearty laughter.

"Am I not right to call you a *fou fieffé?*" said the king. "There is an old proverb, which says of a coward, that his heart lies in his stomach; never before have I heard the soul banished there. But your hymns of praise over the stomach and the pie have made you forget to finish your story; let us hear the conclusion! Did the marriage take place?"

"Sire, I had not quite finished my breakfast when the door was violently opened, and a servant rushed in and announced that the good Van Swiet had had a stroke of apoplexy in the cathedral. The foolish man declared that rage and indignation over my conduct had produced this fearful result; I am, myself, however, convinced that it was the consequence of a good rich breakfast and a bottle of Madeira wine; this disturbed the circulation of the blood, and he was chilled by standing upon the cold stone floor of the church. Be that as it may, poor Swiet was carried unconscious from the church to his dwelling, and in a few hours he was dead! Esther, his daughter and heir, was unfilial enough to leave the wish of her father unfulfilled. She would not acknowledge our contract to be binding, declared herself the bride of the little Mieritz, and married him in a few months. I had, indeed, a legal claim upon her, but Swiet was right when he assured me that so soon as he with-

* La Mettrie's own words.

drew his protection from me, the whole pack of fanatical priests and weak-minded scholars would fall upon and tear me to pieces, unless I saved myself by flight. So I obeyed your majesty's summons, took my pilgrim-staff, and wandered on, like Ahasuerus."

"What! without taking vengeance on the crafty Mieritz, who, it is evident, had carried out successfuly a well-considered strategy with his pie?" said the king. "You must know that was all arranged: he caught you with his pie, as men catch mice with cheese."

"Even if I knew that to be so, your majesty, I should not quarrel with him on that account. I should have only said to my pie, as Holofernes said to Judith: 'Thy sin was a great enjoyment, I forgive you for slaying me!' For such a pie I would again sacrifice another bride and another fortune!"

"And is there no possible means to obtain it?" said the king. "Can you not obtain the receipt for this wonderful dish, which possesses the magic power to liberate young women from intolerable men, and change a miser into a spendthrift who thrusts his whole fortune down his throat?"

"There is a prospect, sire, of securing it, but you cannot be the first to profit by it. Lord Tyrconnel, who knows my history, opened a diplomatic correspondence with Holland, some weeks ago, on this subject, and the success of an important loan which France wishes to effect with the house of Mieritz and Swiet, through the mediation of Lord Tyrconnel, hangs upon the obtaining of this receipt. If Mieritz refuses it, France will not make the loan. In that case the war, which now seems probable with England, will not take place."

"And yet it is said that great events can only arise from great causes," cried the king. "The peace of the world now hangs upon the receipt of a truffle-pie, which La Mettrie wishes to obtain."

"What is the peace of the world in comparison with the peace of our souls?" cried Voltaire. "La Mettrie may say what he will, and the worthy Abbé Bastiani may be wholly silent, but I believe I have a soul, which does not lie in my stomach, and this soul of mine will never be satisfied till your majesty keeps your promise, and relates one of those intellectual, piquant histories, glowing with wisdom and poesy, which so often flows from the lips of our Solomon!"

"It is true it is now my turn to speak," said Frederick, smiling. "I will be brief. Not only the lights, but also the eyes of Algarotti, are burning dimly; and look how the good marquis is, in thought, making love-winks toward his night-cap, which lies waiting for him upon his bed! But be comforted, gentlemen, my story is short. Like La Mettrie, I will relate a miracle, in which, however the eyes were profited, the stomach had no interest. This miracle took place in Breslau, in the year 1747.

"Cardinal Zinzendorf was just dead, and the Duke Schafgotch, who some years before I had appointed his coadjutor, was to be his successor. But the Silesians were not content. They declared that Duke Schafgotch was too fond of the joys and pleasures of the world to be a good priest; that he thought too much of the beautiful women of this world to be able to offer to the holy Madonna, the mother of God, the sanctified, ardent, but pure and modest love of a true son of the church. The pious Silesians refused to believe that the duke was sufficiently holy to be their bishop. The sage fathers of the city of Breslau assured me that nothing less than a miracle could secure for him the love and consideration of the Silesians. I had myself gone to Silesia to see if the statement of the authorities was well-founded, and if the people were really so discontented with the new bishop. I found their statement fully confirmed. Only a great miracle could incline the pious hearts of the Silesians to the duke.

"And now remark, messieurs, how Providence is always with the pious and the just—this desired miracle took place! On a lovely morning a rumor was spread abroad, in the city of Breslau, that in the chapel of the Holy Mother of God a miracle might be seen. All Breslau—the loveliest ladies of the *haute volée*, and the poorest beggars of the street—rushed to the church to look upon this miracle. Yes, it was undeniable! The hair of the Madonna, which stood in enticing but wooden beauty upon the altar, whose clothing was furnished by the first *modistes*, and whose hair by the first *perruquier*—this hair, wonderful to relate, had grown! It was natural that she should exercise supernatural power. The blind, the lame, the crippled were cured by her touch. I myself—for you may well think that I hastened to see the miracle—saw a lame man throw away his crutch and dance a *minuet* in honor of the Madonna. There was a blind man who approached with a broad band bound over his eyes. He was led forward to this wonderful hair. Scarcely had the lovely locks touched his face, than he tore the band from his eyes, and shouted with ecstasy—his sight was restored! Thousands, who were upon their knees praying in wrapt devotion, shouted in concert with him, and here and there inspired voices called out: ‘The holy Madonna is content with her new servant the bishop! if she were not, she would not perform these miracles.’ These voices fell like a match in this magazine of excitement. Men wept and embraced each other, and thanked God for the new bishop, whom yesterday they had refused.

“In the meantime, however, there were still some suspicious, distrustful souls who would not admit that the growth of the Madonna’s hair was a testimony in favor of the bishop. But these stiff-necked unbelievers, these heartless skeptics, were at last convinced. Two days later this lovely hair had grown perceptibly; and still two days later, it hung in luxurious length and fulness over her shoulders. No one could longer doubt that the Holy Virgin was pleased with her priest. It had often happened that hair had turned gray, or been torn out by the roots in rage and scorn. No one, however, can maintain that the hair grows unless we are in a happy and contented mood. The Madonna, therefore, was pleased. The wondrous growth of her hair enraptured the faithful, and all mankind declared that this holy image cut from a pear-tree, was the Virgin Mary, who with open eyes watched over Breslau, and whose hair grew in honor of the new Bishop Schafgotch—he was now almost adored. Thousands of the believers surrounded his palace and besought his blessing. It was a beautiful picture of a shepherd and his flock. The Madonna no longer found it necessary to make her hair grow; one miracle had sufficed, and with the full growth of her hair the archbishop had also grown into importance."

"But your majesty has not yet named the holy saint at whose intercession this miracle was performed," said the Marquis D'Argens. "Graciously disclose the name, that we may pray for pardon and blessing."

"This holy saint was my *friseur*," said the king, laughing. "I made him swear that he would never betray my secret. Every third day, in the twilight, he stole secretly to the church, and placed a new wig upon the Madonna, and withdrew the old one.* You see, messieurs, that not only happiness but piety may hang on a hair, and those holy saints to whom the faithful pray were, without doubt, adroit *perruquiers* who understand their cue."

"And who use it as a scourge upon the backs of the pious penitents," said Voltaire. "Ah, sire! your story is as wise as it is piquant—it is another proof that you are a warrior. You have won a spiritual battle with your miraculous wig, a battle against Holy Mother Church."

"By which, happily, no soldiers and only a few wigs were left behind. But see how grave and mute our very worthy abbé appears—I believe he is envious of the miracle I performed! And now it is your turn, Bastiani: give us your story—a history of some of the lovely Magdalens you have encountered."

"Ah, sire! will not your majesty excuse me?" said the abbé, bowing low. "My life has been the still, quiet, lonely, unostentatious life of a priest, and only the ever-blessed King Frederick William introduced storm and tempest into its even course. That was, without doubt, God's will; otherwise this robust and giant form which He gave me would have been in vain. My height and strength so enraptured the emissaries of the king, that in the middle of the service before the altar, as I was reading mass, they tore me away without regarding the prayers and outcries of my flock. I was violently borne off, and immediately enrolled as a soldier."†

"A wonderful idea!" cried Voltaire, "to carry off a

* Authentic addition to the "History of Frederick the Second."
† Thiébault.

priest in his vestments and make a soldier of him; but say, now, abbé, could you not, at least, have taken your house-keeper with you? I dare say she was young and pretty."

"I do not know," said Bastiani; "I am, as you know, very short-sighted, and I never looked upon her face; but it was a great misfortune for a priest to be torn from the Tyrolese mountains and changed into a soldier. But now, I look upon this as my greatest good fortune; by this means were the eyes of my exalted king fixed upon me; he was gracious, and honored me with his condescending friend-ship."

"You forget there is no king here, and that here no man must be flattered," said Frederick, frowning.

"Sire, I know there is no king present, and that proves I am no flatterer. I speak of my love and admiration to my king, but not to his face. I praise and exalt him be-hind his back; that shows that I love him dearly, not for honor or favor, but out of a pure heart fervently."

"What happiness for your pure and unselfish heart, that your place of canonary of Breslau brings in three thousand thalers! otherwise your love, which does not understand flattery, might leave you in the lurch; you might be hungry."

"He that eats of the bread of the Lord shall never hunger," said Bastiani, in a low and solemn voice; "he that will serve two masters will be faithful to neither, and may fear to be hungry."

"Oh, oh! look at our pious abbé, who throws off his sheep's skin and turns the rough side out," cried Voltaire. "It is written, 'The sheep shall be turned into wolves,' and you, dear abbé, in your piety fulfil this prophecy."

"Your witty illusions are meant for me because I am the historian of the King of France, and gentleman of the bed-chamber to the King of Prussia. Compose yourself. As historian to the King of France, I have no pension, and his majesty of Prussia will tell you that I am the most useless of servants that the sun of royal favor ever shone upon. Yes, truly, I am a poor, modest, trifling, good-for-nothing creature; and if his majesty did not allow me, from time to time, to read his verses and rejoice in their beauty, and here and there to add a comma, I should be as useless a being as that Catholic priest stationed at Dresden, at the court of King Augustus, who has nothing to do—no man or woman to confess—there, as here, every man being a Lutheran. Algarotti told me he asked him once how he occupied himself. The worthy abbé answered: '*Io sono il cattolica di sua maestà.*' So I will call myself, '*Il pedagogue di sua maestà.*'* Like yourself, I serve but one master."

"Alas! I fear my *cattolica* will not linger long by me," said the king. "A man of his talent and worth cannot content himself with being canon of Breslau. No, Bastiani, you will, without doubt, rise higher. You will become a prelate, an eminence; yes, you will, perhaps, wear the tiara. But what shall I be when you have mounted this glittering pinnacle—when you have become pope? I wager you will deny me your apostolic blessing; that you will not even allow me to kneel and kiss your slipper. If any man should dare to name me to you, you would no longer remember this unselfish love, which, without doubt, you feel passionately for me at this moment. Ah! I see you now rising from St. Peter's chair with apostolic sublimity, and exclaiming with praiseworthy indignation: 'How! this heretic, this unclean, this savage from hell! I curse him, I condemn him. Let no man dare even to name him.'"

"Grace, grace, sire!" cried the abbé, holding his hands humbly, and looking up at the king.

The other gentlemen laughed heartily. The king was inexorable. The specious holiness and hypocrisy which the abbé had brought upon the stage incensed him, and he was resolved to punish it.

"Now, if you were pope, and I am convinced you will be, I should, without doubt, go to Rome. It is very important for me to ascertain, while I have you here, what sort of a reception you would accord me? So, let us hear. When I appear before your holiness, what will you say to me?"

The abbé, who had been sitting with downcast eyes, and murmuring from time to time in pleading tones: "Ah, sire! ah, sire!" now looked up, and a flashing glance fell upon the handsome face of the king, now glowing with mirth.

* "Œuvres Complètes de Voltaire," p. 376.

"Well?" repeated the king, "what would you say to me?"

"Sire," said Bastiani, bowing reverently, "I would say, 'Almighty eagle, cover me with your wings, and protect me from your own beak.'" *

"That is an answer worthy of your intellect," said the king, smiling, "and in consideration of it I will excuse you from relating some little history of your life.—Now, Duke Algarotti, your time has come. You are the last, and no doubt you will conclude the evening worthily."

"Sire, my case is similar to Bastiani's. There has been no mystery in my life; only that which seemed miraculous for a priest was entirely natural and simple in my case. I have travelled a great deal, have seen the world, known men; and all my experience and the feelings and convictions of my heart have at last laid me at the feet of your majesty. I am like the faithful, who, having been healed by a miracle, hang a copy of the deceased member upon the miraculous image which cured them. My heart was sick of the world and of men; your majesty healed it, and I lay it thankfully and humbly at your feet. This is my whole history, and truly it is a wonderful one. I have found a manly king and a kingly man." †

"Truly, such a king is the wonder of the world," said Voltaire. "A king, who being a king, is still a man, and being a man is still a noble king. I believe the history of the world gives few such examples. If we search the records of all people, we will find that all their kings have committed many crimes and follies, and but few great, magnanimous deeds. No, no! let us never hope to civilize kings. In vain have men sought to soften them by the help of art; in vain taught them to love it and to cultivate it. They are always lions, who seemed to be tamed when perpetually flattered. They remain, in truth, always wild, bloodthirsty, and fantastic. In the moment when you least expect it, the instinct awakens, and we fall a sacrifice to their claws or their teeth." ‡

The king, who, up to this time, had listened, with a smil-

---

* Bastiani's own words.—See Thiébault, p. 43.
† Algarotti's own words.   ‡ Thiébault.

ing face, to the passionate and bitter speech of Voltaire, now rose from his seat, and pointing his finger threateningly at him, said, good-humoredly: "Still, still, monsieur! Beware! I believe the king comes! Lower your voice, Voltaire, that he may not hear you. If he heard you, he might consider it his duty to be even worse than yourself.* Besides, it is late. Let us not await the coming of the king, but withdraw very quietly. Good-night, messieurs."

With a gracious but proud nod of his head, he greeted the company and withdrew.

CHAPTER V.

ROME SAUVÉE.

THE whole court was in a state of wild excitement. A rare spectacle was preparing for them—something unheard of in the annals of the Berliners. Voltaire's new drama of "Catiline," to which he had now given the name of "Rome Saved," was to be given in the royal palace, in a private theatre gotten up for the occasion, and the actors and actresses were to be no common *artistes*, but selected from the highest court circles. Princess Amelia had the *rôle* of Aurelia, Prince Henry of Julius Cæsar, and Voltaire of Cicero.

The last rehearsal was to take place that morning. Voltaire had shown himself in his former unbridled license, his biting irony, his cutting sarcasm. Not an actor or actress escaped his censure or his scorn. The poor poet D'Arnaud had been the special subject of his mocking wit. D'Arnaud had once been Voltaire's favorite scholar, and he had commended him highly to the king. He had the misfortune to please Frederick, who had addressed to him a flattering poem. For this reason Voltaire hated him, and sought continually to deprive him of Frederick's favor and get him banished from court.

* The king's own words.

This morning, for the first time, there was open strife between them, and the part which D'Arnaud had to play in " *Rome Sauvée* " gave occasion for the difficulty. D'Arnaud, it is true, had but two words to say, but his enunciation did not please Voltaire. He declared that D'Arnaud uttered them intentionally and maliciously with coldness and indifference.

D'Arnaud shrugged his shoulders and said a speech of *two words* did not admit of power or action. He asked what declamation could possibly do for two insignificant words, but make them ridiculous.

This roused Voltaire's rage to the highest pitch. "And this utterance of two words is then beyond your ability? It appears you cannot speak two words with proper emphasis!" *

And now, with fiery eloquence, he began to show that upon these words hung the merit of the drama; that this speech was the most important of all! With jeers and sarcasm he drove poor D'Arnaud to the wall, who, breathless, raging, choking, could find no words nor strength to reply. He was dumb, cast down, humiliated.

The merry laughter of the king, who greatly enjoyed the scene, and the general amusement, increased the pain of his defeat, and made the triumph of Voltaire more complete.

At last, however, the parts were well learned, and even Voltaire was content with his company. This evening the entire court was to witness the performance of the drama, which Voltaire called his master-work.

Princess Amelia had the *rôle* of Aurelia. She had withdrawn to her rooms, and had asked permission of the queen-mother to absent herself from dinner. Her part was difficult, and she needed preparation and rest.

---

* In a letter to Madame Denis, Voltaire wrote: " Tout le monde me reproche que le roi a fait des vers pour d'Arnaud, des vers qui ne sont pas ce qu'il à fait de mieux ; mais songez qu'à quatre cent lieues de Paris il est bien difficile de savoir si un homme qu'on lui recommende a du mérite ou non ; de plus c'est toujours des vers, et bien ou mal appliqués ils prouvent que le vainqueur de l'Autriche aime les belles-lettres que j'aime de tout mon cœur. D'ailleurs D'Arnaud est un bon diable, qui par-ci par-là ne laisse pas de rencontrer de bons tirades. Il a du gout, il se forme, et s'il aime qu'il se déforme, il n'y a pas grand mal. En un mot, la petite méprise du Roi de Prusse n'empêche pas qu'il ne soit le plus singulier de tous les hommes."—Voyez " Œuvres Complètes."

But the princess was not occupied with her *rôle*, or with the arrangement of her toilet. She lay stretched upon the divan, and gazed with tearful eyes upon the letter which she held in her trembling hands. Mademoiselle von Haak was kneeling near her, and looking up with tender sympathy upon the princess.

"What torture, what martyrdom I suffer!" said Amelia. "I must laugh while my heart is filled with despair; I must take part in the pomps and *fêtes* of this riotous court, while thick darkness is round about me. No gleam of light, no star of hope, do I see. Oh, Ernestine, do not ask me to be calm and silent! Grant me at least the relief of giving expression to my sorrow."

"Dear princess, why do you nourish your grief? Why will you tear open the wounds of your heart once more?"

"Those wounds have never healed," cried Amelia, passionately. "No! they have been always bleeding—always painful. Do you think so pitifully of me, Ernestine, as to believe that a few years have been sufficient to teach me to forget?"

"Am I not also called upon to learn to forget?" cried Ernestine, bitterly. "Is not my life's happiness destroyed? Am I not eternally separated from my beloved? Alas! princess, you are much happier than I! You know where, at least in thought, you can find your unhappy friend. Not the faintest sound in the distance gives answer to my wild questionings. My thoughts are wandering listlessly, wearily. They know not where to seek my lover—whether he lies in the dark fortress, or in the prison-house of the grave."

"It is true," said Amelia, thoughtfully; "our fates are indeed pitiable! Oh, Ernestine, what have I not suffered in the last five years, during which I have not seen Trenck?— five years of self-restraint, of silence, of desolation! How often have I believed that I could not support my secret griefs—that death must come to my relief! How often, with rouged cheeks and laughing lips, conversing gayly with the glittering court circle whose centre my cruel brother forced me to be, have my troubled thoughts wandered far, far away to my darling; from whom the winds brought me no message, the stars no greeting; and yet I knew that he lived, and loved me still! If Trenck were dead, he would appear to me in spirit. Had he forgotten me, I should know it; the knowledge would pierce my heart, and I should die that instant. I know that he has written to me, and that all his dear letters have fallen into the hands of the base spies with which my brother has surrounded me. But I am not mad! I will be calm; a day may come in which Trenck may require my help. I will not slay myself; some day I may be necessary to him I love. I have long lived, as the condemned in hell, who, in the midst of burning torture, open both eyes and ears waiting for the moment when the blessed Saviour will come for their release. God has at last been merciful; He has blinded the eyes of my persecutors, and this letter came safely to my hands. Oh, Ernestine, look! look! a letter from Trenck! He loves me—he has not forgotten me—he calls for me! Oh, my God! my God! why has fate bound me so inexorably? Why was I born to a throne, whose splendor has not lighted my path, but cast me in the shadow of death? Why am I not poor and obscure? Then I might hasten to my beloved when he calls me. I might stand by his side in his misfortunes, and share his sorrows and his tears."

"Dear princess, you can alleviate his fate. Look at me! I am poor, obscure, and dependent, and yet I cannot hasten to my beloved; he is in distress, and yet he does not call upon me for relief. He knows that I cannot help him. You, princess, thanks to your rank, have power and influence. Trenck calls you, and you are here to aid and comfort."

"God grant that I may. Trenck implores me to turn to my brother, and ask him to interest the Prussian embassy in Vienna in his favor; thereby hoping to put an end to the process by which he is about to be deprived of his only inheritance—the estate left him by his cousin, the captain of the pandours. Alas! can I speak with my brother of Trenck? He knows not that for five years his name has never passed my lips; he knows not that I have never been alone with my brother the king for one moment since that eventful day in which I promised to give him up forever. We have both avoided an interview; he, because he shrank from my prayers and tears, and I, because a crust of ice had formed over my love for him, and I would not allow it to melt beneath his smiles and kindly words. I loved Trenck with my whole heart, I was resolved to be faithful to him, and I was resentful toward my brother. Now, Ernestine, I must overcome myself, I must speak with the king; Trenck needs my services, and I will have courage to plead for him."

"What will your highness ask? think well, princess, before you act. Who knows but that the king has entirely forgotten Trenck? Perhaps it were best so. You should not point out to the angry lion the insect which has awakened him, he will crush it in his passion. Trenck is in want; send him gold—gold to bribe the men of law. It is well-known that the counsellors-at-law are dull-eyed enough to mistake sometimes the glitter of gold for the glitter of the sun of justice. Send him gold, much gold, and he will tame the tigers who lie round about the courts of justice, and he will win his suit."

Princess Amelia shrugged her shoulders contemptuously. "He calls upon me for help, and I send him nothing but empty gold; he asks for my assistance, and I play the coward and hold my peace. No, no! I will act, and I will act to-day! You know that only after the most urgent entreaty of the king, I consented to appear in this drama. While my brother pleaded with me, he said, with his most winning smile, 'Grant me this favor, my sister, and be assured that the first petition you make of me, I will accord cheerfully.' Now, then, I will remind him of this promise; I will plead for Trenck, and he dare not refuse. Oh, Ernestine! I know not surely, but it appears to me that for some little time past the king loves me more tenderly than heretofore; his eye rests upon me with pleasure, and often it seems to me his soft glance is imploring my love in return. You may call me childish, foolish; but I think, sometimes, that my silent submission has touched his heart, and he is at last disposed to be merciful, and allow me to be happy—happy, in allowing me to flee from the vain glory of a court; in forgetting that I am a princess, and remembering only that I am a woman, to whom God has given a heart capable of love." Amelia did not see the melancholy gaze with which her friend regarded her; she was full of ardor and enthusiasm, and with

27

sparkling eyes and throbbing breast she sprang from the divan and cried out, " Yes, it is so; my brother will make me happy ! "

" Alas, princess, do not dare to rely upon so false a hope! Never will the king consent that you shall be happy beneath your royal rank ! "

" Tell me now, Ernestine," said Amelia, with a smile, " is not the reigning Margravine of Baireuth as high in rank as I am ? "

" Yes, your highness," said Ernestine, with surprise, " for the reigning Margravine of Baireuth is your exalted sister."

" I do not speak of her, but of the widow of the former margrave. She has also reigned. Well, she has just married the young Duke Hobitz. The king told me this yesterday, with a merry laugh. The little Duchess of Hobitz is his aunt, and I am his sister ! "

" If the king had had power to control his aunt, as he has to control his sister, he would not have allowed this marriage."

Amelia heard, but she did not believe. With hasty steps and sparkling eyes she walked backward and forward in her room; then, after a long pause, she drew near her friend, and laying her hands upon her shoulders, she said: " You are a good soul and a faithful friend; you have ever had a patient and willing ear for all my complaints. Only think now how charming it will be when I come to tell you of my great happiness. And now, Ernestine, come, you must go over my part with me once more, and then arrange my toilet. I will be lovely this evening, in order to please the king. I will play like an *artiste* in order to touch his cold heart. If I act my part with such truth and burning eloquence that he is forced to weep over the sorrows of the wretched and loving woman whom I represent, will not his heart be softened, will he not take pity upon my blasted life? The tragic part I play will lend me words of fire to depict my own agony. Come, then, Ernestine, come ! I must act well my tragedy— I must win the heart of my king ! "

The princess kept her word; she played with power and genius. Words of passion and of pain flowed like a stream of lava from her lips; her oaths of faith and eternal constancy, her wild entreaties, her resignation, her despair, were not the high-flown, pompous phrases of the tragedian, but truth in its omnipotence. It was living passion, it was breathing agony; and, with fast-flowing tears, with the pallor of death, she told her tale of love; and in that vast saloon, glittering with jewels, filled with the high-born, the brave, the beautiful, nothing was heard but long-drawn sighs and choking sobs.

Queen Elizabeth Christine forgot all etiquette in the remembrance of her own sad fate so powerfully recalled. She covered her face with her hands, and bitter tears fell over her slender fingers. The queen-mother, surprised at her own emotion, whispered lightly that it was very warm, and while fanning herself she sought to dry her secret tears unnoticed.

Even the king was moved; his eyes were misty, and indescribable melancholy played upon his lips. Voltaire was wild with rapture; he hung upon every movement, every glance of Amelia. Words of glowing praise, thanks, admiration flowed from his lips. He met the princess behind the scenes, and forgetting all else he cried out, with enthusiasm: "You are worthy to be an actress, and to play in Voltaire's tragedies!"

The princess smiled and passed on silently—what cared she for Voltaire's praise? She knew that she had gained her object, and that the king's heart was softened. This knowledge made her bright and brave; and when at the close of the drama the king came forward, embraced her with warmth, and thanked her in fond and tender words for the rich enjoyment of the evening, due not only to the great poet Voltaire, but also to the genius of his sister, she reminded him smilingly that she had a favor to ask.

"I pray you, my sister," said Frederick, gayly, "ask something right royal from me this evening—I am in the mood to grant all your wishes."

Amelia looked at him pleadingly. "Sire," said she, "appoint an hour to-morrow morning in which I may come to you and make known my request. Remember, your majesty has promised to grant it in advance."

The king's face was slightly clouded. "This is, indeed, a happy coincidence," said he. "It was my intention to ask an interview with you to-morrow, and now you come forward voluntarily to meet my wishes. At ten in the morning I shall be with you, and I also have something to ask."

"I will then await you at ten o'clock, and make known my request."

"And when I have granted it, my sister, it will be your part to fulfil my wishes also."

CHAPTER VI.

A WOMAN'S HEART.

THE Princess Amelia lay the whole of the following night, with wide-open eyes and loudly-beating heart, pale and breathless upon her couch. No soft slumber soothed her feverish-glowing brow; no sweet dream of hope dissipated the frightful pictures drawn by her tortured fantasy.

"What is it?" said she, again and again—"what is it that the king will ask of me? what new mysterious horror rises up threateningly before me, and casts a shadow upon my future?"

She brought every word, every act of the previous day in review before her mind. Suddenly she recalled the sad and sympathetic glance of her maid of honor; the light insinuations, the half-uttered words which seemed to convey a hidden meaning.

"Ernestine knows something that she will not tell me," cried Amelia. At this thought her brow was covered with cold perspiration, and her limbs shivered as if with ague. She reached out her hand to ring for Fraulein von Haak; then suddenly withdrew it, ashamed of her own impatience. "Why should I wish to know that which I cannot change? I know that a misfortune threatens me. I will meet it with a clear brow and a bold heart."

Amelia lay motionless till the morning. When she rose from her bed, her features wore an expression of inexorable resolve. Her eyes flashed as boldly, as daringly as her royal brother Frederick's when upon the battle-field. She dressed herself carefully and tastefully, advanced to meet her ladies with a gracious greeting, and chattered calmly and cheerfully with them on indifferent subjects. At last she was left alone with Fraulein von Haak. She stepped in front of her, and looked in her eyes long and searchingly.

"I read it in your face, Ernestine, but I entreat you do not make it known in words unless my knowledge of the facts would diminish my danger."

Ernestine shook her head sadly. "No," said she, "your royal highness has no power over the misfortune that threatens you. You are a princess, and must be obedient to the will of the king."

"Good!" said Amelia, "we will see if my brother has power to subdue my will. Now, Ernestine, leave me; I am expecting the king."

Scarcely had her maid withdrawn, when the door of the anteroom was opened, and the king was announced. The princess advanced to meet him smilingly, but, as the king embraced her and pressed a kiss upon her brow, she shuddered and looked up at him searchingly. She read nothing in his face but the most heart-felt kindliness and love.

"If he makes me miserable, it is at least not his intention to do so," thought she.—"Now, my brother, we are alone," said the princess, taking a place near the king upon the divan. "And now allow me to make known my request at once—remember you have promised to grant it."

The king looked with a piercing glance at the sweet face now trembling with excitement and impatience. "Amelia," said he, "have you no tender word of greeting, of warm home-love to say to me? Do you not know that five years have passed since we have seen each other alone, and enjoyed that loving and confidential intercourse which becomes brothers and sisters?"

"I know," said Amelia sadly, "these five years are written on my countenance, and if they have not left wrinkles on my brow, they have pierced my heart with many sorrows, and left their shadows there! Look at me, my brother—am I the same sister Amelia?"

"No," said the king, "no! You are pallid—your cheeks are hollow. But it is strange—I see this now for the first time. You have been an image of youth, beauty, and grace up to this hour. The fatigue of yesterday has exhausted you—that is all."

"No, my brother, you find me pallid and hollow-eyed to-day, because you see me without rouge. I have to-day for the first time laid aside the mask of rosy youth, and the smiling indifference of manner with which I conceal my face and my heart from the world. You shall see me to-day as I really am; you shall know what I have suffered. Perhaps then you will be more willing to fulfil my request? Listen, my brother, I—"

The king laid his hand softly upon her shoulder. "Stop, Amelia; since I look upon you, I fear you will ask me something not in my power to grant."

"You have given me your promise, sire."

"I will not withdraw it; but I ask you to hear my prayer before you speak. Perhaps it may exert an influence—may modify your request. I allow myself, therefore, in consideration of your own interest, solely to beg that I may speak first."

"You are king, sire, and have only to command," said Amelia, coldly.

The king fixed a clear and piercing glance for one moment upon his sister, then stood up, and, assuming an earnest and thoughtful mien, he said: "I stand now before you, princess, not as a king, but as the ambassador of a king. Princess Amelia, through me the King of Denmark asks your hand; he wishes to wed you, and I have given my consent. Your approval alone is wanting, and I think you will not refuse it."

The princess listened with silent and intrepid composure; not a muscle of her face trembled; her features did not lose for one moment their expression of quiet resolve.

"Have you finished, sire?" said she, indifferently.

"I have finished, and I await your reply."

"Before I answer, allow me to make known my own request. Perhaps what I may say may modify your wishes. You will, at least, know if it is proper for me to accept the hand of the King of Denmark. Does your majesty allow me to speak?"

"Speak," said the king, seating himself near her.

After a short pause, Amelia said, in an earnest, solemn voice: "Sire, I pray for pardon for the Baron Frederick von Trenck." Yielding to an involuntary agitation, she glided from the divan upon her knees, and raising her clasped hands entreatingly toward her brother, she repeated: "Sire, I pray for pardon for Baron Frederick von Trenck!"

The king sprang up, dashed back the hands of his sister violently, and rushed hastily backward and forward in the room.

Amelia, ashamed of her own humility, rose quickly from her knees, and, as if to convince herself of her own daring and resolution, she stepped immediately in front of the king, and said, in a loud, firm voice for the third time: "Sire, I pray for pardon for Baron Frederick von Trenck. He is wretched because he is banished from his home; he is in despair because he receives no justice from the courts of law, it being well known that he has no protector to demand his rights. He is poor and almost hopeless because the courts have refused him the inheritance of his cousin, the captain of the pandours whose enemies have accused him since his death, only while they lusted for his millions. His vast estate has been confiscated, under the pretence that it was unlawfully acquired. But these accusations have not been established; and yet, now that he is dead, they refuse to give up this fortune to the rightful heir, Frederick von Trenck. Sire, I pray that you will regard the interests of your subject. Be graciously pleased to grant him the favor of your intercession. Help him, by one powerful word, to obtain possession of his rights. Ah, sire, you see well how modest, how faint-hearted I have become. I ask no longer for happiness! I beg for gold, and I think, sire, we owe him this pitiful reparation for a life's happiness trodden under foot."

Frederick by a mighty effort succeeded in overcoming his rage. He was outwardly as calm as his sister; but both concealed under this cool, indifferent exterior a strong energy, an unfaltering purpose. They were quiet because they were inflexible.

"And this is the favor you demand of me?" said the king.

"The favor you have promised to grant," said Amelia.

"And if I do this, will you fulfil my wish? Will you become the wife of the King of Denmark? Ah, you are silent. Now, then, listen. Consent to become Queen of Denmark, and on the day in which you pass the boundary of Prussia and enter your own realm as queen, on that day I will recall Trenck to Berlin, and all shall be forgotten. Trenck shall again enter my guard, and my ambassador at Vienna shall appear for him in court. Decide, now, Amelia—will you be Queen of Denmark?"

"Ah, sire, you offer me a cruel alternative. You wish me to purchase a favor which you had already freely and unconditionally granted."

"You forget, my sister, that I entreat where I have the right to command. It will be easy to obey when through your obedience you can make another happy. Once more, then, will you accept my proposition?"

Amelia did not answer immediately. She fixed her eyes steadily upon the king's face; their glances met firmly, quietly. Each read in the eyes of the other inexorable resolve.

"Sire, I cannot accept your proposition; I cannot become the wife of the King of Denmark."

The king shrank back, and a dark cloud settled upon his brow. He pressed his hand nervously upon the arm-chair near which he stood, and forced himself to appear calm. "And why can you not become the wife of the King of Denmark?"

"Because I have sworn solemnly, calling upon God to witness, that I will never become the wife of any other man than him whom I love—because I consider myself bound to God and to my conscience to fulfil this oath. As I cannot be the wife of Trenck, I will remain unmarried."

And now the king was crimson with rage, and his eyes flashed fiercely. "The wife of Trenck!" cried he; "the wife of a traitor! Ah, you think still of him, and in spite

of your vow—in spite of your solemn oath—you still entertain the hope of this unworthy alliance!"

"Sire, remember on what conditions my oath was given.
You promised me Trenck should be free, and I swore to
give him up—never even to write to him. Fate did not accept my oath. Trenck fled before you had time to fulfil
your word, and I was thus released from my vow; and yet
I have never written to him—have heard nothing from him.
No one knows better than yourself that I have not heard
from him."

"So five years have gone by without his writing to you,
and yet you have the hardihood to-day to call his name!"

"I have the courage, sire, because I know well Trenck
has never ceased to love me. That I have received no letters
from him does not prove that he has not written; it only
proves that I am surrounded by watchful spies, who do not
allow his letters to reach me."

"Ah," said the king, with a contemptuous shrug of the
shoulders, "you are of the opinion that I have suppressed
these letters?"

"Yes, I am of that opinion."

"You deceive yourself, then, Amelia. I have not surrounded you with spies; I have intercepted no letters. You
look at me incredulously. I declare to you that I speak the
truth. Now you can comprehend, my sister, that your heart
has deceived you—you have squandered your love upon a
wretched object who has forgotten you."

"Sire!" cried Amelia, with flaming eyes, "no abuse of
the man I love!"

"You love him still!" said the king, white with passion,
and no longer able to control his rage—"you love him still!
You have wept and bewailed him, while he has shamefully
betrayed and mocked at you. Yes, look on me, if you will,
with those scornful, rebellious glances—it is as I say! You
must and shall know all! I have spared you until now; I
trusted in your own noble heart! I thought that, driven by
a storm of passion, it had, like a proud river, for one moment
overstepped its bounds; then quietly, calmly resumed that
course which nature and fate had marked out for it. I see
now that I have been deceived in you, as you have been de-

ceived in Trenck! I tell you he has betrayed you! He,
formerly a Prussian officer, at the luxurious and debauched
court of Petersburg, has not only betrayed you, but his king.
At the table of his mistress, the wife of Bestuchef, he has
shown your picture and boasted that you gave it to him.
The Duke of Goltz, my ambassador at the Russian court, informed me of this; and look you, I did not slay him! I did
not demand of the Empress Anne that the Prussian deserter
should be delivered up. I remembered that you had once
loved him, and that I had promised you to be lenient. But
I have had him closely watched. I know all his deeds; I
am acquainted with all his intrigues and artifices. I know
he has had a love-affair with the young Countess Narischkin
—that he continued his attentions long after her marriage
with General Bondurow. Can you believe, my sister, that
he remembered the modest, innocent oaths of love and constancy he had exchanged with you while enjoying himself in
the presence of this handsome and voluptuous young woman?
Do you believe that he recalled them when he arranged a
plan of flight with his beloved, and sought a safe asylum beyond the borders of Russia? Do you believe that he thought
of you when he received from this ill-regulated woman her
diamonds and all the gold she possessed, in order to smooth
the way to their escape?"

"Mercy, mercy!" stammered Amelia, pale and trembling, and sinking upon a seat. "Cease, my brother; do you
not see that your words are killing me? Have pity upon me!"

"No! no mercy!" said the king; "you must and you
shall know all, in order that you may be cured of this unholy
malady, this shameful love. You shall know that Trenck not
only sells the secrets of politics, but the secrets of love.
Every thing is merchandise with him, even his own heart.
He not only loved the beautiful Bondurow but he loved her
diamonds. This young woman died of the small-pox, a few
days before the plan of flight could be fully arranged.
Trenck, however, became her heir; he refused to give back
the brilliants and the eight thousand rubles which she had
placed in his hands."

"Oh my God, my God! grant that I die!" cried the
Princess Amelia.

"But the death of his beloved," said the king (without regarding the wild exclamations of the princess)—"this death was so greatly to his advantage, that he soon consoled himself with the love of the attractive Bestuchef—this proud and intriguing woman who now, through the weakness of her husband, rules over Russia, and threatens by her plots and intrigues to complicate the history and peace of Europe. She is neither young nor beautiful; she is forty years of age, and you cannot believe that Trenck at four-and-twenty burns with love for her. But she adores him; she loves him with that mad, bacchantic ardor which the Roman empress Julia felt for the gladiators, whose magnificent proportions she admired at the circus. She loved him and confessed it; and his heart, unsubdued by the ancient charms, yielded to the magic power of her jewels and her gold. He became the adorer of Bestuchef; he worked diligently in the cabinet of the chancellor, and appeared to be the best of Russian patriots, and seemed ready to kiss the knout with the same devotion with which he kissed the slipper of the chancellor's wife. At this time I resolved to try his patriotism, and commissioned my ambassador to see if his patriotic ardor could not be cooled by gold. Well, my sister, for two thousand ducats, Trenck copied the design of the fortress of Cronstadt, which the chancellor had just received from his engineer."

"That is impossible!" said Amelia, whose tears had now ceased to flow, and who listened to her brother with distended but quiet eyes.

"Impossible!" said Frederick. "Oh my sister, gold has a magic power to which nothing is impossible! I wished to unmask the traitor Trenck, and expose him in his true colors to the chancellor. I ordered Goltz to hand him the copy of the fortress, drawn by Trenck and signed with his name, and to tell him *how* he obtained it. The chancellor was beside himself with rage, and swore to take a right Russian revenge upon the traitor—he declared he should die under the knout."

Amelia uttered a wild cry, and clasped her hands over her convulsed face.

The king laughed bitterly. "Compose yourself—we triumphed too early; we had forgotten the woman! In his rage the chancellor disclosed every thing to her, and uttered the most furious curses and resolves against Trenck. She found means to warn him, and, when the police came in the night to arrest him, he was not at home—he had taken refuge in the house of his friend the English ambassador, Lord Hyndforth." *

"Ah! he was saved, then?" whispered Amelia.

The king looked at her in amazement. "Yes, he was saved. The next day, Madame Bestuchef found means to convince her credulous husband that Trenck was the victim of an intrigue, and entirely innocent of the charge brought against him. Trenck remained, therefore, the friend of the house, and Madame Bestuchef had the audacity to publicly insult my ambassador. Trenck now announced himself as a raging adversary of Prussia. He inflamed the heart of his powerful mistress with hate, and they swore the destruction of Prussia. Both were zealously engaged in changing the chancellor, my private and confidential friend, into an enemy; and Trenck, the Russian patriot, entered the service of the house of Austria, to intrigue against me and my realm.† Bestuchef, however, withstood these intrigues, and in his distrust he watched over and threatened his faithless wife and faithless friend. Trenck would have been lost, without doubt, if a lucky accident had not again rescued him. His cousin the pandour died in Vienna, and, as Trenck believed that he had left him a fortune of some millions, he tore his tender ties asunder, and hastened to Vienna to receive this rich inheritance, which, to his astonishment, he found to consist not in millions, but in law processes. This, Amelia, is the history of Trenck during these five years in which you have received no news from him. Can you still say that he has never forgotten you? that you are bound to be faithful to him? You see I do not speak to you as a king, but as a friend, and that I look at all these unhappy circumstances

---

* Trenck's Memoirs.

† Trenck himself writes on this subject: "I would at that time have changed my fatherland into a howling wilderness, if the opportunity had offered. I do not deny that from this moment I did everything that was possible, in Russia, to promote the views of the imperial ambassador, Duke Vernis, who knew how to nourish the fire already kindled, and to make use of my services."

from your standpoint. Treat me, then, as a friend, and answer me sincerely. Do you still feel bound by your oath? Do you not know that he is a faithless traitor, and that he has forgotten you?"

The princess had listened to the king with a bowed head and downcast eyes. Now she looked up; the fire of inspiration beamed in her eye, a melancholy smile played upon her lips.

"Sire," said she, "I took my vow without conditions, and I will keep it faithfully till my death. Suppose, even, that a part of what you have said is true, Trenck is young; you cannot expect that his ardent and passionate heart should be buried under the ashes of the vase of tears in which our love, in its beauty and bloom, crumbled to dust. But his heart, however unstable it may appear, turns ever back faithfully to that fountain, and he seeks to purify and sanctify the wild and stormy present by the remembrance of the beautiful and innocent past. You say that Trenck forgot me in his prosperity; well, then, sire, in his misfortune he has remembered me. In his misfortune he has forgotten the faithless, cold, and treacherous letter which I wrote to him, and which he received in the prison of Glatz. In his wretchedness, he has written to me, and called upon me for aid. It shall not be said that I did not hear his voice—that I was not joyfully ready to serve him!"

"And he has dared to write to you!" said the king, with trembling lips and scornful eye. "Who was bold enough to hand you this letter?"

"Oh, sire, you will not surely demand that I shall betray my friends! Moreover, if I named the messenger who brought me this letter, it would answer no purpose; you would arrest and punish him, and to-morrow I should find another to serve me as well. Unhappy love finds pity, protection, and friends everywhere. Sire, I repeat my request —pardon for Baron Trenck!"

"And I," cried the king, in a loud, stern voice, "I ask if you accept my proposition—if you will become the wife of the King of Denmark—and, mark well, princess, this is the answer to your prayer."

"Sire, may God take pity on me! Punish me with your

utmost scorn—I cannot break my oath! You can force me to leave my vows unfulfilled—not to become the wife of the man I love—but you cannot force me to perjure myself. I should indeed be foresworn if I stepped before the altar with another man, and promised a love and faith which my heart knows not, and can never know."

The king uttered a shrill cry of rage; maledictions hung upon his lips, but he held them back, and forcing himself to appear composed, he folded his arms, and walked hastily backward and forward through the room.

The princess gazed at him in breathless silence, and with loudly-beating heart she prayed to God for mercy and help; she felt that this hour would decide the fate of her whole life. Suddenly the king stood before her. His countenance was now perfectly composed.

"Princess Amelia," said he, "I give you four weeks' respite. Consider well what I have said to you. Take counsel with your conscience, your understanding, and your honor. In four weeks I will come again to you, and ask if you are resolved to fulfil my request, and become the wife of the King of Denmark. Until that time, I will know how to restrain the Danish ambassador. If you dare still to oppose my will, I will yet fulfil my promise, and grant you the favor you ask of me. I will make proposals to Trenck to return to Prussia, and the inducements I offer shall be so splendid that he will not resist them. Let me once have him here, and it shall be my affair to hold fast to him."

He bowed to the princess and left the room. Amelia watched him silently, breathlessly, till he disappeared, then heaved a deep sigh and called loudly for her maid.

"Ernestine! Ernestine!" said she, with trembling lips, "find me a faithful messenger whom I can send immediately to Vienna. I must warn Trenck! Danger threatens him! No matter what my brother's ambassador may offer him, with what glittering promises he may allure him, Trenck dare not listen to them, dare not accept them! He must never return to Prussia—he is lost if he does so!"

Frederick returned slowly and silently to his apartment. As he thought over the agitating scene he had just passed through, he murmured lightly, "Oh, woman's heart! thou art like the restless, raging sea, and pearls and monsters lie in thy depths!"

CHAPTER VII.

MADAME VON COCCEJI.

THE Marquis d'Argens was right. Barbarina and her sister had left England and returned to Berlin. They occupied the same expensive and beautiful hotel in Behren Street; but it was no longer surrounded by costly equipages, and besieged by gallant cavaliers. The *élite* of the court no longer came to wonder and to worship.

Barbarina's house was lonely and deserted, and she herself was changed. She was no longer the graceful, enchanting prima donna, the floating sylph; she was a calm, proud woman, almost imposing in her grave, pale beauty; her melancholy smile touched the heart, while it contrasted strangely with her flashing eye.

Barbarina was in the same saloon where we last saw her, surrounded with dukes and princes—worshippers at her shrine! To-day she was alone; no one was by her side but her faithful sister Marietta. She lay stretched upon the divan, with her arms folded across her bosom; her head was thrown back upon the white, gold-embroidered cushion, and her long, black curls fell in rich profusion around her; with wide-open eyes she stared upon the ceiling, completely lost in sad and painful thoughts. At a small table by her side sat her sister Marietta, busily occupied in opening and reading the letters with which the table was covered.

And now she uttered a cry of joy, and a happy smile played upon her face. "A letter from Milan, from the *impressario*, Bintelli," said she.

Barbarina remained immovable, and still stared at the ceiling.

"Binatelli offers you a magnificent engagement; he declares that all Italy languishes with impatience to see you, that every city implores your presence, and he is ambitious to be the first to allure you back to your fatherland."

"Did you write to him that I desired an engagement?" said Barbarina.

"No, sister," said Marietta, slightly blushing; "I wrote to him as to an old and valued friend; I described the restless, weary, nomadic life we were leading, and told him you had left the London stage forever."

"And does it follow that I will therefore appear in Milan? Write at once that I am grateful for his offer, but neither in Milan nor any other Italian city will I appear upon the stage."

"Ah, Barbarina, will we never again return to our beautiful Italy?" said Marietta, tearfully.

"Did I say that, sister? I said only, I would not appear in public."

"But, Barbarina, he entreats so earnestly, and he offers you an enormous salary!"

"I am rich enough, Marietta."

"No! no one is rich enough! Money is power, and the more millions one has to spend, the more is one beloved."

"What care I for the love of men? I despise them all—all!" cried Barbarina, passionately.

"What! all?" said Marietta, with a meaning smile; "all—even Cocceji?"

Babarina raised herself hastily, and leaning upon her elbow, she gazed with surprise upon her sister. "You think, then, that I love Cocceji?"

"Did you not tell me so yourself?"

"Ah! I said so myself, did I?" said Barbarina, contemptuously, and sinking back into her former quiet position.

"Yes, sister, do you not remember," said Marietta, eagerly; "can you not recall how sad you were when we left Berlin a year ago? You sobbed and wept, and looked ever backward from the carriage, then lightly whispered, 'My happiness, my life, my love remain in Berlin!' I asked you in what your happiness, your love, your life consisted. Your answer was, 'Do you not know, then, that I love Cocceji?' In truth, good sister I did not believe you! I thought you left Berlin because the mother of Cocceji implored you to do so. I know you to be magnanimous enough to sacrifice yourself to the prayers and happiness of another, and for this reason alone you went to London, where Lord Stuart McKenzie awaited us."

"Poor lord!" said Barbarina, thoughtfully. "I sinned greatly against him! He loved me fondly; he waited for me with constancy; he was so truly happy when I came at last, as he hoped, to fulfil my promise, and become his wife! God knows I meant to be true, and I swore to myself to make him a faithful wife; but my will was weaker than my heart. I could not marry him, and on my wedding-day I fled from London. Poor Lord Stuart!"

"And on that day, when, bathed in tears, you told me to prepare to leave London with you secretly; on that day you said to me, 'I cannot, no, I cannot wed a man I do not love. The air chokes me, Marietta; I must return to Berlin; he is there whom I love, whom I will love eternally!' I said again, 'Whom do you love, my sister?' and you replied, 'I love Cocceji!' And now you are amazed that I believe you! Is it possible that I can doubt your word? Is it possible that Barbarina tells an untruth to her fond and faithful sister? that she shrouds her heart, and will not allow Marietta to read what is written there?"

"If I did that," said Barbarina, uneasily, "it was because I shrank from reading my own heart. Be pitiful, Marietta, do not lift the veil; allow my poor heart to heal its wounds in peace and quiet."

"It cannot heal, sister, if we remain here," said Marietta, trembling with suppressed tears. "Let us fly far, far away; accept the offer of Binatelli; it is the call of God. Come, come, Barbarina, we will return to our own Italy, to beautiful Rome. Remain no longer in this cold north, by these icy hearts!"

"I cannot, I cannot!" cried Barbarina, with anguish. "I have no fatherland—no home. I am no longer a Roman, no longer an Italian. I am a wretched, homeless wanderer. Why will not my heart bleed and die? Why am I condemned to live, and be conscious of this torture?"

"Stop, stop, my sister!" cried Marietta, wildly; "not

28

another word! You are right; we will not lift this fearful veil. Cover up your heart in darkness—it will heal!"

"It will heal!" repeated Barbarina, pressing Marietta to her bosom and weeping bitterly.

The entrance of a servant aroused them both; Barbarina turned away to hide her weeping eyes. The servant announced a lady, who desired anxiously to speak with the signora.

"Say to her that Barbarina is unwell, and can receive no one."

In a few moments the servant returned with a card, which he handed to Marietta. "The lady declared she knew the signora would receive her when she saw the card."

"Madame Cocceji," said Marietta.

Barbarina rose up hastily.

"Will you receive her?" asked Marietta.

"I will receive her."

And now a great change passed over Barbarina: all melancholy, all languor had disappeared; her eyes sparkled, her cheeks glowed with an engaging smile, as she advanced to greet the proud lady who stood upon the threshold.

"Ah, generous lady, how good you are!" said Barbarina, in a slightly mocking tone. "I have but just returned to Berlin, and you gladden my heart again by your visit, and grant me the distinction and privilege of receiving in my house one of the most eminent and virtuous ladies of Berlin."

Madame Cocceji threw a contemptuous glance upon the beautiful young woman who dared to look in her face with such smiling composure.

"I have not come, madame, to visit you, but to speak to you!"

"I do not see the distinction; we visit those with whom we wish to speak."

"We visit those with whom we wish to speak, and who are trying to evade an interview! I have sent to you twice, signora, and commanded you to come to me, but you have not obeyed!"

"I am accustomed to receive those who wish to see me at my own house," said Barbarina, quietly. "Indeed, madame, I understand your language perhaps but poorly. Is it according to the forms of etiquette to say, ' I have commanded you to come to me?' In my own fair land we give a finer turn to our speech, and we beg for the honor of a visit." As Barbarina said this, she bowed with laughing grace to the proud woman, who gazed at her with suppressed rage.

"This is the second time I have been forced to seek an interview with you."

"The first time, madame, you came with a petition, and I was so happy as to be able to grant your request. May I be equally fortunate to-day! Without doubt you come again as a petitioner," said Barbarina, with the cunning manner of a cat, who purrs while she scratches.

The proud Cocceji was wounded; she frowned sternly, but suppressed her anger. Barbarina was right—she came with a request.

"I called upon you a year ago," said she, "and implored you to cure my son of that wild love which had fallen upon him like the fever of madness—which made him forget his duty, his rank, his parents. I besought you to leave Berlin, and withdraw from his sight that magical beauty which had seduced him."

"And I declared myself ready to grant your petition," interrupted Barbarina. "Yes, I conformed myself to your wishes, and left Berlin, not, however, I confess, to do you a service, but because I did not love your son; and there is nothing more dull and wearisome than to listen to protestations of love that you cannot return. But look you, gracious lady, that is a misfortune that pursues me at every step. I left Berlin to escape this evil, and fled to London, to find there the same old story of a love I could not return. I fled then from London, to escape the danger of becoming the wife of Lord Stuart McKenzie."

"Why did you return to Berlin?" said Madame Cocceji, in an imperious tone.

Barbarina looked up surprised. "Madame," said she, "for that step I am accountable to no one."

"Yes, you are accountable to me!" cried Madame Cocceji, enraged to the utmost by Barbarina's proud composure. "You are accountable to me—me, the mother of Cocceji! You have seduced him by your charms, and driven him to madness. He defies his parents and the anger of his king, and yields himself up to this shameful passion, which covers his family with disgrace."

Barbarina uttered a cry of rage, and advanced a few steps. "Madame," said she, laying her hand upon the arm of Madame Cocceji, "you have called this love shameful. You have said that an alliance with me would disgrace your family. Take back your words, I pray you!"

"I retract nothing. I said but the truth," cried Madame Cocceji, freeing herself from Barbarina.

"Take back your words, madame, for your own sake!" said Barbarina, threateningly.

"I cannot, and will not!" she replied, imperiously, "and if your pride and arrogance has not completely blinded you, in your heart you will confess that I am right. The dancer Barbarina can never be the daughter of the Coccejis. That would be a mockery of all honorable customs, would cast contempt upon the graves of our ancestors, and bring shame upon our nobility. And yet my unhappy son dares think of this dishonor. In his insane folly, he rushed madly from my presence, uttering words of rage and bitter reproach, because I tried to show him that this marriage was impossible."

"Ah, I love him for this!" cried Barbarina, with a genial smile.

Without regarding her, Madame Cocceji went on: "Even against his father, he has dared to oppose himself. He defies the anger of his king. Oh, signora, in the anguish of my soul I turn to you; have pity with me and with my most unhappy son! He is lost; he will go down to the grave dishonored, if you do not come to my help! If, indeed, you love him, your love will teach you to make the offering of self-sacrifice, and I will bless you, and forgive you all the anguish you have caused me. If you love him not, you will not be so cruel as to bury the happiness and honor of a whole family because of your lofty ambition and your relentless will. Hear my prayer—leave this city, and go so far away that my son can never follow, never reach you!"

"Then I must go into my grave," said Barbarina; "there

is no other refuge to which, if he truly loves, he cannot follow me. I, dear madame, cannot, like yourself, move unknown and unregarded through the world. My fame is the herald which announces my presence in every land, and every city offers me, with bended knee, the keys of her gates and the keys of her heart. I cannot hide myself. Nothing is known of the proud and noble family of Cocceji outside of Prussia; but the wide, wide world knows of the Barbarina, and the laurel-wreaths with which I have been crowned in every land have never been desecrated by an unworthy act or an impure thought. There is nothing in my life of which I repent, nothing for which I blush or am ashamed! And yet you have dared to reproach me—you have had the audacity to seek to humiliate me in my own house."

"You forget with whom you have the honor to speak."

"You, madame, were the first to forget yourself; I follow your example. I suppose Madame Cocceji knows and does ever that which is great and right. I said you had vilified me in my own house, and yet you ask of me an act of magnanimity! Why should I relinquish your son's love?"

"Why? Because there remains even yet, perhaps, a spark of honorable feeling in your bosom. Because you know that my family will never receive you, but will curse and abhor you, if you dare to entice my son into a marriage. Because you know that the Prussian nobles, the king himself, are on my side. The king, signora, no longer favors you; the king has promised us his assistance. The king will use every means of grace and power to prevent a marriage, which he himself has written to me will cover my son with dishonor!"[*]

"That is false!" cried Barbarina.

"It is true! and it is true that the king, in order to protect the house of Cocceji from this shame, has given my husband authority to arrest my son and cast him into prison, provided my prayers and tears and menaces should be of no avail! If we fail, we will make use of this authority, and give him over to General Hake.[†] Think well what you do—do not drive us to this extremity. I say there is a point at which even a mother's love will fail, and the head of our

[*] Schneider, "History of the Opera in Berlin."   [†] Ibid.

house will act with all the sternness which the law and the king permit. Go, then, Signora Barbarina—bow your proud head—leave Berlin. Return to your own land. I repeat to you, do not drive us to extremity!"

Barbarina listened to this with cool and mocking composure. Not a muscle of her face moved—she was indeed striking in her majesty and her beauty. Her imposing bearing, her pallid but clear complexion, her crimson, tightly-compressed lips, her great, fiery eyes, which spoke the scorn and contempt her proud lips disdained to utter, made a picture never to be forgotten.

"Madame," said she, slowly, emphasizing every word, "you have, indeed, driven *me* to extremity. It was not my intention to marry your son. But your conduct has now made that a point of honor. Now, madame, I will graciously yield to the passionate entreaties of your son, and I will wed him."

"That is to say, you will force my husband to make use of the power the king has given him?"

Barbarina shrugged her shoulders contemptuously. "Arrest your son, and cast him into prison, you will thereby add a new celebrity to your name, and quench the last spark of piety and obedience in his heart. Love has wings, and will follow him everywhere, and will waft him to the altar, where he will wed Barbarina. Neither your curse, nor your arrest, nor the will of the king, will now protect him. Before six months are over, will Barbarina the dancer be the wife of Cocceji."

"Never, never shall that be!" cried Madame Cocceji, trembling with rage.

"That will be!" said Barbarina, smiling sadly, and bending low. "And now, madame, I think you have attained the object of your visit, and we have nothing more to say to each other. It only remains for me to commend myself to your grace and courtesy, and to thank you for the honor of your visit. Allow me to call my servant, to conduct you to your carriage."

She rang and commanded the servant to open the folding doors, and carry the large muff of the countess to the carriage. Madame Cocceji was pale with rage. She wished to remain *incognito*, and now her name had been called before the servant. All Berlin would know before night that she had visited Barbarina!

"Give me my muff," she said impatiently to the servant; "it is not necessary you should carry it. I came on foot."

"On foot?" said Barbarina, laughing merrily. "Truly, you wished to remain *incognito*, and you would not leave your equipage with its coat of arms, standing before my door! I thank you once more for the honor of your visit, and commend myself to you with the glad wish that we may meet again."

"Never more!" said Madame Cocceji, casting a withering look upon the gay dancer, and hastening from the room.

CHAPTER VIII.

VOLTAIRE.

VOLTAIRE was now a continuous guest of King Frederick. The latter had written a letter to Louis the Fifteenth, and begged him to relinquish his subject and historian, and this request was supposed to be acceded to. Besides this, the king, who was ever thoughtful of the happiness and comfort of his friends, had proposed to Madame Denis, Voltaire's beloved niece, to follow her uncle to Berlin, dwell in the royal castle at Potsdam, and accept from him an annuity of four thousand francs.

Voltaire himself besought her to come. He wrote to her that, as she had lived contentedly with her husband in Landau, she could surely be happy in Berlin and Potsdam. Berlin was certainly a much more beautiful city than Landau, and at Potsdam they could lead an agreeable and unceremonious life. "In Potsdam there are no tumultuous feasts. My soul rests, dreams, and works. I am content to find myself with a king who has neither a court nor a ministry. Truly, Potsdam is infested by many whiskered grenadiers, but, thank Heaven, I see little of them. I work peacefully in my room, while the drums beat without. I have withdrawn from the dinners of the king; there were too many princes and generals there. I could not accustom myself to be always *vis-à-vis* with a king and *en cérémonie*. But I sup with him—the suppers are shorter, gayer, and healthier. I would die with indigestion in three months if I dined every day in public with a king." *

Madame Denis, however, seemed to doubt the happy life of Berlin and Potsdam. She wrote, declining the proposition, and expressing her fears that Voltaire would himself soon repent that he had left beautiful, glittering Paris, the capital of luxury and good taste, and taken refuge in a barbaric land, to be the slave of a king, while, in Paris, he had been the king of poetry.

Voltaire had the audacity to bring this letter to the king —perhaps to wound him, perhaps to draw from him further promises and assurances.

Frederick read the letter; his brow did not become clouded, and the friendly smile did not vanish from his lips. When he had read it to the end, he returned it, and his eyes met the distrustful, lowering glance of Voltaire with an expression of such goodness and candor that the latter cast his eyes ashamed to the ground.

"If I were Madame Denis," said Frederick, "I would think as she does; but, being myself, I view these things differently. I would be in despair if I had occasioned the unhappiness of a friend; and it will not be possible for me to allow trouble or sorrow to fall upon a man whom I esteem, whom I love, and who has sacrificed for me his fatherland and all that men hold most dear. If I could believe that your residence here could be to your disadvantage, I would be the first to counsel you to give it up. I know I would think more of your happiness than I would of the joy of having you with me. We are philosophers. What is more natural, more simple, than that two philosophers, who seem made for each other—who have the same studies, the same tastes, the same mode of thinking—should grant themselves the satisfaction of living together? I honor you as my teacher of eloquence

* Œuvres Complètes, p. 360

and poetry; I love you as a virtuous and sympathetic friend. What sort of bondage, what misfortunes, what changes have you to fear in a realm where you are as highly honored as in your fatherland—where you have a powerful friend who advances to meet you with a thankful heart? I am not so prejudiced and foolish as to consider Berlin as handsome as Paris. If good taste has found a home in the world, I confess it is in Paris. But you, Voltaire, will you not inaugurate good taste wherever you are? We have organs sufficiently developed to applaud you; and, as to love, we will not allow any other land superiority in that respect. I yielded to the friendship which bound you to the Marquise du Châtelet, but I was, next to her, your oldest friend. How, when you have sought an asylum in my house, can it ever be thought it will become your prison? How, being your friend, can I ever become your tyrant? I do not understand this. I am convinced that, as long as I live, you will be happy here. You will be honored as the father of literature, and you will ever find in me that assistance and sympathy which a man of your worth has a right to demand of all who honor and appreciate him." *

"Alas! your majesty says that you honor me, but you no longer say that you love me," cried Voltaire, who had listened to this eloquent and heart-felt speech of the king with eager impatience and lowering frowns. "Yes, yes, I feel it; I know it too well! Your majesty has already limited me to your consideration, your regard; but your love, your friendship, these are costly treasures from which I have been disinherited. But I know these hypocritical legacy-hunters, who have robbed me of that most beautiful portion of my inheritance. I know these poor, beggarly cousins, these D'Argens, these Algarottis, these La Mettries, this vainglorious peacock Maupertius. I—"

"Voltaire," said the king, interrupting him, "you forget that you speak of my friends, and I do not allow any one to speak evil of them. I will never be partial, never unjust! My heart is capable of valuing and treasuring all my friends, but my friends must aim to deserve it; and if I give them my heart, I expect one in return."

* The king's own words.—Œuvres Posthumes.

"Friendship is a bill of exchange, by which you give just so much as you are entitled to demand in return."

"Give me, then, your whole heart, Voltaire, and I will restore mine to you! But I fear you have no longer a heart; Nature gave you but a small dose of this fleeting essence called love. She had much to do with your brain, and worked at that so long that no time remained to make the heart perfect; just as she was about to pour a few drops of this wonderful love-essence into your heart, the cock crew three times for your birth, and betrayed you into the world. You have long since used up the poor pair of drops which fell into your heart. Your brain was armed for centuries, with power to work, to be useful, to rejoice the souls of others, but I fear your heart was exhausted in your youthful years."

"Ah, I wish your majesty were right!" cried Voltaire; "I should not then feel the anguish which now martyrs me, the torture of being misunderstood by the most amiable, the most intellectual, the most exalted of monarchs. Oh, sire, sire! I have a heart, and it bleeds because you doubt of its existence!"

"I would believe you if you were a little less pathetic," said the king. "You not only assert, but you declaim. There is too little of nature and truth in your tone; you remind me a little of the stilted French tragedies, in which design and premeditation obscure all true passion; in which love is only a phrase, that no one believes in, dressed up with the tawdry gilding of sentiment and pathos."

"Your majesty will crush me with your scorn and mockery!" cried Voltaire, whose eyes now flamed with anger. "You wish to make me feel how powerless, how pitiful I am. Where shall I find the strength to strive with you? I have won no battles. I have no hundred thousand men to oppose to you, and no courts-martial to condemn those who sin against me!"

"It is true you have not a hundred thousand soldiers," said the king, "but you have four-and-twenty, and with these four-and-twenty soldiers you have conquered the whole realm of spirits; with this little army you have brought the whole of educated Europe to your feet. You are, therefore, a much more powerful king than I am. I have, it is true, a hundred thousand men, but I dare not say that they will not run when it comes to the first battle. You, Voltaire, have your four-and-twenty soldiers of the alphabet, and so well have you exercised them, that you must win every battle, even if all the kings of the earth were allied against you. Let us make peace, then, my 'invincible!' do not turn this terrible army of the four-and-twenty, with their deadly weapons, against me, but graciously allow me to seize upon the hem of your purple robe, to sun myself in your dazzling rays, to be your humble scholar, and from you and your army of heroes to learn the secret art of winning battles with invisible troops!"

"Your majesty makes me feel more and more how poor I am; even my four-and-twenty, of whom you speak, have gone over to you, and you understand, as well as I do, how to exercise them."

"No, no!" said Frederick, changing suddenly his jesting tone for one of grave earnestness. "No, I will learn of you. I am not satisfied to be a poor-souled *dilettante* in poetry. though assured I can never be a Virgil or a Voltaire. I know that the study of poetry demands the life, the undivided heart and mind. I am but a poor galley-slave, chained to the ship of state; or, if you will, a pilot, who does not dare to leave the rudder, or even to sleep, lest the fate of the unhappy Palinurus might overtake him. The Muses demand solitude and rest for the soul, and that I can never consecrate to them. Often, when I have written three verses, I am interrupted, my muse is chilled, and my spirit cannot rise again into the heights of inspiration. I know there are privileged souls, who can make verses everywhere —in the tumult of court life, in the loneliness of Circy, in the prisons of the Bastile, and in the stage-coach. My poor soul does not enjoy this freedom. It resembles an *anana*, which bears fruit only in the green-house, but fades and withers in the fresh air." *

"Ah! this is the first time I have caught the Solomon of the North in an untruth," cried Voltaire, eagerly. "Your soul is not like the *anana*, but like the wondrous southern tree which generously bears at the same time fruits and

* The king's own words.—Œuvres Posthumes.

flowers; which inspires and sweetly intoxicates us with its fragrance, and at the same time strengthens and refreshes us by its celestial fruits. You, sire, are not the pupil of Apollo, you are Apollo himself!"

The king smiled, and, raising his arms to heaven, he exclaimed, with the mock pathos of a French tragedian:

> " O Dieu! qui douez les poètes
> De tant de sublime faveurs;
> Ah, rendez vos graces parfaites,
> Et qu'ils soient un peu moins menteurs."

"In trying to punish me for what you are pleased to call my falsehood, your majesty proves that I have spoken the truth," cried Voltaire, eagerly. "You wish to show me that the fruit of your muse ripens slowly, and you improvise a charming quatrain that Molière himself would be proud to have composed."

> " Rendez vos graces parfaites,
> Et qu'ils soient un peu moins menteurs!"

repeated Frederick, nodding merrily to Voltaire. "Look you, friend, I am perhaps that mortal who incommodes the gods least with prayers and petitions. My first prayer to-day was for you; show, therefore, a little gratitude, and prove to me that the gods hear the earnest prayers of the faithful. Be less of a flatterer, and speak the simple truth. I desire now to look over with you my compositions of the last few days. I wish you, however, always to remember that when *you* write, you do so to add to the fame of your nation and to the honor of your fatherland. For myself, I scribble for my amusement; and I could easily be pardoned, if I were wise enough to burn my work as soon as it was finished.* When a man approaches his fortieth year and makes bad verses as I do, one might say, with Molière's 'Misanthrope '—

> ' Si j'en faisais d'aussi méchants,
> Je me garderais bien de les montrer aux gens.'"

"Your majesty considers yourself already too old to make verses, and you are scarcely thirty-eight: am I not

* The king's own words.—Œuvres Posthumes.

then a fool, worthy of condemnation, for daring to do homage to the Muses and striving to make verses—I, the gray-haired old man who already counts fifty-six?"

"You have the privilege of the gods! you will never grow old; and the Muses and Graces, though women, must ever remain faithful to you—you understand how to lay new chains upon them."

"No, no, sire! I am too old," sighed Voltaire; "an old poet, an old lover, an old singer, and an old horse are alike useless things—good for nothing.* Well, your majesty can make me a little younger by reading me some of your verses."

Frederick stepped to his writing-desk, and, seating himself, nodded to Voltaire to be seated also.

"You must know," said the king, handing Voltaire a sheet of paper covered with verses—"you must know that I have come with six twin brothers, who desire in the name of Apollo to be baptized in the waters of Hippocrene, and the 'Henriade' is entreated to be godfather."

Voltaire took the paper and read the verses aloud. The king listened attentively, and nodded approvingly over Voltaire's glowing and passionate declamation.

"This is grand! this is sublime!" cried Voltaire. "Your majesty is a French writer, who lives *by accident* in Germany. You have our language wholly in your power."

Frederick raised his finger threateningly. "Friend, friend, shall I weary the gods again with my prayer?"

"Your majesty, then, wishes to hear the whole truth?"

"The whole truth!"

"Then you must allow me, sire, to read the verses once more. I read them the first time as an amateur, now I will read them as a critic."

As Voltaire now repeated the verses, he laid a sharp accent upon every word and every imperfect rhyme; scanned every line with stern precision. Sometimes when he came to a false Alexandrine, he gave himself the appearance of being absolutely unable to force his lips to utter such barbarisms; and then his eyes glowed with malicious fire, and a contemptuous smile played about his mouth.

* Voltaire's own words.—Œuvres Posthumes, p. 364.

The king's brow clouded. "I understand," said he, "the poem is utterly unworthy—good for nothing. Let us destroy it."

"Not so, sire—the poem is excellent, and it requires but a few day's study to make it perfect. On the Venus di Medici no finger must be too long, no nail badly formed; and what are such statues, with which we deck our gardens, to the monuments of the library? We must, therefore, make your work perfect. There is infinite grace and intellect in this little poem. Where have you found such treasures, sire? How can your sandy soil yield such blossoms? How can such charming grace and profound learning be combined? * But even the Graces must stand upon a sure footing, and here, sire, are a few feet which are too long. Truly, that is sometimes unimportant, but the work of a distinguished genius should be *perfect*. You work too rashly, sire —it is sometimes more easy to win a battle than to make a good poem. Your majesty loves the truth so well, that by speaking the truth in all sincerity I shall best prove to you my most profound reverence. All that you do must be perfectly done; you are fully endowed with the ability necessary. No one must say '*Cæsar est supra grammaticum*.' Cæsar wrote as he fought, and was in both victorious. Frederick the Great plays the flute like Blavet, why should he not also write like the greatest of poets? † But your majesty must not disdain to give to the beautiful sentiment, the great thought, a lovely and attractive form."

"Yes, you are right!" said Frederick; "I fail in that, but you must not think that it is from carelessness. Those of my verses which you have least criticised are exactly those which have cost me the least effort. When the sentiment and the rhyme come in competition, I make bad verses, and am not happy in my corrections. You cannot comprehend the difficulties I have to overcome in making a few tolerable verses. A happy combination by nature, an irrepressible and fruitful intellect, made you a great poet without any effort of your own. I feel and acknowledge the inferiority of my talent. I swim about in the ocean of poetry with my

---

* Voltaire's own words.—Œuvres Posthumes, p. 329.
† Ibid., p. 323.

life-preserver under my arm. I do not write as well as I think. My ideas are stronger than my expressions; and in this embarrassment, I am often content if my verses are as little indifferent as possible, and do not expect them to be good." *

"It is entirely in your majesty's power to make them perfect. With you, sire, it is as with the gods—'I will!' and it is done. If your majesty will condescend to adorn the Graces and sylphs, the sages and scholars, who stumble about in this sublime poem with somewhat rugged feet, with artistic limbs, they will flutter about like graceful genii, and step with majesty like the three kings of the East. Now let us try—we will write this poem again."

He made a long mark with a pen over the manuscript of the king, took a new sheet of paper, and commenced to write the first lines. He criticised every word with bitter humor, with flashing wit, with mocking irony. Inexorable in his censure, indifferent in his praise, his tongue seemed to be armed with arrows, every one of which was intended to strike and wound.

The face of Frederick remained calm and clear. He did not feel that he was a mighty king and ruler, injured by the fault-finding of a common man. He was the pupil, with his accomplished teacher; and as he really wished to learn, he was indifferent as to the mode by which his stern master would instruct him.

After this they read together a chapter from the king's "*Histoire de Mon Temps.*" A second edition was about to appear, and Voltaire had undertaken to correct it. He brought his copy with him, in order to give Frederick an account of his corrections.

"This book will be a masterwork, if your majesty will only take the pains to correct it properly? But has a king the time and patience?—a king who governs his whole kingdom alone? Yes, it is this thought which confounds me! I cannot recover from my astonishment; it is this which makes me so stern in my judgment of your writings. I consider it a holy duty."

"And I am glad you are harsh and independent," said

* The king's own words, p. 346.

the king. "I learn more from ten stern and critical words, than from a lengthy speech full of praise and acknowledgment! But tell me, now, what means this red mark, with which you have covered one whole side of my manuscript?"

"Sire, this red mark asks for consideration for your grandfather, King Frederick the First; you have been harsh and cruel with him!"

"I dared not be otherwise, unless I would earn for myself the charge of partiality," said the king. "It shall not be said that I closed my eyes to his foolishness and absurdity because he was my grandfather. Frederick the First was a vain and pompous fool; this is the truth!"

"And yet I entreat your grace for him, sire. I love this king because of his royal pomp, and the beautiful monument which he left behind him."

"Well, that was vanity, that posterity might speak of him. From vanity he protected the arts; from vanity and foolish pride he placed the crown upon his head. His wife, the great Sophia Charlotte, was right when she said of him on her death-bed: 'The king will not have time to mourn for me; the interest he will take in solemnizing my funeral with pomp and regal splendor will dissipate his grief; and if nothing is wanting, nothing fails in the august and beautiful ceremony, he will be entirely comforted.'* He was only great in little things, and therefore when Sophia Charlotte received from her friend Leibnitz his memoir 'On the Power of Small Things,' she said, smiling: 'Leibnitz will teach me to know small things; has he forgotten that I am the wife of Frederick the First, or does he think that I do not know my husband?'"

"Well, I pray for grace for the husband on his wife's account. Sophia Charlotte was an exalted and genial woman; you should forgive her husband all other things, because he was wise enough to make her his wife and your grandmother! And if your majesty reproaches him for the vanity of making himself king, that is a vanity from which his descendants have obtained some right solid advantages."

"The title appears to me not in the least disagreeable! The title is beautiful, when given by a free people, or earned

* Thiébault.   † Ibid.

by a prince. Frederick the First had done nothing to stamp him a king, and that condemns him."

"So let it be," said Voltaire, shrugging his shoulders, "he is your grandfather, not mine. Do with him as you think best, sire; I have nothing more to say, and will content myself with softening a few phrases." *

When he saw that Frederick's brow clouded at these words, he said, with a sly laugh: "Look you, how the office of a teacher, which your majesty forced upon me, makes me insolent and haughty! I, who would do well to correct my own works, undertake to improve the writings of a king. I remind myself of the Abbot von Milliers, who has written a book called 'Reflections on the Faults of Others.' On one occasion he went to hear a sermon of a Capuchin. The monk addressed his audience, in a nasal voice, in the following manner: 'My dear brothers in the Lord, I had intended to-day to discourse upon hell, but at the door of the church I have read a bill posted up, "Reflections on the Faults of Others." "Ha! my friend," thought I, "why have you not rather made reflections over your own faults?" I will therefore speak to you of the pride and arrogance of men!'"

"Well, make such reflections always when occupied with the History of Louis the Fifteenth," said the king, laughing; "only, I beseech you, when you are with me, not to be converted by the pious Capuchin, but make your reflections on the faults of others only."

CHAPTER IX.

A DAY IN THE LIFE OF VOLTAIRE.

VOLTAIRE enjoyed the rare privilege of speaking the truth to the king, and he made a cruel and bitter use of his opportunities in this respect. He was jealous and envious of the king's fame and greatness, and sought to revenge him-

---

* This conversation of the king and Voltaire is historic. Voltaire tells it in a letter to Madame Denis.

29

self by continual fault-finding and criticism. He sought to mortify the great Frederick, who was admired and wondered at by all the world; to make him feel and confess that he could never equal the renowned writer Voltaire.

Frederick felt and acknowledged this frankly and without shame, but with that smiling composure and great self-consciousness which is ever ready to do justice to others, and demands at the same time a just recognition of its own claims. Voltaire might exalt himself to the clouds, he could not depreciate the king. He often made him angry, however, and this gratified the malice of the great French author.

The other friends of Frederick looked upon this conduct of Voltaire with regret; and the Marquis d'Argens, who was of a fine and gentle nature, soon saw the daily discontent of the king, and the wicked joy of Voltaire.

"My friend," said he, "the king wrote a poem yesterday, which he read aloud to me this morning. He declares that there is one bad rhyme in his poem, and that it tortures him. I tried in vain to reassure him. I know that the rhyme is incorrect, but you will provoke him beyond measure if you tell him so. He has tried in vain to correct it, without impairing the sense of the passage. I have, therefore, withheld all criticism, and read to him some verses from La Fontaine, where the same fault is to be found. I have wished to convince him that the poem is worthy of praise, although not exactly conformed to rule. I beg of you, Voltaire, to follow my example."

"And why should I do that?" said Voltaire, in his most snarling tone.

"Because, with your severe and continual criticisms you will disgust the king, and turn him aside from his favorite pursuit. I think it important to poetry and the fine arts that the great and powerful sovereign of Prussia should love and cherish them; should exalt those who cultivate them, and, indeed, rank himself amongst them. What difference does it make, Voltaire, if a bad rhyme is to be found in the poetry of the philosopher of Sans-Souci?" *

"The king wishes to learn of me how to make good

* Thiébault, vol. v., p. 337.

poetry, and my love to him is not of that treasonable, womanly, and cowardly sort which shrinks from blaming him because it fears to wound his self-love. The king has read his poem to you, and it is your province to wonder at and praise your friend. He will read it to me as '*Pedagogo de sua Maestà.*' I will be true and just, where you have dared to flatter him."

Never was Voltaire more severe in his criticism, more cutting in his satire, than to-day. His eyes sparkled with malicious joy, and a wicked smile played still upon his lip as he left the king and returned to his own apartment.

"Ah," said he, seating himself at his writing-table, with a loud laugh, "I shall write well to-day, for I have had a lesson. Frederick does not know how far he is my benefactor. In correcting him, I correct myself; and in directing his studies, I gain strength and judgment for my own works.* I will now write a chapter in my History of Louis XIV. My style will be good. The chapter which I have read this morning, in Frederick's '*Histoire de Mon Temps*,' has taught me what faults to avoid. Yes, I will write of Louis XIV. Truly I owe him some compensation. King Frederick has had the *naïveté* to compare his great grandfather, the so-called great Prince-Elector, to the great Louis. I was amiable enough to pardon him for this little compliment to his ancestors, and not to strike it from his '*Histoire*.' And, indeed, why should I have done that? The world will not be so foolish as to charge this amusing weakness to me! After all, the king writes but for himself, and a few false, flattering friends; he can, therefore, say what he will. I, however, I write for France—for the world! But I fear, alas, that fools will condemn me, because I have sought to write as a wise man." †

Voltaire commenced to write, but he was soon interrupted by his servant, Tripot, who announced that the Jew Hirsch, for whom Voltaire had sent, was at the door. Voltaire rose hastily, and called him to enter.

"I have business with you, my friend," said he to the Jew. "Close the door, Tripot, and see that we are not disturbed."

Voltaire hastened with youthful agility through the sa-

* Voltaire's own words.—Œuvres, p. 363.   * Œuvres, p. 341.

loon, and beckoned to the Jew to follow him into his bed-room.

"First of all, friend, we will make a small mercantile operation." So saying, he opened the door of a large *commode*. "See, here are twelve pounds of the purest wax-lights. I am a poor man, with weak eyes. I have no use for these lights; I can never hope to profit by them. Here, also, are several pounds of sugar and coffee, the savings of the last two months. You will buy all this of me; we will agree upon a fixed price, and the last day of every month you will come for the same purpose. Name your price, sir."

Hirsch named his price; but it seemed that the great poet understood how to bargain better than the Jew. He knew exactly the worth of the sugar and the coffee, he spoke so eloquently of the beauty and purity of the thick white wax-lights, that the Hebrew increased his offer.

"And now to more important business," said Voltaire. "You are going to Dresden—you will there execute a commission for me. I wish to invest eighteen thousand thalers in Saxon bonds. They can now be purchased at thirty-five, and will be redeemed at a hundred."

"But your excellency knows that the king has forbidden his subjects to buy these bonds. He demanded and obtained for his subjects a pledge that they should be paid at par for the bonds they now hold, while the subjects of the King of Saxony receive only their present value. The king promised, however, that the Prussians should make no further investments in these bonds. You see, then, that it is impossible for me to fulfil this commission."

"I see that you are a fool!" cried Voltaire, angrily. "If you were not a fool, you would know that Voltaire, the chamberlain of the king, would not undertake a business transaction which would stain his reputation or cast a shadow on his name. When Voltaire makes this investment, you can understand that he is authorized to do so."

"That being the case," said Hirsch, humbly, "I am entirely satisfied, and will gladly serve your excellency."

"If you fill this commission handsomely and promptly, you may feel assured of a reward. Are you ambitious? Would you not like a title?"

"Certainly I am ambitious. I should be truly happy if I could obtain the title of 'royal court agent.'"

"Well, buy these bonds for me in Dresden *cheap,* and you shall have this coveted title," said the noble author of the "*Henriade,*" and other world-renowned works.

"I will buy them at thirty-five thalers."

"And you will invest eighteen thousand thalers at this rate. Our contract is made; now we will count the gold. I have not the ready money—I will give you drafts—come into my study.—There are three drafts," said he, "one on Paris, one on your father, and one on the Jew Ephraim. Get them cashed, good Hirsch, and bring me my Saxon bonds."

"In eight days, your excellency, I will return with them, and you will have a clear profit of eleven thousand thalers."

Voltaire's eyes sparkled with joy. "Eleven thousand thalers!" said he; "for a poor poet, who lives by his wits and his pen, that is a considerable sum."

"You will realize that sum," said Hirsch, with the solemn earnestness of a Jew when he has made a good trade.

Hirsch was about to withdraw, but Voltaire hastened after him, and seizing his arm, he cried out threateningly: "You are not going without giving me your note? You do not think that I am such a fool as to give you eighteen thousand thalers, and have nothing to prove it?"

"You excellency has my word of honor," said the Jew, earnestly.

Voltaire laughed aloud. "Your word! the honorable word of a man for eighteen thousand thalers! My dear friend, we do not live in paradise, but in a so-called Christian city—your worthy forefathers obtained for us this privilege. Do you believe that I will trust one of their descendants? Who will go my security that you will not nail my innocence and my confiding heart upon the cross, and slay them if I should be unsuspicious enough to trust my money with you in this simple way?"

"I will give you ample security," said Hirsch, taking a morocco case from his pocket. "I did not know why your excellency sent for me. I thought perhaps you wished to buy diamonds, and brought some along with me. Look, sir!

here are diamonds worth twenty-two thousand thalers! I will leave them with you—I, the poor Jew, do not fear that the great poet Voltaire will deceive and betray me."

"These diamonds are beautiful," said Voltaire—"very beautiful, and perhaps if my speculation succeeds, I may buy some from you. Until then, I will take care of them."

Voltaire was about to lock them up, but he paused suddenly, and fixed his eyes upon the calm countenance of the Jew.

"How do I know that these are real diamonds?" he cried; and as Hirsch, exasperated by this base suspicion, frowned and turned pale, he exclaimed fiercely: "The diamonds are false! I know it by your terror. Oh, oh, you thought that a poet was a good, credulous creature who could be easily deceived. Ah! you thought I had heard nothing of those famous lapidaries in St. Germain, who cut diamonds from glass, and cook up in their laboratories the rarest jewels! Yes, yes, I know all these arts, and all the brewing of St. Germain will not suffice to deceive me."

"These diamonds are pure!" cried Hirsch.

"We will have them tested by a Christian jeweller," said Voltaire.—"Tripot! Tripot! run quickly to the jeweller Reclam—beg him to come to me for a few moments."

Tripot soon returned with Reclam. The diamonds were pronounced pure and of the first water; and the jeweller declared they were fully worth twenty-two thousand thalers. Voltaire was now fully satisfied, and, when once more alone, he looked long and rapturously upon these glittering stones.

"What woman can boast of such dazzling fire in her eyes?" said he, laughing; "what woman can say that their color is worth twenty-two thousand thalers? It is true they glisten and shimmer in all lights and shades—that is their weakness and their folly. With you, beautiful gems! these changing hues are a virtue. Oh, to think that with this handful of flashing stones I could buy a bag of ducats! How dull and stupid are mankind—how wise is God! Sinking those diamonds in the bowels of the earth was a good speculation. They are truffles to tempt the snouts of men; and they root after them as zealously as the swine in Perigord root after the true truffles. Gold! gold! that is the magic word with which the world is ruled. I will have gold—I will rule the world. I will not give place to dukes or princes. I will have my seigneuries and my castles; my servants in rich livery, and my obedient subjects. I will be a grand seigneur. Kings and princes shall visit me in my castle, and wait in my antechamber, as I have been compelled to wait in theirs. I will be rich that I may be every man's master, even master of the fools. I will enslave the wise by my intellect—I will reduce the foolish to bondage with gold. I must be rich! rich! rich! therefore am I here; therefore do I correct the poor rhymes of the king; therefore do I live now as a modest poet, and add copper to copper, and save my pension of five thousand thalers, and sell my wax-lights and my coffee to the Jew. Let the world call me a miser. When I become rich, I will be a spendthrift; and men who are now envious and angry at my fame shall burst with rage at my fortune. Ah, ah, it is not worth the cost to be a celebrated writer! There are too many humiliations connected with this doubtful social position. It gives no rank—it is a pitiful thing in the eyes of those who have actual standing, and is only envied by those who are unnoticed and unknown. For my own part, I am so exhausted by the discomforts of my position, I would gladly cast it from me, and make for myself what the *canaille* call a good thing—an enormous fortune. I will scrape together all the gold that is possible. I will give for gold all the honor and freedom and fame which come to me. I am a rich gainer in all these things by my residence with King Frederick. He has this virtue: he is unprejudiced, and cares nothing even for his own royal rank. I will therefore remain in this haven, whither the storms, which have so long driven me from shore to shore, have now safely moored me. My happiness will last just as long as God pleases." *

He laughed heartily, and took his cash-book, in which he entered receipts and expenditures. It was Voltaire's greatest pleasure to add up his accounts from time to time, and gloat over the growth of his fortune; to compare, day by day, his receipts and expenses, and to find that a handsome

* Voltaire's own words.—Œuvres, p. 110.

sum was almost daily placed to his credit. The smallest necessary expenditure angered him. With a dark frown he said to himself: "It is unjust and mean to require of me to buy provender for my horse, and to have my carriage repaired; if the king furnishes me with an equipage, he should not allow it to be any expense to me. The major-domo is an old miser, who cheats me every month out of some pounds of sugar and coffee, and the wax-lights are becoming thinner and poorer. I will complain to King Frederick of all this; he must see that order prevails in his palace."

Voltaire closed his account-book, and murmured: "When I have an income of a hundred and fifty thousand francs, I will cease to economize. God be praised, I have almost reached the goal! But," said he, impatiently, "in order to effect this, I must remain here a few years, and add my pension to my income. Nothing must prevent this—I must overcome every obstacle. What! who can hinder me? my so-called friends, who naturally are my most bitter enemies? Ha, ha! what a romantic idea of this genial king to assemble six friends around him at Sans-Souci, the most of them being authors—that is to say, natural enemies! I believe if two authors, two women, or two pietists, were placed alone upon a desert isle, they would forget their dependence upon each other, and commence intriguing at once. This, alas! is humanity, and being so, one must withdraw from the poor affair advantageously and cunningly.* No one can live peacefully in this world; least of all, in the neighborhood of a king. It is with kings as with coquettes, their glances kindle jealousy—and Frederick is a great coquette. I must, therefore, drive my rivals from the field, and enjoy in peace the favor of the king. Now which of my rivals are dangerous to me? All! all! I must banish them all! I will sow such discontent and rage and malice and strife amongst them, that they will fly in hot haste, and thank God if I do not bite off their noses before they escape. I will turn this, their laughing paradise, into a hell, and I will be the devil to chase them with glowing pitchforks. Yes, even to Siberia will I drive this long-legged peacock, Maupertius—him, first of all; then D'Argens, then Algarotti, then this over-wise

* Voltaire, Œuvres, p. 375.

and good Lord Marshal, and all others like him! When Voltaire's sun is in the ascendant, not even stars shall glitter. It shall not be! I will prove to them that Voltaire's fiery rays have burned them to ashes!"*

He laughed aloud, and seated himself to write a poem. He was invited that evening to a *soirée* by the queen-mother, where he wished to shine as an improvisator. Above all other things, he wished to win the heart of the Princess Amelia. Since she had played the part of Aurelia, in "Rome Sauvée," he had felt a passion for the princess, who had betrayed to the life the ardor and the pains of love, and whose great flaming eyes seemed, from their mysterious depths, to rouse the soul of the poet. Voltaire had promised the Princess Amelia to improvise upon any subject she should select, and he relied upon his cunning to incline her choice in such a direction as to make the poem he was now writing appropriate and seem impromptu.

While thus occupied, his servant entered and announced a number of distinguished gentlemen, who were in the parlor, and wished to make the great author a morning visit. "Let them all wait!" said Voltaire, angrily; declaring that this disturbance had cost him a piquant rhyme.

"But, gracious sir," stammered the servant, "some of the most distinguished men of the court and the oldest generals, are there!"

"What do I care for their epaulets or their excellencies? Let them wait, or go to the devil—if they prefer it."

Well, the eminent gentlemen waited; indeed, they waited patiently, until the great Voltaire, the favorite of the king, the universal French author, in his pride and arrogance was graciously pleased to show himself amongst the Dutch barbarians, and allow some rays of his intellect to fall upon and inspire them!

The saloon was indeed crowded with princes, generals, and nobles. Voltaire had just returned to Berlin from Potsdam, and all hastened to pay their respects and commend themselves to his grace and favor.†

* Voltaire, Œuvres, p. 378.
† Forney writes thus in his "Memoirs": "During the winter months which Voltaire spent in the palace of Berlin, he was the favorite of the court. Princes, ambassadors, ministers, generals, nobles of the highest rank,

Voltaire was very gracious this morning. As he was to play the part of improvisator that night, he thought it politic to make favor with all those who would be present. He hoped that all the world would thunder out their enraptured applause, and that Maupertius, D'Argens, Algarotti, La Mettrie, and all other friends of the king, would be filled with envy and rage. He smiled, therefore, benignantly, and had kind and flattering words for all. His *bon-mots* and piquant witticisms seemed inexhaustible.

Suddenly his servant drew near, and said it was necessary to speak to him on a matter of great importance. Voltaire turned with a winning smile to his guests, and, praying them to wait for his return, entered his private room.

"Well, Tripot, what have you to say that is important?"

"Gracious sir, the court is in mourning."

Voltaire looked at him enraged. "Fool! what is that to me?"

"It is of the utmost importance to you, sir, if you are going this evening to the *soirée* of the queen-mother."

"Will you run me mad, Tripot? What has the court mourning to do with the queen's *soirée?*"

"Gracious sir, the explanation is very simple. When the court is in mourning, no one can appear there in embroidered clothes; you must wear a plain black coat."

"I have no plain black coat," said Voltaire, with a frowning brow.

"It is necessary, then, for you to order one, and I have sent Monsieur Pilleneure to come and take your measure."

"Are you insane, Tripot?" cried Voltaire. "Do you regard me as so vile a spendthrift, so brainless a fool, as to order a new coat for the sake of one evening's amusement—a coat which will cost an immense sum of money, and must then hang in the wardrobe to be destroyed by moths? In eight days this mourning will be over, and I would be several hundred francs poorer, and possess a black coat I could never wear! I will not go this evening to the *soirée* of the queen-

went to his morning receptions, and were often received by him with contemptuous scorn. A great prince was pleased to play chess with him, and allowed him every time to win the stake of two louis d'or. It was declared, however, that sometimes the gold disappeared before the end of the game, and could not be found."—"Souvenirs d'un Citoyen."

mother; this is decided. I will announce myself sick. Go and countermand the tailor."

He turned to leave the room, but paused suddenly. "I cannot decline this invitation," murmured he. "It is widely known that I have promised to improvise. The world is looking on eagerly. If I do not go, or if I announce myself sick, they will say I shrink from this ordeal. My enemies will triumph!—Tripot, I am obliged to go to the *soirée* of the queen."

"Then the tailor must come to take your measure?"

"Fool!" cried Voltaire, stamping furiously. "I have told you I have no gold for such follies. Gather up your small amount of understanding, and think of some other expedient."

"Well, your excellency, I know a mode of escape from this embarrassment, but I scarcely dare propose it."

"Speak out—any means are good which attain their object."

"Below, in the court, dwells the merchant Fromery. His servant is my very good friend. I have learned from him that his master has just purchased a beautiful black coat. I think he has about the figure of your excellency."

"Ah, I understand," said Voltaire, whose countenance became clearer. "You will borrow for me, from your friend, the coat of his master?"

"Yes, if your excellency is not offended at my proposal?"

"On the contrary, I find the idea capital. Go, Tripot, and borrow the coat of Fromery."

Voltaire returned once more to his distinguished guests, and enraptured them again by his witty slanders and brilliant conversation. As the last visitor departed, he rang for his servant.

"Well, Tripot, have you the coat?"

"I have, your excellency."

Voltaire rubbed his hands with delight. "It seems this is a happy day for me—I make the most advantageous business arrangements."

"But it will be necessary for your grace to try on this coat. I fear it is too large; since I saw Fromery, he has grown fat."

"The ass!" cried Voltaire. "How does he dare to fatten, when all the people of intellect and celebrity, like myself, grow thinner every day?" So saying, he put on the coat of the merchant Fromery. "Yes, truly, it is far too large for me. Oh, oh! to think that the coat of a pitiful Dutch tradesman is too large for the great French poet! Well, that is because these Dutch barbarians think of nothing but gormandizing. They puff up their gross bodies with common food, and they daily become fatter; but the spirit suffers. Miserable slaves of their appetites, they are of no use themselves, and their coats are also useless!"

"Does your excellency believe that it is impossible to wear the coat?"

"Do I believe it is impossible? Look at me! Do I not look like a hungry heir in the testamentary coat of his rich cousin the brewer? Would it not be thought that I was a scarecrow, to drive the birds from the cornfields?"

At this moment Monsieur Pilleneure was announced.

"Good Heaven! I forgot to countermand the tailor!" cried Tripot.

"That is fortunate!" said Voltaire, calming himself. "God sends this tailor here to put an end to my vexations. This coat is good and handsome, only a little too large—the tailor will alter it immediately."

"That will be splendid!" said Tripot. "He will take in the seams, and to-morrow enlarge it again."

"Not so!" cried Voltaire. "The coat could not possibly look well; he must cut away the seams."

"But then," said Tripot, hesitatingly, "Fromery could never wear his coat again."

"Fromery will learn that Voltaire has done him the honor to borrow his coat, and I think that will be a sufficient compensation. Tell the tailor to enter."

Thanks to the adroitness of Pilleneure, Voltaire appeared at the *soirée* of the queen-mother in a handsome, well-fitting black coat. No one guessed that the mourning dress of the celebrated French writer belonged to the merchant Fromery, and that the glittering diamond *agraffes* in his bosom, and the costly rings on his fingers, were the property of the Jew Hirsch. Voltaire's eyes were more sparkling than diamonds, and the glances which he fixed upon the Princess Amelia more glowing; her pale and earnest beauty inspired him to finer wit and richer hymns of praise.

No one dared to say that this passionate adoration offered to the princess was unbecoming and offensive to etiquette. Voltaire was the man of his age, and therefore justified in offering his worship even to a princess. He was also the favorite of the king, who allowed him privileges granted to no other man. There was one present, however, who found these words of passion and of rapture too bold, and that one was King Frederick. He had entered noiselessly and unannounced, as was his custom, and he saw, with a derisive smile, how every one surrounded Voltaire, and all were zealous in expressing their rapture over his improvised poem, and entreating him to repeat it.

"How can I repeat what I no longer know?" said he. "An angel floated by me in the air, and, by a glance alone, she whispered words which my enraptured lips uttered as in a wild hallucination."

"The centuries to come are to be pitied if they are to be deprived of this enchanting poem," said the Princess Amelia. She had remarked the entrance of the king, knew that his eye was fixed upon her, and wished to please him by flattering his beloved favorite.

"If your royal highness thinks thus, I will now write out a poem which I had designed only to recite," said Voltaire, seating himself at the card-table; and, taking a card and pencil, he wrote with a swift hand and handed the card, bowing profoundly.

The king, who was a silent spectator of this scene, looked at the Princess Amelia, and saw that she blushed as she read, and her brow was clouded.

"Allow me, also, to read the poem of the great Voltaire, my sister," said the king, drawing near.

The princess handed him the card, and while Frederick read, all stood around him in respectful silence.

"This poem is sublime," said the king, smiling. He saw that the princess was no longer grave, and that Voltaire breathed freely, as if relieved from a great apprehension. "This little poem is so enchanting, that you must allow me to copy it, my sister. Go on with your conversation, messieurs, it does not disturb me."

A request from the lips of a king is a command; all exerted themselves therefore to keep up a gay and animated conversation, and to seem thoughtless and unoccupied. Frederick seated himself at the table, and read once more the poem of Voltaire, which was as follows:

> " Souvent un peu de vérité
> Se mêle au plus grossier mensonge.
> Cette nuit dans l'erreur d'un songe,
> Au rang des rois j'étais monté,
> Je vous aimais alors, et j'osais vous le dire,
> Les dieux à mon reveil ne m'ont pas tout ôté,
> Je n'ai perdu que mon empire."

"Insolent!" cried the king, and his scornful glance wandered away to Voltaire, who was seated near the queen engaged in lively conversation. "We will damp his ardor," said he, smiling; and, taking a card, he commenced writing hastily.

Truly at this moment the stern master Voltaire might have been content with his royal pupil; the rhymes were good and flowed freely. When Frederick had finished his poem, he put Voltaire's card in his bosom and drew near to the princess.

"The poem is piquant," said he; "read it yourself, and then ask Voltaire to read it aloud."

Amelia looked strangely at the king, but as she read, a soft smile lighted up her lovely, melancholy face. Bowing to her brother, she said in low tones, "I thank your highness."

"Now give the card to Voltaire, and ask him to read it," said the king.

Voltaire took the card, but as he read he did not smile as the princess had done—he turned pale and pressed his lips tightly together.

"Read it," said the king.

"I beg your pardon," said Voltaire, who had immediately recovered his self-possession; "this little poem, so hastily composed, was not worthy of the exalted princess to whom I dared address it. Your majesty will be graciously pleased to remember that it was born in a moment, and the next instant lost its value. As I now read it, I find it dull and trivial. You will not be so cruel as to force me to read aloud to your majesty that which I condemn utterly."

"Oh, *le coquin!*" murmured Frederick, while Voltaire, with a profound bow, placed the card in his pocket.

When the *soirée* was over, and Voltaire returned to his rooms, the gay and genial expression which he had so carefully maintained during the evening disappeared; and his lips, which had smiled so kindly, muttered words of cursing and bitterness. He ordered Tripot to arrange his writing-table and leave the room. Being now alone, he drew the card from his bosom, and, as if to convince himself that what he saw was truth and no cruel dream, he read aloud, but with a trembling voice:

> " On remarque, pour l'ordinaire,
> Qu'un songe est annaloque à notre caractère,
> Un héros peut rêver, qu'il a passé le Rhin,
> Un chien qu'il aboie à la lune ;
> Un joueur, qu'il a fait fortune,
> Un voleur, qu'il a fait butin.
> Mais que Voltaire, à l'aide d'un mensonge,
> Ose se croire roi lui que n'est qu'un faquin,
> Ma fois ! c'est abuser du songe."

"So I am already a scoundrel?" said Voltaire, grinning. "My enemies triumph, and he who a short time since was called the wise man of the age, the Virgil of France, is nothing but a scoundrel! This time, I confess, I merited my humiliation, and the consciousness of this increases my rage. I am a good-humored, credulous fool. Why was I so silly as to credit the solemn protestations of the king that I should never feel his superior rank; that he would never show himself the master? If I dare to claim an equality with him for an instant, he swings his rod of correction, and I am bowed in the dust! Voltaire is not the man to bow patiently. The day shall come in which I will revenge with rich interest the degradation of this evening. But enough of anger and excitement. I will sleep; perhaps in happy dreams I shall wander from the chilly borders of the Spree to my own beautiful Paris."

He called Tripot, and commanded him to announce to Fredersdorf that he was ill, and could not accompany the king to Potsdam in the morning.

He then retired, and the gods, perhaps, heard his prayer, and allowed him in dreams to look upon Paris, where the Marquis de Pompadour reigned supreme, and the pious priests preached against the Atheist Voltaire, to whom the great-hearted King of Prussia had given an asylum. Perhaps he saw in his dreams the seigneurie of his glittering future, and his beautiful house at Ferney, where he built a temple, with the proud inscription, "*Voltaire Deo erexit!*"

At all events, his dreams must have been pleasant and refreshing. He laughed in his sleep; and his countenance, which was so often clouded by base and wicked passions, was bright and clear; it was the face of a poet, who, with closed eyes, looked up into the heaven of heavens.

The morning came, and Voltaire still slept—even the rolling of the carriages aroused him but for a moment; he wrapped himself up in his warm bed, the soft eider down of his pillow closed over his head and made him invisible. Tripot came lightly upon tiptoe and removed the black coat of the merchant Fromery. Voltaire heard nothing; he slept on. And now the door was noisily opened, and a young woman, with fresh, rosy cheeks and sparkling eyes, entered the room; she was dressed as a chambermaid, a little white coquettish cap covered her hair, and a white apron with a little bodice was laced over her striped woollen robe. Upon her white, naked arm she carried linen which she threw carelessly upon the floor, and drew with rash steps near the bed. Voltaire still slept, and was still invisible.

The young chambermaid, believing that he had gone with the king to Potsdam, had come to arrange the room; with a quick movement she seized the bed with her sinewy hands and threw it off. A wild cry was heard! a white skeleton figure rose from the bed, now lying in the middle of the chamber, and danced about the floor with doubled fists and wild curses. The girl uttered a shriek of terror and rushed from the room; and if the form and the nightcap had not been purely white, she would have sworn she had seen the devil in person, and that she had cast him out from the bed of the great French poet.[*]

CHAPTER X.

THE LOVERS.

THE day of grace was at an end. The four weeks which the king had granted to his sister, in order that she might take counsel with herself, were passed, and the heart of the princess was unmoved—only her face was changed. Amelia hid her pallor with rouge, and the convulsive trembling of her lips with forced smiles; but it was evident that her cheeks became daily more hollow, and her eyes more inflamed. Even the king remarked this, and sent his physician to examine her eyes. The princess received this messenger of the king with a bitter, icy smile.

"The king is very good; but I am not ill—I do not suffer."

"But, your royal highness, your eyes suffer. They are weak and inflamed: allow me to examine them."

"Yes, as my brother has commanded it; but I warn you, you cannot heal them."

Meckel, the physician, examined her eyes with the closest attention, then shook his head thoughtfully.

"Princess," said he at last, in low, respectful tones, "if you grant your eyes no rest; if, instead of sleeping quietly, you pass the night pacing your room; if you continue to exhaust your eyes by constant weeping, the most fatal consequences may result."

"Do you mean I will become blind?" said Amelia, quietly.

"I mean your eyes are suffering; that, however, is no acute disease; but your whole nervous system is in a dangerous condition, and all this must be rectified before your eyes can be healed."

[*] Thiébault, v., 281.

"Prescribe something, then, as his majesty has commanded it," said Amelia, coldly.

"I will give your royal highness a remedy; but it is of so strong and dangerous a nature, that it must be used only with the utmost caution. It is a liquid; it must be heated, and you must allow the steam to pass into your eyes. Your highness must be very, very careful. The substances in this mixture are so strong, so corrosive, that if you approach too near the steam, it will not only endanger your eyes, but your face and your voice. You must keep your mouth firmly closed, and your eyes at least ten inches above the vessel from which the steam is rising. Will your highness remember all this, and act as I have directed?"

"I will remember it," said Amelia, replying only to the first part of his question.

Meckel did not remark this. He wrote his prescription and withdrew, once more reminding Amelia of the caution necessary.

As has been said, this was the last day of grace. The princess seemed calm and resigned. Even to her confidential maid she uttered no complaints. The steaming mixture was prepared, and, while Amelia held herself some distance above it, as the physician had commanded, she said laughingly to Ernestine: "I must strive to make my eyes bright, that my brother may be pleased, or at least that he may not be excited against me."

The prescription seemed to work wonders. The eyes of the princess were clear and bright, and upon her cheeks burned that dark, glowing carnation, which an energetic will and a strong and bold resolve sometimes call into life.

"Now, Ernestine, come! make me a careful and tasteful toilet. It seems to me that this is my wedding-day; that I am about to consecrate myself forever to a beloved friend."

"Oh, princess, let it be thus!" cried Fraulein von Haak, imploringly. "Constrain your noble heart to follow the wishes of the king, and wed the King of Denmark."

Amelia looked at her, amazed and angry. "You know that Trenck has received my warning, and has replied to me. He will listen to no suggestions; under no pretext, will he be influenced to cross the borders of Prussia, not even if full pardon and royal grace are offered him. I need not, there-fore, be anxious on his account."

"That being the case, your royal highness should now think a little of your own happiness. You should seek to be reconciled to your fate—to yield to that which is unalterable. The king, the royal family, yes, the whole land will rejoice if this marriage with the King of Denmark takes place. Oh, princess, be wise! do willingly, peacefully, what you will otherwise be forced to do! Consent to be Queen of Denmark."

"You have never loved, Ernestine, and you do not know that it is a crime to break a holy oath sworn unto God. But let us be silent. I know what is before me—I am prepared!"

With calm indifference, Amelia completed her toilet; then stepped to the large Psyche, which stood in her boudoir, and examined herself with a searching eye.

"I think there is nothing in my appearance to enrage the king. I have laid rouge heavily upon my cheeks, and, thanks to Meckel's prescription, my eyes are as brilliant as if they had shed no tears. If I meet my brother with this friendly, happy smile, he will not remark that my cheeks are sunken. He will be content with me, and perhaps listen to my prayers."

Ernestine regarded her with a sad and troubled glance. "You look pale, princess, in spite of your rouge, and your laugh lacerates the heart. There is a tone, a ring in it, like a broken harp-string."

"Still," said Amelia, "still, Ernestine! my hour has come! I go to the king. Look, the hand of the clock points to twelve, and I ask an audience of the king at this hour. Farewell, Ernestine! Ernestine, pray for me."

She wrapped herself in her mantle, and stepped slowly and proudly through the corridors to the wing of the castle occupied by the king. Frederick received her in his library. He advanced to the door to meet her, and with a kindly smile extended both his hands.

"Welcome, Amelia, a thousand times welcome! Your coming proves to me that your heart has found the strength which I expected; that my sweet sister has recovered herself, her maidenly pride, fully.

" The proud daughter of the Hohenzollerns is here to say to the king—' The King of Denmark demands my hand. I will bestow it upon him. My father's daughter dare not wed beneath her. She must look onward and upward. There is no myrtle-wreath for me, but a crown is glittering, and I accept it. God has made both heart and brain strong enough to bear its weight. I shall be no happy shepherdess, but I shall be a great and good queen; I will make others happy.' "

" You have come, Amelia, to say this to the king; but you have also come to say to your brother—' I am ready to fulfil your wishes. I know that no selfish views, no ambitious plans influence you. I know that you think only of my prosperity and my happiness; that you would save me from misfortune, humiliation, and shame; that you would guard me from the mistakes and weaknesses of my own heart. I accede to your wish, my brother—I will be queen of Denmark?' Now, Amelia," said Frederick, with an agitated voice, " have I not rightly divined? Have you not sought me for this purpose?"

" No, my brother, no, no!" cried Amelia, with wild, gushing tears. " No; I have come to implore your pity, your mercy." Completely beside herself, mad with passion and pain, she fell upon her knees and raised her arms entreatingly to the king. " Mercy, my brother, mercy! Oh, spare my poor, martyred heart! Leave me at least the liberty to complain and to be wretched! Do not condemn me to marry Denmark!"

Frederick stepped backward, and his brow darkened; but he controlled his impatience, and drew near his sister with a kindly smile, and gently raising her from her knees, he led her to the divan.

" Come, Amelia, it does not become you to kneel to a man—to God only should a princess kneel. Let us be seated, and speak to each other as brother and sister should speak who love and wish to understand each other."

" I am ready for all else, I will accommodate myself to all else—only be merciful! Do not compel me to wed Denmark!"

" Ah, see, my sister, although you are struggling against me, how justly you comprehend your position!" said the king, mildly. "You speak of wedding Denmark. Your exalted and great destiny sleeps in these words. A princess when she marries does not wed a man, but a whole people; she does not only make a man but a nation happy. There are the weeping, whose tears she will dry; the poor, whose hunger she will assuage; the unhappy, to whom she will bring consolation; the sick and dying, with whom she will pray. There is a whole people advancing to meet her with shouts of gladness, stretching out their hands, and asking for love. God has blessed the hearts of queens with the power to love their subjects, because they are women. Oh, my sister, this is a great, a noble destiny which Providence offers you—to be the beneficent, mediating, smiling angel, standing ever by the side of a king—a bond of love between a king and his subjects! Truly one might well offer up their poor, pitiful wishes, their own personal happiness, for such a noble destiny."

"I have no more happiness to offer up," sighed Amelia. "I have no happiness; I do not ask so much. I plead for the poor right of living for my great sorrow—of being faithful to myself."

"He only is faithful to himself who lives to discharge his duties," said the king. "He only is true to himself who governs himself, and if he cannot be happy, at least endeavors to make others so, and this vocation of making others happy is the noblest calling for a woman; by this shall she overcome her selfishness and find comfort, strength, and peace. And who, my sister, can say that he is happy? Our life consists in unfulfilled wishes, vain hopes destroyed, ideals, and lost illusions. Look at me, Amelia. Have I ever been happy? Do you believe that there is a day of my life I would live over? Have I not, from my earliest youth, been acquainted with grief, self-denial, and pain? Are not all the blossoms of my life broken? Am I not, have I not ever been, the slave of my rank?—a man, 'cabined, cribbed, confined,' though I appear to be a great king? Oh, I will not relate what I have suffered—how my heart has been lacerated and trampled upon! I will only say to you, that, notwithstanding this, I have never wished to be other than I am, that I have been always thankful for my fate; glad to be

born to a throne, and not in a miserable hut. Believe me,
Amelia, a sublime misfortune is better, more glorious, than
a petty happiness. To have the brow wounded, because the
crown presses too heavily upon the temples, is more desirable
than to breathe out your sorrows in the midst of poverty and
vulgarity, then sink into a dark and unknown grave. God,
who has, perhaps, denied us the blessing of love, gives fame
as a compensation. If we are not happy, we are powerful!"

"Ah, my brother, these are the views of a man and a
king," said Amelia. "I am a poor, weak woman. For me
there is no fame, no power!"

"Isabella of Spain and Elizabeth of England were also
women, and their fame has extended through centuries."

"They, however, were independent queens. I can be
nothing more than the wife of a king. Oh, my brother, let
me remain only the sister of a king! Let there be no change
in my fate—let all remain as it is! This is my only hope—
my only prayer! My heart is dead, and every wish is buried
—let it suffice, my brother! Do not ask the impossible!"

The king sprang from his seat, and his eyes glowed with
scorn. "It is, then, all in vain!" said he, fiercely. "You
will listen neither to reason nor entreaty!"

"Oh, sire, have mercy—I cannot wed the King of Denmark!"

"You cannot!" cried the king; "what does that mean?"

"That means that I have sworn never to become the wife
of another than of him whom I love; that means that I have
sworn to die unmarried, unless I go to the altar with my beloved!"

"This wild, mad wish can never be fulfilled!" said the
king, threateningly. "You will marry—I, the king, command it!"

"Command me not, my brother!" cried Amelia, proudly,
"command me not! You stand now upon the extremest
boundary of your power; it will be easy now to teach you
that a king is powerless against a firm, bold will!"

"Ah! you threaten me!"

"No, I pray to you—I pray wildly to your hard heart for
pity! I clasp your knees—I pray to you, as the wretched,
the hopeless pray to God—have mercy upon my torment,

pity my unspeakable anguish! I am a poor, weak woman—oh, have mercy! My heart bleeds from a thousand wounds—comfort, heal it! I am alone, and oh, how lonely!—be with me, my brother, and protect and shield me! Oh, my brother! my brother! it is my life, my youth, my future which cries out to you! Mercy! grace! Drive me not to extremity! Be merciful, as God is merciful! Force me not into rebellion against God, against Nature, against myself! Make me not an unnatural daughter, an unthankful sister, a disobedient subject! My God! My God! Oh, let your heart be touched! I cannot wed the King of Denmark—say not that I shall!"

"And if I still say it? If, by the power of my authority, as your brother and your king, I command you to obey?"

"I may perhaps die, but your command will have no other result," said she, rising slowly, and meeting the enraged glance of the king with a proud and calm aspect. "You have not listened to my prayers; well, then, I pray no more. But I swear to you, and God in heaven hears my oath, I will never marry! Now, my king, try how far your power reaches; what you may do and dare; how far you may prevail with a woman who struggles against the tyranny of her destiny. You can lead an army into desperate battle; you can conquer provinces, and make thrones totter to their base, but you cannot force a woman to do what she is resolved against! You cannot break my will! I repeat my oath—I swear I will never marry!"

A cry of rage burst from the lips of the king; with a hasty movement he advanced and seized the arm of the princess; then, however, as if ashamed of his impetuosity, he released her and stepped backward.

"Madame," said he, "you will wed the King of Denmark. This is my unchangeable purpose, my inexorable command! The time of mourning for his dead wife is passed; and he has, through a special ambassador, renewed his suit for your hand. I will receive the ambassador to-morrow morning in solemn audience. I will say to him that I am ready to bestow the hand of my sister upon the King of Denmark. To-morrow you will be the bride and in four weeks you will be the wife of the King of Denmark!"

"And if I repeat to you, that I will never be his wife?"

"Madame, when the king commands, no one in his realm dare say 'I will not!' Farewell—to-morrow morning, then!" He bowed, left the room, and closed the door behind him.

Amelia sighed heavily, then slowly and quietly, even as she had come, she walked through the corridors, and as she passed by her maids she greeted them with a soft smile. Ernestine wished to follow her to her boudoir, but she nodded to her to remain outside; she entered and closed the door. She was alone; a wild shriek burst from her lips; with a despairing movement she raised her arms to heaven, then sank powerless, motionless to the floor.

How long she lay there; what martyrdom, what tortures her heart endured in those hours of solitude, who can know? It was twilight when Princess Amelia opened the door and bade her friend, Fraulein von Haak, enter.

"Oh, princess, dearly-beloved princess," she said, weeping bitterly, pressing Amelia's hand to her lips, "God be thanked that I see you again!"

"Poor child!" said Amelia, gently, "poor child! You thought I would destroy myself! is it not so, Ernestine? No, no, I must live! A dark and sad foreboding tells me that a day will come when Trenck will need me; when my life, my strength, my assistance will be necessary to him. I will be strong! I will live, and await that day!"

With calm indifference she now began to speak of trifling things, and listened kindly to all Ernestine related. There was, however, a certain solemnity in her movements, in her smile, in every word she uttered; her eyes turned from time to time with an indescribable expression to heaven, and anxious, alarmed sighs fell trembling from her lips.

At last the long and dreary hours of the evening were over. It was night. Amelia could dismiss her maids and be once more alone. They brought the spirit-lamp, upon which stood the vessel containing the steaming mixture for her eyes; she directed them to place it near, and go quietly to sleep. She would undress herself and read a while before she went to bed. She embraced Fraulein von Haak, and charged her to sleep peacefully.

"You have promised," whispered Ernestine, lightly, "you will live!"

"I will live, for Trenck will one day need me. Good-night!"

She kissed Ernestine upon the brow and smiled upon her till the door closed—then pressed the bolt forward hastily, and rushed forward to the large mirror, which reflected her image clearly and distinctly. With a curious expression she contemplated her still lovely, youthful, and charming image, and her lips lightly whispered, "Farewell, thou whom Trenck loved! Farewell, farewell!" she greeted her image with a weary smile, then stepped firmly to the table, where the mixture hissed and bubbled, and the dangerous steam ascended.

The next morning loud shrieks and groans were heard in the bedroom of the princess. Amelia's maids had come to arrange her toilet, and found her stretched upon her couch, with disfigured face, with bloody eyes, which, swollen and rigid, appeared almost torn from their sockets! They ran for the physician, for the queen, for the king; all was confusion, excitement, anguish.

Ernestine knelt weeping by the bed of the princess, and implored her to say what frightful accident had so disfigured her. Princess Amelia was incapable of reply! Her lips were convulsively pressed together; she could only stammer out a few inarticulate sounds.

At last Meckel arrived, and when he saw the inflamed, swollen face, the eyeballs starting from their sockets, and then the vessel containing the powerful mixture upon the table, he was filled with horror.

"Ah, the unhappy!" murmured he; "she did not regard my warning. She drew too near the noxious vapor, and it has entered not only her eyes but her windpipe; she will suffer much, and never be wholly restored!"

Amelia understood these words, which were addressed to Fraulein von Haak, and a horrible wild laugh burst from her bloody, skinless lips.

"Will she recover?" asked Fraulein von Haak.

"She will recover, but her eyes will be always deformed and her voice is destroyed. I will hasten to the apothecary's and prepare soothing ointments."

He withdrew, and now another door opened, and the king entered. With hasty steps, and greatly excited, he drew near the bed of the princess. As he looked upon her deformed countenance, her bleeding, rigid eyes, he uttered a cry of horror, and bowed down over his sister.

She gazed up at him steadily; tried to open her lips; tried to speak, but only a dull, hollow sound was heard. Now she slightly raised herself up with a powerful effort of strength, and moved her hand slowly over the white wall near her bed.

"She wishes to write," said the king; "perhaps she will tell the cause of her sufferings. Give her something quickly! there—a coal from the chimney!"

Fraulein von Haak brought the coal, and Amelia wrote, with trembling hand, in great, irregular letters, these words upon the wall:

"Now I will not wed the King of Denmark!—now I shall never marry!" then fell back on her pillow with a hollow laugh, which deformed her swollen and convulsed features in a frightful manner.

The king sank on a chair near the bed, and, clasping his hands over his face, he abandoned himself to despair. He saw, he comprehended all! He knew that she had intentionally disfigured herself; that she had offered up her beauty to her love! For this reason she had so piteously pleaded with him!—for this reason had she clamored for pity!—pity for her youth, her future, her life's happiness! Love and faith she had offered up! Greater, braver than Juliet, she had not given herself up to death, but to deformity! She had destroyed her body, in order to treasure love and constancy in her heart for her beloved! All this the king knew, and a profound and boundless sorrow for this young woman, so strong in her love, came over him. He bowed his head and wept bitterly.[*]

---

[*] La partie de l'histoire de la Princesse Amélie qui a été la moins connue, et sur laquelle le public a flotté entre des opinions plus diverses et moins admissibles, c'est la cause de ses infirmités. Heureusement constituée sans être grande, elle n'aurait pas dû savoir à les craindre, même dans un âge très-

CHAPTER XI.

BARBARINA.

THE visit which the proud wife of the High-Chancellor Cocceji had made to the still prouder dancer, had brought the trembling and irresolute heart of Barbarina to a conclusion. This heart, which had not been influenced by her own wishes or the eloquent prayers of her young lover, was wounded by the insane pride of Madame Cocceji, and forced to a final resolve. The visit was unfortunate, and its results exactly the opposite of her hopes.

She had come to prove to Barbarina that she should not even dare to think of becoming the wife of her son. By her wild passion and abusive words she had so exasperated her, that she determined to do that for revenge which she had firmly refused to love. In flashing scorn she had sworn this to the proud wife of the high chancellor; and her honor and her pride demanded the fulfilment of her oath.

avancé; et elle en a été atteinte bien avant l'âge, qui peut les faire craindre. Encore, ne les a-t-elle pas eues partiellement, elle en a été spontanément accablée. Il n'est pas douteux qu'elle ne les ait cherchées. J'en donnerai pour preuve un fait qui est certain. A une époque où elle avait les yeux inflammés, M. Meckel, qui était son médecin, lui ordonna une composition liquide, qu'il fallait faire chauffer, pour en faire parvenir la vapeur jusqu'aux yeux, mais en tenant ce liquide aux moins à sept ou huit pouces de distance; et lui recommanda bien de ne pas l'approcher davantage; et, cependant dès qu'elle eut cette composition, elle s'empressa de s'en frotter les yeux, ce qui produisit un si funeste effet, qu'elle courut le plus grand danger de devenir aveugle; et que depuis elle a toujours de lès yeux à moitié sortis de leurs orbites, et aussi hideux qu'ils avaient été beaux jusque là. Frédéric, à qui on n'osa pas dire combien la princesse avait de part à cette accident, n'a jamais eu depuis qu'une aversion très-marquée et un vrai mépris pour M. Meckel, que la princesse fut obligée de quitter, et qui n'en était pas moins un des meilleurs médecins de Berlin, et un des plus célèbres anatomistes de l'Europe.

Une autre infirmité plus étonnante, encore, c'est que cette princesse perdit presque totalement la voix; aussi de sa faute à ce qui l'on a prétendu il lui était difficile de parler, et très-pénible aux autres de l'entendre. Sa voix n'était plus qu'un son vague, sourd et sépulcral, semblable à celui que forme une personne qui fait effort pour dire comme à voix basse qu'elle étrangle.

Je ne parlerai pas de sa tête chancelante et se soutenant à peine de ses jambes, pour lesquelles son corps appauvri était un poids si lourd de ses bras; et de ses mains plus d'à moitié paralysé; mais quels puissants motifs ont pu amener cette belle et aimable princesse à se faire elle-même un sort si triste? Quelle philosophie a pu lui donner assez de force pour le supporter, et ne pas s'en plaindre? quelle énergie tous ces faits ne prouvent-ils pas?—Thiébault, ii., 287–289.

And now a fierce contest commenced between them—carried on by both parties with bitterness and energy. The high chancellor threatened his son with his curse. He solemnly declared he would disinherit him. Cocceji only loved the Barbarina the more glowingly; and, as his mother spoke to him of the dancer, and uttered passionate and abusive words, he replied respectfully but decisively that he would not listen to such accusations against the woman who was to be his wife, and must forbid them positively. Madame Cocceji was beside herself with rage; by her prayers and persuasions, she induced her husband to take refuge in the last and most violent resource that remained—in the power of arrest which the king had granted him. He resolved to confine his son in the castle of Mt. Landsberg, and thus break the magical bands of Ariadne.

One day, the Councillor Cocceji did not appear in the halls of justice, and no one knew what had become of him. The servants stated that a carriage stopped at his dwelling in the middle of the night; that General Haak with two soldiers entered Cocceji's room, and remained with him some time. They had then all entered the general's carriage, and driven away.

Cocceji had, however, found a secret opportunity to slip a piece of paper into the servant's hand, and to whisper, "Quick, to the signora!"

The faithful servant obeyed this order. The paper contained only these words: "I am arrested; make all necessary preparations; expect me daily. As soon as I am free, our marriage will take place."

Barbarina made her preparations. She undertook frequently little journeys, and sometimes remained away from Berlin several days. She bought a costly and beautiful house, to prove to the wife of the chancellor that she had no thought of leaving Berlin and returning to Italy.

Some months went by. The king, who had yielded to the prayers of the Coccejis, and allowed them to arrest their son, would not consent to his longer confinement. He had no trial; had committed no offence against the laws or the king; was guilty of no other crime than wishing to marry the woman he loved.

So the young councillor was released from the castle of Landsberg. He returned to Berlin; and his first visit was not to his parents, but to Barbarina, who received him in her new house in Behren Street.

A few hours later, a carriage stood before the door, which Barbarina, accompanied by her sister and Cocceji, entered, and drove rapidly away. No one knew where they went. Even the spies of the Coccejis, who continually watched the house of the dancer, could learn nothing from the servants who were left behind. A few days after, they brought the intelligence that Barbarina had returned; and the councillor dwelt with her in her new house; and the servants were commanded to call the signora *Madame Cocceji*, as she was his well-beloved and trusted wife.

The wife of the high chancellor laughed contemptuously at this narrative, and declared it to be only a *coup de théâtre*. Suddenly an equipage drove to the door. Somewhat curious, Madame Cocceji stepped to the window; she saw that the coachman and footmen were dressed in liveries glittering with gold, and that the panels of the carriage were ornamented with the Cocceji coat-of-arms.

The Signora Barbarina was to be seen at the window. Horrified, the wife of the chancellor stepped back; a servant entered with a card, which he handed her respectfully.

"I am not at home; I receive no visits!" cried she, after looking at the card. The servant retired, and the carriage rolled away.

"Yes, it is true. She has triumphed!" groaned the countess, still gazing at the card, which had these words: "Monsieur de Cocceji and Madame de Cocceji, *née* Barbarina."—"But she shall not succeed; the Barbarina shall never be called my daughter; this marriage shall be set aside, the ceremony was not lawful, it is contrary to the laws of the land. Barbarina is a *bourgeoise*, and cannot wed a noble without the express consent of the king. I will throw myself at the feet of his majesty and implore him to annul this marriage!"

Frederick was much exasperated, and inclined to yield to the entreaties of his high chancellor. A short time before, he had commanded the Catholic clergy not to perform any marriage ceremony without special permission and legitimation; and his anger was aroused at their daring to disobey him, and in secrecy and silence to marry Barbarina and Cocceji.

He commanded his cabinet minister Uhden to ascertain by what right the dancer Barbarina dared to call herself Madame Cocceji, and, if she could establish her claim, he wished to be informed what priest had dared to bless the holy banns. He was resolved to punish him severely.

The minister Uhden was a warm personal friend of the high chancellor, and more than willing, therefore, to carry out sternly the king's commands. The next day he ordered Barbarina to appear before him, stating that he had the king's permission to pronounce judgment upon her.

When Barbarina read this order, she was lost in painful silence, and a profound melancholy was written upon her pale face.

"What will you do, sister?" said Marietta.

"I will go to the king!" replied Barbarina, rousing herself.

"But the king is at Potsdam."

"Well, then, I will go to Potsdam. Order my carriage; I must go in a quarter of an hour."

"What shall I say to your husband when he returns home?"

Barbarina looked at her steadily. "Tell him that Madame Cocceji has gone to Potsdam, to announce her marriage to the king, and ask him to acknowledge it."

"Barbarina," whispered her sister, "hear me! Your husband is troubled and sorrowful; he has confided in me. He says he fears you did not marry him from love, but for revenge, and that you love him not."

"I am resolved to love him! I will learn how," said she, sadly. "I have a strong will, and my heart shall obey me!"

She smiled, but her lovely face was overcast with grief, and Marietta's eyes were filled with tears.

Frederick was alone in his study in the castle of Potsdam; he was busily engaged in writing. The door was lightly opened, and the Marquis d'Argens looked in. When he saw that the king had heard nothing, he beckoned to a lady who stood behind him to draw near. She entered the room silently and noiselessly; the marquis bowed to her, and, smiling kindly, he stepped back and closed the door.

The lady, who up to this time had closely concealed her features, now threw back her veil, and exposed the pale but lovely countenance and flashing eyes of Barbarina. She gazed at the king with a mingled expression of happiness and pain.

The king still heard nothing. Suddenly he was aroused by a low sigh; it seemed to him that a soft, sweet, long-silent voice whispered his name. He rose hastily and turned; Barbarina was kneeling at the door; it was that door before which, five years ago, she had kneeled bathed in tears and wild with despair. She was now, as then, upon her knees, weeping bitterly, and raising her hands importunately to the king, pleading for grace and pity.

Frederick was at first pallid from surprise, and a frown was on his brow; but, as he looked upon her, and saw once more those great, dark, unfathomable eyes, a painful but sweet emotion overcame him; the cloud was lifted up, his countenance was illuminated and his eyes were soft and misty.

With a kindly smile he drew near to Barbarina. "Rise," said he, and the tones of his voice made her heart beat wildly, and brought fresh tears to her eyes. "You come strangely and unexpectedly, Barbarina, but you come with a beautiful retinue, with a crowd of sweet, fond remembrances—and I—of whom men say, 'He has no religion'—have at least the religion of memory. I cannot be angry with you, Barbarina; rise, and tell me why you are here."

He bowed, and took her by the hands and raised her; and now, as she stood near him, lovely as ever, her great eyes glowing with warmth and passion, intoxicating the senses with her odorous beauty, the king felt anguish in his heart which he had no words to express.

They stood silently, side by side, their eyes fixed upon each other, Frederick holding Barbarina's hand in his; they seemed to be whispering mysterious fairy tales to each other's hearts.

"I see you, surrounded by smiling, sacred genii," at last,

said Frederick. "These are the genii of the rosy hours which have been. Ah, Barbarina, thus attended, your face seems to me as the face of an angel. Why were you not an angel, Barbarina? Why were you only a woman—a passionate woman, who, not satisfied with loving and being loved, wished also to govern; who was not content to be worshipped by the man, but wished to subject the king, whom you thus forced to forget his humanity, to trample upon and torture his own heart in order to remain king? Oh, Barbarina, why were you this proud, exacting woman, rather than the angel which you now truly are?"

She raised her hands, as if imploring him to be silent. "I understand all that now, I have thought of it, night and day; I know and I confess that you acted right, sire. And now I am no longer an imperious woman, but a humiliated one! In my helplessness, with my pride subdued, I come to you! I come to you, sire, as one goes to God, weary and heavy laden. I come to you, as a poor sinner goes into God's holy temple, to confess his sins; to have his burden lightened; to pray for help that he may subdue his own heart! Oh, sire, this is a sacred, consecrated hour for me, and what I now say to you, only God and yourself may hear!"

"Speak, Barbarina, and may God hear and answer!"

"Sire, I come for help!"

"Ah, for help!" exclaimed the king, and a mocking expression played upon his lips. "I had forgotten. You wish to be called Madame Cocceji?"

"I am called thus, sire," said she, softly; "but they are about to declare my marriage illegal, and by the power of the law to set it aside."

"And for this reason you come to me?" said the king. "You fear for your beautiful title?"

"Ah, sire, you do not think so pitifully of me as to suppose I care for a title?"

"You married the Councillor Cocceji, then, from love?" said the king.

Barbarina looked at the king steadily. "No, sire, I did not marry him for love."

"Why, then, did you marry him?"

"To save myself, sire—to save myself, and because I

could not learn to forget. Your majesty has just said that you have the religion of memory. Sire, I am the anguish-stricken, tortured, fanatical priestess of the same faith. I have lain daily before her altar, I have scourged my heart with remembrances, and blinded my eyes with weeping. At last a day came in which I roused myself. I resolved to abandon my altar, to flee from the past, and teach my heart to forget. I went to England, accepted Lord Stuart's proposals, and resolved to be his wife. It was in vain, wholly in vain. Whatsoever my trembling lips might say, my heart lay ever bleeding before the altar of my memory. The past followed me over the wide seas, she beckoned and greeted me with mysterious sighs and pleadings; she called out to me, with two great, wondrous eyes, clear and blue as the heavens, unfathomable as the sea! These eyes, sire, called me back, and I could not resist them. I felt that I would rather die by them than relinquish them forever. So, on my wedding-day, I fled from England, and returned to Berlin. The old magic came over me; also, alas! the old grief. I felt that I must do something to save myself, if I would not go mad. I resolved to bind my wayward heart in chains, to make my love a prisoner to duty, and silence the outcries of my soul! But I still wavered. Then came Madame Cocceji. By her insolent bearing she roused my pride, until it over-shadowed even my despair, and I heard no other voice. So, sire, I married Cocceji! I have taken refuge in this mar-riage, as in a safe haven, where I shall rest peacefully and fear no storm.

"But, my king, struggle as I may to begin a new life, the religion of memory will not relinquish her priestess; she extends her mystical hands over me, and my poor heart shouts back to her against my will. Sire, save me! I have fled to this marriage as one flies to a cloister-cell, to escape the sweet love of this world. Oh, sire, do not allow them to drive me from this refuge; leave me in peace to God and my duty! Alas! my soul has repented, she lies wearied and ill at your feet. Help her, heal her, I implore you!"

She was silent. She extended her hands toward the king. He looked at her sadly, kindly took her hands in his, and pressed his lips upon them.

31

"Barbarina," said he, in a rich, mellow voice—"Barbarina, I thank you. God and the king have heard you. You say that you are the priestess of the religion of remembrance; well, then, I am her priest, and I confess to you that I, also, have passed many nights in anguish before her altar. Life demands heavy sacrifices, and more from kings than from other men. Once in my life I made so rich an offering to my royalty that it seemed life could have no more of bitterness in store. The thoughtless and fools consider life a pleasure. But I, Barbarina, I say, that life is a duty. Let us fulfil our duties."

"Yes, we will go and fulfil them," said she, with flashing eyes. "Sire, I will go to fulfil mine; but I am weak, and have yet one more favor to ask. There is no cup of Lethe from which men drink forgetfulness, and yet I must forget. I must cast a veil over the past. Help me, sire—I must leave Berlin! Banish my husband to another city. It will be an open grave for me; but I will struggle to plant that grave with flowers, whose beauty and perfume shall rejoice and make glad the heart of my husband!"

"I grant your request," said the king, sadly.

"I thank you, sire; and now, farewell!"

"Farewell, Barbarina!"

He took again her hands in his, and looked long into her fair, enchanting face, now glowing with enthusiasm. Neither spoke one word; they took leave of each other with soft glances and melancholy sighs.

"Farewell, sire!" said Barbarina, after a long pause, withdrawing her hands from the king's and stepping toward the door. The king followed her.

"Give me your hand," said he, "I will go with you!"

Frederick led her into the adjoining room, in which there were two doors. One led to a small stairway, which opened upon a side-door of the castle; the other to the great saloon, in which the cavaliers and followers of the king were wont to assemble.

Barbarina had entered by the small stairway, and now turned her steps in that direction. "No, not that way," said Frederick. "My staff await me in the saloon. It is the hour for parade. I will show you my court."

Barbarina thanked him, and followed silently to the other door. The generals, in their glittering uniforms, and the cavaliers, with their embroidered vests and brilliant orders, bowed profoundly, and no one dared to manifest the surprise he felt as the king and Barbarina entered.

Frederick led Barbarina into the middle of the saloon, and letting go her hand, he said aloud: "Madame, I have the honor to commend myself to you. Your wish shall be fulfilled. Your husband shall be President of Glogau! it shall be arranged to-day." The king cast a proud and searching glance around the circle of his cavaliers, until they rested upon the master of ceremonies. "Baron Pöllnitz, conduct Madame Presidentess Cocceji to her carriage."

Pöllnitz stumbled forward and placed himself with a profound salutation at Barbarina's side.

Frederick bowed once more to Barbarina; she took the arm of Baron Pöllnitz. Silence reigned in the saloon as Barbarina withdrew.

The king gazed after her till she had entirely disappeared; then, breathing heavily, he turned to his generals and said: "Messieurs, it is time for parade."

CHAPTER XII.

INTRIGUES.

VOLTAIRE was faithful to his purpose: he made use of his residence in Prussia and the favor of the king to increase his fortune, and to injure and degrade, as far as possible, all those for whom the king manifested the slightest partiality. He not only added to his riches by the most abject niggardliness in his mode of life, thereby adding his pension to his capital, but by speculation in Saxon bonds, for which, in the beginning, he employed the aid of the Jew Hirsch. We have seen that he sent him to Dresden to purchase eighteen thousand thalers' worth of bonds, and gave him three drafts for that purpose.

One of these was drawn upon the banker Ephraim. He thus learned of Voltaire's speculation, and, as a cunning trafficker, he resolved to turn this knowledge to his own advantage. He went to Voltaire, and proposed to give him twenty thousand thalers' worth of Saxon bonds, and demand no payment for them till Voltaire should receive their full value from Dresden. The only profit he desired was Voltaire's good word and influence for him with the king.

This was a most profitable investment, and the great French writer could not resist it. He took the bonds; promised his protection and favor, and immediately sent to Paris to protest the draft he had given the Jew Hirsch.

Poor Hirsch had already bought the bonds in Dresden, and he was now placed in the most extreme embarrassment, not only by the protested draft, but by Voltaire's refusing to receive the bonds and to pay for them.

Voltaire tried to appease him; promised to repair his loss, and yet further to indemnify him. He declared he would purchase some of the diamonds left in his care by Hirsch, and he really did this; he bought three thousand thalers' worth of diamonds and returned the rest to Hirsch. A few days after he sent to him for a diamond cross and a few rings which he proposed to buy. Hirsch sent them, and not hearing from either the diamonds or the money, he went to Voltaire to get either the one or the other.

Voltaire received him furiously; declared that the diamonds which he had purchased were false, and in order to reimburse himself he had retained the others and would never return them! In wild rage he continued to raise his doubled fist to heaven in condemnation, or held it under the nose of the poor terrified Jew; and to crown all, he tore from his finger another diamond ring, and pushed him from the door.

And now the Jew indeed was to be pitied. He demanded of the courts the restoration of his diamonds, and payment for the Saxon bonds.

A wearisome and vexatious process was the result. Voltaire's plots and intrigues involved the case more and more, and he brought the judges themselves almost to despair. Voltaire declared that the Jew had sold him false diamonds.

The Jew asserted that the false diamonds exhibited by Voltaire were not those Voltaire had purchased of him, and which the jeweller Reclam had valued. No one was present at this trade, so there were no witnesses. The judges were, therefore, obliged to confine themselves to administering the oath to Voltaire, as he would not consent to any compromise. But he resisted the taking of the oath also.

"What!" said he, "I must swear upon the Bible; upon this book written in such wretched Latin! If it were Homer or Virgil, I would have nothing against it."

When the judge assured him, that if he refused the oath, they would administer it to the Jew, he exclaimed: "What! you will allow the oath of this miserable creature, who crucified the Saviour, to decide this question?"

He took the oath at last, and as the Jew Ephraim swore at the same time that Voltaire had shown him the diamonds, and he had at once declared them to be false, the Jew Hirsch lost his case, and Voltaire triumphed. He wrote the following letter to Algarotti:

"If one had listened to my envious enemies, they would have heard that I was about to lose a great process, and that I had defrauded an honest Jewish banker. The king, who naturally takes the part of the Old Testament, would have looked upon me with disfavor. I should have been lost, and Fréron would have derisively declared that I sickened and died of rage. Instead of this, I still live; and during my last illness the king manifested such warm and affectionate interest in me, that I should be the most ungrateful of men if I do not remain a few months longer with him! I am the only animal of my race whom he has ever lodged in his castle in Berlin; and when he left for Potsdam, and I could not follow him, his equipage, cooks, etc., remained for my use. He had my furniture and other effects removed to a beautiful country-seat near Sans-Souci, which was, for the time being, mine. Besides this, a lodging was reserved for me at Potsdam, where I slept a part of every week. In short, if I were not three hundred leagues away from you, whom I love so tenderly, and if I were in good health, I would be the happiest of men! I ask pardon, therefore, of my enemies; these men of small wit; these sly foxes, who cry out because I have a pension of twenty thousand francs, and they have nothing! I wear a golden cross on my breast, while they have not even a handkerchief in their pockets. I wear a great blue cross, set round with diamonds, around my neck; for this they would strangle me. These miserable creatures ought to know that I would cheerfully give up the cross, the key, the pension; these things would cost me no regret, but I am bound and attached to this great man, who in all things strives to promote my welfare." *

But this paradise of bliss, so extravagantly praised by Voltaire, was not entirely without clouds, and some fierce storms had been necessary to clear the atmosphere.

The king was very angry with Voltaire, and wrote the following letter to him from Potsdam:

"I knew how to maintain peace in my house till your arrival; and I must confess to you, that if you continue to intrigue and cabal, you will be no longer welcome. I prefer kind and gentle people, who are not passionate and tragic in their daily life. In case you should resolve to live as a philosopher, I will rejoice to see you! But if you give full sway to your passion and are hot-brained with everybody, you will do better to remain in Berlin. Your arrival in Potsdam will give me no pleasure." †

Only after Voltaire had solemnly sworn to preserve the peace, was he allowed to return to Potsdam. Keeping the peace was not, however, in harmony with Voltaire's character; plotting was a necessity with him; he could not resist it.

After he had succeeded in setting Arnaud aside and compelling him to leave Berlin, he turned his rage and sarcasm against the other friends of the king. One of them was removed by death. This was La Mettrie; he partook immoderately of a truffle-pie at the house of the French ambassador, Lord Tyrconnel, and died in consequence of a blood-letting, which he ordered himself, in opposition to the opinion of his physician. He laughingly said, "I will accustom my indigestion to blood-letting." He died at the first experiment. His death was in harmony with his life and his principles.

* Voltaire, Œuvres, p. 442.
† Œuvres Posthumes, p. 338.

He dismissed the priest rudely who came to him uncalled, and entreated him to be reconciled to God. Convulsed by his last agonies, he called out, " O my God! O Jesus Maria!"

" He repents!" cried the delighted priest; "he calls upon God and His blessed Son."

" No, no, no, father!" stammered La Mettrie, with dying lips; "that was only a form of speech."*

Voltaire's envy and jealousy were now turned against the Marquis d'Argens, who was indeed the dearest friend of the king. At first he tried to prejudice the king against him; he betrayed to him that the marquis had privately married the actress Barbe Cochois.

The king was at the moment very angry, but the prayers of Algarotti, and the regret of the poor marquis, reconciled him at last; he not only forgave, but he allowed the marquise to dwell at Sans-Souci with her husband.

When Voltaire found that he could not deprive the marquis of the king's favor, he resolved to occasion him some trouble, and to wound his vanity and sensibility. He knew that the marquis was an ardent admirer of the French writer Jean Baptiste Rousseau. One day Voltaire entered the room of the marquis, and said, in a sad, sympathetic tone, that he felt it his duty to undeceive him as to Jean Baptiste Rousseau, to prove to him that his love and respect for the great writer were returned with the blackest ingratitude. He had just received from his correspondent at Paris an epigram which Rousseau had made upon the marquis. It was true the epigram was only handed about in manuscript, and Rousseau swore every one who read it not to betray him; he was showing it, however, and it was thought it would be published. He, Voltaire, had commissioned his correspondent to do every thing in his power to prevent the publication of this epigram; or, if this took place, to use every means to excite the public, as well as the friends of the marquis, against Rousseau, because of his shameful treachery.

At all events, this epigram, which Voltaire now read aloud to the marquis, and which described him as the Wandering Jew, was as malicious as it was mischievous and slanderous.

* Nicolai, p. 20.

The good marquis was deeply wounded, and swore to take a great revenge on Rousseau. Voltaire triumphed.

But, after a few days, he suspected that the whole was an artifice of Voltaire. In accordance with his open, noble character, he wrote immediately to Rousseau, made his complaint, and asked if he had written the epigram.

Rousseau swore that he was not the author, but he was persuaded that Voltaire had written it; he had sent some copies to Paris, and his friends were seeking to spread it abroad.*

The marquis was on his guard, and did not communicate this news to Voltaire. He resolved to escape from these assaults and intrigues quietly; with his young wife he made a journey to Paris, and did not return till Voltaire had left Berlin forever.

The most powerful and therefore the most abhorred of the enemies against whom Voltaire now turned in his rage, was the president of the Berlin Academy, Maupertius. Voltaire could never forgive him for daring to shine in his presence; for being the president of an academy of which he, Voltaire, was only a simple member. Above all this, the king loved him, and praised his extraordinary talent and scholarship. Voltaire only watched for an opportunity to clutch this dangerous enemy, and the occasion soon presented itself.

Maupertius had just published his "*Lettres Philosophiques*," in which it must be confessed there were passages which justified Voltaire's assertion that Maupertius was at one time insane, and was confined for some years in a madhouse at Montpellier. Maupertius proposed in these letters that a Latin city should be built, and this majestic and beautiful tongue brought to life again. He proposed, also, that a hole should be dug to the centre of the earth, in order to discover its condition and quality; also that the brain of Pythagoras should be searched for and opened, in order to ascertain the nature of the soul.

These ridiculous and fabulous propositions Voltaire replied to under the name of Dr. Akakia; he asserted that he was only anxious to heal the unhappy Maupertius. This

* Thiébault.

publication was written in Voltaire's sharpest wit and his most biting, glittering irony, and was calculated to make Maupertius absurd in the eyes of the whole world.

The king, to whom Voltaire had shown his manuscript, felt this; and although he had listened to the "Akakia" with the most lively pleasure, and often interrupted the reading by loud laughter and applause, he asked Voltaire to destroy the manuscript. He was not willing that the man who stood at the head of his academy, and whom he had once called "the light of science," should be held up to the laughter and mockery of the world.

"I ask this sacrifice from you as a proof of your friendship for me, and your self-control," said the king, earnestly. "I am tired of this everlasting disputing and wrangling; I will have peace in my house; I do not know how long we will have peace in the world. It seems to me that on the horizon of politics heavy clouds are beginning to tower up; let us therefore take care that our literary horizon is clear and peaceable."

"Ah, sire!" cried Voltaire, "when you look at me with your great, luminous eyes, I feel capable of plucking my heart from my breast and casting it into the fire for you. How gladly, then, will I offer up these stinging lines to a wish of my Solomon!"

"Will you indeed sacrifice 'Akakia?'" said the king, joyfully.

"Look here! this is my manuscript, you know my handwriting, you see that the ink is scarcely dry, the work just completed. Well, then, see now, sire, what I make of the 'Akakia.'" He took the manuscript and cast it into the fire before which they were both sitting.

"What are you doing?" cried the king, hastily; and, without regarding the flames, he stretched out his hand to seize the manuscript.

Voltaire laughed heartily, seized the tongs, and pushed it farther into the flames. "Sire, sire, I am the devil, and I will not allow my victim to be torn from me. My 'Akakia' was only worthy of the lower regions; you condemned it, and therefore it must suffer. I, the devil, command it to burn."

"But I, the angel of mercy, will redeem the poor 'Aka-kia,'" cried the king, trying to obtain possession of the tongs. "Truly this 'Akakia' is too lusty and witty a boy to be laid, like the Emperor Guatimozin, upon the gridiron. It was enough to deny him a public exhibition—it was not necessary to destroy him."

"Sire, I am a poor, weak man! If I kept the living 'Akakia' by my side, it would be a poisonous weapon, which I would hurl one day surely at the head of Maupertius. It is therefore better it should live only in my remembrance, and be only an imaginary dagger, with which I will some-times tickle the haughty lord-president."

"And you have really no copy?" said the king, whose distrust was awakened by Voltaire's too ready compliance. "Was this the only manuscript of the 'Akakia?'"

"Sire, if you do not believe my word, send your servants and let them search my room. Here are my keys; they shall bring you every scrap of written paper; your majesty will then be convinced. I entreat you to do this, as you will not believe my simple word."

The king fixed his eyes steadfastly upon Voltaire. "I be-lieve you. It would be unworthy of you to deceive me, and unworthy of me to mistrust you. I believe you; but I will make assurance doubly sure. The 'Akakia' is no longer upon paper, but it is in your head, and I fear your head more than I do all the paper in the world. Promise me, Voltaire, that as long as you live with me you will engage in no written strifes or controversies—that you will not employ your bitter irony against the government, or against the authors."

"I promise that cheerfully!"

"Will you do so in writing?"

Voltaire stepped to the table and took the pen. "Will your majesty dictate?"

The king dictated, and Voltaire wrote with a rapid but firm hand: "I promise your majesty that so long as you allow me to lodge in your castle, I will write against no one, neither against the French government nor any of the for-eign ambassadors, nor the celebrated authors. I will con-stantly manifest a proper respect and regard to them.

I will make no improper use of the letters of the king. I will in all things bear myself as becomes an historian and a scholar, who has the honor to be gentleman in waiting to the King of Prussia, and to associate with distinguished persons." *

"Will you sign this?" said the king.

"I will not only sign it," said Voltaire, "but I will add something to its force. Listen, your majesty.—I will strictly obey all your majesty's commands, and to do so gives me no trouble. I entreat your majesty to believe that I never have written any thing against any government—least of all against that under which I was born, and which I only left because I wished to close my life at the feet of your majesty. I am historian of France. In the discharge of this duty, I have written the history of Louis the Fourteenth, and the campaigns of Louis the Fifteenth. My voice and my pen were ever consecrated to my fatherland, as they are now subject to your command. I entreat you to look into my literary contest with Maupertius, and to believe that I give it up cheerfully to please you, sire; and because I will in all things submit to your will. I will also be obedient to your majesty in this. I will enter into no literary contest, and I beg you, sire, to believe that, in the hour of death, I will feel the same reverence and attachment for you which filled my heart the day I first appeared at your court. VOLTAIRE."

The king took the paper, and read it over, then fixed his eyes steadily upon Voltaire's lowering face. "It is well! I thank you," said Frederick, nodding a friendly dismissal to Voltaire. He left the room, and the king looked after him long and thoughtfully.

"I do not trust him; he was too ready to burn the manuscript. And yet, he gave me his word of honor."

Voltaire returned to his room, and, now alone and unobserved, a malicious, demoniac exultation was written on his face. "I judged rightly," said he, with a grimace; "the king wished to sacrifice me to Maupertius. I think this was a master-stroke. I have truly burned the original manuscript, but a copy of it was sent to Leyden eight days since.

* Preus, "Friedrich der Grosse."

While the king thinks I am such a good-humored fool as to yield the contest to the proud beggar Maupertius, my 'Akakia' will be published in Leyden. Soon it will resound through the world, and show how genius binds puffed-up folly, which calls itself geniality, to the pillory."

CHAPTER XIII.

THE LAST STRUGGLE.

It was Christmas eve! The streets were white with snow; crowds of people were rushing through the castle square, seeking for Christmas-trees, and little presents for their children. There were, however, fewer purchasers than usual. The small traders stood idle at the doors of the booths, and looked discontentedly at the swarms of laughing men, who passed by them, and rushed onward to the Gens d'Armen Market.

A rare spectacle, exhibited for the first time during the reign of Frederick, was to be seen at the market to-day. A funeral pyre was erected, and the executioner stood near in his red livery. What!—shall the holy evening be solemnized by an execution? Was it for this that thousands of curious men were rushing onward to the scaffold? that groups of elegant ladies and cavaliers were crowded to the open windows?

Yes, there was to be an execution—a bloodless one, which would occasion no bodily suffering to the delinquent. The eyes of this great mass of people were not directed to the scaffold, but to the window of a large house on Tauben Street.

At this open window stood a pale old man, with hollow cheeks and bent, infirm form; but you saw by the proud bearing of his head, and his ironical, contemptuous smile, that his spirit was unconquered. His whole face glowed with flaming scorn; and his great, fiery eyes flashed amongst the crowd, greeting here and there an acquaintance.

This man was Voltaire—Voltaire, who had come to witness the execution of his "Akakia," which had been published in Leyden, and scattered abroad throughout Berlin. Voltaire had broken his written and verbal promise, his word of honor; and the king, exasperated to the utmost by this dishonorable conduct, had determined to punish him openly. And now, amidst the breathless silence of the crowd, a functionary of the king read the sentence—that sentence which condemned the "Akakia," that malicious and slanderous publication holding up the noble, virtuous, and renowned scholar Maupertius to the general mockery of Paris.

Voltaire stood calm and smiling at the open window. He saw the executioner throw great piles of his "Akakia" into the fire. He saw the mad flames whirling up into the heavens, and his countenance was clear, and his eyes did not lose their lustre. Higher and higher flashed the flames! broader and blacker the pillars of smoke! but Voltaire smiled peacefully. Conversation and laughter were silenced —the crowd looked on breathlessly.

Suddenly a loud and derisive laugh was heard, and a powerful voice cried out: "Look at the spirit of Maupertius, which is dissolving into smoke! Oh, the thick, black smoke! How much wood consumed in vain! The 'Akakia' is immortal—you burn him here, but he still lives, and the whole world will know and appreciate him. That which is born for immortality can never be burned." *

So said Voltaire, as he dashed the window down, and stepped back in the room.

"Farewell, Herr von Francheville," said he, quietly. "I thank you for having allowed me to be present at my execution. You see I have borne it well; all do not die who are burnt. Farewell, I must go to the castle. I have important business there."

With youthful agility he entered his carriage. The people, who recognized him, shouted after him joyfully. He passed through the crowd with an air of triumph, and they greeted him with kindly interest.

The smile disappeared from his face when he entered his room at the castle, and the scorn and tumult of his heart

* Thiébault, p. 265.

were plainly written on his countenance. He seized his port-folio, and drew from it the pension patent signed by the king; tore from his neck the blue ribbon, with the great badge surrounded with brilliants, and cut the little key from his court dress, which his valet had laid out ready for his toilet. Of these things he made a little packet, which he sealed up, and wrote upon it these lines:

> " Je les reçus avec tendresse,
> Je vous les rends avec douleur ;
> C'est ainsi qu'un amant, dans son extrême fureur,
> Rend le portrait de sa maitresse."

He called his servant, and commanded him to take this packet to the king.

Voltaire did not hesitate a moment. He felt not the least regret for the great pension which he was relinquish-ing. He felt that there was no other course open to him; that his honor and his pride demanded it. At this moment, his expression was noble. He was the proud, independent, free man. The might of genius reigned supreme, and sub-dued the calculating and the pitiful for a brief space. This exalted moment soon passed away, and the cunning, miserly, calculating old man again asserted his rights. Voltaire re-membered that he had not only given up orders and titles, but *gold*, and measureless anguish and raging pain took pos-session of him. He hastened to his writing-desk, and with a trembling hand he wrote a pleading letter to the king, in which he begged for pardon and grace—for pity in his un-happy circumstances and his great sorrow.

The king was merciful. He took pity on the old friend-ship which lay in ruins at his feet. He felt for it that sort of reverence which a man entertains for the grave of a lost friend. He returned the " bagatelles " with a few friendly lines to Voltaire, and invited him to accompany him to Potsdam. Voltaire accepted the invitation, and the journals announced that the celebrated French writer had again re-ceived his orders, titles, and pension, and gone to Potsdam with the king.

But this seeming peace was of short duration. Friend-ship was dead, and anger and bitterness had taken the place of consideration and love. Voltaire felt the impossibility of remaining longer. Impelled by the cold glance, the ironical and contemptuous laughter of the king, he begged at last for his dismissal, which the king did not refuse him.

One day, when Frederick was upon the parade-ground, surrounded by his generals, he was told that Voltaire asked permission to be allowed to take leave.

The king turned quietly towards him. " Ah, Monsieur Voltaire, you are resolved, then, to leave us ? "

" Sire, indispensable business and my state of health compel me to do so," said Voltaire.

The king bowed slightly. " Monsieur, I wish you a happy journey." * Then turning to the old Field-Marshal Ziethen, he recommenced his conversation with him. Voltaire made a profound bow, and entered the post-chaise which was waiting for him.

So they parted, and their friendship was in ashes; and no after-protestations could bring it to life. The great king and the great poet parted, never to meet again.

* Thiébault, p. 271.

(40)

THE END.